The Severed Vow

James Runge

To Kaitlyn
**Thank you for all your love and support. I could never
have accomplished this without you. I love you.**

The Severed Vow

Contents

Prologue

The world was forged without mercy. It was carved from blood, shaped by war, and ruled by those who wielded power with an iron fist. Kingdoms rose and fell like waves upon a storm-tossed sea, each grasping for dominance in an endless struggle. The strong ruled, and the weak suffered. Such was the way of things.

What came to pass was seen by many as a divine intervention. Children were born with strange markings on their bodies, signs of the Valasar, the power of the gods themselves. It began with whispers, tales of infants who survived where others perished, of boys who outran wolves and girls who manipulated objects without touching them. Myths, the rulers claimed, until those myths became undeniable. In the beginning, those blessed with the Valasar were seen as saviors, champions chosen to bring order to a broken world. The ones who bore the gods' blessings became kings and queens, their families exalted, their power absolute. With their abilities, they carved new empires from the ashes of the old. A ruler with a forehead blessed with the Valasar could out-think any foe, his mind sharper than a thousand blades. A queen bearing the divine symbol upon her hands could command unseen forces, turning the battlefield itself into her weapon. A warrior with the Valasar's touch upon his back could not be broken, not by blade, nor fire, nor time itself.

But power breeds fear. And fear left to fester turns to desperation. More children were born with the gods' blessings—too many. Not just of noble blood, but from commoners and peasants, those who toiled in the fields and begged in the streets. The nobles saw what they had not dared to fear before. The Valasar was not their birthright alone. It could appear anywhere, in anyone. Their power—their rule—was at risk.

And when that fear bore desperation that desperation, in turn, birthed the Black Vow. This brotherhood of silence, an order of assassins raised from childhood, was a shadow in the dark. Some were taken as infants, stolen from their cradles, but others were chosen—the lost children from the slums and the streets, the ones no one would miss. Belaric Kelmor was among those chosen. A poor peasant boy, barely ten years old. He fought when they took him—wild, hungry, desperate. He tried to run, to escape the cold stone corridors and the whispered promises of pain, but the Black Halls swallowed all who entered.

The Black Vow forged their recruits into killers, breaking them down and reforging them into something cold and efficient. Childhood was stripped away, burned from their bones like impurities in steel. Pain was their teacher, discipline their religion. Hunger taught them patience, agony taught them endurance, and death became something to be delivered, never feared. Belaric earned his place. He proved himself a dozen times over. Yet sometimes, in the stillness of night, he would wake with the phantom taste of rain on his tongue—an echo of a childhood before the Black Vow. The memory of a storm rolling over the slums, the wet scent of dirt, his mother's voice—too faded to recall in words, but still there, somewhere in the back of his mind. He had buried that child long ago. Or so he had thought.

He had served the Black Vow for two decades, killing for them without question, without hesitation. He had slaughtered children in their cradles, burned homes with families still inside, snuffed out futures before they had a chance to unfold. The weight of his deeds settled into his bones, pressing heavier with each life he took. The cold stones of the Black Halls still pressed against his skin in his dreams, their unyielding presence a reminder that the Order had shaped him in ways he could never undo.

Even now, the cries of the innocent no longer faded with time—they lingered, clawing at the edges of his mind. He had always told himself it was a holy mission. But now, as something darker brewed beneath the surface, he could no longer maintain the façade. The whispers in the halls spoke of a shifting tide, the scent of change clinging to the air like the metallic tang of blood. The nobles who wielded the Black Vow as their enforcers were turning their sights inward, culling not only the common-born child who bore the Valasar but their own who dared to question them. Belaric had heard the rumors in taverns and in the darkest alleys: names of minor noble houses, entire bloodlines marked for erasure. No infants. No marks. No divine will. Just men and women who had spoken too loudly, who had dreamed too greatly. He wanted to leave this life behind, but the Black Vow would never allow it. And soon, fate would come for him.

Because the moment his child was born, everything would change.

The Black Vow had raised him. Had forged him. Had turned him into the perfect blade. But even the sharpest blade can break. And when the Black Vow turned their knives upon him, he would not run.

He would sever the vow.

Even if it meant war.

Even if it meant death.

For the boy who had fought, and the child who would never have to.

And when the blood began to spill, the nobles would remember why they first feared the marked. Not because of their power. Not because of their gifts. But because one day, a blade sharpened in their service might turn against their throats.

1

The hill rose steep and steady beneath him, but it was the stench of burning thatch and the ghosts clinging to his clothes that truly weighed him down. He crested the ridge and stopped, lowering his head, breathing deep.

The world whispered around him. Wet grass clung to the soles of his boots, the trees groaned against the wind, and insects droned in lazy circles above him. Somewhere in the distance, an owl called. Beneath it all, curling like a serpent through the damp air, came the scent of smoke.

He turned back.

Flames leapt from the thatched roof, gold and furious against the black sky. Sparks chased the night wind as the fire fed, devouring the walls, the beams, the home. Shadows rushed below—neighbors, wild with panic, forming a desperate chain of hands and buckets. They did not understand.

But Belaric did.

There was no saving them. The father. The mother. The young boy. The newborn girl. The fire was just a funeral pyre, a distraction, a precise way to turn horror into an accident.

A better man would have rushed to help, he knew. But not him, though it pained him not to.

He watched for a time, just long enough. The firelight caught the edges of his cloak, dancing over leather and steel. He was a shadow against the hilltop. That was all he was now.

Finally, he turned his back on the flames and walked toward the treeline, his steps determined. The forest loomed ahead, waiting. He passed between the first trunks, and the darkness closed around him, cool and absolute. Behind him, the burning house flickered one last time before vanishing beyond the black tangle of trees.

He told himself it was necessary, that he had no choice—that he was serving the greater good. But the words rang hollow, the lie so old it tasted like ash.

Once, long ago, he had taken the vow. A whisper over an iron dagger. A covenant of blood given and blood taken. The promise was sealed in silence, unbroken by time or mercy. To defy it meant worse than death. A bond carved into the very bones of the world, older than memory.

And so he killed. And so he burned. And so he walked away before the screams started.

The forest deepened around him, the damp earth muffling his steps, branches shifting overhead like restless hands. The only sounds were the soft rustle of leaves and the faint sigh of wind through the trees. Smoke still clung to his clothes, the heat of the fire lingering on his skin. He exhaled slowly, steadying his breath.

For a moment, there was only silence.

But the quiet was a lie. It never lasted. The stench of ash, the heat still on his skin—these were hooks, dragging him back. His mind rebelled, but it was useless. It drifted—back to the house, back to the faces—as it always did. He was there again, cursed to relive every agonizing detail.

He saw again the cold night air trailing behind him as he slipped inside. The house was quiet now, save for the low crackle of wood shifting in the hearth.

Tonight, the plan took shape. As the moon overtook the sun and the festival came to an end, he slipped inside. Not a single sound betrayed him.

Moving like a shadow, he stepped onto the wooden floor. The firelight reached only so far, leaving the corners cloaked in darkness—and that was where he stayed. Watching. Waiting.

The family returned shortly after, tired from the day's celebration and unaware of the danger waiting inside. They had been at the village's naming ceremony—three days of music, food, and laughter to welcome their newborn into the world. Her parents named her Kessa after her grandmother, beaming with pride as they accepted well-wishes from neighbors and friends. The revelry had stretched into the evening, and by the time they crossed the threshold, exhaustion dulled their senses to the faint wrongness in the air.

The scent of freshly baked bread still lingered, masking the faint trace of oiled leather and steel—the only signs that another presence had entered their home.

He remained hidden in the shadows. Waiting for the moment.

As he watched, he took in every detail. Their faces stayed with him. His mind never let him forget.

He watched the young boy, no older than six—wide-eyed—staring at his baby sister cradled in their mother's arms. Unsure of what to say, the boy shyly offered one of his wooden toys, holding it out to her with both hands.

Their mother chuckled. "She is a bit too young to play, but soon you two will be running and chasing each other through the fields," she told him.

The boy beamed and looked up at her. "I will teach her how to play soldier!" he said excitedly.

Both parents laughed at that, their smiles full of warmth.

He remembered the father's voice as he called the boy over, placing a hand on his shoulder.

"You are her older brother," the man had said, ruffling his son's hair. "One day, you will have to be there for her—when we no longer can. Keep her safe. Especially from the village boys when they come sniffing around."

The father had smiled at that. So had the boy.

Belaric had felt a sharp pang of guilt then—not because the words were wrong, but because they no longer mattered. There would be no one left to protect. No one to grow, to remember, to carry those promises forward. They would all die at his hand.

The mother's voice had come softer, warm as the candlelight that once filled their home. "You are more beautiful than any princess," she had whispered, brushing a wisp of hair from the infant's brow. "And remember, no matter what the world says, no matter how hard it gets—we love you. You are ours."

The words ate at Belaric, but his mind refused to grant him peace. This was his punishment—and he deserved it, and far worse. Again and again, he relived their final moments.

The father sat in his chair, one arm draped over the back, relaxed, unaware of the blade that would soon find his spine. The mother cradled the infant, rocking gently, humming a song under her breath. The boy played near the hearth, stacking wooden figures in a row, his eyes heavy with sleep.

The father shifted, pushing himself up from the chair, stretching out his shoulders as if shaking off the weight of the day. That was when Belaric struck.

He stepped out of the shadows, silent as death itself. His hand moved fast, the dagger already free from his belt as he crossed the floor. The blade spun through the dim light, steel catching the fire's glow for the briefest instant before sinking into the father's back.

The man gasped, his hand shooting out, grasping at empty air as his body stiffened. Before he could utter another word, Belaric was behind him. One hand clamped the man's chin; the other cupped the back of his skull. With a sharp, practiced twist, the vertebrae gave way—snapping with a sound that cracked through the room.

The mother's head shot up, her eyes going wide, horror written on her face as she took in the sight of her husband now lying motionless on the floor.

The boy turned, hands frozen mid-play, his small frame trembling as fear took hold. He stared at the dark figure standing over his father's limp body. His mouth worked silently, trying to form a word—or a cry—but no sound came. Tiny fingers clutched a carved wooden toy to his chest like a shield, knuckles pale. He did not run. He did not scream. Fear had rooted him in place, locking his limbs with the cruel weight of instinct betrayed.

Then Belaric stepped forward, and instinct finally shattered the stillness. The boy's expression twisted in horror, his mouth opening in a sharp, panicked scream. Belaric closed the distance in a heartbeat and seized him, pinning him down hard onto the floor. The boy flailed and kicked, fists pounding against leather, his screams rising into frantic, broken wails as he twisted beneath the assassin's grip.

But the struggle was meaningless. He was too weak, too small.

With his free hand, he reached into his cloak and retrieved a small leather pouch, flicking it open with practiced ease. He pinched a measure of the fine white powder between his fingers and raised it to his lips.

The boy screamed again, shrill and desperate.

Belaric blew the powder into the child's face.

The effect was immediate. The boy coughed violently, his throat constricting as the dust scorched its way into his lungs. His cries turned to choking gasps, fingers clawing at his own neck as though trying to pull the air back into his body.

Belaric let go and leaned back, watching the child's body twitch as he struggled for breath.

The mother continued to watch in horror, frozen as her son's screams turned to choking gasps. She clutched the baby tighter, her eyes wide, lips trembling. Her body twitched—as if some part of her wanted to move, to lunge, to scream—but nothing came. No sound. No step forward.

The fear held her fast. Not just fear of the man, but of what was happening—so sudden, so monstrous, it did not yet feel real.

Then she saw it—his fingers gave one last twitch, his chest gave no rise. He was gone.

Belaric rose to his feet slowly, deliberately, as if the act held no more weight than drawing breath. His hood obscured his face, yet his gaze remained heavy and unrelenting upon her.

That was when the fear cracked.

Something in his stillness told her the truth. He had not come to rob them or threaten them.

He had come to kill them all.

She surged to her feet, clutching the baby tight, and bolted for the door. Instinct took over—a desperate need to flee and protect what remained.

But Belaric was faster.

He crossed the space between them in three strides and caught her by the wrist, yanking her back with ease. She shrieked, twisting in his grip, her free hand clawing at his arm. Nails raked across leather and skin, but it did nothing. Her sobs came in frantic bursts, the words tumbling out between gasps.

"Please—please, do not—we will leave, I swear, we will go, just let us go," her voice cracked, thick with panic. "We did not mean to offend you—whatever we did, I am sorry, we are sorry—just let us go," she begged.

Her grip tightened around the baby. She was sobbing now, her whole body shaking beneath his grip.

"I will tell no one," she gasped. "No one will ever know you were here. I will take her and go—we will disappear. You will never see us again. I swear it to the gods, on my life. Just... just do not hurt her." She said, her voice trembling.

Gods, he thought, do not make me do this.

Her knees buckled, and she half-fell against him, still clutching the child as if she could shield her with nothing but bone and desperation. She buried her face against the infant's head, whispering frantic words only the baby could hear.

He could let them go. Right now. Just open his hand, step aside, and vanish into the dark. No one would ever know. But they would.

The masters would know. And he would pay the price. One slip, one flicker of disobedience—and everything he had built would be torn away.

Then, with a broken cry, the mother tried once more to pull away—but his grip held fast, unyielding as iron. There was no escaping him.

Belaric said nothing. His gaze had locked onto the child in her arms, the tiny face peeking from the bundle of cloth—peaceful, unaware.

She has not even seen her first winter; he thought. And I am here to end it before it begins.

The mother, still clinging to the infant, lifted her head slowly. Her tear-streaked eyes followed his.

And then she saw it.

A sharp inhale, a moment of stillness—then her shriek tore through the room, raw and piercing. Not a cry of pain, but of terror, of desperate understanding. Her fight renewed, her body twisted and thrashed against his grip, her screams turned wild, animalistic. She clawed at his arm, kicked at his legs, wrenched with everything she had—anything to break free, to put distance between him and the baby.

He felt the frantic struggle, the desperate clawing at his arm, but it was like a kitten against hardened steel. Belaric's grip tightened, unyielding.

"Please," she gasped, her voice breaking between sobs. "She is just a baby—please—"

He wanted to say yes. Gods, he wanted to say yes.

But the words had barely left her lips before he blew the powder into her face. Her body jerked, muscles seizing as the toxin took hold. Her arms tightened around the child in one last, desperate attempt to hold on, but the strength bled from her limbs as her knees buckled. She sagged against him, breath ragged, her grip faltering until the baby slipped from her grasp.

Belaric caught the child before she could fall.

For a moment, he just held her. She was so small.

The mark beside the baby's eyes was barely noticeable, a faint blemish that most would mistake for a birthmark. The family had assumed as much. Belaric recognized the truth. He had trained his eyes to see them, to recognize them before they became undeniable.

He sighed, his breath slow, controlled. A deliberate inhale, a careful exhale.

"I am sorry," he murmured, though he did not know if it was the mother, the child, or himself.

He leaned down and placed the baby beside its mother. The woman's chest still rose and fell, but it was shallow, slowing. He reached into his pocket, pulling a small vial of liquid free. Tilting the baby's head back, he uncorked the vial and let a single drop fall onto her tongue.

"It does not hurt," he whispered. It was the least he could do for her, he thought.

The baby stirred faintly in his arms, a soft noise escaping her lips—more breath than sound. Her tiny fingers curled reflexively, clutching at nothing. For a heartbeat, she looked up at him, eyes unfocused but wide, searching without understanding.

Then the poison began to work.

Her body tensed briefly, a flicker of discomfort, before the tension slipped away. Her breathing grew shallow, then shallower still. No cry came. No struggle. Just a slow, inevitable stillness spreading through her small frame.

Belaric closed his eyes, exhaling through his nose. He had done this so many times before—and yet something about it now weighed differently. The Black Vow had trained him to be efficient, to be precise. But no amount of precision could stop the rot that had begun to fester inside him.

His fingers curled tighter around the vial before he tucked it away. The work was not finished; he told himself.

He moved to the father, the silent body a dark shape on the floor. With a quick, practiced motion, he plucked his dagger free from the man's back, wiped the blade clean on his tunic and sheathed it. Then, moving to the pack he had stashed near the window earlier in the night, he pulled free a large flask of oil. He spread it carefully, methodically—across the floorboards, onto the support beams, over the cooling bodies. He made sure the flames would be hungry, insatiable.

When everything was ready, he turned to the hearth. The fire the father had built earlier that evening still burned, its embers red-hot. Belaric reached down, plucking a burning log from the pit.

He touched the flame to the oil.

The fire leapt to life instantly, licking across the floor, eager to consume everything it touched. The scent of burning wood filled the air, thick and suffocating. Soon, it would be something else—flesh, bone, memory.

Belaric slung the pack over his shoulder before climbing out the window. As he did, the flames spread behind him, heat licking at his back as he dropped silently into the cold night. He landed with practiced ease; the earth was damp beneath his boots, the night air sharp against his skin. Smoke curled into the sky behind him, a dark stain against the stars.

By morning, nothing would remain but charred bones buried beneath the ashes, nameless and forgotten. The smoke would rise toward the heavens, carrying away lives that no longer existed, erasing them as though they had never been.

His jaw tightened, the muscles stiff beneath his skin. It was what they demanded, he thought, his teeth gritted.

His thoughts soured further, bitter as old blood on steel. He hated them—the gilded, the privileged, who deemed a common-born child with the Valasar mark a threat to their divine lie. Their fear, a cold, dry rustle like dead leaves, whispered through the land, demanding more and more innocent blood. For years he had silenced the truth for them, putting innocent children born with the Valasar to the blade, upholding a deception wrapped in silk and scripture. If the gods had truly chosen the nobles, they would not need men like him.

A single tear traced his cheek, warm against the sharp night chill, before vanishing into the damp earth. His jaw ached from clenching, his shoulders rigid with tension that refused to ease. He let out a slow breath, willing the tightness in his chest to fade, but it remained—a dull, unshakable weight pressing down on him. He let it go. Weakness had no place here, he told himself. Not for men like him, not if he wanted to live. His fingers curled into a fist at his side, nails pressing into his palm, grounding himself in pain as if it could strip away the doubt.

The Black Vow did not suffer weakness.

The bray of Eddaross pulled him from the dark coil of his thoughts. He looked up, exhaling slowly. The storm-gray stallion pawed at the ground, impatient as ever. Moonlight slipped through the tangle of branches overhead, silvering his coat until he looked pale as a ghost—a spirit from the old songs, restless and waiting.

His oldest companion. His only friend, save for her.

He ran a hand along the horse's neck, feeling the steady rise and fall of breath beneath his palm. Solid. Reliable. Unshaken.

"Well, old boy, it is done now," he murmured. "We can go home. Are you ready?"

Eddaross brayed again and stomped a hoof in reply.

A small smile found its way onto Belaric's lips, brief and fleeting. He strapped the pack onto Eddaross's saddle, cinching the straps tight. He swung into the saddle, settling his weight. Eddaross knew the way. He always did. The reins were little more than a formality.

They rode in silence, save for the steady rhythm of hooves against damp earth. The forest thinned, giving way to open land, the dirt road winding toward home. Ahead, the path stretched long and unbroken, cutting through a world that felt emptier with every mile.

Several days of travel. Long enough for the scent of burning wood to fade—though the memory never did.

Several days to try and forget the father falling lifelessly to the ground.

The young boy, thrashing and screaming, as if any of it could save him.

The mother, who fought back even in desperation just for the chance to protect her child.

And the baby.

Whose only crime was being born with the gift of the gods.

It sickened Belaric to his core. He had become what they wanted him to be—a blade without a sheath, a monster with a human face.

But despite it all, he had done it.

His eyes, fixed on the unchanging road, sometimes lost their focus, the distant landscape dissolving into the same repeating horrors that played behind his lids.

He exhaled slowly, pressing his knuckles against his thigh as if pain might drive the thoughts away. They clung to him. The road stretched ahead—endless, unchanging—cut through lands that had long since blurred together. Eddaross needed no guidance. Belaric let the horse find the path while he focused on the only thing that mattered: getting home. Not just to a place, but to the life he had carved out, to the only person he trusted. He needed to shake off the stench of ash and blood to find a moment of solace.

He reached into his saddlebag, his fingers closing around the smooth, cool skin of an apple. He pulled it out, its unassuming presence a stark contrast to the inferno still burning in his mind. Taking a bite, the crisp sweetness exploded on his tongue, and he clutched onto that simple, clean sensation, willing his thoughts away from the ashes and screams. He needed a different warmth, a different truth to hold on to.

He needed to be with the only woman he had ever loved. Renna.

His mind, seeking refuge from the weight of his deeds, clung to her. The image of her face bloomed in his memory, and he was back in

Greymoor, standing in the hushed morning light, watching the way she moved with flawless grace.

Back to a morning after another job. It had been one of those that left a weight behind, the kind that clung to his bones long after the blood had dried. He had not intended to linger in Greymoor—just another town, another blur of unfamiliar faces—but the ache in his muscles told him to rest, and for once, he listened.

He had just stabled Eddaross, brushing the sweat from the stallion's flanks, when he saw her.

She stood behind a wooden stall, half in shadow, half caught in the hush of morning light. Tall for a woman, but not in a way that invited notice—she carried her height with the ease born of knowing her own shape in the world. Straight-backed, still. Not idle, but present. There was a quiet certainty in the way she stood, the kind that did not ask for attention but often got it.

Her hair caught the sun like a struck match—auburn, streaked gold at the edges. A loose braid hung over one shoulder, already unraveling from wind and work. Not careless, but unconcerned. There was nothing polished about her, nothing that felt rehearsed. The red of her hair made him think of autumn leaves clinging to their branches, of fire before it dimmed, wild and fading all at once.

Then her eyes found his—green, not the dark hush of the forest, but something gentler. Spring's first bloom, or rain settling over moss. Bright enough to catch, soft enough to keep. They held him for a breath longer than they should have, watching not with caution or coyness but with the kind of interest that felt... earned.

And then there were the freckles.

They ran wildly across her nose, her cheeks, her collarbone where her blouse hung open at the neck. Not dainty or sparse, but a scattershot mess of gold dust, like stars thrown from careless hands. He imagined tracing them, not to count, but to follow—wondering if they led somewhere worth the trouble.

But it was her smile that undid him.

Not the trained simper of court girls. Not the angled flirt of tavern women with practiced hands and sharper aims. Hers was brighter than both, and far more dangerous. There was no artifice in it. It rose without hesitation, as if she had never learned the cruelty of withholding warmth.

And it landed like a blow.

Men like him did not get smiles like that. They got nods. Glances. Measured courtesy. But never warmth. Never something meant to reach past the eyes and into the ribs.

And gods, it reached.

He was tired, blood still dried beneath his fingernails, the weight of his work pressing on his back. He had come here to forget, to let exhaustion dull his edges before the next job dragged him back into the dark. But standing there, looking at her, he realized something strange—he was hungry.

Not just for food, though the ache in his stomach reminded him that it had been too long since his last meal. No, this was something else. Something deeper. Something he had not let himself feel in a long time, something he had buried beneath steel and silence.

He swallowed and forced his feet to move. The closer he got, the more his mind scrambled for something to say, the words slipping through his fingers like water.

He cleared his throat. "How much for the pears?"

She looked up from stacking apples, her green eyes flicking over him, weighing him the way merchants did—not just the cloak and the coin purse, but the wear in his boots, the way he stood, the scars on his knuckles. Most would have been wary. She was not. Instead, she smiled.

"Two coppers each," she said. "Unless you are buying a dozen. Then I will pretend I like you and make it twenty."

His brow lifted slightly. "Are you that generous with all your customers?"

She shrugged. "Only the ones who look like they need feeding."

He tried asking about plums, but she simply tapped a finger against the edge of a crate. "You strike me as more of an apple man."

His eyes flicked to the stack beside her. "How much for the apples?"

"Three coppers. But for you? Four," she said with a small grin forming on her lips.

That made him pause. He narrowed his eyes slightly. "You just said you liked feeding people."

"I do. But I enjoy charging people even more," she told him, the grin widening.

His lips twitched. He reached into his pouch, handed her the coins, and took the apple. A nod. A quiet thanks. He turned to leave.

But he did not leave.

Instead, he hesitated, glancing back as she moved on to another customer. The curve of her cheek when she laughed. The way her hands moved—quick and confident—as she weighed fruit in a cloth sack.

When she noticed him still standing there, she came back to him.

"How much for an apple?" he asked.

She blinked, then let out a soft giggle. "You just bought one."

He stared at her, then at the apple in his hand, then back at the stack. What in the gods' names was he doing? His face burned. He had fought men twice his size, slit throats in the dark, cut down anyone who got in his way. And yet, he did not know what to do with this girl laughing at him.

"Right." He cleared his throat. "Then I will take another."

She shook her head, biting her lip as if holding back laughter. He handed her more coins, took the apple, and retreated, his face still burning.

But he looked back.

And when she caught him staring, he swore her smile lingered just a little longer.

That was the moment. The decision, though unspoken, settled deep within him: he would return.

After that, he took every assignment that brought him near Grey-moor.

A noble whispering about a common-born child born with the Valasar? He was there. A quiet job in the dead of night, ensuring a nameless infant never saw its first winter? Consider it done.

He told himself it was the same as always. Just another order, another loose thread cut away before it could unravel the nobles' lies.

But it was not the same.

Because every time he left the blood behind, every time he slipped from shadow into town, he found himself drifting toward the market square.

Toward her.

He told himself it meant nothing. That he was just playing a role, blending in like he always had. That stopping at her stall, buying her apples, watching the way she tucked her hair behind her ear when she laughed—it was just habit.

But he was not fooling himself

Because for a few stolen moments, standing there with the apples in his hands and her voice in his ears, he almost felt like something other than a killer.

The memory drifted like mist through his mind, clinging even as the night pressed in around him.

The road ahead was swallowed by darkness, with the moon a sliver of silver above the trees. Eddaross moved steadily beneath him, hooves muffled by damp earth, the scent of pine and moss sharp in the cool air. It should have been refreshing. A relief from the thick stench of smoke that refused to leave him.

But it was not.

The fire might be behind him, but its presence lingered, settling into his skin like something that would not wash away.

He tried to hold on to the warmth of Renna's memory—the way the morning sun turned her hair to fire, the way her laugh had slipped so effortlessly between the cracks of his walls.

But tonight, the dead were louder.

The boy's wide, terrified eyes. The father's strangled last breath. The mother's whispered words meant for a daughter who would never hear them.

He dragged a hand down his face, pressing his fingers into his brow as if he could knead the thoughts away. It would not stop. Not for days. Maybe weeks. The memories always clawed their way back, a persistent ache that settled in the quiet hours. So he forced his mind back to her—to a moment untouched by blood. The first time she had asked him to take a walk with her.

It had taken him weeks—weeks of lingering at her stall, weeks of clumsy conversation, weeks of waiting for a moment that never seemed to come. She had smiled at him, teased him, sold him more apples than any man could reasonably eat. He had not found the courage to ask. But fate, it seemed, had been kind to him that day, he remembered thinking.

It had been a quiet afternoon, the air thick with the scent of cut hay and river water. He had been leaning against a half-rotted post near the blacksmith's shop, watching her pack away the last of her unsold fruit. She moved with the same quiet efficiency she always did, tucking apples and pears into baskets, wiping down the old wooden stall as if it were something precious. He had meant to leave. He always did. But that day, his feet did not move.

"Closing early?" His own voice startled him, cutting through the murmur of the square.

She glanced up, pushing a loose strand of copper hair behind her ear. "It is a slow day."

He hesitated. He hesitated every time he spoke to her.

She did not.

"You could walk with me," she said, as if the thought had just occurred to her, as if it were the simplest thing in the world.

His throat went dry. He had killed men without blinking, cut through flesh and bone without hesitation, but this—this was something else entirely. And yet, he heard himself say, "Okay."

She led the way, basket in hand, past the last few vendors and down the worn dirt path that followed the river's edge. He walked beside her, silent at first, uncertain of what he was supposed to say. The town stretched behind them, the market square shrinking in the distance, until it was just the two of them—the slow lap of water against the shore, the hum of insects thick in the air.

But as they walked, the silence softened. One question turned into another, a quiet smile into a shared laugh. They had talked. About nothing. About everything. He remembered the way her voice had softened when she spoke of her mother, the way she laughed when he admitted he had never learned to swim. He remembered how light he had felt, how unburdened. Like, for the first time in his life, he had been someone other than the Black Vow's shadow.

The road jolted beneath him as Eddaross stumbled slightly over a rut in the dirt, dragging him back into the present. He exhaled. That had been years ago. Another lifetime. And yet, he still carried the memory with him.

Two hours later, he saw the glow of torches in the distance. Mosswick. The place men rode through without stopping, a town wedged between nowhere and nothing, where the roads forked like an old scar. It had never been prosperous, never been grand—just a cluster of weathered buildings leaning against one another like drunks at the end of a long night. A place where travelers stopped when they had no better option, and where those who had nowhere else to go stayed.

The town slumped against the riverbank, its buildings a patchwork of old stone and splintering wood, the streets uneven, littered with deep wagon ruts and the remnants of yesterday's rain. The only light came from the torches along the main road and the dull glow of the Broken Tusk Inn, the town's only establishment worth mentioning. Mosswick was not the place men built dreams in—it was the kind of place they fled to when dreams had failed them. Which made it the perfect place for a man like him.

Belaric dismounted, swinging stiffly from the saddle. He led Eddaross into the stable, moving quietly, carefully. The stallion snorted as he loosened the straps, large dark eyes watching him in the dim light.

"Rest now, old boy," he murmured, brushing his hand along the horse's flank. "We will be gone before anyone starts asking questions."

He pulled the saddle free, setting it on the rail beside the stall, then unbuckled the reins and hung them neatly over a hook. He unstrapped his pack from the saddle, the familiar weight settling on his shoulders. Eddaross gave a slow, heavy exhale in reply, shifting in the straw as Belaric stepped away.

He wasted no time. He moved like a shadow, keeping to the edges of the buildings, his boots silent against the muddy ground.

The Broken Tusk Inn loomed above him, its timber beams blackened with age, the windows thick with grime. The sign above the door—once a proud carving of a great boar—was now splintered, its tusks worn down to little more than jagged stumps. He did not enter through the door. He climbed. The stone wall was uneven, pockmarked with years of decay, making the ascent easy. Hand over hand, he pulled himself up, his boots finding purchase along the old wooden beams. Within moments, he reached the second floor, his fingers curling over the window ledge of the room he had rented earlier.

A quick glance. No movement inside. Satisfied, he slid the window open, slipped inside, and closed it behind him.

The room was small, the air heavy with the scent of damp wood and old ale. A single candle flickered atop a rickety desk, its flame swaying in the draft from the window. Belaric exhaled and stripped away the night's work. His armor was black as pitch, stitched from layers of supple leather, reinforced where it mattered most—across the chest, the ribs, the forearms. Years of use had worn and scarred the surface, yet it remained flexible enough for silent movement. The buckles, tarnished bronze, were dulled to avoid catching the light.

A dagger was strapped to his thigh, a second hidden along the small of his back. He also wore a half-dozen small throwing knives, each tucked into a separate sheath woven into the lining of his tunic. He removed them all methodically, setting the collection of steel on the bedside table. Tools of his trade. The only thing as familiar as the ghosts that followed him.

Once he peeled away the armor, he reached for his dark brown robe and pulled it over his head. The fabric was soft, worn, and entirely unremarkable—the kind of thing that made men forget his face. He fell onto the bed with a heavy sigh, letting exhaustion take hold.

But sleep did not come easily. His mind was a traitor. It conjured images he did not want—the charred ruins of the house; the boy reaching for a sister who would never reach back; the smell of burning flesh sticking to his skin. They would haunt him. A relentless tide of ghosts.

He stared at the ceiling, willing them away, until, at long last, his mind dulled and the quiet came. And finally, he slipped into a much-needed sleep.

Belaric's rest was brief. Sleep never stayed long, and when the first light of dawn crept through the window, it found him already awake, eyes open, staring at the ceiling. He exhaled, pushing himself up. He needed to move. The family's home in Brindlewood was now nothing more than a smoldering ruin, and the more distance he put between himself and that place, the better.

He dressed quickly, pulling on his traveling gear—a sturdy, well-worn tunic of dark brown wool, layered beneath a thick, patched cloak that had seen more miles than most men. His trousers were re-inforced at the knees, the leather boots scuffed and dirt-streaked but built for the road. A belt cinched at his waist, holding a small pouch, a skinning knife, and a waterskin. Nothing fine. Nothing that would draw attention. Just the clothing of a man used to long roads and rough living.

His packs were already waiting, packed the night before out of habit. He slung one over his shoulder, checked for the weight of his coin pouch, then made his way downstairs to the common room.

The innkeeper was exactly as he remembered him—a large man, built more like a barrel than a man, his gut stretching the seams of his stained tunic. His long black beard, streaked with gray, hung past his chest, thick and unruly, as if he had not trimmed it in years. His arms, despite the layer of fat, carried the strength of a man who had spent his youth swinging hammers and hauling kegs.

The man barely looked up from scrubbing a plate. "Already off, are you?" His voice was deep, rough from years of shouting over drunken patrons.

Belaric gave a small nod. "Need to get moving." He settled at a table near the hearth, though the fire had long since burned to embers. "Best to eat first."

The innkeeper grunted, wiping his hands on his apron before shuffling toward the kitchen. A moment later, he returned with a wooden plate bearing a simple breakfast—two eggs, their edges crisp from the pan, a few strips of thin-sliced pork, and a biscuit smeared with butter that was already beginning to melt. He set it down with a mug of ale and held out a meaty palm.

Belaric wordlessly placed four coppers in it.

The innkeeper glanced at them before pocketing the coins. "Eat fast. The weather's dry now, but the roads will be a mess if the storm they are talking about rolls in."

Belaric smirked slightly. "Always looking out for your customers?"

"Looking out for my coin," the man corrected, scratching his beard before returning to his work.

The food was simple but filling, and Belaric wasted no time finishing it. He chased it down with a swig of ale, wiped his mouth with the back of his hand, and pushed back from the table. "Good meal."

The innkeeper gave a grunt that could have meant anything.

Outside, the town was just beginning to stir. A thin mist clung to the streets, curling in the dips between cobblestones. The baker, visible through his shop window, was already at work, rolling out dough under the glow of a single lantern. Across the road, the blacksmith had kindled his forge, stretching his arms as he prepared for another day of hammering steel.

Belaric moved toward the stables, spotting a boy mucking out the stalls. The kid—freckled, thin, maybe twelve at most—paused as he approached.

"Fetch my saddle," Belaric said.

The boy wiped his nose on his sleeve and hurried off without a word.

Belaric turned to Eddaross. The stallion flicked his ears forward, letting out a low huff as he stepped closer. "Morning," Belaric murmured, reaching into his pocket. He pulled out an apple and held it out on his palm. Eddaross took it eagerly, crunching into the fruit, juice running down his thick lips. He let out a satisfied neigh, bobbing his head.

By the time the stallion had finished, the boy had returned, saddle in hand, still slightly too small for the job but working fast. He tightened the straps, checking them twice as Belaric watched. The kid was good—efficient and precise.

When Belaric finished, he tossed the boy a copper. "Good hands."

The boy caught the coin and grinned, wiping his forehead with the back of his sleeve before ducking back into the stable.

Belaric secured his packs, double-checking the weight of everything. It would not do to forget something here. Satisfied, he pulled himself into the saddle, shifting his weight before patting Eddaross' flank. The horse responded instantly, stepping forward, his hooves dull against the dirt road.

Mosswick was easy enough to move through at this hour. Most doors were still shut, and the streets only lightly traveled. Of the few that were awake, even fewer paid him any mind, too preoccupied with their own business.

That was what he had always liked about this place. It was quiet. Unassuming. People left you alone.

And that was why he could never stay.

With a last glance over his shoulder, he nudged Eddaross forward, and the two of them disappeared down the road, leaving Mosswick behind.

2

Belaric pressed on, Eddaross's hooves tapping out a steady rhythm against the dirt road. The journey was one familiar to him—it was carved into memory by habit and necessity. He had stayed a night in Branloch village, where the roofs sagged under their own weight and the innkeeper forgot names but never a coin. Another night at Tarinnhill, where the stone buildings clung to the hillside like stubborn moss. He had lodged there more times than he cared to count, and the innkeepers always found him a bed and a fair price without questions.

The road narrowed and widened in turns, winding through hills lined with frost-limbed trees and fields brittle with the last breath of winter. Smoke from distant chimneys curled against a pale sky. He passed farmers mending fences, traders with tired eyes, children bold enough to ask what he carried in his packs. Trinkets, mostly. Things bought cheap and sold dear. A few villagers took them off his hands, enough to justify the weight.

He kept moving. Roads changed, faces blurred, but the path to Vorinfall never lost its shape. The city waited like a question he did not want to answer.

After many days of travel, he was well into the late afternoon; the sun bled across the horizon, Vorinfall emerged from the distant haze. Its formidable walls rose like the jagged crest of a great stone beast, a testament to its wealth and the constant flow of trade that made it the kingdom's pulsing heart. Even from this distance, the port was a forest of masts and sails, ships from every known land crowding its harbors, the towering cranes ceaselessly moving cargo under the watchful eyes of dockmasters.

Beyond the bustling port, Vorinfall's walls loomed high—weathered but unbroken—a testament to both its wealth and the dangers that came with it. The banners of Vorinfall hung heavy over the ramparts, deep red cloth bearing the image of a steel-clad knight, sword drawn, shield raised, a dozen arrows buried in its battered face. A symbol not of untouched glory, but of the strength to endure.

The city bore the name of Lord Bastan Vorinfall, the last to stand in a doomed retreat. With his shield shattered and his men fleeing behind him, he held the line alone—unmoving, unbowed, unbroken. His death had not been in vain, and the city built in the wake of his sacrifice wore his name like armor.

The city's defenses were more than mere ornament; mercenaries, city guards, and royal guards patrolled the gates and streets to ensure order—and they were not afraid to break bones to maintain it.

Within the walls, the city itself was a tangled sprawl of trade districts, grand merchant halls, and teeming slums that clung to the edges like barnacles on a ship's hull. The wealthiest sat atop the terraces, their stone manors overlooking the chaos below, while the poor waded through the filth of the lower streets, scraping by on whatever coin the tides of commerce left behind.

Belaric took in the sight, inhaling the salted air thick with the scent of fish, brine, and damp wood. He leaned forward, patting Eddaross's thick neck.

"Not much longer, old boy," he murmured. "Fresh apples and a dry stall. You have earned it."

Before the promise was even made, the horse started galloping and quickly covered the final stretch of road. Within minutes, the city's towering gates loomed ahead, set into high walls of weathered stone.

The guards stood in their polished half-plate, a mix of steel and chain glinting in the fading light. Their dark red surcoats bore the crest of Vorinfall. Each man had a longsword strapped to his hip and a spear in hand. Above, more men paced the ramparts with bows across their backs, their eyes trained on the throng below: merchants fretting over ledgers, travelers squinting against the sun, peasants clutching the last of their coin as they waited for entry.

Belaric dismounted without thought, a fluid motion carved into the muscle by repetition. The line of people crawled forward, a trickle of movement in the dust and heat. He understood this place—its noise, its rhythm, the way it pretended order while teetering on the edge of collapse.

When he reached the front, one guard peeled off the line, a grin already forming.

"Belaric," the man said, voice rough with smoke and memory. "The famous traveling merchant returns from yet another grand venture."

Jorric. Same slouched stance, same weathered grin. He stood with the casual readiness of a man who had seen more fights than he bragged about—and lost fewer than he should have.

Belaric smirked, brushing the dust from his coat. "Famous? That is generous. But I will not argue about the grand venture."

Jorric gave a knowing nod, his spear resting easily across one shoulder like an old friend. "Sell all your wares, then? Or did some poor fool actually haggle you down?"

Belaric patted Eddaross's flank. "Nearly. Just a few trinkets left—for the soft-hearted or slow-witted."

Jorric clicked his tongue. "You could sell water to a drowning man." His gaze drifted to the stallion, lingering. "You will never convince me that beast's just a horse. Moves like he knows he is better than the rest of us."

Belaric ran a hand down the stallion's neck. "He probably is. You would have better luck sweet-talking a dragon out of its hoard than getting him to leave my side. Besides, Renna is fonder of him than of me."

Jorric barked a laugh. "Hells, Belaric, that is hardly an achievement. I have met lizards more charming than you."

He leaned in, exaggerated the motion, and sniffed. Then winced. "Gods, man. Did you bathe in the saddle?"

Belaric raised an arm, sniffed cautiously, and grimaced. "Fair."

"Do us all a mercy and wash, will you? There is only so much stench the city walls can hold." Jorric clapped him on the shoulder, firm and familiar. "Go on. Renna will be waiting. Tell her my wife's coming by tomorrow for apples. Says they taste better from her hands than from mine."

"They probably do," Belaric said, a smile tugging at his mouth despite the wear in his bones. "I will tell her."

He gave Jorric a nod, mounted his horse and led him through the gates. The checkpoint noise faded behind him, swallowed by the city's broader hum—a hundred streets alive with the business of surviving. But for a moment, that shared laughter, the dust, the old soldier's grin, it almost felt like home.

The stench hit him first.

The lower district was as it had always been—clogged with unwashed bodies, the sour tang of sweat and refuse thick in the air. Narrow streets twisted like tangled veins, lined with crooked houses of timber and crumbling brick. The gutters ran slick with filth, and the stagnant puddles reeked of rot. Beggars sat hunched in doorways, their hands outstretched, their eyes hollow. Children darted through the crowd, quick-fingered and barefoot, weaving through merchants barking their wares in hoarse voices.

Belaric rested a hand on his coin pouch, not out of fear, but habit—one born of the merchant class like he pretended to be. A man with coin should act as if he feared losing it, especially in this part of the city. In truth, no beggar or cutpurse on these streets could lay a finger on him without losing a hand. Still, the role required more than clothes and wares; it demanded mannerisms, instincts dulled just enough to seem real. The feigned fear felt like a bitter taste on his tongue, a lie that chafed more than any chain.

His gaze flicked toward a woman in tattered and filth-covered robes, crouched beneath the awning of a collapsed stall, cradling a bundle of rags to her chest. A child, he realized. The small, thin hand curled around her wrist was barely more than bone. She was not begging and was not even looking up. Just sitting there, rocking slightly, staring at nothing.

He took a slow breath through his nose and pressed forward. He had long since learned that pity was worth little in places like this. Coin was the only kindness these people could use, and even that had a way of finding the wrong hands. He had given before—paid for meals, left a few coppers in a street child's palm—but it never seemed to make a difference. For every mouth fed, there were a hundred more left empty.

That was Vorinfall.

He rode slowly through the district, his horse picking its way carefully over refuse and sidestepping outstretched hands. Their eyes followed him—measuring not him, but his horse, the cut of his cloak, the coin they imagined tucked inside his satchel. To them, he was just another merchant with a fine horse and a heavier purse than sense. And maybe he was—until one of them tried to test it.

It was not long before he reached the great iron gate that separated the lower city from the middle district—a clear divide between those who clawed for survival and those who had already won it.

The guards stood rigid, faces set like carved stone, their eyes scanning for the desperate and the unworthy. The rules were simple—no beggars, no vagrants, no filth past these gates. Any peasant caught trying to slip into the wealthier district under false pretenses would find themselves shackled in a cell by nightfall, or worse, dead, and tossed into the street as a warning.

Belaric kept his gaze forward, his thoughts lingering as he neared the gate. How many men beyond these walls had once clawed their way out of the dirt, only to forget what it felt like to be buried by it? How many had pressed trembling hands against the iron, desperate to be seen—only to one day stand on the other side and pretend they never had?

He knew because he had lived it. Born with nothing, unwanted even by the woman who bore him, he had grown up a gutter rat with no name and no chance. He had never known his father. No one ever gave him the luxury of dreaming. And while he loathed the Black Vow for what it had taken from him, he could not deny what it had given. Coin. Skills. A home—cold and cruel as it was. Without it, he never would have found Renna. Never would have known love.

That was the curse of it all. The Black Vow had shaped him into something dangerous, something feared—and in doing so, had handed him the very things he now fought to keep. His hands were stained with its blood, but his heart still carried the pieces it had not managed to break.

He pushed the thoughts aside as he moved closer to the gate.

A guard caught sight of him and gave a curt nod, stepping aside without question. Belaric barely slowed, crossing the threshold into the middle district as the gate loomed behind him, shutting out the world of the forgotten.

The shift was immediate.

The middle district was clean, its streets swept and wide, paved with well-laid stones that did not threaten to trip a man with every step. The houses here were finer, built of solid oak and pale stone, their windows adorned with glass instead of ragged cloth. Stalls lined the main thoroughfare, offering everything from exotic spices to masterfully crafted blades. Jewelers displayed their finest pieces, their gemstones catching the last of the day's light, while perfumers lured passing women with delicate vials of imported oils. The air smelled of roasted meat and fresh bread, a welcome reprieve from the rancid musk of the lower city.

Belaric navigated the crowd with the ease of a man who no longer needed to look where he stepped. The city had changed, grown louder and heavier, but the rhythm of the streets still beat in time with his boots. He passed merchants shouting their final bargains, customers haggling like breath was currency, and children weaving through legs with sticky fingers and sharper eyes.

He turned into the stables, where the scent of hay, sweat, and horseflesh folded around him like an old cloak.

Darius was there, as he always was.

The old stable master moved like a man built from rope and iron—worn but still holding. His beard had surrendered to age, a wild, tangled white, and his shoulders stooped under decades of labor, but his hands were steady. Strong. The kind of strong that did not need proving anymore.

He looked up at the sound of hooves, squinting through the gloom. Then, that familiar, half-crooked smile crept across his weathered face.

"Back already?" he asked, voice a gravelly rasp. "Trade must have been good. Or maybe you finally ran out of honest folk to swindle."

Belaric slid from the saddle and tossed him the reins with practiced ease. "A little of both. The honest ones paid better, though."

Darius gave a grunt of approval, running a hand down Eddaross's flank like he was checking the grain of fine wood. "You have kept him well. Most merchants treat their horses like coin purses—useful until emptied."

Belaric's hand found the stallion's neck, the warmth beneath his palm as steady and familiar as a heartbeat. "He is more than a horse. Never let me down. Not once."

Darius did not answer at first, just nodded as he began unfastening the saddle straps with the precision of muscle memory. "Loyal beasts are rare," he muttered. "Better than most men I have known."

Belaric did not argue.

He drew his coin pouch—worn soft; the leather thinned at the edges—and pressed a few coppers into Darius's calloused palm. The old man did not count them. Just nodded again, and tucked them away like they had always been his.

"I will see him fed and brushed," Darius said. "He will sleep better than you will tonight."

Belaric smirked faintly and reached into a saddlebag, fishing out two red apples. He held one out, and Eddaross took it with a crunch loud enough to echo off the stable walls.

"You spoil him," Darius said, shaking his head.

"He has earned it," Belaric replied, offering the second. The stallion did not hesitate.

With a grunt, Belaric slung the packs over his shoulder. The weight of travel always felt heavier at the journey's end.

Darius watched him for a long moment, thumb brushing his beard in thought. "That wife of yours," he said, almost absently. "She has been pacing since you left. Said, if you do not return on time, she will come drag you back herself."

Belaric let a ghost of a smile pass across his face. "She would too."

"Then do not keep her waiting," Darius replied.

The old man gave a half-hearted wave, already turning back to the next stall. His work never ended, only paused between hoofbeats.

Belaric stepped back onto the street as dusk settled like ash across the city. The market was winding down, merchants pulling in awnings, locking coin boxes with weary sighs. The smell of roasted meat still lingered, clinging to the cobbles with the last warmth of the day. Light thinned and stretched between buildings, shadows lengthening like old debts, and Belaric moved among them like someone who belonged.

As he walked, his grip on the pack slung over his shoulder tightened. Not the one carrying trinkets and goods from his journey, but the other—the one that never saw the inside of his home.

He turned down a narrow side street, his movements deliberate but unhurried. The alley ahead was the same as always, tucked between a seamstress's shop and a storehouse, where the stacked crates and shadows provided cover. He slowed, glancing once over his shoulder, scanning the street for lingering eyes.

Empty.

The city had already begun to settle for the night, the last of the merchants retreating behind bolted doors, the scent of fresh bread and cooking fires replacing the day's dust and sweat. Still, habit demanded caution.

He stepped into the alley, pressing deeper between the crates, where the darkness swallowed him whole. With practiced ease, he knelt, pulling a loose stone free from the base of the wall. Beneath it, a hollow just large enough to conceal the pack waited undisturbed. He stowed it carefully—the weight of leather, steel, and silence settling into the space before he replaced the stone, smoothing dirt over its edges.

Hidden. Forgotten. Just as it should be.

Belaric exhaled slowly, rolling his shoulders before stepping into the street. He kept only his merchant's pack—the one filled with harmless things, the mask of the man he should be.

Before long, he reached his home.

It was two stories of dark timber and pale stone, its windows framed with shutters painted a deep forest green. The roof sloped at a sharp angle, a design meant to shed the heavy rains that swept in from the western sea. A small garden curled along the side, though the colder months had stripped it bare save for a few stubborn herbs. A lantern hung by the front door, its flame flickering gently against the growing night.

Belaric paused for a moment, taking it in. The sight of it, the sheer familiarity, settled something deep in his chest.

He stepped forward, fishing the key from his pocket and fitting it into the lock. The door swung open smoothly, and at once, warmth wrapped around him, the kind that seeped into bone and chased away the last remnants of travel. The scent of home followed soon after, drifting from the kitchen and filling the air with something rich and familiar.

He inhaled deeply, and a slow smile tugged at his lips. Chicken stew. Renna's best—the kind that clung to the core, thick with herbs and simmered for hours until it could make a man forget the weight of the road. Beneath it, something sweeter lingered, woven into the air like a quiet promise. Apples, sugar, and spice, baked into golden perfection.

Apple pie.

He let out a slow breath, letting the silence press in. A strange stillness, deeper than the quiet of the house, settled over him—the kind he knew only from waiting in the dark before a kill. The ache in his limbs dulled, but the weight never truly left. He had crossed kingdoms soaked in blood, bartered with killers for secrets best left buried, and spent nights beneath stars that watched without mercy. But here—within these worn walls, beneath the scent of herbs and hearth smoke—he was not an assassin, not a ghost in the dark. Not yet. For a few hours more, he was just a man. Pretending peace had not already made him soft.

This place—this fleeting warmth—it was the closest thing he had to home. But it was a fragile thing, and he understood it would not last.

As Belaric stepped into his home, the familiar warmth of the hearth greeted him, driving away the last traces of the cold night air. The house was modest but well-kept, a space built for comfort rather than grandeur. The kitchen took up much of the ground floor, its sturdy wooden table surrounded by well-worn chairs, the marks of countless meals and quiet conversations etched into the surface. A large hearth dominated the far wall, casting flickering light over the room as a blackened pot hung above the fire, its contents bubbling softly.

To the left, a door led to the small bathing room, where a wooden tub sat waiting. A narrow staircase climbed upward toward their bedroom, the faint scent of dried lavender wafting down from the loft above. A half-knitted blanket rested over the back of a chair, soft blue wool threaded through the needles—Renna's work, no doubt. She had been preparing in the quiet moments between worry and waiting, filling the space with small pieces of the life they were building.

Belaric's gaze lingered on it for a moment before shifting to her.

Renna stood with her back to him, stirring the stew with practiced ease. Her loose auburn hair framed her face, and though she was turned away, he pictured her quiet concentration in her eyes, the way she always seemed completely at ease in the kitchen.

Belaric let the door close behind him with barely a whisper, creeping forward on silent feet. He had made it halfway across the room before she spoke.

"Stop goofing around and get over here and kiss me," she demanded.

He chuckled. "How do you always know?"

She turned, a slow smile spreading across her lips. "I could smell you." She wrinkled her nose in playful disgust.

Belaric laughed, crossing the remaining distance in two quick strides before pulling her into a firm embrace. Her arms curled around him as he lowered his head, their lips meeting in a kiss that carried the weight of absence and longing. It was slow, deep, the kind of kiss that made a man forget the road entirely.

When he finally pulled back, he dropped to one knee, coming eye level with her swollen belly. He placed a gentle hand over it, warmth blooming beneath his palm.

"And how is our future merchant doing?" he murmured, pressing a kiss to the curve of her stomach.

Renna giggled, running her fingers through his hair. "He has been missing you."

Belaric tilted his head, arching a brow. "He? And how do you know it is a boy?"

She smirked, resting a hand on her hip. "A mother always knows."

He gave her belly another affectionate kiss before rising back to his full height. She reached up, brushing her thumb along his jaw, her touch soft but searching.

"I am glad you are home," she said, quieter now. "I was worried I would have him without you here."

Belaric cupped her face, brushing his thumb over her cheek. "I would never let that happen," he promised. "Neither would Ed."

She smiled, resting her forehead against his chest for a moment before stepping back. "That is sweet—but right now, we need to do something about this smell." She gave him a teasing nudge toward the bath. "Go clean up before dinner. There is hot water waiting."

Belaric grinned. "It is almost like you knew I would be home to-day."

She turned back to the stew, stirring lazily. "Like I said," she mused, "I always know."

He let out a low chuckle as he made his way to the bathing room. Inside, steam curled from the wooden tub, the scent of lavender and cedar rising from the heated water. The small room was plain but practical—wooden shelves held a few neatly folded cloths, and a basin of fresh water sat near the tub.

Belaric stripped out of his road-worn clothes and lowered himself into the bath, letting the heat seep slowly into his sore limbs. The water stung at first, teasing old wounds—some fresh, most long healed. He washed in silence, methodically scrubbing away the dirt and sweat of the road, but no amount of soap could touch what lay beneath the skin.

His fingers paused over the jagged line above his ribs, a wound from a curved blade in Ashendral. Another, fainter one across his thigh from a rooftop fall in Duhwrath. Most of the scars had come from the Black Vow, from training meant to break the weak and harden the rest. A few had come before that—earned in back-alley scraps when he was just a boy with nothing but rage and bone to his name.

He remembered the first time Renna had seen them. She had gone still, eyes tracing the map of old violence across his chest and arms. She had not spoken at first, had not needed to. He had told her quietly that growing up poor in Vorinfall meant fighting for everything—and not always winning. She had reached for him anyway. That memory lived in him like warmth on a cold night, untouched by blood or shadow.

He dried himself with a cloth, slowly and carefully, then dressed in the clothes Renna had left for him. Simple, comfortable—wool pants, a white linen shirt, and soft, fur-lined boots that hugged his feet like warmth itself. He ran a hand through his damp hair, rolled his shoulders, and let the steam fall away with a long breath before stepping back into the kitchen.

The kitchen was just as he had left it, filled with the rich scent of simmering stew and the soft glow of the hearth. Renna stood at the table, slicing thick pieces of bread with practiced ease. The firelight flickered across her auburn hair, strands slipping loose from where she had tied it back.

She glanced up as he entered, a smirk curling at the corner of her lips. "Much better," she said, giving an approving nod. "Now I will not have to douse you in lavender before bed."

Belaric chuckled, stepping beside her. "If you wanted me smelling like flowers, you should have married a noble."

Renna playfully swatted his hand away before passing him a knife. "You can start with the potatoes. I cannot risk you getting near my apple pie—you will eat half before we have even had dinner."

"I would never," he said, feigning innocence.

She raised an eyebrow. "You absolutely would."

He did not argue; instead; he set to work. His hands moved with precision, the blade sliding through the potatoes in smooth, measured strokes. Renna stirred the pot, occasionally tossing in herbs, her rhythm as natural as breathing. Once he finished, she scooped up the diced potatoes and added them to the bubbling stew.

"You may be a lousy cook," she teased, "but you cut those perfectly, dear."

Belaric smiled at her words, but his mind flickered to another memory—one where his knife did far worse things than slicing vegetables. He forced the thought away before it could settle.

"I would never give you anything less than perfect potatoes, my love," he told her.

Renna rolled her eyes in mock exasperation. She continued to stir the bubbling stew for a few moments; the spoon scraping softly against the pot. She gave it a final taste, then turned to him. "Grab the wine, dear—the stew's ready."

Belaric nodded and reached for two wooden cups, setting them gently on the table. He uncorked the wine and let it breathe—the scent of cherry curling up like a ghost. Renna had always preferred the sweet ones, said they reminded her of the orchards outside Vorinfall.

He poured them each a cup, the dark red liquid sloshing gently as he set the bottle down. Renna ladled the stew into bowls, steam curling in the warm air as they carried their meal to the table. The fire crackled softly behind them as they settled in.

They ate in comfortable silence for a while before Renna finally spoke, tilting her head slightly. "Well?"

Belaric pretended not to understand, taking another bite before smirking. "Well, what?"

She shot him a knowing look.

Letting the act drop, he leaned back in his chair, swirling the wine in his cup. "My journey was good. I went south—farther than I planned. All the way to Karadorn."

Renna's eyebrows lifted slightly. "Karadorn? You have never gone that far before."

He nodded, knowing it was a lie.

He had been there more times than he could count. The Black Vow sent him everywhere—sometimes to steal secrets, sometimes to kill, and sometimes just to watch. Karadorn always left an impression, whether he wanted it to or not. A city three times the size of Vorinfall, its pale stone walls rose like mountains, carved not only for defense but for vanity. Historians etched long tales of conquest and kings into the city's base, as if the city itself were trying to outlive the world.

It sat on the Serpent's River, the water twisting like a living thing, winding through the land in endless coils before breaking into the sea. The smell hit you first—fish and brine, damp wood and spice. Streets churned with life: dockworkers, coin-counters, shouting merchants, the clatter of hooves and wheels echoing off stone. The lower market was noise and sweat and sharp elbows. But the Grand Bazaar... that was something else. Quiet. Clean. No one shouted. Merchants made deals with nods, and fortunes shifted hands silently.

"They built it like a fortress," he said, eyes still on the wine. "Walls taller than anything here. White stone, carved all the way around. You see it long before you reach the gates."

Renna leaned forward slightly. "And the river? Is it as wide as they say?"

"Wider," he said. "Twists like a knot. Smells like fish and foreign spice. The kind of place that remembers everything... even the things you would rather forget."

Renna listened intently, resting her chin on her palm. "Did you meet anyone interesting?"

Belaric considered for a moment, then nodded. "A spice merchant who called me 'my friend' while raising his prices, and a bard who swore he would compose a song in my honor if I gave him a goblet on credit."

She grinned. "And did you?"

"Of course not. Told him to write the song first," he said, smiling.

Renna laughed, shaking her head. "You are impossible."

She took another sip of wine before asking, "Anything else happen on your journey?"

Belaric hesitated. "There was a man I met—an old wanderer in the Karadorn marketplace. He claimed he could see the past... and what is to come." Belaric was not sure why he had mentioned it now. He had met the man years ago, barely more than a passing encounter. But the memory had surfaced without warning, and something about it felt like a sign.

Renna's lips pressed together, a hint of amusement in her eyes. "One of those mystics?"

He nodded. "I thought him a fraud. Most of them are. But then he told me something."

He watched her closely.

"He said we would have a child," he told her, voice low.

Renna stilled.

Belaric chuckled softly. "At first, I thought you must have been in the city without telling me. I spent the rest of the day looking for you."

She giggled, shaking her head. "I would have liked to meet him."

He shrugged. "Then we will go—after the baby is born. Let him see how right he was."

Renna smiled, her fingers absently tracing the rim of her bowl. "I would like that."

She looked up again, her eyes narrowing playfully. "And did you buy anything this time?"

Belaric paused, his fingers brushing against the cool metal in his pocket. He had spent years on the road, trading in things that held no meaning beyond the coin they fetched. But this was different. He had bought the necklace without a second thought, yet now, as he prepared to give it to her, it felt like more than just a trinket—it was proof that he had been thinking of her even when he was miles away. He smiled, pushing aside the old instinct to doubt, and stood.

"As a matter of fact," he said, stepping behind her, "I did."

Renna looked at him, her eyes curious.

"Close your eyes." He whispered.

She did without hesitation.

He slipped the necklace over her head, letting the pendant rest against the hollow of her throat before fastening the clasp. The chain was delicate, silver woven so finely it almost seemed to shimmer in the firelight. The pendant—a small, teardrop-shaped piece of polished blue amber—caught the light as it settled against her skin.

"Open your eyes," he murmured.

Renna did, her gaze dropping to the pendant. Her fingers rose to brush over it, tracing the smooth curve of the amber. "What is it?"

"Tavrosi sea-amber," he said. "The merchants claim it comes from the deepest parts of the ocean, but I am fairly sure they just polish river stones."

She looked up at him. "It is beautiful," she said, her voice soft.

Belaric leaned down, pressing a kiss to her temple. "Figured I owed you something for making you wait."

She smirked. "Well, since you brought me a gift, I suppose I can let you have the first slice of apple pie."

Belaric chuckled and thanked her.

He crossed to the counter, retrieving the pie with a boyish eagerness that made Renna laugh. She took it from him and sliced through the golden crust, releasing a rush of warm cinnamon and sugar into the air. They ate slowly, sipping wine between bites, their conversation meandering through old memories, gentle teasing, and the quiet joy of simply being together again.

When the last crumbs were gone and their cups sat empty, they moved in a quiet rhythm—Belaric gathering plates, Renna rinsing them clean. It was a dance they had done a hundred times, wordless and familiar, as natural as breath.

By the time the sun had fully set, Renna stretched and took his hand, guiding him toward the stairs.

Their bedroom was already warm, the hearth's embers casting a soft orange glow across the walls. She sat at the edge of the bed, and he knelt beside her, fingers moving gently over the leather ties at her sleeves, loosening them one by one. She leaned into him as he worked, her breath brushing against his temple.

He helped her out of her dress, careful with each motion, then rose to shed his own coat and tunic, folding them over the chair in the corner. There was no rush between them—only the comfort of routine, of having done this a hundred times before and hoping for a hundred more.

Renna slipped beneath the blanket with a quiet sigh, and he followed, the bed creaking under their combined weight. She curled into him, her head against his chest, and he pulled her close, one hand settling at her back, the other brushing strands of hair from her face.

For a long while, they lay like that, neither of them speaking. The silence between them was full—not empty. The kind that only came with time and trust. Her warmth seeped into him, a soft, yielding embrace utterly unlike the unforgiving weight of the night, or the bite of a blade against his palm. A slow breath escaped him as he pressed a kiss to the top of her head, his eyes closing as the sound of her breathing steadied his own.

He was home. And for a little while, that felt like enough.

But as her breathing slowed into the rhythm of sleep, the weight returned. He lay still, listening to the soft rise and fall of her chest—peaceful, steady, unguarded. She did not know the man beside her. Not what he had done, nor what his assignment truly entailed. If she knew, truly knew, would she still love him? Would her eyes still hold quiet warmth instead of horror in the morning? The thought gnawed at him, but the Order did not wait, and neither could he.

Carefully, he slipped out of bed, keeping his movements slow so the mattress would not shift too much. He leaned down and pressed a soft kiss to her forehead. She stirred slightly, and he froze, breath caught in his throat. After a moment, she let out a soft sigh and stilled again.

He sighed and then turned toward the window.

The stairs were too risky—each board a traitor waiting to creak beneath his weight. He had learned that years ago. Instead, he unlatched the window and pushed it open, letting the cool night air wash over him. He climbed out with practiced ease, his hands finding the holds he had carved into the side of the house long ago. The descent was swift, silent.

Sticking to the shadows, he moved quickly through the streets, slipping between alleys and avoiding the patrols of the city watch. The streets were quieter now, emptied of merchants and traders, but dangers lurked still—cutthroats who worked for coin rather than loyalty, thieves with sharp knives and sharper eyes. None of them saw him.

He reached the narrow alley where he had hidden his armor. The stone was cold beneath his fingers as he pried it loose, pulling the pack free from its hiding place. With quick, efficient movements, he stripped out of his tunic and dressed in the armor.

The black leather fit like a second skin, reinforced with layered plates along the chest and forearms—light enough to move in, strong enough to turn a blade. He secured the daggers to his thigh and the small of his back, the familiar weight a small comfort. The boots were soft-soled, designed for silence. The mask was the last piece.

It was smooth, featureless, save for the faint etchings of old symbols carved into the sides. The eye slits were thin—not enough for anyone to see in, only to see out. The first time he had worn it, he had felt smothered, like he had vanished beneath it. Now, he felt nothing at all.

The Black Vow had many rules, but none more sacred than this:
Never show your face.
Not to strangers. Not to allies. Not even to each other.
It was one of the few rules he broke.
He wore the mask only when necessary. He had grown tired of it—of the weight it carried. Even on most jobs, he went without it. Those who saw his face never lived long enough to speak of it. The last thing they saw was the face of death.

His face.

Once dressed, he left the alley and moved deeper into the city, slipping through empty streets until he reached the towering stone wall that separated the poor district from the rest of Vorinfall. He scaled it in seconds, fingers and feet finding the worn grooves in the stone. With one pull, one pivot, and he dropped soundlessly into the slums.

The abandoned house sat on the far side of the district, nestled between two crumbling buildings. It had once been an inn, long ago, but fire had gutted it, leaving only charred beams and blackened stone. The second floor had collapsed inward, taking the roof with it, but the lower level still stood—a hollowed-out shell, its windows dark and empty.

The beggars and the poor knew to stay away from it. Some whispered that the house was cursed; others claimed a specter inhabiting it walked the halls at night. But Belaric was privy to the truth—it belonged to the Order.

He slipped inside through a side entrance, moving over warped floorboards and stepping around broken furniture. The air smelled of damp wood and rot—the scent of a place long forgotten. He found the basement door, pried it open, and descended into the dark.

The air was colder here. Still. Waiting.

At the far wall, he reached for the stones, pressing them in a precise sequence. A dull click echoed through the chamber, followed by the groan of hidden gears as a section of the wall slid back. He pushed it open and stepped through, pulling it shut behind him.

Darkness swallowed him whole.

The tunnels beneath the city were a labyrinth, built not just for secrecy, but for deception. Extra passages led to dead ends, false doors, and endless loops designed to confuse anyone foolish enough to follow. Belaric had gotten lost once, as a boy. He had learned quickly. He had not gotten lost since.

His steps were sure; his path unwavering. Left, right, right, down. Through the narrow arch, past the empty alcove. He moved like a shadow through the maze until he reached the door.

The Black Door.

It loomed before him, heavy and unyielding, its surface engraved with the sigil of the Order—a hollow circle with a dagger through the center. He remembered the first time he had stood before it, a child barely tall enough to reach the handle, his hands shaking with fear.

He was not afraid now.

He straightened and knocked once. The heavy silence swallowed the sound beyond. A heartbeat passed. Then another.

A panel slid open, revealing nothing but darkness. Then, at last, the voice came—low and rasping, like breath scraping over stone.

"What is the weight of a life?" the voice asked.

The answer came easily. "Less than a feather. More than a soul."

A pause. Then the sound of a latch being drawn back.

The Black Door opened.

The man at the door shifted as Belaric approached, his masked face tilting slightly before he spoke.

"Varros. The Black Council is waiting," the man told him.

Belaric gave a slight nod, not slowing his stride.

The weight of the door pressed against his palm as he passed through. Less than a feather. More than a soul. He had drilled those words into himself since childhood, yet only now, as he left the world behind and entered the darkness, did he feel their weight.

A life was nothing to the Order. A name even less.

And yet, his name meant everything to the woman sleeping in his bed.

3

The halls swallowed sound. The only noise was the faint flicker of candle flames, their weak glow casting feeble halos of light on the stone walls. No portraits adorned these corridors. No statues of heroes stood in alcoves. There were no heroes here. Only killers. Only shadows that bled.

He walked those halls as one of them. A shadow they called Varros.

He hated the name the moment they gave it to him.

It was the one they had given him when he was first taken into the Order, carved into him as deeply as the blade that had marked his initiation. It was not his—it had never been his. The Order assigned names as they stripped away pasts, binding men and women to a life where they did not own even their own reflection. He had learned to answer to it. To obey when someone spoke it. But he had never learned to accept it.

Beyond these walls, he would be Belaric once more. His face, voice, and life were his own, even if built on lies. But here, beneath the weight of the Black Vow, he was only Varros.

He let out a slow breath, pushing the thought aside. This was not the place for such indulgences.

He moved through the darkness, his steps silent. The air was thick with the scent of cold stone and old blood, memories pressed into the walls like ghosts that refused to leave. He flexed his left hand as he walked. They broke his bones when he was thirteen—a master snapped them beneath his boot, teaching him a lesson in failure. It still ached in the cold.

He stopped at the mouth of a tunnel and looked in. Inside, a group of children—no older than eight or nine—knelt in a tight semicircle, backs straight, eyes forward. A man in dark robes moved between them, his voice level, his tone precise.

"The liver will kill, but slowly. The heart is fast, but you must puncture the left side. The throat is silent, but messy. The spine here," he tapped a wooden knife against a boy's neck, "will drop them instantly, but you must be sure."

A small girl with hollow cheeks and a shaved head raised her hand. "What if we need them to talk first?"

The instructor chuckled beneath his mask. "Then you start with the fingers, child. One joint at a time."

Belaric forced himself to look away. The smell of oil and sweat clung to the air, mingling with memory. He had knelt there once, listening. Learning. A phantom ache bloomed in his own small, forgotten hand, recalling the terror of those lessons, the way his fingers had trembled even as he learned to steady them for the kill.

Survive. Serve. Kill. The words pressed against his ribs like a knife turned inward. He had done all three, and yet he felt no victory.

Further down, past another open archway, the sound of steel on steel rang out. A fight. Not practice. Not drills. A tall, wiry man danced across the floor, his movements precise, controlled. His opponent, a stocky woman with a low center of gravity, she did not move with the same grace—she absorbed. She met every strike. Every slash he sent at her was turned away. The man's dagger flashed toward her throat—she twisted, slamming an elbow into his ribs. He staggered, only for her to sweep his legs out from under him with brutal efficiency. She lunged onto him, pinning him down.

For a moment, she had him. Her knee pressed into his chest; dagger poised above his throat. She hesitated. A mistake. The man's legs snapped up, locking around her neck. He twisted, using the momentum to throw her to the ground. In a breath, he was on top of her, her own dagger pressed to her throat. Then he drove his blade down—not into her throat, but into her forearm, pinning her to the stone floor. A sharp, ragged breath escaped her, but she did not cry out. Blood pooled beneath her, dark and slow.

"Never hesitate," the master observing told her. The man twisted the blade before yanking it free and stepping back.

Belaric shook his head. This is what the Order did. It made monsters who felt nothing. He sighed before moving on.

The master's chamber loomed ahead, marked by a thick wooden door. Belaric knocked once.

The door swung open, revealing Dainrik. Nearly as tall as Belaric, but built for war—broad shoulders, thick arms, scarred hands. He had seen the man crush a skull with his bare fingers. He had seen him fight three assassins at once, armed with nothing but the weight of his own body. One of them never stood again. The other two had taken weeks to mend.

"Varros," Dainrik offered as a greeting.

"Dainrik," Belaric replied simply.

They nodded to each other, a silent exchange. Acknowledgment. Nothing more.

Dainrik stepped aside.

Belaric entered. The five masters sat in a half-circle above him, their thrones carved into a raised platform of black stone. Their masks caught the firelight, expressionless but watching. The high placement of their seats forced all who entered to look up—to kneel before them. They sat in silence; the shadows stretching long across their robes, pooling like ink. Three men. Two women. Ageless. Untouchable. The hand that guided the blade. The voice that decided who lived and who bled.

They were the masters of Vorinfall. Every major city had its own masters, its own assassins, its own reach. But here in Vorinfall, they were the will of the Order. And the masters ruled without mercy or the care of others.

Belaric knelt, pressing his forehead to the ground. He waited. To rise without permission was an insult. And those who insulted the masters ceased to exist. The silence stretched, thick as a hanging blade. Then a voice cut through it.

"Rise."

The command came from Kaelen, the central figure, the one who spoke the least but whose words carried the most weight of all five masters.

To his left, Lyessa leaned forward slightly, her mask tilting just enough to suggest scrutiny. Tassian, beside her, exhaled softly through his nose—a sound almost like a sigh, though with him, it could have been amusement or impatience. Vendreth, at the other end of the half-circle, drummed gloved fingers against the arm of her chair—slow, deliberate. Salrik, the largest of the five, remained still, but there was a presence to him, as if his silence was as much a test as his words would be.

"Report," Kaelen ordered.

Belaric did not hesitate. "I reached Brindlewood and scouted the town for several days. At the child's naming ceremony, I confirmed the mark. I identified the family's home and made my preparations. The celebration lasted for three days. On the night of the third, when they finally rested, I struck." His voice remained measured, emotionless.

"I entered through the kitchen window, as planned. I had loosened the hinges the previous night to ensure there would be no resistance. The father was in his chair, unaware. The mother was awake, holding the infant. Playing near the fire was the young boy. I waited in the dark, watching. When the father moved to stand, I struck."

He let the words settle before continuing.

"The blade took him in the spine. He gasped, but before he could call out, I was behind him. I locked my hand onto his chin and the other onto the back of his head. With a sharp jerk, his neck broke." The masters remained still. Watching. Listening.

Tassian was the first to respond. "The mother?"

"The mother did not move, unable to understand what had just happened and what was going to happen. The boy saw me kill his father as well. He did not run. Panic seized him after a brief moment of stillness. When I moved towards him, the fear broke. He flailed, scrambling back, but it did not matter. I caught him before he could scream. He thrashed, kicked, clawed, but it made no difference. I forced him down and administered Death's Whisper."

A pause. No hesitation—just precision.

"He inhaled deeply. The pain took him immediately—his throat closed, his lungs burned. He clawed at his own neck, gasping, choking, until he could not anymore." Still, no reaction from the five above him.

"The mother ran." A faint shift in the shadows above. Not a question—approval.

"She was close to reaching the door," Belaric started but was interrupted.

"She almost reached the door?" Vendreth asked, her voice light but edged, as if humored by the attempt.

Belaric hesitated only a breath. Most would have lied, spun some tale to spare pride or shift blame. But lies here were not just wasted—they were punished. The masters heard all lies. And when they did, the one who dared speak that lie suffered.

"I stopped her. She begged. She swore they would flee. I ignored her. When she realized I was after the child, she fought harder. It made no difference. I dosed her next." He paused.

A silence stretched between them.

Belaric continued, "She collapsed. Her arms tightened around the infant, but her strength bled from her. I put them together. Then I administered Mother's Tear. One drop. No pain. No suffering. Just sleep."

Belaric paused once more, only briefly, before continuing.

"I confirmed their deaths, then poured oil over the bodies and the walls. The fire spread quickly. I watched until the flames took hold, until the smoke thickened and the villagers began to stir. Then I left."

Belaric let the silence linger for a moment longer before adding, "By now, they will think it was a terrible accident. The father was known to drink—some will say he must have knocked over a lantern, that he mistakenly set the blaze himself. There are no bodies to be found now. Nothing left but ash. And no one to prove the fire was not the killer."

After he finished, no one said anything. Salrik tilted his head slightly. He watched Belaric closely. Lyessa tapped her fingers on the arm of their chair—slow, deliberate, as if considering the weight of every word.

Tassian leaned forward slightly. "Efficient," he mused. "But I wonder—I hear you are fond of Mother's Tear, Varros. Why use such a costly poison on a child marked for death? Should the corrupted blood not suffer?"

Belaric did not blink. A test. They always tested.

"The child did not choose to be born. The curse was not of its doing," he said evenly.

"Hmm." This time it was Lyessa who spoke. "And yet, you let the boy choke on his own breath. A painful way to go."

Belaric kept his face still. "The boy struggled. I could not risk wasting Mother's Tear should the drop miss his tongue. As Master Tassian noted, it is costly and difficult to craft. I would not waste it without need."

Salrik cleared his throat before speaking. "You have completed your task. See the quartermaster and receive your payment."

Belaric nodded and bowed, preparing to leave.

"Ah, not so fast," Vendreth cut in, sharper, carrying the weight of command. "We have another job for you."

A rare thing.

For a moment, Belaric was caught off guard. The masters rarely assigned new missions immediately after completing one. All members of the Black Vow led double lives, and frequent disappearances invited suspicion. Even his cover as a traveling merchant would not explain another sudden departure.

"This one is different," Kaelen said, his voice measured, final. "Lady Marvella Haldren and her daughter Lyra must be silenced. The girl's curiosity has become a threat—she questions the origin of the Valasar marks. And worse, the mother encourages it."

A noble target. That alone gave Belaric pause. The Order had killed others who were not marked, but seldom nobles. His mission had always been to preserve the lie—silencing whispers, erasing doubt, ensuring the noble houses remained untouchable.

Now, they wanted blood from within.

Lyessa leaned forward, her voice smooth, cold. "The girl possesses the Valasar—bright and persistent. Dangerous. Her questions have spread. Others have started listening. The high houses will not allow one of their own to fracture the illusion."

Belaric felt something shift deep inside him.

A noble target was rare—but this? A noble girl with a Valasar mark. That was something else entirely.

In all his years under the Order's shadow, he had never heard of such a thing. They protected the nobles who bore the Valasar marks—even enshrined them. They were called symbols of divine favor. Tools of control. No one laid a hand on them, let alone spilled their blood.

But now, he was being asked to do exactly that.

Was he the first?

Had the Order grown so desperate—or so confident—that they would murder one of the blessed to protect the lie?

Belaric's thoughts turned to House Haldren. Lady Haldren had only one daughter—Lyra. No older than fifteen. Her forehead bore the Valasar mark. He remembered the rumors surrounding the girl.

She was known for her brilliance, a mind too sharp for the world she lived in.

But brilliance alone had never made someone a target. Not until now.

The shock passed—but not the weight of it. Belaric turned the names over in his mind, drawing from what else he knew, what he had heard in passing through court whispers and trader routes.

Lady Haldren was a minor noble by blood—a distant cousin to one of the great houses—married to a lesser lord from another minor line. Most had expected her influence to fade after her husband died in a border skirmish a few years prior—a clash between two highborn rivals that had nothing to do with her, yet left her widowed and vulnerable.

But she had surprised them all.

Rather than collapse, House Haldren had held—and even grown. She had proven herself a capable steward of her estate, forging quiet alliances, earning the respect of nearby towns, and keeping her household intact. Many whispered that she wielded more subtle power now than she ever had at her husband's side.

It made sense now. A clever daughter raised by a quietly ambitious mother. A Valasar mark on the forehead—a symbol of insight, of intellect sharpened to a blade's edge. And worst of all, they were asking questions together.

The masters did not fear questions. They feared what might be found.

"You leave in three days," Tassian instructed, his voice calm, as if this were routine. "They are at their family estate in Brookhaven."

Belaric hesitated. He was not a man easily shaken, but this order unsettled him. He needed to be sure. "Master, to confirm—the targets are both of noble birth. And the girl... she is Valasar-blessed?"

They all nodded.

Vendreth was the one to reply, her voice cool, final. "The request comes from the Vow Keeper himself. And his will is not to be delayed."

Belaric kept his posture still, but his mind reeled. The Vow Keeper. The unseen leader of the Black Vow, a figure whispered about even among the assassins. He rarely gave orders. Rarely showed himself. For him to demand this meant something far greater than a child's curiosity was at stake.

Belaric moved to accept. The words almost left his mouth. To defy them was madness. Death, swift and absolute, without so much as a final breath. He had seen it. Known it.

Then his fingers twitched. A small thing. A meaningless thing. And yet, his body had betrayed him before his mind had.

Renna would have the baby any day now. He had done his duty for the Order, taken life in its name more times than he cared to count. But he could not leave her now. He did not want to.

He steeled himself. What he was about to say would decide whether he lived or died. If they denied his reasoning, he would not leave this chamber alive. He was not sure if he could take Dainrik at the door—but with five masters before him, he would never reach the exit.

He took a slow, steady breath. "Masters, I have only just returned to the city early today. Many have seen me already. To leave again so soon would raise suspicion. You have taught us to avoid such risks—to blend, to move unseen. People will ask questions. The risk to our order is great. I humbly request that someone else be assigned to this mission."

Belaric knelt again, lowering his forehead to the cold stone floor. Not out of respect, but to watch Dainrik at the door from the corner of his eye. Belaric's hand slid slowly and deliberate toward the dagger in his boot.

The silence that followed was not instantaneous. It stretched thick and suffocating, filling the chamber like smoke from an unseen fire.

The masked figures did not move, but something about them felt heavier, as though the room itself had turned against him.

Dainrik shifted—just slightly, but enough. Belaric felt the weight of his breath. He kept his forehead pressed to the floor, his fingers barely brushing the hilt of his dagger.

A long, slow exhale from Kaelen. Not quite a sigh. Not quite disappointment. "Caution is our strength," he finally said. "Your absence will not be noticed on this mission, but do not mistake patience for leniency."

Belaric remained still, but inwardly he exhaled.

Salrik let out an inaudible sigh before speaking. "The mission is important, and we must handle it, but protecting the Order comes first. Get up. Your groveling is tedious."

He did as commanded.

Lyessa was the next to speak. "We will find another for the task. In five days, you will return here and instruct the Vow-sworn in poisons. Since you have such vast knowledge of poisons, we will not waste it."

"Yes, Master," Belaric replied.

He rose and bowed once more and left the chamber.

As he stepped into the corridor, the shadows swallowed him once more. He did not quicken his pace. He did not look over his shoulder. Only when he was sure he was alone did he release a slow, measured breath.

Belaric continued down the corridor with measured steps, each one a quiet rehearsal of control. The quartermaster's chamber loomed just ahead. He paused at the door, drawing a slow breath.

The masters were all cold, calculating monsters—but the one behind this door? He did not scheme. He did not command. He enjoyed.

Belaric exhaled and knocked.

"Who is it?" came a muffled voice from beyond the thick wooden door.

"Varros," he replied.

The door creaked open, revealing the man within.

"Ah, it is you, Varros," Orris said, his voice as slick as oil. "Come in. I figured you would be by soon. Come for payment, have you?"

"You know I have, Orris," he told him, his voice clipped.

Belaric stepped inside, keeping his movements deliberate, forcing himself to remain composed. He had long since learned to bury his contempt, but this was one of the few men in the Order he would gladly kill—even if the punishment was death.

Orris was a sickness. He had always begged for contracts, not to serve the Black Vow, but for the twisted pleasure of prolonging death, of stretching each victim's last moments, making them feel every cut, every stolen breath. The masters, wary of such dark indulgence, had long ago forbidden him from leaving the Order's halls. His work lacked precision; his mind was too sick to infect the young ones they trained. So they made him the quartermaster instead.

Orris moved toward the candlelight, plucking a piece of parchment from the desk. "Let us see now—total payment for four deaths. But of course, I must subtract the cost of the herbs I provided for your poisons. Ahh, perfect. I owe you three gold pieces, ten silvers, and four coppers."

He stepped toward the shelf, unlocking a heavy iron box with a key from around his neck. The coins clinked as he counted them out—slow, deliberate, precise.

He hesitated for a fraction longer than necessary.

Waiting.

Then, without a word, he turned, holding the payment out.

When he faced Belaric again, he could hear the smile beneath his mask.

"Do you want to count them?" Orris asked, his voice dripping with amusement.

"No," Belaric said quickly, snatching the coins from his palm and shoving them into his pocket. He turned to leave.

"Oh, wait, friend," he said.

Orris's hand clamped onto Belaric's shoulder. His touch, warm and lingering, felt like a violation.

"Will you tell me about the job? I want to hear all the details. I will even throw in some extra silver for you," Orris told him.

The rage came fast, curling hot beneath Belaric's ribs. He could feel Orris's gaze, hungry and waiting for him to break.

He craved the details—the blood, the begging, the final breath. Not for the report. For pleasure. Orris was a carrion beast draped in coin and shadow, and he knew exactly how much Belaric despised him. That was the game—poke the hound and see if it bites.

Belaric jerked his shoulder away. "No, Orris. I will not. And never touch me again, or you will lose the hand that does."

Orris laughed, low and amused. "So angry Varros is. Does not want to talk with his friend Orris."

Belaric did not respond. He turned on his heel and marched out of the chamber, slamming the door behind him.

Orris's laughter slithered through the wood, low and amused.

He walked purposefully now. He was tired—bone-deep, soul-weary tired—and needed rest. Needed Renna.

The corridors stretched long before him, empty and silent. At the main door, the same man stood on guard. As Belaric approached, the man opened the door without a word, and the two exchanged a simple nod as he stepped past. The heavy door shut behind him, and the lock clicked into place.

He sighed, finally able to relax.

The city felt different at night—quieter, slower, as if the weight of its own sins dulled the air. He moved carefully, navigating the shadows on his way to the middle district, stopping only when a patrol passed too close. When he reached the familiar alley, he scaled the wall with practiced ease, dropping soundlessly into the narrow passage below.

His clothes were right where he had left them.

He pulled off his black armor, piece by piece, and set it aside before reaching for the mask. That cursed thing.

Turning it in his hands, he stared for a long moment. He hated the thing. Every inch of his soul wished he could destroy it.

He took a sharp breath and tucked the mask away with the rest of his gear. He worried about someone finding it, but after years of hiding it here, the worry had lessened. Not completely. But more than if he had kept it at home.

Renna.

If she ever found it, the Order would not hesitate to kill them both. He would never allow that to happen.

He straightened, casting one last glance at the hidden bundle before making his way home.

He climbed through the window, his movements instinctive, silent. The house was dark, the only light a faint glow from the dying embers in the hearth.

He stood there for a moment, just listening.

Renna's breathing was slow, steady. One hand rested against her belly, curled protectively. He let out a breath he had not realized he was holding.

This. This was real.

He stepped closer, standing at the bedside. The firelight flickered over her skin, casting soft shadows across the curve of her belly. Soon—any day now—he would be a father. The thought stirred something deep within him, something sacred and terrifying all at once. For the first time that night, he felt something solid beneath his feet. Not the hollow triumph of a completed mission or the cold relief of survival—but joy. A family. His family.

Warmth crept through his chest, slow and unfamiliar. Peace. Or something close to it. But even as it settled in, he knew how fragile it was. Peace was never meant for men like him. Not for killers. Not for those who built their lives on silence and blood.

The thought coiled in his mind like a sickness, sharp and unwelcome. What right did he have to this life? To her? To the child she carried?

He tried to shake it off.

Instead, he crawled into bed beside her and wrapped his arms around her, pulling her close. Just for tonight. Just for one more night.

The smell of cooking meat woke him. He blinked against the morning light, surprised to find the bed empty. He had been more exhausted than he realized—Renna had gotten up without him even stirring.

He pushed himself up and made his way downstairs.

In the kitchen, Renna stood at the hearth, tending to breakfast. A pan of eggs sizzled in lard, their edges crisping in the heat. Thin strips of pork crackled beside them, curling as they browned. Fresh bread sat on the wooden table, torn from a larger loaf, and a clay cup of steaming tea rested nearby.

She wore a simple linen dress, dyed a soft shade of blue, its hem brushing her ankles. A well-worn apron was tied around her waist, smudged with flour from yesterday's baking. She loosely braided her auburn curls, a few stray strands falling free as she moved.

Belaric smiled. This was home.

He stepped behind her, wrapping his arms around her waist and pressing a kiss to the side of her neck, then another, and another.

She giggled. "Stop it, you brute—if I burn the meat, you are eating it anyway."

He smirked against her skin before letting her go.

"Did you sleep well, dear?" she asked, glancing at him over her shoulder.

He nodded. "Of course. How could I not, with the most beautiful woman beside me?"

She rolled her eyes, but the corners of her lips twitched. "Oh, hush. Go wash up before breakfast."

"Yes, dear," he said in mock obedience, ducking just as an eggshell sailed past his head.

He grinned and strode out of the room, laughing as he went.

As he entered the washroom, a fresh bowl of hot water waited for him. He rolled his shoulders, stretching the stiffness from his muscles, then set to washing his face. The warm water was a relief, washing away the sweat and grime of the night. After drying himself off, he picked up the knife beside the bowl, running his thumb along its edge before turning to the mirror. He hated letting his facial hair grow too long—it made him look unkempt, like a man who had lost control.

He brought the blade to his neck, carefully shaving away the stray hairs with slow, practiced strokes. His hand moved with the precision of a trained killer, but now he used the blade to preserve the shape of a man he wanted to remain. Each pass of the knife demanded patience. Focus. He took his time, mindful not to nick the skin. He would not give Orris the satisfaction of seeing him marked, even by his own blade.

The mirror reflected a man shaped by discipline, by routine, by blood. His dark blue eyes, sharp and watchful, had seen too much, but they still softened at the thought of Renna. He kept his black hair short and neat, not out of vanity, but practicality. His well-trimmed beard softened his jawline, making him look less severe, less like a killer. A thin scar ran along the side of his nose, barely noticeable unless the light hit it just right. A relic from a fight long forgotten.

He wondered if their child would look like him or like Renna. He whispered a prayer to the gods. Let the child have her face. Not mine. Not this life. He let out a deep sigh, shook the thought away, then stepped back out into the kitchen.

The warmth of the home wrapped around him, so different from the cold of the Order's halls. For a moment, he hesitated, standing at the threshold, watching her move in the kitchen. She belonged here. In the light. In the warmth. He sighed softly and stepped into the kitchen.

Renna had just finished setting the table. In comfortable silence, they enjoyed their breakfast together. The eggs were still warm, the pork crisp, and the bread fresh between them. The tea carried a faint sweetness—honey; he realized.

Between bites, Renna glanced at him. "Are you going to help me sell apples at the market today?"

He looked up, meeting her eyes. "You know you do not have to ask." He took her hand gently. "I will take care of everything. You do not need to be lifting a thing."

She smiled, squeezing his fingers. "Good, because it is getting harder and harder to load the cart."

"Jorric's wife is stopping by the stall as well," he added. "She says they only want the freshest apples."

Renna laughed, shaking her head. "Then you better go pick them straight off the trees out back."

He smirked, but nodded. "Yes, dear."

After finishing his meal, he made his way outside, a basket under one arm.

The morning air was crisp, the sun warming the back of his neck as he reached for the ripest apples. He took his time, enjoying the feel of the sun, the distant hum of the city waking up. He could hear merchants setting up their stalls, neighbors exchanging greetings, and the rhythmic hammering of a blacksmith already at work. Each apple he selected, perfect and unblemished, he handled with the same careful precision he would a poisoned dart, a silent vow to protect this fleeting perfection. For once, the world felt normal.

"No daydreaming around here," Renna teased, pulling him from his thoughts. "Only apple picking."

He grinned, plucking another apple from the branch before taking a large, satisfying bite. The taste was perfect—crisp, sweet, fresh.

"I still do not understand how you make them taste this good," he said, chewing thoughtfully.

She smirked, folding her arms in mock secrecy. "That is a trade secret, love. You are not getting it out of me."

He chuckled and picked another apple from the tree and placed it in his pocket.

She let out a dramatic gasp as he took another bite. "You have to pay for that first!"

He raised an eyebrow, swallowing. "Oh? And how much does an apple cost?"

"Three kisses," she told him.

He laughed, dropping the basket and running to her, pressing four kisses to her cheek. She giggled. "Alright, alright! That is enough. Now grab the baskets before we lose our spot at the market!"

But before he stepped away, her fingers brushed against his wrist, tracing his knuckles lightly. A small moment. A quiet thing. Then she pulled away and swatted at his arm. "Hurry, Belaric."

Still grinning, he hoisted the baskets and followed her inside.

Belaric started loading the apples into the baskets while Renna walked through her small garden, gathering an assortment of fresh vegetables and fruits. She inspected each one carefully, choosing only the best before adding them to a basket. Once satisfied, she stacked everything onto the wagon, filling it to the brim with their produce.

As if sensing they were ready, Darius appeared, leading the mule by its reins. The old beast plodded forward, ears flicking lazily, as Darius grinned.

"Good morning Renna, Belaric. I figured you would need this old girl to help pull," he said, patting the mule's thick neck.

Renna wiped her hands on her apron and smiled. "Thank you, Darius. You have been such a help these past few days. I swear, I do not know what I would have done without you."

Darius waved a hand dismissively. "Well, if you are feeling grateful, you could bake me one of those famous apple pies."

Belaric chuckled along with Renna. "Of course," she said, nodding her head. "But if I make one for you, I will have the entire street knocking on my door for a slice."

Darius smirked. "That is your fault for making them too damn good."

Belaric clapped a hand on Darius's shoulder. "You heard her—if you get a pie, we all get a pie."

Darius shook his head with an exaggerated sigh. "Fine, fine. I will take an extra-large slice, then."

Renna rolled her eyes, grinning. "I will see what I can do."

She turned to Belaric, raising a brow. "Do not be rude, love. Help Darius get the wagon ready while I clean up."

"Yes, dear," he said, exaggerating the words as he shot her a playful look.

She patted his arm before disappearing inside, leaving him with Darius, who had already started fastening the mule's harness to the wagon.

"Thank you, Darius," Belaric said, grabbing one of the leather straps. "You are a good man."

Darius scoffed, waving him off. "I am only doing it for the pie."

Belaric laughed, tightening the last strap. "I will be sure to bring her back after we finish for the day."

"Good. Ed will be happy to see you," Darius said. "He wants more apples."

Belaric nodded. "I will bring extra."

The two men worked in peaceful silence, securing the last of the harnesses before stepping back. Darius gave a satisfied nod, clapped Belaric on the shoulder, then gave a small wave before heading off.

A moment later, Renna stepped outside.

She had changed into one of her nicer dresses, a soft green that hugged her form but flowed freely at the skirts, the fabric light enough to move easily as she walked. The color deepened the warm tones of her skin, making her green eyes seem richer in the morning light. She twisted her hair into a loose, elegant coil at the back of her head, letting a few curls frame her face with careless grace.

Belaric watched her for a long moment, taking in the sight of her, unable to believe how beautiful she was.

She caught him staring and tilted her head. "What?"

He shook his head, still admiring her. "Just wondering how I got so lucky."

She giggled and took his hand, squeezing it gently. "Oh, you are lucky. The luckiest man in all of Vorinfall."

"I believe it," he murmured.

She smirked. "Good answer."

"Only the best for you, my love," he said, pressing a quick kiss to the back of her hand.

She smiled. "Hurry, let us go before the other merchants take all the good spots!"

Together, they led the mule through the streets toward the market, weaving between carts and merchants, all focused on setting out their wares.

The market was already alive with energy. The chatter of vendors filled the air, each calling out to passing buyers, eager to sell their wares. A man in a patched tunic stood beside a wooden cart displaying an array of small trinkets—polished stones, carved figurines, delicate rings of tarnished silver. He jingled a handful of coins in his palm as he called out, "Lucky charms! Gifts for the lady in your life! Keep the spirits at bay, protect your home!"

To the right, a woman in fine but well-worn clothes arranged bolts of dyed fabric across a table. Silks in deep reds, soft blues, and muted golds caught the light as she smoothed them out, her voice warm as she spoke to a customer. "Best quality in Vorinfall! A dress fit for a noble or a lady of the city."

The scent of fresh bread drifted through the air, drawing Belaric's attention to a baker near the corner stall. The man had already stacked several golden loaves, steam still rising from them. Beside him, a young boy—his son, perhaps—worked quickly, arranging pastries dusted with sugar and pies filled with dark berries.

A butcher nearby sharpened his knife against a worn stone, the metallic rasping sound cutting through the morning bustle.

Renna led him to their usual spot, between a spice merchant and a woman selling handwoven baskets. She pulled him toward the cart, already reaching for the baskets of apples. "Come on, love. No time for standing around—set them up neatly this time."

Belaric smirked. "I always do."

She shot him a playful glare. "Last time, you dumped them on the table and let me fix it."

He shrugged. "That is called teamwork."

She huffed, but laughed as she started arranging the apples.

As they worked, Belaric took a moment to take it all in. The sound of laughter, the scent of food, the warmth of the sun on his back. It was a world away from the darkness he had left behind the night before.

4

Belaric moved back to the wagon, his hands finding the last of the crates filled with fruit and vegetables. He hefted it with a practiced grunt and carried it to the stall, setting the final crate beside the others. A slight burn lingered in his arms, and he leaned against the wagon, letting his muscles relax as he looked over the crates—some bound with fraying rope, packed with life's simple offerings.

Clusters of plump grapes, their skin dark as midnight; pears, green and speckled, their shapes imperfect but their scent honeyed and full; deep crimson plums, soft enough that a careless grip would split them open; and root vegetables still dusted with the earth that birthed them. The onions carried a pungent bite in the air, mingling with the crisp, clean aroma of apples and the sun-ripened sweetness of tomatoes, their skins taut and glistening in the morning light.

With a quiet breath, he pushed off the wagon and moved to the crates. He loosened the rope on the topmost one and began handing the produce to Renna, handling each item with care. She took stock with deft fingers, her eye for order turning the simple spread into something warm and inviting—more welcoming than any merchant's stall Belaric had ever seen.

When the last of it was in place, she dusted off her hands and gave him a satisfied smile.

"Thank you, love," she said. "Now, let us see who we can convince to eat well today."

Belaric took a step back, watching her work. She was relentless, her voice carrying over the murmur of the market like a tune people could not help but stop and listen to.

"Fresh apples, the best of the season! Sweet as a maiden's kiss and twice as satisfying!" she called to a passerby, an older man in a patched but sturdy coat. "Ah, you look like a man who enjoys his cider. A few of these, a little patience, and you will have a drink to warm your bones before the cold ever touches you."

The man paused, weighing her words, then nodded and reached for his coin pouch.

A young woman hesitated by the grapes. Before she could turn away, Renna had already fixed her with a knowing smile. "For your sweetheart?" she asked, gesturing to the dark clusters. "They say a handful of these shared between lovers will bring a year of happiness. Of course, if you eat them alone, well..." She winked. "That just means more for you."

The girl blushed, fumbled for her coins, and took the bunch without another word.

A bearded man in a thick leather apron eyed the onions skeptically. Renna, never one to miss an opportunity, tilted her head and sized him up. "Cook, are you?" she guessed.

The man grunted. "I run the butcher's stall down the way."

"Then you know good onions mean the difference between a meal and a masterpiece," she said smoothly. "I will cut you a deal. A dozen for fourteen copper pieces—call it an investment in your customers coming back for more."

The butcher gave a slow nod, rubbing his chin. "And if they do not?"

"Then you come back and tell me I was wrong," Renna countered with a grin.

The butcher looked her over, then let out a brief chuckle. "Ten for the dozen."

"Twelve," Renna said. "And if you are stingy with your stew, do not blame me when folk stop coming."

That earned a genuine laugh, and he nodded. He pulled the coins from his small leather coin pouch and dropped them into her palm.

Belaric watched, caught somewhere between admiration and awe. He had dealt with merchants of all kinds—hardened traders, silver-tongued peddlers, men who made their living off promises as much as goods—but none of them could match Renna. She made people feel like they were not just buying food. They were buying stories, memories, small victories to take home.

The hours passed, the morning market swelling with bodies, noise, and the scent of warm bread carried on the breeze. By the time the sun had begun its slow climb toward noon, they had sold more than half their stock.

It was then that Jorric and Selene arrived.

Jorric was a broad man, the muscle of his youth now buried beneath the comfort of age and too many quiet meals. But the weight was still there—the kind that came from a life spent carrying armor, not just wearing it. His beard was trimmed to uneven stubble, more from habit than care, and his dark hair hung a little too long around the ears, as though Selene had not gotten around to scolding him yet.

He wore a thick wool tunic beneath a weather-beaten coat, the brown so faded it bordered on grey, its seams stitched and restitched like scars. The toes of his thick-soled, solid guard's boots were scuffed; these boots, made for standing watch through rain and boredom, not for chasing down thieves.

There was a slowness to his walk now, a slight stiffness in the knees, but his eyes still watched the world with that same dry wit—half amused, half suspicious. The look that said he had seen enough of life to stop being surprised by it.

Selene was a sharp contrast to her husband. Where Jorric moved with the worn ease of an old blade, she was all quiet edges and precision. Slender, but not fragile. There was a sturdiness in the way she stood, like she was used to holding things together when others came apart.

She braided her dark hair tightly and pinned it at the back of her neck, not for vanity but for utility. She wore a plain, deep-blue dress that fit her well enough, though the hem sat a finger too short—either from wear or disinterest in fixing what still worked. The sort of compromise a practical woman made after too many years of putting others first.

She did not linger or fidget. Her gaze moved across the market with the calm sharpness of someone who noticed more than she let on—measuring faces, weighing moments. Not suspicious. Just aware.

The kind of woman who never raised her voice because she never needed to.

The moment the women locked eyes, they fell into easy conversation, Selene reaching for Renna's hands. "And how are you?" she asked warmly. "Any signs the little one is ready to greet the world?"

Renna laughed, resting a hand on her belly. "Within a few days, if the healer knows anything. I swear this child is waiting for the coldest night to make an entrance."

Selene smiled. "They like to make things difficult from the very start."

As the women chatted, Jorric turned to Belaric. "Walk with me a moment?"

Belaric hesitated. He and Jorric had traded countless jests and barbs over the years, as close as two men who had shared a drink in a thousand different taverns. But a private talk? That was a different kind of closeness. Their conversations were usually about the easy, ordinary things—the price of apples, the state of the guards, who had haggled the hardest. This felt like it would be about something heavy.

He glanced at Renna, who was already waving him off. "Go," she said, laughing. "I can run a market stall without you staring at me in awe."

Jorric led him away, their footsteps whispering over the weathered stone like old secrets.

"Do you enjoy the life of a traveling merchant?" Jorric asked, keeping his voice even.

Belaric glanced at him. "I do. It lets me see the kingdom, meet people worth meeting. Not everyone stays in one place their whole lives."

Jorric nodded, thoughtful. "And there is good coin in it?"

"There can be," Belaric admitted. "But it is not just about what you sell. It is about who you are selling to, knowing what they need before they do. You do not take a fine cut of venison to a man who barely has two coppers to rub together and expect him to buy it."

Jorric chuckled. "I suppose not."

They walked a little further before Jorric let out a breath, as if settling something in his mind. "I have been thinking about a change," he said. "Being a guard is… simple. There is no war, no actual fights. Nobles do not come down to our districts, and most of what I do is separate drunks before they beat each other senseless. The coin is not much, either." He glanced at Belaric. "Watching you return the other day made me think. I could be a merchant."

Belaric raised a brow. "Not just anyone can be one."

Jorric grinned. "That is why I want to ask you about the merchant's guild."

Belaric sighed, but nodded. "The Merchant's Guild is not a simple thing. You have to apply, prove you are worth their time. There are fees and tons of paperwork—more rules than you would expect. But once you are in, you get access to their networks, their warehouses. They sell to you at a discount, expecting a cut of your profits in return. You have to submit travel plans and get approvals. They like to keep their hands in everything."

Jorric was quiet for a moment, digesting the information. Then he asked, "Would you take me with you next time?"

Belaric hesitated. A merchant traveling with a guard was one thing—it was common practice. But Belaric's work required him to travel alone. What if Jorric noticed something? What if he saw him for what he truly was?

He would have no choice but to kill him.

Belaric pushed the thought away.

"I have not planned another trip yet," Belaric said carefully. "With the baby coming, that is my priority. But when I do, I will let you know."

Jorric held his gaze a moment longer, then smiled slightly. "Fair enough."

They walked back in relative silence, pointing out an odd trinket or two as they passed—a knife with an ornate handle, a pendant that looked far older than the man selling it. By the time they returned to their wives, the two women were deep in conversation.

Selene's head was tilted slightly toward Renna, a half-smile playing at her lips, while Renna's fingers idly traced patterns on the stall's wooden surface. When they noticed their husbands approaching, they shared a knowing glance, then let out a low laugh before returning to their conversation.

Belaric and Jorric exchanged looks. Belaric simply shook his head and chuckled.

Shortly after, the women's murmured words faded, and Renna crouched to retrieve something from beneath the stall—a sack of apples she had tucked away. She pressed it into Selene's hands with a grin.

"I picked these this morning," she said. "The freshest apples in the entire city."

Selene smiled warmly, brushing her fingers over the sack's rough cloth. "You always look out for me, Renna."

Jorric gave a nod of thanks as Selene took his hand, leading him away into the market's shifting crowd. He tossed a final wave over his shoulder before disappearing into the sea of people.

The moment they were out of sight, Belaric turned to his wife. "What was that about?"

Renna only laughed. "Nothing you need to worry about."

He feigned insult, placing a hand on his chest. "After all we have been through?"

She giggled, brushing a strand of hair from her face. "You are a stubborn man, Belaric."

His smirk lingered as he leaned against the stall. "Jorric asked about becoming a merchant," he said, voice turning more serious. "Said he is tired of playing guard to drunks and coin-pinchers. Even asked to join me on my next trip."

Renna's expression shifted slightly—curiosity flickering behind her eyes. She leaned in, lowering her voice. "Maybe he does know."

Belaric frowned. "Know what?"

The moment the words left his lips, Renna's hand flew to her mouth, as if trying to catch the words before it was too late.

He narrowed his gaze. "Out with it."

Renna cast a quick glance around, her eyes flicking from one merchant to another, making sure none of them were close enough to overhear. The market was still alive with noise—hawkers calling out, the clatter of hooves on cobblestone, the hum of bartering voices—but even so, she spoke softly.

"Selene thinks she is with child," she whispered.

Belaric's brow lifted. "Jorric knows?"

Renna shook her head. "Not yet. She has not told him, but she is planning to tonight. A special meal, a warm evening. She wants it to be right."

Belaric let out a quiet breath, considering the weight of it. If Jorric had sensed it—even without being told—perhaps that was why he was suddenly so eager for a change. A merchant's life was unpredictable, but it held promise. More coin, more freedom.

Renna searched his face. "Will you bring him with you?"

Belaric let out a sigh and rubbed the back of his neck, fingers pressing briefly into tense muscle. His gaze drifted past Renna and over the crowd, as if the answer might be hidden among the bustling figures.

He did not know what to say. Renna was fond of Jorric and Selene, and rejecting him outright might upset her. Best to avoid the issue—for now.

"I do not know," he admitted finally. His hand drifted to the edge of the stall, thumb running along the rough wood as if searching for certainty in its texture. "I have not even thought about leaving again. My focus is here. On you. On the baby."

She gave him a soft smile before stepping closer, resting a hand lightly against his chest. "You are a great man, Belaric."

He looked down at her, his fingers brushing over hers. He wanted to believe her words. But deep in his mind, a whisper gnawed at him—a truth he could never tell. She would not call him great if she knew the weight of the lives he had taken. He tried to force the thoughts away, but they lingered, unwelcome shadows at the edges of his mind.

Renna's voice pulled him back. "If you do not take him, maybe you could put in a good word for him with the Merchant's Guild? They are good people. I know they would both be thankful."

Belaric exhaled sharply through his nose, running a hand over his jaw. The decision was heavy. Finally, he nodded. "I will do what I can."

She leaned up and pressed a kiss to his cheek before turning back to the stall. With effortless ease, she slipped back into her role—calling out to passersby, drawing them in with a warmth that made every deal feel personal.

The day wore on.

At one point, as the market hummed with midday business, Belaric stepped away from the stall and made his way toward the mule, tied to a wooden post near a low stone wall. The old beast flicked an ear as he approached, shifting its weight as though displeased with being ignored for so long.

Belaric approached, running a hand along the mule's side, feeling the steady rise and fall of its breath. "You are fine," he murmured, though the creature had offered no real complaint.

From a small pouch at his belt, he pulled out a handful of oats and let them spill into his palm. The mule snorted before leaning down to eat, its lips rough against his skin. Belaric let it take its time, absentmindedly stroking its coarse fur while his mind turned over Jorric's words.

Would it be so bad? Letting him come along?

Jorric was not a fool, but he was honest—and honesty was dangerous in the wrong company. If Belaric agreed, he would have to tread carefully. Some things were not for Jorric's eyes; they would have deeply disturbed him if he had seen them.

He exhaled, tossing the last of the oats onto the ground before giving it a firm pat. "You have got it easy," he muttered, watching as the beast continued to chew, unbothered by the weight of decisions Belaric carried.

Renna's voice carried over the market noise, drawing his attention back. A sharp laugh, a string of bartered words. Effortless. She did not know how much he envied her ability to move through life without shadows clinging to her heels.

With a final glance at the mule, he dusted his hands off and made his way back to the stall.

Customers had nearly bought all the produce by late afternoon, leaving only six stubborn pears.

An elderly woman approached, leading a young boy by the hand. The child squirmed, his small fingers tugging impatiently at her sleeve as she scowled at the fruit.

"Six coppers for the lot," Renna said.

The old woman snorted. "Six? I could buy a hen for that."

Renna folded her arms. "Then buy the hen. Maybe it will lay you a pear."

The woman huffed. "Three."

"Five," Renna countered. "I have to make a living, too."

The boy let out a frustrated whine, pulling at the woman's grip. "Gran, I want sweets, not pears!"

She shot him a sharp look. "You will eat what is given to you, or you will eat nothing at all."

The boy pouted, but Renna saw the flicker of hesitation in the woman's gaze.

"Four," the woman muttered.

Renna sighed dramatically. "Fine. But only because you remind me of my grandmother—stubborn as a mule and twice as clever."

The woman smirked and handed over the coins. As she dragged the boy away, he turned back once, scowling at Renna like she had personally offended his future dinner plans.

She only laughed, shaking her head as she sank onto the stool behind the stall. "Finally," she muttered, rolling out her stiff shoulders.

Belaric stepped behind her, rubbing slow circles into her back. "Good job, dear. I was not sure who would win that battle."

She nudged him with her elbow. "You knew I would. I never lose."

He chuckled, shaking his head. "I cannot argue with that."

As the sun dipped lower, they worked together to pack up what little remained. They stacked the empty crates, folded the cloth coverings, and dismantled the stall with the ease of habit. When everything was in its place, Belaric hitched their old mule to the wagon, securing the harness with steady hands.

Renna patted the beast's neck, murmuring something soft, and together, they led it home—a quiet end to another long day, with a future uncertain, but not yet unwritten.

The journey home was quiet, the clatter of wagon wheels and the soft thud of the mule's hooves the only sounds between them. The market's noise had faded behind them, replaced by the distant hum of the city winding down for the evening.

The streets bore the lingering echoes of the day—merchants locking up their stalls, lanterns flickering to life in doorways, and the occasional call of a mother gathering her children inside before night took hold. The scent of baked bread and roasting meat drifted through the air, mixing with the sharper tang of smoke curling from chimneys and the faint, salty dampness that clung to the city's stone from an earlier rain.

Belaric guided the wagon with one hand resting lightly on the reins, his other draped over his knee. The road home was familiar, well-worn, yet tonight it felt different—quieter, softer, like a moment of borrowed peace.

Renna sat beside him, legs tucked under her, one hand resting gently on her belly. She let out a slow breath, her eyes half-lidded with exhaustion, but there was a quiet contentment about her. For all the fatigue, there was something else; anticipation, maybe even a small sense of triumph.

Belaric glanced at her, watching the way she traced slow circles over her stomach with her fingers.

"Tired?" he asked.

Renna smiled, though she did not open her eyes. "Only a little."

"You barely stopped moving all day," he smirked.

"I could say the same about you," she murmured. "But you do not have a child pressing against your ribs."

Belaric huffed a small laugh. "Fair enough." He let the comfortable silence settle between them again, unhurried.

The road curved, their home coming into view. Light from a nearby street lamp spilled across the front wall, casting a golden halo that made the windows glow faintly, as if the house were holding its breath.

As they pulled up, Belaric hopped down first, his boots landing with a dull thud. He moved quickly to her side and offered a hand. Renna took it with a grateful smile, shifting her weight carefully as he helped her down. Her belly strained against the fabric of her dress, and she let out a soft sigh once her feet touched solid ground.

She surveyed the empty crates as she ran a hand along the wagon's edge. "Not much to put away."

"Good," Belaric muttered. "Less to haul back tomorrow."

Renna rolled her eyes. "You think I am going back tomorrow?"

He smirked. "You do not want to?"

She shot him a dry look. "I would rather wrestle a starving wolf than spend another day haggling over onions."

Belaric chuckled, stacking the empty crates while Renna began sorting the few remaining supplies. She worked swiftly, movements practiced, but there was a small hitch to her steps now—fatigue weighing down her limbs despite her stubbornness.

He lifted the last crate and set it aside. As he turned back, he caught her brushing a loose strand of hair behind her ear, smudging a streak of dust across her cheek in the process.

She wiped her hands and turned to him with a small, knowing smile.

"Go take the mule back to Darius," she said. "I will finish up here."

Belaric raised a brow. "And leave you to do all the work?"

"You have done enough," she teased. "Besides, I would like to take a bath before supper."

He smirked. "Good. Because I was going to tell you to do that anyway."

She narrowed her eyes playfully. "Oh? And who is giving orders now?"

He leaned in, voice low. "Me, apparently."

She snorted, crossing her arms. "And what, pray tell, will you be doing while I bathe?"

Belaric brushed the dust from his hands and straightened, expression unreadable for a moment. Then he smirked. "Cooking."

Renna's eyebrows lifted, clearly surprised. "You are cooking?"

"Do not look so doubtful," he said, feigning offense. "I can manage more than burning bread."

She tilted her head, studying him as if trying to determine whether he was joking. "I said nothing."

"But you thought it," he countered.

Her lips quirked. "Perhaps."

Belaric reached for the mule's reins. "Go on, then. I will be back soon."

Renna's eyes danced with amusement. "Very well, then. Impress me."

He chuckled. "That is the plan."

As he led the mule toward the stables, he glanced over his shoulder once. Renna had already turned back to the cart, but he caught the small, secretive smile lingering on her lips.

Darius was exactly where Belaric expected him to be—leaning against the stable doors, chewing idly on a strip of dried meat, the kind so tough it might as well have been leather.

As Belaric approached, Darius let out a small grunt, not bothering to straighten from his slouched stance. His gaze flicked from Belaric to the mule, then back again, brow lifting slightly.

"Figured you would be back soon," the old stable master said.

Belaric handed him the reins, rolling one shoulder to ease the lingering stiffness of the day. "Long day," he muttered. "Figured you would want her back before she decided to lay down in the street."

Darius let out a low chuckle, patting the mule's thick neck, fingers running through the coarse fur. "She is stubborn, but she has good sense. More than some men, I would wager."

Belaric smirked. "I will take that as a compliment."

Darius snorted. "I would not go that far." Belaric chuckled.

He led the mule to its waiting stall, muttering under his breath as the beast flicked an ear but otherwise went along without complaint. "Market treat you well?" he asked over his shoulder.

"Well enough. Renna could sell the rain back to the sky."

"That woman's got a gift," Darius agreed. He latched the stall door, giving the mule a final pat before turning back. "Unlike you, apparently."

Belaric feigned offensive. "What is that supposed to mean?"

Darius grinned, revealing teeth that had seen better days. "Just that the last time I saw you 'help' at the market, you haggled worse than a half-blind beggar."

Belaric snorted. "Which is why I let her handle it."

Darius barked a laugh, nodding approvingly. "Smart man. No shame in knowing your limits."

Belaric shook his head, leaning against the wooden stall railing, inhaling the familiar scent of hay, damp leather, and the musk of horses. The air here was different from the market—calmer, heavier, like the weight of the world did not press as hard inside these walls.

After a moment of silence, he glanced toward the far stalls. "Eddaross still in the back?"

Darius jerked his chin toward the far end of the stable. "Aye. Go on. He has been sulking since you left."

Belaric raised an eyebrow. "Sulking?"

Darius smirked. "Aye. Stared at me as if the apples would not taste as good coming from me. I think he missed you."

Belaric chuckled, shaking his head as he pushed off the stall railing. "Doubt it. He just wants more apples."

Darius crossed his arms, chewing on the last of his meat. "I am sure he does."

Belaric nodded and made his way to the far stalls.

Eddaross stood tall in his stall, his storm-gray coat catching what little light filtered through the stable's wooden slats. Even beneath the dust of the day, a faint sheen clung to his flanks. His ears flicked at the sound of approaching footsteps, nostrils flaring slightly before he let out a quiet huff, acknowledging Belaric's presence.

Belaric stopped at the stall door, arms resting on the top rail as he studied the horse. There was something grounding about Eddaross. A steadiness. A certainty. He was always there, patient and unwavering, waiting without complaint, without judgment.

"Miss me?" Belaric murmured as he stepped inside, running his hand along the horse's powerful neck.

Eddaross nudged his shoulder in response, his breath warm against Belaric's collarbone.

"Or just the apples?" Belaric added dryly.

The horse snorted, the sound almost indignant.

Belaric smirked. "Yeah, that's what I thought."

He reached into his coat, pulling out a small bundle wrapped in cloth. With a flick of his wrist, he unwrapped it, revealing two apples he had set aside earlier. The moment Eddaross caught the scent, his ears perked forward, nostrils flaring again.

"Patience," Belaric muttered, holding one just out of reach for a moment before finally offering it.

Eddaross wasted no time, his teeth sinking into the apple with a loud crunch, the juices glistening as he chewed.

As the horse ate, Belaric grabbed a brush hanging from a nearby post and began working it over Eddaross's flank, each stroke sending up a fine dust that caught in the lamplight.

"You know," Belaric muttered, his voice low, "you have a great life. No taxes, no guild fees, no haggling over coppers. Just eat, run, and glare at people who get too close."

Eddaross flicked his tail in response, sending a stray piece of hay fluttering to the ground.

Belaric let out a chuckle. "Alright, fine. I would trade places with you if I could."

The horse gave another loud, crunching bite, his tail flicking again as if dismissing the idea entirely.

Belaric kept brushing, the rhythmic motion familiar, methodical, almost meditative. For a moment, he let himself sink into it—the simple act of caring for something without expectation, without deception.

His thoughts, however, pulled him back to Jorric and his request to join him. He imagined it—the long stretches of road, the market towns, the quiet nights. But then came the other part. The hidden alleys. The locked doors. The targets. He saw Jorric's face, wide-eyed and terrified, witnessing something no honest man should ever see, or worse, becoming a loose end. A chill colder than the night air traced a path down Belaric's spine. He could protect Renna, his home, this fragile peace, but he could not protect Jorric from the inevitable consequences of his own double life. It was a line that could not be crossed.

After a while, he pulled the second apple from the bundle, holding it up between his fingers.

Eddaross stared at him, then at the apple, then back again.

"You could at least pretend it is me you are happy to see," Belaric murmured.

Eddaross let out a deep sigh, as if enduring an unbearable injustice, before finally reaching forward to take the fruit from Belaric's palm.

The corners of Belaric's mouth twitched upward. "That is what I thought."

He lingered a moment longer, running a hand down the horse's muscular neck before giving a firm pat.

"Keep well, old friend," he whispered, voice softer now, almost as if speaking more to himself than the horse.

Eddaross huffed in response, his dark eyes steady, watching as Belaric turned and stepped away, disappearing back into the cool embrace of the night.

When Belaric stepped inside the house, he caught the familiar scent of lavender and crushed rosemary drifting from the washroom. A light mist curled out from beneath the door, carrying with it the faint sharpness of soaproot.

He paused, listening to the gentle slosh of water. Through the slightly ajar door, he glimpsed Renna leaning back in the tub, her damp hair spilling over her bare shoulders, skin flushed from the heat. Her eyes were closed, lips parted slightly in quiet relief as the day's weight melted from her muscles.

Belaric leaned against the doorframe for a moment, simply watching.

It was rare to see her like this, unguarded, without the weight of haggling, household chores, or the quiet worries of an expectant mother pressing down on her.

Her eyes opened lazily as she sensed him near, a slow smirk curling at the corner of her lips.

"That was fast," she said.

Belaric stepped closer, kneeling beside the tub as he rolled up his sleeves. "Shift forward."

She raised an eyebrow. "Why?"

"Your hair is a mess," he whispered.

She chuckled, her voice soft and sleepy. "Is that your way of saying I look terrible?"

He smirked. "You look like a woman who spent the whole day arguing over the price of pears."

She sighed dramatically but did as he asked, sliding forward in the water, allowing him to settle in behind her.

Belaric dipped his hands into the warm water, gathering a handful before carefully pouring it over her scalp. His fingers moved through her hair with steady, deliberate care, working out the tangles with gentle strokes. The tension in her shoulders eased as he massaged slow circles against her scalp, the pads of his fingers pressing just enough to make her sigh in pleasure.

"Mm," she murmured, tilting her head slightly. "Keep doing that, and I might just forgive you for that mess comment."

He smirked. "That easy to win over?"

"Since it's you…maybe," she murmured, voice thick with drowsiness.

Belaric kept at it, taking his time, listening to the way her breathing slowed, the way she unconsciously leaned into his touch.

She rarely let herself slow down.

She was always moving, working, managing, worrying—but here, in this moment, she simply relaxed.

His fingers drifted lower, brushing against the back of her neck, lingering just for a moment. He felt her shiver—not from the cold, but from something quieter, deeper.

When he was done, he reached for a clean cloth, wringing out the excess water before draping it over her shoulders. She sighed, her head tilting back just enough for her half-lidded gaze to meet his.

"You are full of surprises today," she murmured, a lazy, knowing smirk tugging at her lips.

Belaric smirked back, his thumb absently brushing over the curve of her shoulder before pulling away.

"Go dry off," he said, standing. "I have a meal to cook." Renna let out a soft chuckle, stretching her arms over the edge of the tub. "First you pamper me, then you cook? Are you trying to make me fall in love with you all over again?"

He leaned down, voice low near her ear. "Depends... is it working?"

Renna turned her head slightly, brushing the knots out of her damp hair, her eyes glimmering with something unreadable, something warm.

"Maybe," she whispered.

Belaric smiled, stepping back, rolling his sleeves down again. "Then I suppose I will have to make this meal even better."

She watched him go, shaking her head before reaching for a towel.

"Keep this up," she murmured under her breath, "and I might start expecting it."

Belaric heard her as he stepped into the main room, the echo of her voice trailing behind him like the last curl of steam from the bath. He stoked the hearth, adding a split log, and let the quiet settle in—thick with the scent of pine and the faint traces of lavender from the soap she favored.

As she emerged, dressed and barefoot, the soft crackle of the fire and the first rich smells of dinner filled the room.

The meal was simple but well-made—a roast hen, stuffed with wild herbs and garlic, served with black bread and a thick vegetable stew flavored with bone stock and dried thyme. The high heat crisped the hen's skin to a golden brown, and its juices collected at the base of the wooden tray. Beside it, roasted carrots and turnips, glazed with honey, glistened under the firelight.

They uncorked a bottle of deep-red wine, saved for rare occasions, and placed it between them.

"You really are trying to impress me," she said.

Belaric carved a slice of hen and placed it onto her plate. "I will let you be the judge of that," he said, a quiet challenge in his voice.

She smirked as she took a bite. "Ask me after I finish eating."

They sat together at the small wooden table; the fire casting long shadows against the walls. The sound of the city outside had dulled—only the distant echo of voices and the occasional clatter of hooves on stone remained.

As they ate, Renna leaned back, rubbing her belly. "Have you thought of any names?"

Belaric swirled his wine, watching the way the light caught the dark liquid. "A few."

She nodded. "For a boy—maybe Caelan. Or Orryn."

Belaric smirked. "Orryn sounds like the name that belongs to a man who drinks too much and loses every fight he picks."

Renna snorted. "You just made that up."

He grinned. "Maybe."

She tilted her head. "Any others?"

Belaric pretended to be deep in thought. "Elara, if it is a girl."

Renna blinked, surprised. "You thought of that one yourself?"

He tapped a finger against the rim of his wine cup, eyes fixed on the deep red liquid. "It was a name I heard once. Long ago."

Renna studied him for a moment, her playful smile fading into something gentler. "You do not remember much from before, do you?"

He shook his head, a tight knot forming in his throat. "Not much worth remembering." The lie tasted like ash. He remembered all of it.

Elara had been another starving child scraping by in the gutters. They had stolen food together, hands trembling from hunger. One day, the guards caught them. Belaric had been quick enough to escape. She had not.

They beat her, and he had not seen her again—only heard, days later, that her body had given out from the wounds. He had carried the guilt with him ever since, her name buried like so many others.

Renna reached across the table, resting her fingers over his. "Then maybe this name can be a good memory."

Belaric stared at their hands, her touch light but certain.

He found the idea of naming something irreplaceable and meant to be kept foreign. Dangerous, even. But Renna had a way of dragging warmth into places where only cold belonged.

His fingers curled slightly, just enough to return the touch.

"If it is a girl," Renna continued, "she will be stubborn. Like you. But clever, like me."

Belaric smirked. "Are you sure about that?"

"Oh, absolutely," she said confidently, sitting up straighter. "She will have your temper, but my patience. Your sharp eyes, but my way with people."

Belaric raised an eyebrow. "So all the good parts are from you, then?"

She grinned. "Naturally, but maybe our next child will be a girl, because I already know this one is a boy," she said, rubbing her belly.

He let out a small chuckle, shaking his head.

They sat in comfortable silence for a moment; the fire crackling between them.

Then Renna sighed dramatically. "So I will admit that this is better than your usual burnt bread and over-salted stew."

Belaric leaned back in his chair, taking another sip of wine. "Enjoy it while it lasts. I do not plan on making this a habit."

She raised her glass to him. "To rare occasions, then."

He clinked his own against hers. "To rare occasions."

The fire flickered, the night stretching ahead of them, warm and uncertain.

Later that night, as Renna curled beneath the sheets, her body warm against his, Belaric waited.

He lay beside her, listening to the slow, steady rhythm of her breathing. His hand rested lightly on her stomach, where their child stirred beneath skin and bone. He could stay. Just this once. He could pretend this life was real, that the weight of his past did not press against his ribs like a blade waiting to slip between them, that tomorrow's concerns were nothing more than stock to be counted and coin to be earned.

But the lie would not hold.

Slowly, he pulled away.

He moved with deliberate quiet, dressing in the dark, pulling on a simple tunic and a dark cloak. His boots barely made a whisper as he crossed the room, casting one last glance at Renna before turning toward the window.

With practiced ease, he unlatched it, pressing his weight against the frame as it slid open. The cold air rushed in, sharp against his skin. He climbed through, lowering himself onto the ledge, his grip sure against the worn stone. After a moment of climbing down in silence, his foot found solid ground. And with it, a familiar, unwelcome hollowness settled in his gut, already expecting the silence of the hunt.

He moved between the two houses. The street was empty. The night stretched around him, silent and watchful.

He let out a silent breath, and moved into the street, remaining in the shadows.

The city at night was different—a world apart from the market's noise and the laughter of the day. This was a city of shadows. Of men who did not want to be seen. Of things best left unnamed.

Belaric walked with purpose, but not haste, sticking to the narrow alleyways where the moonlight did not reach. He avoided the main roads, keeping an ear out for the shuffle of boots and the telltale clink of armored patrols.

At one point, he paused at a corner, pressing himself against the rough stone wall as a pair of guards passed by. Their conversation was idle—one complaining about the cold, the other about his wife's new fascination with scented candles.

Belaric waited until their voices faded before moving on.

The herbalist's shop sat wedged between two larger buildings, its windows dark, its wooden sign creaking softly in the breeze. The scent of old roots and damp earth lingered even out here, clinging to the stones beneath his feet.

Belaric scanned the street once more. Empty. Silent.

He crouched before the door, fingers moving with practiced ease. The worn lock resisted at first, stiff from disuse, but a slight adjustment—a precise turn of the pick—coaxed it open with a muted click.

Inside, the air was thick, saturated with the mingling scents of dried herbs, aged wood, and something faintly metallic—traces of ground minerals and distilled extracts clinging to the shelves. The space was narrow but meticulously arranged, with rows of earthenware jars, wax-sealed vials, and bundles of roots tied neatly with twine. The place meant for healers. Or killers.

He moved quickly, scanning the labels scrawled in ink along the glass bottles. Some calmed the nerves. Some dulled pain. Others stopped a heart in its cage.

He took only what he needed—leaves to numb, powders to silence, extracts potent enough that a single drop could tip the balance between life and death.

Before leaving, he ran a hand over the counter, brushing away the faint disturbance his presence had left behind. A habit more than a necessity. Ghosts did not leave footprints.

Then he was gone, slipping back into the night as if he had never been there at all.

The return trip was just as silent, just as careful. By the time he reached home, the city was still, the only sound the distant hoot of an owl perched somewhere on a rooftop.

Inside, he lifted the loose floorboard he had loosened many years ago, where his past lay hidden beneath their present.

A small pouch of coins. A folded letter he had not read in years.

And the Ashen Blade.

The dagger's blackened steel caught the faint glow of the dying fire, its edge still sharp despite the years of disuse.

It had been the symbol of his rise among the Black Vow, proof that he had spilled blood for them, earned his place among the most ruthless of killers.

Now, it was little more than a relic of another life.

His fingers hovered over the hilt, the familiar curve of the grip fitting against his palm like an old sin. He had not touched it for months. But it was always there. Waiting.

Belaric touched the hilt, his fingers lingering for a breath longer than they should have. Memories flickered—faces, names, the weight of a dying man's final breath.

Belaric released a slow breath, forcing it away.

The blade stayed where it was, buried beneath floorboards and old regrets.

He placed the herbs next to the coin pouch and secured the hiding place and slipped back into bed, wrapping his arms around Renna. She stirred slightly, mumbling something incoherent before settling against him.

Belaric closed his eyes. He wished he could live in this moment forever with Renna, but the memory of the cold steel under the floorboards and the whispers of the Black Vow were promises he doubted the gods would ever let him forget.

5

Renna shifted beside him, a slow, lazy movement that barely disturbed the stillness of the room. Belaric's eyes cracked open to slivers of dawn creeping through the wooden shutters, painting thin golden lines across the ceiling. He felt anchored to the moment by her warmth against him and the steady rise and fall of her breath. The blankets had grown cool at the edges, the lingering heat between them the only barrier against the creeping morning chill. Beneath them, the bed's wooden frame gave a soft creak, the only sound in the hush of early light.

Belaric let out a slow breath, letting himself stay there a little longer. It was rare, these quiet moments. Rarer still to wake with no immediate purpose clawing at the edges of his mind. Renna nestled closer, tucking herself into the curve of his body, her fingers tracing idle patterns against his ribs. Her fingertips were slightly rough, calloused from years of tending the garden and weaving. Strands of her hair, loosed from sleep, brushed against his jaw, carrying the faint scent of lavender from the oils she used to keep it from tangling. She was warm, her breath stirring against his collarbone, the slow rhythm of it lulling, almost enough to pull him back into sleep.

"We should get up," she murmured against his skin, though she made no effort to move.

"Not yet," he said, tightening his hold just a fraction.

She let out a quiet laugh, pressing her forehead to his chest. "If we do not, the sun will leave us behind."

"The sun can wait," he murmured.

Renna scoffed, but did not pull away. "You used to rise before the birds."

"That was before I had a reason to stay in bed," he told her.

She smiled, eyes half-lidded as she looked up at him. "You have spoiled me, Belaric."

He brushed his fingers down the curve of her back. "Good."

Another moment passed before she sighed and stretched, the movement slow and deliberate. "If we stay any longer, I will talk myself out of getting out of bed entirely."

Belaric sighed and relented, slipping out of bed and into the cool morning air. The cold hit first, sinking through his skin, tightening the muscles along his back. The wooden floor was rough under his bare feet, chilling him further as he stepped toward his clothes. He reached for them; the fabric worn but sturdy, his movements methodical. The linen shirt was softer in places, thinned by years of wear, but still held strong at the seams. His trousers had stiffened from dried sweat and travel dust, though they fit snug once fastened. The belt, darkened with age, creaked faintly as he pulled it tight. His coin pouch rested light at his hip—lighter than he liked, but enough for today's needs.

Renna dressed beside him, slipping into a simple gown before pulling on her boots. She tied her hair back with absentminded ease, fingers working through the strands with practiced efficiency. Belaric watched, taking in the routine of it, the quiet normalcy that had grown between them.

Together, they moved into the small kitchen, the wooden floor creaking beneath their steps. Morning light filtered in through the single window, stretching pale gold across the table. Belaric stoked the hearth, setting the iron pan over the fire as Renna cracked the eggs, their yolks breaking like liquid gold. Their scent filled the room, mingling with the rich tang of berries on thick slices of bread. The fire let out a low pop, the embers shifting as heat spread through the small room. The scent of iron and smoke curled into the air as the pan heated, a whisper of steam rising when the eggs met the metal. The scent of frying eggs, rich and savory, filled the kitchen as the yolks began to set, while the berries smeared onto the bread left sticky trails on Renna's fingertips.

For a while, there was only the sound of the fire popping in the hearth, the scrape of utensils, the quiet companionship of shared silence. The table—scarred by years of meals and careless knife strokes—felt solid beneath Belaric's forearms as he leaned against it. His fork dragged against the wooden plate, the slight grainy sound barely louder than the fire's breath.

Renna sat across from him, idly dragging a crust through the remnants of jam.

"I do not think I will go to the market today," she said, her voice still thick with sleep. "I am too tired."

Belaric did not question it. She had spent most of the previous day at her stall, selling fruit and vegetables under the weight of a sun that showed no mercy. Even now, she looked worn thin—her shoulders sagged, eyes shadowed with exhaustion, as if finishing breakfast was more effort than she had to give.

"You should rest," he said gently. "The market can manage a day without you. You have been running low on things from the garden anyway. Probably best to tend to that instead."

She smiled—small, but real.

"I was thinking the same. I will check on the plants, water what needs it. Maybe plant a few new things, if the soil's right."

"Just make sure you take it easy," Belaric told her, not trying to sound too stern.

"I am taking it easy." She arched a brow, lips quirking. "It is not like I am hauling crates for the Merchant's Guild."

He smirked. "True. While you tend the garden, I will visit the merchant's guild."

She tilted her head slightly, studying him. "Planning the next trip?"

He shook his head. "No. But new shipments usually come in around this time of the month. I will check the warehouse, see what they have got. And I still need to pay my guild fees."

Renna exhaled, brushing a thumb along the rim of her cup. The wood was warm from the tea, its surface uneven where the glaze had cracked. She did not drink—just traced the edge, eyes distant.

"Be careful in the upper district. They are stopping people at the gates. Must be on edge about something," she told him, her voice filled with warning.

Belaric frowned and set his fork down. Extra guards in the upper district were not a common sight—most knew better than to cause trouble there. The guards gave no warnings; they gave only bruises and broken ribs. They maintained order through fear, not mercy.

But there were no wars on the horizon, no riots in the streets, not even the usual whispers of unrest. Just the same tired nobles clinging to their power.

So what were they afraid of? He thought. He wiped his hands on a cloth and stood.

"I will be careful," he assured her with a smile.

He slung his cloak over his shoulders and turned toward the door.

Renna caught his wrist before he could leave. Her fingers tightened just slightly, the warmth of them lingering even after she let go. Belaric hesitated, just for a breath. He did not enjoy leaving her alone—not out of some foolish need to protect, but because if something happened, she would have no warning. No escape. The walls of Vorinfall were sturdy, but its dangers did not always come through the gates.

"I mean it," she said.

His lips twitched. "I know."

She leaned up and kissed him—soft and sure. Not desperate, not dramatic. Just full of quiet, steady love. The kind that lingered after it ended.

He stayed there a moment longer, feeling the shape settle in his chest. Then she let him go, and Belaric stepped out into the streets of Vorinfall.

The streets were still rousing, heavy with chimney smoke and the clatter of shutters being thrown open. He passed neighbors he barely knew, nodded at the baker setting out loaves, side-stepped a boy chasing a rolling hoop down the lane. All of it familiar. All of it forgettable.

But with each step, the city changed. Cobblestone grew cleaner, homes taller. The scent of morning bread and smoke-dried meat gave way to something sharper—expensive perfumes, polished steel, and the lingering tang of horse sweat from well-bred destriers lined at the roadside. The noise shifted too. Gone were the haggled curses and barked laughter of the lower quarter. Here, voices spoke in measured tones, the kind used by those who had never needed to shout to be obeyed.

Belaric slowed as he neared the gate to the upper district, eyes sweeping over the guards already watching him.

A line had formed at the gate, where city guards in polished helms inspected papers with practiced scrutiny. The crest of Vorinfall, a symbol of the ruling lord's dominion, adorned their breastplates. The men wearing them carried themselves with the air of those who believed in that dominion, their hands resting lazily on the hilts of their swords, as if already assured of victory in any conflict.

Belaric took his place in line, patience thinning with each slow-moving moment. A merchant ahead of him—a squat man with sweat pooling beneath his collar—grumbled under his breath as the guards picked through his satchel. "It is hard enough getting business done without you lot sniffing through my things," the merchant muttered.

The nearest guard, a broad-chested brute with a nose broken more than once, did not look up from his inspection. "Hard enough for us to keep out the likes of you."

The merchant's face darkened, but he said nothing. A wiser man, or simply one who had learned not to test the patience of a bored guard.

By the time Belaric reached the front, the nearest officer—a burly man with a permanent scowl—held out a hand. "State your business in the upper district."

Belaric pulled his merchant's license from his belt, flipping it open with a practiced motion. "Turning in my fees at the Merchant's Guild. Checking their stock."

The guard scrutinized the papers longer than necessary, eyes flicking between the parchment and Belaric's face. Not suspicious, just the sort of man who enjoyed making others wait. At last he grunted, returning the papers with a flick of his wrist. "Do not cause trouble."

"I would not dream of it," Belaric murmured, stepping past as the gate swung open.

The upper district was a world apart. Cobbled streets, so meticulously maintained they looked as though they had never known filth, stretched in perfect symmetry toward the city's heart. The scent of perfume and polished cedar clung to the air, masking whatever ugliness might still exist beneath the surface.

Grand facades of stone and carved wood framed the avenues—shops gleaming with imported silks, jewelers displaying rings that could feed a family for a year, smithies selling blades that had never seen a battlefield. A blacksmith, standing proudly beside his wares, spoke in animated tones to a customer, extolling the virtues of a dagger forged from southern steel.

Belaric doubted the man had ever held a blade with intent.

Even the air seemed different, lighter somehow, though perhaps that was just the distance from the stench of the slums.

He kept to the edges, navigating through the well-dressed crowd with practiced ease. Nobles and wealthy merchants strolled past, clad in fine velvets and silks embroidered with house sigils. Their hands bore rings set with polished gems, their expressions the practiced indifference of those who had never wanted for anything.

A group of young lords, barely men, laughed as they clustered around a weapons vendor, pointing at a selection of ornately crafted swords. One of them, his face flushed with drink despite the early hour, gestured with exaggerated enthusiasm toward a curved dagger with a gold-inlaid hilt.

"Do you think I could gut someone with this?" he joked, the words slurred.

His companions laughed. The vendor did too, but he was more careful, wearing a mask for his wealthier clientele.

Belaric moved on, unwilling to let his temper sharpen against a fool's edge.

He veered around a cluster gathered near a jeweler's stall. At its center stood a woman draped in a finely tailored dark green dress, the stitching along the hem catching the light with each shift of her weight. Rings adorned every finger—emerald, onyx, sapphire—and a ruby pendant hung from her neck like a claim of status. Two armored guards flanked her, their hands never straying far from the hilts at their sides.

Most nobles kept guards, but these were not there for the ceremony. They were muscle. Protection. Warning.

It was her voice that caught his attention—low, smooth, and commanding in a way that did not ask for attention but seized it. The merchant before her leaned in as if drawn by instinct, nodding at every word.

Belaric's eyes flicked to her face as he passed. That is when he saw it—the black Valasar mark, stark against her skin, encircling her mouth.

A wave of nausea, cold and familiar, twisted in Belaric's gut. He knew that mark intimately. Knew the precise, clinical way it was described in the Order's scrolls, and the terrified cries of the common-born children who bore it, their last breaths exhaled around its cruel symmetry.

The ones who bore the Valasar mark were a rare sight, true. Powerful, coveted, feared. But he had only ever seen them within palace halls, behind the gates of grand estates, or in the desolate corners where his work led him. They rarely mingled with the common-born—most considered themselves chosen by the gods, untouchable, too sacred to be sullied by the filth of the lower classes.

He held her gaze for a moment too long. One of the guards caught it and stepped forward just enough to make the message clear.

Belaric turned away before a word could be spoken. In the upper district, even looking too long could be taken as an insult. And insults here had consequences.

At last, the Merchant's Guild loomed before him, a structure built to rival some of the lesser noble houses. Its facade bore intricate carvings of trade ships and coin purses, a silent reminder of who truly controlled the city's wealth. Wide marble steps led to heavy oak doors, each reinforced with thick bands of iron.

Belaric took a breath and stepped inside.

Belaric stepped inside the Merchant's Guild, greeted by the scent of aged parchment, polished wood, and faint traces of expensive pipe smoke. The lobby was expansive yet orderly, a high-domed ceiling casting soft echoes over neatly arranged desks. Tall windows let in slanted beams of morning light, illuminating rows of heavy-bound ledgers stacked along mahogany counters. The room carried the quiet hum of commerce, the type that dealt not in frantic bartering but in deliberate negotiations made with quills and coin.

At the nearest desk sat an older man, hunched not with age but with habit—like someone who had long ago learned the world pressed down harder if you stood too tall. He turned the pages of a ledger with the precision of a man who never wasted motion, each fingertip calloused by ink rather than toil. His white hair was combed back with obsessive care, the part so straight it looked measured by a ruler, not by hand.

He wore a deep blue doublet, finely tailored and without a thread out of place. Three silver rings gleamed on his fingers—deliberate choices, each one likely bearing a quiet story of gain. The kind of wealth that did not shout but waited for you to notice. Belaric did. Most did. Fendral had that effect.

Not just money, but influence—the sort earned not in court or war, but in coin, calculation, and quiet leverage. He was not a man who raised his voice, because he never needed to.

Belaric had dealt with his type before—measured men with tidy desks and untidy ledgers, who kept their smiles close and their knives closer.

Belaric approached with a quiet familiarity and dipped his head.

"Morning, Fendral," he said, his voice cheerful.

The man looked up, pushing his spectacles higher with a precise motion.

"Belaric," he replied, voice even and practiced. "Did not expect you back so soon."

"Had some luck selling. Figured I would press it before it turns."

Fendral gave a dry chuckle. The sound did not warm his face—it was a sound made for ledgers, not people.

"Wise enough. You know the drill. Sign in," Fendral said as he offered the quill to Belaric.

Belaric took the quill offered—still wet, still sharp—and scratched his name into the ledger's thick parchment. Fendral glanced at the signature, then gave a small nod.

"Come," he said. "I will take you to an office while you wait."

They walked deeper into the guild hall, the polished stone giving way to thick carpets that dulled their steps. Tall shelves flanked them, filled with scrolls, ledgers, and sealed contracts bound in leather. Chandeliers hung from carved beams overhead, casting a gentle gold over oil portraits of past trade masters—all with the same tight-lipped gaze. The scent of ink, dust, and aged wood lingered in the air, heavy with generations of kept promises and unspoken debts.

"How were your travels?" Fendral asked without looking, hands clasped behind his back.

"Good," Belaric said. "Saw a few things worth remembering. A few I would rather forget. Roads are worse than before—bandits are hitting smaller caravans."

Fendral let out a sharp, calculating breath through his nose. "They always crawl out of the cracks before winter. Desperation breeds boldness. Did they trouble you?"

"No more than usual," Belaric replied.

Fendral nodded. "No honest merchant lasts long without drawing steel. But you are still walking, so I will assume you handled it."

Belaric allowed himself a faint smirk. "Handled it."

They stopped before a reinforced oak door, its surface carved in intricate patterns that time had softened but not worn away. Fendral pushed it open and gestured for him to come inside.

The office was modest but refined—no wasted luxury. A large desk stood beneath the window, stacked with ledgers and sealed scrolls. Two cushioned chairs faced it, and a side table near the hearth held a crystal decanter of red wine and two glasses.

Fendral stepped inside, eyes sweeping the room as if to ensure it had not changed.

"Drink while you wait?" Fendral asked.

Belaric shook his head. "No, thank you."

Fendral seemed unsurprised. He adjusted the cuffs of his doublet with a small, deliberate motion.

"One of the masters of the ledger will be along shortly," he informed him.

Belaric gave a curt nod and sank into one of the chairs. The wood creaked beneath his weight, soft and familiar, like an old floorboard. His eyes drifted over the shelves, neat and ordered, a life arranged by profit.

Fendral lingered a moment, then gave a final nod and stepped out—quiet as the door he closed behind him.

Left alone in the office, Belaric leaned back in his chair, the fire's warmth doing little to push away the unease settling in his bones. His thoughts drifted to Renna, wondering if she was all right. It was foolish—nothing had changed since this morning—but still; the worry gnawed at his mind. He pictured her tending the garden, fingers working the soil, brushing stray hair from her face as she studied the leaves.

He should have been comforted by the thought of her—safe, tending her garden, untouched by the weight of the life he lived. But the unease lingered, clinging like damp air before a storm. A quiet breath escaped him as he pressed a hand against his knee.

Soon, he would have to teach again.

His mind turned darker at the thought.

He hated training the young ones. Most were too eager to kill, their masks concealing faces that had yet to grow into the weight of the blades they carried. He could not see their expressions, but he heard it in their voices—the eager, breathless way they asked how best to sever a tendon, the too-swift acceptance of cruelty. Some were barely past their twelfth year, yet already hungry for the act of killing itself.

And worse still, it was his task to show them how.

A sharp knock cut through the quiet.

Belaric straightened, instinct already bracing. The door creaked a breath later.

She stepped in with a presence that demanded respect—and would get it. People like her never needed to speak first. Rooms were adjusted to accommodate them.

She was older than him—though not by much—and carried her years like a coin: counted, polished, and never given freely. Her brown hair was pinned into a tight coil streaked with silver, worn openly and without vanity. The lines on her face had nothing to do with laughter or grief. They were drawn by long years of disappointment and the certainty that everyone else would eventually prove her right.

Her cool, dark, unreadable eyes swept the room like a ledger. When they reached him, they stopped, not in surprise or recognition, but in assessment. He had seen better men than he falter under that kind of stare. It was not cruel. Cruelty implied care. This was colder—curiosity reduced to calculation.

She wore a deep red robe, its golden embroidery flowing along the hem and cuffs as if it had been painted with a single perfect stroke. It was not gaudy. It did not need to be. This was the true wealth of nobility, and it demanded notice, and it would never beg for it.

A book rested in the crook of her arm, its spine cracked, its corners worn to leathery nubs. Belaric knew the type: not a symbol, not a prop—just a tool, and one sharpened often.

He rose to his feet. "Master."

Her lips twitched—not in greeting, but in correction.

"Master Deyra," she said, tone flat enough to clip steel.

He inclined his head. "Master Deyra. I am Belaric Kelmor."

She did not answer. Did not nod. Just moved past him with the dismissive grace people usually reserved for flies.

The book landed on the desk with a dull thud, and she sat with the stiff finality of someone delivering a sentence. The chair seemed to straighten to meet her, not the other way around.

She flipped the book open, fingers moving with quiet precision. When she found her page, she stopped.

Her eyes flicked up at him, then back down at the parchment. "List your transactions."

Belaric nodded. "Two crates of dried herbs, one of southern textiles, and a half-crate of iron fittings. I sold half the herbs to market sellers, the textiles to a tailor in the lower district, and the iron to a blacksmith near Eastgate."

She flipped a page in the ledger, fingers tapping once before tracing down a column. Her lips pressed into a thin line as she scanned.

"Small sales," she said at last, her voice clipped. "Low-margin. Fragmented."

Belaric crossed his arms. "They paid in full."

Her nose wrinkled, faint and involuntarily. "Yes, well. Coin is coin. But it does little to cover your guild fee."

He met her stare for a moment longer than courtesy allowed. She was used to merchants bowing their heads, used to them swallowing their complaints to avoid friction with the Guild. He did neither—he only exhaled through his nose and said nothing.

"I pay my fees like any other merchant," he said.

Deyra tapped a finger against the ledger. "Then you will pay them now. Seven gold pieces, four silvers, and ten coppers."

The number was higher than expected. Too high.

Belaric's fingers flexed at his side, but he kept his voice measured. "Fees were lower the last time I bought."

Deyra did not blink. "And now they are not."

A pause stretched between them. He could argue, but it would do him no good. She was not the type to negotiate, and he doubted she would bother listening.

Without a word, Belaric pulled his coin pouch from his belt, counted out the required amount and placed it on the desk. She did not reach for it immediately. Instead, she watched him for a beat longer than necessary, as if waiting for him to hesitate, to complain. When he did not, she finally swept the coins toward herself, counting them again with precise, deliberate movements.

Satisfied, she slid the book toward him. "Sign."

Belaric took the quill and signed his name in the space beneath the tally. Deyra took the quill after him, signing with sharp, deliberate strokes before slamming the book shut.

He nodded. "Thank you."

She ignored him, standing and gathering the ledger, moving toward the door without so much as a parting glance.

The moment she left, Belaric exhaled through his nose, shaking his head before turning and making his way out of the office.

When he reached the front, Fendral glanced up from his desk, took one look at him and exhaled.

"Let me guess," Belaric said, smirking. "She is new."

Fendral pinched the bridge of his nose. "Unfortunately."

Belaric chuckled. "Who the hell decided to let her in?"

Fendral leaned back, folding his arms. "Her family bought the position."

Belaric barked a quiet laugh. "Of course they did."

"No one likes her," Fendral muttered, shaking his head.

Belaric smirked. "No one? Not even her fellow masters?"

"Especially not them," Fendral grumbled.

Belaric let out a low chuckle and shook his head. "With any luck, she will find the work beneath her and move on."

"One can only hope."

Sobering slightly, Belaric leaned against the desk. "Have they restocked the warehouse recently?"

Fendral nodded. "A few shipments came in the past few days. Some good stock, if you are quick about it."

Belaric pushed off the desk. "I will go take a look."

"Try not to clean us out," Fendral said.

"No promises," Belaric replied with a smirk.

He signed out, handed the ledger back, and stepped into the streets of the vast city. The chill bit against his skin, creeping through the seams of his cloak. His coin pouch hung lighter now, but that was Vorinfall—a city where nothing came cheap, least of all survival.

Pulling his cloak tighter, Belaric moved through the streets. He had walked these roads hundreds of times, yet the stark difference between the middle district and the upper district never ceased to surprise him.

Here, everything gleamed—polished stone streets free of filth, the air filled with the rich scents of spiced wine and fresh-cut flowers rather than sweat and coal smoke. Nobles strolled with effortless grace, their hands adorned with rings made from the finest jewels, their laughter light, untouched by hardship. Even the merchants dressed finely, their stalls shaded by silk canopies, their voices smooth as they pitched their goods to well-dressed buyers.

Belaric's steps slowed as he passed one such stall, a vendor displaying fine dresses and embroidered shawls. He hesitated.

Renna would look beautiful in something like that. Something warm, something soft—something to remind her that she was more than the weight she carried.

His fingers brushed the pouch at his belt.

He could afford something modest. Not the silk-draped gowns meant for noblewomen, but something simple, something that would bring her a smile.

Then he met the merchant's eyes—sharp, assessing. Already judging.

Belaric knew the type. The moment he spoke, the price would double, or the man would sneer and call for the guards to have him removed.

His fingers curled, then withdrew. His jaw tightened as he stepped away.

Minutes later, he arrived at the warehouse.

The structure loomed before him, a fortress of stone and timber, its high walls lined with iron brackets holding burning torches despite the daylight. The air here smelled of oil, dust, and damp wood—thick with the scent of trade and storage.

At the entrance stood a cluster of hardened mercenaries, their presence a silent warning to anyone with the wrong intentions.

They were broad-shouldered men, scarred and brutal-looking—muscle hardened by years of bloodshed, not labor. Their armor was a patchwork of steel and leather, strapped tight with no regard for appearance, only function. Longswords, axes, and blunt cudgels hung from belts or rested in calloused hands. A few leaned against the stone wall, eyes sharp and restless, scanning each passerby like they were counting coin—and weighing whether it was worth stealing.

Belaric approached at a steady pace. He saw it happen before it began—the shifting of shoulders, the subtle narrowing of eyes. One of the guards straightened from his post, a thick-necked brute with a lopsided helm and a face that looked like it had stopped more fists than it had dodged.

"Stop right there," the man barked. "State your business."

Belaric halted, hands slowly rising to chest height. Palms out. Non-threatening.

"Merchant," he said evenly. "Guild member. Came to see if anything new had come through the warehouse."

The brute's eyes narrowed. "You do not look like a merchant."

Belaric gave a faint smile. "I get that a lot."

He reached slowly—deliberately—to his belt, drawing out the folded papers with two fingers.

Around him, hands drifted toward hilts. One man shifted his weight, just enough to clear his blade if it came to that. Another rolled his shoulder, adjusting his grip on a cudgel. The air took on a tightness Belaric had known many times before.

He measured the distance between them. Four men. None of them are fast. Not trained the way he had been. He could kill all four if he needed to. Not without blood—but without failure.

But that was not the game today.

The brute snatched the papers and gave them a once-over, lips moving silently as he scanned. Then, with a grunt, he turned his head toward the warehouse doors.

"Aedric!" he bellowed.

Moments later, the heavy warehouse doors creaked open, and a man stepped forward into the daylight.

He was tall, broad-shouldered, and moved with the ease of someone who had spent years learning exactly how not to waste a motion.

His build spoke more of a discipline than brute strength—like every inch of him had been shaped with purpose, not pride.

Long, dirty-blond hair was tied back in a loose knot, a few strands slipping free to frame a face that might have passed for handsome, if it were not for the sharpness of it. The kind of sharp that cuts conversation short. His eyes—light brown, cool, and precise—took in the room like a man marking exits, threats, and weaknesses all at once. He looked like someone who noticed everything and let people wonder how much he had seen.

His armor was leather, fitted and worn, reinforced at the chest and shoulders. It bore scars that told quiet stories—none flashy, none decorative. Just damage survived. At his hips rested twin swords, mirror-polished, the hilts worn by repetition, not neglect.

Then his eyes found Belaric, and a smirk curved his lips. The kind that never meant one thing.

"Ah, Belaric," he said, voice smooth and laced with amusement. "Did not expect to see you again so soon."

Belaric returned the nod, offering nothing else. Aedric was the kind of man who played the room like a board—always three steps ahead, never so careless as to show his hand. He did not need to win every exchange. He just needed you to think he might.

Then Aedric turned to the guards.

"This is Belaric, you idiot."

The brute who had challenged him blinked, brow furrowing.

"I—what?"

Aedric let out a long-suffering sigh.

"He was here a few weeks ago. You really do not remember?" He shook his head. "I swear, you lot spend more coin on ale than on memory."

The others chuckled. The brute just grunted and looked away.

Aedric waved Belaric forward. "Come on. Let us get you inside before one of them tries to charge you a gate fee."

They stepped through the open doors, the scent of dust and timber pressing close. Lanterns hung from the high beams, casting shifting pools of gold over a vast sprawl of crates and barrels. The air smelled of old spice, dry grain, and the faint hint of sea salt carried in from southern ports. Every item bore a mark—trader's seal, port stamp, or merchant cipher—each one a fragment of some far-off journey. A ledger comes to life.

Workers moved between them, tallying goods, hauling sacks over their shoulders, checking shipments against long lists of inventory. The air buzzed with the steady rhythm of trade—men shouting orders, the scrape of crates being dragged across the stone floor, the distant hammering of nails sealing another shipment.

Aedric walked alongside Belaric, his hands resting on the hilts of his swords as he surveyed the room. "Looking for anything specific today, or just pretending you have coin to spend?"

Belaric smirked faintly. "Did not realize I had to report my finances to you."

Aedric let out a short laugh. "Not my concern—unless, of course, you plan on taking without paying."

Belaric's expression did not change. "I think we both know I would not be that sloppy."

Aedric's smirk lingered as he studied him. "Not sloppy, no. But cautious. Too cautious, if you ask me."

Belaric glanced at a crate of bundled pelts, brushing his fingers over the markings. "Good way to stay alive."

Aedric hummed in agreement, watching a pair of workers struggle with an ironbound chest. "Got a trip planned, or are you standing here for the warmth of my company?"

A breath escaped Belaric. "Not yet."

Aedric arched a brow. "That is rare for you. You usually have a plan before you set foot in this place."

Belaric only shrugged, his attention on a set of finely crafted daggers resting in an open crate.

Aedric's eyes flicked over him, unreadable. "Take your time, then. Look around." He clapped Belaric on the shoulder, the weight of his hand firm but brief, before turning toward a group of workers arguing over the tally on a shipping manifest.

Belaric spent the next few hours browsing the aisles. He ran his fingers over a barrel of cured salts, eyed a shipment of leather from the borderlands, and took mental note of the finer steel goods tucked away in the far corner. Belaric knew he would have to decide soon—his coin would not sit idle forever—but today he let himself wander without urgency.

When he was done, he sought out Aedric near the entrance.

"Nothing today," Belaric said.

Aedric snorted. "Figured. You stare at half the stock like you are memorizing it for later. Makes a man wonder if you ever actually buy anything."

Belaric smirked. "Some of us have to be careful."

Aedric shook his head, amused. "And yet, you walk around like you own the place."

Belaric shrugged. "Confidence is free."

Aedric chuckled. "Until next time, then."

Belaric thanked him and stepped back into the street. The guards barely spared him a glance as he passed.

His steps carried him toward home, but his thoughts lingered elsewhere.

Renna.

He was eager to get back to her, to shake the dust of the guild from his shoulders and let her voice pull him back to something simpler, something warmer.

But the moment of anticipation soured as another name crept into his mind. Lady Haldren. And her daughter Lyra. The names brought with them the scent of cold steel, the faint echo of a desperate plea he had heard too many times before. A fresh wave of disgust, sharp and bitter, washed over him.

He had never seen the girl himself, only heard murmurs—young, barely grown, but that would not matter. The Order did not hesitate, and once they set their sights on someone; they were already dead. The only question was how soon someone would discover the bodies.

Would they send someone experienced? A veteran of the Order, swift and cold as the steel they carried, who would end it quickly and efficiently, leaving no trace but the chill of his presence? Or would they send a fresh-faced recruit, someone full of zeal and a desperate need to prove their loyalty? The thought of the latter was a poison in his gut. A seasoned killer might feel nothing, but a new one, full of fire and misplaced conviction, would find a strange, morbid satisfaction in the act. And that, he knew, would be far more damning to his own soul.

His fingers curled at his sides.

There was nothing he could do about it now.

By the time he reached his home, the sun had dipped lower in the sky, casting long shadows over the dirt path leading to his door. He wasted no time stepping inside, closing the world behind him.

Renna was in her chair, the soft candlelight flickering against her face as she worked on the blanket for the baby.

For the first time that day, Belaric allowed himself to breathe.

He closed the door behind him, shutting out the cold and the world beyond. The fire's glow stretched flickering shadows across the wooden walls, the scent of dried lavender clinging to the air, mingling with the faintest trace of crushed berries from breakfast.

Renna looked up from her chair, setting her sewing aside with a tired but knowing smile.

"You are back," she said softly.

Belaric stepped toward her, his boots light against the wooden floor. "Where else would I be?"

She huffed a small laugh, tilting her head. "I could think of a few places."

Belaric smirked and leaned down, brushing a kiss against her lips before resting a hand over her belly. "How are you feeling?"

"Well enough." She stretched, rolling her shoulders. "The baby's been restless today—kicking."

Belaric's expression softened. He knelt, pressing a hand against her stomach, waiting. A moment passed—then another—before a sharp, insistent push met his palm. He smiled, rubbing slow circles over her belly before pressing a light kiss there.

"Already a fighter," he murmured.

Renna chuckled, fingers brushing through his hair. "Or just impatient."

Belaric smirked. "That would be your side of the family."

She scoffed, swatting at his shoulder.

He pushed himself to his feet, grabbed the water pitcher, and poured her a cup, pressing it into her hands. "Here. You need to drink more."

Renna took a slow sip, watching him over the rim of the cup.

Belaric rolled his shoulders and glanced toward the hearth. "I will get dinner started."

Renna arched a brow. "You are cooking again?"

Belaric grabbed a few ingredients, glancing over his shoulder. "Two nights in a row. Imagine that."

She smirked. "Should I be concerned?"

He gave her a mock scowl. "I would say you should be grateful."

"Oh, I am," she said, amusement flickering in her voice. "A husband who cooks? I must have done something right."

Belaric huffed a laugh, shaking his head as he set to work. He sliced thick chunks of meat, dropping them into the iron pot over the fire. The scent of sizzling fat quickly filled the air as he added herbs, a handful of salt, and dried root vegetables. As the stew thickened, he pan-fried fresh greens with oil and crushed garlic; the aroma warming the space.

Renna shifted in her chair, tucking her legs beneath her. "So… how was your day?"

"Eventful," he said, stirring the pot. "The Merchant's Guild has a new master of ledgers. Master Deyra."

She arched an eyebrow. "Deyra? Never heard the name."

"New to the post," Belaric said. "Bought her way in."

Renna's lips twitched. "Oh, I can already tell you two got along well."

Belaric shot her a dry look. "She counts her coins twice before handing them over. I imagine she weighs the air before she breathes it."

Renna smirked. "Sounds like someone I know."

Belaric turned back to the stew, shaking his head. "I count it once and make sure no one tries to take it. There is a difference."

She chuckled, swirling the water in her cup. "And the warehouse?"

"Aedric was there. Stock was good—fine steel, a few shipments of southern spices. Gave me a few ideas for the next journey."

Renna hummed, thoughtful. "Have you decided where that will be?"

"Not yet." He met her gaze. "I have been thinking about it."

She studied him for a long moment, then took another sip of water. "And have you been thinking about Jorric?"

He stirred the stew—smooth, practiced. But at the mention of Jorric, the spoon slowed. Just for a moment. He had thought of Jorric, thought of him with a protective dread. He could not, would not, take him on the road. But the Guild was another matter. "I have," he said, his voice quiet. "But I have not decided the best way forward for him yet."

"You will," she murmured, setting her cup down.

He nodded, silent. The risk of bringing Jorric was high. But maybe—if he planned it right, before the Order assigned another task—there would be no risk at all.

He thought again of the warehouse. The spices. The steel. All of it held potential. One good shipment, and he could line his pockets enough to last the season. Maybe longer.

He pushed the thought aside, scooping a bowl of stew and plating the vegetables before bringing them to Renna.

She accepted it with a grateful smile. "Thank you."

"For what?" he asked.

She smiled back. "You were just planning it in your head—with Jorric coming with you."

He allowed himself a smile. "Maybe. But let us not worry about that right now."

He sat across from her and dug into his own portion. The food was simple but warm—the kind of meal that settled in the belly and softened the edges of a long day.

As they ate, they spoke of the coming days—supplies they needed, repairs around the house. They talked about the baby, about the names they had yet to choose, about whether they would have a boy or a girl.

Eventually, the fire burned low, and Belaric pushed back his chair, stretching. "I am going to bathe."

Renna nodded, finishing the last of her stew. "Do not take too long. I will be asleep before you finish."

He smirked. "No promises."

The bath was quick—a rinse to wash away the dust of the city, the weight of the day. When he returned, Renna was still by the fire, wrapped in a thick wool blanket, her hands resting over her belly.

Belaric sat beside her, stretching his legs toward the flames.

She glanced at him, her expression softer now. "You are quiet."

He sighed, rubbing a hand over his jaw. "Just tired."

Renna continued to study him for another moment, then reached over, lacing her fingers through his. "Come to bed."

She led Belaric upstairs; her warm hand steadied him more than he cared to admit.

As they settled beneath the blankets, he pulled her close, pressing a final kiss to her temple. Her presence was a warmth against the cold, a quiet hope that, for now at least, his night world would leave them be.

6

The days passed in quiet routine, a rhythm both foreign and strangely fragile. Belaric spent his mornings in the garden, turning soil between his fingers, helping Renna pluck weeds from between the roots. In the afternoons, he busied himself with repairs—patching the roof, sealing drafts in the walls, hammering loose steps into submission. The latter had become a necessity. He told himself it was for Renna, that she deserved a home without groaning boards and broken steps.

But stillness was a sharp thing. It cut in places he had not noticed before. With no blades to clean, no orders to follow, his thoughts had begun to crowd him—shadows of the life he had lived, questions of whether this one was ever truly his. The quiet was not a reward. It was a reckoning.

One morning, before the markets had fully shaken off the night, Belaric made his way through the quiet streets, pausing at a vendor's stall. Apples. Firm, red, sun-warmed. Eddaross had little luxury in his life, but he would have this. They would not be as good as Renna's, he knew. No apples ever were. But Eddaross would still eat them, and that was enough.

The stables were dim and still, with the scent of hay and leather thick in the air. Only the distant clatter of hooves echoed from the main yard. Darius was already up, hunched by a feed bin, scratching notes into a small ledger.

He glanced up as Belaric entered. "Did not think you would come this early."

Belaric offered a nod. "Thought he could use the air."

Darius snorted softly and jerked a thumb toward Eddaross's stall. "He has been restless. Nearly kicked down the slats yesterday."

Belaric found the stall door already unlatched. Eddaross lifted his head at the sound of boots, nostrils flaring, eyes steady with the weight of familiarity.

"I did not forget you," Belaric murmured, pulling an apple from his satchel. Eddaross took it greedily, crunching down, flicking his tail like this was no more than his due.

Belaric spent the better part of an hour tending to him—checking his hooves, brushing him down, placing the saddle on his back and tightening it. Things that needed no checking, no brushing, no tightening. But he did them anyway. Not out of duty. Out of need.

When the last strap was pulled taut, he led Eddaross from the stall and out into the waking streets. He mounted Eddaross and moved swiftly through the streets. The guards at the gate barely spared him a glance—just a nod, and a murmured greeting.

The city gave way to morning dew-covered fields and open sky. Belaric loosened his grip, and Eddaross took his freedom as though it had always been his, surging forward into a gallop.

The wind lashed at Belaric's face, stinging his skin, blurring the edges of the world until nothing remained but speed and silence. He leaned into the rhythm, the pounding of hooves, the flex and stretch of muscle beneath him. It was not an escape. It was not atonement. It was motion—pure and untethered. Enough to exist simply in this moment.

The sun climbed higher, warming the damp earth beneath them. The scent of pine and wild grass replaced the wet soil of the dawn. They skirted the edge of a forest, with the deep shadows on his left, the endless fields on his right, before turning back toward the rising sun. Belaric felt the familiar burn in his thighs, the steady ache in his back, a welcome physical reality that chased away the shadows in his mind. For the first time in days, the weight in his chest seemed to loosen.

He eased back on the reins, slowing the stallion to a steady canter, then a trot. Eddaross resisted for a breath, then relented, his sides heaving, foam gathering at the bit.

By the time they reached the stables again, the morning had well and truly settled. Eddaross's coat gleamed with sweat, his breath deep but unlabored—better for the run, none the worse for it.

"Better?" Belaric murmured, patting his neck.

The horse flicked an ear and nudged at his satchel. Searching. Expecting.

Belaric smirked faintly, obliging him with another apple.

The ride had done what it needed to do. Taken the edge off of Eddaross's restlessness, and allowed Belaric to clear his mind of the shadows.

Because it never lasted.

It never did.

By the time they returned to the city, the sun sat high in the clear sky, casting a long, drowsy light over the rooftops. The men guarding the gate gave him the same indifferent nod. Nothing had changed. Nothing ever did.

He spent the last of the afternoon on his hands and knees, replacing a wobbly leg on the kitchen table—the one that had rocked and groaned with every meal for months now. He worked with methodical care, his hands finding the grain of the new wood, fitting it with precise cuts, then hammering it into place with quiet, confident strokes. When he was done, he tested it with his weight, and a small, satisfied breath escaped him when it held without so much as a whisper. Afterward, he climbed a ladder to the roof, finding the small leak he had noticed weeks ago. The air was cool and crisp, a welcome relief from the day's heat. He worked quickly, a hammer in one hand and a few extra shingles in the other, sealing the leak and shoring up the wood against the coming rain. It was simple, honest work. The kind that filled his hands and quieted his mind.

As the afternoon waned and shadows stretched long across the yard, a weight settled in his chest. By nightfall, he would be back within the Black Vow's walls, standing before the young initiates, teaching them the art of poison. How a few grains of powder could hollow a man from the inside. How a single drop could turn breath into silence.

He had planned it out. Keep it simple. Show them the distinction between slow and swift poisons, between agony and quiet death. Demonstrate. Speak little. Leave before the walls closed in again.

But the sun dipped lower, Renna's voice pulled him from his thoughts.

"You have been somewhere else all day," she murmured, her tone gentle, certain. She always knew when his mind had gone wandering. "What is it?"

Belaric glanced up from the whetstone, considering his answer. A dozen truths. None of which he could say. He exhaled slowly.

"The baby," he said. Not a lie. Not entirely. "I have been thinking about the baby. About whether I will be a good father."

Renna stilled, her hands pausing over the kettle. A silence stretched between them, heavy with something unspoken, before she set it aside and crossed the room. She sat beside him, fingers threading through his with quiet certainty.

"Do you know how I knew I loved you?" she asked.

Belaric blinked. He had no answer for her. She seemed to know that, too.

She gave his hand a gentle squeeze before continuing. "It was not because you kept me safe," she began. "Or because you provided for me. It was not even the way you look at me when you think I do not notice." Another squeeze, firm, certain. "It is because you are always there. No questions. No hesitation. You show me every day that you love me, and you do not even need to say it."

Belaric frowned, shaking his head. "You see what you want to see."

She arched an eyebrow. "Do I?" Her gaze sharpened, seeing right through the defenses he had spent a lifetime building. "Then tell me, why do you do these things? Why fix the stairs, tend the garden, mend the roof—like a man who intends to stay forever? You think that because you are away, you are an evil man? That is a story you tell yourself. I know the truth." She stepped closer, her hand rising to cup his cheek. "Even when you are not physically here, you are still here with me. You are here in the way I feel safe. You are here in my heart."

The words landed where no blade could reach.

Renna's voice softened. "I have known men who do not care. They take what they need and leave the rest. But you—you build. You fix what is broken. You take care of what is yours, without hesitation, without question."

His jaw tightened. "That does not make me a good man."

She did not flinch. "I think it makes you a great one. One who will love and support your child every day. Will you make mistakes? Of course—we both will. But we are only human. We will learn. Remember, only the gods are perfect."

Her words sat heavy on his chest, a weight he did not know what to do with. She saw something in him he could never quite grasp. A man who could be more than the blood on his hands. A man who could build rather than destroy.

Belaric squeezed her hand. A rare thing. A quiet thing.

"Thank you," he murmured.

Renna smiled, pressing a kiss to his knuckles before standing. "Come to bed. You will worry yourself into an early grave at this rate."

He did as she asked, lying beside her in the dim candlelight, listening to the slow rhythm of her breathing as she drifted to sleep.

But sleep never came for him.

The room darkened. The night stretched on.

Outside, the wind whispered through the trees, rattling the shutters. A dog barked in the distance. Somewhere in the city, a bell tolled the hour.

Belaric exhaled slowly, shifting onto his back, eyes tracing the ceiling. He felt the weight of it all in his chest; it was settling deeper. It always did.

With careful, practiced movements, he slipped from the bed. Renna shifted, but did not wake.

He crouched beside the bed, fingers brushing along the wooden floor. Finding the loosened board, he pried it free. The scent hit him first—bitter, sharp, familiar. A memory wrapped in dried leaves and crushed roots.

He untied the cloth bundle, checking the contents. Everything untouched. Everything waiting.

For a moment, he sat there, the bundle resting heavy in his hands.

How easy it would be to burn them.

To let the fire swallow them whole. To bury this piece of himself and never look back.

But he had never been that foolish.

Silently, he rose and dressed, buckling his belt, fastening the heavier garments against the cold. His cloak came last, the fabric whispering as he pulled it over his shoulders. The bundle vanished beneath it.

One last glance at Renna. Then, he was gone.

The house barely stirred as he moved through it, each step measured, each breath quiet. He unlatched the door and stepped into the night.

The cold met him first, biting through fabric, curling around his skin like an old companion. The street was quiet, the usual late-night murmurs reduced to the distant echo of footfalls on stone. He kept to the edges, slipping through the narrow passageways behind the rows of houses.

A few turns. A shadowed path between two buildings.

The alley was empty, save for the distant hum of the city beyond. His old life waited where he had left it—a bundle wrapped in dark cloth, patient and inevitable.

His fingers found the leather, stiff from disuse. With each buckle tightened, each blade slid into place, each motion was a step back into something he had once shed but never truly lost.

Then, at last, his hands found the mask.

He hesitated.

It was always heavier than he remembered. The smooth wood bore no features, no warmth—just a reflection of the thing he had become.

He stared into its empty eyes and, for the briefest moment, wondered.

If he would ever escape this. If the weight of this life would ever leave his shoulders.

But the answer had been written long ago.

With a slow, measured breath, he lifted the mask to his face.

The night swallowed him whole.

His body went through the motions. No thought. No hesitation. Muscle and memory guiding every step.

He scaled the crumbling stone wall with ease, fingers seeking familiar grooves, feet light against weathered stone. At the top, he crouched, scanning the alley below. Empty. Silent. He dropped, landing without a sound.

The abandoned house loomed ahead, its wooden beams warped with age, the air thick with mildew and rot. He slipped inside, keeping to the edges where the floor held strongest. Dust swirled in the moonlight, stirred by something long past breathing.

Down the steps. To the far wall.

Belaric stood there for a moment, exhaling slowly. He had done this countless times. Yet tonight, it settled heavier in his bones.

But weight meant nothing.

He pressed his palm to the stone in the precise sequence, just as he had since he was a boy. A deep, grinding shift rumbled through the silence. The hidden door slid open.

He stepped inside, boots soundless against the cold stone.

At the passage's end, the black door waited. Unmarked save for a single iron knocker, its shape twisted into a serpent's head. He lifted it, rapping twice.

A voice, low and rasping, spoke from the other side. "What is the weight of a life?"

The answer came easily. "Less than a feather. More than a soul."

A pause. The scrape of shifting metal. The quiet exhale of an unseen breath.

Then the lock clicked.

The door swung inward.

The guard barely looked at him, offering a curt nod. Belaric returned it with equal indifference.

Anything less would be noticed.

If he hesitated, if he let the weight press too hard against his ribs, the masters would hear of it. And if the masters suspected weakness, even a fracture in the mask he wore, they would kill him. And they would not stop with him.

Belaric let the rhythm take hold.

He moved through the corridors, steps steady, shadows jagged against the stone walls. The air smelled of damp rock, of oil, of something faintly metallic—the scent of steel, waiting.

At the entrance to the tunnels, he stopped.

The children were already there. Waiting. Watching. Expecting.

They sat in small clusters, their voices hushed but eager. Some sat cross-legged on the floor. Others leaned against the walls.

Waiting for him.

Waiting for the lesson.

Waiting for the knowledge that had been driven into him since childhood.

His stomach coiled. Not in fear. Not quite.

He hated this part. Hated the way their eyes lit up when he spoke of poison, of pain. Hated the way they leaned forward, hungry to learn how to make others suffer. They were too young to carry that kind of knowledge. Too young to have been shaped into what he had become. But here they were. And here he was.

He stepped inside.

As he entered, the children's attention snapped to him. In unison, they rose to their feet.

"Master."

The word grated on him.

He moved past them, his expression carved from stone. "I am no master. You will address me by my rank—Ashen Blade. Do you understand?"

"Yes, Ashen Blade." The answer came crisp, rehearsed, drilled into them.

He hated it. The title, the rigid discipline they had. The way they had already begun to shape themselves into the same mold he had been forced into. A muscle twitched, barely perceptible, in his jaw. Under the heavy fabric of his cloak, his hand clenched, a tremor fighting to rise.

But there was no room for anything else.

A single misstep, a misplaced word, and the masters would demand answers.

He could already see it—dragged before them, their masks impassive, their silence heavier than their questions. The words would come slowly, deliberately, each one a blade pressed to his throat.

"Why do they call you Master, Varros? Which of us did you kill to claim the title?"

And he would have no answer.

The thought coiled in his mind, tightening like a noose. He forced it aside.

He spoke in a measured tone. "I am Ashen Blade Varros. I am one of the most proficient with poisons, and that is what your lesson will be on tonight." His gaze swept over them. Their sharp, waiting eyes. Their quiet hunger.

"I will teach you the difference between poisons that put a man to sleep and those that stop a heart. Use the wrong one, and your target may live. And if that happens, you will expose the Order."

His tone turned sharper. "And that will result in death. Your death."

None of them flinched.

"Now, gather around me." He reached beneath his cloak, retrieving the cloth bundle. He commanded.

"Yes, Ashen Blade." The children moved as one, forming a tight circle around him.

For a moment, all was still.

Too still. The air stretched thin, waiting.

Then a voice cut through it.

"I could not agree more, Varros. Exposing the Order will always result in death."

Belaric's attention snapped toward the figure moving into the chamber.

Master Lyessa.

He straightened, forcing his expression into something unreadable. "I was not expecting you to join us this evening, Master Lyessa." A measured pause. "But yes, I wanted to impart our most sacred rule—never expose the Order. Our secrecy is our greatest strength."

His thoughts darkened.

He already hated this—watching these children twist into something unrecognizable, shaping them into what he had once been. What he still was.

But now, a master watching? His night had found a way to get worse.

"How right you are, Varros." Lyessa's voice was smooth, almost amused. She moved slowly, letting the flickering torchlight stretch shadows across the black silk of her robes. "I thought it might be useful to refresh my knowledge of poisons. And who better than you to teach me?"

A pause. A small, deliberate thing.

"And of course, I have a special treat for them."

A murmur spread through the initiates. Not fear. Not uncertainty. Excitement.

Master Lyessa clapped her hands, the sound sharp as a whip-crack. "Come forth," she commanded.

Dread settled low in Belaric's gut.

The sound came first.

Chains clinking. Metal scraping against stone.

He knew what was coming. Knew what she had planned. Could almost see the cruel smile beneath her mask.

"While showing them the herbs is important," Lyessa continued, voice smooth, measured, "we felt that allowing them to witness the true effects of these poisons would be an even greater opportunity. Would not you agree, Varros?"

He bowed. A small thing, precise, exact. "Of course, Master. Since they will need to use these poisons in the near future, witnessing their effects firsthand will be invaluable."

"Indeed," she replied. While Belaric could not see her face, he knew she was smiling behind the mask.

Belaric's gaze flickered past her as Dainrik entered, leading four prisoners into the chamber. A woman. Three men. They were a pathetic sight—heads covered in rough cloth sacks, hands bound in rusted chains. The metal rattled as they stumbled forward, shoulders hunched, steps unsteady.

Their clothes were barely more than rags. The woman's dress was threadbare, its once-dark fabric faded to a dull, lifeless grey. One man wore a tunic held together by stitches, seams barely clinging to the fabric. The other two were in patchwork coats, sleeves uneven, hems muddied from the filth of the streets.

Beggars.

Victims of the city's unyielding cruelty, plucked from the gutters and offered up to children who would be taught this was justice.

Lyessa turned toward them.

"These four were condemned to death this morning." Her tone was idle, conversational, as if she were discussing the price of grain. "Caught attempting to sneak into the Upper District. No doubt looking to steal from their betters."

The first prisoner stiffened, a sharp breath waiting in his throat

"That is not—" the man started.

Dainrik's fist buried itself in his stomach.

The prisoner collapsed, chains snapping taut, dragging the others forward with him. He coughed, breath rattling in his chest. No more words escaped him.

Belaric did not move. Did not react.

She was lying.

No beggar was foolish enough to try the Upper District. The guards would gut them before they ever got close. These people were here because they had been seen at the wrong time, in the wrong place.

The children sat unmoving, masked faces turned toward the prisoners. Then the whispers started.

"Will we get to use them soon?" A boy asked softly.

"I hope we get to watch them die," another whispered back.

A third child leaned forward. "I wonder how long it takes."

Soft voices. Steady voices. Not uncertain—eager.

Belaric forced his hands to remain loose at his sides, his shoulders still. But something cold twisted inside him. Not anger. Not grief. Something quieter. Something worse. A slow, creeping revulsion buried beneath the mask he wore—both the one on his face and the one he had lived behind for years.

Master Lyessa let the whispers linger a moment longer before lifting a hand.

The chamber fell silent.

The children leaned forward, their masked faces tilted toward the prisoners. Not with hesitation. With excitement.

Belaric swallowed down a sigh before it could form.

Then he stepped forward. "Form a half-circle."

The children obeyed at once. Silent. Orderly. They moved into place, a ring of eager shadows.

"Dainrik, if you do not mind—lay them down in the circle." He asked.

Dainrik nodded and yanked the kneeling man forward. The chains pulled taut, metal scraping metal, a sharp protest that went unheard.

The children parted, their masked faces turning as one. Watching. Waiting.

The prisoner stumbled, breath ragged behind the cloth sack.

Reaching the center of the formation, Dainrik placed a heavy hand on his shoulder and shoved him down. The others followed—dragged, positioned, forced into place like pieces in a game where they did not know the rules.

The rusted chains rattled as they twisted against their restraints. One began to sob softly beneath the sack. Another muttered broken prayers between choked breaths. None dared scream. Not here.

A gesture of defiance. Nothing more. Nothing useful.

Dainrik stepped back, leaving them in the circle's center.

Belaric turned to one of the children. "Stone and pestle."

A girl no older than ten perked up at the command.

"Yes, Ashen Blade." She darted toward the stone desk, small hands careful as she lifted the mortar and pestle. She returned swiftly, presenting it with both hands.

Belaric took it and knelt beside the first prisoner.

"We will start with Dreamrot."

From his cloak, he pulled the bundle of herbs, unwrapping the tightly bound leaves.

"This poison places the target into a deep sleep—a dream sleep." His voice was steady. Detached. "But it is known to give them nightmares."

The children leaned in slightly. Not nervous. Not hesitant. Curious.

"To prepare it, you mix three leaves of nightshade, three inches of Dreamvine, and two leaves of Twilight Myrrh."

He dropped the herbs into the stone bowl and began grinding them down.

"You must crush it into a fine powder. If any part remains unground, the full effect will not take hold. And if that happens, the target may wake too soon."

The slow, rough scrape of stone against stone filled the chamber. Rhythmic. Unhurried.

The pungent aroma of crushed herbs mingled with the damp, metallic scent of the underground halls.

When the mixture was reduced to dust, Belaric shifted.

He reached forward, grabbed the cloth sack covering the prisoner's face, and pulled it off.

The man's eyes went wide.

Pupils contracted against the firelight. Terror crawled into every inch of him.

Then came the begging.

"Please—please, I did not do anything!"

"I do not belong here—gods, please!"

The words collapsed over each other, cracking, trembling, desperation spilling free. His body jerked, twisting as if it might matter.

It did not.

Belaric's grip tightened. One hand forced the man still. The other plunged into the stone bowl, retrieving a handful of fine powder. He leaned in, blowing the poison into the prisoner's face.

The man jerked back, inhaling on instinct. The dust filled his lungs, clung to his throat. He coughed violently, thrashing as if sheer will alone could undo what had already begun.

His breath hitched. His limbs trembled. His body fought.

It did not matter.

His movements slowed—jerky, desperate twitches before his limbs fell slack.

Then, silence.

The prisoner's breath had slowed. Deep, heavy. A body sinking into black waters.

Belaric released him, watching as he drifted into unconsciousness. "He is now asleep." His voice carried no weight, no emotion. "And he will be plagued by nightmares. We will wake him soon, and he will tell you what he saw."

A hushed ripple spread through the children.

"It worked so fast," a young boy, no older than ten, whispered, his eyes wide.

"What do you think he is seeing?" a girl a little older asked, her voice tight with morbid curiosity.

"I wonder if he will scream when he wakes," another child, giggling nervously, added.

Soft voices, eager voices. Like they were discussing a festival trick, not a man sinking into torment.

Belaric said nothing. The scent of the crushed herbs, sweet and cloying, tasted like bile in his throat.

The man's breath came slowly, heavily. Locked in nightmares he could not wake from.

The children waited, whispering, expectant.

Belaric reached for the next bundle of herbs.

"Now, we move to one of my favorites," he said smoothly. A lie.

"Phantom Mead." He unwrapped the next bundle with measured precision. "This poison mimics drunkenness. One can inhale it or slip it into a drink; the effect is the same. Slurred speech, unsteady legs. Those around the target will assume they have had too much. I have used it to have a man thrown out of a tavern, dragged home by a friend. And that is when you strike."

He let the words settle.

With the last traces of Dreamrot wiped from the bowl, he began again.

His fingers sifted through the dried herbs. Found what he needed.

"First, you grind Ironleaf." The brittle leaves were dropped into the bowl, the pestle moving slowly and deliberate. The rough scraping of the stone pestle echoed in the chamber.

"Once it is a fine powder, you add Blackfire Lily. Extract the drops from its center."

He picked up the delicate flower, dark petals curling at the edges. Pressed. Three drops of thick, inky liquid fell into the dust.

"The more drops, the stronger the effect. Too much, and the target will collapse before you can reach them. Worse, they might taste it in their drink. Blackfire Lily is bitter—we must mask it."

He reached for the last ingredient.

"Sunbloom. It hides the Blackfire Lily's taste without altering its effects." He dropped the pale yellow petals into the mix and resumed grinding. The scent shifted—floral sweetness over something deeper. Something wrong.

It was ready.

Belaric rose and approached the second prisoner.

The man tensed, sensing what was coming. Fear thickened the air, sharpening his breath.

When the cloth sack was yanked from his head, he exploded into motion.

Wild, frantic thrashing. Not an attack—panic. His bound hands swung erratically, his breath a mess of gasps and half-formed words.

The children gasped. Not in fear. In fascination.

Belaric did not move.

Panic was like fire. Let it burn, and it would consume itself.

So he waited.

And when the first signs of exhaustion crept in—the tremors in the prisoner's limbs, the slowing of his ragged breath—he struck.

His hand shot out, fingers locking around the man's throat. Not tight. Not yet. Just enough to remind him he had already lost.

The prisoner froze.

His breath came in shuddering gasps. And then the tears.

"Please… please, no," the man whispered.

Belaric ignored him.

With his free hand, he reached for the mortar, tilting it carefully over the prisoner's open mouth. The powdered mixture tumbled down.

The man jerked his head aside, but Belaric's grip was unyielding. His other hand clamped over the prisoner's mouth.

The body beneath him twisted, struggled. Choked.

But in the end, there was no choice.

The prisoner swallowed.

Belaric let go and turned toward the children. "We will wait a few minutes. This poison works quickly."

The group sat in silence, watching.

The prisoner shifted uneasily on the ground, his breath coming in short gasps. Then—his limbs loosened, his body swaying as if it no longer knew where to put its weight.

Belaric grabbed him by the shoulder. "What is your name?"

The prisoner's mouth opened. Slurred nonsense spilled out.

Belaric pressed further. "Where are you from?"

Another garbled mess of sounds.

He blinked slowly, as if trying to hold on to something already slipping through his fingers.

Turning back to the children, Belaric gestured toward the prisoner.

"He is unable to answer. Those around him would assume he is drunk," Belaric stated.

A ripple of excited murmurs passed through the group. A small boy nudged his friend. "He looks ridiculous."

The second boy snorted, pointing. "He cannot even sit up—look at him."

"Imagine using this on a noble. We could make them collapse in the street," a girl whispered, her eyes shining with mischief.

"Or stumble off a bridge," another giggled, the thought seeming to delight her.

Laughter rippled through them, small but genuine.

Belaric said nothing.

But he raged on the inside. Being made to put on a show for the children. torturing these pathetic beggars. He hated this with every inch of his soul.

The children continued to whisper, already discussing what they would do with such a tool.

What they would make of it.

Belaric grabbed more herbs from the cloth bundle.

"Next is Heartbite." His voice carried no inflection. No weight. It was a lesson. A simple fact, spoken aloud.

"This poison must be ingested and is thicker than most. Once consumed, it works to thicken the blood—so much so that it can no longer flow. Eventually, the heart strains against it. And then, it stops."

The children shifted forward, anticipation humming through them. This one was different. This one was meant to kill.

And that made all the difference.

Belaric remained composed, reaching for the mortar and pestle. "First, we add Ebonmoss." A clump of deep green plant matter dropped into the stone bowl. "You will need a spoonful, but it is too thick alone, so we thin it with Dawnfern." A dried, yellow-tinged leaf followed. "Last, Bloodpetal." He held up the red-petaled flower, plucked it apart, and let the pieces fall.

Then he began grinding.

The motion was steady. Mechanical.

Only the slow scraping broke the silence.

The woman was next.

Unlike the others, this poison would hurt.

As the blood thickened, the heart would fight. Each beat heavier, slower. Like something clawing through mud, dragging itself toward a shore that was not there.

The pressure. The strain. The slow, creeping squeeze of her own body turning against itself.

He rarely used Heartbite himself, but he knew those who favored it. They liked the way it made them watch.

Finishing the mixture, he rose.

Approached her.

Her shoulders trembled beneath the sack. No struggle. No thrashing.

She already knew.

He tore the cloth away.

Tears streaked her dirt-stained face. No begging. No pleas. Just silent, shaking sobs. The kind that knew there was nothing left to ask for.

Belaric brought the mortar to her lips.

She hesitated.

Just for a moment.

Then, without a word, she opened her mouth.

He tilted the bowl. The thick powder tumbled down.

At first, she sat still. Swallowed slow.

Then her fingers twitched.

A shudder ran through her.

Another.

Then, her body convulsed.

Her arms jerked, her spine bowing sharply as the pain took hold. A strangled gasp tore from her lips.

Then came the screaming.

Not a shriek of surprise. Something deeper. Raw. Wrenching.

The kind of sound that tore at itself, that wrung the lungs dry.

Her hands clawed at her chest, grasping at something unseen, as though she could tear the pain free, pull the weight from her ribs.

But there was nothing to grasp.

Nothing but the slow, crushing fist closing around her heart.

The children leaned forward, watching intently.

"It is working fast," a boy whispered, his eyes wide with a strange mix of awe and dread.

Another child, an older girl, nodded slowly. "She is in so much pain."

A third, younger and more detached, simply stated, "This one is incredible."

They were studying her death, not mourning it.

Her convulsions slowed. The fight bled from her body, second by second. Her fingers, once clenched in agony, went limp. Her breath, uneven gasps at first, thinned to something softer.

Then—nothing.

Her heart stopped.

The children turned to each other. Murmuring. Awed.

"That was incredible," a young boy whispered, his face full of admiration.

"She was still alive for so long. Do you think she felt every bit of it?" an older girl asked, her voice tight with excitement.

"Imagine how much someone would suffer before dying... we could make it last longer, could we not?" Another child laughing added, the thought seemed to excite them.

Laughter, small but genuine, rippled through them.

Belaric exhaled slowly. Pressed the mortar back down.

Enough.

He rose and turned back to the first prisoner. "Let us see what effect the Dreamrot had on him."

The children whispered among themselves, speculating, eager. He ignored them.

Without warning, he struck the man across the face.

The reaction was instantaneous.

The prisoner tore from sleep with a scream. His body convulsed, limbs jerking, breath a sharp, ragged mess. His eyes darted wildly around the chamber, as though the horror still clung to him, as though it had followed him back into waking. Then his entire frame collapsed into sobs.

Belaric barely reacted.

He had seen this before.

He pulled his dagger free and brought the hilt down hard against the man's skull.

A strangled whimper. Then silence.

The prisoner slumped unconscious once more.

"As you can see, the Dreamrot did its job," Belaric said, his tone flat.

He was tired.

Tired of this lesson. Tired of their eager stares. Tired of all of it. He wanted it over.

And he knew exactly how to end it.

He turned, stepping toward the last prisoner.

The chamber fell silent. Expectant. Waiting.

"I have shown you several poisons, all of which you will use at some point." His voice was calm. Measured. "But tell me—who here can tell me which is the most effective method we use?"

The children hesitated, glancing at one another. Then—

"Gravewater, Ashen Blade!" a boy shouted, his voice eager.

"No, Moonveil Dust, Ashen Blade!" a girl retorted just as quickly.

Belaric shook his head. "No."

No flourish. No hesitation, he pulled the dagger strapped to his lower back free.

He drove the dagger into the prisoner's heart.

The chamber stilled.

For a breath, nothing.

Just the soft drip of blood onto stone.

Then the children gasped.

They had not expected that.

Blood bloomed across the man's chest. His body tensed for only a second before falling still.

Belaric watched him die. Then he spoke.

"The blade." His voice was steady. Unshaken. "It leaves nothing to chance... it does the job."

A slow, deliberate clap echoed through the chamber.

"Well put, Varros," Master Lyessa said, her voice smooth. "Well put indeed."

"Perhaps we will make you Master of Poisons and have you teach this permanently," she told him.

Belaric turned to her and bowed.

"Thank you, Master, for your kind words. I will carry out any task the Order requires," he stated flatly.

She studied him. Her gaze, cold and calculating, weighed him like a coin, assessing his value, his willingness.

Then, simply nodded. "You are excused, Belaric. I am sure you have other matters to attend to."

Then, turning to the children, her voice lifted, laced with something almost akin to delight.

"Now... who would like to kill the last one?" she asked.

The children erupted. Scrambling to their feet, hands shooting up, voices overlapping in eager desperation. Begging for the opportunity.

As if it were a gift.

As if it were anything but an execution.

Belaric did not wait to hear her choice.

He gathered his bundle of herbs, tucked them under his arm, and left. Quickly. But not too quickly.

Not enough to be noticed.

He did not look back.

The corridors twisted around him, cold and empty. The echoes of voices followed him, dim but persistent. Muffled excitement. The careful debate of children deciding who should take a life.

The air bit at him as he stepped outside. A stark, slicing contrast to the heat of the torches below. The city stretched before him, never silent, never truly asleep. He kept to the shadows, moving steadily, slipping through alleys and side streets.

He had walked this path a hundred times. A thousand.

By the time he reached the Middle District, the streets had emptied. The night watch lingered on corners, pacing the wealthier avenues. He slowed his stride, adjusting his pace to something unremarkable.

Moving too quickly. Looking too certain. That was a mistake of desperate men.

And desperate men were always remembered.

A turn. A narrow alley. A boarded-up shop.

There, beneath a loose stone, lay his escape.

Belaric reached for the fastenings of his assassin's garb, stripping it away. The fabric was cold against his fingers, thick with the scent of tunnels, of damp stone and blood.

Layer by layer, he removed it. Piece by piece, he shed Varros.

Stripping down to tunic and trousers, he folded the dark clothing with precision, tucking it beneath the stone where it would wait. The extra herbs joined it.

For a moment, he stood there, the chill air a stark relief against his skin. Breathing in the stillness. The weight of the cloak was gone. He almost smiled. A fleeting, foolish thought that he had left it all behind. But not from his mind. Rolling his shoulders, he straightened. Adjusted his stance. He was no longer Varros. No longer the Ashen Blade. He was Belaric again. A simple merchant returning home. He stepped back onto the street.

The path was familiar. His feet followed it without thought, but his mind was still elsewhere.

Still in the tunnels.

Still in the chamber.

Still in the echoes of laughter and screams.

Master Lyessa's slow, measured clap.

"Well put, Varros. Well put indeed." He could still hear her saying.

The words clung to him. Like blood under his nails. Like the weight of the mask before it was lifted.

He exhaled, slow and steadily. Counted his breaths. Focused on the cold air in his lungs. One step. Then another.

As he reached his house, the silence had settled again.

Moving carefully, he stepped inside, his footfalls light against the worn wooden floorboards. The fire had burned low in the hearth, casting flickering shadows along the walls.

Renna lay curled beneath the blankets. Breathing slow. Steady.

Belaric undressed with quiet efficiency, slipping beneath the covers without disturbing her.

The warmth of her body was immediate. A contrast so sharp it almost hurt. For a long moment, he lay still, listening to the rhythm of her breath. He had left the Order hall behind. He had returned home. But the weight of the night did not leave him. It settled over him like a second skin—silent, unseen, and always there.

7

The morning light slanted through the shutters, casting golden lines across the room. The air carried the faint scent of tallow and old wood, the kind of smell that settled into a place over years of living. Beneath them, a firm but warm bed was wrapped in a patchwork quilt Renna had sewn herself, its edges frayed from years of use.

Belaric stirred first, though he made no move to rise. His arm rested over the swell of Renna's belly, feeling the slow, rhythmic rise and fall of her breath beneath his palm. She lay curled into him; her back pressed against his chest, the loose folds of her nightdress bunched slightly where she had shifted in her sleep. The fabric was soft, worn thin in places, but it still held a faint scent of lavender—one of the few indulgences she allowed herself.

He closed his eyes again, wishing they could stay like this a little longer.

Renna stirred, a small wince betraying her discomfort. Her fingers pressed gently into his forearm, her skin cool in contrast to the heat of his own. "He is restless this morning," she murmured, eyes still closed.

"Then he takes after you," Belaric said, rubbing slow circles over her belly. "I was hoping for a quiet one."

She huffed a sleepy laugh, though fatigue clung to the sound. "I will remind you of that when he is up crying through the night, and you pretend not to hear."

Belaric smirked, resting his chin lightly on the top of her head. "I will hear it. I just might not move."

Renna turned slightly, tilting her face toward him. Her lips brushed his jaw, warm and soft. "You will move," she whispered.

There was something in her voice, something distant. Not sadness, but a kind of quiet acceptance, as if she were already looking beyond the moment.

Belaric let his fingers trail along her arm, following the curve of her wrist, the rise of her knuckles. Memorizing her warmth, the way her breath hitched slightly when he touched her ribs.

"How do you feel?" he asked.

She sighed, shifting slightly. "Like I am carrying a full sack of grain up a mountain." A pause, then a wry grimace. "And the mountain is angry about it."

Belaric sat up, sliding an arm around her to help her upright. Even that slight movement seemed to drain her, her shoulders slumping the moment she was fully seated. Her nightdress clung to her in places, wrinkled from sleep, the ties at her collarbone coming loose.

"Come, let us get you moving," he said, keeping his voice light. "Staying in bed too long will not help."

She groaned but did not argue, letting him pull the quilt away. She reached for the bed, attempting to push herself up, but Belaric was already there, steadying her with a firm grip beneath her arm.

She dressed slowly, slipping into a deep blue woolen dress that draped over her belly, the fabric stretched taut around her growing form. Belaric laced up the bodice for her, his fingers deft and practiced from years of helping when the ties grew too tight.

"Too snug?" he asked.

She shook her head. "Just right."

When they reached the stairs, he clasped her hand, guiding her down each careful step. Renna gripped his fingers harder than usual, as if she were afraid of falling. When they reached the bottom of the stairs, she was breathless.

She sank into the chair with a small sigh, brushing a stray lock of hair from her damp forehead. "I think he is punishing me for something."

Belaric smirked, pouring her a cup of water from the earthen jug on the table. "Maybe he already knows his mother is stubborn."

She took the cup, rolling her eyes over the rim. "And his father is insufferable."

Belaric only grinned, reaching for his belt where his coin pouch hung. "Rest. I will go to the baker, get fresh bread, and then come back and make eggs and meat."

Renna tilted her head, eyes half-lidded with exhaustion. "I think I love you most when you are bringing me food."

He chuckled, tying the coin pouch securely. "I will be sure to remind you of that next time you are angry with me."

She smiled faintly as he left, but as he stepped through the door, a flicker of hesitation passed through him—an irrational pull to turn back, to stay.

He shook it off and set off into the city.

The streets were already alive, filled with merchants calling their wares, the scent of fresh bread and roasting meat thick in the morning air. Horses clattered over the stone roads, and children weaved between carts, their laughter mingling with the steady hum of the waking city.

Belaric moved quickly, but when he rounded the corner to Thalrin's bakery, he let out a quiet curse under his breath. A line had already formed, spilling onto the street. He did not enjoy being away from Renna for long. Every moment felt like a tether stretched too thin.

With a sigh, he stepped into place, arms crossed.

The bakery squatted low against the cobbled street, a broad stone structure with smoke curling from its chimney and a wooden counter thrown open to the morning air. The smell hit him first—warm yeast, rich butter, and the golden sweetness of honey glazing fresh loaves. It was a scent that made a man forget his worries for a moment, the kind that promised comfort in the form of crisp crusts and soft, steaming insides. Inside, baskets brimmed with fresh loaves: dark rye thick with crust, barley bread speckled with seed, and rolls glistening faintly with melted butter.

At the center stood a long wooden table dusted white with flour. Dough rose in neat mounds along its edge, and at its heart, two broad hands worked a fresh batch with slow, practiced rhythm—hands that had known the same task for decades and never once hurried it.

Thalrin moved behind the counter with surprising agility for a man of his girth. His round belly pressed close to the table's edge, the strings of his flour-stained apron drawn tight against his sides. Stray flour clung to his thick grey beard, and his forearms—bare to the elbow—were marked with old burn scars and calluses that spoke of long hours near flame and stone.

But it was his eyes that gave him away—light brown, keen, and always watching. There was mischief there, but not of the kind born of youth. It was the careful, measured kind—that of a man who had seen too many lies in the marketplace to be fooled by new ones, and chose laughter over bitterness.

He nodded to an older woman who passed by, pressing a still-warm loaf into her hands with a soft word. She smiled in return, murmured something about her grandson, and moved on. Thalrin did not charge her.

By the time Belaric reached the front, the baker was already grinning.

"Ah, if it is not my favorite customer," Thalrin said, voice deep and thick as the bread he sold. "Or at least the one that does not haggle like an old fishwife."

Belaric smirked. "Maybe I should start."

Thalrin laughed, his belly heaving with the sound. "Not today, I promise you that. I have got something special for you—sweet honey bread, fresh from the oven."

Belaric arched a brow. "Is that so?"

"As sure as my wife's temper in the morning," Thalrin said with a wink, reaching beneath the counter for a wrapped bundle still warm to the touch.

As if summoned by his laughter, Tessira appeared from the back room with a presence that made the air shift. She was near her husband's size, though she carried herself with a different kind of weight—one born of command, not bulk. She tied her long brown hair back in a thick braid, streaked with silver that caught the light like thread. A dusting of flour clung to her apron, along with faint smudges of honey and spice that hinted at a morning spent in hurried preparation. She held a large wooden spoon in one hand, tapping it against her palm in a slow rhythm that was less idle and more deliberate—like a warning not yet spoken.

"I heard that," she said dryly, aiming a look at Thalrin that could curdle milk. Then her attention shifted to Belaric, and the sternness gave way to warmth. "And how is Renna?"

Belaric shifted his weight, unsure why the question unsettled him. Tessira had always had a way of seeing past answers.

"She is well. Tired," he said. "The baby should come any day now."

Tessira's face lit up, her hands coming together with a soft clap. "Wonderful news. You be sure to bring that little one by once he is born—you hear me?"

Belaric forced a smile. "I would not dare do otherwise."

"You had better not," she said, wagging the spoon at him—but there was no real menace behind it. Only the kind of love that remembered too many faces lost too young. She turned back toward the ovens, trailing the scent of cinnamon and roasted nuts as she went, already barking instructions at someone out of sight.

Thalrin returned, holding out a wrapped loaf still warm from the stone. "Three coppers for the best bread you will eat all week."

Belaric fished the coins from his pouch and dropped them into the baker's hand. "We will see if it is worth the claim."

"You will be back," Thalrin said, waving him off. "They always are."

Belaric gave a faint nod, tucking the loaf under one arm as he stepped out into the street. The air was cooler now, the morning haze beginning to lift, casting soft light across the cobbles. He walked without hurry, the warmth of the bread seeping through the cloth and into his fingers. A few passersby offered nods, but he returned none. His thoughts were already home—on the slow way Renna moved now, on the flickers of pain she tried to hide, on how close the moment had come.

When he stepped inside, the warmth of the loaf still clung to his hands. The scent of smoldering ash lingered near the hearth, mingling with the honeyed sweetness rising from the cloth-wrapped bread. The room was dim, the fire reduced to a faint orange glow beneath the charred logs. Renna sat near the small window, its weak morning light catching on the thread in her hands, the needle moving through the fabric in slow, methodical strokes.

Belaric raised a brow. "Another blanket?"

She did not look up. "You can never have too many."

Belaric set the bread down on the table and crossed the room, bending to kiss her forehead. Her skin was cooler than he expected. He brushed his fingers over her temple, pushing a few strands of hair back. "At this rate, the baby will be swaddled in a fortress of wool."

Renna huffed a small laugh, but it was faint, almost distracted. Her hands kept moving, but he noticed the tremble in her fingers, the way the thread slipped once before she caught it.

He frowned. "Renna—"

"I am fine," she said too quickly. She glanced up at him then, the shadow of exhaustion dark beneath her eyes.

He did not push. Instead, he ran a hand over her shoulder and gave it a light squeeze before moving toward the hearth. The fire had burned low—only a faint orange shimmer beneath a layer of ash. He set the bread aside, grabbed a few sticks of split wood from the basket, and fed them carefully into the embers. It took only a few breaths before the kindling caught, flames licking up with a soft whoosh.

He reached for the iron pan. Soon, the sharp crack of eggs echoed in the quiet, followed by the sizzle of meat curling in hot fat.

The rich scent of cooking filled the small house, warming the air with something familiar, something safe. He listened to the rhythmic pull of thread behind him, the soft scrape of a needle through cloth.

By the time he brought her plate, she looked half-asleep again, her head tilted slightly to one side, her needlework resting in her lap. He nudged her gently with his knuckles. "Eat before you doze off."

Renna stirred and stretched, taking the plate with slow, deliberate movements. "You spoil me," she murmured, setting the cloth aside and balancing the plate in her lap.

Belaric smirked, tearing off a piece of bread. "Well, a queen deserves nothing less than to be spoiled."

She smiled drowsily and took a bite. They ate in comfortable silence for a while, the only sounds being the occasional clink of forks against wood, the quiet hum of the fire.

After a while, Renna glanced up. "What are your plans for the day?"

Belaric leaned back in his chair, chewing thoughtfully. "Stay here. With you."

She gave him a look, amused but knowing. "That is sweet, but you will go mad sitting around."

Belaric shrugged. "Then I will go mad."

She reached out, her fingers brushing his wrist before curling around his hand. "I would rather you checked on the garden. Water the plants, see how the fruit and vegetables are doing."

He squeezed her fingers gently. "Consider it done."

She smiled, but something lingered in her expression—a flicker of something unspoken. He saw it in the way her grip lingered, the way her gaze dipped briefly to their joined hands before she released him.

And for a moment, it felt like everything was as it should be.

But he knew better than to believe in peace.

The sun was beginning its climb, warm but not overbearing, casting a golden hue over the small garden as Belaric stepped outside. The scent of damp earth and fresh greenery filled the air, mingling with the faint smoke curling from the chimneys of neighboring homes. A light breeze rustled the leaves, carrying the distant murmur of market stalls and the occasional call of a vendor hawking wares.

The garden itself was modest but well-kept—a patch of fertile soil fenced in with wooden slats, vines curling along the posts where peas and beans clung like desperate hands. Rows of vegetables stretched neatly before him: plump red tomatoes hanging heavy on their stems, thick bundles of carrots waiting beneath dark soil, broad cabbage heads with their waxy leaves glistening from the morning dew. A few apple and pear trees stood at the back, their fruit ripening in dappled sunlight, their low-hanging branches swaying ever so slightly.

Belaric crouched, running a calloused hand through the soil. It was still damp from the last watering, but needed more. He fetched the wooden bucket near the well and began his work, careful not to drown the roots. He picked a few ripe tomatoes, rolling one between his fingers before placing it in a small basket. A stray weed crept along the edge of the bed, and he pulled it free. His movements were methodical, practiced—the simple work that required no thought, only routine.

The sun had climbed higher, and its warmth deepened from a gentle caress to a steady heat on his back. The shadows, once long and thin, now huddled close to the garden walls. The sounds of the market grew louder, the voices more distinct. He heard the clang of a blacksmith's hammer from down the lane and the distant cry of children at play. He worked on, pulling weeds, mending a loose fence post, and watering the thirsty cabbage. For a brief moment, he allowed himself to believe this peace was permanent.

He wiped the sweat from his brow and stepped inside. The house was still. Upstairs, Renna lay curled beneath the blankets, her breaths slow and deep, the afternoon light painting soft shadows across her face. The morning's tension faded into rest. Belaric smiled, leaning down to brush his lips against her forehead before pulling away.

He moved to the wooden chest, pulling out simple linen, dark trousers, a loose tunic, worn soft over the years. He heated a basin of water downstairs—a small luxury. Scrubbing the dirt from his arms, he ran wet fingers through his hair and dressed swiftly. Renna remained asleep as he settled at the table, pulling an old leather-bound book from the shelf. He bit into a crisp apple, the soft crunch and faint sweetness a fleeting distraction as he turned the pages.

The peace shattered in an instant.

"Belaric!"

Renna's voice—sharp, urgent—cut through the house like a blade.

Belaric shot up, the book tumbling from his hands with a dull thud. His heart slammed against his ribs as he was already moving, boots pounding against the wooden boards as he sprinted up the stairs.

He burst into the bedroom. Renna sat upright, her face pale, sweat already beading along her brow. Her hands clutched the blanket, knuckles white.

"It is happening," she breathed, eyes wide. "You need to fetch the healer. Now."

Belaric froze, his body tensing. He thought it would still be days until the baby came. For half a second, he nearly stepped toward her, nearly reached out to steady her.

"Go!" she gasped. "I need Kaedra—now!"

That broke his daze. Without another word, he spun on his heel and sprinted down the steps, and barreled into the street.

The city blurred around him as he ran, his boots striking the cobblestones with enough force to rattle his bones. He shoved past merchants and townsfolk, barking for them to move, barely registering the curses flung his way.

The healer's house loomed ahead—a squat stone structure tucked between the warped timbers of an apothecary and the scorched shell of an old blacksmith's shop. Moss crept along the base of the walls, and the shutters hung slightly crooked, as if the building had weathered more years than it should have.

Belaric reached the door and hammered his fist against it.

"Kaedra!" he shouted, his breath coming hard, his voice raw with desperation. He struck again, louder this time. "Kaedra, open the damn door!"

A long pause. Then the scrape of wood, the slow drag of feet.

The door creaked open to reveal a woman hunched in the frame, swaddled in a heavy gray robe too large for her wiry frame. Her silver hair escaped its braid in fine strands. Her eyes—deep-set beneath thick, overgrown brows—narrowed, then widened as they found him.

"Belaric?" she rasped, the surprise brief before her gaze sharpened with grim understanding. "What is it?"

"The baby is coming now. Renna needs you. Now!" he choked out, the words tearing from his chest.

Kaedra did not hesitate. Her face, a map of lines and creases, hardened with professional focus. She clapped her hands, the sound sharp in the still air. "Well, do not just stand there, lad. My brown bag—inside, second shelf from the window!"

Belaric pushed through the narrow doorway into a room steeped in age and herb-smoke. The scent of dried lavender, bitterroot, and damp stone filled his nose. Shelves lined every wall, crowded with glass vials, leather-bound journals, and bundles of plant stalks suspended from the ceiling. Near the hearth sat a low table, scattered with half-crushed petals and a bloodstained, unwashed cloth.

He found the brown leather bag where she said and turned back to see Kaedra already outside, one hand braced against the doorframe.

"Well?" she said. "I do not walk as fast as I used to, but I am not dead yet."

He slipped her arm through his and started toward the house. Her pace was maddening—every step a crawl—but she did not complain once.

Belaric kept his eyes ahead, to the distant rooftops, whispering a silent plea that they would not be too late.

Renna's scream was still echoing in his head.

Kaedra must have felt the tension in his grip because she gave a quiet chuckle. "No use dragging me along like a sack of potatoes, lad. The baby will come whether we run or crawl."

He did not reply—he just clenched his jaw and forced himself to slow.

By the time they reached the house, the screams were not just in his head anymore. Renna's cries tore through the walls, raw with pain.

Belaric's gut twisted.

They hurried upstairs.

Sweat plastered Renna's hair to her forehead as she hunched forward in the bed. Renna breathed raggedly, her hands gripping the sheets in white-knuckled fists.

Kaedra moved swiftly despite her age, kneeling at Renna's side and taking her hand. "Do not worry, dear, I am here now."

She turned to Belaric. "I need fresh water, linens, and my bag."

He thrust the bag toward her, watching as she unlatched it and pulled out several small vials. One caught his eye.

Heartrest.

A lump formed in his throat, but he said nothing, moving quickly to fetch the other supplies. When he returned, Kaedra was grinding herbs in a bowl, her movements precise. She took the cup of water from him and mixed the crushed herbs in smooth, practiced motions.

"Here, dear," she said, pressing the cup to Renna's lips. "This is Heartrest. It will help with the pain."

Renna drank deeply, her hands trembling. Together, he and Kaedra positioned fresh linens beneath her, preparing for what was to come.

Then Kaedra straightened, turning to him. "Now, step outside, lad."

Belaric stiffened. "No. I should stay—"

Kaedra shot him a sharp look. "This is not a battle, Belaric. Your wife needs focus, and I need space."

He turned to Renna, expecting a protest, but she nodded.

His shoulders sagged.

With a reluctant step back, he left the room, closing the door behind him.

Downstairs, he began pacing. Every scream from upstairs twisted inside him like a blade.

He wanted nothing more than to rush back.

But all he could do was wait.

Several hours had passed. The sun had long since dipped beneath the rooftops, casting long, unmoving shadows across the room. Lanterns burned low, their flames wavering slightly as they cast soft halos against the walls, dimming against the dull orange of the hearth embers. The air hung heavy with sweat and the bitter scent of crushed herbs, undercut by the sharper, metallic tang of blood.

Belaric had spent those hours pacing, his ears straining with every cry from upstairs. Renna's screams had dulled into ragged gasps, broken only by Kaedra's steady, unshaken voice.

Then, at last, that voice cut through the house again. "Belaric! Get up here—now!"

His heart lurched. He was moving before he could think, his boots hammering against the steps.

The moment he entered the room, he froze. Renna lay back against the pillows, her legs bent, a linen draped over them for modesty. Strands of damp, dark hair clung to her flushed face, her chest rising and falling in exhausted, shallow breaths. But as soon as she saw him, she smiled.

Kaedra, stationed at the foot of the bed, turned sharply. "Hold her hand—the baby is almost here."

Belaric nodded, his throat dry. He crossed the room in three long strides, kneeling beside Renna and taking her trembling hand in his. Her fingers curled weakly around his, but her smile remained. "You are here," she whispered, voice rasping.

"I am here," he said, pressing a kiss to her sweat-slicked forehead. "Everything is going to be alright."

Kaedra snapped her fingers. "Time to push, girl. Hard as you can."

Renna sucked in a breath and bore down.

Belaric felt it instantly—her grip turning to iron, nails digging into his skin. She gasped, then pushed again. And again. Kaedra remained focused, hands steady, her voice commanding but calm. "You are doing fine. Keep going. Almost there."

Renna let out a sob, her entire body trembling as she gave another push. Kaedra suddenly straightened. "I see the head! One more!"

Renna's breath hitched—her lips curled back as she clenched her teeth and let out one last piercing scream. Then—a wail, high and thin, split the air.

The tension in the room shattered. Renna gasped—a sob of relief, of pure, exhausted joy. Her body went limp against the pillows, fresh tears spilling over her cheeks. Belaric let out a ragged breath, his forehead dropping against hers. He wrapped his arms around her, holding her tight.

Kaedra lifted the tiny, bloody infant, its limbs flailing, its cries filling every corner of the room. A small, wrinkled body—fragile, yet full of life. She let out a tired chuckle. "It is a boy."

Renna let out a breathless laugh, blinking up at Belaric. Even through the haze of exhaustion, her triumph was unmistakable. "Told you," she murmured, her voice thick with emotion.

Belaric huffed a quiet laugh, shaking his head. "You did." But his eyes were not on her anymore. They were on his son.

Kaedra moved quickly, cleaning the infant with practiced efficiency. For the briefest moment, Belaric saw himself in that small, wrinkled face—the same strong nose, the same shape to his eyes. Then Kaedra wrapped the baby in soft linen and held him out. "Go on, then," she said, smirking. "Hold your son."

Belaric hesitated, his hands hovering for a moment before taking the bundle. The weight was so much less than he expected—warm, small, impossibly delicate. The baby squirmed, his tiny fingers curling instinctively. Without thinking, Belaric extended his own finger, and—gods, he barely fit his entire hand around it. Something cracked inside his chest. He swallowed hard and bent down, pressing his lips to his son's forehead before carefully handing him to Renna.

She cradled the baby close, sobbing quietly as she rocked him. Belaric kissed her temple, letting his hand rest on her hair. In this moment, he let himself believe that this—this was safe. This was right.

Renna sniffled and glanced up at him. "Do you have a name for him?"

Belaric faltered. A name. They had spoken of them before—softly, in the quiet hours, when everything still felt certain. But now, with the weight of the moment pressing down on him, only one came to mind. One that felt right. Like it had always been waiting.

"One came to me earlier," he said quietly. "Eryndorr."

Renna smiled, then looked down at the tiny bundle in her arms. "Our little Eryndorr," she whispered. She tested the name on her tongue, soft and reverent, as if it had already belonged to him. Then she looked back at Belaric, her eyes shining. "I love it."

Kaedra, who had been wiping her hands clean, nodded approvingly. "A strong name. Good and proper for the lad." She leaned forward, running a careful hand over the baby's head, her fingers gentle for someone so gruff. "He is healthy and strong. You did well, girl."

Renna beamed. And for a few blissful moments, the world felt whole.

Then Kaedra's voice cut through it all. "Belaric."

Something was different. He looked up immediately, uneasy. Kaedra's face had shifted. Gone was the small smirk, the confidence, the ease of a healer who had seen a hundred births. Instead, she was digging through her bag—frantic, precise, but unmistakably concerned.

"Take the baby," she said, voice sharp. "Step back."

Belaric blinked, confused. "What?"

"Now."

The command snapped through the air like a whip.

Renna's brow furrowed, the joy in her expression giving way to confusion. "What is wrong?"

Kaedra did not answer. She was already working, already moving faster than her old bones should have allowed, already pressing linens against—blood. Too much of it.

Belaric hesitated.

"Take the baby now!" The sheer force of Kaedra's voice jolted him. He gently lifted Eryndorr from Renna's arms, stepping back as she let out a weak protest.

Kaedra muttered a curse under her breath and pressed harder against Renna's stomach. Renna flinched, panic flickering in her tired eyes. "Kaedra?"

Belaric held his breath. "What is happening?"

Kaedra did not look up. "She is still bleeding."

The words hit Belaric harder than a blade. His throat tightened. "What does that mean?"

Kaedra's lips thinned. Her hands did not stop working. "It means," she said, grim and unflinching, "we have a very serious problem."

Renna's breath stuttered, fear creeping into her gaze. "Belaric—"

He took a half-step forward, his pulse roaring in his ears. "Fix it," he demanded, his voice not quite steady. "You are a healer. Fix it."

Kaedra let out a sharp breath. "I am trying, lad."

Belaric's arms tensed around Eryndorr, suddenly aware of how fragile, how real, how fleeting this moment was. Renna's trembling fingers reached for him, but he could not move.

He could do nothing but watch.

Kaedra worked with growing desperation, her hands moving swiftly as she ground more herbs into a fine powder, mixing them with warm water before thrusting the cup into Renna's hands. "Here—drink this," she commanded, her voice sharp with urgency. "It will slow the bleeding."

Renna did not hesitate. She took the cup and drank, wincing at the bitterness, but she was in no position to argue. She swallowed hard, then coughed slightly, the acrid taste making her throat tighten.

Kaedra pressed fresh linens between Renna's legs, muttering beneath her breath as she worked, hands steady despite the blood soaking through. She mixed pastes, packed herbs deep against the bleeding, whispered prayers to gods Belaric had long since abandoned.

Nothing worked.

Her frustration boiled over, and she slammed a hand against the bedframe. "Damn it," she hissed, her voice cracking. "I should have been better prepared. Should have had more of the right herbs, should have—" she cut herself off, her jaw tightening as she looked down at Renna.

Belaric stood there, frozen, helpless, clutching their son as he watched Kaedra struggle. He was not a healer. His knowledge of herbs came from a different world—one of poisons and pain, not of healing and hope. And now it was useless. He was useless.

His heart broke further with every shallow breath Renna took. She had always been strong, the most stubborn woman he had ever known, but now—now she was fading before his eyes. He saw it in her face—the way her skin grew paler by the minute, the way her strength dwindled as fear crept into her expression.

After what felt like an eternity, Kaedra exhaled shakily and called him forward. Her hands trembled as she took his and Renna's, her face no longer fierce but broken. Tears welled in the old healer's eyes as she shook her head.

"I am so sorry, Renna," she whispered, her voice a raw, thin thread of sound. "There is nothing more I can do. I—I cannot risk cutting you open to try and stop the bleeding. You will only bleed faster."

The words were not loud, but they struck Belaric like a physical blow. Nothing. He, who could always find a way to kill, who could always escape, could do nothing. The world tilted. His grip tightened on Eryndorr, suddenly the only solid thing in a collapsing universe.

The words hung in the air like a death sentence.

Kaedra squeezed her eyes shut, trying to hold back the flood of emotions, but when Renna's weak hand squeezed hers in return, the dam broke. A sob tore from her throat. "I—I should have been able to save you," she choked out. "I should have—"

Renna's voice, though faint, was gentle. "Kaedra… you did everything you could. And more." She exhaled slowly, a weak smile touching her lips. "You delivered my baby boy into this world. That is a gift I could never repay."

Kaedra's shoulders shook, and she bowed her head, gripping Renna's fingers as if she could keep her tethered here just a little longer.

Renna turned to Belaric, her arms outstretched. He hesitated, just for a breath, before stepping forward and placing their son into her arms. Holding Eryndorr close, she sighed softly, as if a great weight had lifted from her soul.

Belaric sank to his knees beside the bed. His body felt too heavy, his limbs sluggish. Slowly, tears slipped down his face. His mind refused to believe this was real. He had spent a lifetime fighting, killing, surviving—but now he was powerless. All his training, all his strength, and none of it could keep her with him. How could the gods be so cruel? How could they give her this moment—this happiness—only to rip it away?

A gentle touch beneath his chin startled him, and he flinched slightly as Renna lifted his face, forcing him to meet her gaze.

He resisted at first. He did not want to look. Because if he did, it became real. And he was not ready for goodbye. But she was always stronger than him in the ways that mattered.

Tears shimmered in her eyes, but she fought them back. "My love," she whispered, her voice softer now, fading. "You are the greatest man I have ever known." She smiled, though it wavered. "You have always been there for me... protected me... loved me. Now, our son will need that. He will need you."

Belaric clenched his jaw, struggling to breathe, struggling to stay whole when everything was falling apart. The words cut deeper than any blade. Not because they were cruel—but because they were final.

"Protect him. Always. Give him enough love for both of us," she continued, her fingers brushing his cheek, memorizing the feel of him one last time.

He clutched her hand, pressing it to his lips. He tried to speak, to promise her he would, but he lost his voice. Every vow he had ever taken had meant nothing compared to this one.

Renna leaned forward and kissed him, slow and lingering, as if trying to press a lifetime's worth of love into a single moment.

She pulled away just enough to look down at their son. As if sensing something was wrong, Eryndorr whimpered, then let out a small, broken cry.

Renna rocked him gently, brushing her fingers over his tiny face. "It is all right, my love," she murmured, her voice soothing even as it trembled. "Daddy will protect you... He will always be there for you." She kissed his forehead, her tears falling onto his soft skin. "I love you, little one. And I will always be with you. Always."

Renna turned back to Belaric, her strength waning fast now. Tears streamed freely down her face. Her breath came in shallow, ragged pulls, each word a visible effort.

"Next time we meet, my love… do not wait so long to take me on a walk." A small, fading laugh slipped from her lips, though her breath caught halfway through.

Belaric forced himself to smile. "I would never dream of making you wait."

But the smile broke almost immediately. It was not strong enough to hold back the grief rising inside him like a tide.

Her fingers went limp in his grasp.

Her breathing slowed.

Her eyes fluttered once, twice—then closed.

Belaric stood, cradling the back of her head, pressing one last kiss against her damp hair. His throat locked as he whispered against her skin.

"Goodbye, my love."

He swallowed hard, forcing the words past the ache in his chest. "My Renna."

The name felt like a blade drawn across his throat.

A final, fragile breath left her lips.

And just like that, she was gone.

8

Belaric exhaled slowly, trying to swallow down the tide of grief clawing at his chest. The air in the dimly lit room felt too thick, pressing against his ribs like an iron band.

"Belaric," Kaedra's voice wavered, rough from exhaustion and sorrow of her own. He looked up to see her dabbing at her wet cheeks, her mouth opening as if to say more, but he raised a hand, stopping her. He did not want words—not now. Not when grief still clung to his chest like a blade lodged too deep to pull free.

"As Renna said, we owe you a debt we can never repay," he said, his voice raw but steady. "You brought our son into this world, and we will always be grateful to you."

Kaedra tried to smile through the sorrow lining her face. "You are a good man, Belaric. If you ever need help with the child, I will be there."

He nodded, murmuring his thanks, but his mind had already begun to slip away from the moment, drawn into the weight of the tiny body wrapped in cloth before him. His son. The only thing left of Renna.

Belaric reached out, hands trembling, and lifted the baby from Renna's arms. The blanket slipped away, and he cradled the infant against his shoulder, pressing his cheek against the downy-soft hair. His eyes shut as he tried to grasp the impossible—how everything had changed in a single night, how her life had been stolen, just as she had given life to their son. The scent of blood and birth, usually a symbol of new life, now mingled with the cold tang of death, a stark, agonizing reminder of what he had lost.

Then Kaedra's voice cut through the fragile quiet.

"What is that?" Her tone sharpened with unease.

Belaric blinked, frowning as he followed her gaze to the baby's back.

"Is it a bruise? Oh, gods, please tell me I did not hurt him," she whispered, horror creeping into her voice. She reached out, her finger hovering, then tracing the faint, dark line.

A sick, twisting sensation curled in Belaric's stomach. His throat tightened, chest constricting as if a fist had closed around his ribs. No, it was not possible. It could not be.

His arms trembled as he shifted, turning the tiny body carefully despite the way his fingers felt numb and useless. The baby let out a thin, wailing cry, as if he could already sense the weight of his father's fear.

Belaric swallowed hard, squeezing his eyes shut for a moment. Please let it be nothing. A trick of the light. A shadow.

But when he opened them, the truth stared back at him.

The mark was there. A Valasar mark on his spine.

A deep, shuddering breath left his lips. His knees felt weak.

"Gods, no," he whispered.

Kaedra shot him a confused glance. "Belaric… what is it?"

She took a step closer, voice cautious. "Is it a—"

A whisper in the air—then a sickening thwack.

Kaedra let out a strangled, wet gasp as her body jerked violently. Her eyes widened in disbelief. She staggered back, hands rising instinctively to her chest. When they came away, they were slick with blood. She looked down, then up again, as if trying to understand. Her lips parted, trembling around a single, broken word.

"Belaric."

She collapsed in a heap; the breath leaving her in a soft, final sigh.

He froze. For half a heartbeat, the world narrowed to the sight of her crumpled form—Kaedra, who had stood beside Renna while she bled, who had wept for the child as deeply as he had. Who had whispered prayers when he had none.

And now she lay still. Gone. Another light snuffed out while the gods watched in silence.

A bitter heat surged through his chest, but he could not scream. Could not mourn. Not yet.

The weight of his son suddenly seemed unbearable in his arms.

Belaric turned—jaw clenched, eyes burning.

Two figures stepped from the doorway, shadows peeling away from the gloom, moving with quiet certainty.

They had not come just for him.

They had come to finish everything.

They moved with the surety of men who had already decided how this night would end.

The first figure tilted his head slightly, voice light, almost amused.

"Varros. It has been a while," he said. "Shame about the old woman. Messy."

Belaric gritted his teeth. He knew that voice.

"Vorin," he said, his tone flat, edged with something dangerous.

Vorin chuckled, stepping further into the dim glow of the room. "Ah, so you have not forgotten me. I was beginning to worry."

The man behind him shifted, his presence just as sure, just as unwelcome. "Told you he would recognize your voice," the second figure said, amusement laced through his words. Then, with a smirk, he added, "But what should we call you? Varros? Or should I say... Belaric?"

Belaric turned his gaze toward the second man, his jaw tightening. "I know your voice too, Morrell."

Morrell clapped his hands together, slowly and mocking. "Very good, Varros. We were told that you were smart."

Belaric did not rise to the bait. His focus remained sharp, cutting through the smirks and casual arrogance. "Why are you here? How did you find me?"

The two assassins looked at each other before breaking into laughter.

"While it is true, we all keep our second lives hidden from each other," Vorin said, voice like sand dragged across stone. "The masters see more than they ever let on. They always have."

He took a step closer, boots scuffing softly against the floorboards. "But you—you thought you were different. Thought you could love, build a life, hold a child… and they would not notice?"

Vorin scoffed. "Fool. They watched. They waited. They saw your weakness—taking only the contracts assigned, never requesting your own. They saw the hesitation, the reluctance creeping in."

He tilted his head slightly, as if studying a dying animal. "And now they have sent us to clean up your mess."

Morrell sighed, shaking his head as if in disappointment. "They planned to kill you months ago, but for some reason, they held off. Until now." He tilted his head, considering. "Our orders were simple—kill you, take the baby. But now…" His gaze flickered toward Eryndorr. "Now that we know he is marked, that changes things."

He shrugged carelessly. "Shame, really. The masters wanted the child. Now we will just have to leave two corpses instead of one."

Belaric shook out his shoulders, the familiar tension settling in. He let the breath slip through his teeth, slow and measured. The old instincts never left—only slept, waiting. A part of him had softened over the years, lulled by something resembling peace. But peace was a lie, and tonight proved it.

"You dare come into my home," he said, voice like iron. "The day my wife dies. The day my son was born. And you expect to walk out of here after threatening him?"

His grip on Eryndorr tightened, careful but trembling with rage. "You will find only death here."

He stepped forward, slow and deliberate, his presence filling the room like a shadow stretching long before a storm. "I will send your heads back to the masters—and any other fool who dares to challenge me."

Eryndorr whimpered, a small, fragile sound in the heavy silence.

Belaric took a breath and forced himself to turn, setting his son gently back onto the bed and wrapping him in the blanket. His fingers lingered for a fraction of a moment, a silent promise made to Renna.

He would protect their child. No matter the cost.

Straightening, he shifted his gaze back to the two assassins, stepping past them toward the corner of the room. They did not move, but their posture shifted, hands hovering near their weapons, sensing the change in the air.

He moved towards the false floorboard.

Belaric knelt, fingers slipping beneath the edge of the worn floorboard. He found the groove by instinct; the wood lifted with a soft creak.

The ashen blade gleamed in the low light.

He had taken many lives with this blade—quiet deaths in darker corners than this. Now, he would take two more.

With cold, steady purpose, he lifted it free.

Then he stood, turning to face them, his grip firm, unwavering. His mask of the detached assassin, "Varros," had shattered along with his world. Tonight, he was something far more dangerous: a man with nothing left to lose but the one thing he swore to protect.

"I am Belaric Kelmor," he said, voice like the promise of a storm. "And tonight, you two fools die."

The air had shifted.

A heartbeat before the first move, Belaric saw the fight unfold in his mind. The rhythm of death—strikes, counters, blood. Vorin and Morrell were skilled—fast, precise, dangerous.

But they were not Ashen Blades.

He was.

Trained in the darkest halls of the Black Vow. Tempered by years of silent war. Every motion honed to kill.

And that made all the difference.

They drew steel in unison, the whisper of sharpened edges cutting through the tense quiet. Vorin stood loosely, confidently, arrogant as a man never challenged by a superior opponent. Morrell was tighter, cautious, the stance of a fighter who understood risk but had never faced something beyond it. Belaric unsheathed the ashen blade, dark and wicked in his grip, and with the same motion, snapped the sheath toward Morrell, sending it spinning through the air. Morrell flinched instinctively, raising an arm to deflect it—just as Belaric struck.

He moved fast, lunging for Vorin, meeting him mid-strike. Their blades clashed, steel shrieking as they locked for a breathless instant.

Belaric struck first—short, brutal movements meant to over-whelm. Vorin barely kept pace, parrying a flurry of blows that came fast and unrelenting.

Then they broke apart.

Vorin retaliated immediately—slashes toward Belaric's ribs, his throat, his legs. Belaric parried, sidestepped, deflected, the flick of his wrist sending each attack just wide enough to miss. A thrust came for his gut, but he turned with it, letting the dagger's tip slice nothing but air.

Belaric countered, driving his blade toward Vorin's exposed shoul-der, but Vorin twisted, catching the attack on his own dagger. He barely held against the force of it, stumbling back a half step. Then Morrell moved for Eryndorr.

Belaric saw it the moment he shifted, that subtle pivot of weight that gave his intention away. Morrell lunged toward the bed, the dag-ger aimed at something far more vulnerable than him.

A mistake.

Belaric pivoted, throwing his weight into a sharp, brutal kick. His boot crashed into Morrell's ribs, the impact reverberating up his leg. Bone cracked, the sound unmistakable. Morrell grunted, the force of the blow sending him careening into the wall, where he clutched his side in pain.

Vorin took advantage of the moment, his blade whipping toward Belaric's throat. He barely jerked back in time, feeling the cold whis-per of steel as it grazed his skin, sharp enough to sting. A flicker of warmth ran down his neck, a shallow cut, but he ignored it. The next strike came even faster—a diagonal slash aimed for his ribs.

He twisted, but not fast enough.

A thin line of pain flared across his stomach. He hissed through clenched teeth, stepping back, feeling the warmth spread beneath his tunic. It was not deep, but it was there.

They spread out, forcing him between them. Two against one. A cornered animal.

Belaric let them believe that, just for a moment.

They attacked together. Vorin struck high, an overhead arc meant to force Belaric back, while Morrell lunged low, blade flashing toward his ribs. Belaric was already moving before their strikes landed, twisting his body in a tight motion.

Vorin's dagger carved through the empty space where his head had been—but Morrell's blade caught the edge of his retreating leg, slicing a harsh line across his right thigh.

Pain flared, hot and sudden. He stumbled a step, breath hitching. Not deep enough to cripple—but deep enough to slow.

He gritted his teeth, forced the pain down, and struck back.

His elbow smashed into Morrell's masked face, the force sending a sharp crack through the room. The assassin grunted, staggering back, his breath sharp and ragged behind the cloth. Belaric turned in the same motion, slamming a knee into Vorin's gut, the blow folding him in half. A choked wheeze escaped through his mask as he stumbled back, gasping for breath. Although wounded, they remained standing. Not dead. Not yet.

A sharp sting lanced through his arm—Vorin's blade had found him again, a quick slashing cut across his left bicep. The pain flared, hot and bright, but he did not let it slow him. He moved with it, turning the momentum into another strike, catching Vorin's blade with his own and wrenching it aside.

Warmth trickled down his arm, the sting blending with the burning sensation in his stomach. But the worst was his right leg—the gash Morrell had opened was bleeding freely now. Every step sent a pulse of pain up his thigh, but he did not have time to feel it. He shifted his stance, keeping the weight off it as best he could.

Vorin ran a gloved hand over the front of his mask, as if wiping away sweat that was not there, his arrogance slipping into something more wary. Beside him, Morrell tilted his head slightly, his muscles tensing as if trying to shake off the pain, his silence speaking louder than words. They were not laughing now.

Then they rushed him.

Vorin lunged high, blade flashing forward—sharp, forceful, but too eager. He had over-committed.

At the same time, Morrell veered to the side, circling for an opening, his dagger aimed low.

Belaric turned sideways, just enough to let Vorin's dagger pass him. In the same instant, he drove his own blade forward—straight into Vorin's chest.

Vorin let out a wet, choking groan, his body freezing on the blade, his dagger slipping from limp fingers. His lips trembled, mouth forming words that never came—only blood.

Belaric wrenched the weapon free, twisting as he did. Vorin stumbled, clutching uselessly at the open wound, as if he could hold his life inside him. His knees buckled, and he collapsed.

One down. One to go.

Morrell froze. His breath came fast, shallow. His fingers tightened around his blade, but they were trembling. He took a step back, his foot shifting in Vorin's pooling blood. He had never seen Vorin fail. Never thought he would.

The hesitation lasted less than a heartbeat.

But it was long enough.

Belaric closed the distance in two quick steps. Morrell barely had time to lift his blade before Belaric was on him, steel flashing in a storm of strikes. He blocked once, twice, but his defenses were crumbling, his mind still reeling from the shock. A parry turned weak. An opening.

Belaric slashed low, his blade carving through Morrell's wrist. A cry of pain ripped from the assassin's throat as his dagger fell, fingers severed cleanly from his hand. He stumbled, his breath hitching in agony, but he had one blade left. His right hand shot forward in desperation, aiming to drive his last dagger into Belaric's gut.

Belaric was faster.

He caught Morrell's wrist in a brutal grip, twisting it. Morrell's dagger clattered to the floor. The assassin's mask was a blank slate of emotion, yet Belaric could feel the man's sheer panic—a raw, desperate energy that radiated from him in the last seconds before the ashen blade plunged into his throat.

Morrell staggered, hands flying up, blood gushing between his fingers. A gargled breath, a choked gasp, and then his legs failed him. He collapsed beside Vorin.

Belaric let out a slow breath, his body finally registering the pain—the sting of open wounds, the warmth of blood trailing down his skin. His arm throbbed, his stomach ached, and his leg sent a sharp pulse of fire through his nerves with every step. He adjusted his stance, shifting his weight off his leg. It did not matter. He was still standing. And they were not.

Without a word, he wiped his blade clean on Morrell's tunic and turned toward the small bundle on the bed.

Belaric moved with slow, measured steps, his body aching in protest. The adrenaline that had carried him through the fight was fading, and now the wounds made themselves known—stinging, burning, throbbing reminders he was still alive.

He knelt by Kaedra's bag, his fingers searching through its contents until he found what he needed—strips of linen, a small bundle of dried herbs, a vial of bitter-smelling oil. He unwrapped the linen and laid it across his lap, grinding the herbs between his fingers, their scent sharp in the air.

His hands worked on instinct. He had done this before—on rooftops, in alleyways, in bloodied rooms like this one. Clean, press, bind. He poured the oil over the gash on his leg, gritting his teeth as it burned the open wound like fire, the pain momentarily blotting out everything else. The cut across his stomach was shallower, but still a danger. He packed it with herbs before wrapping a bandage tightly around his torso, each pull of the fabric sending a fresh bolt of pain through him.

His arm came last. The slice was clean, but deep enough that blood still slicked his fingers. He pressed a folded cloth against it, tying it off with his teeth.

It was not perfect, but it would do. It had to.

Belaric reached for Kaedra's mortar, pouring the remaining herbs inside, crushing them into a fine dust. He mixed them with water from a nearby pitcher, stirring the dark, murky liquid with two fingers before drinking. Heartrest. A blend to dull the pain, to steady his mind, to keep him moving when the body wanted to stop.

The bitterness curled against his tongue as he swallowed.

He sighed deeply, rolling his shoulders, testing the limits of his injuries. His body protested, but not enough to stop him. He had fought through worse. He would fight through this.

His eyes drifted to Eryndorr, still lying quietly on the bed.

"Your mother always said I was a good man," he murmured, voice rough. "I never believed it. She never saw the other side of me. Now you have. I wonder—will you say your father is a good man?"

The words hung in the air, heavy with exhaustion.

He lowered his head, inhaling slowly. That was when he heard it.

They were not trying to sneak.

Footsteps on the stairs. Slow. Measured. Deliberate. Whoever was coming wanted him to know they were coming.

Belaric exhaled through his nose and reached for the ashen blade, feeling its familiar weight settle into his palm. He rose to his feet, ignoring the stiffness in his leg, the fire in his ribs. He had fought injured before, and now he would fight again.

The figure stepped into the doorway.

Taller than the other two. Broader. He felt no fear.

Dainrik.

His shadow fell long across the room, stretching over the bodies of Vorin and Morrell. He stopped just inside the threshold, his masked face turning down to regard the corpses. A beat of silence passed before he spoke.

"The masters thought these two would be enough." His voice was steady, unreadable. "They thought you had grown too weak. They thought you would roll over. But not me."

He lifted his gaze, fixing Belaric with a look that was not cruel, but was not kind either.

"I knew the old Varros was still in there. I knew when they threatened your baby, this would be the outcome. So, I thank you for killing these two fools. I hated them."

A dry chuckle left Belaric's lips before he could stop it. "I never imagined I would hear 'thank you' from you, Dainrik."

Dainrik shrugged, unconcerned. "I have orders. I am to bring you and the child back to the Order Hall." His body shifted slightly, his stance still relaxed, as if this were nothing more than an exchange of words. "But before you give another speech like you did with them, we both know how this will end."

Belaric's grip tightened on his blade, but he said nothing.

Dainrik took a slow step forward. "We will fight. And you will lose. You are injured. I wish you were not. I would prefer a fair fight."

He paused, gaze steady. "We fought often back then. Most ended in ties."

His voice lowered, with a hint of something almost like regret beneath the weight of duty.

"It is your lucky day, because the masters prohibited me from killing you."

He drew his blade.

"I always wondered who would win if it were to the death," Dainrik said, his voice calm, confidence radiating from him.

He lifted a gloved hand, gesturing toward the fallen assassins. "But much like the outcome with those two…" His voice carried no malice, only certainty. "This battle is already determined."

Then, without hurry, Dainrik stepped forward. He nudged Vorin's corpse aside with his boot, then dragged Morrell's body clear of the floor with a single effortless motion—clearing the space between them. When he looked back at Belaric, there was no triumph in his eyes. Only the grim weight of duty.

"They believed you were finished. I knew better. You were always the best of us—at least, before you let yourself believe in something else," he told Belaric.

Belaric exhaled slowly, a wave of exhaustion settling over him like a shroud. He shifted his stance, testing his footing, his injured leg still steady beneath him.

"You know I will not go back," he murmured. "I am left with one choice. I will kill you here and now."

Dainrik let out a low chuckle.

For a brief second, neither moved.

Then steel flashed, and the room exploded into motion.

Their blades met with a thunderous clang. The force of the collision sent a sharp vibration up Belaric's arm. Dainrik was strong—stronger than Vorin or Morrell—and his first strike was meant to break through, not test.

Belaric held firm.

Muscles bunched. Tendons strained. He poured what strength he had left into resisting the blow, every inch of him screaming with effort. The pain in his leg flared, the cuts along his torso and arm throbbed with heat—but he locked it all away. For now.

A contest of strength. Both men pushing forward, neither giving ground. The air between them seemed to freeze, heavy with the weight of what was about to come.

The fight had begun.

Belaric barely had time to brace before Dainrik drove into him again, a brutal shove that sent him stumbling. His boots scraped across the wooden floor as he fought for balance, breath ragged in his throat. Dainrik was not just stronger than those other two fools—he was stronger than Belaric even on his best day.

And today was not his best day.

Pain coiled in his muscles, his wounds burning with renewed fire. His leg ached, the deep cut pulsing with every shift of his stance. The bandages were tight, but they could not erase the truth—he was bleeding, slowing, fading. This was a fight he could not win.

His grip tightened on the ashen blade, his free hand clenching and releasing, trying to keep the feeling in his fingers. He glanced toward Eryndorr. The child remained still, wrapped in blankets on the bed. Helpless. He would not fail his son; he could not fail his son.

Belaric focused on Dainrik. The two assassins held their silent stances for a long, tense moment—a shared stillness that acknowledledged the fight, and what it meant. Then, their heads lowered in a curt, shared nod.

Dainrik moved first, his blade darting forward in quick, probing strikes—not to kill, not yet. Testing. Measuring. His movements were precise, forcing Belaric to dodge rather than parry, making him expend energy he could not afford to waste. As Belaric shifted, favoring his wounded leg, Dainrik's eyes—even behind the mask—seemed to register the tell. A flicker of grim acknowledgment passed over his face before his next strike pressed even harder against the weakness. Belaric evaded the first strike, twisting his body just out of reach. The second came for his ribs—he leaned back, feeling the steel whisper past his tunic. His wounds throbbed, sweat beading at his temple. The pain was growing, his body betraying him with every breath.

He needed to end this.

Dainrik feinted left, then swung a sideswipe at his ribs—a killing strike if it landed. Belaric shifted. His feet moved without thought—one step out of reach, one step back in. Dainrik's blade whistled past him. In that instant, Belaric caught Dainrik's elbow with his free hand, locking the limb in place. With the ashen blade still gripped tightly in his right hand, he pressed the dagger's tip under Dainrik's chin—a killing blow. The fight was over. His muscles tensed. He was about to drive it in—

And then he stopped.

A sharp sting pressed against his chest. He looked down. Dainrik had switched his blade to his other hand, its tip pushed against Belaric's heart.

A sigh left Belaric's lips. "I should have known it would not be that easy."

Dainrik gave a small, knowing nod. Both men held their positions for a breath longer, then they stepped back.

"Shall we get on with it now?" Dainrik asked.

"I suppose so," Belaric replied, adjusting his stance.

A heartbeat later, Dainrik lunged. His blade became a storm—slashes, thrusts, cuts flowing together in a deadly rhythm. Belaric had mere seconds to react, dodging by inches, the steel flashing in the dim candlelight. A downward slash—Belaric twisted away. A thrust toward his gut—he sidestepped, feeling the air shift past him. Then another, faster than before. Belaric parried, but Dainrik's strength was overwhelming—the impact sent a shock of pain up his arm.

The big man pressed the attack. Belaric countered, slicing toward Dainrik's ribs, but Dainrik easily slapped his blade away. He was too fast for his size. Too strong.

Belaric launched another attack, his blade slicing upward, aiming for the gap beneath Dainrik's arm. Dainrik dodged. Before Belaric could react, a brutal kick crashed into his injured leg. The impact was like an axe splitting through his thigh. His vision exploded with white-hot pain, his balance snapping out from under him. He barely felt the crack of his knee hitting the floor before he forced himself up again, but the damage was done. Blood leaked through his bandages. His leg screamed with every movement.

"I hope you can forgive the underhanded tactics," Dainrik said, loosening his stance. "But we are assassins."

Belaric did not respond. He only steadied himself. He knew he could not last much longer.

He forced himself to stand and then lunged at Dainrik again. The two men moved in a deadly dance, blades flashing, feet shifting, bodies twisting. Each attack met a counter; each feint met a block. Dainrik was stronger. Belaric was faster. But he was slowing. His wounds bled, and his breath came harder. His hands trembled around the hilt of his dagger.

Then—a chance.

A single misstep brought him exactly where he needed to be. Dainrik swung—Belaric sidestepped. His free hand snatched the linen sheet from the nearby bed and in one motion, he flung it toward Dainrik's face.

For the first time, Dainrik hesitated. The fabric unfurled midair, blocking his vision.

Belaric did not think. He threw the ashen blade.

The blade vanished into the air, swallowed by the dim light of the room. For a breath, he thought he had him.

Then—THUNK—it struck wood. His hope shattered.

A sharp, searing pain followed. He gasped, looking down. Dainrik had buried his blade deep in his right thigh. Somehow, in the fraction of a second beneath the sheet, he had moved—dodged low, seen through the trick.

Belaric gasped, a shuddering sound as he dropped to his knees, his vision swaying. Blood pooled beneath him, a dark stain spreading across the floor.

Dainrik stood over him, a calm strength radiating from him, his voice as steady as ever. "You almost had me," he admitted. "But I knew you had a trick up your sleeve."

He reached down and wrenched the blade free.

Belaric's breath hitched, pain exploding anew through his leg. He could not reply. He could barely breathe.

Dainrik wiped the blade clean on the edge of Belaric's tunic, then sheathed it with deliberate calm. "It was a good fight. But like I said—the outcome was determined."

Belaric nodded weakly, his strength failing. His gaze drifted to the bed—to Eryndorr. He had failed. His jaw clenched, forcing his fingers to curl into fists. He tried to push himself up—but his body refused. His vision blurred. He had nothing left.

The last thing he saw was Dainrik's fist coming toward his head. The world cracked apart.

Then—nothing.

9

Warm sunlight bathed the grassy hillside, golden beams cascading through scattered clouds. A gentle breeze carried the scent of summer—wildflowers, rich earth, the distant whisper of river water. Belaric sat cross-legged beside Renna on a thick woolen blanket, the warmth of her presence sinking into him deeper than the sun's glow.

A plate lay between them, the remains of their feast still steaming—roasted meat, charred at the edges, crisped vegetables glistening with oil, thick slices of bread slathered in melting butter. A clay jug of red wine rested by Renna's knee, the taste of it still on his tongue—ripe, full-bodied, with that faint burn that lingered at the back of his throat. Birds chirped on a nearby branch. The world felt still, content, whole. It had been perfect.

She laughed, the sound like the wind through autumn leaves. Gods, she was beautiful. Even now, after all the years, after all the horrors his hands had known, her smile was enough to leave him breathless. He reached across, taking her hand in his, rough fingers tracing the smoothness of her skin. She squeezed gently, tilting her head, a lock of chestnut hair slipping over her shoulder, catching the light like silk.

And then the world shattered.

A cry—thin, distant, aching.

Belaric tensed, the peace draining from his body like water through cupped hands. He turned his head, scanning the hillside, the distant tree line, and the far-off bend of the river. Nothing. The cry came again, louder now, cutting through the golden afternoon like a jagged blade.

He turned to Renna. "Did you hear that?"

She said nothing. Just sat there, her hand still in his, staring at him. Her expression had not changed, but something in her eyes had gone empty—hollow in a way that set ice creeping along his spine. The warmth drained from her hand, her skin chilling to the touch as if the sun had vanished from her. Her lips parted slightly, as though she meant to answer, but no words came.

She could not speak. A whisper of thought crept through his mind. She is trying, but something will not let her.

His chest tightened. The baby's cries grew sharper, raw with fear. He pushed to his feet, scanning the landscape, turning in circles. There was nothing. No crib. No child.

He turned back to Renna—to pull her up, to tell her they needed to find him—but she was gone. The blanket was gone. The food, the wine, the sun's warmth. All of it stripped from the world in the blink of an eye.

Belaric stood alone on the hilltop. The air itself felt thin, brittle, as if the dream was cracking around him.

The wind had changed, carrying a chill, dry as bone dust. The sky, once vibrant, had turned an ashen gray. Shadows pooled along the edges of the grass, stretching like fingers. He swallowed hard, panic swelling in his chest.

The cries came again. Belaric felt his heart drop. He knew at that moment it was his son. It was Eryndorr.

"Eryndorr!" he shouted, his voice ragged, torn from him by something deep and primal. He ran, feet pounding against the brittle grass, the sound of his own breath loud in his ears.

He crested the hill and saw it—a stone table standing alone, carved from dark granite, stark against the lifeless earth. Eryndorr lay upon it, wrapped in his blanket, his tiny body writhing as he wailed.

Belaric surged forward, but before he could reach him, a force slammed into his back, sending him sprawling to the dirt. The impact stole the breath from his lungs. He gasped, pushing up on trembling arms, but something held him—an unseen weight pressing him down as if the very ground had grown hands to bind him.

A shadow stretched across the ground before him, long and thin, cast by nothing he could see. The air turned brittle, cold, pressing against his skin like unseen claws.

Boots crunched against the dead earth. A figure stepped past him, clad in a flowing black robe, the hood drawn low, swallowing their face in shadow. Where their feet touched the ground, the grass blackened and curled inward, dead in an instant.

"The boy will die."

The voice was a whisper—thin as smoke, thick as certainty. It echoed inside his skull, not just heard, but felt.

Belaric thrashed, the veins in his neck bulging, his arms straining until his joints popped. The invisible force tightened around him, pressing into his ribs, his lungs. It was not just holding him—it was crushing him, grinding him into the earth like a forgotten thing.

"Stay away from him!" His voice was raw, torn from the depths of his chest. "Take me! Leave the boy!"

The figure ignored him, gliding toward the stone table. The folds of its robe barely stirred, as though the wind itself recoiled.

Belaric's breath caught as the figure reached into its sleeve and withdrew a blade—his blade. The ashen steel caught no light, swallowing it whole. The air rippled with a low, metallic hum, and the faint scent of ash filled Belaric's nose.

Eryndorr screamed, tiny fists trembling in the air.

The figure raised the blade.

Belaric roared, thrashing, tearing at the unseen chains, but they did not yield. He watched as the dagger came down, a swift arc of blackened steel.

He screamed.

In the instant before the blade pierced his son's chest, the world fractured around him.

Belaric shot upright, breath coming in ragged gasps, sweat slicking his back. Darkness. Stone walls. Cold air was pressing in. The scent of damp rot and old blood.

He was no longer on the hill. Eryndorr no longer lay on the table. The dream had broken, and he was pulled back into reality.

The sound of Eryndorr's final scream still rang in his ears, so sharp it might have been real. Belaric's chest heaved, each inhale dragging fire through his lungs. He groaned as he shifted, the rough stone beneath him biting into his skin, the chains around his wrists cold and unforgiving.

Pain reminded him where he was. His right leg throbbed, a dull ache beneath a tight, professional bandage that had clearly been applied while he was unconscious. They had not wanted him to bleed out.

The Order Hall—where oaths were forged, and lives were ended.

His eyes adjusted to the dim light, and as they did, he saw the five masters standing before him—not in their elevated seats as usual, but mere feet away, towering over him like the grim specters of his fate. Nearby, Dainrik stood, his broad form casting a long, immovable shadow. Belaric's thoughts flickered toward the next encounter with the brute. It would end differently next time.

The masters turned their gaze toward him, the weight of their stares pressing down like stones stacked on his chest. It was Kaelen who spoke first, his voice thick with mockery. "Ah, look who has finally joined us."

Tassian's voice followed, deeper and colder. "Your son has been crying for you."

A fresh spike of dread curled in Belaric's gut. His eye darted past the masters, searching—until he saw her. Vendreth stood just beyond them, cradling Eryndorr in her arms. The boy was alive.

A deep sigh of relief escaped Belaric's lips, but the sight of his son in their hands twisted the moment into something darker. Vendreth stepped forward, holding the child out toward him. "Would you like to hold him?" she asked.

Belaric tried to move, but his legs were bound tightly, his arms tied behind his back. The restraints bit into his flesh as his muscles strained against them. His body betrayed him—helpless as a man shackled in a nightmare.

The masters laughed—a sharp, mocking chorus.

"You fool," Kaelen spat, stepping forward. "Did you really think you would get to live your happy little life with your whore wife and this boy?"

Belaric's blood ran hot, fury tightening his throat. He forced himself to remain still, even as his hands clenched into fists behind his back.

Kaelen stopped just before him. Then, with slow, deliberate disdain, he crouched—bringing his mask down to Belaric's level, mere inches from his face.

He tilted his head, studying him in silence.

"Oh, how I wish she had not died," he murmured. "We would have had such fun together. You know, I tried her apples once. They were disgusting. Took me days to get the taste out of my mouth." The laughter that followed was hollow and grating, the sound of a man savoring his own cruelty.

Something inside Belaric snapped. He surged forward with the speed of a striking viper, smashing his forehead into Kaelen's mask. A sickening crack filled the hall. The movement tore at the wounds along his side, sent fresh agony up his spine—but it was worth it. Kaelen staggered back with a strangled grunt, clutching his face. Blood seeped through his fingers, dripping down the front of his robe. His breathing turned ragged, more snarl than gasp.

Belaric smirked, blinking away the sting. "You did not care for the taste of that either, did you?"

Kaelen roared, a guttural sound of pure rage, and lunged forward. His fist, wrapped in black leather, connected with Belaric's jaw. The blow sent a jolt of white-hot pain through Belaric's head, his teeth clashing together with a sickening crunch. His head snapped back, his body swaying dangerously to the side as he strained against the chains that held him fast. A thin trickle of blood ran from the corner of his mouth, down his chin.

He gave me a taste of his rage, and Belaric did not regret a second of it.

For a heartbeat, the hall stood still. Vendreth instinctively pulled Eryndorr tighter to her chest, her grip protective—too protective. Belaric saw it, even through the haze of pain.

Tassian's hand hovered near his belt. None of the masters moved, but the tension was a taut wire, ready to snap. Kaelen's hand trembled as he reached for the blade at his hip. Slowly, deliberately, he pulled it free, the dim light glinting off the edge. His breaths came in sharp hisses through clenched teeth.

"You bastard," he seethed, voice thick with pain. "You will suffer for that." His grip tightened on the blade at his side. He took a step forward. Then another. The moment stretched thin. No one moved to stop him.

A voice—deep, slow, and edged with danger—cut through the silence. "Now that was funny." The words carried weight, not just in tone but in presence—thick as iron, cold as the grave. Footsteps followed, steady and unhurried, their rhythm deliberate. A figure emerged from the gloom, clad in flowing black robes, a hood drawn low over his face. The mask underneath was smooth, featureless, save for its sharp edges.

The air in the hall shifted—not colder, not heavier, but thicker, as if the very walls had stiffened at his arrival. Even the torches seemed to burn quieter. He passed by Belaric without a glance, stopping just before Kaelen. The knife in Kaelen's hand wavered, fury flickering into doubt.

The figure tilted his head. "What did I tell you?"

Kaelen swallowed. "Not to touch him or the boy," he muttered. "You would decide their fate."

The hooded man inclined his head slightly. "And yet," he mused, "you were about to do just that, were not you?"

Kaelen hesitated for only a heartbeat before pressing forward. "He broke my—"

The figure struck without warning. His hand lashed out in a blur, catching Kaelen across the side of the head with a force that sent him staggering. Kaelen gasped, clutching his temple as he fought to remain upright.

The figure's voice remained calm, almost bored, but there was no mistaking the steel beneath it. "Remember your place, Kaelen. I command here. Disobey again, and you will die. Do you understand?"

Kaelen hesitated, then dropped to one knee. Blood trickled from beneath his mask. "Yes, master," he whispered.

The hooded figure turned toward the remaining masters. His gaze swept across them like a blade. "Do you all understand?"

Tension gripped the room. A pause followed, then, one by one, the others knelt. Even Vendreth, though she clung to the child as she did. "Yes, Master," they murmured in unison.

The silence that followed was dense, unyielding. The figure sighed, as if this display bored him. "Rise." The masters obeyed, their movements stiff. The balance of power had been reasserted. Belaric remained where he was—bloodied, but unbowed.

Then the figure turned to him, his masked face unreadable. "My apologies for them," he said, his tone shifting to something almost conversational. "I am sure you are wondering who I am."

Belaric stared at the mask but spoke to the man behind it. "You are the Vowkeeper."

A low chuckle followed. "Ah, yes. I always heard you were sharper than most." He paused. "That is correct. I am the Vowkeeper—the leader of our order."

A dark chill settled in Belaric's chest. He had never seen the Vowkeeper before—no one had besides the masters. But every assassin in the Order had heard the rumors about him. If the Vowkeeper came in person, it meant your fate was already sealed. Belaric understood in an instant. His life was meant to end here.

The Vowkeeper took a slow step forward, his black robe whispering across the stone like dead leaves blown through a tomb. The torchlight flickered low, shadows thickening as he moved. A single drop of water fell in the distance, the sound echoing like a falling hammer in the stillness.

He stood above Belaric now, and the shadow that spilled from him seemed to swallow the room.

"We have been watching you, Belaric," he said, his voice low and measured, as if reading from a book long forgotten. "Every job you carried out. Every kill made in our name. Every night spent beside your wife in that little house with its stone walls and garden out back. We even saw the little wooden bird you carved for her, remember? Left it on her bedside table, did you not? So domestic. We were there, watching."

He let the silence stretch, letting the weight of the words press in like a tightening noose.

"We saw how close you became to her. How your loyalty thinned with us but grew with her. Each assignment was longer than the last, spending days scouting when hours would do. You began taking off your mask mid-job—almost begging to be seen. Begging to be caught." He tilted his head, just slightly. "And now, here you are caught, just like you wanted."

He paused as though savoring the moment, letting it steep in Belaric's pain. "Do you have anything to say for yourself? And if you are planning to beg for your life, I suggest you make it good."

Belaric chuckled—dry and cracked, like stone splitting under frost. The sound scraped from his throat, blood bubbling at the corner of his mouth. His vision swam, torches swaying like ghosts behind a veil. But he blinked, forced the blur away, and raised his head.

"Beg?" he rasped. A smear of blood ran down his chin as he shook his head. "Do not insult me. I know how this ends. I am not leaving this place alive. But I will not beg for mercy—not from you."

He spat blood and bile, spattering at the Vowkeeper's feet.

"You think you broke me? That you own me. But I found something you will never understand. I found her." His voice cracked, thick with pain. "Renna was real. The love we shared was real. The Order gave me nothing but shadows. Pain. A blade to press into the throats of children. A vow soaked in blood and silence. But she gave me breath. She gave me a reason to live."

His arms strained against the shackles, muscles trembling with effort. His chest heaved. Still, he looked up—hair matted to his brow, one eye burning with fury, the other clouded with grief.

"My only regret," he whispered, "is not taking her far away from this cursed place when I had the chance."

The Vowkeeper stood still for a beat, then let out a deep laugh, low and guttural, echoing through the hall like something dredged from a crypt. The sound was joyless—like a wolf baring its teeth before the kill.

"Fool you are not, Belaric," he said. The laugh died in an instant, cut off like a breath before a blade. "But you are right; you will die. Slowly. Painfully. And you will have no one to blame but yourself."

He stepped closer, his tone dropping lower, more intimate. "Still... I envy you."

Belaric narrowed his eyes. The confusion was plain on his face. Why would this man envy me? He thought.

"In a world built on shadows," the Vowkeeper murmured, breaking Belaric's thoughts, "you found light." He let the words linger, then twisted them. "But we are assassins. And we hate the light."

Belaric's face hardened. If I am going to die, he thought, I will die bleeding truth into the cracks of their precious Order.

He wet his lips. His voice, when it came, was steady as steel. "Then why am I still breathing?"

The Vowkeeper looked at him but said nothing.

Belaric leaned into the silence. "Why is my child still alive?"

He watched the Vowkeeper closely, gauging even the smallest shift.

"You—the great Vowkeeper—saw a marked child and did not kill it. Why?" His voice was rising now, but sharp, deliberate. "Could not do it? Maybe those eyes reminded you of something you buried long ago. Maybe these five masters behind you—so loyal, so silent—are wondering why you hesitated. Why you, our great Vowkeeper, faltered when it counted."

He let the words settle. He saw it—the flicker. One of the masters shifted. Another turned their head, just slightly, as if to glimpse the Vowkeeper from the corner of their eye.

Doubt.

The Vowkeeper's masked face tilted a fraction. His gloved hand clenched. The silence twisted.

Then came the blow.

He moved in a blur, and his boot slammed into Belaric's chest. The force lifted him from his knees and drove him down like a broken statue. Bone cracked. Breath fled. Pain burst white across his vision.

Belaric hit the stone hard, gasping, choking on blood. He was sure at least one rib was broken—he knew the feeling of that particular agony—but he pushed through it. Belaric dragged air into his lungs, each breath causing a spasm of pain. He lifted his head slowly, grinding his teeth to keep from groaning.

He would not give them the pleasure of watching him stay down.

The Vowkeeper loomed above, breath steady, voice cold.

"You may be clever, Belaric," he said, voice as calm as ever—but now there was ice beneath it. "But clever men still die. I will be sure we take our time with you."

Belaric coughed, tasting blood and grit. "You gave me a blade," he rasped. "She gave me something to sheath it for."

His smile was small. Sharp.

The Vowkeeper turned, his gaze settling on Eryndorr, still wrapped in Vendreth's arms. The infant let out a soft cry, limbs shifting beneath the folds of the blanket.

"As for your son," the Vowkeeper said, his voice unnervingly calm, "yes—he will live."

He stepped closer; his black robe moved silently across the stone like falling ash. "I have plans for him. I will shape him into a great man… our greatest weapon."

Belaric ensured he remained still, to keep his breathing even—but confusion twisted in his gut. What did he mean? The Order was built to erase children like Eryndorr—common-born and marked with the Valasar. They hunted them. Killed them. This… this went against everything the Black Vow stood for.

A ripple passed through the circle of masters—barely visible, but there. A flicker of discomfort in posture, a sideways glance quickly suppressed. The weight of the Vowkeeper's words hung like a gathering storm, just beyond the horizon.

Tassian stepped forward, uncertain but firm. "Master… that is not our way. We have a duty."

The Vowkeeper turned like a drawn blade. His boots echoed off the stone as he advanced on Tassian, each step deliberate and sharp with menace.

"Your duty," he said through clenched teeth, "is whatever I say it is, you fool. You forget yourself."

He stopped inches from Tassian's mask, breath calm but laced with heat.

"Never question my authority," he commanded.

Tassian bowed his head and stepped back. The line reasserted—but the crack was made, and it ran deep. No one else moved. Even Kaelen remained still.

Belaric shifted. He saw one last chance to sow discord among them.

Belaric let out a dry, blood-choked laugh. "You are nothing but pawns to him," he rasped. "He will take what he can from you—and when you are no longer useful, he will slit your throats and leave your corpses in the dark."

The Vowkeeper's head snapped toward him.

A flick of the wrist. Steel sang.

Belaric twisted, but too slow. The throwing knife sliced through the meat of his upper arm and clattered against the stone. Pain flared, sharp and immediate. Warm blood soaked through his sleeve, and he hissed between his teeth.

Before he could recover, the Vowkeeper was on him. A gloved fist tangled in his hair, yanking his head back until his face met the smooth black mask.

"Oh no, Belaric," the Vowkeeper said, voice low and curling with disdain. "I protect those around me. You? You stood there and watched her die. Did nothing. Just knelt there while she bled out like a gutted pig."

He leaned in closer, breath a whisper of rot and spice behind the mask.

"She did not scream. She did not beg. She just looked at you—silent, bleeding, dying—and you looked back, helpless. You were all she had left."

He leaned in, the mask close enough for Belaric to feel the heat of his breath through the metal.

"And what did you do? Whispered nonsense. Clutched her hand. Cried like a child."

A beat passed—quiet, heavy, deliberate.

"She held your son for the first and last time while you sat there, weeping. Not a sword in your hand. Not a plan in your head. Just tears. You were not a man in that moment—you were a failure. Blood on your hands. And no courage to stop it."

He paused, letting the words settle like poison in a wound.

"Tell me—when her body went cold beneath your touch, did you finally understand what it means to be powerless? Did you finally see what you really are?"

Belaric growled low in his throat, eyes blazing. The pain did not matter. Not compared to the cold fury hardening inside him.

"She told you to protect the boy—and you failed. Utterly. She is watching now. She sees who you really are, and you disgust her... she already hates you. You are a murderer, Belaric. And you lost her son."

Belaric remained silent. He would not give him the pleasure. His fists clenched behind his back, nails biting into his palms. He would kill this man.

The Vowkeeper snorted and released him. Belaric slumped to one knee, panting, blood dripping from his arm to the floor in slow, rhythmic beats. Each drop echoed louder than it should have in the heavy silence.

The Vowkeeper turned back to the masters. "Give him to Orris," he said. "Let him have his fun."

Belaric's stomach churned.

Not that. Anything but that. Even death would be a mercy.

Orris did not just break bodies—he hollowed men out and left the shells grinning. Belaric had seen the aftermath once. He still remembered the eyes of that poor soul—empty, but somehow still screaming.

As the Vowkeeper approached Vendreth, he reached for the child. She hesitated—just for a breath. Her grip tightened almost imperceptibly before she released him with careful, practiced ease.

Belaric saw it. That flicker. That pause. It was not fear. It was not defiance. It was something else. For a heartbeat, he wondered—Had she once held a child of her own?

The Vowkeeper took Eryndorr into his arms. The infant whimpered once, confused, but did not cry. Belaric's body tensed violently. His limbs jerked against the bindings, muscle memory and madness screaming for him to rise, to fight, to do something. His heart pounded like a war drum, the sound thundering in his ears.

But he could not move. Could not even scream. He was useless—rage, grief, and helplessness trapped inside broken flesh.

"Say goodbye to Daddy, Eryndorr," the Vowkeeper said softly. "You will never see him again."

Belaric wanted to lunge. To tear them apart with his bare hands. To claw and bite and kill his way through anyone between him and his son. But he could only kneel, jaw clenched, muscles twitching against restraints that would not yield.

The Vowkeeper turned, vanishing into the dark with the child in his arms, swallowed by the shadows like a nightmare fading at dawn.

Silence followed. Heavy. Absolute.

Then Kaelen stepped forward. Though his mask hid it, Belaric could feel the grin behind it—smug and venomous.

"Dainrik," he said, voice casual. "You heard the Vowkeeper. Take him to Orris. Tell that disgusting filth to enjoy his new plaything. Ensure he makes it as long as possible. I want Belaric to truly suffer. Make him understand the price of his foolish decisions."

Heavy boots thudded across the stone. Dainrik said nothing. He did not need to.

His grip found Belaric's shoulders—rough, ironlike—and lifted him as though he weighed nothing at all.

Stone scraped beneath Belaric's boots as Dainrik dragged him from the master's chamber.

Into the dark.

And toward something worse.

The only sound was the scrape of Belaric's boots against the cold stone. Dainrik dragged him without a word, the rhythm of his steps unchanging, steady as death. The hallway pressed close around them, thick with damp and shadow. Somewhere above, a droplet fell, the sound echoing off the ceiling like a ticking clock.

Belaric's hand shifted slightly as he moved, brushing the inside seam of his trousers. His fingertips found it—a narrow hilt, hidden in the slit-pocket near his hip. The knife the Vowkeeper had thrown. No one had seen it. Not even him.

He had tucked it there in silence, shifting it down his leg as Dainrik led him through the hall. Now it pressed against him like a promise. He could use it. Drive it into Dainrik's spine. Make his escape. Find Eryndorr. His hand moved slightly, preparing to twist just enough to grip it—

"I would save that blade for Orris," Dainrik muttered, voice low and gravel-rough. "You will need it."

Belaric froze. His gaze sharpened.

How?

He had been careful. Precise. The blade had barely been visible, even to him. But Dainrik had noticed. And more importantly... he had not stopped him.

Belaric opened his mouth, but Dainrik's grip clamped down—firm and wordless.

They reached the chamber—bare stone walls, damp air, a single slab of a bed bolted to the floor. A rusted ring of chains hung from one wall. Belaric's stomach turned at the sight.

Dainrik tossed him onto the slab—rough, but not cruel. The impact drove a fresh wave of pain through Belaric's ribs, but he shifted just slightly as he landed, rolling onto his side so the blade was beneath him. Hidden. Pain bloomed in his chest and shoulder, but he welcomed it. Pain meant he was still alive.

Dainrik began strapping him down. Tight leather bindings looped around his ankles and biceps. Not his wrists. Not his chest. He knows, Belaric thought. He is helping me.

Without a word, Dainrik stepped toward the door. "Orris. He is ready for you."

A wooden door creaked open. Footsteps followed—shuffling, gleeful.

"Good, very good," came the voice. High, too cheerful. "I cannot wait to play with my friend."

Orris stepped into the chamber, dragging two heavy packs behind him. He was squat and thick-bodied, his bald head glistening with sweat, eyes too wide. His grin twitched at the edges as he turned back toward the hallway. "Do you want to stay and play too, Dainrik?"

A beat passed. Then, without turning, Dainrik muttered, "Have fun with the rat," and left.

Belaric's brow twitched. Rat. That is what the others called Orris—never to his face. Dainrik wanted him dead. That much was clear now. But why?

Orris turned back. "I brought so many toys," he sang, setting the packs beside the slab. "Would you like to see them?"

Belaric stared past him, silent.

"Aww," Orris pouted. "He does not want to play with me. That is fine. I still will."

He opened the first pack and began laying out tools—a curved gut-hook blade, a serrated flensing knife, a narrow stiletto made for slipping between ribs, a barbed awl, a scalpel gleaming like glass, a rusted paring knife with a cracked leather grip. He placed each one carefully, reverently. An altar of pain.

Then came the pouches. Orris untied them, and the sharp scents of crushed roots and bitter herbs filled the room. Some Belaric recognized—nerve stimulants, pain enhancers, poisons. Others were unfamiliar, their colors too bright, their smells too sweet.

"Which one first?" Orris murmured, pacing the row of knives like a man choosing fine wine. "Ahhh, yes, you." He plucked the flensing knife from the collection and stepped close, breath reeking of rotted fruit and iron. "Are you ready to play, my friend? Where should I cut first?"

Belaric gave him nothing. His jaw was tight, eyes locked on the ceiling above. Orris slumped in mock disappointment.

"Okay."

His hand lashed out like a snake, the blade slicing into Belaric's palm from thumb to wrist. Belaric grunted, the sting immediate and deep, but bit down on the pain.

"Oh, we will have fun," Orris giggled, moving to his feet. He carved behind the knee, then down the calf, across the ankle—each cut deliberate, testing, as though mapping nerve and resistance. Belaric stared upward, unflinching. Silent.

Orris chuckled through the blood. "Now, this is where the real fun begins." He picked up one of the pouches and began sifting through it. "I know how much you love to use poison," he said, voice dropping to a murmur. "Let us see how you like them used on you."

Belaric's pulse quickened. His breathing slowed, narrowed to focus. The blade pressed faintly against his hip, warm from skin and blood—hidden in the seam of his trousers, exactly where he had tucked it.

He shifted, slow and steadily, masking the movement with a labored breath. His fingers found the hilt. Slick. Familiar. He gripped it tight and eased it free, the steel whispering against the cloth.

He exhaled softly.

He pressed the dagger to the straps binding his wrists and, with a careful twist, sliced through the first. Then the second. The leather gave with a quiet hiss.

The stone beneath him stayed silent—cold, unmoving—as he shifted into a crouch. A drop of blood hit the floor.

Orris paused. Turned slightly.

Belaric moved.

He surged off the slab, silent and fast. His arm snapped around Orris's throat, dragging him back into the dark.

"You were right," Belaric whispered into Orris's ear, his breath hot and shaking. "This is where the fun starts."

He slipped his hand beneath Orris's mask and clamped it over his mouth, muffling the first cry. Then, he drove the knife into his kidney.

Orris thrashed, eyes bulging. The scream died against Belaric's palm, replaced by a strangled, wet gasp.

Belaric pulled the blade free and stabbed again—lower this time, then higher, twisting. Blood poured down Orris's robes in thick sheets. He sagged, but Belaric held him upright, his grip iron, his arm a blur.

Shoulder. Throat. Chest. Gut. The blade punched through muscle, scraped bone. Again. Again.

This was not killing.

This was obliteration.

Every thrust spoke of the scars Orris had left on others. Every rip of flesh paid back a scream. Belaric's body moved on fury and instinct, not stopping even when Orris began to slide from his grasp, barely alive.

He let the body drop, flipped it onto its back, and stared down at the blood-soaked face.

Still not enough.

He drew the blade across Orris's throat in one long, savage pull—then reached for the hatchet he had once so proudly displayed.

The first strike crushed skin and cartilage. The second split the spine. The third made the corpse twitch.

Belaric did not stop.

He hacked, over and over, until with a final, wet snap, the head tore free in a spray of blood.

He staggered back, chest heaving, arms trembling from exertion. Blood dripped from his hands, his boots, his jaw. For a dizzying moment, the room seemed to spin, the clang of the hatchet still echoing in his ears, every splash of blood feeling like a hammer blow against his senses. The stench of iron and viscera was suffocating, threatening to choke him. The room swam around him, a tunnel of red and silence.

But there was no triumph. No release.

Only emptiness.

He bent down and picked up Orris's head by his greasy hair, staring into lifeless eyes and a frozen grin. "Still want to play, friend?" he muttered, then hurled the head across the chamber. It struck the far wall with a wet crack and vanished into shadow.

Belaric steadied himself against the blood-slick stone, breath ragged. He was bleeding, exhausted, and every muscle in his body screamed for rest—but rest meant death. He needed to move. Needed to vanish. The way out lay deep within memory—every hallway, every turn etched into his mind. But if anyone saw him, they would kill him on sight.

His eye drifted down to Orris's corpse. The robe. It might work. Another assassin would be questioned. But Orris? No one would stop a man like him. No one wanted to. Belaric moved quickly. He peeled off his bloodied shirt and trousers, ignoring the raw pain of movement. The damp, blood-covered robe came next—he tore it from Orris's cooling corpse and wrapped it around himself. It was warm with the man's blood, thick and sticky, but he forced down his revulsion.

He wiped the blade on the dead man's robe before placing it in his sleeve. Then, with a practiced hand, he unbuckled the worn leather belt from Orris's waist, freeing the second dagger, and strapped it to his side.

The mask had fallen off when he had severed the head. He found it slick with gore and strapped it on. The stench hit him instantly—sweat, blood, rot—and bile surged up his throat. He swallowed it down, steadying himself. Hood up, face hidden, he checked the straps. The dagger slipped into his sleeve. It would have to do.

He left the chamber and entered the hall, footsteps careful, movements practiced. He did not limp—he could not. Limping would draw eyes. Blood still dripped from the wounds on his leg and hand, and every breath dragged fire through his cracked ribs, but he forced himself to walk tall. Orris was sick. Unpredictable. No one would question if he wandered.

He moved quickly, from shadow to shadow, hugging the edges of the corridor. Once, voices echoed from around the bend. He froze, breath caught sharply in his chest, ribs screaming, and slipped behind a pillar. Only when silence returned did he move again.

Finally, he saw it—the door. Salvation. And the man who stood before it, arms crossed, watched the hall with practiced boredom.

As Belaric approached, the guard straightened. His head tilted. "Orris?" he asked, voice uncertain. "Is that you?" Belaric said nothing. Two paces left. The guard frowned, stepping forward. "What are you doing? You know you are forbidden to leave. Go back to your room." The man's hand touched Belaric's chest. It never got the chance to push.

In one motion, Belaric slapped the arm aside and lunged. His shoulder slammed into the man's chest, driving him back against the door. As the guard grunted, Belaric shoved his hand beneath the mask, clamping down over his mouth. With the other, he drew the blade and dragged it across the throat in one clean, practiced stroke.

The man jerked violently, limbs flailing. A wet, choking sound gurgled behind the mask as he clutched at his throat, blood spilling in hot streams through his fingers. He staggered once, then collapsed, twitching at Belaric's feet.

Belaric did not wait to watch him die. He slipped past the slumping body and pushed open the door.

He staggered through the winding corridors, one hand on the wall to keep himself upright.

At last, he emerged through the hidden passage in the abandoned house.

The cool night air hit him like a blessing.

He was outside.

But not free.

His legs shook beneath him, blood soaking through the makeshift wrappings he had tied in haste. Every step pulled at open wounds, each breath a saw blade in his ribs. He could not afford to fall. Not yet. Not here.

He moved through the alleys, weaving toward the city's middle district. The climb over the wall left him nearly faint, hands shaking as he hoisted himself over the edge. He dropped into the dirt with a grunt, the world spinning. Above, the stars blinked down indifferently—clear and cold. He hated them for shining. For pretending nothing had changed.

Eventually, he found the alley—half-forgotten, piled with crates and littered with broken stone. He dragged the crates aside slowly and clumsily until he saw it: his assassin gear. Folded. Waiting. Hidden like a second skin he never wanted to wear again. He hated it—but it would protect him more than the stinking robe. Quickly, he stripped off Orris's blood-soaked garments and changed. He kept the mask.

I might need it, he thought. To move unseen among them. Let them think I am one of the hounds sent to hunt me. He slid the mask into his satchel.

Then his thoughts drifted to Renna—her still body in the bed. Her eyes closed. Her hands still warm when he had left her. He clenched his fists. I will bury her in the garden. She loved it there. Always said it was the one place she could breathe. It will be her peace, if nothing else.

He moved through the sleeping streets like a phantom, gliding from shadow to shadow. The closer he came to home, the slower he moved. Something in him twisted—dread blooming with every step.

Then the smell hit him. Smoke. Burning wood.

He froze, then raised his head. A faint orange glow painted the sky beyond the rooftops. His stomach turned to stone. No.

He ran, pain forgotten. Turned the last corner—and stopped. His home was ablaze. Flames clawed through the roof, belching smoke into the night. The windows glowed with firelight. Embers drifted skyward like red snow. A small crowd had gathered, faces lit with sorrow and fear.

He almost fell to his knees. Almost screamed. But the grief locked inside his chest was too heavy to move. A guttural sound, part sob, part growl, tore at his throat, but no air could escape. He remembered Renna laughing with flour on her face. Her hands reached for his. The sound of Eryndorr's first breath. Gone—all of it, eaten by fire. She died in pain. Now she would vanish in smoke. They had not just taken her—they had erased her.

There would be nothing left of her to bury. Nothing left to return to.

He did not realize he was shaking until he saw Jorric standing at the edge of the crowd, arms around his wife, Selene. She wept on his chest. Belaric's mind flashed with a memory: Selene, laughing with Renna over a pot of stew, the two of them friends, companions. They had cared for one another. The grief on Selene's face was for her friend Renna.

Belaric's heart hardened to stone. They had taken everything from him. The masters, the Vowkeeper, and every assassin who served them. In a single night, his wife had died, his son was stolen, and his home was burned to ash. They had destroyed his life, and now he would do the same to theirs.

Belaric turned away from the light. He looked down at the mask in his hand—the one that had helped him escape, the one that marked him as theirs. It was slick with dried blood, its weight heavier now than when he first put it on.

Let them hunt. Let them come. I will kill every single one.

He drew the dagger he had taken from Orris, held the edge to his palm for a moment, as if weighing what was left of himself. Then he walked to the wooden wall beside him. He placed the mask against it like a corpse prepared for burial and drove the blade through the center of its brow—pinning it there like a severed oath.

He stepped back, breathing hard, and stared into the mask—into the hollow eyes of the life he had abandoned.

"I sever my vow," he whispered.

"They will suffer as I have suffered—and not even the gods will save them from my vengeance."

His voice dropped, rough and low. Fierce.

"Eryndorr... I am coming."

And in the silence that followed, with blood on his hands and fire in his chest, he made a vow no one else would hear:

My life is no longer a vow to the Order. It is to vengeance, and to my son.

10

The fire still roared behind him, a red wound on the night. Belaric did not look back.

Smoke clung to his clothes, the stench of ash and ruin thick in his lungs. Each step away from the blaze felt like walking through the remains of a life already buried. His boots sank slightly into the softened ground, blood trailing from wounds he had long stopped feeling. Somewhere behind him, wood cracked and collapsed with a groan—the roof, maybe. Or the bed where Renna had once slept.

He clenched his jaw and kept moving. There was nothing left to save.

Hate burned hotter in his chest than the flames swallowing his home. Every lick of fire seemed to sear a new line of purpose into his very bones. But beneath the rage was something colder—something hollow. Grief clawed at his ribs like a beast left starving.

Vengeance gnawed at him too, but it was quieter. Crueler and more patient. It was the only thing keeping him upright. Not strength. Not hope. Just the promise of retribution—sharp-edged and certain.

His legs trembled, but he did not stop. There was no home to return to. No grave to weep beside. Only fire behind him. And a name ahead.

The Vowkeeper.

Belaric had never laid eyes on the man until tonight. Just a name, whispered through stone halls and bloodied corridors—power cloaked in ritual, unseen, untouched. But now the Vowkeeper had taken his son. Had burned the home where he and Renna had built a life out of love and fleeting peace.

He had taken everything.

Belaric would return the favor—gladly, and without mercy.

The Vowkeeper loved the shadows. So Belaric would drag him into the light—and make sure the world watched him burn.

He stopped and inhaled deeply, letting the cold bite his lungs. The air reeked of soot and blood, but it steadied him all the same. Rage clouded judgment. He needed clarity. He needed to think.

What would the Vowkeeper do next?

He would not linger—not after tonight. He would leave the city after he received word of Belaric's escape. Not out of fear, but to avoid unnecessary complications. Attention. Uncertainty.

Still, even he would not risk the roads at night. They were notoriously poorly kept, riddled with deep, unseen ruts and treacherous with loose stones. One wrong step could snap a horse's leg or crack the wheel of a wagon. Bandits stalked travelers on the road at night, drawn to the promise of a hobbled horse or broken-down cart, but they would pose no threat to a man like the Vowkeeper.

The true danger came with urgency. And with haste came mistakes. Tracks left behind. Patterns rushed. Trails are easier to follow.

So he would not flee—yet. But he would be preparing to.

Belaric ground his teeth and looked up at the twisting alleys before him. Where would a man like that begin?

He would not steal a horse. A man like that did not need to.

The Vowkeeper controlled the Order—every coin it earned, every secret it bartered. He had access to coffers deeper than most noble houses and the connections to match. If he wanted a mount, it would already be arranged. Swift. Bred for distance. Handpicked from bloodlines meant for kings and couriers. No risk. No questions. A sealed deal with a merchant lord. A favor owed to a noble with too many secrets and too little spine.

Belaric could almost picture it: the stable doors opening, the finest mare already saddled, reins in gloved hands. The best horse in the city.

That is when it hit him.

Only one place in Vorinfall kept the best.

The stables in the Upper District.

Belaric had been there once, years ago—shadowing a noble with a taste for fast horses and faster losses. The stables had smelled of sweet hay, oiled leather, and pride. Even the stable hands wore silk at their wrists, sleeves too fine for the work they did.

A man like the Vowkeeper would not settle for less. He might be Order-forged—shaped by blood, silence, and ritual—but he wore the arrogance of wealth like a cloak. Nobles and killers were not so different. Both liked to rule from behind high windows. Both believed themselves untouchable.

If he meant to flee, that is where he would start. With a fresh mount. With the best.

It was only a guess. But a good one.

And it was all Belaric had left to chase.

He turned north, pain flaring in his side as he moved. The alley swallowed him whole.

He made it only a few streets before the world tilted. His boot caught on uneven stone, and his shoulder slammed into a cold wall. He slid down it in a half-collapse, air rasping in a ragged choke.

A cough tore free—wet and violent. Pain followed like fire behind broken ribs.

He raised a shaking hand to his mouth.

Blood.

Dark. Viscous. Fresh.

He stared at the smear on his palm, his lungs burning with short, stabbing pulls.

Worse than I thought.

The bleeding had not stopped. Maybe it was deeper than he realized. Maybe something inside had torn. His body was not just wounded—it was failing.

He shoved off the wall, spine scraping rough stone. His legs quivered, barely obeying him. Another step. Another cough.

His vision warped at the edges, the world bending and rippling like heat rising off scorched iron.

Then his balance gave again, and he crashed to one knee. The street blurred—gray shapes and flickering torchlight, distant roofs hunched like crouched beasts. Voices drifted from shuttered windows, faint and far away, part of a world that no longer felt real.

Belaric bared his teeth in a soundless snarl, low and feral.

Weakness will not save him. Will not bring her back.

He forced himself up again, legs trembling, joints stiff with pain. But even as he stood, he felt it—the weight pressing in, not just from blood loss, but from the truth.

He would not make it to the stables tonight.

He let out a long sigh. Not quite a curse. Not quite surrender.

He needed shelter. A place to breathe. To stop the bleeding.

Somewhere to survive—just long enough to kill the man who had done this.

He thought of friends—but the thought died quickly. He did not have friends. Only people who had once known him. Like Jorric.

But even Jorric believed he and Renna were dead. To show up now, bloodied and hunted, would raise questions no one could afford to answer.

The inns would be worse. Once word got out that he had escaped, if it had not already, every inn would be watched. Looking for him.

And he needed more than rest. He needed bandages. Healing herbs. A fire that had not burned down to ash.

He exhaled through his nose, low and bitter. There was only one place that made sense.

Kaedra's house.

She would have had what he needed—salves, poultices, clean water. And now… she would no longer need them.

She had died trying to help Renna. A knife to the chest. Blood soaked through the floorboards. He would never get the chance to bury either her now.

But he remembered the rafters lined with drying herbs, the sharp scent of crushed roots, the firelight dancing against stone walls. A place of healing once. Now just another empty house.

It was a risk. A fool's choice, maybe.

The Order knew he would be wounded. They would expect him to seek treatment.

He only hoped that they would overlook it—that they would see it for what it was: too obvious. A desperate man's mistake.

And Belaric was not desperate. Not yet.

Or so he told himself.

He sighed, set his jaw, and pushed off the wall.

He would go to Kaedra's house.

He had to reach it before the blood loss claimed him.

It took several long minutes of staggering through alleys before Kaedra's house came into view.

A squat stone building nestled between shuttered shops, its windows dark, its door still unbroken. Belaric leaned against the edge of a wall across the street, half-shadowed, half-folded in on himself. He waited and watched.

He heard them before he saw them—boots scuffing uneven cobbles, the low murmur of voices rising between the walls.

Belaric ducked into the shadows, pressing his back to the cold stone, holding himself still.

Two guards passed a moment later, their steps lazy, their tone light. They spoke of a card game, and one of them bragged about a woman he had enjoyed the night before. Easy. Careless.

Nothing of burned houses.

Nothing of dead healers.

Nothing of missing assassins.

Why would they look for a killer hiding in the dark? The Order would want to keep this quiet. They would never risk exposing themselves.

When the voices faded and silence took the street once more, Belaric pushed off the wall. He crossed quickly, crouched at the door, and drew a thin length of iron from inside his bracer.

The lock was simple—worn from years of gentle use, the tumblers soft with time. He slid the pick in, listening, feeling for the subtle shift of pressure. One by one, the pins clicked into place beneath his touch. He tilted the pick, nudged the final pin, and the bolt gave way with a quiet snap.

He released a breath he had not realized he was holding, tucked the pick away, and stood.

The door creaked slightly as he slipped inside. He shut it behind him and turned the bolt gently, locking it again. For a long moment, he leaned against the wood, body sagging, the last of his strength bleeding out of him.

But there was no time for rest.

They would come looking. He knew that much. And if they came here—if they found him—he would make sure they paid for the trouble in blood.

He forced himself upright and moved through the house.

The front room was narrow but clean, a simple kitchen taking up most of it—shelves lined with clay jars, a basin in the corner, dried roots strung above the counter. To the left, a door opened into a study filled with books, their spines worn, their corners bent. A chair sat beside the hearth, a thin blanket folded across its back.

He stepped deeper in. Another room—her workroom. Herbs dangled from ceiling hooks like strange, dry flowers. Bottles and vials cluttered the shelves. The scent of lavender and rot lingered in the air.

He climbed the stairs.

The bedroom was modest; the bed was dressed in deep red linens. She had always liked bold colors, even in her quiet way. The sight of it hit harder than he expected.

She would never sleep there again.

Because of him.

For a moment, he saw her as she had been hours ago—slumped beside Renna's still body, a knife buried deep in her chest, her eyes wide with shock and pain that had already passed. She had not screamed. She had not had time.

He inhaled slowly and shook the image off.

Guilt could wait. Survival could not.

It took time, but he gathered what he needed—a coil of string, metal hooks, a few sharpened kitchen knives. He set traps quickly but carefully: a wire strung across the hall to drop a blade from the rafters, a string of bells tied to the window latch, a few nastier surprises tucked into doorframes—enough to wound, enough to kill. Nothing perfect. But good enough.

His hands were numb by the time he finished the last one. His shirt stuck to him with sweat. Every step felt like walking uphill with a blade in his side.

Still, the house was ready. Or as ready as it could be.

He moved through the workroom again, fingers brushing labels until he found them—Ashroot Brew, thick and bitter, meant to numb the pain. Fleshmend, pungent and pale, used to draw wounds closed and harden the skin beneath. He took both, along with a bundle of clean bandages.

Kaedra's room was waiting.

He paused in the doorway, eyes drawn to the bed once more. The linens were neat, untouched. There was something cruel in how still it all was.

She would never lie there again. That truth settled deep in his chest like a knife turned inward.

He locked the door behind him and stripped off his assassin's garb, letting the bloodstained fabric fall to the floor. Sitting on the wooden boards, he uncorked the Ashroot and drank. The taste was bark and bile, sharp enough to make him gag. He almost did not finish it.

Almost.

Then came the Fleshmend. He dabbed the salve into each cut, each gouge, gritting his teeth against the sting. The bandages came last—tight, methodical, done with hands that barely shook.

Relief followed. Faint, but real.

He needed rest.

But he could not bring himself to lie in her bed. Not tonight. Not ever.

He pulled the blanket from the foot of the bed, moved to the far corner of the room, and wrapped it around himself.

He kept his ears open for the sound of bells, for the creak of a window or for the groan of the floorboards below. Traps or no traps, he did not expect sleep to come easily.

But it did.

Darkness pulled him under like deep water, and this time, he did not fight it.

Belaric woke to sunlight pouring through the window—warm, golden, too gentle. It painted soft lines across the wooden floor, and birdsong drifted in through the open shutters. The air smelled of spring: fresh bread, lilacs, and a faint trace of honey. Belaric opened his eyes, disoriented, the pain in his body strangely absent. A strange stillness clung to everything. Familiar, but not quite right. Like a song played just slightly out of key.

He turned his head. And there she was.

Renna sat in the chair beside the window, rocking gently—though the chair made no sound, and the floor beneath it did not move. Eryndorr lay bundled in her arms, tiny fingers twitching in sleep. Her hair fell loose over her shoulders, catching the light like strands of firegold. She looked up and smiled.

"Hello, my love. Did you sleep well?"

He chuckled softly and rubbed a hand over his face. "I did. Though I had a nightmare."

Her smile faded slightly, something shifting behind her eyes—not fear, but sorrow. A knowing sort of sadness. "That does not sound pleasant, dear. What was it about?"

He sat up slowly, turning his back to her as he looked out the window. The sheet beneath his hands was soft and smooth, untouched by blood. The air felt light. Safe. "I saw horrible things," he said, voice quieter now. "But let us not dwell on that. It was only a dream. Nothing more."

He rose to his feet, intending to walk toward her—but something had changed. The air had gone still. The warmth receded. The scent of lilacs warped, replaced by the faint, cloying sweetness of blood. The sunlight outside the window seemed to dim, casting the room in a sickly gray light. He turned, and the chair was empty.

Renna now stood in the center of the room, barefoot, her nightgown soaked with blood that ran in dark rivulets down her legs and pooled on the wooden floor. Her arms were empty. Her face, once serene, had grown pale and haunted, streaked with tears.

"Where is my son, Belaric?" she asked, her voice cracked and hollow. "Why did they take him?"

His heart lurched as he took a step forward, but she recoiled from him, flinching as if he had raised a blade. "Renna… what happened?" he asked, the words trembling in his mouth.

"You lost him," she said, voice rising, shaking. "You let them take him."

He reached toward her, but she pulled away. Her eyes burned now with something sharper than sorrow—accusation. "You let them take him," she repeated, louder this time, as if daring him to deny it. Then she shoved him hard, her hands cold and slick with blood. He stumbled back as the room seemed to darken around them.

"You sat there," she said through gritted teeth, her voice shaking with rage and grief. "And you did nothing."

The words cut deep. The warmth of the dream peeled away like old skin, replaced by smoke, shadow, and the stench of death. Memory surged back—her scream, the blood flooding the floor, Kaedra's lifeless body, the child in his arms, and the Vowkeeper walking into the night with his son.

Belaric collapsed to his knees, the weight of it leaving him gasping. "I am sorry," he gasped. "Gods, I am so sorry. I failed you. I failed him." Tears streaked down his face, bitter and hot, as he bowed his head, the shame too heavy to carry.

A hand touched his shoulder—soft, warm.

He looked up.

Renna stood before him again, the blood gone, her face calm once more. She wore the simple brown dress she always favored in the garden. There was no anger in her now, only an ache, as if sorrow had hollowed her out and left something deeper behind.

"Find him," she said gently. "Save our son, Belaric."

He swallowed hard and nodded. "I will, Renna."

She parted her lips, about to speak again—then the world tore itself away.

Belaric jolted awake, breath ragged, heart hammering in his chest. The room was dark again, the kind of dim that came just before dusk. Cold sweat clung to his skin, his pulse thudding in his ears.

Someone was pounding on the front door.

"Kaedra! Kaedra!" a man shouted. "You old bat, I need my herbs!"

The pounding came again, heavier this time. Belaric sat up, the blanket sliding from his shoulders, listening.

"You deaf, woman? Open the damn door!"

More banging. Then curses. Then the sound of boots retreating down the street, each step louder than the last in the silence he left behind.

Belaric wiped the sweat from his brow and stood, limbs heavy and aching. The dream still clung to him—like ash after a fire, weightless and inescapable. He moved to the window, eased the shutter open.

Afternoon light poured through—thick, golden, and far too bright.

The sun had already passed its peak.

Too late.

A cold knot twisted in his gut as realization struck. He had slept longer than he should have. Too long.

Dawn. If the Vowkeeper had meant to leave, he would have done it at dawn.

Belaric's jaw tightened. Rage surged through him, raw and useless. He clenched his fists until his knuckles ached. He should have moved sooner. Should have bled on the road if that is what it took. Sleep had been a mistake—a weakness he could not afford.

He exhaled sharply through gritted teeth and turned away from the window.

Pain returned with every movement—dull throbs through his ribs, sharp stings beneath torn skin. He dropped to the floor, peeled away the blood-crusted bandages, and opened the jar of Fleshmend. The salve hissed as it touched raw flesh, the sting immediate. This was a payment. A reminder. He would use every ounce of it.

Good. Let it burn.

He re-wrapped the wounds slowly, methodically, jaw clenched against the pain. When he finished, he stood, opened Kaedra's closet. Dresses, robes—most of them too small. But one gray cloak looked serviceable. He pulled it on, hood low.

It would do. Until nightfall.

And if he had not missed his chance entirely, he would make damn sure he did not miss the next.

He drew a breath, forcing the anger down where it belonged—buried beneath the calm, cold focus the Order had drilled into him. No room for regret. Not now.

Downstairs, he moved with care, slipping through the house without disturbing the traps he had laid. Wire triggers, hanging blades, bells strung along doorframes—they waited in silence, poised for any who entered uninvited. He passed them like a ghost, each step deliberate, heading to the medicine shelf.

Another bottle of Ashroot waited there. He downed it quickly, gagging on the bitter taste. It dulled the worst of the pain, but not the hollow gnaw in his gut.

Hunger twisted in him—low and sour, a hollow ache that gnawed at the edge of his strength. He could not risk a fire. The scent, the smoke—it would betray him, send wordless signals to anyone watching. But something cold might be safe.

In the kitchen, he searched the shelves and cabinets until he found a few bruised apples, a pair of withering pears, and a half-loaf of stale bread left wrapped in cloth. It was not much, but it would have to be enough. He set the food on the small wooden table, filled a cup from the water jug beneath the counter, and sat down.

The bread was hard enough to crack a tooth, and the fruit had gone soft in spots, but he chewed through it slowly, methodically, his mind drifting with each bite.

The silence pressed in around him—thick, heavy, too complete. No footsteps overhead. No wind rattling the shutters. No sound of life but his own. The quiet did not comfort him. It accused.

Belaric stared at the cold hearth, its silence louder than it should have been.

For a moment, his mind betrayed him. He imagined Renna there, stirring a pot with her back to him, humming that low tune she always did while cooking. Half melody, half memory.

He used to tease her about it. She used to tease him for eating like a starving beast.

The clatter of spoons, the warm smell of garlic and herbs—it all pressed at the edges of his mind, fragile and uninvited. A dream bleeding into the quiet of someone else's home.

He closed his eyes and let the weight of it settle on him for just a moment.

Her laugh. Her hands. Her warmth. Gone.

His hand clenched around the wooden cup until his knuckles went white. He forced his eyes open.

This was not his home. That warmth was dead. All that remained was a grave someone had left standing.

He could not afford to think like that. Not now. Not here.

The Order would come. Maybe not tonight. Maybe not tomorrow. But soon. They would search until they found him. It was only a matter of time before they searched Kaedra's house.

He had to move. He had to plan. Before the wolves found the scent.

He knew the Vowkeeper was gone—already outside the city, most likely. Belaric did not know the man's face, did not know his name. He did not know where he would go.

But someone had to.

The Black Vow had always served the nobility—shielded them in secret, silenced their enemies, severed threats before they could bloom. Their true power did not lie in the shadows they moved through, but in the coin that paid for those shadows. In names. In influence. In the nobles who kept their coffers full and their hands clean.

The Order could not monitor every birth across the kingdom. But the nobility could. Midwives, servants, records—quiet channels of information, all under noble control. If a child with a mark had been found and taken, someone had to know. Someone had to have helped.

But who?

There were too many names. Too many banners. The city crawled with petty lords, merchant barons, old blood and new wealth, all vying for favor. Most of them were noise.

Only the High Houses would have the resources, the reach—and the arrogance—to be involved.

Belaric leaned back in the chair, hands clasped as he stared at the cracked ceiling above him. He ran through the names in his mind. Considered what he knew.

House Draven, the ruling bloodline of Vorinfall. Their seat was the palace itself, built on stone and gold. Half the family bore Valasar marks. The other half were all masters of one blade type or another. They were a fortress draped in velvet. Even if they were tied to the Order—and he suspected they were—he would never get inside without a bloody fight and possibly his death.

House Ardwynne, cousins to the king himself, sat just beneath Draven in power and coin. He had watched them from the shadows before—too many guards, too many locked gates. And their son, Lord Corven, was a threat unlike the rest. He possessed a Valasar mark on his ear, and rumor claimed he could map a room by sound alone. They said he did not need eyes to hunt. Belaric had no desire to test truth against legend. Not yet.

House Tenebral—old money, colder hearts. Too private. Too quiet. He knew too little.

House Virel—generals and knights. All steel and glory. They might back the Order with coin, but they did not traffic in secrets. Not the right kind.

He sifted through each option, sorting names like blades on a table—some too sharp to handle, others too dull to matter.

Then his thoughts landed on one name.

House Sarrivane.

They were the fourth most powerful family in Vorinfall, seated just beneath the others and the blood that supported it. They ran the trade—every shipment, every caravan, every coin that crossed the gates. If the Black Vow needed to make a child disappear, no one could grease the wheels faster or quieter than the Sarrivane's.

Lord Sarrivane was a calculating man. Rarely seen in public, his influence was everywhere—in deals signed behind curtains, in markets that bowed to his coin. His wife, Kiaraa, bore a Valasar mark on her hand, but rumor said she had never trained with it. More inclined to fine dresses and expensive art than discipline or power.

They were wealthy, proud, and just foolish enough to believe themselves untouchable.

He crossed to Kaedra's desk, found ink, quill, and parchment, and began to draw from memory—sketching the outline of House Sarrivane's estate. The order kept records and layouts of every noble house in Tavros.

He had seen it before in passing—high stone walls, twin gates flanked by brass lions, terraced gardens that spilled into a marble courtyard. A smaller servant's gate behind the western wall. Two balconies overlook the side wing. A third floor that caught moonlight like silver teeth.

He studied the sketch for over an hour, refining the lines—courtyard walls, entry gates, servant quarters, garden paths. The study was the most likely target. That is where records would be kept—letters, sealed documents, shipping manifests, maybe even correspondence with the Order.

If the documents held nothing, he would go further.

He would not leave without answers.

The light outside faded from gold to gray. Shadows stretched along the walls. He stood and retrieved his assassin's garb from upstairs. The fabric reeked of fire, smoke, and blood. He filled a basin and began to scrub.

The blood was stubborn—dried into the seams, clinging to the black fabric like it had taken root. Belaric dipped the cloth again, scrubbing harder as the basin of water turned reddish brown, clouded with ash and memory. His arms ached, muscles screaming from the exertion, but he ignored it. His fingers stung from the cold and friction, the skin rubbed raw as he worked with the urgency of a man trying to undo the past by force of will. The scent of blood clung to the robe, clung to him, no matter how hard he tried to wash it away.

The cloth slipped in his hand, and he cursed under his breath, twisting it tighter, grinding it into the fabric with renewed fury. Water sloshed over the rim, soaking the floorboards. His knuckles split, red lines blooming on pale skin, but still he kept going. Scrubbing harder. Faster. As if he could erase everything that had happened—Renna's last moment, Kaedra's broken body, his son's cries.

He could still hear that sound—the thin, desperate wail of a newborn torn from the only warmth he had ever known. Eryndorr's cries echoed through his skull, mingling with the memory of the Vowkeeper's silhouette vanishing into darkness, the infant wrapped in cloth, carried like spoils from a battlefield. Belaric's chest tightened as he imagined what was being done now—his son would be given a new name, a new life, one fed on obedience and sharpened like a blade. Would they raise him to serve the Order? To kill in its name, as Belaric once had? Would he grow up never knowing what had been stolen from him?

Rage surged, hollow and helpless. Belaric slammed the cloth into the basin, splashing blood-tinged water across his arms. His muscles trembled from exhaustion, from fury. He stared down at his hands—split, shaking, and red—and felt a rawness deeper than skin. They were a killer's hands. A father's hands. Hands that had failed everyone who mattered.

He bowed his head for a moment, gasping through clenched teeth as the sting grounded him. This pain he could use. This pain had a purpose. He would not let the Vowkeeper bury Eryndorr's name beneath an oath and a mask. Would not let his son be twisted into a weapon for the same cause that had stolen Renna's life.

No matter how far the Vowkeeper fled, no matter how many bodies had to fall along the way, he would find him. And when he did, he would take back what was his.

When the hardened leather was finally clean and laid out to dry, he turned to his blade. Even dry, the faint metallic tang lingered in the air, a phantom reminder. He passed the time sharpening each one with slow, careful strokes, letting the rhythm steady his thoughts.

He searched the house again—methodically this time—and discovered a chest beneath the stairs. Inside, wrapped in old cloth, lay a dagger. It was simple and unadorned, but its blade was honed to a wicked sharpness, clearly forged for cutting and slicing. It was a weapon, not a tool for a healer's work, kept hidden for a day she hoped would never come.

Even Kaedra, gentle as she had been, had prepared for blood.

Maybe she had always known—peace was a luxury bought with blades.

He crossed to where his armor hung on the wall near the cold hearth. He had not risked a fire—not with the Order hunting him. Darkness was safer. Silence, even more so.

The leather was dry now, stiff and cool from the air. He dressed slowly, piece by piece, testing the fit, adjusting each buckle. Pain flared with every motion, but he made no sound.

Once the armor was secured, he turned to the dagger. The leather of the scabbard was slick and cool, the hilt familiar to his palm. He strapped it to his belt, the clink of the buckle a sharp, final sound in the quiet room. He checked the balance, the easy slide of the blade, and the perfect placement on his hip. Everything was in place.

He was as ready as he could be.

Night had fallen. The streets outside whispered with wind and the faint echo of distant footsteps.

Belaric moved to the window, pulled his hood low, and slipped out into the dark.

He dropped into the alley behind the house, landing in a crouch. Pain lanced through his ribs, but it was nothing compared to the searing agony that erupted in his leg, a deeper and more vicious tear of muscle and sinew. He clenched his jaw, breathing through his nose, willing himself not to cry out.

He steadied himself but was slow to rise.

He turned north, toward the Upper District. Toward House Sarrivane.

Toward the first thread that might lead him back to Eryndorr.

Belaric moved through the narrow arteries of Vorinfall, sticking to the shadows and avoiding the pools of light cast by taverns and street torches. Laughter and music drifted into the alleys—men singing off-key, tankards raised in drunken rhythm, women's voices trailing laughter and flirtation through the smoke-thick air. The scent of roasted meat carried on the wind. He felt the pull, the ache for something simpler. A drink. A warm voice. A night without blood.

But tonight, he had work to do.

He slipped past a trio of guards near the artisan quarter, their idle chatter echoing off the stone. They did not see him—just a shadow passing between buildings, unnoticed and silent.

By the time he reached the outer wall of the Upper District, the sky had darkened and the moon had taken its place high in the sky. The wall was lined with torches, flames casting long shadows between the parapets. Armored guards moved in practiced rhythm—four pacing the battlements, two stationed at each iron-gated entry. Belaric slipped into a shadowed alley and crouched low, watching.

There—a weak link.

A heavyset man slouched in a wooden chair just beside the eastern parapet. Belaric raised an eyebrow. The man still wore his cuirass, but barely. His gut spilled over the beltline, and he gripped his spear more like a walking stick than a weapon. In his free hand, he clutched a thick strip of pork, chewing slowly, grease running down his wrist.

Lazy bastard. Fortunate for me.

Belaric waited, eyes tracking the rotation of the other patrols. The rhythm was slow—predictable. That made it dangerous. Predictability bred complacency, but it also meant any break in the pattern would be noticed.

He counted silently.

One. Two. Three—pause.

Now.

He sprinted low to the base of the wall and pressed his back against the stone, feeling the heat of nearby torches bleeding through the granite. He paused and searched the ground before quickly finding what he was looking for—a small rough stone. This would do the trick, he thought. He placed the stone in his pocket.

He inhaled deeply; braced himself, then climbed. The rough-hewn stones of the lower wall offered just enough grip to ascend, but each movement flared pain in his side. He gritted his teeth, swallowing the grunt that climbed his throat. Blood pulsed in his ears. Halfway up, he paused beneath the lip of the wall, heart hammering.

He reached into his pocket and gripped the stone.

He raised himself just high enough to peer over the edge.

The heavyset guard was still seated, still gnawing. His helmet rested on the ground beside him. He did not even look up.

Belaric arced the stone high.

It clanged against a metal bracket several feet to the guard's left—just as he had hoped, though he knew it was more luck than precision. The sound rattled through the quiet, then the stone skittered out of sight.

The man jolted, nearly dropping his pork. He struggled to rise, clanging against his armor as he waddled over to the edge, peering into the darkness.

"What the hell...?" the guard muttered, lifting his spear with effort. "Oi! You hear that?"

From the far side of the wall, a second voice replied, muffled. "Hear what?"

Belaric moved.

He pulled himself up, getting to the top of the wall in a single swift motion, landing in a crouch. His boots met stone with barely a whisper. He darted across the platform, hand brushing the ledge as he dropped over the far side.

It was only a six-foot drop. He landed on gravel and rolled once to deafen the sound—pain flaring sharply in his ribs and leg as he hit. He clenched his jaw, forcing himself still in the shadows of a hedgerow.

No shouts. No alarms. The fat guard was still searching the far edge, confused but not alert.

Belaric let out a slow, quiet sigh, lips curling into a faint, satisfied smile. Then he moved again, slipping through narrow paths and moonlit gardens.

The city's wealth wrapped itself around him here—marble benches, silvered fountains, hedges sculpted into animals no one had seen in a hundred years. It was beauty built atop bones, and it sickened him.

After several minutes of weaving through alleyways and merchant courtyards, the Sarrivane estate came into view—massive and walled in polished stone, its silhouette broken only by decorative spires and tiled rooftops.

Belaric found a tree near the outer wall and climbed quickly, the bark rough beneath his fingers. He crouched among the leaves and watched.

The estate grounds were wide, wrapped in torchlight and guarded walkways. The main gate had two guards posted beside an iron lantern stand, their helms reflecting the firelight. Others walked the perimeter in pairs, slow and steady. No door was unguarded.

He watched. Measured.

A pair passed below.

"...told him not to take the whole coin purse," one said, voice hushed. "But you know Jerrin. He is nothing but a fool and a drunk."

"He is lucky Lord Sarrivane did not cut off his damn hand," the other voice replied.

Belaric made note of their pace, their spacing. Every patrol ran on a loop—tight, tight enough that a single body out of place would draw notice.

He would have to go above.

At the far end of the garden stood a towering tree, its thick limbs stretching like fingers over part of the estate. One branch caught his eye—wide, low, and curved directly toward the second-story balcony of the side wing. That was the path.

After another hour of watching, memorizing the rhythm of the guards, Belaric slipped down from the tree and moved toward the estate wall.

The gate's iron bars loomed before him—black and cold. He gripped one, pulled himself up and over, sliding silently into the garden beyond. He crouched low among the shrubs, eyes flicking to the nearest torch-lit path. One pair of boots passed. He waited. Counted.

Then moved again.

Each time the guards passed, he halted behind trimmed hedges or crouched beneath archways. Once, he was forced to flatten himself against the base of a fountain while two guards paused nearby, grumbling about their aching feet. He waited until they moved on.

Finally, he reached the great tree. He climbed quickly, pain screaming in his leg again, ignored. He reached the broad limb, edged out onto it, and crouched.

The grounds below were quiet. A guard rounded the far corner. Belaric's fingers curled around the bark. He waited.

The man turned the corner and vanished from sight.

Belaric moved.

He crossed the branch with slow, measured steps, the wind tugging at his cloak. Every movement was deliberate. The branch dipped under his weight, groaning faintly.

At the end of the branch, he paused. The balcony was just a few feet away.

He let out a low, steady breath.

Then jumped.

He landed hard on the stone balcony with a thud, knees bent to absorb the impact. Pain shot up his body, sharp and immediate—but he ignored it. Rolled into a crouch, knife already in hand.

He held still, listening—every muscle taut.

No footsteps. No voices. No alarm.

Only silence.

He sheathed the blade and pulled a slender lock pick from his belt pouch. Kneeling beside the ornate door, he set to work. The lock was old, finely made. No rust. The pins were stiff but responsive.

After a minute of careful work, there came a faint click.

Belaric turned the handle, pushed the door open, and slipped inside.

11

Belaric shut the balcony door behind him with a soft click. The air inside was still, heavy with the scent of ink, smoke, and the dry musk of old paper.

Shelves lined every wall, sagging under the weight of books and scrolls. A cluttered desk sat beneath the glow of dying embers in the hearth—quills, ink-stained parchment, and a broken wax seal scattered across its surface. The fire in the hearth burned low, casting flickering shadows that danced like ghosts against the stone.

A bed loomed on the far side—ornate, too large even for him, its carved posts rising like watchful sentinels in the gloom. A small shape lay nestled in the center, wrapped in heavy covers, barely visible in the faint spill of moonlight through the curtains. A pale tangle of hair marked the head. The rise and fall of quiet breathing was the only sound, steady and soft—punctuated now and then by a faint, childlike snore. The air in the room seemed to shimmer with that innocence, a stark contrast to the grit and blood that clung to Belaric's own skin.

Belaric watched her for a moment. Not for threat. Not even guilt. Just the strange weight of seeing something untouched.

He thought of his son—just days in the world, stolen. He had barely even had the chance to hold him properly. There was no peace in that memory, only a hollow ache. But seeing this child now, safe in sleep, he felt something stir—hope, perhaps. That somewhere, somehow, his son might know such safety too. That he might live long enough to watch over him from the shadows... and one day, step into the light.

Not now. Not here.

He forced the thought away, steadying his breath.

Then he moved—silently and low across the floor.

At the door, he paused, and pressed his ear to the door listening.

He waited another moment until he was sure there was no sound. He tested the handle. It groaned, just barely, as he cracked it open. Light spilled through, a thin golden blade cutting across the floor. He waited. No sound. No movement. He slipped into the corridor.

The hall stretched ahead, regal in its quiet. Tapestries hung between candle sconces, each one a scene of battle or bloodsport. Faces stared from gilded portraits on the opposite wall—cold, sharp-featured, born into power.

Belaric shut the door quietly behind him, careful not to let the latch click.

He knew he was on the second floor. The study would be on this level—he had studied the layout carefully, committing it to memory. But memory and reality often diverged in the dark.

He moved with measured steps, slow and deliberate, each footfall placed to avoid the louder groan of floorboards. The hall stretched long and quiet, broken by closed doors and branching corridors. Shadows clung to the corners. Tapestries stirred faintly in the draft.

He paused at each turn, listening.

Then he rounded the next corner—and froze.

A voice. Soft. Singing.

"Sweet is the night when no one weeps,

Dreams come fast and secrets keep..."

The sound grew louder, closer.

No time.

He glanced up. Support beams crossed the ceiling like ribs. Without thinking, he ran two steps up the wall, kicked off, and caught the edge of the nearest beam. His fingers slipped—then caught. Muscles screamed in protest. He grunted softly, hauling himself up. Pain lanced through his side as he wrapped his legs around the beam and went still.

A woman passed beneath him, arms full of linen. Short, with long blonde hair tied back in a loose braid. She wore a servant's robe—simple wool, dusted at the hem from a day's work. She kept singing, unaware.

"Lock the door and hush your breath,

Let no soul wake death..."

She paused, turned into the first room on her left, and closed the door behind her.

Belaric exhaled through clenched teeth. He unwound his legs and dropped to the ground with a soft thud. The jolt sent fresh pain up his spine and into his ribs.

He grimaced. Should have brought some Ashroot. Stubborn pride had no place on nights like this.

But pain was a familiar companion, and he had work to do.

Belaric moved with purpose, footsteps slow, controlled. Without pausing, he passed closed doors; he had memorized the layout, tracing it repeatedly in his mind until he knew it by heart. Two turns past the main stairwell, just beyond the narrow window slit. That was where it should be.

Then he saw it.

A broader frame, iron-braced, set deeper into the stone than the others. Exactly where it had been marked on the layout. A study according to the records. Private. Only for Lord Sarrivane to use.

His breath caught—just for a moment. This could be it. The first step toward answers. Toward finding where they took his son.

He reached for the handle and met resistance. Locked. He figured it would be.

Kneeling swiftly, he pulled a leather pouch from his belt and worked a pick into the keyhole. It fought him—an older lock, finely crafted. Slower than he liked. Sweat beaded on his brow as the seconds slipped by.

Click.

The bolt slid back with a faint, satisfying shift.

He opened the door just a crack and peered inside. Rows of shelves lined the walls, heavy with books. A thick wooden desk sat at the center, scattered with parchment and ink. The air held the scent of wax, old paper, and dust.

Still, he did not move. He waited. Listened.

No breathing. No footsteps. No rustle of hidden danger.

Only silence.

He slipped through and closed the door behind him, slowly enough not to make a sound. Then, with practiced care, he slid the bolt back into place from the inside—just enough to keep out anyone curious.

Now that he was in, the shape of the room sharpened—walls heavy with knowledge, the desk strewn with maps and correspondence. Ink stains bloomed across loose pages like bruises. A globe sat in one corner, cracked and worn, half-forgotten.

Belaric crossed the room and took a candle from one of the small tables by the desk. He struck a match and lit the wick. The flame flared to life, soft and flickering. A risk, yes—but one he had to take. He brought the candle to the desk and sat, the old wood groaning beneath his weight.

Papers lay scattered across the surface, ink still fresh on some. He started with the topmost letters—half-sealed scrolls from merchants across the region. One wanted steel ore in exchange for rare spices from the eastern isles—cardamom, dried citrus, and nightroot. Another offered three dozen goats and two prize rams for Sarrivane's stockpile of fine timber. Others proposed trades in salt, wool, and glasswork, all dressed up in polite language and hidden intentions. Barter, bribes, or both. All of it stank of desperation and subtle threats.

Further down the pile, he found letters from other noble houses, each one oozing with overly formal pleasantries, asking for the Sarrivanes' daughter to visit during the summer season. Some promised lavish feasts. Others hinted at "friendships" with young heirs. The girl in the bed—that was her.

He shook his head. There would be no choice for her. No freedom. Her future would be traded off like grain or ore, wrapped in ribbons and smiles. She would marry for power, not love. It was the way of their kind. Still, it soured his stomach. He pushed the thought aside and turned to the drawers.

Each creaked as he opened them. Inside—ledgers. Books marked with neat lines and columns, entries spanning years of transactions. He skimmed quickly, flipping through pages. Nothing useful. Just routine trade and tax records. All too clean. Frustration crept in. He shoved the book back into the drawer with more force than he meant to—and paused. A sound. Subtle. Something shifted.

He pulled the book out again, then the loose sheaves beneath it. His fingers swept the base of the drawer until they caught the difference—a change in pressure. One side sank slightly under his touch; the other rose. A faint smile touched his lips. He pried up the false bottom.

A narrow compartment lay beneath, hidden in the hollow frame. Inside were several sealed letters and a single ledger bound in dark brown leather, the corners cracked with use. He started with the letters. The first was between Lord Sarrivane and Lord Caervoss—an odd pairing. Caervoss was one of Tharamoor's high noble families, known for its military prestige, not for merchant dealings. Their sons were all married and served as generals or knight-commanders. There were no obvious gains to be had from these exchanges.

He scanned the text, but the meaning eluded him—tight script, carefully coded, impossible to break without a cipher. The next letter was the same. So was the next. Dozens of them, each addressed to a powerful noble house, each encrypted. He set them aside and opened the book.

Another ledger. But this one read differently. The format was similar, but the content told another story. Numbers were inflated, shipments duplicated, purchases hidden behind vague notes. He flipped back through one of the earlier ledgers for comparison. The difference was obvious. This was the truth—the rest, smoke and polish.

Lord Sarrivane had been skimming. Not just from peasants and tradesmen, but from other nobles. Overcharging for rare goods, falsifying records, rerouting coin to vanish beneath layers of false dealings. Belaric was not shocked. Corruption was the language of the nobility. This was not why he was here—but it might still be useful.

He slid the book and letters back into the compartment, lowered the false bottom, and snuffed the candle between his fingers. Darkness returned like the tide.

He waited a moment, letting his eyes adjust, then rose to his feet.

No names. No orders. No mention of the Black Vow. Whatever answers this study held, they were not the ones he needed.

A flicker of frustration burned in his chest. He had risked much for this—and found only rot he already expected.

Fine, he would get the truth from Lord Sarrivane directly.

He moved to the door, jaw set, hand flexing once at his side. The lord might need persuading—but that would be simple enough with a knife to his throat.

He pressed his ear to the wood. Metal on stone—footsteps approaching. Voices, low and familiar.

"Another late night, my lord."

A tired sigh followed. "Ahh, Halvek… that damn woman never lets me sleep. There is always another story, even if I have heard the same one ten times. I figured if I must suffer, I may as well get some work done."

The man called Halvek chuckled. "I can always tell you a story, if you wish, my lord."

"Do not even try it," the other voice said, chuckling.

The footsteps grew louder, stopping just outside the door. Then came the jingle of keys.

"Halvek," the other voice said, "you do not have to stay. It is late. Go see that maid you are so fond of. She is better company than me."

"You are sure, my lord? I do not mind—" Halvek started.

The other voice cut him off. "Yes, yes, I am sure. Go on."

Belaric allowed himself a quiet breath. Perhaps the gods were feeling generous tonight. His target had come to him.

He smiled in the dark and stepped back into the shadows, just as the key slid into the lock.

There was a soft click—the quiet turn of metal tumblers—and then the door creaked open.

Lord Jastor Sarrivane entered, heavy-footed and mumbling. Middle-aged and thick around the middle, he was balding on top, with a short grey beard that curled toward his throat. A dark blue robe hung around his shoulders, the belt pulled too tight around his belly.

He shut the door behind him and started towards his desk.

Belaric moved like smoke. One step, two. His hand clamped down over the man's mouth, the other pressed a blade to his throat. The lord froze.

Belaric leaned in close, his voice cold and quiet—measured, rehearsed, like the lines of a well-used script.

"Lord Jastor Sarrivane. If you scream, you and your family die. If you run, you all die. If you fight, you all die. If you disobey me in any way... you all die."

He felt the man's body tremble under his grip.

"Nod if you understand." Belaric whispered in his ear.

Sarrivane whimpered, then nodded once. Then again, slower, more certain.

"Good," Belaric said, his voice even as he pulled the dagger away and seized the man by the back of the neck. His grip was deliberately rough, and Sarrivane winced at the sudden pressure. Belaric leaned back just long enough to relock the door, then forced him forward in silence. As they reached the desk, he shoved the man toward it.

"Sit," he commanded.

Lord Sarrivane stumbled, caught himself on the edge of the table, then rubbed his neck and eased into the chair. Belaric gestured to the candle, and the noble quickly reached for a box of matches. His fingers trembled as he struck one and lit the wick, the flickering light casting shadows across the books and scrolls that lined the room. Sarrivane squinted into the darkness beneath the hood, trying to get a look at his visitor, but the angle and light revealed nothing.

"Do you know who I am, my lord?" Belaric asked.

Lord Sarrivane let out a forced, humorless chuckle. "No one knows who you are. The better question is—do I know what you are? And yes, I do. Assassin."

A thin smile played on Belaric's lips. "Careful. You would not want to make me angry."

The noble's confidence vanished. His face paled. "No offense meant, of course. I was not told anyone would be dropping by tonight. I have done everything they asked."

Belaric raised a hand and cut him off. "Good. Now it is my turn. Where is the Vowkeeper?"

Confusion flickered across Sarrivane's face. "I—I do not know. Why would I know that?"

Belaric moved before the man could even shift in his seat. The dagger came out in a whisper of steel and stopped just short of Sarrivane's outstretched hand; the tip hovering over his knuckles.

"Please," Lord Sarrivane gasped, frozen in place. "Please, no—do not hurt me. I swear, I do not know. I do not know!"

Stepping around the desk, Belaric closed in. "I know when people lie." He grabbed the man's hand, pressing it to the desk. "Maybe I will start by breaking each bone, one at a time. Or maybe I drag your daughter in here and do the same. Then your wife. Would you prefer that?"

The words came hard. Belaric hated saying them. Hated invoking a child's pain. But he would do whatever it took to find his son.

Lord Sarrivane flinched as if struck. His lips trembled, and the blood drained from his face. "Please…" he choked, voice thin and wavering. "I have met him only a few times. I swear it."

The words stumbled out, raw and pleading. Tears welled in his eyes, and his hands shook at his sides—too afraid to raise them, too terrified to keep them still.

Belaric reached forward, grabbed the collar of the man's robe, and yanked him forward until their faces were inches apart. "You are one of their masters of coin. Everyone knows what coin buys—food, loyalty, silence. Do not insult me by pretending you know nothing."

He shoved Sarrivane back into the chair.

"They do not trust me," the noble stammered. "They think I am weak. I am weak. I get only letters. Sealed ones. A guard from House Draven delivers them. The last one told me to send payment in order to pay off ship captains and caravan leaders. They move him quietly. Always quietly. They do not leave trails."

"After he left Vorinfall," Belaric asked, narrowing his eyes, "where was he going?"

"I did not pay anyone off here. If he is in the city now… it is new to me. Maybe even Lord Draven does not know."

"Where has he been?" Belaric demanded.

"Everywhere," Lord Sarrivane said, nearly whispering now. "I do not know all the places. He is always on the move."

"Why?" Belaric asked.

Lord Sarrivane hesitated, gaze darting toward the floor. "Rumor is… that he is ensuring their alliances, reminding the other nobles that they could end up hanging from a noose if he so chooses."

That made Belaric pause, confusion settling in. "Why would he do that? Why would he kill the nobles he has protected for decades?"

"I do not know," Sarrivane said quickly. "More rumors. Nobles are dying. The ones who speak out—who question the ruling families—have accidents. Lord Draven thinks the king's using him… using the Vowkeeper to silence dissent and unrest. To lock in power."

Belaric stepped back, unsettled. This was no longer about one missing child or a rogue assassin. This was bigger—vast and unseen, stretching beneath the feet of kings and traitors both. The Vowkeeper was not just hiding. He was working.

He refocused. "What else?"

"That is all. That is everything," Lord Sarrivane whispered. "I would never lie to the Order." He tried to force a smile onto his face.

Belaric did not believe him. But he did not think the man was hiding anything useful—at least not about the Vowkeeper. That kind of knowledge would not be entrusted to a coward.

He stepped forward and unsheathed his dagger once more, placing the tip gently against Lord Sarrivane's chest. The noble flinched, trying to shrink away, but the chair pinned him in place.

"You will say nothing of this. If you do, the Order will kill you themselves. We both know it," Belaric told him.

Lord Sarrivane nodded frantically, breath coming in short bursts.

Belaric sheathed the blade and turned toward the door. He had one hand on the handle when the noble found his voice again.

"Wait… I have one question," Lord Sarrivane said, voice low.

Belaric did not turn, but paused.

"Why do you not wear a mask? Is it forbidden to show your face?" his voice trembled as he asked.

A dry laugh escaped Belaric. "I no longer serve the Vow."

Before the man could respond, Belaric moved behind him, slipped an arm beneath his chin, and locked it tight across the throat.

"Why are you—?" Sarrivane choked out.

"Stop moving. I am not killing you," Belaric said softly. "Just helping you sleep. Now… forget this conversation."

The man tried to relax, but panic fought him. After a brief struggle, his limbs sagged. Belaric held him a few moments longer to be sure, then eased him back into the chair.

He looked at the slumped form, shook his head once. Lord Sarrivane would wake to a nightmare of his own making, caught between the wrath of the Order and the phantom threat of Belaric's return. He would keep silent not out of loyalty, but out of absolute, gut-wrenching terror. That was enough. Then turned toward the door.

Something was shifting in the dark—bigger than vengeance, older than the Black Vow. And he was already standing in its shadow.

Belaric eased the door open, every movement measured. The light from the candle still flickered faintly behind him, casting a soft glow over the unconscious noble slumped at the desk. No sign he had been there. No trace left behind but silence and fear.

He slipped into the hallway and closing the door behind him, turning the handle with practiced ease. The corridor was empty, still wrapped in the heavy hush of nobility at rest. Candle sconces burned low along the walls, casting a dim light across portraits and woven tapestries. The air carried a mix of beeswax, wine, and perfumed oils—noble comforts, thick enough to taste.

Belaric moved swiftly but low, retracing his path with careful steps. The quiet creak of the floor beneath his boots was masked by the whisper of distant voices—a man and a woman, somewhere around the far bend.

He paused, pressed himself into a shadowed alcove beneath a mounted boar's head. The voices grew clearer.

"...and I told him, if he wanted the contract honored, he had best not speak to me like some hedge-born scullion," the man said, his tone dripping with wine and arrogance.

The woman giggled softly. "And what did he say?"

"He bowed. Like a beaten dog," the man said.

They were close now—too close. Belaric's muscles tightened.

Without a sound, he slipped out of the alcove and crossed the hall in a single stride, disappearing once more into the room. The tiny figure still lay nestled in blankets at the center of the large bed, pale hair spilling across the pillow. A stuffed rabbit rested loosely in one arm, its ears drooping over the edge of the coverlet.

Belaric moved like fog across the floor, careful to avoid the creaky board near the hearth, and made his way toward the balcony.

He crouched low and eased the balcony door open, slipping outside.

The night air was cold against his skin, sharpened by altitude. A breeze rustled the treetops below, carrying with it the faint scent of dew, distant fires, and something sour from the lower wards. The estate grounds stretched wide, painted in moonlight—cobblestone paths, neatly trimmed hedges, a fountain that had not flowed in weeks. The wall surrounding it all stood high and iron-topped, an imitation of safety.

Belaric waited. A full minute stretched to two. The voices faded behind him, swallowed by the manor's stone and velvet.

He rose, placed one foot on the balcony rail, and stood without wavering. Pain flared in his thigh, a deep, throbbing pulse that reminded him of the wound beneath the wrappings. He gritted his teeth and steadied himself.

The tree was just beyond reach—a towering sycamore whose branches scraped the stonework. He studied the sway in the breeze, timed it.

Then he jumped.

The tree groaned as he caught a thick branch with both hands, the bark tearing at his gloves. The weight dragged the limb down slightly, but it held. He hung for a moment, muscles tensed, leg burning, then swung one over and climbed to straddle the branch, balancing with the ease of long practice.

Somewhere below, a voice rang out.

"What was that?"

Belaric froze. Another guard. Sounded like he was near the stables. No line of sight.

Belaric held still for a moment, then slid from the branch and dropped. He landed in a crouch, rolled with the fall, and came up behind a hedge.

"I said, what was that?" the guard called again, his boots crunching gravel. A dog barked once, far off.

Belaric moved. He stayed low, following the rear path that curved beneath an overgrown arbor. Vines dragged at his sleeves, and thorns scraped at his side, but he did not slow. He crossed the southern lawn in quick bursts, moving from hedge to statue to empty servant post, slipping through shadows like spilled ink.

The iron gate came into view—a tall structure entwined with ivy, rusted at the corners, its lock glinting faintly in the dark. The grounds were too quiet. If another guard came from the side house, he would be seen.

No time.

He sprinted the last ten paces, leapt, and scaled the gate without hesitation. The iron bit into his hands, cold and rough. At the top, he swung a leg over, braced his weight, and dropped into the alley beyond with a soft grunt. The noble quarter now lay behind him—but his way out was not over yet.

The true barrier loomed ahead—the outer wall of the Upper District. Belaric had already climbed it once tonight, but that did not lessen its weight. Cold stone rose high into the dark, torches burning steadily along the battlements. Shadows still moved between the flames—slow and deliberate—the guards above pacing in practiced rhythm.

Belaric crouched in the shadow of a low-roofed warehouse, the scent of smoke and tallow thick in the air. This was no forgotten stretch of wall—this was watched, reinforced, and sharp with consequence.

He moved south, skirting the edge of a tannery's outer yard until he found what he needed—a delivery cart half-buried in refuse and crates stacked haphazardly behind a row of boarded-up stalls. The wall curved here, close to a disused guard access stair that had long since been bricked up. The mortar was fresh, but the stones above it were not.

Belaric climbed onto the cart, then onto the crates. They wobbled beneath his weight, the wood groaning in protest. He pressed close to the stone and scanned upward, eyes catching the rhythm of the guards' steps above. Fifteen seconds of blind spot. Just enough.

He launched upward.

Fingers found a thin seam between stones, a decorative ridge halfway up the wall that broke the otherwise smooth face. He climbed fast and silently, relying on balance and memory. Every reach was precise. Every foothold chosen. His shoulder burned from the estate fall, and his breath came shallow, but he refused to slow.

A guard passed overhead, torchlight flaring just above him. Belaric flattened his body against the stone, holding his breath. Ash drifted down from the flame. The guard kept walking.

Three seconds.

Two.

Now.

He surged upward, gripped the lower edge of the parapet, and vaulted silently over the top. The iron spikes were clustered at the gated entry points—not along the patrol route. He crouched, heart hammering, and watched the second guard vanish around the next corner tower.

He did not hesitate.

Dropping to the far side, he caught the ledge with both hands, lowered himself just enough, then let go.

He hit the ground hard, knees flexing into a crouch. Pain lanced through his body, but he rolled and came up behind the crumbling wall just as a torch flickered behind him.

No shout. No alarm.

He stayed low and moved quickly, slipping between the backs of shuttered shops, where lanterns glowed faintly behind drawn curtains. Now finally, the Middle District.

Here, the city felt older—more human in its ugliness. Buildings leaned together like drunken conspirators. Stone gave way to plaster and wood, patchwork rooftops tilting with age. The streets were narrow, littered with broken crates, the occasional smear of old blood. Someone coughed in the shadows. Someone else laughed too hard. A baby cried from an upper window.

He passed the bakery long since closed for the day, its chimney still warm. A tailor's shop where moonlight glinted off silk in the display. A meat stall with hooks still swaying from the wind. The night was a tapestry of half-heard sounds and half-seen lives.

Belaric ducked into a narrow alley, climbed a broken stairwell three levels up, and crossed a walkway of rotted boards to a rooftop ledge. From here, he stopped. Finally.

The noble estate was a memory now—its towers distant shapes behind the haze. A place of masks and whispers. Of secrets and rot.

He adjusted his armor and pulled his hood tighter over his face. His limbs ached. His shoulder throbbed. But worse than all of it was the taste of his own words, still fresh on his tongue—threats he never wanted to say. Things he never wanted to become.

He had escaped.

But part of him had not.

He crouched in shadow, the damp wall behind him slick with midnight sweat. He had not been followed—he would have known—but the Order would come. It was only a matter of time before someone found Lord Sarrivane, and when they did, the net would close fast.

He needed to be gone before the sun touched the towers.

Above him, the stars had begun to pale—just a few hours before dawn. Enough time, if he hurried.

He took one last breath, then slipped back down the broken stairwell, careful with each step. At street level again, he kept to the narrowest lanes and deepest shadows, cataloguing what he needed in silence. Clothes. Food. Herbs. Coin. He would leave a note for Darius to ready Ed at the stables, and with any luck, be gone before the bells tolled first light.

The tailor's shop came first.

He made his way through the lower lanes, counting steps. The shop sat on the corner of a quiet side street, its sign swaying gently above the closed shutters. He waited beneath the overhang until the road cleared—a stray drunk passed, muttering to himself—then silence again.

Belaric moved to the back of the building and found the service door, and knelt beside the lock. His pick moved with practiced ease, each twist precise. The tumblers clicked. He pushed the door open just wide enough to slip inside.

He closed it behind him and stayed low, moving through the dark like he belonged there.

Shelves of folded fabric lined the walls—dyed wool, linen, and the rare sheen of imported silks. He found a stack of large sacks near the cutting table and pulled one open. Into it he stuffed shirts, trousers, and tunics—simple clothes, sturdy enough for the road. Nothing that would draw the eye. He grabbed a single set of finer garments—a doublet with a subtle gold weave and a pair of high-quality boots, polished but unworn. If he needed to bluff his way through the gates of some noble estate, appearances could matter.

Lastly, he took two pairs of boots—one made of soft, fur-lined hide for quiet travel, the other reinforced leather with iron-toed caps. Winter was creeping closer, and coin would not always buy comfort.

As he slipped the last item into the sack, he hesitated—just for a moment. These were not nobles. Not corrupt lords bleeding the city dry. Just people doing honest work, trying to keep their heads down. He hated stealing from them. The bitter taste of it rose in his throat, sharper than any Ashroot.

But there was not time for kindness. Not tonight.

He slipped back out the way he had come, locking the door behind him.

The butcher's shop lay two streets over. On the way, he passed a trio of drunk men weaving their way out of a tavern. Their laughter echoed down the alley.

"—and I told her," one slurred, "I was not paying for that mess, gods be damned."

"You paid anyway," the second chuckled. "Your purse was empty and your pants still down when we found you."

"Was worth it!" the third shouted, stumbling into a stack of barrels.

They roared with laughter and wandered off, voices fading.

Belaric crossed behind them like a ghost.

The butcher's shop had no back door, but he had seen the window before, narrow and tucked behind the smokehouse. He approached carefully, scanning the rear alley for signs of life. The butcher lived above the shop, and while the windows were dark, sleep was not safety.

Belaric ran his hand along the window frame. Old wood. Dry but tight. He drew his dagger and worked the tip into the seam where the latch would be. The blade whispered against the grain.

A soft creak betrayed the age of the wood.

He paused, listening.

Silence.

He worked again. Two minutes passed like hours. Then, at last—the soft click of the latch giving way.

He eased the window open and slipped inside.

The shop was cool and thick with the scent of blood and spice. Hooks lined the rafters, some still bearing dried strips of meat. He moved quietly, careful not to jostle the display cases. He took several pieces of preserved meat from the racks, wrapped them in cloth, and tucked them into a second sack. Dried sausage. Smoked jerky. Salt-cured strips wrapped in waxed paper. Enough to last a week, maybe more.

Again, the hesitation came. He did not want to take from people who scraped by. But survival had no room for pride—and the ache in his gut reminded him that this, too, was a necessity. His son would not be found on empty promises and an empty stomach. This was not about him anymore.

He climbed back out the window, making sure to close it behind him. Without another sound, he vanished into the alley once more.

By the time he reached Kaedra's house, his limbs were beginning to stiffen, legs aching, hands raw from scaling the wall. But the worst of it was not pain—it was the slow, grinding exhaustion that came from too many nights like this one.

He slipped through the back door without a sound. Inside, the house was still and dark; the coals in the hearth had long since faded to embers. He moved quickly, knowing exactly where to go.

The shelf in the workroom held what he needed. He grabbed a roll of bandages, two jars of fleshmend, and a few vials of Ashroot. He removed the stopper from the vial and downed it. The bitter taste made his tongue curl, but within moments, the edge of the pain began to dull.

He shoved the rest of the supplies into a sack, tied it off, and slipped outside again.

The stash spot was behind the root cellar, buried under an old tarp and broken crates. He crouched low, set the sack in place, and covered it with practiced care.

One more stop.

He still needed coin.

Breaking into the merchant bank was suicide. Even if he could get inside, the front was watched—mercenaries posted at the doors, more inside. Paid well. Loyal enough.

The risk was not worth the payout.

But he knew somewhere else.

Hask.

The man called himself a lender. In truth, he was a wolf wrapped in fish gut cloth. He offered coin with impossible terms, and when debtors could not pay, he sent his brutes to collect—breaking fingers, lives, and sometimes worse.

Belaric's jaw tightened as he moved.

He told himself it was a necessity. He told himself the man had it coming.

But the truth was simpler.

Hask had coin.

And Belaric had none.

As he slipped through the alleys toward the dockside, a faint glow began to climb over the eastern rooftops—soft, pale, and merciless. The city was waking. And when it did, the hunt would begin.

The scent of fish and saltwater drifted thick on the air, clinging to the damp boards beneath Belaric's boots. Most found the smell disgusting—rank with rot and brine—but he had lived in Vorinfall long enough that it barely touched him. If anything, it was almost soothing. A constant. Something the sea never failed to provide.

He walked more freely here. The guards rarely came to dockside, and when they did, they kept their eyes forward and their mouths shut. Everyone knew Hask ran the dock's underbelly—extortion, smuggling, and the quiet disappearances of anyone foolish enough to cross him. Occasionally, a body turned up face-down in the channel. The guards just shrugged and muttered that someone must have angered Hask. That was the end of it.

As Belaric moved deeper, the city changed around him. The narrow stone lanes of the inner districts gave way to warped planks and sloped mud tracks. Homes here were little more than shacks—one-room shelters built from mismatched lumber, hammered tin, and the bones of other houses torn apart by sea storms. There were no second stories. Too many had learned the hard way that what stood tall did not stay standing long.

The air buzzed with low voices and shifting shadows. Sailors argued over coin; beggars muttered beneath their breath. The dockside was never truly quiet. The rhythmic slap of water against hulls, the groan of ropes, the distant shouts of drunken sailors; it was a constant, grimy symphony. Belaric slipped past them all, unnoticed and unbothered, but as he neared his destination, the roads narrowed, and the tavern lights poured out into the streets. With drunk men stumbling between buildings and too many open eyes, the shadows became scarce.

He picked up speed, timing his stride as he approached a crooked hut on the far side of a small alley. With a running start, he hit the wall—one step, two, three—then kicked off, launching upward. His fingers caught the edge of the roof, splinters biting into his palms as he hauled himself up. He rolled flat onto his back and let out a breath, chest rising and falling with quiet, steady pain. The wounds from the estate climb still ached, each movement slower than he wanted it to be.

After a moment, he rose to a crouch and moved low along the rooftops. The planks creaked beneath him, but the sound was masked by the noise of dock life below. He crept forward until he saw it.

The shack sat hunched near the far edge of the docks. No back door. Every window was boarded from the inside. Just one entrance. A single man stood out front—clearly not there for decoration.

He was taller than Belaric by half a head, lean but powerful, his frame roped with muscle. His head was completely bald, his nose crooked and long since broken. Small scars marked his face like tally marks, and his bare chest was broad and hairy, pocked with old burns and bruises. He wore patchwork pants and simple leather boots.

He looked like a man who had wrestled a bear once—and killed it just to see if he could.

In one hand, he held a dagger, slowly cutting strips from a thick hunk of pork in the other. He chewed as he worked, relaxed and slow—the type of man who had never been surprised in his life.

But Belaric knew better. This was not laziness. It was confidence. And confidence meant danger.

He scanned the surroundings. The street had emptied without anyone saying a word. No drunks, no beggars, no curious stares. People knew what this place was. And they kept their distance.

Belaric circled back two houses behind the shack and dropped into a narrow alley, boots landing softly in the muck. The air here smelled of fish guts and wet timber. He crept forward slowly, avoiding puddles and patches of loose mud. A single wrong step would ruin everything.

The ache in his leg flared with each crouched movement. His hands were still raw from the climb, and his legs burned. He needed this to end quickly.

After several long, silent minutes, he crouched just two feet behind the man. The butcher of a guard tore another strip from the pork and chewed noisily, still utterly at ease.

Belaric moved fast.

In one smooth motion, he drew both blades—one pressed to the man's throat, the other buried just behind his kidney, the tip touching flesh.

The man froze instantly.

Belaric leaned in, his voice quiet but sharp. "Evening. I am here to see your boss. Is he in?"

The man's voice was deep, gravel-coated. "You must have a death wish. You know who lives here? What he will do to you?"

Belaric smiled faintly. "I know his reputation. Sadly, he does not know mine."

A rough chuckle rumbled from the man's chest. "Boss does not care about a dead man's reputation. He will skin you from head to toe. Might even cut your cock off, just for good measure."

Belaric's tone dropped into something darker. "He does not care?" He pressed the dagger deeper into the man's side. "Let us go ask him."

The man grunted and moved—slowly, carefully. Belaric stayed just behind, both blades steady as they reached the door. The man fumbled with the key, and the lock clicked open.

Belaric shoved him forward into the shack.

12

He stepped across the threshold and paused. The contrast hit him like a slap.

Outside, the place had looked like every other hovel on the eastern edge of the lower quarter—sagging roof, cracked stone, shutters hanging limp like a drunk's arms. But inside? A different world. A lord's sitting room, if the lord had an appetite for polish and pretense.

Fine rugs lay draped over polished hardwood floors, the fibers thick and well-kept beneath the dust of boots. Chairs lined the walls—high-backed, carved from dark walnut, upholstered in crimson velvet. A round table stood in the room's center, silver-banded and gleaming. On top of it was a pristine bowl of fruit. Real fruit. Not bruised, not dried. Oranges. Figs. A pomegranate split open like a wound. A painting hung over the mantle—a seascape, waves breaking gold beneath a painted sun. The artist had known what they were doing.

Belaric stared at it a moment too long, then rolled his eyes. He should not have been surprised. Hask was the unofficial ruler of the Vorinfall scum—of course, he would try to live like a noble. Pretend at refinement. Play lord in a city that would never let a man like Hask rise above anything but the other beggars and whores.

Belaric had always been mildly surprised the Order had not sent someone to slit Hask's throat years ago. But the man had his uses. And the Order valued utility more than principle.

He let out a quiet scoff. "Your boss is not one for subtlety, is he?"

The brute ahead of him turned slightly, just enough to glance back—a sliver of his thick neck visible above the collar, scalp gleaming under the candlelight. "Gonna have to replace it all after your blood gets on it."

Belaric rolled his eyes again, slower this time. "Careful. Yours might get there first if you keep testing me."

He shoved the man between the shoulders—harder than necessary. The brute grunted, stumbling a step, but did not resist. He reached for the far door with a kind of slow, deliberate defiance. The kind that begged for steel in the back.

Belaric's fingers itched.

Beyond was a hallway, just as richly appointed. Oil lamps hung in polished sconces along either side, throwing soft light across more rugs, more varnished wood, more excess. Doors lined the corridor. Belaric's eyes moved from left to right, studying the layout.

Clever bastard. Hask had knocked out the walls between several shakes and turned them into one seamless den of luxury. From the outside, you would think it was just another run-down slum house. But within? A criminal king's keep.

"Which door?" Belaric asked, keeping his voice low.

"Fuck you," the man said without turning.

Belaric sighed—and moved faster than thought. The dagger in his left hand drove into the brute's shoulder, sliding through muscle like a hot blade through ice-fat. The man grunted but did not cry out.

Belaric wrenched the blade free, then pressed its tip to the base of the man's spine.

"Try again," he commanded.

A twitch of the brute's chin. "End of the hall."

Belaric did not take him at his word.

They walked. Blood dripped in slow taps onto the wooden floor. At every door they passed, Belaric checked the handle—careful, quiet. Most were locked. One opened into a kitchen, dark and empty, the scent of roasted meat still hanging in the air like smoke from a dying fire. Another revealed a narrow closet, shelves lined with folded cloth and spare boots.

Irritation gnawed at the edge of his calm.

Then they reached the final door, standing alone at the end of the hall. Belaric halted, raised a hand.

He stepped in close behind the brute, pressing his dagger tight to the man's throat. The tip nestled just beneath the jawline, angled with quiet promise.

"If you move or speak, and you die before the second word leaves your mouth," Belaric murmured.

Then he leaned past him, tilting his head toward the door. His ear brushed the wood.

There—a sound. Faint. Metal. The soft clink of coins being counted. Unhurried. Unaware.

Belaric shifted the blade slightly, keeping pressure against the brute's back as he reached past him and tested the handle.

It turned.

Unlocked.

He stepped behind the brute again, repositioning the dagger. "Open it."

The man reached out and placed his hand on the handle. He hesitated—just a fraction too long.

Belaric drove a boot hard into his spine.

The big man stumbled, crashed through the doorway, and hit the floor on his knees with a grunt. His palms slapped the stone to catch himself, but the impact rattled the fruit from his lungs.

Belaric followed, silent and sharp. He seized the brute by the collar, yanked him upright just enough, and pressed the blade back to his throat. The edge bit skin this time, drawing a thin line of red.

"Did not say you could fall," Belaric said.

The brute froze, jaw clenched.

Two men waited inside.

The first remained seated in the corner, tall and lean, with long blond hair tied back behind his shoulders. He wore full black leather—the kind stitched for quiet and speed. A loaded crossbow rested by his feet, his hand far too close for comfort. Another sell-sword, by the look of him—and not one hired on the cheap.

The second had already risen from behind a grand desk of polished oak, stacked high with ledgers and loose coins. Hask.

Belaric recognized him at once. Taller than he was, broader too—though not as thick as the brute bleeding beside him. His head was shaved smooth, the scalp marked with old nicks and a faint scar curving behind one ear. His pale, washed-out green eyes burned with long-stored fury. One hand braced the desk's edge; the other hovered near a half-eaten plate of lamb and figs, fingers curling like they were itching for a blade. Mid-forties, maybe. The kind of face that had spent more years taking than building.

Belaric smiled thinly. "Good evening, gentlemen."

He gave a small nod to each, then turned his gaze to the man behind the desk.

"I take it you are, Hask?" he asked.

The room held its breath for a beat too long.

Belaric angled his blade just slightly against the brute's throat and gave Hask a subtle gesture with his free hand—two fingers flicked downward, commanding without words.

"Sit," Belaric commanded.

It was not a suggestion.

"Do you know who—" Belaric began, but Hask cut him off.

"Before we do introductions," he growled through clenched teeth. He reached to the desk, plucked a napkin from beside the half-eaten plate of food, and hurled it across the room. "Stop bleeding on the fucking rug, you idiot."

The brute caught it mid-air, grunted, and clumsily reached back to press the cloth against the wound in his shoulder. "Sorry, boss," he muttered, eyes lowered.

"Shut your mouth," Hask said, voice low and sharp as glass. "You will be lucky if I let you live through the night."

He turned back to Belaric, his face a controlled snarl.

Belaric raised a brow, more amused than wary. Odd, he thought. A man who would bury a knife in your back without blinking, and yet here he was—furious over blood on a rug. Either Hask had a twisted sense of civility, or the rug cost more than the man bleeding on it.

"Now," Hask said, "what do you want?"

Belaric met his gaze. "Do you know who I am?"

"Of course I do," Hask said. "Black Vow assassin."

A slow smile tugged at Belaric's lips. "You are well-informed."

Hask snorted. "I paid half my fortune for that scrap of truth. And once I knew someone like you existed, I had to know more. Obsession's expensive."

Belaric's smile thinned. "And how did you know we existed?"

"I saw one of you. Few years back. Smoke in the air, a house burning just down the road. A woman and a baby died inside—one of my better whores, actually. Shame. Had good teeth."

He said it as if discussing livestock.

"I was outside, the moon overhead, and then—something moved. Fast. Silent. Shadow skimmed the rooftops like a ghost. One breath, and it was gone. But I knew. Spent the next year dragging gold behind me like bait, trying to catch that shadow."

He leaned forward, voice dipped in something darker than menace.

"And now one of you walks right into my home. Must be my lucky night."

Belaric did not blink. "Ah, yes. I was not the one who carried out that job, but I know who did."

He was about to continue when he caught it—a flicker in the corner of his eye.

The mercenary in the corner. His hand inching toward the crossbow.

Belaric moved—instinct taking over, years of training guiding his hand. His free arm flashed, grabbing the concealed blade. The dagger cut through the air. It struck with a wet thunk, driving through the man's hand and into the wooden wall behind him. The crossbow dropped, forgotten.

The man screamed, trying to wrench free, but the blade had pinned him in place. Blood poured down his arm, spattering the floor.

Belaric tilted his head. "He is bleeding on your rug again. Might want to hire smarter."

Hask's face went red with fury. "You brainless little shit," he snapped, storming toward the wounded man. "Did I tell you to move? Did I tell you to so much as twitch?"

The mercenary whimpered, trying to cradle his impaled hand and failing.

"I just said the word assassin, and you thought you could be faster than him?" Hask's voice was a blade, every word a fresh cut. "You arrogant fucking whelp. You are lucky you crawled out of my sister or you would be dead on the floor."

He raised one hand, the other sliding toward a drawer.

"Ah, not so fast," Belaric said, another dagger already drawn, leveled at his chest.

Hask did not flinch. "If you came to kill me, you would have done it already. You want something. Fine. Say it. But know this—"

His voice turned into a roar.

"—I will not have blood on my goddamn floor!" Hask shouted.

He yanked open the drawer slowly and deliberately, and pulled out a black linen shirt. He hurled it at the wounded man without sparing him a glance.

"Wrap it up. And stop crying like a kicked dog. You bleed again. I will have the rest of your hand nailed to the fucking ceiling," Hask snarled at him.

The nephew whimpered, clutching the shirt to his wound. Blood soaked through it quickly, but the screams died down to whimpers.

Hask turned back to Belaric, eyes narrowed like a man who would skin you for smiling wrong.

Belaric stared at Hask for a long moment. "Ruthless, brutal, and smart. It seems everything I have heard about you is true."

Hask snorted, a low sound like a dog clearing its throat. "I will take that as a compliment. But you did not come here to flatter me, assassin. What do you want?" His voice sharpened with agitation.

Belaric's gaze dropped—not that Hask could see it under the hood—but his head tilted just enough to draw attention to the neat stacks of coin on the desk.

Hask followed the gesture and smiled like a snake. "Ahhh. You want what everyone wants. Coin." A sick grin spread across his face.

Belaric returned it with calm ease. "Correct. I figured a man of your wealth could part with a few."

"And I suppose if I say no, I get a dagger through the heart?" Hask chuckled, nodding slowly.

"I thought about it," Belaric said with a shrug. "But that sort of mess draws too much attention. You are a businessman. I assumed we could strike a deal."

Hask's laughter came deep from the belly, his head rolling with the motion. Then it stopped cold. "You are right," he said, smile vanishing. "Depending on the amount, I will determine the interest on the loan—"

"No loan," Belaric interrupted, lifting a hand. His voice was steady, measured. "You like to buy secrets. I have one. Priceless."

That made Hask lean forward, the grin returning wider this time—too many teeth showing. "An assassin selling secrets about assassins? That is a tale worth hearing. And why would you be willing to do that?"

"Questions are not part of our agreement," Belaric replied flatly.

The smile did not fade, but the gleam in Hask's eyes darkened. He did not like being in the dark. Hask was a man who owned information, who expected leverage. But Belaric stood untouched by the usual games—unimpressed, unafraid. The silence between them stretched.

Belaric knew what was crawling through the man's thoughts: *If I kill him now, can I make it clean? Quiet? Will it cost me more than I gain?*

"How much?" Hask asked at last, voice tight.

"Ten gold. Twenty silver. Twenty-five copper," Belaric replied.

Hask leaned back slowly in his chair. "And if I am not satisfied with this so-called priceless secret?"

Belaric shrugged. "You can try your luck with that dagger strapped to your back. But I doubt it will do much. You will end up like your nephew—screaming, pinned to the wall."

He saw the flicker. A barely there shift in Hask's eyes. Surprise. He had not expected Belaric to notice the blade. He also had not expected to feel powerless.

Hask sighed like a man swallowing poison. He opened another drawer, retrieved a thick leather pouch, and dropped it onto the desk. The clink of coins followed—gold, silver, copper. He counted them out in tense silence, then slid the small pile to the edge of the desk with two fingers.

Belaric stepped forward—but not before flipping the dagger still pressed to the brute's neck. He reversed the grip and slammed the hilt into the man's temple. The brute collapsed with a grunt.

Hask threw up his hands, his face twisted in fury. "Stop getting fucking blood on my floor!"

Belaric tilted his head slightly as he stepped forward and swept the coins into his pouch without looking up. "He is still breathing. That is the part you should be grateful for."

He turned to go.

"And my secret?" Hask demanded, his voice tight behind him.

Belaric paused and turned just enough for his voice to carry back. "The Order has one mission. One purpose. To kill every child—and every family—that bears a Valasar mark outside noble bloodlines."

Hask's eyes widened, just for a moment. "That is a priceless secret if it is true," he said, voice low.

Belaric nodded. "And if anyone finds out you know it, they will kill you." His tone turned almost cheerful. "Every last man, woman, and rat you have ever spoken to."

Hask's face tightened with restrained fury. But he said nothing.

Belaric turned and made for the door.

"Do not let our paths cross again, assassin," Hask called after him, his voice sharper than steel and twice as cold.

Belaric stopped, turned, and snapped his arm forward. The dagger sang as it flew, slicing past Hask's cheek. A fine line of red bloomed across the man's face.

Hask did not flinch. Did not blink. Only his jaw tightened almost imperceptibly, and his eyes, cold as winter stones, locked onto Belaric. But as Belaric turned back to leave, he muttered under his breath, bitter and low, "Bastard."

"Next time," Belaric said, not looking back, "you will never see me coming."

Then he stepped out and closed the door behind him.

Belaric moved through the house and slipped back onto the street, shadows folding around him like an old cloak. Fear would keep Hask in place—for now. But not forever. The man was too proud, too rich, and too angry to let it go. Belaric had no doubt he would spend the other half of his fortune trying to find him. That would be a problem for another day.

He had what he needed. Supplies, coin, a way out. He only wished he could leave tonight.

But if he was seen taking Ed from the stables without Darius present, the guards would brand him a horse thief. And if—by some luck—they did not see him, questions would come when he tried to leave the city. The Order would be watching. Of that, he was certain.

The last detail was a note for Darius. Just a few lines, telling him to have Ed ready at first light. Darius would not see him—not until the moment mattered. Belaric would give the call. Ed would do the rest.

Sliding through the alleyways, he scaled a narrow wall and climbed to the rooftops, moving low and fast through the night. Smoke from cook fires curled through cracked chimneys, mixing with the faint stink of rain-damp stone and the sour tang of waste. He passed a crumbling gargoyle where someone had stuffed a dead rat between its jaws—an old warding against ill luck. The city breathed foully and slowly beneath him.

He glanced up—dawn crept closer. Time was bleeding out.

He reached Kaedra's house not long after and slipped inside. His two daggers were gone, thrown at the mercenary and Hask, leaving him unarmed. His hand closed around the wooden handle of a kitchen knife on the counter. It was a flimsy thing, no match for a proper blade, but it could still cut a throat if it had to. He grabbed his bag of supplies and threw it over his shoulder. His legs ached, and his shoulders burned where the weight of the day still clung. Once the door was locked behind him, he fetched a scrap of paper and ink from the side room and scrawled a quick message for Darius. Nothing detailed—just enough to set the wheels in motion.

With the note in hand, he crept out again, keeping low, watching for torchlight and the heavy stomp of patrols. At the stables, the horses stirred as he entered, sensing the predator in their midst. He calmed them with a quiet word, then moved to the farthest stall.

Ed was already waiting, staring straight at him like he had been expecting him. He flicked his ears, pawed the straw once, and let out a low, scolding huff.

"Hey, old boy," Belaric murmured, voice softer than it had been in days. "Miss me?"

Another huff, this one heavier.

"I know. I am sorry I did not come sooner," he whispered.

He stepped forward and pressed a hand to the side of Ed's face, rubbing gently between his eyes. The warmth there steadied him more than he cared to admit.

"I do not have long," he whispered, "but I will be back in the morning. Alright?"

The horse blinked at him, then nudged his arm as if to say you had better be.

"I know, I know," he told the horse.

He stepped back, crouched near the sack of apples Darius kept at the rear of the stall, and pulled out three. He placed the note beneath them—Darius would come early to feed him and find it. Belaric ran a hand along Ed's neck once more, then turned to go.

"Be good, old boy. I will be back soon," he said before turning.

He slipped out of the stables, pausing in the shadows to listen. No voices. No metal on stone. When the way was clear, he moved—quick and silent—back through the alleys until Kaedra's house took shape in the dark.

Inside, he checked each lock, each trap, each hidden blade and snare he had prepared. He would not sleep tonight. He could not. Dawn was too close, and one mistake would see him gutted before he ever reached the gates.

He gathered the sack of supplies and sifted through it, pulling out a pair of padded black pants and a simple linen shirt—practical, unassuming, perfect for riding. Slowly, he stripped off his assassin's garb, piece by piece. When the last of it came off, he looked down at the armor in a heap at his feet.

He hated it. Hated what it had made him. Hated even more what it had taken from him. But he could not throw it away—not yet.

Not while his son still breathed.

He stuffed the armor into an empty sack, double-checked the rest of his gear, then stepped into the kitchen. There was fruit left, and wine on the shelf. The scent of dried lavender clung faintly to the corner where Kaedra kept her things—something delicate tucked in beside all the blood and steel. He poured a cup, sat at the table, and drank slowly.

His mind drifted first to Renna.

He missed her. Gods, he missed her. He did not have the chance to mourn her, and he knew he would not for some time yet. Not until their son was safe. She would never forgive him if he gave up.

Hot tears threatened, pressing at the corners of his eyes, but he forced them back. Not now. Not with so much left undone.

He needed a plan. He knew how to get out of the city—but then what? He still did not know where the Vowkeeper was, and those who did were too well-guarded to question. He slammed his hand down on the table, the cup rattling as wine sloshed over the rim.

He should have gotten more from Sarrivane. That craven bastard. Maybe he should have killed him. Nobles were already turning up dead—maybe they would assume he had an accident like the others.

That is when it struck him.

Nobles were dying. The ones who asked questions. The ones who spoke when silence was safer.

Lady Haldren. Her daughter, Lyra. They would be next.

They would not know who the Vowkeeper was—not yet. But they would want to. Especially after someone tried to kill them. And if Belaric saved them?

They would owe him.

He could use that—use their influence, their reach, their resources—to find his son. The plan had holes, more than he wanted to count, and it all rested on one fragile hope: that the Order, in their hunt for him, would delay sending someone else.

It was a slim chance.

But it was a chance.

Belaric had spent the last two hours pacing Kaedra's house like a caged animal. He went over every thread of the plan, turning each possibility over in his mind until the edges bled. No matter how he approached it, two outcomes kept rising above the others: either the assassin reached Lady Haldren first, or Belaric killed the assassin and was rewarded with a sword in the ribs from her guards. Both felt equally likely.

He had little to go on when it came to House Haldren. There were too many noble families to track, and most blended together in his memory—titles, crests, names passed around like coin. What he remembered of Lady Haldren was vague. Proper. Reserved. A widow, but he could recall nothing else.

Which meant he could not predict how she would react to him.

Would she scream? Call for the town watch? Or worse—put a knife through him herself?

He might be riding straight to his death.

But the alternative was silence. Inaction. Doing nothing while the Order tightened its grip and his son slipped further out of reach.

If there was even a whisper of a chance this plan could work, he had to take it.

He moved to the window and pulled the cloth aside just enough to peer out. The moon was sinking low now, its pale light fading, and the first hints of sunrise brushed the eastern rooftops with ash-colored gold.

It was time.

He moved through the house and began dismantling the traps one by one. The weighted knife over the doorframe. The thin cord stretched across the pantry. The glass shard wedged under the windowsill. Sooner or later, someone would come here looking for Kaedra—most likely bleeding, desperate, or both—and it would not do to have them impaled for their trouble.

When every snare had been cleared, he returned to his gear and checked it all one last time. Weapons in place. Packs secure. Nothing left behind.

He crossed to Kaedra's closet and pulled a dark grey cloak from the back—one he had nearly missed, half-hidden behind heavier garments. It fit snugly across the shoulders, tighter than he would like, but the hood came low enough to hide his face. It still carried a faint scent of herbs and old smoke—Kaedra's presence, clinging like a memory. He fastened the cloak, slung his packs into place, and stood in the middle of the quiet home, staring at the door.

He was leaving Kaedra's for the last time.

No moment of silence. No words spoken.

Just the weight of it sitting in his chest as he stepped out into the dark.

He moved swiftly through the city, navigating alleys and back lanes, staying clear of the main roads where the guards still patrolled—sluggish in the pre-dawn hours, but dangerous all the same. The streets were damp from the night's mist, cobblestones slick beneath his boots.

Eventually, he reached it.

The Rusted Tankard Inn sat squat and steady at the edge of the eastern row, only a few buildings down from the stables. A two-story structure made of dark, well-oiled timber, it stood prouder than most of its neighbors. A wide balcony stretched across the upper floor, ringed with heavy railing and low tables—meant for patrons who liked to eat under starlight or smoke their pipes in the open air. The sign above the door creaked slightly on its hinges, painted in the likeness of a battered, rust-streaked tankard spilling golden ale.

It was quiet now, the windows dark and the doors locked. No voices, no light. Only the hush of a city still asleep.

Belaric slipped into the narrow alley beside the inn and waited in stillness, watching. When he was sure the street was clear, he leapt, caught the lip of the balcony, and pulled himself up in one smooth motion. His boots made no sound on the wood. He crouched low and moved toward the far end, pressing himself against the shadows. The wood beneath him was cold with dew, soaking through the knees of his pants.

No one would see him here. No one would come out to smoke or drink before the sun rose.

He pried one narrow board from the side of the balcony railing—just enough to create a thin slit of visibility—and peered through. From this angle, he had a clear line of sight to the stables.

Now he waited.

Several minutes passed. Belaric felt the ache in his knees, and deeper still in the rest of his body. His wounds were healing—slowly—but Kaedra's tonics had dulled most of the pain. He forced the discomfort aside and kept his focus on the stables.

Then, at last, he saw him. Darius shuffled into view with the same steady gait Belaric remembered. The old man was always up before the city—his pride in caring for the horses left no room for laziness. Belaric watched as he slipped into the stables and disappeared from sight. All he could do now was wait and hope Ed would be the first to be fed.

The street below was beginning to stir. He heard the scrape of boots, the clatter of a cart, a dog's barked greeting between vendors still hoarse from sleep. But Belaric's eyes never left the stable doors. The minutes dragged, heavy and sharp.

Then Darius emerged, reins in hand—and Eddaross behind him.

Belaric allowed himself a quiet exhalation and the faintest smile. It was working.

Darius brought Eddaross out and began looking around, clearly scanning for Belaric. He must have read the note. But before Belaric could rise, another figure entered the street.

A city guard.

Jorric.

Belaric tensed. He had not expected the man—but of course he would come. They likely thought he had died in the fire with Renna. His body tensed further as Jorric stepped toward Darius, clearly asking questions. Then, after a moment, the guard's posture shifted—his head turning slowly, searching the rooftops.

Belaric swore under his breath. Jorric was a good man. Kind. But now was not the time for questions. And certainly not for answers.

He stood, pressed two fingers to his lips, and gave a sharp, piercing whistle.

Heads turned across the street. People stopped, stared. Darius and Jorric both turned toward the sound—and Eddaross, too. The horse perked his ears, nostrils flaring. He started stomping and pulling against the reins, agitated and eager. Darius tried to calm him, but something shifted in his expression. He remembered.

The reins dropped.

Eddaross surged forward, hooves ringing off the cobblestones as he galloped toward the inn. Belaric smiled again. Good boy.

As the horse reached the balcony, he slowed to a stop. Belaric dropped the packs down first, then vaulted over the railing. It was only a short fall, but the landing jarred his ribs and leg, and a grunt escaped his lips. He hit mud, scrambled upright, grabbed the packs, slung them across Ed's back, and swung into the saddle in one fluid motion.

Just as he took up the reins, a voice called out behind him.

"BELARIC!"

He did not need to turn; he knew.

Still, he looked back.

Jorric stood there, eyes wide with disbelief. Confusion was carved on his face like a wound. Belaric met his gaze and held it.

"I am sorry, Jorric," he said. "One day I will explain. But for now... just know—I will find the one who took her from me."

Jorric did not respond. His head tilted slightly, trying to make sense of it. But there was not time.

Belaric turned, snapped the reins, and Eddaross lunged into motion. Behind him, he heard his name again—called by a voice filled with questions he could not afford to answer. A familiar ache settled in Belaric's chest—the price of this path, paid in silence and goodbyes.

He did not look back.

He had a noblewoman to save. And a son to find.

The streets blurred as Eddaross charged forward. Belaric shouted warnings, scattering merchants and early risers. Some dove out of the way; others cursed and shouted back. He ignored them all. The city could curse him later.

The guards at the gate spotted him and moved to block the road, calling for him to stop. Belaric did not stop. He barreled straight toward them. At the last moment, they threw themselves aside—one drew a sword, another raised a horn and blew a sharp, panicked blast—but the warning came too late.

One guard took a few steps, seeming to give chase before realizing the futility. No horses were ready. No rider could catch him now.

By the time they responded to the alarm, Belaric would be long gone.

He spurred Eddaross harder.

Brookhaven waited.

13

Belaric drove Eddaross hard through the first day, riding as the light thinned behind the trees and the shadows stitched themselves thick across the road. His limbs felt carved from stone—each hour in the saddle grinding him down further. He had not slept, and the strain was catching up. His eyes stung, lids heavy, thoughts drifting too easily into memory when they needed to stay sharp. But he kept going.

Stopping was not an option. Not yet. He told himself that with every mile. Every ache. Every time his head dipped lower, and snapped upright again.

He kept glancing over his shoulder, half-expecting a shape to slip from the woods and follow. Nothing came. Still, he watched.

Earlier that day, he spotted a lone rider on a distant ridge—a silhouette framed against the horizon. It did not move. Not forward, not back. When he looked again, it was gone. Imagination, perhaps. Or not. Men like him did not afford the luxury of doubt.

Soon after, as the road curved around a low rise, he saw them. A family. A man and a woman, their backs to him, walked beside a laden mule with a small child riding perched on the mule's back. The boy's laughter, light and carefree, carried on the breeze, a sound Belaric had not realized he had forgotten. His grip tightened on the reins, the leather biting into his raw hands. For a searing moment, he saw Renna, her smile, the weight of their son in her arms. He clenched his jaw, forcing his gaze to the horizon, urging Eddaross to pick up the pace, leaving the innocent joy behind him like dust.

Brookhaven lay days ahead, nestled in the rolling hills southeast of Tavros. It was a small, quiet town, or so people claimed. He aimed to reach it quickly, though the roads forked more than once between here and there. He could skirt the towns, lose himself in the wilds. Safer, perhaps. But not for Eddaross. He needed grain, and grass alone would not carry them far. The horse was loyal—but even loyalty broke when the body failed. There were other roads. Riskier ones.

Norvalth lay to the east, a longer route, but not without appeal. A city larger than Vorinfall, its walls rose like cliffs of black stone, crowned with catapults and bowstrings strung tight. Its forges birthed blades that sang through steel; its stables bred horses meant for war. It was a place that honored strength and buried the weak in silence.

General Thaylore Tannic ruled Norvalth—a name forged from iron itself. Tactician. Warrior. A man of honor. Wed to one of the king's nieces, not for love, but for reach. He did not parade his victories—he tallied them in graves. It was said he could see the outcome of a battle before it began—and shift its course with the swing of his sword.

Belaric could disappear there. Just another ghost among thousands. But the Black Vow had a long reach. Norvalth held its own Order Hall, its own masters. Word would have spread—his name, his face—he would be marked as a traitor in their eyes now. The Black Vow would not stop hunting him until he was lying dead at the feet of the masters. The Vowkeeper would not leave a thread like him to flap loose in the wind.

He considered using the smaller villages and towns to hide in. But he knew the smaller villages were not safer. In towns where everyone knew every face, his would be the one that did not belong. The kind people remembered.

He ran through the risks, each path a different gamble. Danger shadowed every road, but only one promised what he truly sought: not safety, not peace, but retribution.

Somewhere behind him, a branch cracked—sharp and sudden. He froze, pulling on Eddaross's reins. The horse stopped instantly. Belaric scanned the trees, every muscle drawn tight, his breath held against the silence. Nothing moved. No sound followed.

Still, he did not trust it.

He kept his hand near the hilt of his dagger as he nudged Eddaross forward again, each step measured. For miles, his fingers twitched with the promise of violence.

The threat passed, but the tension remained.

He needed to choose his path—and soon.

Brookhaven might offer the answers he sought, and he needed to reach it quickly. But Norvalth might offer answers too—closer ones. Sharper ones. That city knew the Order well. If the Vowkeeper had left a trace anywhere, it would be there.

He exhaled through clenched teeth.

In the end, he turned Eddaross east, toward Norvalth. Towards one of the strongholds of the Black Vow.

He would watch the Order Hall from the dark. Count the ones who came and went. Trace their patterns. Study the gaps. Maybe—if the gods stopped cursing him—he might glimpse the Vowkeeper.

And if not... then he could still move on to Brookhaven and have a chance to find something. Answers. Blood. Vengeance. It all spilled the same.

The sun was sinking fast now, the last light fading. He needed to find shelter for the night. Eddaross moved slower with each step, sides lathered with sweat. Belaric's own limbs felt hollowed out, his thoughts drifting too easily, too far.

They needed rest.

The Hollowood offered cover, a place to vanish from sight—but it was no haven. Belaric had heard the stories. Trees that collapsed without warning. Predators that moved without a sound. Still, he guided Eddaross off the road and towards the woods.

Better the forest than open ground.

As they slipped beneath the canopy of tree branches, the sky had dimmed to brass, and the trees ahead swallowed the remaining light.

Once a lush and living forest, Hollowood now groaned beneath its own decay. The trees still stood tall and defiant, but their hearts were gone—devoured from within by the Wyrmhusk, a pale parasite that hollowed trunks like a sickness. The bark remained smooth, untouched, a lie of health. But inside, the wood was lacework and dust. Entire groves collapsed at the mere whisper of wind. Travelers said the forest moaned in its sleep, dreaming of a life it no longer had.

Belaric kept to the edges at first, careful not to brush too near the trees. When the ground grew uneven, he dismounted and led Eddaross by the reins, boots crunching against a layer of brittle leaves and dead twigs. Eddaross followed without complaint, though his ears twitched at every distant groan of timber. There was no reaching the nearest town before nightfall—not without riding blind. Even here, beneath the boughs, light filtered through in dying slivers, like the forest was trying to remember the sun.

After a few minutes, he found a small clearing—just wide enough to make camp, just hidden enough to stay unseen. He let the reins fall from his hand.

"Stay," he murmured. Eddaross flicked an ear but made no move to wander, already nosing at a patch of grass like he had earned the rest.

Belaric moved through the clearing in silence, tapping trees with his knuckles, then with the palm of his hand. He listened for the sound that meant death—a deep groan, a crack in the dark.

One trunk gave it to him. The creak came first, slow and warning. Then a brittle snap, like old bone. The tree shifted with a sound like thunder muffled under blankets, and Belaric leapt clear just as it toppled backwards. It did not fall far, caught by the tangled arms of its brothers, branches locking it upright at a sick angle. Like a corpse still standing.

He turned, breath caught in his throat.

Eddaross looked up, blinked once, snorted, and returned to chewing his grass.

Belaric shook his head, a dry smile tugging at his lips.

"Glad one of us has faith," he muttered.

But as he looked around the clearing, at the standing dead trees that loomed like silent sentinels, something in him shifted. The trees were hollowed, gutted beneath the surface. He felt a sudden, familiar ache in his chest, a memory of a voice that was calm, distant, already half gone.

He shook the thought away and moved among the trees, gathering what firewood he could. Most of it was brittle and worm-eaten, bark crumbling beneath his touch. After searching for a few minutes, he believed he had enough to last the night.

By the time he returned to the clearing, it was almost completely dark. He set the bundle near the center and began arranging the driest sticks with care. Flint and steel struck once, then again—until a thread of orange flame took hold and spread. The fire rose slowly and low, curling smoke into the quiet.

Only then did he walk to Eddaross, running a hand down his neck. The horse let out a low breath, steady and warm. Belaric unbuckled the saddle and lifted it off with care, setting it near the edge of the clearing.

The leather was damp with sweat; the padding crusted with a long day's ride. He loosened the straps and gave Eddaross a few slow strokes along the flank before unfastening the pack. The straps had grown stiff with dried sweat and trail dust. He slung it to the ground, unrolled it, and pulled free two strips of dried meat. No spices, just smoke and salt. He held them over the fire with his knife; the flames licking the edges until the fat hissed.

He sat cross-legged, the knife still in his hand, chewing in rhythm with the slow, wet grinding of Eddaross munching on his patch of grass. The sound was oddly comforting—something ordinary in a world that had long since lost its taste for such things.

As the silence pressed, the memories of Renna came unbidden.

Quiet days in their house, picnics by the river where the reeds whispered like gossiping old women, the nights they lay in bed talking until the candles burned out. She had always asked too many questions; he had always found ways to answer without telling the truth.

He thought about their wedding—a small thing, just her mother and the priest. Her mother, already pale and fading with pain, had still smiled brightly at Renna that day. Belaric had held her hand, promising to keep her daughter safe.

He looked down at his own hand, still gripping the kitchen knife. His knuckles were white. The promise felt like ash on his tongue.

He closed his eyes and took another breath.

The fire crackled, low and cautious. Deep within the Hollowood, a tree groaned and fell with the sound of a dying man. Eddaross shifted uneasily, his ears twitching toward the noise, then settled.

Belaric rose and moved to one of the thicker trees at the edge of the clearing—one that had not groaned or shifted when he tested it. He settled there, placing his back against the trunk, its bark cold but solid. He hid the blade within his shirt, his hand still near the hilt.

His breathing slowed. Steadied.

Sleep came slowly, not like a closing door but like a fog creeping in—quiet, cold, and unwelcome.

He found himself standing in the master's chamber again. The stone beneath his feet glistened with a strange dampness, cold and clinging, though no water had fallen. Around him, torches burned with an unnatural green light, casting warped shadows that made the walls seem farther away than they should have been. It was the same place he had known for years—but something about it felt hollow now, subtly wrong, as if time or memory had eaten away at the edges.

Before him stood a stone table, its surface smooth and grey, worn by generations of blood and silence.

And atop it—Eryndorr.

Small. Still. His skin held a faint blue cast beneath the flickering green light, and his chest did not rise. He looked like a doll carved from ice.

Belaric's hand moved without command, rising slowly and stiffly until it hovered over the boy's heart. His fingers curled around the hilt of an ashen dagger. He did not remember drawing it.

He tried to speak, but the words died in his throat. He tried to pull the dagger back. But his body refused.

The dagger began to descend—not by his will, but by some invisible force pressing down, inch by inch. He fought against it, muscles strained, every breath ragged with the effort to resist.

An icy breath traced the edge of his ear, and a voice—smooth, patient, intimate—slipped into his thoughts like poison in wine. "You know what he is," said the Vowkeeper. "What he will become." Belaric gritted his teeth, jaw clenched so hard it ached. "No." The voice coiled tighter. "He bears the mark. You saw it. You know what that means. Let it end before it begins."

"I said no." The dagger continued to lower. Every ounce of strength he had went into holding it back, but it was not enough. His arms trembled. His legs locked in place. He could not even look away from the tip of the blade.

Then—a touch. Gentle. Steady. A hand closed over his, warm and sure, grounding him to the world that had begun to slip away. Heat bled into his fingers—real, familiar.

He turned his head and saw Renna standing beside him.

She wore a flowing green dress, soft and radiant, her dark hair loose around her shoulders, eyes clear and steady as they met his. Her smile did not tremble. It anchored.

"You are not the monster they say you are," she said softly. "You are my husband. My love. And his father."

He reached for her, needing to feel her, to hold on to the last good thing he remembered—but she was already looking down at the table.

So he followed her gaze.

The dagger was gone. Eryndorr's eyes were open, bright and alive. He smiled up at his father with a joy that seemed untouched by the world. Belaric felt something break inside—not in pain, but relief. Tears blurred his vision, hot and sudden, and he leaned forward to lift the boy into his arms, but before he could reach him the dream shattered.

A sharp snort dragged him back. His eyes flew open. Embers pulsed low in the fire, painting the clearing in a weak amber glow. Instinct took over. He crouched, blade in hand, breath tight in his chest. Eddaross stood a few paces away, head raised, ears forward.

At the treeline stood a deer, small and calm, blinking curiously at the firelight. It took a tentative step back, more wary than afraid.

Belaric let out a breath he did not know he was holding, lowering the knife. "Really?" he muttered, casting a look toward Eddaross. "You are scared of a deer?" Eddaross snorted again and shook his mane, as if to defend his honor.

Belaric sat back down beside the fire. The night was still thick around them, but the dream lingered behind his eyes—Renna's hand, her voice, the peace in their son's smile.

The fire had burned low, nothing but a bed of glowing embers now, pulsing faintly in the dark. He reached for a few of the thicker logs he had set aside earlier and laid them gently across the coals. A moment passed, then another—until orange licked up the wood's edge and the fire stirred back to life with a soft crackle.

He watched the flames grow, slow and steady, and then leaned back, letting the warmth settle into his skin.

He stared into the fire for a long while, the silence pressing in again.

The forest groaned in the distance. Quiet. Almost thoughtful.

Sleep did not come again that night. The dream had left too much behind—shadows in his mind, weight in his chest. He continued to add more branches to the fire and sat beside it, silent, eyes flicking toward the darkness that filled the clearing. Hours passed like slow-moving clouds. When the faintest hint of orange began to bleed through the trees, he rose with a groan, saddled Eddaross, and rode on. Hollowood groaned behind them, fading into the mist.

The next few days were hard riding. He pushed Eddaross where he could, stopping only when Eddaross needed to rest. He was fortunate to find several small creeks and streams for Eddaross to drink and rest at. Belaric avoided the small villages along the way. Too many eyes. Too many questions. Instead, he found what cover he could—one night tucked into a field of high grass, where the stalks reached his shoulders and masked the light of the small fire he lit. Another night in an abandoned farmhouse, with the roof half-collapsed and moss creeping up the beams. He was grateful for it all the same. There was dry hay in the corner and a half-barrel of grain left untouched. Eddaross ate well, and for once, Belaric slept on something that did not bruise the bone. His wounds itched under the bandages, and his muscles protested with every step, but he endured.

On the morning of the sixth day, the sun rose in front of him, and there—on the far edge of the horizon—stood Norvalth.

The black walls gleamed like polished obsidian, towering high and proud. Catapults lined the parapets, motionless but watchful. Even from a distance, the banners of House Tannic snapped in the wind, blood-red against the pale sky. Belaric guided Eddaross forward, eyes tracing the walls that were said never to have fallen. He had not seen Norvalth in years. Not since before Renna. Back then, it had felt distant. Imposing. Now it loomed like a tomb built by kings—beautiful, unfeeling, and ready to bury him.

He entered through the southern gate. The eastern gate was for the highborn nobles, wealthy merchants, and soldiers of rank. The southern entrance bore fewer guards, and the ones stationed there barely gave him a second glance as he passed beneath the stone archway. Dust cloaked his clothes and face, and the limp in his step helped sell the illusion: just another worn traveler among hundreds.

Norvalth reminded him of Vorinfall in some ways—the way the city was divided, the clear line between the rich and the forgotten. Beggars crowded the corners near the gate, their hands outstretched and eyes hollow. Vendors barked halfheartedly from makeshift stalls, their wares sun-faded and half-rotten. He moved through it quickly, keeping his head low, until he reached the lower district inns.

He could have afforded better. The coin in his pack could buy him a room in the middle district for many nights, a bath and supper with wine to spare. But coin was not the only thing that mattered. In the lower district, no one asked questions. No one remembered faces. And no one noticed if a man vanished.

He found an inn not far from a crooked smithy and a boarded-up chapel—the Green Stag, the name carved above the door and half-faded with time. He dismounted and pulled the packs from Eddaross's sides. One of the stable boys—a lanky youth with straw-blond hair and a nervous smile—approached and took the reins.

"Water him, brush him down, and feed him," Belaric said, handing over a copper piece. "He has been worked hard."

The boy nodded eagerly. "He will be well looked after, I promise." He gave Eddaross a gentle pat and led him away.

Belaric watched until the gelding disappeared into the stable, then stepped through the inn's warped doorway. The common room smelled of sweat, onions, and stale ale. Flies circled a plate of crusted bread and congealed fat near the hearth. A handful of older men sat hunched at the tables or leaned over mugs at the bar—men too worn or broken to still work, killing the days as best they could. Their eyes followed Belaric for a moment, but he did not meet their gaze, and they did not hold his.

Behind the bar stood a man who looked more bear than human—tall, thick-necked, with forearms like tree trunks and a belly that strained his apron. He chopped onions with a cleaver that looked more fit for war than cooking. His hands did not pause as Belaric approached.

"Room for one. Supper and something in the morning," Belaric said.

The innkeeper grunted, not looking up. "Ten coppers."

"Nine," Belaric replied, calm as coin sliding across a table.

"Roof does not patch itself," the man said, finally meeting his eye.

Belaric set nine coppers on the bar. "Nine—and I will not be trouble."

The man studied him a moment longer, then scraped the coins into a tin. "Third door on the left. The water basin is in the hall."

Belaric gave a brief nod and climbed the narrow staircase. The room was small but clean enough, with a straw mattress and a shuttered window. He set his pack's down beside the bed and checked the lock. It clicked into place, but he did not trust the locks.

Then he returned to the common room and placed two more coppers on the bar. "For a bath."

The innkeeper barked at one of the boys scrubbing pans in the corner. "Heat some water. Move like your mother's chasing you with a belt."

Belaric took a seat at the bar and let out a slow breath. His muscles throbbed, his wounds pulsed under the fresh wrappings, and the ache behind his eyes had not dulled in days. He kept one hand near his mug, the other resting loosely near the dagger at his hip. When the ale came, he drank slowly, letting the bitterness settle.

For now, this would do.

Belaric had just finished the last sip of his ale when the boy returned, cheeks red from the heat and effort. "It is ready, sir," he said, voice thin with youth and steam.

Belaric nodded, tossed a copper toward the innkeeper, and followed the boy down a narrow hall. The bathing room was small, paneled in old wood stained dark with time. Steam clung to the walls, curling from the surface of the tub like mist from a quiet lake. The heat was welcome.

He closed the door behind him and stripped down, every movement stiff with the dull ache of travel. The bandages had held—barely. He unwrapped them one by one, careful not to reopen the skin, and dropped the blood-stiffened cloth into a nearby basin.

Then he lowered himself into the water slowly and cautiously, biting back a groan as the warmth touched bruised flesh and torn muscle. The burn came sharp and immediate—but then came the release. His limbs loosened. His back settled. The pain faded to a dull, bearable throb.

As he lay there, eyes half-lidded, his thoughts turned to the Order Hall.

Norvalth's order had hidden its entrance well. Most would not know it was there. It lay beneath the city, tucked into one of the sewer tunnels in the lower district, masked by rot and runoff. The stench alone kept people clear. No homes had been built near it. No shops, no stables. Just a stretch of crumbling stone and weedy flagstones where even dogs did not linger.

But he remembered something else. A guard post sat near the sewer's edge—half-forgotten, barely manned. If he timed it right, and if the guards avoided the stench like everyone else, it might give him the vantage he needed. A line of sight. A place to watch who came and went. It was not perfect, but it was the best he had. And if a guard returned early, or lingered too long, he would adapt.

He shifted slightly and winced as the wound along his ribs pulled beneath the water. Not deep enough to kill, but deep enough to matter. He ran a hand through his hair and leaned back again, closing his eyes.

He was close now. Closer than he had ever been in the last few days. Brookhaven still waited—but here, in Norvalth, there was the chance of something else. A glimpse of the Vowkeeper. Maybe even a face. And a part of him, the part that had been forged in the dark, already knew: if he saw that face again, there would be blood.

The water began to cool. Belaric reached for the bar of soap, ran it through his hair and across the line of his beard. The sting where it met the cuts on his side was sharp but clean. He dunked his head beneath the surface and let the world disappear in silence for a few brief seconds. When he rose again, his skin steamed in the cooler air.

He dried off with a rough towel left folded on a stool and dressed in simple clothes: grey patchwork trousers and a white linen shirt that clung damply to his shoulders. It was enough to pass unnoticed.

He left the room without a word and climbed the stairs, footsteps heavy with exhaustion. Once inside, he checked the door, then wedged a stool beneath the handle for good measure.

Before lying down, he retrieved a fresh length of cloth and re-wrapped his wounds, working slowly, jaw clenched against the sting. When it was secure, he flexed carefully, testing the bandage. It held—but only just.

He would need to be careful.

He needed rest. If he were to watch the Order Hall through the night and leave before dawn, rest was a weapon he could not afford to waste.

Sleep came quickly. This time, no dreams followed.

A soft knock stirred him from the dark. His eyes opened slowly, heavy with rest. He rubbed the sleep from them and rose, joints cracking as he stood. He removed the chair and opened the door. The same young boy stood there again, arms full, with a tray balanced carefully against his chest. On it sat a steaming bowl of stew, two thick slices of buttered bread, and a tin cup of ale.

"Father figured you were not coming down," the boy said.

Belaric nodded, murmured thanks, and took the tray. The boy turned and padded away, bare feet quiet on the floorboards.

He shut the door, crossed the room, and sat on the edge of the bed with the tray across his lap. The smell hit him first—meat, onion, something green. Simple food, but warm and real. He exhaled slowly and picked up the spoon.

The sun was almost gone. Only the last sliver of light touched the rooftops beyond the window as night began its slow crawl across Norvalth.

Soon it would be time to work.

After he finished eating, Belaric gathered the tray and empty bowl and made his way downstairs. The inn had changed with the fall of night—no longer the quiet, half-empty room he had walked into earlier. Now it pulsed with life.

The common room was packed shoulder to shoulder. Dozens of men and women sat at the tables or on the wooden stools at the bar, mugs in hand and laughter in the air. Platters of roasted meat were passed down benches, tankards clinked together, and the smell of sweat and ale tangled with the warmth of spiced broth rising from every table.

Near the hearth, a man played a flute—lean, quick-fingered, with a battered hat turned upside down before him. Beside him stood a woman with copper hair and a voice that silenced even the rowdiest drinkers. She sang with her eyes half-closed, swaying with the notes as if the music itself were dancing through her.

"Lay me down on a bed of green,
Where no kings come and no blade's gleam.
Let the river forget my name.
Let the stars say who I have been."

A few in the crowd joined in softly, their voices cracked from age or drink, but no less sincere. When the last verse faded, the room broke into applause. Coins clinked into the flute player's case—coppers, mostly, along with a few tarnished silvers.

Belaric stood near the steps, a fresh ale in hand, letting the warmth soak into him as he listened. The woman's voice lingered in his thoughts, delicate and steady, like something remembered from another life. When the noise began to swell again, he moved through the crowd and dropped a single silver coin into the case.

The flute player looked up, smiled in thanks—then blinked as the coin caught the firelight.

"That is—uh—sir, this is…" he stammered, glancing from the coin to Belaric, clearly unsure whether to thank him or question his judgment.

The woman stepped closer. "You are too kind, stranger," she said. "That is more than generous."

Belaric gave a slight nod. "I liked the song."

"Are there any you would like to hear?" she asked, brushing a lock of hair behind her ear. Her voice still held its musical lilt, but there was a quiet sincerity behind it now.

He paused, thinking. "Do you know The Maiden and the Beast?"

She tilted her head, curiosity flickering behind her eyes, but she nodded. "I do."

"Then I would like to hear it," Belaric said.

He returned to his place near the steps. The flute player shifted to a slower rhythm, deep and haunting, and after a few mournful notes, the woman began to sing:

"In shadowed wood where wild things tread,

A maiden walked where most would dread.

Her voice was calm; her step was light.

And all the beasts gave way to night.

But one remained—a fearsome thing.

With bloodied claws and a broken wing.

It snarled and snapped, and yet she stayed.

Her voice, the balm that sorrow made.

She sang not fear, but hope instead.

And touched the crown upon his head.

No monster lives where love has grown,

She whispered low. You are not alone.

And so, the beast became her shield.

His wrath, the sword her heart could wield.

And in that wood, where legends meet,

They carved a home with hands and teeth."

As she sang the last verse, Belaric stood unmoving, his hand wrapped loosely around his mug. A knot formed low in his chest—something old, something buried. She whispered low. You are not alone. His grip tightened slightly. Just words, just a song—but it left something behind.

The crowd clapped when it ended—louder than before. A few cheers rose from the back of the room. The woman's eyes met his.

Belaric stepped forward again and placed another coin—this time a copper—into the flute player's case. A small gesture, but one meant for the song rather than the crowd.

Before he could turn away, the woman leaned in slightly, her voice lowered now to something more personal. "Few ask for that song."

He held her gaze for a breath, then gave a faint nod. "Most forget why it matters."

She smiled—soft, genuine, touched with something more than thanks.

Belaric returned to the stairs without another word and climbed them slowly, the last verse echoing in his thoughts like a truth he did not know he needed to hear.

After a few minutes, Belaric entered his room and let out a deep breath. The warmth from the common room still lingered faintly in the wood, but it offered no comfort. He wished he could rest—just lay back and forget everything for a few hours. But if there was even the slimmest chance the Vowkeeper was in Norvalth, he could not let it pass.

He pulled his pack from beneath the bed and unrolled the bundle of black leather within. Piece by piece, he dressed. The gear smelled faintly of oiled steel and cold nights. As he tightened each strap, the soft creak of worn leather was the sound of ritual, familiar and quiet. The armor clung to him like a second skin, snug across his shoulders and chest. He slipped the knife into place; he hoped it would be enough if he needed to fight. Every strap was double-checked. Every buckle cinched.

He pulled the hood over his head, casting his face in shadow, then crossed to the window and unlatched it. The hinges groaned softly as it opened. A gust of foul-smelling air crept in—the rot of the lower district's gutters and the sour reek of cheap ale and old piss. He was thankful his window faced a narrow side alley rather than the street.

Belaric leaned out slowly. The alley below was empty. No footsteps. No flicker of lantern light. He swung a leg over the sill and began his descent, bare fingers gripping brick and warped timber with the practiced ease of long habit.

On the ground, he kept to the shadows, moving like a wraith through the sleeping city. Most shops had long since closed, their windows shuttered tight. The only light came from taverns and inns, spilling gold into the streets through warped glass. He gave them a wide berth, avoiding doorways and torchlight. Patrols passed at intervals—two guards at a time, armor dulled with use, swords loose at the hip. He stopped in alcoves or behind crates, always still, always silent, until they passed.

Soon, he reached the abandoned stretch of the lower district.

No house's stood here. No stalls, no carts, no voices. Just silence and decay. Even the rats had grown thin. Weeds cracked through the cobblestones. Ash collected in the corners of the broken stone. He moved along the wall, stopping before a thick wooden door set into its base—a forgotten guard post nestled near the sewer entrance.

He had not heard anyone nearby, but he placed his ear to the wood, anyway.

Silence.

He tested the handle. Locked, as expected.

He knelt, pulling his lock pick set from a pouch on his thigh. The lock was old, simple, and rusted with neglect. After a few seconds of work, he heard a soft click, and the door creaked open.

Dust greeted him first. A stool sat in the corner beneath a cob-webbed arrow slit. No scent of oil, no footprints, no heat. Nobody had used the post for some time. He stepped inside and shut the door behind him, leaving it slightly ajar—just enough to maintain a view of the sewer entrance across the alley.

He climbed the narrow steps to the upper ledge and rigged a string to a broom at the base of the stairs. Crude, but it would work. If someone entered behind him, he would hear the broom drop. Maybe not in time—but better than nothing.

He returned to the gap in the door and settled into the shadows.

And he waited.

Time passed in aching silence. The kind that stretched, folded in on itself, and slowed thought to a crawl. Once or twice, he heard distant voices. Once, a bottle shattered a few streets over. But no one came near the sewer gate. No movement. No sign of the Vowkeeper. Not even a masked wretch skulking on their master's behalf.

Hours passed.

He sighed, quiet as a breath. Part of him had known. It was a fool's errand. The Vowkeeper would not be found this easily. Still… he needed to hope. Just a little.

Belaric removed the string, pocketed the bell, and slipped back out into the night. The city was quieter now. Even the taverns had dimmed.

He returned the same way he had come, scaling the wall in silence and slipping through the window. He latched it behind him and stood in the dark for a moment, unmoving.

Then he undressed, folding the black leather neatly before tugging his grey patchwork trousers back on. There was no time to sleep. Two hours until first light. He lay back on the bed, arms behind his head, eyes half-lidded.

He had not found the Vowkeeper.

But the silence still whispered more softly than regret.

14

Belaric lay still on the bed, eyes fixed on the ceiling, listening to the silence pressing in. The last of the patrons had long staggered to their rooms, and even the floorboards seemed to hold their breath.

He turned over the next steps in his mind. If the roads held and Eddaross kept pace, he would reach Brookhaven in a few days. But what then?

He shut his eyes, trying to summon the estate from memory. Lady Haldren's estate was modest—just a few rooms, a narrow hall, and an iron gate that barely counted as a defense. He exhaled sharply, annoyed. He should have known better. Brookhaven had always been beneath notice. A few hundred souls, no garrison, no walls. Just her and a handful of personal guards. That would work to his advantage—no patrols to stop him, no questions asked by half-bored watchmen.

Still, he would stand out. An outsider always did.

He sat up, rubbing the heel of his palm into his temple. The Order would strike soon. That much was certain. But how?

A commoner's death would not stir the dust. A noblewoman's might. Questions would be asked. Nobles love questions—especially when they are not the ones bleeding.

An accident? No, a mother and daughter dead while the rest of the house lives? Too neat. Too loud in its quietness. Even the dimmest lord would squint at that.

Fire, then. Fire told no truths, left no witnesses. But fire was a gambler's tool. They might escape before it swallowed them.

Or maybe subtlety was not the plan. Slit throats, red from ear to ear. A message written in blood: this is the price of disobedience.

He leaned forward, elbows on knees, hands steepled beneath his chin. He needed time—time to learn their habits. Which lanterns burned past dusk. Who walked which halls and when.

He needed luck.

And luck had stopped answering the door.

If he failed—if he was too late, or made the wrong move—then the path ahead would narrow to one.

War with the Order.

No banners and horns. No charges across open fields. A slow war, one corpse at a time. Blood in the gutters. Names crossed off lists. He would kill them, every last one, until the Vowkeeper had no place left to hide.

He exhaled slowly. Morning light crept along the window's edge—pale, gold, and unaware of the kind of world it was waking up to.

Belaric stood and stretched the ache from his limbs. The stiffness of the last few days of riding clung to his muscles like frost. He unwrapped the soiled bandages from his hand and re-wrapped it with clean linen from his pack, the fresh cloth a small, cool comfort against the wounds. He pulled on his shirt, tightened the buckles of his worn leather, and checked his packs—twice, then once more. It was a habit, a ritual.

He slung the packs over his shoulder and descended the stairs in silence. Below, the innkeeper stood behind the bar, already cutting carrots into clean, practiced slices. They thunked against the board before he swept them into a pot bubbling over the hearth.

The two men locked eyes. A nod passed between them—neither warm nor cold. Just two men doing what needed doing.

"Boy," the innkeeper called. "Roasted pork strips and some bread."

Belaric took a seat near the door, setting his packs down with care.

"Ale or water?" the man asked.

"Water. Long ride ahead."

Another nod. The innkeeper moved to fetch a mug and filled it from the clay jug resting on the sideboard.

The boy arrived moments later with a plate and a nervous energy, dropped the food in front of Belaric, then darted back to fetch the mug. He returned, set it down, then vanished again—like all things, the boy was too young to understand the weight of the world.

Belaric ate quickly. The meat was salted and sharp, the bread thick and covered in butter. He swallowed it all and washed it down with the water. He rose and placed the plate and mug on the bar.

"Thank you," Belaric said.

The innkeeper took the coins without looking. "Come back any-time. Wish I had more guests like you."

Belaric paused. "Guests like me?" A faint smile touched his lips. "Foolish to wish for more ghosts."

The innkeeper blinked, brow furrowing. "Pardon?"

But Belaric was already walking away.

He stepped outside. Dawn greeted him like a blade drawn slow—light creeping in slivers across the stones, the sky beginning to pale. A beautiful day to ride, if he had anything beautiful to ride toward.

The stable smelled of hay, sweat, and manure. The same boy from the day before was already mucking out the stalls, arms thin and calloused from work too large for him. He spotted Belaric and moved quickly, shovel abandoned. Without a word, he crossed the straw-littered floor and began to saddle Eddaross.

The horse snorted the moment he saw Belaric, ears pinning back, breath flaring with judgment.

Belaric arched a brow. He half-expected Eddaross to nip at the boy's arm, but the beast only swished his tail and stood still. Too tired to care, maybe. Or saving the bite for him.

"Well. Good morning to you too," Belaric muttered.

He turned to the boy. "Any trouble with him?"

The boy shook his head. "No trouble. Ate, then slept."

Belaric nodded. "Smart beast."

Eddaross was led out, saddle secured, gear fastened. Belaric tied down his packs, checked the straps. "Time to earn your oats. Ready?"

Eddaross stamped his hoof.

"That is what I thought," Belaric said with a dry chuckle.

Belaric mounted. The leather groaned beneath him. He took the reins, offered the boy a nod, and guided Eddaross through the early streets. A few souls wandered, heads down, eyes quick to look away. He passed through the southern gate without a word.

With a flick of the reins, Eddaross surged forward, hooves hammering the road like war drums.

Belaric leaned low over the saddle, the wind pressing against him.

"Good job, old boy," he murmured, and the horse galloped on into the waiting dawn.

Belaric pushed hard through the day, the road unfolding in long, empty stretches that whispered of old wars and forgotten travelers. Eddaross gave everything he had, muscles taut, breath steady—but by late afternoon, his stride had slowed, and the fatigue began to show in the way his head dipped between steps.

At the base of a wide, sloping hill veiled in soft green, Belaric pulled the reins and dismounted. The moment his boots hit the grass, Eddaross lowered his head and began tearing mouthfuls from the earth like the land owed him something.

Belaric stretched slowly, rolling the stiffness from his shoulders and back. The saddle left a deep ache in his spine, and his legs buzzed with the numbness of too many unmoving hours.

"You have done well, old boy," he said, stepping close and patting Eddaross's neck with slow, steady hands. "We will take it slower now."

The horse snorted, as if to say he had earned that much, and did not lift his head from the grass.

Belaric pulled the waterskin from his pack and took a few measured sips before tipping it gently toward Eddaross, who drank greedily from his cupped hands. For a while they simply stood—man and beast beneath a sky streaked with dusk—no sound but chewing grass and the distant call of birds making for their nests.

After a brief rest, Belaric mounted again. Eddaross climbed the hill at a measured pace, hooves sinking slightly into the damp, yielding ground. They walked for miles, the silence of the world pressing close, until Belaric leaned forward and muttered, "Ready to go?"

Without warning, Eddaross surged forward, a burst of life returning to his limbs. Belaric gripped the reins as the horse flew across the open fields, a streak of muscle and breath, the wind whistling past like laughter.

They rode until dusk melted into full darkness.

That night they camped in the wild, beneath a scatter of stars mostly hidden by cloud. Belaric avoided a fire—no need to invite eyes from the road or worse from the trees. He chewed cold meat and lay beside Eddaross; the horse lying in the grass with one ear flicking at flies.

Sleep took him like a hand closing over his eyes.

He woke to the kiss of rain.

Droplets tapped against his face like fingers urging him back into the world. He opened his eyes to find a sky of dull, endless grey above. Clouds hung low and full, a ceiling that promised misery.

Belaric sighed. "Of course," he muttered, already reaching for his saddle straps.

They were soaked within the hour.

The rain came steadily, never violent, but merciless in its patience. Belaric let Eddaross walk, unwilling to risk injury on the wet, uneven ground. He rode hunched beneath his cloak, water sliding down the back of his neck and seeping into everything.

Caution kept them crawling. By early afternoon, the clouds began to break apart—only slightly, but enough to let the sun peek through in golden shards. An hour later, the rain softened into a mist, and then stopped altogether. The world steamed. Every leaf and blade glittered with water.

Belaric turned east and guided Eddaross toward the rising edge of Rosewood Forest.

It grew before them like a painting—ancient trees stretching into the sky, their trunks thick with age, bark the color of iron and shadow. The canopy overhead shimmered with emerald and amber light, filtering the sun in shifting hues. Rosewood was no ordinary forest—it was a place where the kingdom's finest lumber was harvested, where beasts still ruled in the underbrush and birds sang with voices older than men.

It was a sanctuary for man and creature alike. A cathedral of bark and root.

Belaric knew it well. A creek ran through the heart, cold and clear. He needed water. And a fire. And dry clothes.

They entered beneath rustling boughs and the hush of rain-dripped leaves. He found the creek not long after—its water winding through stones with the sound of soft laughter. He refilled his water skin and took several long gulps, grateful for the water. Belaric set about making camp a few paces from the bank.

Belaric stripped off his soaked clothes and wrung them out before laying them across a low-hanging branch to dry. Steam rose from his skin in the fire's heat. He crouched beside his pack, hands steady but slow, and pulled out what remained of his bandages.

The wounds were nearly closed now—raw lines across ribs and thigh, reminders of Dainrik and Orris's handiwork. He cleaned them with water from the creek, teeth clenched, then bound them again with the last of the linen. No more after this. If they split open again, they would stay open.

When the wrappings were done, he pulled out the kitchen knife he had taken from Kaedra's house. The blade was dull and thick, and he spent several minutes running it against a smooth river stone, the scrape and rasp of steel against grit a rhythmic counterpoint to the crackling fire. It would never be a proper weapon, but by the time he was done, the edge was sharp enough to do its work. He sat back on his heels and let the fire warm his bones.

Fresh clothes. Dry skin. A moment's breath.

Eddaross drank from the creek with lazy gulps. The horse looked up once, ears twitching, then returned to the water as if to say wake me when it matters.

Belaric cooked a portion of pork over the flames, letting the fat hiss and crackle. He ate slowly, chewing with care. Nearby, he found several berry bushes—deep blue with a tart bite. He picked them in silence and let the taste settle on his tongue.

Night fell quiet.

Brookhaven lay ahead now—close enough to reach by midday, if the road held. Lady Haldren. Her daughter Lyra. The knife was meant for both.

He leaned back against Eddaross, the horse's slow breath rising and falling behind him.

Morning came quicker than he liked. The soft chirping of birds pulled him from sleep, dragging him out of the only place that did not ache. Belaric opened his eyes to a pale sky and the breath of the forest around him. He shifted and groaned—every root and stone beneath him had left its mark. His back felt like it had been beaten in his sleep.

He rose stiffly and coaxed life back into last night's fire, feeding it the driest wood he had stashed beneath his pack. He speared a cut of venison and held it over the flame, letting the heat do its quiet work. While it cooked, he returned to the berry bush and picked several more—some for himself, most for Eddaross. He ate quickly, then walked over to the horse, which now stood with ears twitching and tail swaying.

Belaric held out the berries. Eddaross took them gratefully, chewing with the kind of joy only animals and children seemed to know.

The scent of sizzling meat pulled him back to the fire. He retrieved the venison before it blackened, sliced it into strips, and chewed slowly. Not the finest meal he had eaten, but it would do. He drank from his waterskin, then refilled it at the creek—cold water, clean. A rare thing in a world soiled by men.

When the fire was out and camp packed, he turned to find Eddaross buried in a patch of wild grass, chewing like the ground owed him something. Belaric clapped his hands softly. "Enough of that, lazy beast."

Eddaross did not move.

"Oh? That is how it is?" he muttered as the horse kept eating, tail flicking in defiance. "I was going to buy you apples in Brookhaven. But if you prefer grass, that saves me coin." He turned and began walking away.

Eddaross snorted and bumped him in the back with his nose.

Belaric chuckled, reaching back to pat the horse's nose. "Thought so."

He saddled the horse, cinched the packs, and led it out beneath the thinning canopy of Rosewood.

The days that followed passed slowly and hard, marked by cold nights, quiet roads, and the steady ache of old wounds. Eddaross remained stubborn as ever, though he tolerated Belaric more as the miles wore on—too tired to argue, or perhaps simply choosing his battles.

By the time Brookhaven's modest rooftops crested the horizon, the horse was limping slightly, and Belaric was not much better.

The town was modest. Neat rows of timber and stone buildings spread across the valley floor. Merchant stalls lined the main road—blacksmith, baker, tailor, a tavern with weathered shutters and a hand-painted sign. Smoke drifted from chimneys, and carts rumbled over hard-packed dirt. Brookhaven was known for its mill—one of the kingdom's finest—its lumber sent to build keeps, warships, and palaces alike. The scent of fresh-cut wood hung in the air, sharp and clean.

Above it all, seated on a low hill, was the Haldren estate. Gabled rooftops, grey stone, well-cut lumber and an iron gate half-swallowed in ivy. Modest, well-maintained. Like most noble homes—it was built to keep the world out, and the secrets in.

Belaric rode in at a calm pace. The townsfolk were friendly enough—nodding, offering soft greetings as he passed. He returned them with a brief smile and kept moving. No reason to linger. He could not afford to draw attention.

What struck him most was the quiet. No shouts, no weeping, no signs of alarm. If Lady Haldren and her daughter were already dead, he doubted the town would be this calm. Someone would be crying. The guards would be stirring.

Hope stirred in his chest—unwelcome, but stubborn. Maybe he was not too late.

The estate still needed scouting. He had to learn its weaknesses, its servants, its entry points. And he had to do it in daylight.

First, he needed to see to Eddaross. Then, a room for the night.

He found The Singing Maiden just off the main road—a tidy structure of pale stone with a solid wooden roof and a pair of flower boxes beneath the windows. It looked well-kept, not rich, but proud of itself.

Around the back, he found the stables. An older man lay snoring on a stack of hay, a wide-brimmed hat pulled down over his face. His clothes were dust-streaked, work-worn. A short white beard clung to his jaw like frost on a stump.

Belaric kicked the hay.

The man jolted up, spitting curses. "Who the hell—?"

Belaric raised a hand. "Apologies, sir. Did not mean to wake you. Just need to stable old Ed here."

The man squinted at him, then at Eddaross. He rubbed a hand down his face and grunted. "Well, why did not you just say so? Sorry 'bout my mouth—we do not get many fancy visitors like yourself," he said before his eyes shifted to Eddaross again. "Fine horse. He need hay or grain?"

"He could use a good brushing. And he loves apples if you have got any," Belaric said.

The man grinned. "I have a few lying around. Copper a night to stable him. Give your coin to Amara inside—she runs the place."

Belaric nodded and thanked the man before turning and patting Eddaross on the neck once more. "Be good," he told him. The horse flicked his tail in reply.

Belaric smiled before turning and stepping into the inn.

The Singing Maiden was quiet and warm. A hearth crackled low to his right, with a small stage tucked beside it. Tables and chairs filled the space—nothing fancy, but all in good condition. The scent of bread and herbs lingered in the air, clean and inviting. Only one man sat in the common room, nursing an ale in the corner. He glanced up as Belaric entered, eyes sharp beneath bushy brows, then dropped them again without a word.

Behind the bar stood a woman—short, round, and undeniably in charge. She had the settled confidence of someone who had been managing drunkards and debt-dodgers long before Belaric ever learned to hold a blade. Her black hair was neatly braided, trailing down her back like a banner, and her deep red dress—clean and pressed—seemed to defy the grime of the room around her.

She hunched over a book, one finger gliding beneath the lines as she read, her lips moving faintly. She did not look up when the door opened, only when footsteps stopped at the bar.

Then her eyes lifted—sharp, assessing, and her face softened. "Hello, dear," she said, setting the book aside with care. Not the greeting of a woman caught off guard, but one prepared to handle whatever sort of man had just walked in.

"Afternoon," Belaric said. "Need a room. My horse is in the back. Not sure how long I will be staying."

She beamed, with the kind of smile that had likely defused many bar fights. "Oh, we have not had a traveler in weeks! One copper for the horse, four for the room. Comes with meals and a bath each day—if you are the sort that likes to stay clean."

He handed over the coins without comment.

She passed him a key. "First door on the right, up the stairs. Sheets are fresh. If you need the water warmed, just let me know."

He gave a small nod, turned, and climbed the narrow steps. The room was small but clean. A single bed, a writing desk, and a scuffed storage trunk. One window overlooked the rooftops of the town, with the distant trees of Rosewood visible beyond.

Belaric shut the door behind him, slid his packs beneath the bed, and sat with a quiet grunt. He leaned forward, extending his arms, then stretched out his limbs one at a time—stiff from the ride, sore in ways he had been in many years.

The easy part was done.

After several minutes, he sighed. It was time to scout the estate and its grounds.

Daylight work. He did not like it. Shadows were fewer; the world louder. At night, he knew how to move unseen. But in the sun, every step risked notice. Every glance carried weight.

Belaric stood and opened his pack. From its depths, he drew the kitchen knife—sharpened the night before, the edge clean and mean. He lifted his shirt and strapped it across his lower back, snug against the base of his spine.

He left the room, locking the door behind him with a quiet click.

Amara was still behind the bar, reading from her book with the same look of mild disinterest she had worn when he first arrived. As he passed, he offered her a nod.

She looked up and smiled. "Back already, dear?"

"Just going on a walk," Belaric said. "Will not be long." He turned back, offering her a smile.

The sunlight poured in as he opened the door. He paused at the threshold, letting it warm his face for a breath—eyes closed, breathing slow. Despite all the killing the world held, the sun still rose. A small mercy.

He stepped outside, then cut around the side of the inn, boots crunching lightly over the hard-packed dirt. Behind the building, the old stable master was brushing down Eddaross with long, deliberate strokes. The horse looked up at Belaric, ears twitching, head raised as if to ask, "Going somewhere?"

Belaric lifted a hand. Stay.

Satisfied, he turned and made his way back around front, then started down the main street.

The merchants spotted him instantly. A stranger was a gift to their quiet lives, and they descended like crows on a fresh corpse.

"Fine cloak, sir! But I have got better—imported from Valorim!" one man shouted.

"You there, friend! New trousers for the road? These will last you ten winters!" another said.

"A gift for the lady in your life?" a woman called, holding up a glittering necklace of glass beads. "Every man should have something waiting at home."

"You look hungry!" another man barked. "Best chicken stew in the realm. I swear it on my mother's bones!"

Belaric weaved past the stalls, giving a few polite nods, but his eyes swept over the goods, cataloging them all. One cart in particular caught his attention, its proprietor a plump man with a beard full of crumbs. On a velvet cloth, among jars of dried herbs and spices, sat a small, dark vial. Belaric's gaze lingered for only a second before moving on.

Belaric gave a few polite nods and kept walking, weaving past the stalls without pause. Friendly folk, and harmless. But noise all the same.

At the edge of town, where the road gave way to grass and old trees, he turned west—toward a grove that shadowed the Haldren estate. The trees grew thick there, close enough to hide in, high enough to climb. He moved with care, always glancing over his shoulder. No one followed. Still, he kept to the edges, watching for movement between buildings and hedgerows.

He entered the woods in silence.

He circled around the estate slowly, searching. It did not take long to find what he needed. A tall tree with a clean trunk and branches that arched toward the estate like arms reaching for shelter. It would offer a perfect vantage point of the estate grounds. He climbed swiftly, every movement practiced. The bark bit into his hands, but the pain meant little.

He reached the branch he had picked out and crawled across it, ensuring he kept his balance. He crouched on a thick branch and steadied himself with the limbs around him. Slowly, he pushed forward until he found a gap in the leaves—an opening just wide enough to see the rear grounds.

A riding pen came into view.

Inside it, a young girl circled on horseback—tall for her age, dressed in fine riding clothes. Her long brown hair was tied back in a neat braid, and laughter escaped her lips as she guided the animal with surprising ease. She did not ride with the stiff posture of a noble, but with a natural grace that spoke of hours in the saddle. Lines curved across her forehead in intricate patterns—a Valasar mark, unmistakable. Not just noble blood, but power.

Lyra Haldren, Belaric realized.

The horse beneath her was large and black, with a powerful gait and a gleaming coat. It moved with control, every motion crisp under the girl's touch.

A man walked alongside them—tall and thin, dressed in similar riding gear. His short black hair was slicked back, and he called out instructions as the girl rode past him, correcting her posture, urging better form. The horse trainer, no doubt. He moved with the smooth confidence of a man who had trained more than animals.

Near the edge of the pen stood an older woman, wrapped in a deep blue robe trimmed with silver thread. Her dark brown hair was pinned up in an elegant twist, streaked with grey, but her features mirrored the girl's almost perfectly. She smiled as she watched, eyes filled with a quiet pride. She held herself with an unshakable poise that Belaric recognized. It was the stance of a woman who had given orders her entire life—and expected them to be obeyed.

Lady Marvella Haldren.

Belaric exhaled—slow, steady, but deeper than before. A weight eased from his chest.

They were alive. He had made it in time.

A faint, unexpected warmth stirred within him. It was not a victory. Not yet. But it was something.

He let it pass.

Because alive did not mean safe.

Behind Lady Haldren stood a man who was more statue than servant—towering, broad-shouldered, wrapped in polished steel. His breastplate gleamed in the sunlight, and his greaves and boots were thick enough to turn aside a war hammer. A long forest green cape hung from his shoulders, and a sword rested on his hip. His helmet—also steel—masked his face entirely.

Belaric frowned. That was not parade armor. That was battlefield plate.

The man did not move. Did not shift. He was not scanning the field like a guard trained to assess threats—no restless glances, no twitch of the neck. He simply watched, his posture radiating a quiet, unassailable confidence. The way he held his longsword, not casually but with a focused ease, hinted at a lifetime of battle. The distinctive forest-green of his cape, the weight of his plate, the unmoving silence of his stance—all of it spoke of one man.

Belaric's mind supplied the name, one he had heard in hushed whispers and dark corners of taverns. Sir Marius Tolman. A famed knight, known for his unwavering honor and loyalty. He was also a man who had mastered the sword not with flourishes and pomp, but with a brutal, pragmatic efficiency honed on the battlefield.

Then, just for a second, the helmet tilted—no more than a hair's width—toward the trees.

Belaric froze, breath held.

But he did not move again.

A warrior. A knight. A man of honor. Her personal bodyguard—and he was not just for show.

He would kill for her without hesitation. Belaric could see it. But assassins did not come for sword fights. They came like a sickness—quiet, unseen. And when they struck, men like that died without ever knowing where the blade came from.

He stayed in the tree motionless, watching as the lesson drew to a close. The trainer called a halt, and the girl slowed her horse to a trot before swinging her leg over and dismounting. She ran to her mother, and the two embraced. Words passed between them—laughter, maybe. The armored man turned and followed as they walked toward the estate, disappearing behind its stone walls. The trainer remained, leading the horse away toward the stables.

Once everyone was out of view, Belaric dropped from the tree, landing in a crouch.

It was too risky to act now. If the assassin was already in position, he would not strike during the day—not with so many eyes on the grounds, and certainly not with that steel-clad sentinel guarding them.

Belaric had seen the man—head to toe in plate, every joint covered or reinforced. You did not fight that kind of armor with a dagger. Assassins were not made for brute contests. Slipping a blade between the gaps was possible in theory—but only a fool would count on it.

And the man was not just armored. He was trained.

No, the attack would come after dark. That is when armor mattered less. When discipline could falter. When shadows turned even heavy steel into just another silhouette.

Belaric would need to be ready.

He took careful stock of the estate as he moved—watching the rotation of guards, noting gaps in their patrols, measuring angles, timing steps.

The guards were professionals. That much was clear in their movements—silent, precise, scanning with trained eyes. Their armor was fitted, uniforms clean, hands never far from their blades. They did not wander. They watched. The kind of men who would not hesitate when steel was drawn.

Near the rear of the house, a servant worked briskly, hanging damp linens on a stretched rope. She did not look toward the trees—too focused on her work to notice, and he was careful enough to stay invisible.

The hedges near the back corner grew taller than the rest—decorative, but thick enough to break sightlines. Just enough room for a man like him to slip through unnoticed.

There were entry points. Not many. But enough.

But first, he needed information.

If another assassin had arrived, someone in town would have noticed. And if anyone knew the rumors worth hearing, it was the innkeeper. He needed to speak with Amara.

Belaric turned and headed back toward The Singing Maiden.

Belaric kept to the outskirts on his return, slipping between houses and side alleys to avoid the market. The last thing he needed was another swarm of cheerful merchants trying to dress him, feed him, or marry him off.

As he stepped inside the inn, a warm, sweet aroma greeted him—rich with herbs and something faintly spiced. The common room had filled since morning. Locals sat clustered at tables and along the bar, drinks in hand, conversation humming low. Several pairs of eyes followed him as he passed, curious more than cautious.

He ignored them.

Belaric took a seat at the bar, the same spot as earlier. A moment later, Amara appeared, bright as ever.

"Welcome back," she said with a smile. "We have got ale, dark red wine, water... oh, and my favorite—a sweet honey mead."

That surprised him. Most inns offered little more than watered-down ale and cloudy well water. Mead was something you found in noble halls and city taverns with silver-gilded signs.

"I will take the mead," he said.

Amara nodded and turned to fetch it. She returned with a clay mug filled to the brim and set it gently in front of him. Before she could step away, he leaned in slightly.

"What is that scent?" he asked.

She beamed, clearly pleased. "That would be my sweet pork stew. Been in the family for years. My mother taught it to me when I was just a girl. Would you like a bowl?"

"Yes, please," he said without hesitation.

She vanished into the kitchen, and Belaric took a sip of the mead. It was smooth and golden, with just enough bite to keep it from being cloying. He took another sip, slower this time.

Delicious.

Still, he reminded himself why he was here. He let his ears do the work as he listened to the conversations swirling around him.

Two men debated their crops—whether the rain had helped or hindered. Another muttered about the difficulty of getting ore from the northern passes. A woman was scolding her husband for not listening, which was punctuated by him making the fatal error of replying with, "Huh?"

Belaric almost chuckled.

Then the stew arrived.

Amara placed a steaming bowl and a soft roll in front of him. "Enjoy, dear," she said before moving off to help another customer.

He ate slowly, savoring every bite. The pork was tender and sweet; the broth thick and hearty. For a moment, he wondered if Amara had written the recipe down—and if he might ask for it.

The thought made him chuckle softly. He pushed it aside.

It felt strange, smiling. He had not done it much since Renna died. Lately, every good thing came with blood behind it. But here, for a moment, he let himself have it.

Amara caught the sound and drifted back over to him, smiling. "You know, dear, you never gave me your name."

Belaric had been waiting for that.

Of course she would ask. People always did—eventually.

"I am Relinn," he said, extending a hand. "Nice to meet you, Amara."

She took it. "Pleasure's mine, Relinn. What brings you all the way out to Brookhaven?"

He met her eyes with practiced calm. "Just passing through, actually. I am on my way to Raskamoor. My sister sent word—our father's fallen ill. I was hoping to get home quickly, but the old boy out in the stable is not as fast as he used to be. Needed to rest, and I knew Brookhaven was close. Figured I would stay the night."

He imagined Eddaross's snort at being called slow.

Amara's face softened. "I am sorry to hear that, dear. I hope you reach him in time."

"Thank you," Belaric said, then lowered his voice just a touch. "Though... tell me, do I have something on my face? Feels like everyone has been watching me since I walked in."

She giggled. "Oh, no, dear. We just do not get many visitors. Only the merchant caravans that bring our supplies. You are a rare sight."

He raised his eyebrows in mock surprise. "Really? In a town like this—and with stew this good—I am shocked there is not a line out the door."

That drew a louder laugh from her. "You are too kind, Relinn. No, we have not had a real visitor in months. We would not have any at all if it were not for Lady Haldren. She keeps this town going. Very kind woman. Not like those city nobles who think gold makes them gods."

Belaric nodded thoughtfully. "I have heard good things about Lady Haldren."

He paused, then offered a warm grin. "Also, could I have another bowl of this stew?"

Amara grinned widely. "Of course, dear."

She swept the empty bowl away and scurried back to the kitchen.

No real visitors in months, Belaric thought. That either meant the assassin had arrived silently and kept to the shadows... or they were not here yet. He prayed for the latter.

He needed to get into the estate tonight.

Amara returned soon after with a second steaming bowl. He thanked her and ate more quickly this time, focused now. Once finished, he slid two copper coins onto the bar and gave Amara a final nod before heading upstairs.

Inside his room, he closed the door and locked it behind him.

Then he crossed to the bed, dropped to one knee beside his packs, and began to prepare for the night's work.

15

Belaric sat cross-legged on the floor, his gear laid out in neat rows beside the bed. He moved in silence, each motion practiced—tugging leather straps, testing seams, checking buckles for signs of wear. Shadows flickered across the walls as the lone candle guttered low, wax pooling thick at its base.

His armor was old—dark leathers, worn smooth with use and quiet against movement. No crest. No ornament. Just function.

The kitchen knife lay before him. The edge held a slight chip. It was simple, unremarkable. But it could still open a throat.

He ran the whetstone along the edge of the blade, each stroke methodical. Sparks hissed once, then vanished.

It was not the blade that mattered. It was how you used it.

He set the stone aside and turned the weapon in his hand, thumb brushing the worn grip. Not too loose. Not too tight. The weight was familiar. Reassuring. Like an old scar.

The cloak came next. He shook it out once, the fabric whispering as it settled across his lap. Still carried a faint scent of pine and smoke.

Unacceptable.

He uncorked a small vial and tipped a few drops of clear liquid into his palm. No fragrance. No residue. He rubbed it briskly between his hands, then worked it into the cloak, pressing deep into the seams. It lifted every trace—wood smoke, sweat, blood, even the faint oil of his own skin. Gone.

He repeated the motion over his gloves, collar, and the underarms of the armor. Quick, methodical strokes.

Scents could linger. Scents could betray. And in a noble estate where perfumes marked everything, even a breath of wrong air could turn a head.

He would leave nothing behind. Not even a trace.

His thoughts drifted to the estate. No walls, only iron fencing. Easy enough to cross if you knew where the trees leaned close. He would enter through the rear. The guards favored the front—habit, not strategy.

But his mind did not linger on the estate for long. It drifted, as it always did, back to the Order.

They would come. Blades drawn, ready to kill anyone who got in their way.

The Order would hunt him, yes—but not only him. They would not risk Lady Haldren or Lyra stirring things further. He hoped their focus stayed on him for now, that their pride would demand retribution before precision. If they spent their resources chasing shadows through the city, it might buy him more time to save her.

He did not know who would be sent to silence them. But it would not be long.

He considered warning her. Walking through the gate and speaking plain. But what would she see? A killer at her door, spinning stories of danger and betrayal. She would call for guards and have him locked up—or worse, she would deem him a madman and send him away.

No, she would not believe words. She needed proof. She needed to see it.

And when she did…

She would have no choice but to listen.

Outside, the sun had vanished behind the rooftops, leaving only the faintest ember of light along the horizon. Downstairs, laughter had faded to the occasional clink of cups and the last tired bursts of chuckling.

Belaric rose from the edge of the bed. The moment had come.

He stretched slowly and carefully, testing limbs for weakness. His muscles answered with a quiet ache of readiness.

He dressed without hurry. Each piece felt heavier than he remembered. As he tightened the buckles along his wrist and on his boots.

He pulled the last strap tight, pulled the hood over his head, and stood. Cloaked again in a life he thought he hoped to bury.

"Let this be the last time," he told himself.

He crossed to the window and unlatched it with deliberate care. The hinges dared not squeal. Outside, the town had gone still, lit only by the lonely glow of lanterns in the upper windows. Somewhere in the distance, a dog barked once and was silenced.

Belaric climbed out and hung from the ledge with one hand. The other reached back to pull the window shut until the click sealed the world behind him. He let go.

His boots struck the ground in a roll, smooth and silent. Pain flared along his thigh as he crouched—the wound from Dainrik's blade still ached, still angry. He ignored it. Pain was a language he spoke fluently.

He slid into the nearest shadow, still as stone, listening.

Nothing. No alarm. No prying eyes. He moved.

Before the estate, he had one stop to make.

Belaric cut through the alleys like a ghost, avoiding the light. He remembered the merchant's booth, the small glass vial tucked behind false wares. He had known the moment he saw it what it was—and what it would cost him. An item like that was not just a tool. It was a final decision sharpened to a point.

He could not risk the merchant knowing who wanted it.

The shop was not far. He circled around the back, found the rear door, and crouched low. Through the small pane of dusty glass, the inside looked still—shapes of barrels, cloth, and the glint of steel catching moonlight. No movement. No sound.

He drew a slender pick from his belt and knelt. The lock yielded in seconds—Brookhaven craftsmanship was built for show, not secrets.

The door opened without so much as a groan. Inside, he moved like a shadow over stone—silent, deliberate.

His eyes swept the room with practiced ease. Fingers ghosted across jars and boxes, pausing only when they found what he was after. He found the plump man's cart, left just inside the door, its wares covered with a thin sheet of cloth. He pulled the cloth back, his gaze immediately falling on the small, dark vial nestled between rolled parchments and half-forgotten trinkets. It waited—unmarked, and easy to overlook.

He picked it up, weighing it briefly in his hand.

So small a thing, but worth the risk.

Then he slipped it into his cloak and vanished the way he came, locking the door behind him.

Back into the dark.

He made for the edge of town with the patience of a stalking panther, every footstep placed with care. When the buildings thinned and the land turned to hedgerows and fields, he gave the estate a wide berth, circling until he reached its rear wall.

An entrance within the iron gate located directly behind the stables. He had seen it earlier in the day—unguarded, likely forgotten. A place for horses, not men.

The gate's lock looked thick but honest, forged to keep out thieves, not killers. He worked on it for a full minute before it gave way with a soft groan. He winced, eyes flicking to the shadows. No one came.

He unwound the chain and slipped through. Once inside, he re-secured the lock. A loose chain would raise questions. A locked gate looked like nothing at all.

He moved toward the stables, hugging the wall. Off to the right, a guard leaned against the far fence, bored enough to yawn with his mouth wide open. Belaric stilled.

One of the horses inside snorted, loud and sharp. It stepped back, hooves clacking against the wood. Belaric froze, hand already on the hilt at his side.

The guard turned, half-looking.

A heartbeat passed.

Then another.

The man muttered something, spat, and turned away.

Belaric exhaled through his nose and moved fast, slipping from cover to cover, using every tree, every clump of brush to stay unseen. The servant's door was not far.

He crouched low and listened. The guard yawned again, and the sound of his boots shuffled away down the path.

Belaric tested the handle.

It turned.

He slipped inside and eased the door shut behind him. A narrow stone corridor stretched ahead, lined with unmarked doors. The air was damp, tasting faintly of stone and soot. Somewhere distant, water dripped in a slow rhythm. The corridor smelled of sleep and secrets.

No voices. No footsteps.

He had made it in.

He stayed low as he crept to the first door. It hung slightly ajar, spilling a sliver of light onto the stone floor. He eased forward and peered inside—a kitchen, clean and orderly. The hearth was cold. There was not a soul in sight.

His hopes rose. If they all slept, he could move more freely.

He padded to the next door and pressed his ear against the wood. No sound. The handle turned with a careful twist, and he opened it just wide enough to peer into the dark. For a moment, he saw only shadows—then a soft gleam caught his eye.

Steel.

He slipped inside, not making a sound. He stuck to the shadows, the only friend he still had. Moonlight from a narrow window reflected off the weapons lining the far wall—swords, spears, pole arms—all crafted well and kept ready. Polished blades, leather-wrapped grips, edges that had not dulled from neglect. A small armory, and not ceremonial.

In the corner stood a suit of steel plate—the same one worn by the big man he had seen earlier in the day. The armor stood on a wooden stand like a sentinel watching over its brothers.

Belaric was about to turn away when something on the back wall caught his eye.

This version emphasizes the difference between the weapons, which makes Belaric's choice feel more deliberate and intelligent.

He crossed the room, weaving between racks and blades. A section of the wall was dedicated to more personal weapons—smaller, faster, made for precision rather than strength. Daggers, throwing knives, and a short row of hatchets, each held in place by iron hooks.

He pulled the kitchen knife from its sheath. The edge still chipped, and the balance was slightly off in his grip. Good enough for a street kill, but a liability for what came next.

His eyes settled on the new ones. The daggers were finely made—several inches long, narrow-bladed with a slight curve at the tip. Forged for quick strikes and clean exits. Not too heavy. Balanced for speed. He ran a thumb along the edge of one and smiled. This was a tool of his trade.

He took two. He strapped them to his hips, feeling the familiar, comfortable weight of a proper weapon. The kitchen knife was now useless; he slipped it into a sheath on his lower back, a last-ditch option.

Next, he turned to the throwing knives. Simple, elegant tools. No gilding. No pointless decoration. Forged from dark steel, honed to perfection. Each was nearly identical in length and weight—designed by someone who understood what they were for.

He picked one up and tested the balance with a flick of the wrist. The weight was perfect; the grip secure. He moved with the ease of a man who had done this a thousand times. He grabbed several, tucking one up each sleeve, securing two to his ribs with a thin leather strap, and sliding a final one into each boot. They vanished from sight, their weight a familiar, comforting presence.

Once he was satisfied, he slipped back into the corridor and eased the armory door shut, the quiet click of the latch echoing loudly in the sudden silence. He held his breath for a long moment, listening for any shift in the air, any whisper of a response from the house. When nothing came, he let out a slow, silent breath.

The next door offered no resistance. He pushed it inward, and a dense, earthy scent of damp wood and old straw greeted him. He could feel the bristled heads and smooth handles pressed together in the dark.

A broom closet.

He sighed through his nose, a sound of bitter amusement more than annoyance. "Why do I always find the damn brooms?" he muttered, a wisp of a joke he had told himself a thousand times. He shook his head, a ghost of a smile on his lips, and kept moving, his steps hushed and deliberate, his mind already recalculating the layout of the manor.

At the end of the corridor, the hall turned sharply. The floor changed—stone giving way to a plush rug woven in deep reds and golds. The walls were polished stone, smoother here, touched by wealth. A portrait hung in a bronze frame—Lord and Lady Haldren, younger, standing beside each other in high fashion. Lady Haldren held a baby in her arms. The child's eyes were bright, even through paint.

The corridor opened wide. To his left, a set of stairs climbed upward into shadow. Across from them stood a grand door, oak and iron-banded, slightly ajar. Beyond that, another corridor stretched deeper into the estate.

He started toward the stairs, but a sudden creak of wood froze him in place.

"Come, Mother. You promised! One game of Crown's Fall," the voice was young, excited.

An older woman laughed gently. "It is never just one game with you, and you know it."

"But you said—" the younger voice started.

"Fine, fine. I will not take it easy on you this time," the older woman said.

The girl snorted. "Oh, you mean you will not lose in fifteen moves again?"

"I only let you win that time," the woman countered.

Footsteps creaked above—they were coming down.

He had no time to think. Belaric moved fast.

He slipped to the grand door, pushed it just enough to slide inside, and closed it behind him. Softly. Quiet as a breath.

He turned and took in the room.

A hearth flickered at the far end, orange light casting warmth across the space. Bookshelves lined the left wall, tall and full. A polished table sat near the fire, and on it was a Crown's Fall board—each square laid with glass tiles, the wooden game pieces arranged mid-match. The board was a thing of beauty, carved to make war seem elegant—soldiers, siege towers, keeps, and kings.

Two high-backed chairs faced the table.

The room smelled faintly of old parchment and lavender smoke.

Belaric moved right toward the shadows near the wall. Several thick beams rose to support a narrow balcony that overlooked the room. He eyed the lowest beam, took two steps, and jumped.

His fingers caught the edge. His shoulder flared in protest, but he pulled himself up, hand over hand, and slipped onto the balcony floor. He crouched low, tucked into shadow.

Moments later, the door creaked open.

A young girl entered barefoot and smiling, tugging her mother by the hand. The faint torchlight caught the intricate lines etched across her forehead. The Valasar mark was unmistakable even in the dimness.

Lady Haldren and her daughter Lyra.

They wore flowing nightgowns, white and soft, trailing behind them as they walked. The girl moved impatiently, dragging her mother toward the board like a commander leading a charge.

Belaric watched, breath low, muscles still. His hand never strayed far from his dagger—but not for them. He was here to protect, not to harm.

He tilted his head. Crown's Fall. He hated the game. He always had. A mess of rules and counters, walls and sieges, and no room for instinct. But this child looked excited to play, as if it were the grandest thing in the world.

Lady Haldren laughed. "Always so eager."

"Of course, Mother. You and Sir Tolman are the only ones who can challenge me. He almost won a few times." Lyra told her.

Lady Haldren smiled faintly. "He is a bright man. I hope he feels better soon. It is not like him to fall sick."

Lyra's face fell slightly. "Yeah… he seemed fine, then almost collapsed. Maybe I can bring him some soup tomorrow. Might help."

Lady Haldren placed a hand on her daughter's shoulder. "He would like that, I am sure. Now go on—set the board."

Lyra grinned and dashed to the table, immediately rearranging pieces with both hands.

Her mother moved to the hearth and added several logs. Sparks flared, and shadows danced across the walls.

"What defense will you go with this time, Mother?" Lyra asked.

Lady Haldren turned, eyes glinting. "Oh, you will see, dear."

The two sat across from each other, game pieces in hand, as the fire cracked and the game began.

Belaric watched from the shadows above as the two played. He but quickly set to making his final preparations.

The first game lasted twenty-seven moves. Lyra won.

"Ha! Got your queen again," she grinned, sliding a carved soldier into the heart of her mother's defenses.

Lady Haldren leaned back with a mock sigh. "Again? And here I was, thinking I had you cornered."

"You always think that. Then I take your keep and end it," Lyra said, grinning.

"Remind me never to let you near the war table when you are older," her mother told her.

Lyra grinned. "Too late."

They laughed—light and genuine, something rare and golden in a world too eager to smother such things.

Lady Haldren leaned forward, gathering the pieces. "One more. And this time, I will not let you win."

"You say that every time," Lyra teased, already setting her defense.

He watched them for several minutes. Belaric found himself smiling. Not for the game, but for the ease of it. He watched Lyra with something close to longing, and for the first time in days, he let himself wonder.

Would I ever sit like that with my son? Teach him a game? Lose on purpose and pretend I did not?

He almost missed it. A flicker—barely more than a breath—in the corner of his eye. Movement. Low. Shadow within shadow, slipping through the doorway.

Belaric's muscles tensed. He rose slowly from his crouch, staying tucked in the dark. Below, Lyra leapt from her chair with both arms raised.

"Yes! I win!" the young girl shouted.

His eyes snapped to her—then back. There. A glint of steel cut through the firelight.

Belaric drew a throwing knife in one smooth motion and hurled it downward—not at the figure, but at the arc of steel glinting through the air. A heartbeat later, metal rang out—his blade struck true, deflecting another in mid-flight. Two daggers clattered to the floor.

Lady Haldren jolted to her feet, eyes wide. She shoved Lyra behind her and stepped forward, gaze fixed on the fallen weapons. "Who is there?" she demanded. Her voice firm and unwavering.

A low laugh answered her. Slow. Seductive. Dripping with confidence. "Well… I did not expect that one. Who could have done that, I wonder?"

The voice stepped forward.

She emerged from the shadows like mist given shape. A dark cape trailed behind her, boots silent on the wood. She wore the same garb as Belaric—stitched leather, tight at the joints, weighted for speed and death. The only difference was the mask she wore, pale and smooth, with a cruel smile carved into the wood. Belaric no longer wore one.

Her eyes lifted, finding him easily in the dark above.

"Will you not come down?" she purred. "We can play a game like theirs."

Belaric sighed and stood. He stepped toward the railing, looking down at them.

Lady Haldren followed her gaze, eyes climbing toward the balcony. She froze.

Her mouth parted slightly, breath shallow, a flicker of fear crossing her face. One arm extended in front of Lyra beside her—reflexive, protective. Her gaze darted between the two strangers—one above, one ahead—each dressed in death's clothing.

"Who are you?" she demanded, voice tight with alarm. "What is this?"

Neither figure answered.

He stepped onto the railing and dropped. He hit the ground with a heavy thud, then rolled to his feet with the grace of old training. Belaric refused to show weakness. Not here. Not now.

His eyes swept to Lady Haldren and Lyra, then locked on the assassin. The woman tilted her head, the carved grin on her mask unmoving—but her laughter spilled through it, sharp and musical.

"Ahhh... Varros," she said, her voice curling around the name. "How lucky for me. We all thought you had found a hole to crawl into and die. But instead... you came to me."

Belaric sighed. "Aeryn Kael."

One of the Order's deadliest. Swift as the wind, precise as poison. She had risen faster than any before her, and many whispered she would be the next First Shadow—heir to the Vowkeeper's mantle. She was no bluff. No amateur.

The image of the training hall flared in his mind. The way she had stood over the boy, no more than thirteen, his face bloody and his ribs likely broken. She had not offered a hand, only a cold rebuke for his weakness. He had known then the boy would not live through the night. She was a weapon that felt no remorse, a blade that never dulled. He had always hated her for it, and now he was reminded why.

"Still sick as I remember. But I see madness has joined you," he spat.

She laughed louder now. "Madness? No. Just purpose. You always mistook the two." She stepped lightly over the fallen daggers. "We thought you were dead. The Vowkeeper offered a reward to whoever found your body. Imagine his joy when I return with your head."

Belaric's grip tightened.

Lady Haldren's voice cut through the tension. "What is the meaning of this?"

Belaric did not turn fully—his eyes never left Aeryn—but he spoke clearly. "My lady... this is Aeryn Kael. She has come to kill you. And Lyra. And anyone else in her way. I am here to see that does not happen."

Lady Haldren stared at him, her arms tight around Lyra, as if the name alone could explain the madness unfolding in front of her. Her mouth opened, but no words came.

Before she could speak, Aeryn interrupted. "Oh, they will die tonight. And you, Varros—you betrayed the Order. You know the price for failure."

Belaric felt the heat rise in his chest but forced it down. "My only failure was not leaving years ago. Tonight, you and the Order will know the weight of what you have done. I will carve my vengeance into your bones. And when I find him—he will die screaming for what he took from me. For the blood he spilled. For the child he stole."

Aeryn's laugh turned sharp. "Still dreaming, I see. You are a fool, Varros. But I will be a hero when I bring back your head."

She drew her twin blades in one smooth motion. Steel sang as it left the sheath.

Belaric turned slightly, speaking low and fast. "Lady Haldren—you have no reason to trust me. But if you call your guards, they will only die trying to help. She is not a foe they are ready for. Let me do what I came to do."

Lady Haldren said nothing. Her arms tightened around Lyra.

Belaric stepped forward and drew the twin daggers he had taken from the armory. Their weight felt right in his hands.

Aeryn tilted her head. "You always did look the part—pity you never fought like it."

Belaric spat at her feet.

Aeryn's laughter died.

The room went still.

Two assassins stood facing one another—past and present, betrayal and devotion. Then, without warning, they exploded into motion.

They met in a blur of steel.

Aeryn struck first—two quick slashes aimed low and rising. Belaric turned with them, letting her blades kiss the air. He countered with a feint to the ribs, but she pivoted, already gone, sliding past him like smoke. Their daggers hissed as they moved, fast and sharp, the air between them whistling with missed death.

Aeryn was faster.

She pressed in again—high, then low, then a spinning cut toward his throat. Belaric ducked the first, caught the second on the flat of his blade, and dropped under the third, rolling across the rug and coming up in a crouch. He knew her grin widened beneath the mask.

"Is this your grand new life, Varros?" she hissed, her voice cutting through the air. "A lapdog for a noblewoman? You used to be an Ashen Blade. Now you are just a beggar wearing a stolen cloak. The old life was not good enough for you, was it? Or did you just lack the guts for it in the end? I hear you are soft now. The whispers say you have a conscience." She spat.

Belaric refused to rise to her taunt.

She came again. Left, right, left—strikes too fast to track. Belaric retreated one step at a time, absorbing the rhythm, watching for flaws. There were none. She flowed from form to form, each motion honed by years under the Order's cruel eye.

They had sparred once, years ago. Then, she had grinned when she drew blood. Now? She wanted his throat.

He blocked a thrust toward his heart and pivoted around her shoulder, slashing low. She twisted, avoided it, and drove her elbow toward his head. He ducked. Her knee came up. He caught it with his forearm, gritting his teeth as pain surged through the bone—just as her blade flashed and nicked across his ribs.

He hissed. A shallow cut, but it burned like fire.

Then he struck—two jabs toward her midsection. She caught one with her blade, deflected the other, and kicked at his legs. He hopped back narrowly, avoiding a sweep that would have taken him down.

They broke apart.

Across the room, Lady Haldren stared in wide-eyed horror.

She had seen blades drawn before—guardsmen sparring, a drunken duel once in her youth—but never anything like this. This was not combat. This was death in motion. Silent, precise, practiced.

She stepped back, trying to shield Lyra with her body, one arm outstretched as if that alone could protect her daughter from what was happening in front of them.

Lyra clutched at her mother's gown, eyes fixed on the two figures locked in deadly rhythm.

The fire cracked. Shadows danced across the stone.

Belaric was breathing harder now. Not ragged, but controlled. She did not seem winded at all.

"You have slowed," Aeryn said, pacing around him like a cat playing with a mouse. "The Order was right to take the boy. Look at you. This is what weakness looks like. Your son will never be as pathetic. One day, he will wear the mask and curse your name, and the whore who birthed him."

The words sank deep, sharper than any blade.

Belaric's jaw clenched. Rage stirred in his chest—hot, immediate—but he crushed it down. She wanted him reckless. Unthinking. Easy. He gave her none of it.

His voice was low. Controlled. Meant to hurt.

"You were never a true assassin, Aeryn. Just a whore with a blade—crawling into every master's bed, hoping they had mistaken sweat for talent. The only reason the Order kept you around was how easily you spread your legs," he spat.

That got a reaction. Her stance stiffened, only for a moment, but he saw it. She came in hard, her anger driving the speed.

Belaric dropped low beneath her strike and kicked out, sweeping her ankle. She jumped over it, caught herself, and flipped into a reverse stab aimed at his gut. He parried just in time. The force of it vibrated through his wrist—just as her off-hand dagger slipped in and carved a line across his upper thigh.

He grunted, the warmth of blood soaking into the fabric. Still shallow. Still bleeding.

They broke apart.

Then clashed again. Blades met with sharp, ringing notes. He twisted to avoid her first cut, leaned back from the second. He caught a strike on his crossguard, shoved it wide, and jabbed—missed. Her dagger slashed across his chest. He blocked. Another jab. Another dodge. With a flick of her wrist and he felt a sting across his forearm.

Each strike was faster than the last. They were no longer thinking—just reacting, instinct ruling the space between them.

Sweat beaded on his brow. His shoulder ached. His thigh flared with heat. His forearm was bleeding now, lines of red soaking through the wrap. None of the wounds would kill him. Not yet. But they were adding up.

He had to end this. Soon.

She lunged—overextended, greedy. He saw it a breath before it came. This was the opening.

Belaric stepped into it.

He turned his body just enough to narrow his profile and drove his dagger in a tight arc toward her ribs. Her blade came across his shoulder—he felt the sting, the bright flare of pain as steel cut deep. Heat bloomed. Blood ran in thick pulses down his arm—but he did not stop.

His blade struck true. A line of red bloomed along the side of her arm, cutting through leather and flesh alike.

Aeryn hissed, her first sound of pain.

Then, her boot slammed into his chest.

He stumbled back, breath knocked from him. His shoulder screamed. He caught himself before he fell, one foot skidding on the rug as he slid into a crouch near the hearth.

She flexed her wounded arm, testing it; he knew the smile behind her mask was gone.

They stared at each other. Then a slow grin formed on Belaric's face as his eyes moved to the cut on her arm. She tracked his gaze, looking at the gash.

"You think that matters?" Aeryn spat, chest heaving. "One lucky cut from a coward who ran from the vow. I have already won. You will die bleeding, and your son will be made in my image."

Belaric rubbed the ache blossoming across his ribs, feeling the throb of bruised bone where her boot had landed. He did not answer. Not yet. She was faster. Her blade work cleaner. She had drawn more blood.

But she had made a mistake.

He started to laugh—low and bitter.

Aeryn stepped forward, daggers loose in her hands, flickering with the last of her confidence. "Is your death funny?" she hissed. "I will make it slow. I will carve your screams into the stone."

Belaric chuckled again. Darker this time. "You are the fool, Aeryn. I have already won," he said, sheathing the daggers.

Her head tilted. That mask of arrogance faltered. "You have won nothing, you bastard." She turned her blade toward Lady Haldren and Lyra. "Maybe I will kill them first… make you watch."

The laughter vanished from his voice.

"You thought I was slow. You thought I was broken. But you misjudged me." His voice dropped, cold and sharp. "I knew they would send someone good. So I prepared. You should have remembered."

"Remembered what?" she snapped, suddenly breathing heavier, sweat beading at her brow.

"That I was Varros… the master of poison," he declared.

Her head jerked at the gash on her arm. She stared at it, wide-eyed, as if only just now feeling the burn in her veins.

"No," she whispered. "It is not… possible…" she stammered.

Belaric smiled. It was a cruel thing. "Look who is scared now," Belaric said cruelly. "You feel it, do you not? The heat crawling into your muscles. The weakness in your hands. Your strength is fading second by second."

"You… you lying piece of—" She staggered, breath hitching.

"I only needed one cut," he said. "And you gave it to me."

Aeryn screamed in defiance and rushed forward, blades extended. It was a wild charge—sloppy, desperate.

Belaric slapped her weapon aside and caught her by the throat, slamming her to the ground with a grunt of effort. Her body hit hard, the air wrenching from her lungs. He straddled her chest and pinned her arms down, forcing her twitching wrists against the floor as she thrashed beneath him.

"Get off me!" she shrieked. "I will kill you—!"

He tore the mask off her face.

The poison was doing its work. Her skin had gone pale. Her eyes wept red—thin trails of blood leaking down her temples. Her lips trembled as she tried to curse him, but her voice cracked.

"Remember my face, Aeryn," he growled, voice low and trembling with fury. "Know that it was I who killed you. And know this—I will kill every one of you. One by one. For Renna. For my son."

"Die, bastard!" she screamed.

He leaned close.

"Enjoy death, bitch." He snarled.

He pulled one of the daggers free. Then he drove it straight into her stomach.

She howled, arching beneath him, blood pouring from her mouth. She tried to speak, to curse, to spit—but the words gurgled into a moan.

Belaric twisted the blade and drove it up—through ribs, through lung.

She coughed blood onto his face.

He did not blink.

With both hands, he wrenched the dagger higher into her heart. Her scream died in her throat. Her back arched one final time before her body went limp. Her eyes fluttered, then closed, blood still leaking from the corners.

He held there a moment longer, breath heaving. Then he pulled the blade free with a wet, tearing sound and wiped it clean on the dark folds of her cloak.

Slowly, he rose to his feet. His shoulder throbbed. His thigh burned. Blood trickled down his arm in steady drops. He swayed for a moment, lightheaded, his breath dragging through clenched teeth.

But he did not fall.

He turned.

Lady Haldren and Lyra stood frozen in the corner. Lyra still clung to her mother's gown, face pale and eyes wide. Lady Haldren's expression was harder to read—shock, yes, but something deeper ran beneath it.

She flinched when Belaric's eyes met hers. Not fear—not entirely. But something close.

He wondered then if anything he said could make them believe him.

Belaric stared at them in silence. Then, with a slow breath, he pulled back his hood, revealing his full face.

Lady Haldren flinched. "Stay back, monster," she snapped, her voice cracking under the weight of fear. She stepped back and pulled Lyra behind her, arms spread protectively. Lyra's head peeked out from behind her mother, watching him with wide, unblinking eyes.

Belaric lowered his gaze. "My lady... I swear to you, I mean neither you nor your daughter harm. I acted only to ensure your survival." He saw the rage building behind her eyes. "You are a killer. An assassin," she hissed. "I will never believe a word from your mouth."

"You do not have to believe my words," he said quietly. "Believe my actions. She was the first they sent. She will not be the last. You are a threat to them now."

For a brief moment, something cracked through her anger. "Who are they?" she demanded. "And who the hell are you?"

"My name was stripped from me when I was a boy. To the Order, I was Varros. But in the world beyond them, I was once Belaric Kelmor. And they... they are the Black Vow—an order of assassins hidden beneath centuries of blood and silence."

Lady Haldren blinked, processing. She swayed slightly on her feet, a hand rising to her temple as if to steady herself against the shock. "The Black Vow? I have never heard of it. Why would assassins be targeting me?"

Belaric did not answer. Instead, he looked at Lyra. The girl's mouth opened slightly. "Me?" she whispered.

Lady Haldren followed his gaze, then looked back at him. "Yes," Belaric said softly. "Their true target is Lyra."

The words landed like a physical blow. Lady Haldren's face went slack with horror, and she stumbled backward, pulling Lyra with her. "But... why? She is a child."

"She is dangerous to them," Belaric said. "She is digging too deep into the Valasar. They fear what she might uncover—what she might expose. The two greatest secrets the nobility has kept hidden for generations."

"What secrets?" She asked, barely above a breath.

Belaric sighed. "The first is the Black Vow itself. Founded centuries ago to protect the lie—the illusion that only noble children can be born with a Valasar mark."

Lady Haldren's head snapped up. "What?" Her eyes, wide with fear, went to the intricate mark on her daughter's forehead. Her hands trembled as she stroked the child's brow.

"It is true. I served the Black Vow for twenty years. Their mission was simple: eliminate any common-born child that bore a Valasar mark—preferably before the mark could even be identified. I have killed more than I can count... families, infants... all to protect that lie. But your daughter, she has been asking the wrong questions. Questions that made them afraid. The upper nobility ordered her silenced."

Lady Haldren stepped back. "You... godless abomination." Her voice was trembling now, horror spreading across her features. "Leave this house and never return. If you do, I swear on the graves of those you have damned—I will see you hunted like the beast you are."

Belaric nodded slowly. He had not expected gratitude. Only the slimmest chance.

He turned to leave—but Lyra spoke up. "Why did you say it was for Renna and your son? Who is Renna?"

He paused. He had not expected that. "She was my wife," he said quietly.

"Was?" Lady Haldren scoffed. "What, did you kill her too?"

The words cut deeper. "No," Belaric said, voice tightening. "She died in childbirth."

Lady Haldren's eyes narrowed. "And your son?"

"They took him from me," Belaric said, his voice low, steady. "And I have sworn to kill every last one of them. The Order has branded me a traitor. They hunt me now."

He paused, letting the words settle like ash.

"The one who leads them—the Black Vow—he is known only as the Vowkeeper."

Lyra's eyes went wide. "Vowkeeper? The one who holds the vows?"

Lady Haldren turned sharply. "What are you talking about?"

"I saw it, Mother," Lyra said. "In that old book we found in the capital's library. It had strange entries—old stories, maybe. But one mentioned someone called the Vowkeeper."

Belaric's voice turned urgent. "Destroy that book. If it holds other truths, they will hunt you even harder."

He took a painful step forward, his weight shifting onto his good leg. "I do not know why they took my son," he admitted. "But he was born with the Valasar mark on his spine. The Vowkeeper said he would use him. For what, I do not yet fully know for what. But I must find him before it is too late."

Lady Haldren crossed her arms. Her initial rage was gone, replaced by a cold, calculating fear. "So why come here? We do not have your son. We do not know this Vowkeeper."

Belaric smiled faintly. "You are as clever as they say. I hoped that if I saved you, your mother might agree to work with me."

"Work with an assassin?" Lady Haldren scoffed. "Never. I would never order a death. I am not like you."

"I would never ask that of you," Belaric said. "I have heard much about you. The town speaks well of you, my lady. You have their trust. Their respect."

Her voice hardened. "Then what do you want from us?"

"They will come again. Once she does not report in, they will send others. I know how they think. I know how they kill. I can protect you both."

Lady Haldren let out a dry laugh. "We do not need an assassin. We have Sir Tolman. One of the greatest knights I have ever known."

Belaric's tone dropped. "If I do not get to him soon, he will be dead. She poisoned him."

Lady Haldren stiffened. Her hands, which had been fisted at her sides, fell limp. "That is not possible," she said, though a flicker of doubt crossed her face. "When did he fall ill?"

Lyra looked up. "We had just finished lunch."

Lady Haldren looked between her daughter and Belaric. "How do I know you did not poison him? You admitted you were a master of it."

Belaric shrugged, wincing as the motion sent a jolt of pain through his shoulder. "I did. But I had no reason to poison Tolman. And I can save him. If I do not, he will be dead within five hours."

Lady Haldren did not respond. She was weighing it all, fighting against her instincts—and her fear.

"Please, Mother," Lyra said, voice quiet now. "He has always protected us. Let us protect him."

Lady Haldren closed her eyes. When they opened, they were colder. Sharper. "If you save him… then what? Will you leave us in peace?"

"If that is your wish," Belaric said. He leaned against a bookshelf for support. "But they will return. I wish to work with you. I will protect you both, and in return, I ask for your help in finding the Vowkeeper—and my son."

Lady Haldren studied him, silent for several breaths. "You have said much tonight, assassin. I do not know how much is true. But if you save Tolman, I will listen. Just know—if you lie to me, I will use every contact I have to find you and see you dead."

Belaric lowered himself onto one knee. It was a slow, painful descent, not a sign of deference. "My lady," he said quietly, "I swear to you, on my vengeance and on the memory of my wife and son, I will not fail."

There was a beat of silence.

"Spare me the theatrics," Lady Haldren said. "Save your oaths for the gods."

Lyra giggled.

Belaric rose slowly, still aching, blood drying on his arms. But there was something steadier in his breath.

"Thank you, my lady," he said.

"Do not thank me yet," she muttered. "Now go. Save Tolman."

16

Aeryn Kael lay lifeless on her back, arms at her sides like a soldier laid to rest—though there was no peace in her expression, only the slack-jawed silence of a failed killer. The wound was a brutal thing, a single upward tear that had opened her from belly to breast, tunic riven and clinging crimson to her skin. Blood had spread beneath her, thick and glistening, pooling into the grooves of the wooden floor like black roots seeking soil. From Aeryn's mouth, the final spill of red had dried in a broken line across her cheek. Blood still wept from the corners of her eyes and ears, slow and stubborn, as if her body had not yet accepted the truth.

Belaric stood over her without ceremony, breath still unsteady. A line of pain pulsed through his shoulder, warm and wet beneath the leather. He reached up, winced at the sting. Aeryn's blade had bitten deep, and he would need to bind it before he lost too much blood.

He knelt beside her body. With his blade, he cut a strip from the edge of her cloak—just wide enough to wrap. The fabric was thick but intact, one of the few parts of her clothing untouched by blood. He wound it tightly around his upper arm and shoulder, binding the cut with one hand and clenched teeth. It was not pretty, but it would hold.

Then, with his wound compressed and breath steadied, he began his search.

His hands moved with calm precision, fingers checking beneath her belt, inside her sleeves, and under the lining of her tunic—places only someone trained in death would think to look. Lady Haldren stepped closer, silent in her approach, watching him closely. Lyra tried to follow, but her mother caught her by the wrist and held her back.

At last, Belaric's fingers found a hidden seam near Aeryn's waist. He dug into the false lining and retrieved a small glass vial, no larger than a thumb joint. He uncorked it and brought it to his nose, inhaling.

No scent.

"Ah well, that answers that question," he muttered.

"I thought you said you knew what it was," Lady Haldren said, arms folded tightly across her chest.

"I did," he said, standing. "Needed to be certain. It was either Whiteshade or Cinderbane. One smells like damp earth. This has no scent. That makes it Cinderbane."

Lady Haldren frowned. "I do not know the name."

"It is a rather unpleasant poison. Most describe it as a fire in the blood—an agonizing heat that coils in the gut and spreads outward, searing nerves and soft tissue alike. The fever comes fast, violent and sudden, drenching the skin in sweat as the body tries—and fails—to purge the toxin. Muscles cramp. Vision blurs. Some scream; others choke on their own breath. And through it all, the burning never stops. It only deepens," he told them, his voice flat.

Lady Haldren stared, pale and motionless, her lips parted in stunned silence. One hand rose slowly to her mouth as if to keep from retching. Behind her, Lyra's eyes had gone wide, fixed on Belaric with a mixture of fear and awe—as if for the first time, she truly understood the kind of man who stood in their company.

Belaric held their gaze for a moment too long, then looked away. He had not meant to speak in such detail. Not here. Not like this. There was no pride in it—only memories better left buried. He drew a breath through his nose, sharp and shallow, and let it go.

He stood and turned toward the door, voice firmer now, more practical. "We can counter the effects. But I will need boiling water. And your garden."

She nodded grimly and shielded Lyra's eyes again as they moved past the corpse. "We will boil the water. No sense waking the others."

Belaric followed in silence, their footsteps softened by rug and stone. At the kitchen door, Lady Haldren and Lyra disappeared inside. He turned away, slipping into the cold night.

The air outside cut colder than he expected. Night still hung thick over the estate, the garden bathed in silver light from a half-veiled moon. Dew clung to everything—petals, leaves, even the stone underfoot—making each step slick and silent.

Belaric exhaled and scanned the garden. Beds of carefully arranged flora stretched out before him, wild in places, but not neglected. Someone tended them—someone who understood what lived and thrived and could kill here.

He moved to the edge of the nearest bed and crouched low beside a Velwyn Rose—its deep crimson petals curled inward like clenched fists, the dark green center swaying with the breeze. Its thorns were long and pale, like teeth pulled from something that should have stayed buried. He clipped a single bloom, careful to avoid the thorns, and wrapped it in cloth.

The movement sent a sharp pulse through his shoulder. He hissed through clenched teeth and pressed a hand against the makeshift wrap. The warmth of blood trickled through it. He ignored it. No time for tending wounds.

The Windfern grew just beyond clustered, unruly fronds. Its long fronds brushed against his arms as he stepped through. He reached out and stripped several of the leaves, the damp texture cool against his fingertips. Every twist of his arm made the muscles around the wound flare, but he worked through it with a grim efficiency.

Last came the Ironbud. He knelt again—slower this time, breathing measured. The unopened flower was tucked low beneath the others, its dark blue bud gleaming like ink in the moonlight. It bloomed only once a year. He found one still sealed and plucked it carefully.

For a moment, he remained crouched there in the moonlight, holding the flower, the scent of blood and iron mixing with the crisp smell of earth. His shoulder throbbed in time with his heartbeat. The wind stirred, cold and clean.

One more life to save.

He stood with a grunt, pain blooming fresh in his side, and walked back toward the manor.

Inside, the pot was already boiling. Lady Haldren and Lyra spoke in hushed tones, but fell silent when Belaric reentered. He said nothing, only took a bowl from the shelf and set it down.

The two ladies watched him closely. Lady Haldren with suspicion and Lyra with curiosity.

He began with the Velwyn Rose. Thorns first—plucked with care, though the strain in his shoulder made every movement slower, tighter. Then he squeezed the stem over the bowl, and dark sap bled in sluggish drops.

Next came the Windfern, torn by hand and dropped in. His fingers trembled slightly, not from nerves, but from the pull of torn muscle and blood loss.

The unopened Ironbud took the longest. He set it down carefully and worked the blade's edge beneath its sealed petals, prying them apart with painstaking care. When the seed at last came free, he let it fall into the bowl like a final offering.

He took a spoon and began crushing the mixture—slow, deliberate strokes, each one sending pain down his back like a jolt of fire. But he did not stop. Would not stop. The paste thickened as he worked; the scent rising—bitter, sharp, medicinal.

He stepped to the pot, scooped three spoonfuls of boiling water, and poured them in. Steam curled up in fragrant spirals as he stirred.

Then, without hesitation, he reached into one of his pockets and withdrew a tiny glass vial filled with fine white powder.

Lyra tilted her head. "What is that?"

"Bone dust," Belaric said with a faint smile. "And no, it is not made from bones."

She looked a little disappointed.

"It is a poison," he added.

Lady Haldren's tone sharpened. "We said save him, not kill him faster."

"I am," Belaric replied, not looking up. "It is powerful, yes—but in small amounts, it counters other toxins. Like striking a match in smoke. Burns, but clears the air."

He pinched two flecks of the dust into the bowl and stirred again. "It is ready. Where is he?"

Without a word, Lady Haldren took Lyra by the hand and led the way. Belaric followed, the bowl still warm in his grip.

They left the kitchen and entered the corridor beyond, dimly lit by sconces burning low with orange flame. The hush of the manor pressed around them—stone floors softened by carpet, long shadows stretching from every doorway. No servants. No guards.

Too quiet.

Belaric's steps were light, but each one made his shoulder flare with pain. He shifted the bowl to his uninjured side, jaw clenched against the throb.

Lyra glanced back over her shoulder. "Why did you join the Order?"

Belaric let out a low chuckle, but there was no humor in it. "I did not," he said.

"My mother left me." His voice had grown quiet, edged with something brittle. "She was a beggar—barely enough coin to feed herself, let alone a child. She used to tell me my father was a drunk bastard. He vanished the moment he found out she was pregnant. Never saw his face. Never even knew his name."

He paused, jaw tightening.

"And when I got old enough to beg on my own, she disappeared, too. No goodbye. No warning. Just gone. Left me to rot in the gutters of Vorinfall, like I was nothing. Like I had never mattered at all," he said.

His voice was calm, flat—like someone reciting another man's life.

"The Order found me not long after," he said. "Told me I would be fed. Said I would be safe. I believed them. For a day."

Lyra's hand tightened around her mother's, knuckles pale.

"Then I saw the truth. Saw what they were. What they made us do. What they trained us to become." His voice thinned. "I ran."

"The first time… they beat me with cords until I could not stand. Said I would not last a week beyond their gates."

Lady Haldren's jaw clenched. She said nothing, but her eyes, fixed on Belaric, were hard with fury.

"The second time, they shattered my fingers. Locked me in a pit so dark I forgot what my hands looked like. No food. No light. Just the sound of my own breathing."

"Third time, they did not bother with threats. Just told me the truth." He swallowed. "That I had no choice."

He paused, jaw clenched, breath uneven.

"I still tried to run, anyway."

"They caught me at the door. One step from the wind and the sun. They broke my ribs, split my lip, crushed something inside I never got back. I pissed blood for days. Could not move for a week."

Their footsteps echoed now as they climbed the stone stairs. A steady rhythm. Like a drumbeat before a hanging.

"After that… I stopped running. Stopped thinking like a person. I feared death more than I feared them. So I did what they wanted."

He looked down, voice barely a breath.

"I became the thing they needed."

Lyra had stopped walking. Shock and sadness plainly showed on her face.

Lady Haldren turned sharply, voice tight. "While your story is… enlightening, I would prefer you not share it with my daughter."

Belaric lowered his gaze. "My apologies, my lady. I was not thinking."

Lady Haldren stood still for a breath, then resumed walking. Her grip on Lyra's hand did not loosen.

She said nothing else as they reached the top of the stairs. The hall stretched left and right—silent, empty. He noticed again the lack of posted guards and wondered if Aeryn had left more than one corpse in her wake.

Lady Haldren turned left and approached the first door. She knocked softly. "Sir Tolman? Are you awake?"

No answer.

She hesitated, then eased the door open.

The room was simple. A large bed, a chest, a writing desk, and a few weapons lined neatly on the wall. Sir Tolman lay atop the covers, bare-chested, his skin slick with sweat. His arms were thick with muscle, his chest broad and hairy. His head was shaved clean—not from age, but from ritual, on purpose. A soldier's look. And yet now, all that strength trembled faintly beneath the fever.

Belaric moved past them and knelt beside the bed. He checked Sir Tolman's brow, his eyes, his tongue, then looked back at Lady Haldren.

"He will live. But he will need rest to recover. Someone has to watch him."

"I will assign—"

"No," Belaric cut in. "It has to be me. If he changes, I need to act right then. A delay could kill him. You will not have time to send a runner to the inn or the dungeon."

Lady Haldren exhaled. "Fine. Just save him."

Belaric sat beside the bed and lifted the bowl to Tolman's lips. "Sir Tolman," he said softly, "this will help. It will burn, but you need to drink."

He tilted the bowl slowly. The liquid slipped past Sir Tolman's lips. He gagged but managed to swallow. Then again. And again. Belaric watched his throat, saw the tension ease slightly.

"Good," he murmured. "Now we wait."

Lady Haldren's voice was tight. "We will talk in the morning. Come, Lyra. You are with me tonight."

Lyra groaned. "What about the body?"

"We will lock the door. Let the dead wait," Lady Haldren said.

As they turned to go, Lyra lingered. "Thank you, Belaric. For saving us. And him."

He gave her a tired smile. "Thank you, Lyra."

"That is enough," her mother said, and led her out.

The door shut behind them with a quiet click.

Belaric let out a breath and moved to the far wall, sliding down until his back met the cold stone. The bowl sat beside him, still faintly warm.

The first part of his plan had worked.

Somewhat.

But the cost had not finished being counted yet.

Belaric sat for hours, the dark pressing close around him. His eyes drifted often to the slow rise and fall of Sir Tolman's chest, to the bowl cooling beside him, to the closed door that separated them from the rest of a world gone quietly hostile. But his thoughts refused to settle.

He needed to decide what came next. Something more than survival. Influence. Leverage. He sifted through possibilities, none perfect. Several workable. But would Lady Haldren even agree to any of them?

His thoughts drifted unbidden to Renna.

He closed his eyes and saw her—standing barefoot in his empty home, laughing at the bare walls and silence. She had filled it with warmth and color before the first week had passed. Their first kiss. The first time he had told her he loved her, awkward and fumbling, spoken like it was a confession of guilt instead of affection. She had smiled then—tucked her hand into his and said it back like it was the simplest truth in the world.

He missed her so deeply it hurt.

His lips moved in silence, offering a prayer not to gods but to her. *I will find him, Renna. I will take our son away from this. From all of it. I swear it.*

The moon shifted through the window slats, dragging pale light across the stone floor. Occasionally, Belaric stood to stretch the stiffness from his joints. Every movement sent a dull ache through his left side.

He sat back down with a quiet breath, then peeled away the blood-dried edge of the cloak cloth tied around his shoulder. The bleeding had stopped, but the wound still burned—deep and angry beneath the skin. He re-tied it with slow, practiced fingers, pulling the knot tight with a grimace.

He would need a proper bandage soon. Aeryn's cloak had done enough to stop the bleeding, but it was not a long-term solution. The other wounds still needed tending, and for that, he would need his packs—though he could afford to wait a little longer. He sat back against the wall and let the silence reclaim the room.

Sir Tolman's breathing remained steady—he had made it through the night. The worst was behind him.

Now came the slow climb back.

It was just before dawn when the door creaked open.

Belaric was on his feet in an instant, hand resting on the hilt at his side. He relaxed when he saw the familiar figure slip through the doorway and close it quietly behind her.

Lady Haldren's eyes flicked to his weapon. "Must you?"

He eased his hand away. "Old habits," he said. "My apologies, my lady."

She said nothing, only crossed the room and placed a hand gently on Sir Tolman's brow. "He is still warm. Are you certain he will live?"

Belaric nodded. "He is through the worst. He will need rest and water, but he will recover. My only concern is a delayed reaction. Rare, but it happens."

She nodded once, eyes lingering on Tolman. "He has been with me for years. Protected my husband until his last breath. Then me. Then Lyra. I leaned on him more than I knew." She turned to face Belaric. "Thank you—for saving him. For saving us."

He said nothing, but offered her a small nod.

"I could not sleep," she continued, voice dropping. "Every time I closed my eyes, I imagined another shadow in the corner. Another dagger coming towards us, coming towards her."

"I am sorry you had to feel that," Belaric said quietly. "I knew they would come—I just did not know who, or when. But I figured they would go for her first. That is why I was waiting there." He told her, his voice low.

Lady Haldren's eyes sharpened. "And Lyra? Did you expect her to see it?"

He hesitated, jaw tight. "I did… but not like that. I lost control. It was not just the fight. It was everything. Losing my son, my wife. My life was collapsing around me. And then Aeryn standing there—mocking me, trying to finish what the Order started. She did not take everything, but she represented it. And in that moment, I—"

He looked away; the words catching on his tongue.

"I did not want Lyra to see what I was. No child should have to watch something like that. I wish she had not." He murmured.

Lady Haldren studied him for a long moment. "What you are… sickens me, Belaric. The lives you have taken. The things you have done—there is no excuse for any of it. No mercy in me for men who kill children."

Her voice wavered—not with uncertainty, but with restrained fury. Then softened, just barely.

"But I would not wish the life you have endured on anyone. And gods help me... a part of me is grateful you survived it. Because if you had not, my daughter and I would be dead."

She took a breath. "I can not say I trust you. I do not know if I ever will. But I said I would listen. So—speak. What would you have me do?"

A flicker stirred in his chest. Not quite hope. But close enough.

"I have thought it through. First, we need to explain Aeryn's body. We say an assassin came for you. Sir Tolman fought her off and killed her, but was wounded in the fight."

She frowned. "Why Tolman? Why not the truth?"

"Because it gives us time. The Order will not believe Sir Tolman bested one of their top assassins. They will send more—quietly at first—to investigate. But if word spreads of another assassin, they will assume it was me. No need for questions. No need for subtlety. They will come in force with one goal—to kill us all. This way, the lie slows them down."

Lady Haldren tilted her head, confusion written on her face. "Time for what?" she asked.

Belaric looked at her, his face serious. "Time to prepare for the next attack, build alliances where we can, and gather as much information as we can."

Lady Haldren nodded, understanding his plan. She turned and looked at Sir Tolman lying on the bed.

"Tolman will not lie. His honor will not allow it," she said.

"I understand. But this lie protects you and your daughter. If he refuses, ask him if his honor is worth your life," Belaric countered.

Lady Haldren continued to look at Sir Tolman, saying nothing.

Belaric continued, "Once word spreads of what happened, they will rally to you. The common folk trust you—many love you. This will not just spark outrage. It will feel personal. Like someone attacked one of their own. They will demand justice. And they will stand with you to see it done," he paused, watching her closely.

Lady Haldren turned to him and raised a brow. "And the nobles?"

"The highborn will feign outrage," he said. "They will come offering concern, protection, sympathy. But they will test you. Probing for weakness. Trying to gauge what you know—who you suspect."

"The minor houses will be different. More afraid than curious. If they think nobles are being targeted, they will wonder if they are next. That fear is something we can use. Push the idea of unity—safety in numbers. Offer them a place at your table, a voice in your decisions. They will come, not out of loyalty, but survival."

He stepped a little closer. "You will claim you are being cautious. That another attempt might come. You will need more guards—I will be among them. I will need to be close; you will need to name me as one of your personal bodyguards, serving alongside Sir Tolman."

She tilted her head. "You are good with daggers. But can you use a sword?"

Belaric gave a short laugh. "Trained in most weapons. Maybe not like Tolman, but I will not embarrass you."

She nodded slowly. "And Tolman? If we say he succeeded where he failed, he will see that as a deeper shame."

"I know. But the truth is riskier. This lie buys us time," he told her.

Lady Haldren sighed. "I will speak to him when he wakes. I just hope he forgives me." She looked back at Belaric. "That is not the entire plan, is it?"

He shook his head. "You will play the grieving noble, seeking answers. That is what they will expect. They will invite you into their homes, offer support, but always with questions beneath their smiles. You give them just enough to feel in control. And while you talk, I will be listening. Finding leverage."

His eyes darkened.

"Then we hunt," he said, voice low and sharp. "We find every Order loyalist, every name tied to the Black Vow, and we cut them down. No mercy. No exceptions. We carve a path in blood to the Vowkeeper himself—and when he falls, I take back what they stole. I take back my son."

She shook her head faintly. "You make it sound so easy."

"There is nothing easy about it," he said. "They will come for you. Again and again. You will need to be strong. For Lyra. And for yourself."

She was quiet for a moment, then looked him in the eye. "What is your son's name?"

The question had caught him off guard. Belaric lowered his gaze. "Eryndorr."

A small smile touched her lips. "It is a beautiful name. Did you or your wife choose it?"

"I did," he said softly. "It came to me a few days before he was born. She liked it right away."

"I am sure you will find him," she said. Her voice was gentle, but her next words came sharper. "But what happens if I say no?"

The answer sat heavy in his chest. "Then I will keep my word. I will leave you in peace. But I still suggest hiring more guards."

She stepped closer, morning light catching the tired strain in her eyes. "I believe you. But I do not have an answer. Not yet. I need time."

Belaric gave a slow nod. "Of course. I will honor whatever you decide."

She turned toward the door. "Thank you, Belaric. I will have food and water sent up for both of you."

She was halfway out when he cleared his throat. "My lady—one more thing."

She turned back, brow raised.

"I hate to ask, but could you send someone to the inn? My packs are there. I would rather not spend the day dressed like this." He gestured at his bloodstained leathers.

She nodded in understanding. "I will send someone."

"I told them my name was Relinn," he added, pulling a small key from his pocket. "You will need this."

She took it with a soft sigh. "Why the false name?" She hesitated, then shook her head. "Never mind. I do not want to know."

She lingered at the door. "Please keep me informed of his condition."

"I will," he said, nodding.

She left without another word; the door clicking softly shut behind her.

Belaric sat again and watched the sunlight creep across the stone floor, slow and golden through the window's glass panes. It was the kind of morning that promised beauty—clear skies, birdsong in the garden, a breeze warm enough to make the flowers turn.

But all he could think of was the night.

The fight with Aeryn replayed in his mind, again and again. Lyra's face had paled when she had seen what he had done. Blood dripped from his blade. He could still hear the sound of his blade splitting flesh. He had gone too far in front of her—shown too much. Not just what he could do, but what he was. At his core.

He lowered his head into his hands, fingers pressing hard against his temples as if he could squeeze the shame out of his skull. Would he ever be anything more than this? A killer wrapped in borrowed names. A weapon dressed as a man.

When Renna was alive, he believed he could be. She had made a home from scraps, from broken walls and quieter mornings. She saw something in him—something good—when all he could see was the ruin.

She made him want to be better. And for a time, he almost was.

But she was gone now. Burned out of the world like a candle left too long in the dark.

For her, he thought. For Eryndorr.

He would become the man she believed in, even if that man never truly existed. Even if it broke him to pretend.

Even if it killed him.

The silence of the room settled around him. He took a long, slow breath, steadying the tremor in his hands, before a quiet knock stirred him from the thought. He stood and was surprised to see the door creak open.

Lyra stepped inside, a tray in her hands, with a jug of water balanced carefully atop it.

Belaric moved toward her immediately. "My lady—please, allow me," he said, taking the tray and jug from her arms with care.

She wrinkled her nose. "My mother is the lady. You do not need to call me that. I hate it when the others do."

Belaric smiled faintly. "You are still a lady, Lyra. But I am surprised you are the one bringing food. You surely have others for that."

She closed the door behind her. "We do. But I insisted. Figured it would not do much good for Fennra or Roth to come in and see a man dressed like that." She pointed to his assassin's leathers.

Belaric glanced down at himself. "Ah. Very smart." He set the tray and jug down on the desk. "I asked your mother to send someone to the inn for my packs—my clothes are in there."

"She already did," Lyra said, stepping beside him. "One of the guards left not long after. He should return shortly."

She looked past him then, to where Sir Tolman still lay on the bed, his chest rising and falling with steady breath.

"How is he doing?" she asked softly.

Belaric stepped beside her, keeping his voice low. "Better. His body is strong. He will recover. It will take time, but he made it through the worst of it."

Lyra exhaled slowly, as though she had been holding the breath all night. "That is good. I do not know what we would do without him." She paused. "But… it is only because of you that any of us are alive. I still can not believe it. All this, just because I asked questions."

She turned to face him, her eyes uncertain.

"They have guarded these secrets for centuries," Belaric said. "And they believed you were close to uncovering them. I am sorry, Lyra, but they will kill to protect what they know."

He hesitated for a beat, then met her eyes. "I have some questions I would like to ask you, my lady."

She raised an eyebrow, clearly amused. "Questions for me? I will answer—but only if you stop calling me lady."

Belaric smirked. "I will address you as Lyra in private. But around others, it will still be 'my lady.' You are a noble, and I am a commoner. If your mother hears me calling you by name in front of others, she will have me thrown in chains—or worse, forced to attend dinner."

She giggled and tapped a finger against her chin, pretending to ponder. "Hmm… I think I can agree to those terms."

Belaric extended his hand. "Then we have a deal."

She grinned and shook it. "Alright. What are your questions?"

His expression turned serious. "Last night, I told your mother what I am, what I have done. She sees me as a monster, and rightly so. I expected you to be no different. Yet you came here. You stand a few feet from me now, unafraid. Why? Why are you not disgusted by me?"

Lyra did not flinch. She simply looked at him, her gaze clear and unwavering. "My Valasar lets me see things differently," she said softly. "Not without feeling, but without emotion. I understand what you did, and why. I know it is horrible. But I also understand why we need you and your knowledge. Mother is afraid, and that is a normal response, but it keeps her from seeing the truth."

"What truth?" Belaric asked, his voice low with surprise.

"The truth is that you and I are on the same side, Belaric," she said. "We both want the Black Vow destroyed. You told us you are trying to find your son. I believe you. I believe you will do whatever it takes to protect us to find him."

He looked at her, truly seeing her for the first time—not as a child, but as an ally. Her wisdom was a weight she carried with grace. "I was a fool to ever doubt your intelligence," he murmured, more to himself than to her. "You are far beyond your years."

"And your other question?" she prompted.

His tone shifted, just slightly. "How did you find a book about the Vowkeeper? I would have sworn the Order would never risk putting anything in writing. But somehow, you found one."

Her smile faded into something thoughtful.

"It was luck," she said. "I had been spending a lot of time in the capital's library while Mother was in meetings at the palace. Reading anything I could get my hands on. Then one day, I was putting a book back and slipped. Fell right onto the stone. Hurt my arm, but when I reached out to steady myself, I noticed the board at the bottom of the shelf had come loose. Rust had eaten through the nails."

She paused. "I tried to push it back into place, but as I did, I lifted the edge just a little—and that is when I saw it. Just the corner of something tucked underneath. Covered in dust."

Belaric stood still, listening.

"It was a book. Old, brittle, nearly falling apart. It looked as if no one had touched it in decades. I forgot all about the shelf and pulled it out. I started reading."

She looked down. "Most of it made little sense. Pages missing. Ink faded. But I saw the name—the Vowkeeper. And a symbol I did not recognize. I started asking questions, and... then you showed up."

She paused. "I did not mean to cause trouble."

Belaric crouched slightly so their eyes met. "You did not. They did."

She held his gaze. And for a moment, she looked like someone older than her years—shouldering a weight she had not asked for but would not set down.

Belaric stepped closer, his voice lowering into something steadier, firmer. "Lyra, do not trouble yourself with shadows. Not tonight. Your mother needs you—needs your strength beside her. I will handle the shadows. That is my burden now."

His eyes held hers, unflinching. "And I swear to you, Lyra—I will die before those shadows ever reach you or your mother."

She studied him for a breath, her expression unreadable at first. Then she gave a quiet nod. "Thank you, Belaric," she whispered. "I feel safer knowing you are here."

He offered a small smile, the weariness in his body not quite able to dull it. "Now go," he said gently. "Attend to your mother. She needs you more than you know. I need to feed Sir Tolman."

Her gaze drifted to the sleeping knight. She nodded once more, then turned to the door. As her fingers touched the handle, she stopped, turning back to him.

"I hope you find your son, Belaric," she said, her voice low.

His throat tightened. He gave her the faintest smile. "As do I."

She smiled back, then slipped through the door and closed it softly behind her.

Belaric exhaled, his shoulders sagging with the weight of her words. Lyra was a good child—brighter than most grown nobles he had met, and far more compassionate. She did not deserve this. To be hunted. Forced into secrecy. Forced into fear.

I will find him, he thought. But what kind of man would my son believe I was if I let them die while I ran?

No. The Black Vow would not take another innocent—not while he still had blood in his veins. His son remained the goal, but this... this too had become a vow.

The room was quiet except for Sir Tolman's slow, rasping breaths. Belaric moved to the tray Lyra had left behind—bread still steaming, eggs cooling fast. He poured a cup of water and crossed to the bed.

The knight's brow glistened with sweat, but the fever had not worsened. Belaric eased an arm behind his back, lifting him just enough.

"Come on, old bear," he murmured. "You are not done yet."

He brought the cup to Sir Tolman's lips. The man stirred, coughed once, and then drank—slow, clumsy gulps. Some of it spilled down his chin, but most went down. When the cup was empty, he slumped back, murmuring something incoherent before settling again.

Belaric stayed beside him a moment longer, listening to the rhythm of his breath.

Then finally he allowed himself to eat.

He sat at the desk and made short work of the meal. Hot bread with grape jam. Three hardened eggs. The smoked meat was tougher than it should have been. He did not savor it. He chewed, swallowed, and moved on. The warmth helped, but it was not comfort—just something to keep the weight from dragging him under.

He was still wiping his hands when the door opened again.

Lyra stepped in, a key dangling from her fingers. "They found your packs," she said. "I had them brought up."

She set them down just inside the door and turned to go.

"Oh—and Eddaross is doing well. Apparently, he has been eating every apple in sight," she said, smiling.

Belaric managed a small smile. "That sounds like him. Thank you, Lyra."

She nodded and slipped out again.

Belaric moved to the packs, fingers finding the familiar stitching and weather-worn leather. He stripped out of the assassin's garb without ceremony, the dried blood on his shoulder tugging at the fabric. He winced as it peeled free, checked the wound—still sealed, still sore.

He dressed quickly in his travel clothes—wool and leather, plain but clean. They felt strange now, like clothes meant for another man. One who had not killed. One who had not bled.

He tied the last buckle and let out a slow breath, the ache in his shoulder a dull throb beneath the fabric. But for the first time in hours, he felt almost human again.

Kneeling beside the pack, he dug deeper until his fingers brushed a small leather roll. He pulled it free and unwrapped it—bandages, thread, a half-used tin of fleshmend salve. The smell hit him—earthy, sharp, familiar.

He cleaned the worst of the wound with water from the cup, then smeared a thin layer of salve across the angry red line. His fingers moved with practiced ease, though the pain made his jaw tighten. The bandages came next—tight, efficient wraps to hold it all in place.

When it was done, he sat down and let out a deep sigh. The pain was still there, but dulled now. Manageable.

Like everything else.

There would be more pain before this was over.

But the pain he could endure.

17

Belaric opened the window and leaned out into the morning light. It warmed his face, though not enough to thaw the cold beneath his skin. The breeze carried the scent of pine and sweat—training grounds, likely. The distant clash of wooden swords rang out in a staggered rhythm. Practice.

They would need more than practice.

The Order would come again—quiet and sure. When they learned he was here, they would come in force with knives dipped in shadow and poisoned words. There would be no warning next time, no challenge. Just a dead woman. A dead girl. And him, torn to pieces before the last breath left their lungs.

He exhaled, the sound a sharp hiss through his teeth.

Maybe I should go before I get them killed. I could draw the Order's attention—buy them time.

It was a foolish notion, and he knew it. Noble perhaps in some wasted corner of his heart. But it would cost him his life. And worse—it would end any hope of finding Eryndorr.

Still, the thought lingered.

She does not need me.

Sir Tolman was older, but his name still carried weight. There were stories—half-whispered, half-worshiped—of what he had done with a blade. If even a few of them were true, then he was a man who could kill without mercy. A monster in the right light.

But stories did not matter.

Assassins did not fight with honor. They did not meet you blade to blade. They struck in the quiet between heartbeats—when your back was turned, when your guard dropped, when you thought the danger had passed.

And Lady Haldren had only four guards. Good men, maybe—but not enough. Not even against two well-trained killers.

And the walls? Just an iron fence. Ornate. Decorative. Meant to impress guests, not repel shadows.

They were all illusions that would crumble under the Black Vow.

And if Tolman found out what he was—what he had been—there might not be a choice. He would kill Belaric just to keep the house clean, or he would try to.

He sighed, jaw tight with indecision. Leaving might save them. But it might doom them too.

A low groan cut through his thoughts.

Belaric turned sharply. Sir Tolman stirred beneath the sheets, body sluggish but alive. He crossed the room in two strides and crouched beside the bed.

"Sir Tolman, can you hear me?" Belaric asked.

The man's eyes opened slowly, wincing against the light. His voice was like gravel poured into a cloth. "Who… are you?"

"My name is Belaric," he said softly. "You were poisoned. I countered most of it, but your body's still recovering. You need to stay calm."

Tolman coughed—dry, hacking, painful. "Lady Haldren?"

"She and Lyra are safe," Belaric said, raising a hand to still him. "With her permission, I have been watching over you. They are worried about you, but I assured them you would live."

That seemed to reach him. His shoulders slackened, only slightly.

"What happened?" he rasped.

Belaric hesitated. "That story's best told by Lady Haldren. I will fetch her. Can you sit up?"

Sir Tolman's eyes narrowed. He said nothing, but tried. His limbs betrayed him, and Belaric stepped forward to help, steadying the man's back until he was upright.

He moved to the tray near the hearth, placing a few strips of dried meat on a plate and refilling the water cup. "You need to eat—a little at a time. And drink. The poison has not bled entirely from your body."

Sir Tolman took the plate with hands that trembled. "Thank you... Belaric."

A rare warmth stirred in Belaric's chest. He gave a small, tired smile. "Call if you need me. I will bring her."

He stepped out of the room and shut the door behind him, the weight of it pressing briefly in his hand.

The manor was still. Sunlight slanted across the stone, catching the dust in slow spirals. At the base of the stairs, a figure emerged—a house guard in Haldren's colors. Broad-shouldered, with a steel helmet shadowing his brow. Hardened leather across the chest, reinforced linen at the joints, and stiff leather boots scuffed from long patrols. The man's hand crept to the hilt at his side.

Belaric moved toward him, fast but calm. "Where is Lady Haldren? Sir Tolman's awake."

The man blinked. "She is out back," he said. "Are you the healer?"

Belaric nodded and brushed past him, already walking.

The guard followed, boots thudding softly in his wake.

Down the corridor, past shuttered windows and closed doors, to the back. He pushed open the door, and sunlight lanced across his eyes.

In the courtyard, Lady Haldren stood near a half-dug grave. Her dress was simple—deep green, unadorned—but it caught the light as she moved, like ivy climbing through stone. She had tied back her hair, though a few strands had escaped, curling against her sweat-damp skin. A short man stood beside her, mid-motion with a shovel. Sweat made his shirt cling to him; he had rolled his sleeves to the elbow. Dirt streaked his grey linen pants.

At their feet lay a shape wrapped in linen. Aeryn.

Belaric paused, a strange numbness settling in his chest. He would have burned her—let fire eat the last of her name, her face, her secrets. That was the Order's way. Fire left no bones for memory to cling to.

But here she was. Wrapped like a child in sleep. Laid to rest among gardens.

The gravedigger straightened, eyes finding Belaric's.

"He has woken up," he said, and nothing more.

Lady Haldren turned. Her eyes widened, and she was already moving. She passed him in silence, and together they climbed the stairs. At Sir Tolman's door, she paused.

A breath. A heartbeat.

Then she knocked once and stepped inside.

Sir Tolman's eyes found her at once. He struggled upright with a groan, pain etched deep into every line of his face, but it was shame that clung to him more than the fever.

"My lady…" His voice cracked. "I have failed you."

Lady Haldren was at his side in an instant, pressing a steadying hand to his shoulder. "Sit, Tolman. You have never failed me. Not once." Her voice was soft, but it carried the finality of a sealed verdict. "An assassin poisoned you. The intent was clear—leave you dead in your bed."

He froze. The weight of it settled on him, slow and brutal. His eyes cut to Belaric, and the confusion behind them twisted into something far uglier.

"I see," he said, voice rough. "Belaric, is it? I would ask you to step outside. My lady and I have words to share—in private."

Belaric's mouth opened, but Lady Haldren raised her hand without even glancing his way. "Belaric stays."

Sir Tolman gave her a confused look. "My lady?" he asked.

Her gaze shifted to Belaric—just a flicker of hesitation behind her mask—but she said nothing.

Belaric sighed and stepped forward, eyes on Sir Tolman. He would be honest and straightforward with the man. "I am a former assassin of the Black Vow, trained from a young age to kill," he said. "Our order is a secret one most do not live long enough to whisper about."

Sir Tolman's face twisted. "You are joking."

He looked from Belaric to Lady Haldren, his eyes searching for the flicker of a smile, a sign of a jest. But her face was a cold, emotionless mask. The truth of the situation settled in his gut like a stone. The light in his eyes died as he understood the full scope of their betrayal.

He surged forward only to collapse back with a gasp. Fury filled the cracks in his voice. "You… you snake-hearted bastard. Are you the one who poisoned me? Is this some twisted game?"

Belaric did not flinch. His voice was cool, tired. "If I had wanted you dead, you would not have made it to morning."

Sir Tolman snarled and reached again, but Lady Haldren slammed a palm into his chest, pinning him to the bed.

"Enough," she commanded.

Her voice rang through the chamber like steel drawn in a quiet hall. When she spoke again, it was cold and deliberate—each word sharp as a blade's edge.

"You will listen, Sir Tolman. You will not interrupt." Her tone left no room for argument.

The silence that followed was taut as a drawn bow.

"Belaric did not poison you," she said. "The woman who did is being buried behind this house as we speak."

Sir Tolman blinked. "Woman?"

"Her name was Aeryn. She came from the same Order—but unlike Belaric, she was loyal to them. She poisoned your food to leave me and Lyra defenseless, then returned to finish the job," Lady Haldren said.

Sir Tolman's stare bored into Belaric as if he could strike him dead with will alone.

Lady Haldren did not look away. "He fought her. He killed her. If not for him, I would be cold in the ground. Lyra too. And you—gods, you would have died choking in your sleep."

She turned toward him fully, voice rising now—not in volume, but in gravity.

"I know what he is. I know what he has done. He has lied. He has killed. He has committed acts that cannot be undone. But he is also one of the few with the skills to stop another assassin—and right now, we do not have the luxury of turning him away."

Her eyes flicked to Belaric again. That shadow of doubt was still there—haunting the corners of her gaze. A man like him did not earn trust. He bought it with blood. Still, she pressed on.

"His wife died in childbirth. His order took his son. Branded him a traitor and marked him for execution, but he escaped and came here. He came to me not as a beggar, but with a proposition: protection for information. Help in exchange for help. He seeks only to find his son," she said, her tone flat now.

Sir Tolman's lip curled. "You would trust a man like this? You would gamble your house, your daughter, everything—on him?"

This man has no right to judge me as he lay in a bed dying, leaving his lady and her heir defenseless. The thought was a sharp, hot blade in Belaric's mind. He knows nothing of my sacrifice, of what I did to keep his house—and him—intact.

Belaric took a step closer, his voice quiet but full of fire. "You speak of trust while I bled to keep her breathing. You lie in that bed breathing because I stood where you could not."

"You—"

"Belaric." Lady Haldren's voice cracked across the room like a whip.

Sir Tolman tried to rise again. She slammed him down, harder this time.

"Enough," she said, her voice like winter frost. "You are not well, Sir Tolman. And your judgment—right now—is clouded by pain and pride."

She turned to Belaric with a final, imperious nod. "Go. Tend to your horse."

Belaric held Sir Tolman's glare a breath longer than was wise, then gave the slightest bow.

"As you command, my lady," he said, voice clipped.

He stepped out, closing the door behind him. The sound echoed like the end of a sentence too long delayed.

He stood there for a moment. Behind the door, Sir Tolman's voice rose in protest—furious, wounded, pleading.

But she did not raise hers.

That silence said more than words.

He descended the stairs, his boots thudding against stone. The front door opened to morning light and the scent of dew on the grass. Brookhaven stretched below in quiet stillness. A clean town. Peaceful. Unbloodied.

Renna would have loved this place.

He smiled at the thought, though it hurt to do so, and began walking down the hill toward the inn.

The walk through Brookhaven eased Belaric's thoughts more than he expected. Each step pulled him further from the estate, from the weight pressing on his shoulders. The cobbled streets were warm beneath his boots; the sun bright above softening the edges of the world.

He wondered what choice Lady Haldren would make. Listening to Sir Tolman would be the smart choice, the right one. Sir Tolman was not one to ignore his instincts lightly. But Lady Haldren did not strike him as someone who let others think for her. There was a quiet steel to her—she made her own decisions. Damn the consequence.

He sighed, trying to focus on the world around him instead. The market buzzed with life—stalls bursting with woven cloth, baskets of dried fruit, jars of spice and honey. Birds called from tiled rooftops. Laughter echoed between shopfronts. Several merchants called to him again, waving familiar wares and hopeful smiles. He gave them a faint grin and waved them off.

Soon the inn came into view, its old stone and timber unchanged. In the stable beside it stood Eddaross, half-dozing in the sun. When the horse noticed him, its ears perked and its gaze locked with Belaric's. The corner of Belaric's mouth lifted.

"How are you doing, old boy?" he asked as he approached.

Eddaross snorted in response.

Belaric chuckled and ran a hand along his flank. "I figured. We will be staying at Lady Haldren's estate for a while. You alright with that?"

The horse stamped a hoof in approval.

"Good." He gave him a pat. "Do not bite anyone while I am gone."

As he turned, a voice greeted him from the stable door. "Ahh, Sir Rellin. Good to see you again."

It was the same old stableman—broad-shouldered and dusty, with wind burnt cheeks and a bristle of white beard. Belaric recognized him at once.

"You did not tell me how stubborn this one was," the man said, nodding at Eddaross. "Nearly took my hand off more than once."

Belaric gave the horse a sidelong glare. "My apologies for his behavior. He has always been ill-tempered and ill-mannered."

The man laughed. "Ah, he is just loyal. There was no harm done. And please call me Bram."

"Thank you, Bram. Would you mind getting him ready while I settle with the innkeeper?" Belaric asked.

"Of course. He will be saddled and waiting," Bram said cheerfully.

Belaric stepped inside the inn. The scent of warm bread and old wood greeted him, unchanged. Behind the bar, Amara stood with a book in hand. When she looked up and saw him, her face lit with surprise.

"Relinn. I was not sure I would see you again."

She came around the bar, eyes still scanning him like she was counting bones.

"I was confused when one of Lady Haldren's guards came asking for your packs. Said you were at Lady Haldren's estate and needed them. Then we heard about the attack... and that you helped. They said Sir Tolman was injured, and you saved him," Amara said, her tone curious.

Belaric blinked. So, Lady Haldren was already shaping the story. Clever woman.

"I am sorry, Amara. I know it is confusing. And I wish I could explain. I hope one day I can," he told her.

Amara gave a single thoughtful nod, her expression softening. "That sounds troubling. But I trust Lady Haldren's judgment. Just… take care of yourself, alright?"

"I will. For you, Amara," Belaric told her, a slight smile forming on his lips.

She laughed, shaking her head. "Oh, stop that, Relinn."

He leaned in. "There is something I can tell you if you promise to keep it between us."

Her eyes widened with excitement, and she leaned closer. "I can always keep a secret."

He glanced around, then said quietly, "My name is Belaric." He slid a few copper coins across the counter.

Her eyes widened, but he raised a finger to his lips. She nodded, solemn now, and took the coins without another word.

He figured the whole town already knew his real name, and if things played out the way he suspected they would, his name would be the least of his worries.

"Thank you, Amara. I am sure we will see each other again," he said.

"I am sure we will… Relinn," she said, her smile returning.

He turned and stepped back into the light.

Outside, Bram stood with Eddaross already saddled, reins in hand. "He is all ready, sir."

Belaric approached and extended his hand. Bram shook it—and blinked in surprise when he felt the weight of coin pressed into his palm.

"Thank you," Bram said, quieter now.

Belaric nodded and took the reins. With one smooth motion, he swung into the saddle and settled his weight.

"Let's go, old boy," he murmured.

As they rode, the quiet of Brookhaven trailed behind them like mist burning away in the sun. A peaceful town. Simple. Unbloodied.

Moments like this made him dangerous. They made him forget what he was. Or worse—what the Order would never let him become.

He did not look back.

Belaric rode at a measured pace up the hill toward Lady Haldren's estate, with the reins loose in his grip, the road quiet but for the soft clop of Eddaross's hooves. The manor crested into view—stately, unmoved by all that had happened within its walls. He passed the stone markers at the edge of the estate, sunlight catching the tips of the iron gate ahead.

A familiar guard stepped forward, the same one who had met him before. His helm shaded his face, but his tone was relaxed.

"Lady Haldren said you would be back," he said. "Told me to have you put him in the stables out back."

He pulled the gate open without waiting for a response. Belaric gave a nod and led Eddaross through.

The estate grounds were quiet, hushed in the afternoon's warmth. He spotted the man who had been training Lyra days earlier—a lean figure with a trimmed beard and a scar that crossed his chin like an unfinished sentence. He moved with a practiced economy of motion, every step deliberate and quiet. He stood beside a trough, wiping his hands with a rag, but straightened as Belaric approached.

The man's eyes flicked to the horse. "Is this the stubborn horse I heard about?"

He spoke in a clipped, precise voice, a voice that was used to giving commands and expecting them to be followed.

Belaric smiled faintly. "Yes, sir. This is Eddaross."

He dismounted smoothly and looped the reins in one hand. The man stepped forward, his eyes sharp and intelligent, already assessing the horse.

"I am not a sir; my name is Rusk," he said, already moving to inspect the horse.

Belaric simply nodded to the man.

Rusk walked the perimeter of Eddaross with a practiced eye. He ran his hand down the legs, checked the hooves, tapped the iron shoes to test their fit. He did not touch the horse with the soft familiarity of a stable hand, but with the cool, professional detachment of a man who understood a weapon as well as an animal. Eddaross shifted once, but did not resist, seeming to recognize the authority in Rusk's touch.

"He is a bit restless," Rusk said, brushing dust from his palms. "I will put him in the pen. Let him run."

He extended a hand for the reins.

Belaric hesitated. "Perhaps I should. He is not fond of others."

Rusk let out a sigh and stepped directly in front of Eddaross, locking eyes with him. The moment stretched.

"I am going to let you run," he said, calm as still water. "Then I will brush you down and feed you. Do you understand?"

Eddaross did not move. Then he snorted.

Rusk looked back at Belaric. "I understand them. And they understand me."

Belaric chuckled and handed over the reins. "I am impressed. The first time we met, he tried to run me down."

"They say horses match their rider's temperament," Rusk said, glancing over his shoulder with the faintest smirk.

Belaric gave a low laugh. "You are not wrong."

Rusk led Eddaross into the circular pen, unfastened the saddle with smooth efficiency, and set it over the rail. Then he gave the gelding a firm slap on the flank. "Go on."

That was all he needed.

Eddaross took off in a burst of dust and muscle, thundering around the pen in wide, looping arcs. Rusk leaned on the far rail, watching him closely.

Belaric stayed, leaning against the pen rail, arms crossed. He watched the way Eddaross moved—purposeful, wild, but controlled. There was peace in the rhythm of it, the kind that came only when no one was trying to kill you.

This might be the last peaceful moment I have with you, he thought. Enjoy it, old boy.

The wind shifted. He heard quiet footsteps behind him—too measured to be a servant.

He turned his head slightly and saw Lady Haldren approaching from the manor, her green dress catching the light with each step. She walked at a deliberate, unhurried pace.

He exhaled and looked back at the pen.

Eddaross was still running, his gait even, his power undiminished. Rusk stood at the far edge, calling sharp, practiced commands.

He wondered if she had come to send him away—or ask him to do something worse.

Lady Haldren stepped beside him without a word. They stood in silence, with the dust and hoofbeats between them.

Then she turned and met his gaze.

"We will work together," Lady Haldren said, her voice level, her gaze fixed forward. "For the time being."

Belaric waited, watching her carefully.

"You will assist Sir Tolman in protecting this estate," she continued. "Not just me and Lyra—everyone beneath this roof. Second, you will not kill again unless I say so. If someone threatens the lives of those in this house, you may act. Otherwise, no blood without my command."

Her tone had the weight of authority, stripped clean of warmth.

"You will follow my lead. You will advise me when your knowledge of the Order proves useful. You are not alone in this—Sir Tolman will advise me. And Lyra will be part of it as well."

Belaric blinked, caught off guard. "My lady, she is still a child."

Lady Haldren motioned for silence, and he fell silent.

"She bears the mark of the Valasar on her forehead," she said calmly. "She sees more than most. Understands more than most. I have made my choice."

She turned to face him fully now, her expression carved from marble.

"I intend to stop these attacks—on my house, and on others. You will help me do that. In return, I will use every resource at my disposal to find your son."

Her eyes narrowed, voice sharpening.

"But hear me, Belaric. If you betray me—or endanger what I am building—I will see you imprisoned. Or buried."

The air thickened, heavy with unspoken risk.

"Do you understand?" she asked, her voice as sharp as steel.

Belaric stepped forward. His voice was low, tight as a drawn wire.

"If we are speaking plainly, then hear this as well. If anyone—you, Sir Tolman, even Lyra—tries to stand between me and my son, I will strike them down. Without hesitation. I am not your hound to be leashed."

The threat felt hollow even to his own ears. He knew he could never raise a blade against Lyra, much less her mother. But he could not let Lady Haldren believe she held all the cards.

She did not flinch. But her fingers curled at her sides—barely. "I expect loyalty," she said coolly. "Not obedience."

"You will have my loyalty," he replied, his voice low and firm. "But know this."

He took another step, close enough for her perfume to mingle with the scent of steel and sweat clinging to him. "I served the Black

Vow for years. I will not be ruled again. Not by masks. Not by kings. Not by you."

Her gaze did not waver. "Then rule yourself wisely, Belaric. Because if you fall out of line, I will not hesitate to stop you."

They stood in silence—two blades unsheathed, not yet crossed.

Finally, Belaric offered his hand. "Then we have an agreement."

She looked at it, eyes unreadable. Then—reluctantly, deliberately—she placed hers in his. Her grip was surprisingly firm, almost calloused, a subtle testament to the hidden strength beneath her noble bearing.

"Yes. We do," she said, her voice tense.

Belaric's smile was a flicker, sharp-edged and joyless. Despite himself, he found he liked her. "And how does Sir Tolman feel about this agreement?" he asked.

She turned toward the pen, watching Eddaross thunder through the dust, Rusk's voice still barking orders.

"He hates it," she said. "And he hates you. But he will do as I command. He has agreed to say he killed Aeryn. For now, I suggest you stay out of his path. He will be furious in the coming days."

Belaric followed her gaze, watching Eddaross run.

"I figured," he said. "I will keep my distance."

She turned back to him. "What is our first move, Belaric?"

He did not hesitate.

"Send word to every noble house you can—high and low. Tell them there was an attempt on your life, and that you demand answers. Their replies will tell us what they fear. And who we need to worry about first."

Lady Haldren studied him for a breath, then nodded once. "Very well. We will see to it."

Lady Haldren lingered at the fence for a few quiet minutes, watching Eddaross move. The horse's hooves thudded softly against the dirt, his breath steady, his muscles flowing like water under pressure.

"Have you had him for a long time?" She asked, her gaze still fixed on the pen.

"I have," Belaric said, arms resting along the wooden rail. "He was about to be sold to a farmer. The merchant said he was too stubborn to ride, so he planned to sell him cheap to pull a plow for the rest of his life."

He smiled faintly at the memory.

"We looked at each other once. That was all it took. I paid double what the farmer was offering, but it was worth it in the end," he said.

"He is in excellent hands with Rusk," she said, finally glancing his way. "Do not worry."

She turned toward the manor. "We should get started on those letters."

Belaric looked up at the sky. The sun was beginning its slow arc downward.

"I will be in shortly," he said. "I am going to scout the woods. See if I can trace Aeryn's route. She must have hidden her pack somewhere nearby—it could be useful. And I need to identify the estate's weak points. We need to be prepared."

He turned to meet her eyes. "I would also recommend speaking with Sir Tolman. Ask if he knows anyone he trusts—mercenaries, soldiers. We need more than guards."

Lady Haldren held his gaze for a long beat, expression unreadable.

"Agreed," she said simply, then turned and walked back toward the house.

Belaric exhaled and watched Eddaross one last time as the horse slowed to a trot, responding to Rusk's commands with near-military discipline. He smiled, then turned and made his way through the back gate, slipping into the woods.

The forest greeted him with birdsong and shadows. Sunlight pierced through the canopy in shifting columns, casting dappled patterns across the moss-covered ground. The air was rich with damp earth and pine. Insects buzzed lazily through the golden beams. Every few steps, he passed claw marks in bark or the remnants of old nests. Deer had moved through here recently—fresh droppings, bent grass—but nothing human.

Aeryn had been good. Careful.

Hours passed. He worked in widening spirals, noting faint depressions in the dirt, paths broken by foxes and crows. But no footprints. No scent of a camp. Just forest, silent and undisturbed.

Then, as he angled slightly north, something shifted.

Near the base of an old, gnarled tree, a patch of dirt sat oddly beneath a loose scatter of leaves. The pattern was too clean—too intentional. The rest of the forest floor was natural chaos, but this... this had been placed.

Belaric crouched low and examined the area. The dirt was softer here. A faint tug of thread caught his eye—a torn strip of leather reins tied around a thick branch overhead, the fibers frayed and sun-bleached.

She came on horseback; he thought. Tied it off here. The horse must have broken free.

He scanned the surrounding brush but saw no sign of the horse's body. Likely wandered off when it got free, or someone found it.

He turned back to the tree, kicked aside the leaves, and began to dig.

After a few minutes of careful work with his dagger, he struck cloth—canvas. He pulled free a small black pack, worn but intact. Kneeling, he opened it.

Inside: a spare change of female clothes, neatly folded. A throwing knife. A small belt dagger. Three vials of dark liquid—poisons, likely. A length of bandage, and beneath it all, a folded letter with a cracked wax seal.

He stared at it for a moment longer than he had expected.

He unfolded it. The ink was clean, tight, and unmistakably coded. But he recognized part of the cipher immediately—one of the simpler patterns the Order used when secrecy bowed to urgency.

Orders, he thought. Of course. Finding it should have pleased him—but all he felt was cold certainty. The kind that never left.

He returned everything to the pack and slung it over his shoulder. He would crack the cipher back at the estate.

The walk back was shorter. The light had softened, casting the trees in hues of copper and fading gold. The sounds of the woods shifted—birds settling, insects growing bolder. Evening was near.

When he returned through the back gate, he spotted Rusk bent beside Eddaross. The man was crouched near one hoof, carefully hammering a new horseshoe into place. Eddaross stood still, watching the man with the patient expression of a war veteran tolerating a medic.

Rusk barely looked up as Belaric passed, focused on aligning the iron just right.

It had taken Belaric three days the first time he tried to shoe the horse. Eddaross had tried to kick his ribs into a pulp.

Belaric chuckled under his breath and stepped inside the manor.

He found them in the same room where Aeryn had died.

Lady Haldren and Lyra sat at a long table, papers and inkwells spread between them. A young guard stood a few feet away—alert, rigid, one hand resting near his blade. The guards had changed since the attack. Everyone had. They were watching now. Listening.

All three looked up as he entered.

"That took a while," Lyra said with a grin. "All that time just to find a pack?"

Belaric chuckled, making his way across the room. "She was skilled. Buried it deep. I found it more by luck than anything else."

His steps slowed as he passed over the rug—darkened, stiff where the blood had dried. Aeryn's blood. This was where she had fallen. The memory flickered in his mind—steel clashing, breath hitching, a final gasp—and then it passed.

"What was in the pack?" Lady Haldren asked, drawing his attention back.

Belaric set the worn black pouch on the table and took a seat beside them. "Her orders. It is coded, but I should be able to break it." He pulled the folded parchment free and reached for a clean sheet of paper and ink. The letter itself was sparse—no greeting, no signature—just four disconnected words spread across the page like wounds. To someone untrained, it would look meaningless.

Lyra leaned in with interest. "What kind of code is that? It just looks like a mess of letters."

"That is the point," Belaric replied, already scanning the page. "It is designed to be meaningless unless you know what to look for. They use symbol substitution with a shifting alphabet, layered with anchor intervals. Crude, but quick. Meant to be memorized and destroyed." He began decoding. The quill scratched steadily across the page as he marked lines, counted intervals, and cross-referenced the patterns.

After several minutes, Belaric set the quill down, a frown creasing his brow. "The cipher's been changed," he murmured. "The anchor intervals are off. I cannot break it."

Lyra leaned closer, her eyes tracing the lines he had drawn. "What if it is not a change?" she asked. "Look here." She pointed to a sequence of symbols that repeated near the bottom of the page. "You said the anchor was every sixth letter, but what if the whole word is the anchor?"

Belaric's gaze sharpened. He looked at the page, then at Lyra. "You are not looking at the symbols," he said, a new respect in his voice. "You are looking at the pattern." He looked back at the parchment, his fingers now moving faster as he applied her theory. The quill scratched again, this time with a new sense of purpose.

Minutes passed before Belaric set the quill again and reviewed his notes. Then, with a slight breath, he read the decoded message aloud.

"Haldren.

Hidden.

Robbery.

Draskmarr."

He looked up. Both Lady Haldren and Lyra were staring at him. Lyra was beaming.

"Is that it?" Lyra asked, clearly underwhelmed.

"That is enough," Belaric said. "She was ordered to eliminate the Haldren family—you. Told to remain hidden. That fits—someone hiding in plain sight draws more attention in a town this size. The robbery angle's odd, though. With Sir Tolman here, it is not a believable cause of death. Then there is the final word—Draskmarr. The capital. That is where she was told to go next."

Lady Haldren studied him. "Why would she go there?"

"Likely to report on her mission," he said. "Probably to the Vowkeeper or one of his agents. If he is tied to the nobility, it makes sense he would stay close to the king and the high houses. But it is only a guess."

"You got four words from a whole letter?" Lady Haldren asked skeptically.

"That is the brilliance of it. Anyone who found the letter would expect a full page—paragraphs, names, details. Not four scattered words. It is exactly why it works." He told them.

Before Lady Haldren could respond, Lyra straightened in her chair. "We do not go to the capital."

The room stilled. Belaric and Lady Haldren both turned to her.

"We were just attacked," Lyra continued. "They will expect us to be scared, maybe even hiding. Not traveling openly to Draskmarr, where we would be exposed. If we show up at the same time our letter does, it will look suspicious. And we are a low house—who is going to grant us an audience with the king?"

Belaric studied her. She was composed, confident, and right. Lady Haldren had said she was sharp. That was not a mother's pride—it was a fact.

"You are absolutely right, Lady Lyra," he said with a respectful nod. "We must play the part we are expected to."

Lady Haldren said nothing, but Belaric caught the barest nod of approval in her posture. She reached for one of the letters on the table and held it up.

"Thank you for the insight, Belaric. While you were out playing in the dirt, we were crafting messages of our own." She tapped the letter once. "These will do their part just fine."

She turned toward the guard standing nearby, a smirk playing at the corner of her lips.

"Oh, and since you are playing a part as well..."

"Staven," she said, "escort Belaric to the armory. He will need to be outfitted in proper guard attire."

Belaric raised a brow. "You cannot be serious."

Lady Haldren glanced at him. "If you are to play the role of one of my personal guards, you must look the part," she said, her voice flat.

Staven hesitated, his eyes darting between Belaric and his lady. He was young, no more than twenty, with a face still soft with youth and a posture that was a little too stiff. He held his spear with the nervous rigidity of a recruit, and his knuckles were white where he gripped the shaft.

"My lady... Sir Tolman ordered me not to leave your or Lady Lyra's side."

Lady Haldren turned to him, her tone like frost.

"Tell me, Staven. Do I command this house—or does Sir Tolman?"

A beat passed. Staven swallowed hard, the movement visible in his throat. His gaze dropped to his boots, a clear sign of his discomfort. "You do, my lady."

"Good. Then take Belaric to the armory and see him properly dressed. Oh, Belaric, please leave the pack. I would like to see its contents as well."

"...Yes, my lady," Staven said, his voice laced with nervousness, and with a slight tremble to his words.

Belaric sighed as he rose from his chair, leaving the pack behind.

"Bye, Belaric," Lyra said sweetly, clearly enjoying herself.

He glanced back with a mock smile. "Goodbye, Lady Lyra."

Her grin faltered. Her eyes narrowed.

"Enough," Lady Haldren said without looking up. "Belaric—go. Lyra—back to writing."

Belaric chuckled softly before he turned and followed Staven from the room, the young guard leading the way with nervous, hurried steps.

18

As they walked down the narrow corridor, Belaric slowed for a moment, eyes drifting to the faded banners lining the stone walls—sigils half-erased by time and dust. One bore the talon-mark of House Aldenmoor, its crimson thread now dulled to rust. Another showed a black tower split by lightning, the emblem of some long-dead war host he could no longer name. Most were tattered, their meanings lost to all but memory.

He had not stopped to notice them the previous night he came through—too focused on staying silent, staying hidden.

He was drawn back to the present as Staven reached the armory door, opened it, and turned to look at him expectantly.

Belaric nodded to the man and entered.

The smell of oiled leather and cold steel had not changed. Racks lined the walls, each holding blades polished to a near-mirror sheen. Some were works of art—daggers with jeweled hilts, sabers etched with curling silver script. Others were brutal in their simplicity. Killers' tools. He still carried the twin blades he had taken on that first night—balanced things, truly perfect in a way only assassins could appreciate.

Staven moved toward a series of heavy storage chests at the back of the room. He threw them open one by one, pulling out pieces of armor and laying them across a nearby bench with practiced haste. Each piece landed with a dull thud or a faint clatter, the sounds echoing through the quiet space like distant thunder.

"Reinforced linen," he muttered, holding up a pair of dark grey trousers stitched thick at the thighs and knees. "Hardened leather boots... same for the chest piece. Flexible, but it will hold against most blades." He added them to the pile, then placed a steel helm on top—its polished surface catching the torchlight. It covered the skull and brow, leaving the jaw exposed, but extended low enough to shadow most of the face.

Finally, he unfolded a deep forest green cloak—the color of old pines and tradition. Embroidered across the back in fine, silvery thread was House Haldren's sigil: a lone rider atop a rearing horse, bow drawn and aimed toward the horizon. The lines were long and elegant; the style deliberate—noble, but not ostentatious.

Staven nodded toward the weapon racks lining the far wall. "Not sure what you used before, but there is plenty to choose from. Sword, axe, spear—just grab what feels right."

While Staven looked over the gear, Belaric wandered toward the blades. He tested a few—lifting them one by one, letting the weight settle into his hand. Most were nearly perfect, as if forged by smiths who had known the feel of blood on their hands. He admired that.

He was reaching for another when Staven's voice cut through the stillness.

"Is it true?" he asked softly, almost swallowed by the stone around them.

Belaric turned slowly, finding the man standing still, hands idle, eyes wary. Fear sat at the corners of his mouth.

"Is what true?" Belaric asked, setting a short sword back in its cradle.

Staven gave a nervous laugh, rubbing the back of his neck like he wished he had not spoken. "That you are... actually an assassin. You killed the other one, right?"

Belaric let the question hang there. Then he stepped closer, just enough to make Staven flinch.

"I was," he said. "But not anymore. Now I am a father who will do anything to find his child."

Belaric's eyes moved to the armor laid out before him.

"Is that all of it?" he asked.

Staven nodded quickly. "Yes, sir."

"Just Belaric," he said, lifting the hardened chest piece and testing its weight. Not bad, he thought.

"I am Staven—but you already know that," the man added, fumbling for something like courage. "The old one is Tarnel. And Kedd—you met him at the gate."

Belaric gave a nod of acknowledgment.

The boy looked young for a guard. Too stiff in the shoulders. Too many glances, like every shadow might move. Veterans did not act like that. But Belaric did not blame him. It was likely his first time seeing—let alone speaking to—an assassin.

Belaric turned back to the blades. His eye caught on a sword near the far wall. It was longer than most, forged of blackened steel that drank the light rather than reflecting it. Strange, curling patterns were etched along the blade—lines like coiled smoke or the paths of spiders. The crossguard and grip were dark grey, unadorned, but the pommel ended in a sharp spike of the same steel, like it had been shaped to punch through plate.

He lifted it. Felt it settle into his hand like it belonged there.

When he swung it, the weight followed without resistance. It did not just cut air—it parted it.

Belaric smiled and grabbed the blade's sheath before hooking it to his side, replacing the dagger.

Staven watched him, eyes wide. "Good choice. Is there anything else you need, Belaric?"

Belaric shook his head. "Just a soft bed. Where do the guards sleep?" he asked Staven.

The young man smiled. "Oh—yes, follow me. I will show you."

Together, they gathered the armor and left the armory.

As they stepped out into the hall again, they passed Lady Haldren's study. The door stood slightly ajar, the faint golden flicker of candlelight painting lines across the stone floor. The quiet scratch of a quill on parchment drifted through the opening—measured, focused. Even unseen, she cast a long shadow in these halls.

They turned down another corridor until they reached a heavy oak door bound in iron.

"We already moved your packs in here," Staven said, pushing it open with a grunt.

The room beyond was simple, meant for soldiers rather than guests. Four beds, each framed in dark wood. Modest wardrobes stood beside them. A chest rested at the foot of each bed, scuffed and dented. One small writing desk, its ink bottle tipped on its side. The smell of sweat and oil lingered.

Staven gestured to a corner. "That one is yours. Your gear is on the bed."

Belaric stepped in and moved toward his bed. He placed the armor down and opened one of the packs. Everything was still there. Even the assassin's garb. He was surprised. He would have stripped it from someone like him.

Staven laid the rest of the armor down beside him. "Lady Haldren said you were fine with the night shift. I hope that is alright."

Belaric looked up from the pack, his mouth twitching into something close to a grin.

"Perfect. I work better in the dark," he told Staven.

The young man hesitated. His voice dropped as if admitting something dangerous. "If men like you are standing guard now... I am guessing more assassins are coming."

Belaric did not answer.

Staven took a step back, faltering. "I—I should get back. Sir Tolman will be... well, he notices when I am gone. Good luck, Belaric."

He turned quickly and left, shutting the door with a soft thud.

Belaric chuckled under his breath. People always assumed assassins were monsters until they needed one.

He sorted through the rest of the pack, checked straps and blades, then stowed everything with quiet care. He unbuckled his sword and laid it on the floor beside the bed, then removed the daggers from his belt. He left only a single throwing knife, its handle barely visible against his skin, tucked into a concealed sheath on his forearm.

He doubted Lady Haldren would send the other guards to capture or even kill him, but the years had taught him that the best way to survive was to prepare for betrayal—even from those who had offered a truce.

He stretched out on the bed—rough blanket, straw-stuffed mattress—better than most places he had slept. He folded his arms behind his head and stared at the wooden ceiling.

Night was coming. And with it, the only peace he had ever known. His eyes drifted closed, and sleep took him.

A fence beneath his arms, the scent of wildflowers and horsehair on the breeze—Belaric stood smiling, hands entwined with Renna's. Sunlight bathed the field in gold. Beyond the fence, Darius moved slowly through the paddock, one hand on the reins of Eddaross, the other steadying Eryndorr, who grinned from ear to ear atop the dappled gelding. Six years old now, the boy had begged for this moment for weeks.

Renna had taken more convincing. She had made them all promise—the boy would be safe. Even Eddaross had to swear, her hands on his bristled snout, whispering to the horse like it understood. Maybe it did.

"See?" Belaric said, watching the paddock.

Renna leaned into him, warm against his side. "You were right, dear."

"I usually am," he stated confidently.

She snorted. "You only wish you were," she laughed, the sound soft and full of life. He turned to her—those green eyes had always undone him. They still did. He leaned down and kissed her, the world narrowing to the softness of her lips and the calm they carried. For a moment, there was nothing but sunlight and summer.

Then the sky cracked, and the scent of death and wet earth filled the air.

Thunder rolled across the fields like a beast stirring from sleep. Belaric's head jerked up as the clouds thickened unnaturally fast, gold fading to gray, then black. Shadows crawled across the paddock like ink through water.

"Darius," he called, already moving. "Bring him in."

But Darius was gone.

In his place stood a tall figure, draped in black robes, gripping Eddaross's reins. Eryndorr still sat on the horse, still staring ahead, unmoving. Panic rose cold in Belaric's gut.

"He is taking him," Renna whispered.

Belaric turned. She stood beside him, pale as moonlight. Her nightgown was white and soaked with blood that bloomed across her belly. Her voice trembled—soft, but certain. "He is taking him."

"Renna..." It was all he could manage.

She pointed.

The robed figure began to turn, slow as death. His face was hidden behind a mask—black iron, twisted into the shape of a grinning skull. Belaric did not need to see his eyes to know. The Vowkeeper.

"NO!"

He vaulted the fence, boots thudding into mud, and sprinted across the paddock. The Vowkeeper was already mounting the horse behind Eryndorr, arms closing around the boy like shackles. Eryndorr remained still, his eyes fixed on Belaric, unblinking.

"No, Eryndorr!" Belaric shouted, legs driving hard through the muck.

The Vowkeeper laughed, the sound warped and hollow. Then he flicked the reins.

Eddaross surged forward.

Belaric lunged, arms outstretched, but the horse thundered past. Mud struck his chest as he hit the ground hard. Scrambling to his knees, he watched helplessly as the Vowkeeper rode off into the darkness with his son.

"NOOOO!"

His scream shattered the dream. He woke to the sound of his own ragged breathing, his heart hammering against his ribs. A hand—cold, not his own—reached for the reins. The reins vanished, but the hand remained, a cold emptiness in his own fist. His heart hammered against his ribs as he stared into the blackness of the ceiling.

He lunged, his arm moving on instinct—a throwing knife appearing as if by magic in his hand, its honed edge already slicing through the air.

He stopped a heartbeat before the point found flesh.

He had sworn to protect her. Swore to stop any blade that came for her. Now here he was, merely a few inches from taking her life.

Lyra stumbled back, eyes wide as the tray in her hands clattered to the floor. Food scattered. The clang of metal rang out like a blow.

Belaric stared at the blade, horrified, then flung it aside. "Lady Lyra..." His voice was hoarse, barely formed. "I am... I am sorry." He wiped the sweat from his brow, hands trembling.

To her credit, she did not scream. She took a cautious step back, but her voice stayed calm. "Belaric... are you alright?"

He could not meet her eyes. "A nightmare."

"I knocked," she said gently. "You did not answer. When I came in, you were shaking."

He nodded, still breathing hard. "It is my fault. I am just grateful you are not hurt."

She stepped forward, her gaze steady, then sat beside him on the edge of the bed. "We will find him."

He looked up at her. She smiled, hesitant but sincere—and something about the way she said it gave him pause. There was no fear in her voice, no doubt. It did not sound like a child's hope. It sounded like a vow.

How could she have known? And why did he believe her? He wondered.

"Thank you, my lady... for your kind words," he told her.

She grinned. "Well, since you dropped the food, we will have to go get more."

She crouched beside the mess, already gathering the scattered meat and vegetables.

"No, please—my fault." Belaric moved quickly to help her, the edge of shame still burning. "Let me, my lady."

"Oh, enough with the 'lady,'" she said with a wave of her hand. "And we need to hurry. Your shift starts soon, and you cannot stand guard on an empty stomach."

He blinked, surprised. She had not come to scold or check on him. She had come to make sure he ate.

He did not know what to say. So he simply nodded.

"Thank you... Lyra."

Together, they gathered the last of the food, then stepped quietly into the hallway. The dream still clung to him like ash, but her words had steadied his hands.

The hallway was quiet as they walked, their footsteps soft against stone. No words passed between them. Lyra kept her hands tucked against her stomach, still cradling what remained of the tray. Belaric carried the rest, and the silence between them was not strained—it was understood.

The kitchen greeted them with warmth and the smell of roasted meat. A spit turned slowly over a low flame, the fire crackling faintly beneath it. Fat dripped from the browning skin of a chicken, sizzling as it hit the coals. Rosemary and crushed garlic clung to the skin, filling the air with a savory, mouthwatering heat. Beside it, a broad platter of vegetables steamed—thick-sliced carrots and potatoes, blistered and softened, glistening with oil and dusted with herbs.

They each took a plate and filled it, working side by side without a word. Belaric carved clean slices from the chicken, placing portions on Lyra's plate before filling his own. At a side table, he poured two cups of water from a cool clay jug, and they sat at a long wooden table opposite one another.

They ate in silence for a while. The only sounds were the soft clink of cutlery and the gentle hiss of the fire. Lyra was the one to break the quiet.

"What was Renna like?" she asked.

Belaric paused, a forkful of vegetables halfway to his mouth. He set it down.

"She was strong," he said after a moment. "Not in the way most people use the word. She lifted neither blades nor broke bones. But she carried things. Carried me. Carried hope, even when everything around us gave her reason to let it go."

Lyra looked at him quietly, listening.

"She teased me constantly. Said I talked like a man twice my age and twice as foolish. She had stolen the last bite of every meal and swore she did not. She loved apples—she could not go a day without one. Would drag me halfway across the market to get them, but she never doubted her apples were better. And she made this pie…" He let out a small breath. "Best thing I ever tasted. Swore I would stay with her for the rest of my life after the second slice."

Lyra smiled faintly. "You loved her."

"I still do," he replied, looking back down at his food.

There was nothing more to say. She did not press further, and he was grateful for that. They finished the meal in companionable quiet. When they were done, Lyra rose and started gathering their plates.

"Well," she said, turning toward the door, "do not fall asleep out there."

"I will not," he assured her.

She gave him a tired, genuine smile. "Good night, Belaric."

He smiled. "Thank you, Lyra, now off to bed, young lady". He chuckled as she rolled her eyes at him.

He watched her go. When she disappeared around the corner, he gathered the dishes, cleaned them quickly, and left the kitchen. The quiet of the manor had deepened—sunset gone, the hush of night pressing in.

He left it untouched.

Instead, he opened his pack and drew out the black assassin's garb. The cloth was soft and worn, the leather light, the buckles and straps molded to his shape. Familiar. Silent. Deadly. He dressed quickly, the motions automatic, and strapped the heavy sword to his hip, the familiar weight a grim comfort. He slid a pair of daggers back into their sheaths on his belt, then tucked a series of throwing knives into concealed holsters along his boots and inside his sleeves. He slipped into the hall with barely a sound.

The house was still. No servants moved through the corridors now. Even the guards outside seemed distant, their steps muffled behind the thick walls.

In the front chamber, candlelight glowed low. Lady Haldren sat at her desk, posture rigid but upright, her hand steadily moving a quill across the parchment. She was still pale, but stronger than before—her recovery was no longer in doubt. In a worn armchair beside her sat Sir Tolman, arms crossed, mouth tight, his leg tapping idly against the floorboards.

They had not noticed him yet.

"He is late," Sir Tolman muttered. "First night on duty, and he cannot even show up on time. That tells you all you need to know."

Lady Haldren did not look up.

He snorted. "We should never have brought him in. The longer we keep him here, the worse this will get. Sooner or later, we will regret it. He is one of them. You do not unmake a killer like that. We should be rid of him."

She dipped her quill again, the scratching of ink on parchment her only reply.

He stood abruptly, paced two steps, then slapped a hand against his thigh. "Where is that damn fool?"

A hand settled on his shoulder.

"Here," Belaric whispered.

Sir Tolman jumped, spinning around so quickly he nearly tripped over himself. When he saw Belaric—half in shadow, dark eyes catching the candlelight—his face twisted red with rage.

"You bastard!" he shouted.

Lady Haldren finally looked up from her work, her eyes cold and steady. "Enough, Sir Tolman," she said, her voice clear and final. "He saved my daughter's life. He is to protect us. Go rest."

Sir Tolman stood frozen, seething. He turned and stormed from the room, his muttering curses growing fainter with each heavy footfall.

Belaric watched him go, then let out a low laugh, more amused than anything.

Lady Haldren looked up, brow slightly furrowed. "Must you?"

"I find it hard not to," Belaric told her.

She sighed and returned to her writing. Belaric stepped forward, pulled out a chair opposite her, and sat without invitation. He reached for one of the letters on the table and quietly began to read.

The letter was well-crafted—measured and deliberate in tone. It described the attack with enough drama to draw concern, but not panic. The assassin, it said, had been overconfident in her skill, brazen enough to challenge Sir Tolman directly. She had lost. Sir Tolman had sustained injuries but recovered fully—a reassuring note for those who might still doubt his ability to protect House Haldren.

Lady Haldren's portion was more personal, almost desperate in places. She expressed concern that more attacks would come and confessed confusion about why she had been targeted at all. There were pleas woven into her words—requests, even begging, for any information about who the assassin was or why she had come. It was not just a letter. It was a call for help.

Belaric set it down gently.

"It is good," he said, glancing at Lady Haldren.

"I know," she replied, still writing. "Lyra has a brilliant mind for this. She crafted different versions depending on the recipient—some more emotional, some more political."

"She is very smart," he murmured.

Lady Haldren paused, setting down the quill. Her eyes met his, steady and sharp.

"These next few days... weeks... maybe years—they will be dark," she said. "I still do not trust you. But I sleep better knowing you are here to protect her."

Belaric held her gaze. "I will protect her," he said. "But I would be lying if I said I did not wonder whether I do more harm by being here. Yes, they will come for you. But once they know I am with you... they may send worse."

She gave a tired shrug. "Then you will have to stop them all. It is too late to second-guess. The plan is in motion—we have already sent letters to a few nobles. More go out tomorrow. Sir Tolman sent word to men he trusts. He hopes they will arrive soon." Her lips tightened. "I am sure he will urge me to send you away once they do. But we are in this now. Whether or not we like it."

A faint smile tugged at Belaric's mouth. "Yes. We are."

He pushed the letter back toward her. "Now, Lady Haldren, I think it is time for you to rest. You will need your strength for the days ahead. And I have work to do."

She arched an eyebrow. "Work?"

He gave a slight wave. "Just the kind that keeps blades out of your ribs."

She exhaled slowly, amused in spite of herself. "Fine. I am tired. I think I will."

She gathered her pages and turned to go. At the doorway, she looked back. "Try not to give Sir Tolman a reason to say, 'I told you so.'"

Belaric smiled without warmth. "No promises."

She shook her head and left him then, and he sat for a while longer as the house fell deeper into silence. The candle burned low. The ink dried on her parchment. Outside the windows, the moon had crept high and cast long shadows.

Then he stood.

Let's get to work.

Through the night, he moved like a shadow through the manor, taking silent stock of what could break—and what might already be broken. He checked the windows, testing each frame with a cautious hand. Too many were loose. A few could be wedged shut for now, but most would need iron splints or bolts to keep them from being pried open.

In the stone hearth tunnel that led from the great room to the garden beyond, he measured the space with his eyes, fingers brushing the mortar lines. A trap could be rigged there—a tripwire anchored between stones, tensioned to trigger a blade. He made a note of it. That one would need wire, anchors, and a clean edge.

He walked the halls, jotting down the flaws in his mind. Rusted nails needed pulling. Warped doors would need new hinges. The gate outside was not just weak—it was an invitation. The metal rusting in some places, it would never hold against any real opponent.

Locks. Oil. Reinforcements. Tools.

By the time the sky began to pale, he had a list longer than he liked. But now he knew what needed fixing—and where death might slip in if he did not move fast.

He made one final round, checking the locks and listening for any sign of movement.

Then, without a sound, he climbed the stairs and stopped outside Lady Haldren's chamber. He knew she still had Lyra staying with her.

He stood silently in the hallway, listening. The house remained still. No footsteps echoed through the halls. No creak of wood. No whisper of wind.

He doubted an attack would come tonight—or in the next few nights. The capital was days away. Whoever had sent Aeryn would assume the job was unfinished, or at least delayed. That ignorance gave him time. He intended to use it.

The first light of dawn stretched into the hallway when Staven came trudging toward him, rubbing sleep from his eyes. He slowed when he saw Belaric in full assassin garb—face bare, but unmistakable.

"How was your first night?" He asked, trying for casual, though his gaze flicked nervously to the twin blades at Belaric's side.

"Easy enough," Belaric replied.

Staven gave a small, uneasy smile. "That is good. I am here to relieve you. You can go rest."

Belaric nodded and made his way back through the manor.

The guards' quarters were dim, touched only by the soft gray light bleeding in through the high window. Tarnel and Kedd still slept, undisturbed.

Belaric entered without a sound. He unbuckled his sword; the leather creaking softly as he placed it on the floor, then slid the daggers from his belt. Finally, he removed the throwing knives hidden in his boots and sleeves, placing each one in a neat row beside the rest of his gear. He packed it all away in practiced silence. Then he dropped onto the bed, exhaustion pulling at every muscle.

Sleep came quickly.

And, thankfully, without dreams.

Belaric stirred at the sound of movement—boots on stone, soft murmurs. He did not open his eyes, but listened as Kedd and Tarnel shuffled around the room.

"Did you see his armor last night?" Tarnel whispered.

"I saw it," Kedd replied. "Dark as pitch. That sword, too... he moves like he is made of smoke."

"He scares the piss out of me," Tarnel murmured.

"Good. Maybe he scares off the bastards trying to kill us," Kedd told him.

Belaric forced himself not to smile. A moment later, the sound of their footsteps faded down the hall, and the room fell silent. He eased back down, the aches in his body a heavy weight that finally won the argument against his mind. He was asleep before his body had fully settled.

When he finally rose, the morning light had tilted higher through the window. He stretched once, then turned to the neatly folded guard uniform. Time to play his part. He dressed quickly—the reinforced linen and hardened leather fitting snugly—and strapped the black-forged sword to his hip. The air was still; the estate hushed inside.

But outside, it stirred.

He stepped through the back door into the courtyard and found the rhythm of the day already moving. Lady Haldren stood on the steps, arms crossed, her eyes fixed on Lyra, who rode in slow circles on her mare. Rusk walked beside her, holding the reins gently, speaking low words of encouragement. Nearby, Sir Tolman had gathered the three guards in the yard—Kedd, Staven, and Tarnel—each armed with wooden practice swords.

As Belaric approached, Sir Tolman's gaze snapped toward him.

"Finally got out of bed, I see," Sir Tolman spat.

"I am just surprised they are still alive," Belaric replied, his voice calm and even. "Whoever trained them must not have been serious about winning a fight."

The guards' heads turned. Eyes widened. Even Tarnel looked up from tightening his bracers.

Sir Tolman took a step forward, jaw clenched, but before the words left him, Lady Haldren's voice cut through the air.

"Well," she said, not looking away from the riders, "let us see if your skill is more than just daggers."

Everyone turned.

Belaric gave a shallow bow, still smiling. "As you wish, my lady," he said, his voice filled with confidence.

Belaric moved to the rack by the wall, removed his real blade, and selected a practice sword—oakwood, balanced, slightly worn. He returned to the yard, the practice sword feeling light and clumsy after the weight of his real blade. He rolled his shoulders as he stepped into place.

"Staven," Sir Tolman barked. "You face him."

Staven stiffened. "Sir, I—"

"Now," Sir Tolman commanded. His voice left no room for objection.

The two men faced off. Staven took his stance—feet too close, sword angled wrong. His knuckles whitened. Belaric winked at him. Staven visibly gulped.

"Begin!" Sir Tolman shouted.

Staven lunged forward, swinging hard—but off balance. Belaric stepped to the side with fluid ease, pivoted on the ball of his foot, and turned behind him. His blade touched the back of Staven's neck, gentle and precise.

Staven froze. Mouth open.

"Dead," Belaric said.

Kedd stepped forward before Sir Tolman even needed to speak. The older man nodded once, took position, and squared his stance. His eyes stayed locked on Belaric.

"Begin," Sir Tolman commanded.

Kedd was quick. His footwork was sharp; his strikes calculated. He did not overextend, did not wait long between attacks. He came in with a low swing—Belaric blocked it and sidestepped, narrowly avoiding a thrust to the ribs. Another strike came high, then low. Belaric moved like wind between stone, letting Kedd spend his energy. Then, just as the next strike came in, Belaric dipped beneath it, stepped inside, and lifted the wooden blade gently beneath Kedd's chin.

Kedd let out a quiet breath and stepped back.

Sir Tolman's jaw clenched. "Kedd and Staven. Against him."

Kedd glanced at Staven, who looked like he might rather be anywhere else. Still, they both took positions. Belaric set his feet and gave a courteous nod.

"Begin," Sir Tolman growled.

Kedd took the lead, moving in with a flurry of swings, forcing Belaric into a defensive rhythm. Staven circled wide, looking for an opening. Belaric blocked a strike, spun out from between them, and repositioned. Kedd pressed in again, but Belaric sidestepped a lunge and swept low—his leg catching Staven's. The man toppled. Belaric turned on the pivot and tapped the wooden sword against Staven's back before he hit the ground.

One down.

Kedd came again, sharper this time, forcing Belaric into retreat—but Belaric caught the rhythm. A high feint. A parry. Then he stepped close, twisted Kedd's weapon aside, and struck upward. The tip rested against Kedd's chest.

"Dead," Belaric said quietly.

Sir Tolman's face found a new shade of red.

"Tarnel," he snapped. "Get in there. All three of you. Take him down."

The guards hesitated. Kedd frowned. "Sir... that does not seem fair."

"Now!" he yelled, face reddening.

The three guards exchanged glances, then took their stances. Belaric exhaled slowly and shifted his weight.

"Begin," he ordered.

They moved as one—Kedd attacking from the front, Tarnel circling left, Staven hanging back. Belaric did not give them time to surround him. He cut toward Tarnel first, forcing him to block, then pivoted to deflect Kedd's strike. Staven came in late—clumsy, desperate. Belaric turned, caught Staven's wrist, and with a twist, used his own momentum to shove him sideways—straight into Tarnel's path.

Kedd hesitated just long enough for Belaric to press the opening. He turned sharply, drove between the two, and knocked Staven's sword from his hand with a hard parry. Tarnel struck from behind—Belaric ducked, rolled, and swept low, catching Tarnel's knee and dropping him hard. Kedd was already on him—swinging fast, furious.

Belaric blocked high, stepped inside the reach, and disarmed him with a twist and shove. The wooden tip pressed into Kedd's chest.

"Dead," he said, breath steady. A low throb of pain pulsed in his healing shoulder, a reminder of the fight he had survived. He stretched once, hiding the grimace from prying eyes. Silence hung over the yard.

Sir Tolman stood, fists clenched. "Pathetic, three of you, and you cannot even take him down? Fine. I will do it myself."

He stepped forward.

"Enough," Lady Haldren said, her voice firm.

Sir Tolman turned, still fuming.

"You are still recovering," she continued. "You will do no good limping about with cracked ribs and pride. All of you—go about your duties."

The guards bowed slightly and dispersed. "Yes, my lady," they said in unison, though a few cast lingering glances at Belaric as they passed.

Belaric turned back toward the weapon rack and reclaimed his real sword, fastening it at his side. When he looked up, he saw Lyra standing beside her mare, grinning.

She clapped once, then again.

Belaric gave her a smile and offered a slight bow.

Belaric caught up to Staven near the side garden, where the man had paused beside a cart stacked with sacks of grain. Belaric clapped a hand on his shoulder.

Staven jumped slightly, nearly dropping the sack in his arms. "Oh—Belaric. Sorry, I was deep in thought."

He paused, then added with a nervous chuckle, "You fight very well."

Belaric gave a half-smile. "I spent years being trained in most weapons. Daggers are my best, but the Order did not give me the luxury of picking a favorite. You either learned everything, or you did not last long."

Staven blinked. "Right. Makes sense," he said, letting out a nervous chuckle.

"Did you need something?" Staven asked, trying to recover his footing in the conversation.

"I need to run into town," Belaric said. "Pick up a few things. I will return shortly—just in case anyone wonders where I have gone."

Staven nodded. "Of course. I will let the others know."

Belaric gave him a brief nod and set off down the road. The day had warmed since morning, and the breeze carried the scent of dust and river water from the south. As he passed through the outer gates and moved down into town, he felt eyes following him.

A few people paused mid-step. Some whispered. Others pointed. He heard the name Sir Tolman once, and the phrase "the one who fought the assassin." He did not slow.

Rumors moved faster than horses. He had expected as much.

He sighed and kept walking.

After another minute, he reached the blacksmith's forge, a squat stone building tucked along the eastern edge of the market. Smoke billowed from the chimney, thick with the tang of burning coal. The clanging of hammer against steel rang like steady thunder.

Inside, the heat pressed against him like a wall.

At the anvil stood a man of formidable size—tall, thick-shouldered, with a heavy gut beneath a soot-streaked apron. His head was bald, but a long black beard fell past his chest, braided in places, flecked with gray and smelling faintly of smoke and honest sweat. His forearms were thick with old scars, each a testament to a lifetime of working hot metal. The hammer in his hand looked like it could crack skulls as easily as iron, and he held it with a casual ease that spoke of immense strength.

He looked up as Belaric stepped in, slid the half-formed blade back into the coals, and wiped his hands on his apron as he approached.

"I am Oswin," the man said, his voice a deep rumble, offering a thick hand.

"Belaric." He shook it firmly. The blacksmith's grip was like a vise, calloused and firm, a hand that had built and mended with equal force.

Oswin gave a nod. "What can I do for you, Belaric?"

"I need a few things," Belaric said, pulling a small parchment from inside his vest. "Some custom work. Reinforcements for doors, new lock plates, and steel fittings to brace the gate around Lady Haldren's estate."

Oswin took the list and read as Belaric went on.

"The doorframes are old—some of the iron nails are warped or rusted through. I will need thickened hinges, preferably cold-forged. Three sets. The locks need stronger plates and longer bolts—steel, not brass. I want them set deep, hard to reach with any tool. And for the gate—the bars are solid, but the latch and hinges are loose. I will need reinforced corner brackets and a locking mechanism with an interior release. If someone tries to jam it from the outside, I want it to open from within."

Oswin scratched his beard and nodded slowly, clearly impressed. "You know what you are doing."

"I have seen too many gates broken from the wrong side," Belaric replied.

The smith grunted. "Smart man." He eyed the list again. "I can forge the hinges and plates myself. Might take four days, five if my apprentice burns his hand again trying to test steel with his bare fingers."

Belaric arched a brow. "Is that common?"

"More than I like to admit," Oswin muttered, half a smile under the beard. "He means well. Does not think much, but means well."

Belaric reached for his coin pouch, but Oswin waved him off.

"Lady Haldren's always been good to us. Kept taxes fair, fed three families during the lean season. I would not take her coin. And besides..." He shrugged. "You saved Sir Tolman. That is worth more than all the hinges in this forge."

Belaric paused. "Are you sure?"

"Dead sure," Oswin told him.

"Then thank you," Belaric said. "I will return in a few days to check the work."

"You do that," Oswin said, already turning back toward the forge. "I will have it ready."

Belaric stepped out into the afternoon light, the heat of the fire still clinging to his skin. As he walked, more eyes followed him—curious, cautious, calculating. He paid them no mind.

By the time he reached the estate again, the breeze had cooled, and the shadows had stretched across the gravel path.

The walls would hold better once the work was done.

He just hoped the people inside them would, too.

19

The days passed in rhythm, like drumbeats echoing in a long corridor—measured, deliberate, hollow. Belaric moved through them as he always had, not with purpose, but necessity. He drilled the guards until their arms ached and their tempers frayed. Sir Tolman tolerated it the way a hound tolerates a leash—snarling, but not biting. Whatever the man thought of him, he could not deny that Belaric's blade cut clean and his words struck true.

Most of his time went to Staven, a boy with too much fear and not enough footing. He gripped the sword as if it might bite him, swung like he was asking permission. Belaric did not yell. He felt no shame. He corrected—again, and again, and again. Step. Strike. Recover. Guard.

"Confidence is born of familiarity," he said on the fourth morning, tapping the flat of his blade against Staven's shoulder. "Learn the shape of each strike. Let it live in your bones. That is how you stop dying."

And slowly, the boy began to listen. Not just hear—but listen. There was hope in him, hidden like steel beneath rust.

Lady Haldren sent her last letters, the last sealed with deep red wax that shimmered faintly when it caught the light. The letter was addressed to King Aelion Valebran, ruler of Tavros and self-declared Shield of the West. A man of high words and heavier judgment. The kind of king who would let cities burn if it meant preserving the shine on his throne. Still, he was powerful. And if anyone could shift the winds, it was him.

Lyra had crafted the letter with merciless precision. Belaric watched her from the shadows of the hall, the way her ink-stained fingers trembled as she crossed out lines, muttered revisions, rewrote entire paragraphs. She worked through a dozen drafts, maybe more—each one closer to the truth wrapped in the silken language of diplomacy. She wrote of unrest, of rebellion, of the rot blooming beneath gilded surfaces. It was a plea disguised as a warning, veiled beneath compliments sharp enough to bleed.

Her mark glowed faintly when she focused, bright as a coal under wind. It had grown—he was certain of it. More defined. More dangerous. She had become something sharp in her own right. One day, he knew, there would be no one who could match her—not with a pen or mind.

In the late afternoons, when the estate quieted, Belaric took Eddaross riding. The horse grew restless when confined too long, his mood turning mean in the stalls. Rusk, the stablemaster, understood him well and often loosed him into the pen for a few hours of head-tossing freedom. Still, Belaric knew Eddaross needed more than a fence and dirt. He needed space. Wind. Distance. The kind of run that reminded the beast of what he was.

After several days, he returned to the blacksmith.

Oswin met him without a word. The smith had blackened hands up to the knuckles, and his apron was scorched and split. Belaric examined the goods—new bracing nails, thick-barred hinges, iron-banded wood. He had everything he had asked for, and more.

He reached for his coin pouch.

Oswin merely grunted, crossed his arms, and said, "I told you, Lady Haldren has done more for this time than I can ever repay her for. I will not charge her for mere trinkets."

Belaric nodded and said nothing. He carried the weight home on his back.

The work took hours. Nails driven deep, beams notched and slotted into reinforced frames. He carved a locking brace into the front door, thick enough to stop a battering ram for at least a few strikes. Belaric replaced the rusted hinges on the outer gate and lined the interior walls of the estate's perimeter with dull steel tips—not to kill, but to slow.

He did not stop there. Along the interior paths, where shadows pooled, he set small tripwires with bells made from bent copper, and in the grass beside the wall, he hid sharpened caltrops. He knew the traps were simple, obvious to a trained eye, but they were not meant to kill; they were meant to warn.

He knew it would not stop the Order. Nothing would. But it would buy him time, and that might be enough.

He finished as the sun dipped low, its light burning the rooftops gold. Sweat clung to his neck. His knuckles were scraped raw.

In the kitchen, Wess had left him a bowl of stew—thick, spiced, steaming. He did not ask how the cook always seemed to know when he would show up hungry. He devoured it and then went back for another. The smell clung to him as he left, warm and animal.

In the guards' quarters, Kedd was fastening his boots, buckles clinking like distant bells. He glanced up as Belaric entered. They only nodded.

Belaric moved to his bed and knelt, pulling the pack free from beneath it. He undid the leather ties with practiced fingers. Slowly, reverently, he pulled out the armor piece by piece. Shadows clung to it, as though the darkness did not want to let go.

Kedd paused mid-motion. His hands froze. He stared at the gear as if it were cursed.

"You are wearing that now?" he asked, voice low and brittle.

Belaric said nothing. He dressed quickly, the leather whispering against his skin, heavy with the smell of old sweat, oiled hide, and something fainter—like ash. The armor slid on like a second skin. Familiar. Unforgiving. He cinched the last strap. The heavy sword thudded against his hip as he buckled it, and he slid a pair of daggers into their sheaths on his belt, their hilts a grim comfort to his hands. He pulled the hood low; the cloth casting shadows across his face until only the glint of his eyes remained.

When he turned, Kedd had not moved. His fingers hovered near the buckle of his chest strap, forgotten.

"You look like death itself," Kedd muttered.

There was no jest in his voice. No humor. Just the stark, unsettled truth of a man seeing something he did not understand.

Belaric stepped past him, the floorboards creaking under his boots.

"I am," he whispered.

Then he vanished into the corridor, silent as smoke, the night ready to test his claim.

Belaric found them in the front room.

Sir Tolman sat across from Lyra at a small table, with a game of Crown fall between them. He was laughing—genuinely laughing—as Lyra slid a golden piece into position with a smug grin. Lady Haldren sat nearby in a tall-backed chair, a book open in her lap, but only half-read. The fire crackled. For a brief moment, the estate felt like a home.

Then Belaric stepped through the doorway, clad in black, the hood shadowing half his face. All three turned.

Sir Tolman's smile vanished like a snuffed candle.

"Must you wear that?" he snapped, his voice sharp with contempt.

Belaric smiled coldly. "Sir Tolman, I did not think you were capable of laughter. I always figured you were born scowling."

Sir Tolman stood so fast the chair scraped across the floor. "You bastard," he spat. "You dare disrespect me again? I have had enough of your games, Belaric. Just leave—crawl back into the filth you came from. You disgust me."

Belaric's smile faded. He stepped forward, eyes locked, voice low. "Careful. I have got my limits."

Sir Tolman gave a joyless laugh, all teeth and venom. "Limits? You are a fucking coward, Belaric. A ghost hiding in the dark. It would be better if you never found your son. What would you even teach him? How to gut a man from behind?"

The air shifted. Belaric's body went still—not calm, but coiled.

Lady Haldren opened her mouth, rising halfway from her chair, but too late.

Belaric was already in front of Tolman, face inches from his.

"Speak of my son again," he growled, "and you die."

He jabbed a finger into Sir Tolman's chest.

"You can take your 'honor' and shove it straight up your ass. You think I do not know what you are? A minor noble from a piss-poor house. Then someone noticed you had a bit of talent with a blade, and suddenly your family sunk their coffers dry to buy you a sword master and silk sheets."

Belaric stepped closer, voice dropping into a snarl.

"While you sat pretty on your cushioned pillows, learning fancy footwork, I was getting beaten bloody because a floorboard creaked under me. I have had ribs snapped, fingers crushed, lashes down my spine so deep I pissed blood for days. You want to talk about what makes a man?"

He leaned in, voice razor-sharp.

"I survived. And if it were not for me, Lady Haldren and Lyra would be rotting in graves alongside her husband. Your honor did not save them. I did. You have done nothing for them. You are nothing."

He spat the last word like venom.

Sir Tolman's face turned a deeper red, fists trembling with rage. Then he swung—wild, a straight punch meant to break Belaric's nose.

Belaric did not flinch. He sidestepped easily, and with a whisper of motion, the blade in his sleeve snapped free—its tip now pressed against Sir Tolman's throat.

He froze.

"You are no man of honor, Sir Tolman," Belaric hissed. "You hide behind it. Maybe it is time you left, because the only failure in this room is you."

Sir Tolman did not move. His face was burning with fury, veins standing out in his neck.

Lyra sat frozen beside the table. Her mouth was slightly open, but no words came. She looked at Belaric as though seeing someone else—something else. Something darker. Her gaze lingered on the blade at Sir Tolman's throat, then drifted up to Belaric's face. She looked away quickly, her expression unreadable.

"ENOUGH!" Lady Haldren's voice cracked through the room like a whip. Her book slammed shut with a thunderclap.

"I am sick of you two clawing at each other's throats like feral dogs! This cock-measuring contest ends now. I do not give a damn whether you like each other, but you will work together. If either of you so much as looks at the other in a way I find irritating, I will have you removed from my service. Do you understand me?"

The silence that followed was absolute.

Belaric slid the blade back into his sleeve, the metal whispering home like a secret.

"Yes, my lady," both men said, nearly in unison.

Sir Tolman opened his mouth again, some final barb burning on his tongue—but Lady Haldren raised a hand, eyes like sharpened glass.

"I have had enough of both of you tonight. Lyra, come. We are going to bed. Leave these ignorant fools to sulk in their own piss."

"Yes, Mother," Lyra said quickly, pushing herself up from the table. Her steps were hurried; her eyes never touched either man. She passed them as though walking between ghosts.

Sir Tolman glared at Belaric one last time, jaw clenched so tight it looked like it might crack. Then, as he turned to go, he slammed his fist into the doorframe with a dull thud, the wood groaning beneath it. He did not look back.

The room emptied, but the heat of it lingered, like smoke after a fire.

Belaric sank into the nearest chair, the tension bleeding from his muscles in slow waves. The room was still warm with the echo of his anger, and he knew he had let it run too far. Again.

He let out a long breath.

I should not have said it, he thought to himself.

But the words were out now, and they hung between him and Sir Tolman like smoke, refusing to clear. The truth was—part of him believed it. Maybe the bastard was right.

What kind of father would I be?

He knew how to kill a man six different ways before they hit the ground. He knew how to vanish in a crowded market, how to silence screams before they ever rose. But children? He had no answer. He had always counted on Renna for that. She had the grace, the patience, the heart. She would have known how to raise a son.

Now she was gone. And so was Eryndorr.

And it was all his fault.

He buried his face in his hands, letting the thought linger just long enough to sting.

Would his son be better off without him? Safer? Freer?

He shook his head hard, as if trying to physically drive the thoughts out.

No. No. Eryndorr was his son. His blood. He had loved that boy the moment Renna first whispered of him, had imagined what his voice might sound like, whether he would have her eyes or his.

Whatever else he was—killer, coward, failure—he was still a father. And he would not let the Vowkeeper make a weapon out of his son. He would not let Eryndorr become another shadow on someone else's leash.

He would find him. And then they would vanish. Far from this cursed land, far from kings and orders and oaths twisted into chains.

There was only one path left. And he would follow it, no matter how much blood it cost.

Belaric stood resolute. He drew a slow breath, steadying himself, then walked out.

The rest of the night passed without incident.

Belaric moved like a wraith through the halls—checking every door, every latch, every lock. He watched the windows until his eyes burned. He searched the shadows until the shadows stopped hiding from him. No one would get past him.

When the sun rose, Staven came to relieve him.

"You are clear," Belaric said simply, patting the young man's shoulder. "Keep your eyes sharp."

Staven nodded, jaw tight, and took his post. Belaric offered a small nod before slipping back to his room.

Kedd was already in bed, one arm sprawled off the side, snoring like a storm rolling through timber. Belaric gave a quiet chuckle.

The man sleeps like a bear.

He stripped off the assassin's gear, folded it carefully, and packed it away. He climbed into bed, the ache in his shoulders finally settling as he curled under the covers.

He closed his eyes and whispered a silent prayer to Renna—not for strength, not even for guidance.

Just... to be seen.

Sleep took him like a slow tide.

He did not know how many hours had passed before Kedd's voice cut through the haze.

"You coming to drills?" he asked.

Belaric groaned and rolled over. "Not today."

Kedd hesitated at the door. "Suit yourself."

Then he was gone, boots thudding down the hall.

Belaric stared at the ceiling. He did not want another run-in with Sir Tolman. He would rather keep his blood cool for a little longer. He shifted to go back to sleep—but the gods had other plans.

There came a knock at the door. Sharp. Nervous.

He groaned again, dragging himself upright.

He opened the door to find a girl standing there—young, maybe twenty, if that. Short, slight, dressed in simple earth-colored clothes worn by commoners who worked in noble houses. Her dark brown hair hung in soft waves past her shoulders, and her eyes—also brown—were large, deep, and currently full of nervous energy.

"Sorry to disturb you, Sir Belaric. I am Fennra," she blurted. "Lady Haldren wishes to speak with you. She is in her room upstairs."

Belaric blinked once, then waved her off gently.

"Fennra, just call me Belaric. And thank you. I will be up in a moment."

She nodded quickly and turned away, walking faster than she needed to. He watched her retreat with a sigh.

They are all still afraid of me.

He closed the door.

After a pause, he dressed in one of the finer sets he had been given—soft grey linen pants, a white shirt, light as air, and black fur-lined boots that fit snugly. He ran a hand through his hair, pushing it back from his face, and examined the beard he had been growing.

He had never been fond of facial hair. Too much upkeep. Too easy to grab in a fight.

But now? He liked the way it looked. Like a man who had seen things.

He took another breath, let it fill his lungs, then stepped out the door.

He could not keep Lady Haldren waiting.

Belaric climbed the stairs at a steady pace, the boards beneath his boots creaking softly in the morning hush. He stopped before Lady Haldren's door and knocked twice, knuckles light on the wood.

"Enter," came her voice—cool and composed.

The room spoke of nobility without extravagance. A large bed with a dark wood frame stood in one corner, its linens neatly arranged, not a wrinkle in sight. Several bookcases lined the wall, each filled with weathered tomes and ribbon-bound scrolls. A modest hearth crackled faintly in the far corner, embers glowing like fading coals. Multiple wardrobes stood near the back wall, well-kept but un-adorned. At the center sat a finely carved desk beneath the window, the wood polished to a deep sheen. Lady Haldren sat behind it, a letter in her hand.

She did not look up. "Still sulking, I see."

Belaric stepped inside, closing the door quietly behind him. "No, my lady. I figured Sir Tolman and I could use some time apart."

Her gaze finally lifted. "You make it sound as if you are married."

"Just two men who cannot stand the sight of each other," he replied, tone flat.

Setting the letter down, she sighed. "You do not make my life easy, Belaric. He has begged me to send you away more times than I care to count." Her voice softened slightly. "He hates you because you remind him that he failed."

Belaric lowered his gaze. "I should not have said what I did. I let my temper speak for me. It was foolish. But what would you do if Lyra were taken from you?"

Her face tensed, and the silence that followed spoke louder than any words. "I would do many things," she said finally. "Most of them would land me in prison or dead."

She leaned back in her chair. "I understand your point, Belaric. And yes, Sir Tolman can be... difficult. But he is part of this. You both are. You will have to live with that."

"And he will have to live with me," he replied smoothly.

She nodded once. "Thank you for not sharpening your words this time."

"I will refrain from insulting him. For now," he told her.

Her lips twitched with the faintest ghost of approval. Then she lifted the letter again.

"Now, to why I called you. We have received our first reply. Lord Vanis Halmor and his wife, Lady Maranna, wish to meet. They say they are being targeted as well—though they did not say why. They are offering to travel here. Three days' time."

She watched his reaction. "Sir Tolman thinks it is a mistake. He wants to wait until his mercenaries arrive."

Belaric folded his hands behind his back and began pacing. "I agree. Not entirely with him, but on waiting for the extra guards."

That earned a raised eyebrow. "You? Agreeing with him?"

"Only partially. I think we should go to the Halmor's, not wait for them to come to us." He stopped, facing her. "If they are coming under false pretenses—if they are tied to the Order—they will not bring anything incriminating with them. Any proof would be back at their estate, hidden, protected. If we go to them, I can listen to their guards, hear what their people are whispering. I will also be able to search their private rooms, their study, their library—anywhere they would keep a record of their betrayal. If the threat is real, I will hear it. If not, I will find it."

She nodded slowly. "And if they are being hunted?"

"Then we gain allies. But either way, we will learn more going to them than we will letting them walk into our walls," he said.

Lady Haldren's fingers tapped the edge of her desk. "Hosting them here before we understand their position is a risk. If they bring more eyes than answers, we will be handing them the shape of our defenses."

"Exactly," he said, nodding along with her.

She considered that a moment longer, then gave a faint nod. "Logical. So much so that it is what Lyra suggested as well."

Belaric gave a dry chuckle. "Of course she did."

A rare smile touched her lips—small, fleeting, but genuine. It was rare, that smile—and rarer still that it was meant for him.

"I will write back. Tell them we will come to Kerrinwatch. Sir Tolman's men should arrive in a few days. We will leave shortly after."

"A sound plan, my lady," he said. "I will ensure we are prepared."

He turned to go, but she stopped him with a word. "Belaric."

He paused, glancing back.

"Stop hiding from Sir Tolman and go help Staven. Lord knows the boy needs you," she told him.

He allowed himself a grin and opened the door. "Yes, my lady."

Then he was gone, leaving the room as quietly as he had found it.

Belaric took Lady Haldren's advice and joined the other guards for sword drills that morning. Sir Tolman was not pleased to see him—but to his credit, said nothing. Belaric focused on Staven. The boy had improved—less fumbling, less fear. He decided it was time to teach him the next form.

For the next few hours, he worked with him alone, correcting each mistake with a quiet word or a guiding hand—adjusting Staven's feet, shifting his grip, easing the blade into proper alignment. The boy would likely never be a master swordsman, but he would be good enough. Enough to hold his own against an average soldier. Enough to survive.

The following days passed quickly. Belaric oversaw the preparations for the journey. The road to Kerrinwatch would take three days, but planning mattered. He mapped their route, marked defensible rest points, and coordinated supply. Every detail was a layer of armor between Lady Haldren and the shadows that followed them. He knew the Order would expect Aeryn's return. When she did not come back—or worse, when word reached them that Lady Haldren and Lyra had survived—they would send someone else. He only hoped they would be gone before that happened. The longer the Order remained unaware of him, the safer they all were.

He made several quiet trips into town, gathering food, tools, and whatever else was requested. Whispers followed him, and a few glances turned into stares. He ignored them all.

Finally, the answer to their question came when Staven's shout broke the calm.

"Riders!"

Belaric turned from the training yard as Sir Tolman was already striding toward the gate, a rare grin creasing his face. Belaric followed, hanging back beneath the leaves of the outer hall. Lady Haldren appeared moments later, composed as ever, smoothing the folds of her gown as she approached.

Six riders closed the distance, the thunder of their hooves shaking the gate's iron hinges. They were dust-caked, broad-shouldered, and carried the weight of long travel as if it were nothing. Their saddles were worn, their armor practical, and every piece of their gear was scuffed and scarred, telling stories of a life spent on the road.

"Tolman! By the gods, you have gotten old!" the lead rider bellowed. The voice was a booming laugh that seemed to shake the air.

Sir Tolman barked a laugh. "I may be old, Dross, but I will never be as ugly as you!"

The men laughed as one, a rough sound that echoed off the stone walls.

Sir Tolman opened the gate himself. The six rode in without ceremony, heavy stallions snorting as they dismounted in near unison. The air around them was thick with sweat, old leather, and the hard dust of the road. Sir Tolman clasped arms with each man in turn, sharing short words, rough smiles, and harder grips.

Lady Haldren stepped forward with poise, eyes scanning the new arrivals. She gave no hint of emotion, but Belaric saw the small shift in her stance—the practiced stillness of someone watching for tells. Weighing them. Measuring.

"These are the men I told you about," he said, turning to her. "This is Dross, Hasker, Knoll, Ruthan, Nollan, and Jass."

Dross stood as tall as Tolman, thick-armed and broad-chested. Steel breastplate over leathers, his gloves worn and cracked from use. A massive two-handed sword rode across his back, its hilt worn smooth, a blade meant not for duels, but for war. His light brown hair circled a bald crown, and his eyes held the open, unapologetic confidence of a man who was used to being in charge. His black stallion loomed behind him, ears twitching, a creature as powerful and unrefined as its rider.

Hasker was just as tall, though leaner—narrow-shouldered, sharp in profile. He wore light brown leather armor that had been mended and resewn more than once, each patch a mark of its long use. A duelist's sword was at his hip, its hilt gleaming, a blade meant for speed and precision. A shield was strapped to his back. His dark brown stallion shifted, ever alert, its nervous energy mirroring the sharp intelligence in its rider's eyes.

Knoll was a boulder in comparison—short, thick, barrel-chested with two axes at his hips, their heads scarred and nicked from heavy use. Iron armor, dark as coal, protected him entirely, its dents and gashes telling a story of countless fights survived. He removed his helmet to reveal a mess of red hair and a short, bristling beard. He moved with a heavy, purposeful gait, the ground seeming to sigh under his weight. His black stallion tossed its head, stomped once, a beast of pure, unbridled strength.

Ruthan shared Hasker's wiry build, though he was slightly shorter. A longsword was at his side, a crossbow hanging from the white stallion beside him, its wooden stock polished from years of use. His fur-lined leather armor was worn but well-kept, and the quiver across his back rattled as he moved. He carried the bow with the confidence of someone who knew he could kill from a distance, a self-contained silence that spoke of patience and focus.

Nollan was the most forgettable at a glance—average build, average height, shoulder-length black hair hanging loose. A double-bladed axe, a difficult and unwieldy weapon, was strapped across his back. A single metal breastplate protected his chest over soft linen pants. His face was a blank slate, his eyes holding a neutral, unreadable expression. His light-grey stallion looked half-asleep, mirroring its rider's deceptive lack of presence.

Jass mirrored Hasker in height, long-limbed and quiet. He wore dark grey linen armor—meant for silence, not survival—with a cloak draped over his shoulders, the hood up, its folds concealing his face. A bow and quiver were strapped neatly to each side of his brown stallion's saddle, his hands resting on the reins with a stillness that suggested a hunter's patience.

"They are good fighting men," Sir Tolman said. "And loyal to the last."

Belaric watched them carefully. Six loyal men, Sir Tolman had said. But loyalty was a word that bent under pressure. He had seen it sharpen into a blade. He had seen it bought. For now, he said nothing. But he would be watching.

Lady Haldren nodded once. "Gentlemen, I cannot thank you enough for coming. We are in dire need of your help."

Dross stepped forward, grinning. "You certainly are, if Tolman's the one protecting you." He elbowed Sir Tolman in the ribs, and the others laughed again.

Sir Tolman smiled, but Belaric caught the brief tightness in his expression. Words, even old ones, could still cut.

"We are happy to be here, Lady Haldren," Dross added, his grin softening. "We will help however we can."

She inclined her head. "Your presence alone is a comfort."

Each man offered a small bow in turn. Lady Haldren gestured back toward the estate. "Let us get your horses stabled and get you something to eat. I am sure it has been a long ride."

The group gave a cheer and followed after her, boots thudding on stone and voices echoing with relief. Belaric remained behind a moment longer, watching the last of them disappear into the courtyard.

He sighed.

This was going to be fun.

After the horses were stabled, the men joined Lady Haldren, Lyra, and Sir Tolman in the estate's broad kitchen. Belaric did not follow. He lingered in the hall beyond, far enough to stay unseen, close enough to hear every word.

Wess worked like a man possessed, grease hissing and flour flying as he scrambled to feed them all. Eggs, strips of salted pork, thick biscuits with butter—he cooked with furious precision, muttering curses between every pan flip. The smell alone was enough to test Belaric's resolve.

Inside, the men joked with Sir Tolman like old soldiers reunited from war. The laughter was sharp and frequent, rising and falling in waves.

Belaric leaned against the wall, arms folded.

He could not remember the last time he had laughed like that. Only Renna could ever make him truly laugh.

Lady Haldren eventually pulled their focus back to business. She informed them of the plan: they would leave at first light for Kerrinwatch.

Sir Tolman followed with a grim edge to his tone. He told them the danger here was real. That the assassin—Aeryn—had nearly killed them all. He spoke plainly, without exaggeration, detailing how the attack had exposed their vulnerability. With only five trained men, it had been difficult to mount a real defense. He mentioned Staven—young, still green. Then Kedd and Tarnel, both veterans who had seen blood and knew what it meant.

Then came the pause. Dross leaned forward, his voice curious.

"What about the fifth man?" he asked.

Sir Tolman sighed. "Belaric."

The name tightened something in Belaric's chest. He tilted his head slightly, listening harder.

"A truly dangerous man," he said. "If it were my choice, he would not be here."

A silence settled, and Belaric imagined Lady Haldren's eyes turning sharply toward Sir Tolman. A warning.

"But," Sir Tolman added after a breath, "he is skilled with a blade. I doubt anyone here could best him. Even me."

The table fell silent.

Dross let out a low whistle. "Surely I cannot be hearing this right. The fearless Marius Tolman… afraid of another man?"

Sir Tolman's eyes narrowed. "I am not afraid. I have just seen what he is capable of. And I am telling you—heed my warning. Keep your distance. He keeps to himself. Best to let him."

The others grunted their agreement, but Belaric could hear the shift in tone—curiosity now, not fear. The kind that led to testing boundaries.

The men had been fed, their bellies full of Wess's cooking. They were gathered in the guards' quarters, drinking ale and talking in low tones. Belaric stood near the doorway, unseen in the shadows, listening. The air was thick with the scent of ale, sweat, and worn leather.

"Did you hear the old man?" Ruthan said, taking a drink from his mug. "Told us he fought off some assassin, and then his 'savior' is a man we are not to trifle with."

Dross, leaning back against the wall. "He says he won, but he acts like he lost. I have never seen a man give such a warning about someone who supposedly saved his life."

Hasker, his brow furrowed with concern, took a long drink from his mug. "He said he is skilled, but what kind of skill? I just saw a common man. Wears common guard's uniform, he cannot be that skilled with a blade."

"Sounds like a man with a big secret," Knoll replied, his voice a low rumble. "Best to let him be."

"He is still just one man," Ruthan scoffed. "I bet if he's that good, he has got a big head. Probably thinks he is better than us."

"Maybe," Dross said, with a mirthless smile on his face. "But if he is as good as Tolman says, he would probably make a fool of one of you before you would even touch him. So you go first."

The men fell silent, their bravado dying out.

After a moment, Hasker took another drink from his mug. "Did you hear what happened down in Wyvern's Crossing? Lord Marshal Garrick Volkov's house was found burned to the ground. No one knows who did it. The entire city's on lockdown."

"These are dark days in the kingdom when that can happen to a Lord Marshal," Dross said, his voice flat. "Someone's making a statement."

Belaric's eyes narrowed. The Volkov family was a powerful house, with a long history of being at odds with the crown. If they were involved… he tucked the thought away.

Belaric eventually slipped away, leaving the voices behind. He saddled Eddaross and rode out toward the southern hills. The sun was high, the sky clear. He let the wind wash over him, the warm air brushing his face as the scent of pine and wildflowers filled his lungs.

Out here, away from walls and whispers, he could breathe. He did not feel watched. Did not feel judged. For a little while, the silence was not heavy. It was clean.

He thought of Eryndorr.

Of a life beyond this—of finding another town like Brookhaven, quiet and sun-dappled, where no one asked who he was or what he had done. A place to build something different.

If I get him back… maybe.

He held the thought like a fragile thing.

When the sun began to dip, he turned Eddaross toward home. He was hungry, and he had watch that night.

The evening passed quietly. A spare room had been made up for the new arrivals, and they turned in early—exhausted from the road, and aware of what awaited them come morning. The house settled into its rhythm again, just a little more crowded than before.

When dawn broke, Belaric dressed in his guard gear and packed what he needed. The estate stirred to life. Boots thudded on the floorboards. Tack was checked. Provisions were loaded.

The six mercenaries, true to their word, left Belaric alone. No one approached him. But their eyes followed. All of them. He could feel the weight of their curiosity—measured, uncertain.

They were wondering whether the stories were true.

After the last hour of preparation, the group was ready. Dross and Sir Tolman led at the front, their horses side by side, already trading barbed jokes. "What is a man's skull worth these days, Tolman?" Dross grunted, a cynical grin on his face. "I am guessing your family is in debt."

Sir Tolman laughed and shook his head, but the smile never reached his eyes.

Hasker and Knoll followed just behind. In the center rode Lady Haldren and Lyra, wrapped in riding cloaks and flanked closely by Belaric, his eyes scanning every movement. Hasker, looking out across the open fields, said a quiet prayer to himself, his lips moving just enough for a watchful man to notice. Belaric caught the moment and understood. Knoll, his face a silent mask, simply adjusted the reins and stared intently at the path ahead, his gaze missing nothing.

Staven stuck close to him, quiet and nervous. Kedd and Tarnel took the rear ranks, with Ruthan, Jass, and Nollan trailing last.

The path ahead was not long. But blood had been spilled for less than letters, and trust did not ride easy in a saddle. As they rode, a dull ache flared in Belaric's shoulder, a sharp reminder of the battle that had brought him here. He adjusted his posture in the saddle, but the pain persisted, a steady, unwelcome companion on the road to Kerrinwatch.

20

Belaric sat in the saddle, eyes always moving. Watching. Measuring. The road ahead was empty, but that meant little. Quiet roads made for simple deaths. He had chosen this path carefully—not the shadowed trails the Order would favor, but the traveled ones, where others walked and talked and lived. Assassins disliked witnesses.

Sir Tolman was displeased.

"Too exposed," the knight had grunted. "She is a lady, not a peddler. She deserves a proper inn."

"She deserves to live," Belaric had answered.

They had argued, as they often did. Sir Tolman wanted quiet, safe places. Belaric knew there were none. The Order did not need silence to kill. They were silence.

In the end, it was Lyra who had settled it. "His plan makes the most sense," she had said, and that was that.

They rode southwest toward Brayfold, a near-forgotten cluster of farmland with a name just barely clinging to the map. Belaric knew it for what it was: somewhere to sleep with a roof overhead and food that was not dried strips of regret.

The sun climbed as the road unwound, dust curling beneath the hooves of eight horses. The new men rode stiff and jumpy, flinching at every crow's call and snapping branch.

Only Belaric seemed at ease, and even that was a façade.

Jass leaned closer to Hasker. "Long ride today," he muttered. "Think we will make it to the next town before the horses give out?"

Hasker shook his head. "The horses are fine. We are the ones who might not make it."

Belaric heard the words, but he did not react.

"You do not seem worried," Lyra said, her voice low beside him.

"I am not," he lied. "They may have heard about the failed attempt, but getting another blade to Brookhaven in time? Near impossible."

In front of them, Dross leaned closer to Sir Tolman. "How does he know so much?" he asked.

Sir Tolman did not miss a beat. "Do not ask."

But Lyra, seeing no reason to keep Belaric's past hidden, spoke up.

"He knows all of it because he used to be one of them. An assassin," Lyra stated, her gaze steady. "He broke his vow. That means they consider him a traitor, and they will hunt him just as fiercely as they hunt us."

Silence rolled over the group like a sudden wind. The six new men stared, eyes narrowing, fingers twitching toward hilts.

Lady Haldren gave Lyra a sharp look, but the girl only shrugged. "They were going to find out eventually. Better now than when their throats are already cut." She told her mother.

Questions came like hail—short, loud, and many. Accusations. Demands.

Sir Tolman reined in his horse and raised his voice. "Enough! Yes, he served as an assassin. Now he serves Lady Haldren. That is all you need to know."

The words fell like iron, ending the matter with weight rather than grace.

Belaric blinked, caught off guard by the absence of insult. He waited for the sneer, the spit, the backhanded slight. But Tolman only glanced back at him, then turned forward again with a roll of his eyes.

Progress, then. Or perhaps he simply did not want to be berated by Lady Haldren again.

The rest of the ride passed in silence.

Brayfold revealed itself in pieces—first a thin line of smoke, then tilled fields and groaning fences, then crooked homes scattered like bones across the earth. The buildings leaned with age and indifference. A boy stared from the side of a barn, a wooden spoon in one hand, mouth open.

Belaric led them to the only inn.

The group dismounted, their heavy stallions snorting and shifting in protest. An old stable master with gnarled, calloused hands emerged from the stables, followed by a young apprentice with wide, hesitant eyes. The master took the reins of the other horses, but paused when his gaze fell on Eddaross. The stallion's ears were back, a low rumble in its chest. The master simply nodded to Belaric. Belaric then took the reins himself and led Eddaross away into the stables. The rest of the group waited for him.

The Dancing Mare stood near the heart of town, or what passed for one. Two stories of tired brown timber, patched where the wood had rotted. The sign hung from a single rusted chain, groaning with each breath of wind. The windows had not seen a clean cloth in years, and the door looked like it had survived more fights than it should have.

A cracked barrel sat near the entrance, filled with ash and a single boot.

Inside, the smell of smoke and stale stew hung thick in the air. A handful of tables, all empty. Shadows huddled in the corners like old regrets.

Behind the bar stood a man who did not fit the room. Tall and lean, with long blond hair tied at the nape, and eyes the color of spring leaves. He moved with a kind of restless energy, a readiness to serve that was almost a nervous tic. He was too clean for the dirty work of an inn, and his hands, though strong, were not calloused from heavy labor.

"Afternoon, ladies and gents," he said, smiling. "Welcome to the Dancing Mare."

Belaric stepped forward, suspicious. "I thought Tobin ran this place."

The man's smile faltered just a touch. "He did. My father passed away nearly five years ago. I am Rourke. If you knew him, you might remember me—I was smaller than. I had the rare ability to trip over stools."

A memory stirred. A boy. A spilled mug. A roar of laughter from the broad-shouldered innkeeper.

"I remember. I am Belaric," he told the man.

Rourke's face lit up. "Belaric Kelmor—the merchant! You sold my father that necklace! He gave it to my mother—she still wears it!"

Before Belaric could stop him, Rourke turned and ran toward the back. "Mother! Come quick! Belaric's back!"

Belaric sighed.

Sir Tolman gave him a flat look. "You just had to ask."

Belaric smirked. "We cannot be too cautious."

"Right," Tolman muttered. "You are the picture of caution."

Belaric chuckled again as Rourke came bounding back through the door, a flour-dusted shadow trailing close behind. Brin looked much as Belaric remembered—older now, of course, with her face marked by time and long years in the kitchen. Wrinkles curled around her eyes like delicate threads, and her apron bore fresh stains—sauce, flour, the usual weapons of her trade. Her blonde hair, streaked with gray, was tied back in a no-nonsense bun, but her smile was bright and boyish, and her eyes held a kindness that was hard to find in a world of war.

"See, Mother—it is Belaric!" Rourke said, pointing like he had just caught a rabbit in a snare.

The woman peered at him, narrowing her eyes as she stepped closer.

"It is good to see you again, Brin," Belaric said.

Recognition lit her face. She clapped her hands together. "It is you! Belaric! Saints' mercy, you were always such a kind soul—and always brought the finest little trinkets. Useless mostly, but so lovely."

Belaric smiled. "Sadly, no trinkets this time. But we are in need of rooms."

Brin glanced over his shoulder, eyes widening as she took in the full group. "Oh, love, I am sorry. I have only three rooms upstairs. Doubt that it hold your lot."

Rourke stepped in quickly. "We have extra blankets and a few hay beds stowed out back. If it pleases you, we can push the tables aside tonight. The rest could sleep down here near the hearth," he spoke with a newfound confidence, a man finding his place in the world.

Brin beamed at her son. "That is a fine idea, Rourke." She turned back to Belaric. "Would that suit you, hun?"

Belaric nodded. "Perfect. Thank you."

She clapped again. "Well? Rourke—get these folk something to drink. I have got a pot of stew in the back that has been calling for company."

Sir Tolman gave a stiff bow. "Your hospitality is appreciated."

Brin waved a flour-caked hand at him. "Any friend of Belaric is welcome under my roof."

Sir Tolman eyed Belaric sidelong. "You have strange friends."

Belaric shrugged. "I have found them more reliable than most enemies."

The group settled—Dross and his men at one table, Kedd, Tarnel, and Staven at another. Belaric joined Lady Haldren and Tolman in a quiet corner. Lyra, ever curious, sat with Dross, her laughter already rising above the hum of voices.

Rourke returned with mugs of ale and a light wine for the ladies. He moved with more grace than Belaric remembered, though his eyes lingered too long on Lyra. Belaric caught the stare and fixed him with a warning look—a subtle tilt of the head, a narrowing of the eyes.

Dross, seated across from Lyra, caught the glance and the subtle tension that passed between the two men. He took a long drink from his mug, a cynical smirk playing on his lips. Beside him, Nollan gave a nervous chuckle and lowered his own eyes, pretending not to have seen.

Rourke chuckled nervously and hurried back to the bar.

Lady Haldren leaned in. "What is the plan?"

Belaric kept his voice low. "You and Lyra take one room. Dross and his men get the others—they have been on the road longer. Kedd and Staven take the back. Tarnel and I will stay down here by the stairs. You will be covered on all sides. Tolman should keep watch in the upstairs hall."

Sir Tolman nodded, but frowned slightly. "Staven's willing, but green. Let Dross swap with him. He can take the watch and still ride at sunrise."

Belaric agreed with a curt nod. Lady Haldren gave no protest.

For the first time since Brookhaven, the tension seemed to bleed from the group. Dross launched into a tale about a drunken bear and a half-naked knight, and Lyra giggled so hard she nearly spilled her drink. Lady Haldren watched her daughter quietly, a wistful smile tugging at the edge of her mouth. Despite everything—the threats, the shadows, the weight of noble blood—Lyra could still find joy. That was something.

Stew arrived in heavy clay bowls—roasted chicken with potatoes and carrots, swimming in a thick broth. Bellies filled, and for a time, the inn felt almost like a home.

Afterward, Belaric stood and motioned to Staven. "Training," he said.

The young man rose without complaint. Kedd and Tarnel joined, unwilling to miss the lesson. They stepped into the cool air as the last light slipped behind the hills. Belaric worked them hard—corrections here, redirection there. Kedd and Tarnel caught on quickly, refining footwork and edge control.

Staven struggled.

"Strike, recover. Now again. Step... stop—your weight's too far forward."

Staven adjusted, sweat streaking down his neck.

Belaric moved beside him. "A poor strike kills slowly," he said, voice flat. "You want it fast. You want them dead before they scream."

Staven swallowed and nodded. "Again," Belaric barked.

They practiced until their arms hung heavy, and their shirts clung to their backs. Belaric felt a familiar strain in his shoulder, the old wound protesting the exertion. He hid it behind a weary mask. Finally, he called a halt. The sun was gone now, replaced by a silver sliver of moon.

Back inside, a few villagers had trickled in—old friends of Brin or curious strangers drawn to the warmth. The room filled with laughter and the clink of mugs. Sir Tolman watched from the corner, still as stone.

Belaric approached him. "I will take the next watch. Go rest."

He studied Belaric for a moment before giving a muttered, "Keep an eye on the boy."

He had noticed it through the night, the way Rourke's eyes kept drifting toward Lyra, a hungry, adolescent gaze that made his gut twist. Not malice, but a callow, lustful curiosity that set Sir Tolman's teeth on edge.

Belaric smiled but agreed.

The evening passed easily. Eventually, the villagers took their leave. Brin and Rourke brought out the spare blankets and laid down the hay beds with care. After some final goodnights, they stepped out the back, heading for the small home next door.

Belaric bolted the door behind them.

Dross and Kedd took up their places at the back. Tarnel and Belaric settled near the fire, one on the floor, one hidden in a dark corner. The rest climbed to their rooms. The fire crackled low. Shadows deepened, stretching long and distorted across the worn floorboards.

The hours stretched, each moment a quiet hum in the stillness.

Then—a sound.

Faint. Almost delicate. The soft, careful click of the tumblers, then the barely audible scrape of a key turning in the lock.

Belaric's breath hitched, not from fear, but from the sudden surge of adrenaline that always sharpened his world. Every other sound in the inn—the settling timbers, the faint hiss of the embers, even his own heartbeat—receded. Someone was letting themselves in. Not forcing entry, but slipping inside. Too quiet for a guest. Too deliberate for a simple misstep. An intruder. And a cautious one.

Belaric stood, preparing himself. Tarnel tensed, hand drifting to his sword.

The front door creaked. Slowly. Carefully. A shadow slipped inside, a lean form silhouetted for a fleeting moment against the fainter moonlight beyond before melting into the inn's deeper gloom.

Belaric moved from the shadows and lunged before the figure could react.

He slammed the figure against the door, dagger at the man's cheek, pressing it just beneath the eye socket. Tarnel was already there, sword angled to gut.

From the back of the inn, the shuffle of boots—Dross and Kedd emerging from the shadows near the rear door. Sir Tolman came storming down the stairs, sword half-drawn, eyes sharp.

"What is it?" Sir Tolman demanded, voice sharp as steel.

Belaric did not glance back. His blade held firm. "It is Rourke."

Sir Tolman crossed the room in three long strides, eyes narrowing as he grabbed the young man by the collar and yanked him back. Belaric released his hold, stepping aside with practiced ease, the dagger still clutched in his hand.

"What in the nine hells are you doing here?" he growled, his grip tightening.

Rourke looked like a trapped animal, blinking against the firelight, breath ragged. "I—I am sorry. I just wanted to speak with her. Lyra. She is... she is beautiful."

He swallowed and then went on, voice quick and shaking. "Not just her looks. She is... different. Kind. The way she laughed—gods, I have not heard a sound like that in years. Not here. Not in a place like this." His gaze flicked between the men holding him. "I know what she is. I know she is a noble, a Valasar blessed, and I am just the son of a barkeep... but I was not trying to hurt anyone. I just—wanted to talk to her. To see her smile again."

Sir Tolman's jaw clenched, knuckles white around the boy's collar. "That is Lady Lyra, you miserable pissant. Not someone for you to gawk at like a tavern girl."

Belaric stepped forward, calm but cold. "Where was Tobin's famous scar?"

Rourke blinked in confusion. "What?"

Sir Tolman's brow furrowed, a flicker of confusion in his own eyes at the abrupt question. What did Tobin's old wound have to do with this?

"Where?" Belaric snapped.

But before Sir Tolman could speak, Belaric raised a hand, a subtle gesture that cut through the noise, and suddenly Tolman understood. It was a test.

Rourke stammered. "Above his right hip—he got it years ago. Two drunk farmers started brawling one night. One broke a bottle and tried to stab the other with it. He missed. Caught my father instead."

Belaric held his gaze for a beat longer, then nodded. "He is telling the truth. He is Tobin's son. That is the story Tobin always told."

Sir Tolman did not relax. "She is a noble. You are a boy with loose hands and looser thoughts. If I catch you even glancing at her again, I will make sure you never glance at anything again."

"Tarnel, get the door," he added without turning.

Tarnel moved, opening it swiftly. Sir Tolman, still holding Rourke like a sack of spilled grain, flung him outside. The boy hit the dirt hard and scrambled up, fleeing toward his home without a word.

The five men looked at each other, breath steadying.

Then, one by one, they broke into laughter.

It cut off as Lyra's voice rang from above. "He was handsome."

All heads turned. She stood at the top of the stairs in her night-clothes, arms crossed, smirking faintly. Behind her, Lady Haldren loomed like a thundercloud, silent and unimpressed.

Sir Tolman sighed, running a hand over his face. "Everyone back to bed."

They obeyed. One by one, the guards returned to their posts and rooms; the fire crackling low once more.

The rest of the night passed without incident.

Morning came swiftly.

Golden light crept through the smeared windows of the Dancing Mare, pooling across wooden floors and warming the scent of old stew, damp ash, and worn linens. The inn stirred with slow movement—armor shifting, boots scraping, tired men blinking away sleep as the hearth crackled faintly behind them.

Staven and Hasker stretched first. Then Lyra descended the stairs in a swirl of morning energy, followed more sedately by Lady Haldren, Jass, and the rest. They gathered around the long table in silence, the weight of travel settling across them again like a familiar cloak.

Brin entered through the back door, a basket of herbs in her arms and hesitation on her face. Her eyes swept the room before settling on Lady Haldren.

"My lady," she said, voice quiet. "I am so sorry for how that foolish boy behaved last night. If I had known what he planned, I would have beaten him senseless myself."

Lady Haldren raised a hand. "Brin, you have nothing to apologize for. I was young once. The heart is a powerful thing. I am just glad he was not harmed. My men can be... overprotective."

Brin offered a nervous chuckle. "They put the fear of the gods in him, that is for sure. We have decided he will spend the day with the farmers—working off the foolishness in sweat."

Sir Tolman's mouth twitched, but he held his tongue.

"There is no need," Lady Haldren said, her voice warm. "We only have time for breakfast, then we must leave. No harm was done."

Brin nodded visibly relieved. "You are too kind, my Lady. I will fetch the boy. We will have your breakfast soon." She bowed slightly and slipped into the back room.

Belaric leaned closer to Tolman. "We should send two to get the horses ready."

Sir Tolman agreed with a nod. "Staven, Jass. You know what to do."

The two men rose without a word and made their way outside.

Belaric unrolled the map across the table, its worn parchment crackling softly as he smoothed it flat to reveal the route he had painstakingly planned. "If we push hard today, we can make Goldmeadow before the sun dips. No long stops. If we manage it, we will reach Kerrinwatch by early tomorrow."

Sir Tolman folded his arms. "Long ride, but it can be done." He hesitated, a slight frown creasing his brow. "The inn in Goldmeadow... it is a small place, is not it? Just like this one. Cramped quarters for Lady Haldren and Lyra after such a journey. Perhaps we should consider another route. Crowmere, maybe? Bigger city, easier to vanish into the crowd, and better accommodations."

Belaric frowned. "Normally, I would agree. But the Order has a presence there. Several assassins live there. If they have heard that Lady Haldren and Lyra survived, we risk walking into a nest."

Lady Haldren and Sir Tolman exchanged glances before the knight turned back to Belaric. "Very well. Goldmeadow it is, if you agree, my Lady?"

Lady Haldren nodded. "Lower risk is worth a sore back. I only hope Lyra is ready for the pace."

All three turned to glance at her. She was seated across from Hasker, laughing over a shared story and utterly unaware that half the table had just plotted her day around the shadows of death.

Brin returned with Rourke in tow. The boy looked smaller than the night before. He kept his head down and made a quiet retreat behind the bar. The men's eyes followed him. Rourke did not lift his gaze once.

Lyra giggled. Lady Haldren shook her head with an exhale that might have been a sigh or a smile.

Moments later, Jass and Staven returned. "The horses are ready—except yours, Belaric," Jass said. "Damn thing would not let us near it."

Amusement flickered across his face. "He does not take to strangers. I will handle him."

Breakfast followed—hot toast spread with butter, eggs cooked firm, and strips of roasted pork still steaming. It was the kind of meal you only noticed you missed once it was in front of you. They ate quickly, and the table slowly cleared.

When he finished, Belaric rose and approached the bar. He placed three silver coins on the counter.

Brin's eyes widened. "Oh no, Belaric—I could not possibly."

He smiled. "You have been a kind host. Just do me one favor—if anyone comes asking about us, tell them you do not remember."

He added a small wink.

She hesitated, then nodded. "I will tell them nothing. You have my word."

Belaric's eyes dropped to the necklace around her throat. "Still wearing it?"

Brin smiled, brushing it with her fingertips. "Every day. Tobin always said I had no love for jewelry—he was not wrong. But this one... I never take it off."

Her smile softened. "Gods, I miss that fool of a man."

Belaric's hand lingered on the counter as he looked at her.

He imagined Renna in Brin's place—older, a touch of silver in her hair, a smudge of flour on her cheek, still laughing at his bad jokes. Maybe they would have run an inn like this. One day, passed it on to their son. A quiet life full of wood smoke and warm bread. He liked the thought. More than he wanted to.

"He was a good man," Belaric said gently.

Brin nodded, her eyes glistening. "Safe travels, Belaric."

The group began to move toward the door. At the kitchen entrance, Rourke stood, half-hiding. Lyra paused, then darted toward him.

"I thought it was sweet," she whispered—and kissed him on the cheek.

Rourke froze, eyes wide. His mouth opened to speak, but then he spotted Sir Tolman across the room. The knight was staring at him—expression blank, hand resting on the pommel of his sword.

Rourke blinked, swallowed, and wisely turned back to Lyra. He gave a small, stiff bow. "Thank you, my lady."

She grinned and ran back to the others.

Sir Tolman shook his head. "Damn fool of a boy."

The group stepped outside into the cool morning sun. The scent of dew and tilled soil filled the air, and birds called lazily from the rooftops.

Belaric found Eddaross waiting, the stallion pawing at the ground. He fetched the saddle and gear himself, his movements efficient and quiet. The horse snorted, but stood still as Belaric swung the leather over its back and cinched the straps with practiced hands. Eddaross tossed his head in approval once Belaric took the reins himself.

They mounted up in silence.

Sir Tolman took the lead.

It would be a long ride—but Belaric was ready for it.

Sir Tolman pushed them hard. Breaks were rare; the pace unforgiving. The sun climbed, then sagged toward the horizon, and still they rode—saddles creaking, throats dry, bones aching. More than one man muttered under his breath about sore legs and stiffer backs, but no one dared ask for more than a brief stop. Sir Tolman kept them moving, and Belaric agreed with the strategy. He felt a dull ache begin to throb in his mending shoulder, a constant thrum beneath the weight of his saddle. He shifted his weight, trying to ease the pressure, but it was a familiar companion on a long journey. The longer they lingered on open roads, the more likely the Order would find them.

It was near sundown when they crested the last hill and Goldmeadow revealed itself. The town lay in a valley awash in amber light, its thick-timbered buildings casting long shadows across the cobbled main road. Merchant stalls still bustled despite the late hour, colorful cloth canopies swaying in the wind. Goldmeadow was not large enough to be a true trade hub, but it had the look of a town content with itself—peaceful, well-kept, and blessed with breathtaking views. It was known for the vast fields of sun-lilies that surrounded it, flowers that bloomed gold in the spring and gave the valley its name. Compared to Brayfold, it was cleaner, quieter, and easier on the soul.

They entered without trouble, hooves clapping softly against the stone. The first inn they spotted was a two-story place with clean shutters and a sign swinging gently in the breeze. A painted serpent on the wooden plaque held a frothy mug in one clawed hand: The Drunk Dragon. There was another inn farther down the road, but they hoped this one would suffice.

Jass went inside. He returned a moment later, frowning. "Only three rooms."

Hasker volunteered to check the other inn—The Broken Shield. He returned ten minutes later, scowling. "One room. Small. No other space."

Tolman cursed under his breath. "We will have to split."

He, Belaric, and Lady Haldren stood near the horses, weighing options. Belaric was the first to speak. "Lady Haldren and Lyra will take one room. I will sleep now. When they are ready for bed, they wake me, and I will stand guard from inside. Hasker, Dross, and you take the second room. Kedd, Tarnel, Knoll, and Ruthan in the third." He looked towards the road. "Jass, Staven, and Nollan can take the room at the Broken Shield. It will be cramped, but it will do."

Sir Tolman exhaled, but nodded. "It works." He turned to the three men. "No getting drunk. First light we leave." They nodded and rode off toward the second inn.

The rest dismounted and handed their reins to the waiting stablemaster—an older man who looked as if he would rather be doing anything else. He took the horses in grumbling silence, though Belaric had to walk Eddaross into the stable himself. The stallion did not tolerate strange hands.

Inside, the inn was warm, with the comforting scent of roasting meat and fresh bread lingering in the air. The others had already claimed two tables near the hearth. Sir Tolman was at the bar, finishing payment with the innkeeper. Belaric slid into a seat beside Lyra. She looked tired, but she still managed a faint smile.

Sir Tolman returned and dropped the keys on the table. A young woman soon followed, balancing a tray of mugs. Each man took one and drank. The first sips were fast, the second slower. Sir Tolman did not touch his.

"One drink," he said, voice low but firm. "That is all."

The men nodded. Belaric drained his, pushed the mug aside, and stood. "I will go rest now. Wake me when they are ready."

He took the stairs two at a time, weariness tugging at the edges of his thoughts. The room was small, but clean. Two beds, a washbasin, a shuttered window. He settled with his back to the wall between the beds and let sleep take him.

He woke to the click of the door, on his feet before it opened fully. Lady Haldren stepped inside and jumped, pressing a hand to her chest.

"Must you do that?" she said, tone flat.

Lyra laughed behind her. "You startled her."

Belaric exhaled. "My apologies. Habit," he said with a grin.

Lyra tilted her head at him. "Would you mind stepping outside while we change?"

He gave a small bow and stepped into the hallway. Sir Tolman stood nearby, leaning against a doorframe.

"If you need more sleep," he said, "wake me. I will take over."

Belaric nodded. "Thank you. I may take you up on that."

Sir Tolman grunted and stepped back into his room, leaving the door half-open behind him.

A few minutes later, Lyra opened their door. "You can come back now."

The candlelight flickered gently as Belaric stepped back in. Both beds were turned down. Lady Haldren sat brushing her hair. Lyra was already under the covers.

"You do not have to stay in here all night," Lady Haldren said.

"I will be fine, my lady," he replied.

She shrugged and leaned over to blow out the candle. Darkness filled the room. For a long while, there was only silence.

Belaric sat in the corner, listening to the slow rhythm of sleep. The world beyond these walls seemed distant—like it could not touch them here. He did not believe that, of course. But for the moment, he let himself pretend.

Then Lyra's voice broke the stillness.

"Belaric?" she whispered.

"I am awake," he murmured.

"I know I act tough," she whispered. "But I am scared. They tried to kill my mother because of me."

He stood quietly and knelt beside her bed. "Lyra... this is not your fault. It is theirs. The Order. The nobles who give the commands. They are the ones who should be afraid." He took her hand gently. "We will not let them hurt you. Or your mother. You have my word."

She sniffled and squeezed his hand. "Thank you, Belaric. You are a good man."

He gave a dry laugh. "I hope one day I can believe that."

He made to stand, but she held him.

"Will you tell me a story?" she asked.

He hesitated. "My stories are not like Dross's. They are not funny. Not safe."

"They cannot all be bad. Tell me about your wife. Renna," she pleaded.

The name hit softly, like a memory held too long in the dark. He sat back down beside her bed.

"All right. I will tell you how we met," he told her.

He folded his arms over the edge of the bed, resting his chin there like a man laying down a blade.

"It was Greymoor. I had just come off a job—one of the bad ones. The kind that sticks in your bones. I was not even supposed to stay long, but something made me linger. I saw her at the market. Selling fruit. Apples, pears. Hair like fire in the sun. Freckles everywhere. Gods, she smiled at me."

Lyra did not laugh this time—she only smiled into her blanket. It was a gentler sound. She could hear the weight beneath the words.

"I panicked. Asked her the price of pears. She told me. And the plums. She said they were good for thinking, but I was an apple man. And she was right. So I bought an apple, gave her the coin, and then… I just stood there."

He chuckled softly, a ghost of a memory. "Could not bring myself to leave. Before I knew it, I asked her how much another apple was." He shook his head, a wry smile. "She blinked, then said, 'You just bought one.' There I was—killer of men, lost in front of a fruit stall. I could not think of anything to say, so I bought another apple. She laughed the whole time, but from that moment, I knew I loved her."

He smiled faintly. "She finally said, 'You must really like apples.' And I said, 'I do not know.' She must have thought me an idiot; she would have been right to assume so."

The room grew quiet again. Lyra did not ask for another story. She did not have to. Her breathing slowed. She had fallen asleep.

Belaric leaned forward, brushed her hair gently from her forehead, and kissed it. As he did, a sharp twinge of pain shot through his mending shoulder, a physical echo of a memory he still carried.

"Goodnight, Lyra."

He turned and moved quietly back to his corner. He had spent years watching in the dark for blades. Tonight, he watched over something far more fragile.

Moments like this did not come often. And they never stayed.

Then a voice came softly from the shadows.

"Thank you, Belaric."

It was Lady Haldren. He had not known she was still awake.

He stood a moment longer; the words sitting heavy in the dark. Then finally, "Of course, my Lady."

She said nothing else. Soon, her breathing joined her daughter's in a quiet rhythm of peace.

And Belaric kept watch, just as he always had.

First light came with a gray hush, the kind that softened the edges of the world and made it easier to forget what shadows might follow. The group stirred with quiet discipline—the groan of boots, the clink of buckles, the scrape of chairs against floorboards all louder than any spoken word.

The innkeeper brought out breakfast—warm bread, goat cheese, and strips of smoked meat. No time to waste. They ate quickly, saying little, exchanging only nods or tired glances across the table. The air held a different kind of weight. Not fear—something sharper. Purpose.

Jass, Staven, and Nollan arrived from the Broken Shield Inn shortly after, looking half-crushed from their night's sleep but sober and ready. Sir Tolman gave them a curt nod, and that was all the acknowledgment they needed.

They departed without incident, riding beneath a pale morning sky veiled in streaks of gold. The formation stayed tight, hooves drumming steadily over hardened earth. Hours passed in silence.

The road wound on, the terrain rising, the trees thinning until they gave way to highland scrub and jagged stone. Knoll, who had been silent for hours, shifted his weight in the saddle and spoke without looking at anyone.

"These people live in stone, but they are built for war," he said, his voice a low rumble.

Dross grunted in agreement but said nothing else.

By midday, Kerrinwatch came into view.

The town sat nestled like a wedge of granite between two mountain shoulders, smoke curling from squat chimneys, the distant ring of hammers echoing between stone walls. The buildings were low, dark, and heavy, crafted from local ore and capped with slate roofs. Kerrinwatch lived off its mines—its veins of rich metal shaped into fine blades and honest tools.

The group rode through without pause. No merchants flagged them down. No children chased their horses. This was not a place for wandering strangers to linger. People here had iron to bend and coin to earn, and little patience for anything else.

The road curved toward the mountain's base, where the estate of Lord Vanis Halmor waited—a structure carved into the rock itself. The walls were quarried stone, clean and seamless. Only the angled roof was wooden, framed in dark pine. The outer wall was solid and unwelcoming, flanked by two narrow towers and a gate of black iron that looked like it had never once opened in a hurry.

As they neared, a voice called out from atop the wall.

"Hold!"

The group halted.

Belaric scanned the ramparts. A few guards were visible—bows slung, halberds in hand, eyes like stone.

No one moved. The wind stirred dust across the road. Cloth flapped softly from one of the tower slits. No sound came from within the estate. The only noise was the distant ring of a hammer from the town far below.

They waited.

Lyra shifted in her saddle and cast a glance toward Belaric. He returned it with the faintest nod—just enough to say I see it too. She said nothing, but her hand moved slightly toward her cloak's inner seam.

Then, after several long minutes, the gate creaked open.

From the shadowed courtyard beyond emerged Lord Vanis Halmor and Lady Maranna Halmor, arm in arm. They moved with slow, deliberate grace, as though they were statues brought to life.

They were older; that much was plain even from a distance. Lord Halmor's beard was white and sharply trimmed, a symbol of his age and carefully maintained authority. His posture was as stiff as the dark maroon robes he wore, which were lined with gold stitching. His eyes, though old, were sharp and missed nothing—a look that spoke of a life spent in court politics and cunning. His wife stood beside him like a blade in silk: tall, narrow, and precise. Her emerald robes shimmered faintly in the sun, pearls hanging from her ears and wrists like trophies from some bloodless war. The jewels were not just for show; they were a declaration. She held her head at an angle that suggested a constant, subtle judgment of the world around her.

They walked with a kind of practiced grace, as though the road should part for them, not the other way around.

Lady Haldren dismounted and stepped forward, hands open in greeting, shoulders straight. The rest remained mounted, watchful. Belaric shifted slightly, trying to catch the words exchanged between them, but the wind stole them away.

He watched their expressions instead. Lord Halmor's brows lifted as Lady Haldren spoke, a gesture of mild surprise or perhaps skepticism. He turned to his wife, said something, then looked back and nodded. When he finally raised his voice, it carried.

"You are welcome to stay under our roof, Lady Haldren. All of you," he told them.

The gate opened wider, and the group was motioned forward.

They rode into the estate under the watchful gaze of guards and stone. The courtyard was paved, the walls smooth, the structure built more like a fortress than a home. Belaric noted the arrow slits. Reinforced shutters. A murder hole above the gate. All subtle, all intentional.

The iron gate groaned shut behind them. A bolt slid into place with a deep metallic thunk.

He did not look back. Did not need to.

He dismounted beside Eddaross, letting his hand rest on the stallion's shoulder a moment longer than necessary. His eyes swept the estate grounds—guards, doors, corners, places where men could hide steel.

No one had drawn a weapon. No one had said the wrong thing.

And yet...

He kept his voice silent, but the thought pressed in like weight behind his eyes.

Please, he thought, let this not be a cage.

21

Two boys, no older than ten, sprinted from the side of the estate as the company dismounted. Dirt clung to their bare feet, and their tunics hung loose, patched and stained from stable work. Each took hold of a horse's reins with practiced ease—except one.

Belaric was already leading Eddaross by the time a hand reached for the stallion's bridle.

"I will handle him," he said simply, his voice low and flat.

The boy flinched, stepping back.

Belaric offered a half-smile. "He is a grumpy old bastard. He does not like strangers near him. Barely likes me most days."

A few chuckles followed from behind. Eddaross snorted, tossing his storm-gray mane as if offended.

Belaric guided the stallion into a stall padded with fresh straw. "Be good, old boy. No biting, no kicking, no theatrics." Eddaross stomped a hoof, and Belaric let out a quiet laugh. "I will take that as agreement."

With the horses stabled and the men reclaiming their gear, a servant in finely embroidered black and silver led them into the estate. The Halmor house loomed like a carved mountain, all stone angles and silent judgment. Built directly into the rock face, it bore no frills beyond what the stone itself offered—no ornate arches, flawless symmetry, walls that whispered of wealth with no need to shout.

Guards escorted them through echoing halls into the east wing, where rooms had been prepared.

They gave Lady Haldren and Lyra their own chamber, while they offered Belaric, Sir Tolman and Dross another room. The remaining guards were given beds within the barracks.

Lord Vanis Halmor had bid them rest, citing the long road behind them and promising a quiet dinner to mark their arrival.

But before anyone could think of rest, Lady Haldren summoned Belaric and Sir Tolman to her room.

The chamber was carved from mountain stone, seamless and solid. The floor was softened with thick rugs—red, gold, and bone-white—woven in patterns Belaric did not recognize. A massive bed sat against the far wall, its wooden frame dark as midnight and carved with scenes of war and hunt. A trio of wardrobes lined the left wall, each tall enough to dwarf a man. Opposite them stood a stone hearth already burning, the fire casting flickering shadows across a desk carved straight from the room's foundation. Stone shelves were built into the wall, filled with leather-bound tomes, scrolls, and relics. A small table, round and bare, sat beside a narrow window that over-looked the valley below.

They gathered at the table—Lady Haldren, Lyra, Sir Tolman, and Belaric. Outside, dusk was surrendering to full dark.

Lady Haldren did not waste breath on pleasantries. "What is the plan?"

Belaric leaned forward, forearms resting on the table's edge. "We will all be at dinner tonight. I will not be able to move freely with so many eyes watching. After the halls go quiet and sleep settles, I will begin. I will search their private quarters—look for letters, signs, anything they did not intend to show us."

"No killing," Sir Tolman said sharply, unprompted.

Belaric's jaw tightened. "I will kill no one—unless I must."

Lady Haldren watched him with narrowed eyes but said nothing.

"I expect they will want to speak with you tomorrow. Privately. That is when they will press. What happened. What you intend. Who you have spoken to." He glanced at her, then at Lyra. "In their letter, they claimed they were being targeted as well. Try to make them tell you why."

Lady Haldren nodded once. "We will draw out what we can."

Belaric nodded and continued. "I will search again tomorrow night. Depending on what I find, we may need to leave quickly. Or stay longer, though I do not like the thought."

He looked to Sir Tolman. "We will need a man or two in town. Someone who can speak plainly, blend in, draw out rumors without raising suspicion."

Sir Tolman did not hesitate. "Hasker and Ruthan. They have got tongues sharper than their swords. I will have them sent to the local inns and taverns."

Lyra sat forward slightly, her hands clasped on the table. "What about me?"

Belaric smiled faintly. "You help your mother. Listen. Use your mark. Judge what is true and what is not. Most men lie without thinking—they will not expect a child to see through it."

She grinned. "I can do that."

He let his gaze fall on each of them in turn. "We do not know whether these people are allies or if they are simply better liars. Be cautious."

All nodded.

Sir Tolman stood. "We will be in our room, my lady. Call if you need us."

Lady Haldren thanked them. As they departed, Belaric felt the familiar knot return to his stomach. It tightened with every silent footstep down the polished hall. They had ridden into a fortress, and for all his careful planning, they might have just stepped into a prison. He trusted no one here, least of all the smooth-faced lord and his bejeweled wife. Lyra and Lady Haldren were within these walls now, vulnerable, and the thought clawed at him. He walked with purpose, ignoring the intricate tapestries and gleaming armor that lined the corridors, until he reached the heavy oak door that had been assigned to the guard detail.

Their room was nearly identical in shape to Lady Haldren's, but made for soldiers—less grandeur, more practicality. Three beds stood against the far wall, smaller but comfortable. Dross was already collapsed onto one bed, still wearing his boots and snoring softly.

Belaric's first action was to find a place for his pack. He knelt beside the cold hearth and, after a quick sweep to ensure it was empty of cinders, wedged the pack and its contents—the leather armor and silent steel—deep into the unlit chimney. No one would think to look there, not for a long while.

Belaric gave a quiet laugh.

"I am going to rest while I can," he told Sir Tolman, voice low. "If I am to be up all night, I will need it."

Sir Tolman nodded, already unstrapping his belt. "Try not to get yourself killed tonight."

"No promises," Belaric muttered, peeling off the borrowed guard's uniform. His muscles ached, joints sore from riding and the weight of vigilance. He rolled his shoulders, feeling the familiar stiffness in his old wound, but the ache was less than it had been a week ago. He lay back on the thin mattress, the cool air against his skin a brief comfort.

He stared at the ceiling. Stone above, stone below. A house built like a tomb.

He had slept in worse places. The Order had given him the ability to rest anywhere, even with blood still wet on his hands. But this—this false comfort—was harder somehow. Every inch of stone around him felt like it was watching. Waiting.

He did not trust this place. Did not trust the Halmor's, their quiet servants, or the way the halls echoed too perfectly.

Still, he let his eyes close.

Sleep claimed him slowly, as if even rest feared what the night might bring.

Heat struck him like a hammer.

Belaric opened his eyes, and flame consumed him.

The room around him crackled with fire—wood beams overhead sagged and split, coughing embers into the air like dying stars. Smoke curled in every breath. He staggered backward, stumbling into the wall as tongues of fire licked the stone beside him. The scent hit next—burned leather, scorched wood, and something worse. Familiar. The taste of a past he could not outrun.

He knew this place. His house. The sitting room below the loft. The same worn rug beneath his boots. The same chair Renna used to sit in when peeling fruit, now half-consumed, its legs glowing red with heat.

"Belaric!" Her voice cut through the roar of the flames, high and cracked.

His head snapped up toward the stairs. "Renna!"

He surged forward; the fire clawing at his clothes, his skin. Heat blistered his arms as he shielded his face and pressed on. The staircase loomed ahead—splintered and ablaze, each step a trial by fire. He forced his way up, boots charring, breath seared from his lungs.

"Hold on!" he shouted, choking on smoke. He reached the top and kicked the door inward. It exploded open with a spray of sparks.

Renna lay on their bed, her face pale and slick with sweat. She looked just as she had that night—when she had brought their son into the world and bled too much doing it. A crimson pool soaked the sheets beneath her, spreading like spilled ink. And beside her stood a man in black robes, holding a screaming infant in one hand.

Eryndorr. His son.

"No," Belaric breathed, staggering forward.

The robed figure turned slowly. A mask concealed his face—smooth, expressionless, with eye slits like a vulture's stare and no mouth to speak lies or truths. Somehow, that absence made the voice worse. A voice Belaric knew.

"You are a failure," the Vowkeeper said. "Nothing but a rusted weapon. A man broken. Your world will burn."

Belaric reached for his blade—but it was not in his hand. He reached anyway, burning fingers curling to nothing. "Put him down!" he roared. "Let him go!"

The Vowkeeper only laughed—a hideous, hollow sound that rang louder than the fire. Then, quick as a striking adder, he drew a curved blade and swept it across Renna's throat.

Belaric screamed.

Blood spilled down her neck like a red river, soaking the sheets anew. Her eyes locked on his—wet, wide, and full of sorrow. Her lips moved, forming words he could not hear over the fire's roar. A whisper lost to flame. "Save him…"

He charged.

The Vowkeeper sidestepped with an almost casual ease, a hand flashing out to shove Belaric aside.

Too slow.

He hit the wall hard enough to knock the wind out of him. Flames curled along the baseboards now, the room caving inward. He spun, bladeless hands ready to rip the man apart—but the Vowkeeper was behind him, still holding the child. Still laughing.

"As I said… a failure."

Then, he was gone.

The flames surged. The floor beneath Belaric's feet cracked and split. He looked for Renna—but the fire swallowed the bed, swallowed the walls. Smoke rolled in, thick as fog, and his skin screamed from the heat. He turned in frantic circles.

"Renna!" Nothing.

"Eryndorr!" No response.

The flames reached for him like hands. His body burned. His thoughts burned. His scream tore free, raw and broken—

—and he woke with a gasp.

His house was gone, and the fire with it. The stone ceiling above him was unmoving. The air cold. Sir Tolman stood over him, one hand on Belaric's shoulder, eyes narrowed.

"You were dreaming," Sir Tolman said. "Loudly."

Belaric's chest rose and fell in rapid bursts. Sweat soaked his skin. His hands trembled as if still scorched. It took him a long moment to realize the pain was gone, but the echo of it—of her—remained.

He wiped a hand across his face and sat up; the bed creaking beneath him.

"Was it the boy?" Sir Tolman asked, quieter now.

Belaric nodded slowly, his voice low and bitter. "I am cursed with these damn dreams." He clenched his jaw, the heat from the memory still coiling in his chest. "They do not let me rest. They never have."

Sir Tolman stepped closer, arms crossed. "While I hate what you are—" he paused, correcting himself with a grunt, "—what you were... I find it even worse that a man like the Vowkeeper took a child. Whatever monster he is, no child deserves to grow up under that kind of shadow."

Belaric looked up at him. There was no pity in his eyes, only grim certainty.

"Thank you," Belaric said. "You truly are a man of honor."

Sir Tolman rolled his eyes but smiled. "Do not go soft on me now, you miserable pissant. I just want to be rid of you. And this," he gestured vaguely toward the walls around them, "is the fastest way."

Belaric let out a dry laugh. "Then let us hope tonight gives us our first clue—something to stop these attacks on Lady Haldren and Lyra. And something to lead me to my son."

Sir Tolman gave a curt nod, then turned toward Dross's bed. The man was still sprawled across it, boots half on, snoring loud enough to rattle stone.

With a grunt, Tolman walked over and kicked the wooden frame hard. "Wake up, you damn fool. You snore like a bear with a dagger up its ass."

Dross groaned, dragging a pillow over his head. "Fuck off, old man..."

"I will show you, old man." Sir Tolman reached down, gripped the blanket, and yanked it off in one swift motion. Dross shot upright, eyes wide and hair a disaster.

"You have done it now!" he growled, launching himself off the bed.

What followed could barely be called a fight—more a tangle of limbs, grunts, and muttered curses. Dross barreled into Tolman, but the older man sidestepped, grabbing him by the collar and twisting them both into a grapple. Dross tried to hook a leg, but Sir Tolman's experience showed; he turned the motion against him and sent Dross crashing back onto the mattress, straddling him with a triumphant grin.

"That is what a real fighter feels like, boy," Sir Tolman declared.

Dross panted, laughing despite himself. "Your bones creak louder than your voice."

Sir Tolman smirked. "And yet I still put you down."

They both stood up, breathless but grinning. Belaric shook his head.

"We must hurry, old men. We have to get ready for dinner," he told them.

The room went still, like the moment before a storm.

Both men froze. Slowly, in perfect unison, they turned to him.

"Watch your mouth, boy," Sir Tolman growled, a wide smile on his face. Dross snorted in agreement. "We will show you what old men can do."

Belaric backed a step, smirking. "There is no shame in being old. Wisdom, scars, brittle knees—it is all part of the charm."

They exchanged glances, then charged.

Belaric ducked, sidestepped, grabbed a chair and shoved it between them. Dross stumbled but kept going, while Sir Tolman lunged wide. Belaric pivoted, weaving through the room, knocking over a stool and sending a basin clattering. He jabbed Dross in the ribs with an elbow and shoved Sir Tolman into the wall—but they kept coming. Two predators fueled by pride and petty vengeance.

He almost made it to the door.

Almost.

Dross caught his legs just as Sir Tolman wrapped him from behind, and together they dragged him to the floor. Belaric grunted as his back hit stone. Dross pinned his legs while Sir Tolman straddled his chest, grinning like a wolf.

"These old men just beat you," Sir Tolman said, breathless with laughter. "What do you have to say about that, Belaric?"

Belaric opened his mouth to reply—but the door creaked open before he could speak.

Lady Haldren stood in the hallway, framed by golden torchlight, her hair braided intricately and a deep blue dress falling like silk over her form. Lyra stood just behind her in a matching gown, eyes wide with poorly hidden amusement.

Lady Haldren arched a brow. "Why is it that men always act like children?"

Sir Tolman cleared his throat, half-raising a finger—but she cut him off with a wave.

"Get up off the floor. We cannot be late for dinner," she told them.

Without waiting for a reply, she turned away with a swish of fabric, Lyra giggling as she followed. "I swear, you move like old men," Lady Haldren called back, disappearing into her room.

All three men were quiet for a heartbeat before bursting into laughter.

Dross and Sir Tolman helped Belaric to his feet, still grinning like fools. He dusted himself off, nodding toward their packs.

"Come on, you two. Cleanest uniforms. Let us try to look like guards, not drunks dragged from an alley," he told them.

They got to it, trading smirks and muttered threats as they dressed in silence broken only by the sounds of boots pulled on, belts buckled, and the faint echoes of laughter down the hall.

For a moment, Belaric forgot the fire, the blood, the boy. Just men—grimy, sore, and laughing like fools in borrowed uniforms. It did not last. But it was something.

The three men finished dressing quickly, buckling swords and adjusting their collars with varying levels of care. They stepped into the hall, where the rest of the group waited. Lady Haldren stood near the front, Lyra at her side, both dressed in matching deep blue.

"Finally," Lady Haldren said, voice clipped, before turning on her heel and leading them down the corridor.

The halls were quiet, with only the soft tap of boots echoing off polished stone. After a few short turns, they entered a grand dining hall. A massive hearth dominated the far wall, flames crackling beneath an intricately carved mantle. The air smelled of spice and roasting meat. A long wooden table stretched nearly the length of the chamber, clearly the work of a master craftsman—its legs shaped like twisting vines, the surface polished to a mirrored sheen. Paintings hung along the walls, all rich in color and clearly expensive: landscapes, noble portraits, hunting scenes frozen in triumphant stillness. Fine plates of porcelain and polished silverware were already set out, goblets of deep-cut glass standing beside each seat. Off to the side stood a single servant, posture rigid, dressed in black pants and a perfectly fitted black tunic. He looked more prepared for a noble gathering than any of them.

"Good evening, my lady," the man said with a courteous bow.

Belaric could not help but feel underdressed. The servant might not hold a title, but finer hands had stitched his garments than any guard could afford.

Lady Haldren nodded in thanks, and they were shown to their seats. Her place was beside Lord Vanis Halmor's, with Lyra set to sit next to where Lady Maranna Halmor would take her spot. Belaric sat beside Lyra, with Sir Tolman across from him beside Lady Haldren. The other guards took seats farther down the table, exchanging quiet glances and murmured observations.

Knoll, one of the youngest, leaned toward Jass, a man with a thick scar across his lip. "Think we can trust 'em?" he muttered, low enough that only Jass could hear. Jass did not reply, just shook his head slightly.

They waited only a few minutes before Lord and Lady Halmor made their entrance.

They did not walk—they arrived, as if the room had been waiting to acknowledge them. Lord Halmor wore finely cut dark blue pants and a matching tunic lined with silver trim. His boots were fur-cuffed, soft-soled, pristine. A dagger hung from his hip, small and or-nate—meant for fashion, not for war. His wife wore a form-fitting black gown that shimmered slightly in the firelight. Her long silver-blonde hair had been braided into a crown across her head, and a golden necklace, thick and studded with emeralds, glinted at her throat.

Belaric's instincts tightened. The silence stretched, too formal, too controlled. Were they hosts... or hunters?

Then Lord Halmor offered a thin smile and raised a hand.

"Please, all of you—sit. It is an honor to host such brave company tonight."

He clapped twice.

Servant after servant entered the hall, each bearing silver trays that released warm steam into the air. Roasted duck glazed with honeyed wine. A platter of spiced potatoes crisped in oil and sprinkled with flaked salt. Thin cuts of lamb seasoned with rosemary. Fresh loaves of braided bread, still hot from the oven, served with golden butter and sweet fig jam. A final dish of poached pears resting in a pool of dark syrup gave the room a heady sweetness.

Each goblet was filled with a dark red wine, nearly black in the firelight.

Lord Halmor lifted his cup.

"To Lady Haldren and Lady Lyra's health and safety."

The guests raised their goblets in unison, repeating the words before drinking.

Lady Halmor turned almost immediately to Lady Haldren. "Tell us, my lady—how was the journey? I trust the roads were not too unkind?"

Lady Haldren kept her tone even and diplomatic as she recounted their travels—sparse food, restless nights, and the looming threat of unseen danger. She left out nothing essential, but no detail too sharp. Her manner was measured, regal, and precise.

Lady Halmor nodded once, listening intently. Her eyes flicked toward Belaric as the tale continued—just for a moment, a silent acknowledgment, unreadable and gone in a blink.

When the recounting ended, Lord Halmor steepled his fingers and leaned slightly forward. "And the assassin?" he asked. "How did she get in? How did Sir Tolman best her?"

Lady Haldren looked toward Tolman, wordlessly offering the floor.

He nodded, glanced briefly at Belaric, then began. "We discovered she—"

Lord Halmor raised his eyebrows. "She? It was a woman?"

He let out a laugh—dry, more like someone recalling a bad joke than hearing a good one.

Lyra, unfazed, looked directly at him. "I assure you, Lord Halmor—a woman is very capable of slitting throats."

The room froze. Even the fire seemed to dim.

Lady Haldren's eyes widened. Belaric had to force himself not to laugh to maintain the silence, and Sir Tolman simply closed his eyes. Down the table, Staven choked on his wine, while Kedd stared into his cup, pretending he had not heard a thing.

Lady Halmor cleared her throat quietly, glancing at her husband that might have been a reprimand—or a warning.

Lord Halmor offered a dry chuckle. "Right you are, my dear. Of course. Now, Sir Tolman—you were saying?"

"Yes, my lord," Sir Tolman continued carefully. "We believe she entered through the kitchen window late in the evening. Lady Haldren and Lyra were playing a game of Crownfall—I was watching over them—when she came through the door. She acted as if she had already won and did not expect resistance. She challenged me to a duel, though she quickly discovered daggers do not fare well against steel plate. She was quick and skilled, but arrogance undid her. I was able to unbalance her and strike the final blow. I took a few slashes, but nothing that will kill me."

Lord Halmor clapped his hands, genuinely impressed—or at least skilled at faking it. "Wonderful! You truly are the warrior they say you are, Sir Tolman."

Sir Tolman offered a polite nod. "You honor me, my lord."

The evening passed with a parade of stories, mostly centered on wealth and status. Lord Halmor spoke at length about his holdings, his coin, and the rare ore pulled from the mountain's spine. Lady Halmor chimed in often, but carefully—her praise of their son, one of the finest knights in the capital, always seemed timed to keep attention on her husband, but her gaze often wandered.

Belaric watched them closely. Every word weighed. Every phrase studied. Across the table, Lyra did the same, her eyes sharp behind a courteous smile.

Eventually, the hearth had burned low, and the plates had long since emptied. Lord Halmor rose from his seat with a regal stretch.

"I believe that is enough for one evening. We old men need our rest," he said with a thin smile. "Lady Haldren, Lady Lyra, please make yourselves comfortable during your stay. You are under our roof, and under our protection."

As the noble couple turned to leave, Belaric caught Sir Tolman's eye, then Dross's. The three exchanged a look—no words, just the quiet understanding of men who had fought, laughed, and survived the same fire.

Then they all chuckled softly.

"Old man," Dross muttered with a smirk.

Sir Tolman shook his head. "He has no idea."

Belaric just grinned.

Hasker and Ruthan broke away at the stairwell, their cloaks already drawn tight.

"Try not to draw too much attention," Sir Tolman warned.

"We will be shadows," Hasker replied with a wink.

The rest continued on. Before entering her room, Lady Haldren paused, locking eyes with Belaric. She gave a subtle nod. He returned it, and they went their separate ways.

Inside his room, Belaric shut the door behind him. Dross collapsed onto his bed with a groan, while Sir Tolman remained by the door.

"I believe we are safe for tonight," Belaric said as he crossed to the hearth. "If they are enemies, they will not strike while we are still in their home. Too risky. It would stain their reputation."

Sir Tolman nodded.

Belaric knelt and reached into the hearth, pulling free the hidden pack. Black leather, worn and familiar. Within seconds he had stripped down and slipped back into his old life.

Dross stared at him in disbelief. "By the gods. You really were an assassin."

Belaric tugged the last strap into place, the hood drawn low. "Still am."

He crossed over to the window. Sir Tolman followed.

"Why not the door?" he asked.

Belaric smiled faintly. "They may be watching it."

He cracked the window open and peered into the night. No movement. No guards in sight. The drop was not far—but far enough to break a leg if taken wrong.

Belaric turned back to them. "Help lower me down. One arm each."

Sir Tolman hesitated for only a moment before nodding. Dross moved to the other side.

Together, they each took one of Belaric's arms and leaned out the window, gripping tightly.

"On my count," Belaric said, voice barely above a whisper. "Three... two... now."

They let go.

He hit the ground and rolled, coming up low, already moving. In a few swift steps, he vanished into the darkness, swallowed by the night.

It felt too easy.

But the worst traps always did.

Belaric moved across the grounds like a shadow slipping between torches. The guards along the wall paced in predictable patterns, eyes turned outward. No one watched the estate from within. Typical mistake.

He did not know the full layout, but he had gathered enough from dinner talk to know that Lord Halmor's quarters were on the west wing. Circling behind the estate, he stopped abruptly when he discovered something unexpected—an immaculate garden carved into the mountain itself. Symmetrical hedges, polished stone benches, vines trained to perfection. It reeked of control and vanity.

Crouched low, he studied the space from the shadows. Torches flickered along the paths, but they were spaced wide enough to slip between. After a moment of stillness, he moved, crouching and crossing the garden with practiced care. His soft-soled boots made no sound on the stone, and the dark swallowed him whole.

The western wall offered no easy purchase. Smooth, tall, uninterrupted. He scanned for anything useful—drainage pipes, gaps in the stone, low windows. After several minutes, he spotted one—narrow and low to the ground, half-concealed behind a hedge. He tested the frame; it groaned slightly as he lifted it. Belaric froze, listening. Nothing moved inside.

He eased it open fully and peered through the opening. Rows of drying linen swayed faintly in the draft. Laundry. Perfect. He climbed in and landed silently, taking in the room—several washbasins, bundles of cloth, a faint soapy smell. Servants' quarters. Better than stumbling into a barracks.

Crossing the room, he paused at the door and pressed his ear to the wood. Torchlight bled underneath. No footsteps. No voices. He opened it a crack and looked through—a long hallway, stone walls, several closed doors, sconces burning low. He slipped out and stayed close to the wall, sliding until he reached a pocket of shadow.

He moved slowly, boots silent, pausing at every door. Servants' rooms, likely. Nothing useful. The hallway opened into a larger space—an intersection. A stairwell rose on his left, while more doors lined the hall to his right. Another passage stretched forward. He crept toward the stairs and placed a foot carefully.

The wood groaned.

Belaric closed his eyes, cursed inwardly, then kept going. The stairs protested with every step, but he moved lightly, shifting his weight with care. At the top, the hallway split in two. He took the right first—a short passage that ended in a sharp turn. He froze at the sound of a breath. A soft huff, like someone exhaling hard.

He reached into his sleeve and drew a shard of polished glass, angling it carefully around the corner. The reflection showed a bored house guard standing post outside a door. Belaric pocketed the glass and retreated, silent as a shadow.

Returning to the junction, he took the other path. Another turn, this one to the left. He paused, checked the angle with the glass. Three doors. No guards. He smiled faintly and turned the corner.

The first door opened easily—just linen and a broom. He sighed through his nose. "Enough with the damned brooms."

The second room was a bedroom. Empty, neatly made. A painting hung on the far wall—a young man in ceremonial plate armor, sword resting against his leg. The son, no doubt. Belaric crossed to the desk and opened a drawer. Letters. Dozens. All addressed to noblewomen—flirtations, poems, exaggerated affections.

He skimmed a few with a smirk. "Courting half the kingdom," he muttered, returning everything to its place.

The third door was locked. He smiled. That was promising.

He knelt, pulled a small leather pouch from his belt, and selected two thin picks. The lock was good—tight tolerances, well-made. Lord Halmor had spared no expense in securing this one. After several patient minutes, he felt the mechanism yield with a soft click.

Inside, the room was everything he had hoped for: bookshelves lining the walls, a broad desk in the center, neatly stacked papers, unlit candles. He closed the door behind him, relocked it, and then lit a single candle, shielding the flame with one hand.

Drawer by drawer, he sifted through letters—most of them routine. Land disputes. Council notices. Favors owed and favors expected. Nothing. The meticulous order of the papers was almost insulting; the typical, mundane affairs of a lord, with no hint of the shadow he suspected. A muscle twitched in his jaw.

He was starting to think this was a dead end. He ran a hand along the underside of the desk and found nothing. His jaw tightened. He stood and began to examine the bookshelves, running his eyes over the hundreds of leather-bound spines.

Most were thick with dust and age, their covers worn. But on a high shelf, he spotted one that looked pristine—its spine a deep green, the leather unmarked. He reached for it. As his fingers brushed against the books around it, a fine cloud of dust puffed into the air, but the new book remained clean.

He pulled it free. It was a personal journal, with Lord Halmor's name etched on the cover. Belaric opened it and saw the first page was filled with careful, spidery handwriting. As he thumbed through the pages, he found several sealed letters tucked between them. He carefully unfolded them.

The handwriting was different, sharp and angular. The tone—veiled but urgent—and something else. A venomous undercurrent that made his gut clench.

Belaric read each one. And then he read them again.

A cold rage rose in his chest, a quiet swell of power like an incoming tide. The words twisted his features into a grim mask. These were not just "allies" playing a game; they were active participants, wolves in sheep's clothing, inviting their prey into a gilded trap. He gripped the letters tighter, the parchment crinkling under his fingers. So much for "protection." So much for "brave company." His disgust was a bitter taste on his tongue. He wanted to rip the letter, to break something, to put his fist through the carefully polished desk.

There was no question. This would interest Lady Haldren. And it would confirm every dark suspicion he had ever had about noble pronouncements.

He searched the study further—checked behind books, under the desk, for false panels or compartments. Nothing. No hidden chambers. Just well-oiled shelves and a noble's arrogance in thinking a secret drawer was enough to hide treachery. His search was complete. He had what he came for.

He blew out the candle and, with a silent twist of the doorknob, slipped into the hall. He took two steps when he heard it—voices, laughing and whispering, coming from around the corner. He moved back instantly and without a sound, slipping back into the study and closing the door behind him with a soft click.

Footsteps drew closer.

Then a woman's voice: amused, sultry. "Shall we use his study or his son's bed again?"

A man laughed. "The study. Let us see if he notices what happened on his desk."

Belaric moved fast. He opened the window and looked down. No guards, but the drop was long—ten feet at least. A thud hit the door. Laughter followed.

No time.

He climbed onto the ledge, twisted around, and gripped the window with one hand while reaching up to slide it shut with the other.

Just as it clicked into place, he heard the door open behind him—more laughter, the unmistakable sound of kissing.

He let go.

The ground hit like a hammer. He rolled, but pain shot through his leg. Not broken, but close. He gritted his teeth and pushed himself up, using the wall for balance. Limping through the garden, he kept to the shadows, torchlight flickering in the distance.

He reached the wall that led up to the window of his room—still open. Lucky.

He picked up a small stone and tossed it through.

"What the hell?" came Dross's voice.

A moment later, his head appeared. Belaric stepped out of the dark. "I need help up. Two sheets tied together. Now."

Dross vanished. Moments later, the linen rope dropped.

Belaric tested it with a tug and began to climb, every muscle burning. When he neared the top, his hand found the sill. The rope slackened as Tolman and Dross grabbed him and hauled him up through the window.

They shut it behind him and collapsed onto the floor, all three of them breathing hard.

Dross shook his head. "Old man? More like a fat man. You weigh more than a horse."

Sir Tolman raised a brow. "You all right?"

"Needed a quick escape. Jumped out a window." He replied, his breath coming out ragged.

Both men stared at him. Then burst out laughing.

"You are a fool," Dross said, still catching his breath.

Belaric laughed with them, easing himself down onto the mattress, one hand on his sore leg.

After a moment, Sir Tolman leaned forward. "So... what did you find?"

22

B elaric turned to Sir Tolman, his voice rough with suppressed anger, a stark contrast to his earlier controlled movements. "Should we wake Lady Haldren now?"

Sir Tolman's jaw tightened, his brow furrowed with consideration. "It is late. Three men entering her chambers at this hour, especially here... it would raise questions we do not want to answer."

Belaric gave a slow, frustrated nod. "Fair enough. But she needs to know. The Halmor's claim that they are being targeted is true. But it is not by the Order."

Sir Tolman's eyes, sharp even in the dim light, narrowed. "Not the Order? Then who?"

Belaric glanced toward the shuttered window, and the black beyond it, as if the answer lay lurking in the night. "A feud. With Lord Thelron Talveth of Tharnhill. Their lands border each other—Halmor's on the mountain, Talveth's in the lowlands. I found a letter in Halmor's study. Hidden, but not well enough." He paused, the words replaying in his mind like a grim echo. "He has built up a mountain of debt. The mine is not producing. He is desperate for a way to restore his wealth."

Belaric's voice dropped, tinged with a cold disgust. "He appealed to his cousin, Lord Erwin Danvar, for help. Danvar refused, calling Halmor's debts his own doing. But the important part, the truly rotten part, is what Halmor told Danvar. He claimed Talveth's lands once belonged to House Halmor. Said they were stolen generations ago. Fertile fields, clean rivers. He wants them back. And seeks Lord Drelvane's support for his claim."

Sir Tolman's arms crossed, his expression turning to stone. "So, he is going to stir up an ancient land dispute and try to drag Lady Haldren into it?"

Belaric's jaw clenched. "Exactly. He knows about the attack on her life. Knows it will stir sympathy. If he can convince her the attempt came from Lord Talveth—give her just enough reason to believe it—she might speak out. Join his call for 'justice.' And once her name is tied to his cause..."

"... he will use her, rally the commoners against Lord Talveth, then cast her aside when she is no longer useful," Sir Tolman finished, the words like a stone dropping in a well.

Belaric's eyes held a dangerous glint. "Worse. If he can draw her into a feud that weakens her, he may even strike at her while she is exposed. He will paint it as just another retaliation in a war she helped start. A perfect way to remove a rival claimant to the land, disguised as an 'unfortunate' casualty of another lord's greed."

Dross let out a low whistle, shaking his head. "Halmor's been acting strange. Watched us as if we were bleeding his coin purse dry. Too many smiles from a man drowning in debt."

Belaric gave a faint, bitter smile. "I thought the same. His study was neat—too neat. I found a book with a new spine. Inside, tucked away, was a letter. There was only one letter, but it was enough to see the rotten core of the man."

"Are you sure there was nothing else?" Sir Tolman asked, his voice now entirely devoid of his usual disdain for Belaric. The gravity of the situation had erased it.

"I found what I needed in the journal," Belaric replied. "My search was complete. I was leaving when a pair of servants stumbled into the corridor outside the study, heading for the door. Their hushed whispers and lingering touches implied they sought the study for more than just reading. I had to take the window to avoid being seen. The drop was long."

Dross chuckled. "Romance in a stone house full of spies and traitors. That is brave or stupid."

"Both," Belaric said. Then, more seriously, "We need to tell Lady Haldren before her meeting. Whatever Lord Halmor is planning, it starts with her. If she walks in blind, he will have her dancing to his tune before she knows the melody."

Sir Tolman nodded. "First thing in the morning, then."

The three stood in silence for a beat, the weight of it hanging between them.

"Well, if you two old men are done playing spy, I will turn in for the night. I need my rest," Dross told them before letting out a loud yawn and turning towards his bed. Sir Tolman followed, muttering about sore shoulders and treacherous nobles.

Belaric stayed a moment longer, letting the quiet settle.

With a sigh, he stripped down, the motion slower than he liked. The scrape of cloth against his side pulled a sharp breath through his teeth. The bruises were deepening. His leg throbbed from the landing in the garden. He felt every year of training etched into muscle and bone.

The pain was real. Much like the threat they faced now.

He eased into the bed, the cold sheets clinging to him like a shroud. He stared at the ceiling, the dark pressing in from all sides.

He thought of Lady Haldren, walking into a lion's den cloaked in civility. He thought of Lyra, clever and wide-eyed, in a world that would eat her if it could.

He thought of the Order, and how schemes like this had once seemed so distant—noble troubles for noble blood. He had killed to keep those lies buried.

Now he was watching them sprout again.

He hoped tomorrow would require fewer windows.

And fewer leaps of faith.

Sleep came quickly.

For once, it stayed.

When Belaric woke, morning light had already crept through the window, painting pale lines across the stone floor. He lay still for a moment, breathing evenly, testing his limbs. His legs ached, but nothing sharp. Nothing torn. He whispered a quiet prayer to the gods—not of thanks, but of recognition. They had not cursed him with dreams. That was gift enough.

He rose slowly, carefully. His shoulder tugged with dull protest, and the ache in his leg had settled into something familiar. His body had taken worse and kept moving.

Sir Tolman was already dressed, buckling the last strap of his shoulder guard. Dross stood near the hearth, chewing on a slice of apple, his sword hanging loosely from his hand.

"You were right," Dross said, looking up at Belaric. "Old men do like to sleep in."

Belaric smirked. "You mistake stillness for sleep."

Sir Tolman snorted and rolled his eyes. "Both of you move slower than an old man."

He dressed quickly. Belaric pulled on the uniform once more—a disguise worn so often now it was beginning to feel like a second skin. By the time they stepped into the corridor, the estate had already stirred to life. Voices echoed faintly down the stone halls, servants moving in and out of side chambers, the low clatter of a pan in a distant kitchen.

Dross split off toward the barracks to see to the other men. Belaric and Tolman made their way to Lady Haldren's chambers.

Sir Tolman knocked, two sharp raps.

"Enter," came her voice from within.

They stepped into the room to find Lady Haldren seated at a small round table, a book open before her. Lyra sat across from her, curled slightly, legs tucked under her chair, another book resting in her lap. The scent of parchment, wax, and spiced tea hung in the air.

Belaric paused in the doorway.

There was a stillness here—delicate and rare. A mother and daughter, reading in silence. It was not the silence of dread, or plotting, or aftermath. It was peace. Something he had never known. Something he had long stopped believing in. For a heartbeat, he simply stood in it.

Lady Haldren looked up. "A knock so early—I assume it was an eventful night?" she asked.

Sir Tolman stepped forward with a slight bow. "A fruitful one, my lady. And one poorly executed escape through a window."

He looked back at Belaric with a smirk.

Belaric shrugged. "Young love is a dangerous thing, and one I could not afford to interrupt," he replied.

Lady Haldren arched a brow. Lyra giggled behind her book.

"See, Mother? They are friends now." She told her mother.

Belaric and Sir Tolman shared a glance. Not denial. Not quite agreement either.

"We serve a common purpose," Sir Tolman said. "And we have learned to respect each other's strengths. If we mean to keep you safe, we will need both."

Belaric nodded. "And keep each other in check."

Lady Haldren lifted her cup, sipping slowly. "I am pleasantly surprised. All it took was me berating you like children."

Lyra grinned. "That usually works."

Belaric allowed a quiet chuckle, though it held little humor. "We found something," he said, stepping forward, the dark letter still heavy in his thoughts. "And you need to hear it immediately."

Lady Haldren closed her book, her gaze sharp and expectant. She gestured for them to sit. "Tell me."

Belaric took the chair across from her, Sir Tolman settling beside him, his own expression grim. Belaric exhaled, bracing himself for the reveal.

"In Halmor's study, I found a letter. They were tucked inside a journal, a pristine copy hidden among dusty books on a high shelf," he paused, letting the implication sink in before continuing. "This letter confirms our suspicions, Lady Haldren. The Halmor's are not merely cautious allies. They are playing a much deadlier game."

He glanced at Lady Haldren, then at Lyra, who had set her book aside, her eyes wide with curiosity.

"Lord Halmor is deep in debt. His mines are failing, and he is desperate to restore his wealth." Belaric's voice hardened. "He wrote his cousin, Lord Erwin Danvar, seeking support for an old territorial dispute. He claims Lord Talveth's lands—a fertile stretch along the river—were stolen generations ago. Danvar refused to help, calling Halmor's troubles his own doing."

Lady Haldren's expression darkened, her fingers tightening around her cup, though her eyes remained fixed on Belaric.

"The timing matters," Belaric continued, leaning forward. "The letter is dated only two weeks ago. Lord Halmor was already in motion. And when he learned of the attempt on your life, he saw not a tragedy, but an opportunity." His voice dropped, low and bitter. "My guess is he plans to blame the attack on Lord Talveth, to stir your outrage, and to pull you into the war he intends to start."

Sir Tolman leaned forward, his voice like grinding stone. "It is a trap, my lady. One designed to use your name, your reputation, your very voice, as the opening move in his war."

Lyra's brow furrowed, a flicker of outrage in her eyes. "But what does he gain by turning us against Lord Talveth?" she asked.

Belaric met her gaze, a grim respect dawning in his eyes. "Your mother is loved by the commoners, a beacon of justice. He believes he can use her influence to gather forces, to legitimize his claims against Lord Talveth. Once Talveth's lands are taken and weakened, that is when he will make his next move."

Sir Tolman nodded, his hand instinctively going to the hilt of his sword. "Lord Halmor has always been power-driven. We believe his next move will be to claim your lands as well, Lady Haldren."

Lyra's confusion returned, her head tilting. "But our land does not border Lord Halmor's. How could he possibly claim them?"

"No," Belaric said, letting the full implication hang in the air for a moment. "But Lord Drelvane's lands do."

Lyra's eyes lit up, the pieces clicking into place. "And Drelvane is Halmor's friend. I have heard that he is ill. Rumor has it his sons are weak, and the heir is not yet of age. If he dies, that land becomes vulnerable!"

Belaric gave a sharp nod, impressed by her quick grasp. "Exactly. He can use your mother's influence to take Lord Talveth's land. Then, through his influence over Lord Drelvane, or by exploiting Drelvane's weakness, he will find a way to attack your mother. Then, once you are both weakened, he turns on Drelvane's vulnerable estate. He would increase his holdings tenfold, perhaps more. This is not a simple land grab; this is a long game, Lady Haldren, cunning and ruthless. I am certain this is his ultimate goal."

After Belaric finished, a heavy silence fell over the room. All eyes turned to Lady Haldren.

Lady Haldren blinked once, then stared at her daughter a moment longer. She had always known Lyra was sharp, but each day it showed more plainly. There was pride, yes—but fear, too. The girl was learning to read blood and ambition as easily as books. She was adapting far too fast, a dangerous skill in a dangerous world.

Lady Haldren turned to Belaric, her voice cool and steady despite the gravity of the news. "I thank you for this information, Belaric. You have done me a great service indeed. And saved us from walking into a viper's nest."

Belaric nodded. "He might try to force your hand. If you speak against Lord Talveth, then he loses influence and becomes weakened. If Talveth is weakened, Drelvane is exposed. And Halmor? He is waiting. All he needs is one moment where the pieces align to begin his grand conquest."

Lady Haldren stood slowly, her expression hardening, regal and determined.

"Well," she said at last, her voice clear and strong. "I am glad I know precisely what game I am walking into."

Sir Tolman stood as well, placing a reassuring hand on his sword hilt. "We will be at your side, my Lady."

Lady Haldren nodded to both of them, a newfound resolve in her gaze.

She stood and turned towards the door, her tone lightening. "Now... let us see what passes for breakfast in this stone tomb. I find myself in need of something warm. And strong."

Lady Haldren led them through the halls at a calm, steady pace, her expression unreadable. The four of them—she, Belaric, Sir Tolman, and Lyra—entered the same dining hall they had used the night before. Morning light spilled in through narrow windows, casting angled gold across the table.

Belaric was not surprised to see Dross and the other guards already seated and halfway through their meal. Their laughter dulled when Lady Haldren entered.

She took her place at the head of the table; the others settling near her. A servant approached and placed warm food in front of them—soft eggs, a biscuit drenched in thick gravy, still steaming.

Belaric filled his cup from the water jug but waited to drink until the servant had left. Only after the doors shut behind the man did he lean slightly toward Lady Haldren.

"I imagine Lord Halmor will arrive soon," he said, voice low. "When he does, remember—you know nothing of the feud. You are here seeking answers. Trying to understand why you were attacked. Nothing more."

Lady Haldren nodded slightly, her eyes on her plate.

"He will probably want to speak with you alone," Belaric continued. "If there is an opening, I suggest taking Lyra with you. But Sir

Tolman and I will not be able to follow. If you go in unguarded, stay guarded all the same."

"I understand," she said softly. "And do not worry. I have dealt with the greed of nobles before." She lifted her cup, paused. "I am half tempted to send word to Lord Talveth—tell him what Halmor's doing. Might push him to our side."

Belaric shrugged. "Never met the man. What kind of ally would he be?"

Lyra did not look up from her food. "He spends half his coin on wine and the other half on whores. His wife wants to leave him, but she was not born noble. If she does, she will be just another commoner."

"Lyra," Lady Haldren warned. "We do not speak down about others. It only puts us on their level."

Lyra sighed. "Yes, Mother. I will try to do better."

Belaric fought down a laugh, covering it with a sip from his cup.

He was about to speak when the doors opened, and Lord Halmor stepped in.

"Ah, good," he said, smiling thinly. "I see you are all enjoying breakfast."

The smile did not reach his eyes.

He turned to Lady Haldren. "My lady, would you care to join me in my study? I believe I have some information that may interest you."

She looked to Sir Tolman, then to Belaric. Both men rose with her, as did Lyra.

There was a pause—a breath of stillness as Lady Haldren considered the request. Alone, with a man who wore a smile like a veil. She masked the hesitation with practiced ease, then returned the smile.

"Of course, my lord." She told him smoothly.

She turned back to the others. "I will not be long."

As she stepped toward him, Lord Halmor added, "If you like, Lady Halmor is taking tea in the garden. Perhaps the young lady would enjoy joining her?"

Lady Haldren glanced at Lyra. "That is a wonderful idea. Come, Lyra—you always speak so highly of your love for tea."

Belaric caught the twitch of Lyra's eye as she smiled sweetly.

"I would love to," she said, syrup in her voice. "But I have not left my mother's side since the attack. I am still frightened. I would feel so much safer if Belaric came with me."

Lord Halmor's smile tightened, but it held. "Of course, dear. How could I deny such a sweet request?"

Lyra offered a small curtsy. "Thank you, my lord."

As he turned and led Lady Haldren away, Lyra looked over her shoulder and stuck her tongue out at Belaric.

Belaric narrowed his eyes. He would get her back for that.

He rose from his seat just as Ruthan called down the table, "Enjoy your tea, Belaric."

Belaric turned slowly, expression unreadable. In one smooth motion, he drew the hidden throwing knife from beneath his cloak and let the morning light catch along its edge. He did not say a word.

The laughter stopped on cue.

Ruthan's grin faltered. Staven choked softly on a piece of biscuit. Another leaned back as if he expected the blade to fly.

Belaric gave them a long look, then sheathed the knife with a soft snick.

"I take my tea seriously," he said, and turned to follow Lyra.

She was already a few steps ahead, glancing back at him with a sly smile.

"That was a bit much," she whispered, rolling her eyes.

"Oh, I can do much more," he whispered back while smiling.

They found their way to the garden easily enough. The path curved gently through rows of clipped hedges and flowering shrubs, each step muffled by the gravel beneath their boots. The air smelled of damp earth, trimmed rose, and the distant sweetness of crushed lavender.

Lady Halmor was already seated at a stone table beneath a trellised arch, the iron wrapped in blooming vines. A book rested in one hand, a steaming teacup in the other. Around her, servants moved like quiet shadows—watering potted plants, trimming back ivy, brushing petals from the stonework.

She looked up as they approached. "Ah, Lyra. What a lovely surprise!"

Lyra offered a small bow. "Lord Halmor said you were taking tea and suggested I join you. I hope that is all right."

Lady Halmor waved her off with a gentle smile, polished and insincere. "Of course, dear. I am always grateful for company. Please—sit."

Lyra took the seat beside her. Lady Halmor clapped once, and a servant girl came rushing over. She could not have been older than sixteen. Her dress was plain; her sleeves were damp from watering. She kept her head bowed.

"Fetch another cup for Lyra," Lady Halmor said.

"Yes, my lady," the girl murmured, before hurrying off.

Lady Halmor turned to Belaric, her gaze lingering just a beat too long. "And who is this?"

Belaric dipped his head with the minimum of courtesy.

"He is one of our protectors," Lyra replied easily. "He and Sir Tolman are our personal guards."

Lady Halmor's eyes narrowed slightly. "Just Belaric? Not Sir Belaric?" She let the words hang, her tone like velvet wrapped around a dagger. "Odd for a bodyguard to lack a title. I had expected more of Lady Haldren."

Belaric did not flinch. He had been looked down on by nobles for most of his life—usually before they bled. Still, something in him shifted when Lyra spoke up again.

"Oh, I would not be surprised if he is knighted soon," she said, her voice light, charming. "There is no man I have seen who can match his skill. He sparred with three men at once and did not even sweat. Even Sir Tolman admits he could not beat him."

Belaric felt the faintest flicker of surprise. Not at her words—but at her tone. Confident. Loyal. Unapologetic. People did not usually speak for him, let alone speak well of him.

Lady Halmor blinked, just for a moment, before her mask settled back into place. "Oh, child. Knights are chosen for more than skill with a sword. Men like Sir Tolman have proven themselves in battle. I doubt someone of his standing would struggle."

She set her teacup down just a bit too hard. Not enough to seem clumsy. Just enough for Belaric to notice.

Lyra did not blink. "He would not struggle," she said.

Lady Halmor smiled, as if she had won the exchange.

"He would lose," Lyra finished.

A single rose petal drifted down from the trellis above, landing between the cups.

"I know Sir Tolman is a fine fighter," Lyra went on, still smiling, "but I would wager Belaric is better. Perhaps your House's protector, Sir Elandor, would care to prove me wrong? I have heard much of his skill; it would be fascinating to see them spar."

She turned to Belaric, still smiling as if it was all a pleasant suggestion. "You would not mind, would you?"

Belaric gave her a sideways glance. "I—"

Lady Halmor cut in with a thin laugh, though her eyes had a distinct chill. "Sir Elandor is away at the King's Court with my son, I am afraid, and quite occupied. Let us not turn this garden into a training yard. Let us enjoy the morning while we can."

"It is a shame he is away," Lyra said, giving Lady Halmor a wide grin. "I would have loved to see that duel, however short it would be."

Lady Halmor's smile remained fixed, but her eyes narrowed to icy slits, and a faint flush rose on her pale cheeks. For a fleeting moment, the carefully constructed elegance seemed to crack, revealing a sliver of raw annoyance beneath.

Right on cue, the servant girl returned, placing the cup carefully in front of Lyra before vanishing again, silent as smoke.

The rest of the time passed at a crawl. Lady Halmor stuck to safe, empty conversation. How was Brookhaven? Was the road comfortable? Had they tried the honeyed pears from the market? Belaric stood behind Lyra, arms crossed, barely listening. His muscles were stiff, his mind drifting. This was not his world. Too many words. Too little action.

At last, Lady Halmor stood. "Well, my dear, I have a few matters to attend to. But enjoy the garden as long as you wish."

Lyra bowed politely. "Thank you, my lady."

Once Lady Halmor disappeared behind a hedge wall, Lyra rose with a sigh.

They walked in silence for a few steps before Belaric said, "Do you always try to start duels before tea?"

"Only when the company's dull," she replied, flashing him a grin.

He shook his head, chuckling under his breath. He walked her back to her chambers, then turned to find Sir Tolman—hoping the man had survived his own round of politeness.

It did not take long for Belaric to find them. Out in front of the estate, the men had cleared a space in the yard for drills and sparring. The morning sun warmed the stones, but the mountain breeze still cut through the open air. The clash of wood against wood rang out across the courtyard, rhythmic and sharp. Several of the House Halmor guards stood nearby, watching in silence. A few had even lent out worn sparring blades, scarred from years of use.

Kedd and Hasker circled each other in the ring, their shirts damp with sweat, blades low and tense. Hasker lunged with a sudden thrust, but Kedd met it with a clean parry and a pivot. They were evenly matched—neither reckless, both reading and responding. No wasted effort. No easy advantage.

Belaric stepped up beside Sir Tolman, arms crossed.

Sir Tolman glanced over at him with a crooked smile. "Enjoy the tea?"

Belaric gave a faint smirk. "Was not offered any. Got a few insults instead."

Sir Tolman chuckled. "Sounds about right. Lady Halmor's charm is mostly ornamental."

"She may polish it more carefully after the way Lyra talked to her," Belaric said. "She did not hold back."

Sir Tolman sighed and rubbed the back of his neck. "That girl… she needs to learn that timing matters."

Belaric shrugged. "The Halmor's are not enemies, but they are not allies either. They want to use Lady Haldren. That puts them close enough to the wrong side."

"Aye," Sir Tolman muttered. "Close enough."

Belaric glanced back at the sparring. "Did Hasker or Ruthan learn anything in town?"

Sir Tolman huffed. "Not much. Word was that a few Lord Talveth guards had passed through two weeks back. Some say they were scouting. Others claim they were just moving between outposts. No one agrees."

"Better than bad news, at least," Belaric replied.

Before Sir Tolman could respond, a cheer rose from the yard. Kedd was flat on his back, chest rising and falling as he laughed. Hasker offered him a hand and pulled him to his feet. A feint, well-timed, had earned him the win.

Then all eyes turned to Belaric.

"Well then," Dross called out with a grin. "You up for a round?"

Belaric raised a brow. "Sorry. I am still full from tea."

Sir Tolman shoved him forward with a hand on his back. "Of course he is."

Belaric turned to glare at him. "You will regret that."

"They did not believe me when I said you would win. Prove it," Sir Tolman told him.

With a sigh, Belaric stepped into the ring. Staven jogged over, handing him a worn wooden blade and taking his real one with care. Dross loosened his shoulders, cracking his neck. They squared off.

"Begin!" Sir Tolman called.

Dross lunged with force, all size and weight. Belaric moved like water—every strike blocked or slipped, his footwork tight and calm. Dross pressed harder, swinging in wide arcs, hammering with the kind of strength that bruised even through wood. Belaric felt each blow rattle through his arms, but he did not give ground without a reason. He let Dross push, let him spend energy like coin at a tavern.

Then came the moment.

Dross's shoulder dipped too far. His grip loosened for a breath.

Belaric slipped in, twisted his blade down, and struck hard across Dross's wrist. The sparring sword flew from his hand and landed in the dirt. Belaric stepped forward and gave him a soft tap to the forehead with the flat of his blade.

The men burst out laughing. Dross held up his hands and bowed his head, grinning. Kedd clapped Belaric on the shoulder, his face split in a wide smile. "He will be telling everyone he 'almost' beat you, you know."

Belaric smiled and offered his hand. "You nearly cracked both my arms."

"I was trying to crack your ribs," Dross said, a wide grin on his face. "You slippery bastard."

Ruthan stepped forward, grinning. "My turn, then?"

Before Belaric could reply, the tone of the yard shifted.

Lady Haldren and Lyra had stepped out from the estate and crossed the courtyard in silence. Her presence cut through the leftover laughter like a breeze through fog. Belaric stood a bit straighter, brushing sweat from his brow.

"Training so early?" Lady Haldren asked, her voice calm. "I do hope no one has broken anything."

Sir Tolman bowed slightly. "Only a few egos, my lady."

She turned to him and Belaric. "If I could have a moment. Both of you."

Ruthan looked crestfallen. Belaric turned to him with a smile and tossed him the sparring sword. "I will duel you next time."

He crossed the yard to Staven and retrieved his real blade, strapping it across his back. As he moved to follow the others, he looked back at the circle.

"Dross—make sure Staven runs his drills for at least an hour."

Staven groaned. "That is not fair—"

The rest of the men laughed again as Dross clapped a heavy hand on Staven's shoulder and pulled him toward the ring. Belaric shook his head and jogged after Lady Haldren and Tolman, the moment of peace already behind them.

They moved through the halls in silence. Lady Haldren walked ahead of them, her steps clipped and purposeful. Belaric followed with Tolman and Lyra close behind, noting the tension in her shoulders—the kind that did not come from fear, but fury.

When they reached her chamber, she opened the door and ushered them inside without a word. Once it closed, she exhaled through her nose, a long breath as if she had been holding it since leaving Lord Halmor's study. She did not speak right away, only crossed the room and poured herself a glass of wine from the decanter by the hearth. She took a long sip, then set the glass down with more force than necessary, the clink echoing in the stone room. Her fingers lingered on its rim, knuckles pale with pressure.

"You were right," she said, her voice a tight whisper, barely containing a tremor of fury. "He is moving against Lord Talveth."

Sir Tolman stepped forward, his tone careful, sensing the storm brewing. "We expected as much, my lady. But something else happened. You are... incandescent."

Lady Haldren turned, pacing slowly toward the window, her silhouette stark against the fading light. "Lord Halmor is a disgusting man. A pig."

Lyra's expression shifted immediately, her voice rising with raw concern. "Mother... did he do something to you?"

Belaric and Sir Tolman both tensed, a sudden, stony silence falling over the room. Their postures tightened, coils ready to spring. Belaric's hand drifted to his belt unconsciously, already calculating the fastest path to violence.

Lady Haldren turned back around, a strained laugh escaping her. "No. Nothing like that. You two can stop sharpening your blades," she said, trying to smooth her tone, but the tension in the room remained thick enough to cut. She sighed, took another drink, and continued, her voice now clipped with barely contained disgust. "He spun a tale claiming Lord Talveth is demanding the mountain. Cited an ancient, forgotten marriage contract as proof of inheritance. Said Lord Talveth has been harassing traders, sending scouts, preparing for war. That he is training soldiers and hiring mercenaries—all to take what he claims is his."

Sir Tolman folded his arms, his frown deepening into a hard line. "Convenient timing for such a renewed claim."

"It did not end there," she went on, a shiver running through her. "He says Lord Talveth's sights are set on us next. That the assassination attempt on my life was his doing—sent to remove me so Lord Talveth could marry Lyra and claim Brookhaven."

Lyra's reaction was immediate and explosive. "What?!" she snapped, her face flushing a furious red. "I would sooner marry a dung heap than that pig Talveth!"

Lady Haldren raised a hand, a grim humor touching her lips. "I know. It is all false. Every word. He is trying to frighten us into an alliance built on lies."

"And what kind of alliance does he propose?" Belaric asked, his voice low, though the chilling answer was already clicking into place in his mind.

Lady Haldren did not hesitate, her gaze holding his. "He wants to unite the families. He proposed Lyra marry his son."

Lyra's jaw dropped, her earlier outrage replaced by stunned revulsion. "Marry his son?!"

Belaric and Tolman exchanged a glance—confusion melting into shared, cold understanding.

"I did not expect that one," Belaric muttered, a dark chuckle escaping him.

"I figured he would just betray us after we had done his dirty work against Talveth," Sir Tolman added, shaking his head slowly, a grim realization settling over him. "This is… more ambitious."

"It gets worse," Lady Haldren said, her voice dropping to a near whisper, laden with revulsion. "He proposed another match. To himself. Said his wife is barren, and he wants more heirs. Offered to cast her aside… and take me as his bride." Her lips curled in a sneer of pure disgust. "And he reached for my leg while saying it, as if that would seal the deal."

Lyra stepped closer, her eyes wide with outrage. "And you?!"

"I stood. Told him I needed time to consider such… weighty proposals." Her voice dripped with sarcasm. "Then I left before he could sully the air with more of his filth."

Sir Tolman's fingers twitched, clenching into fists. "That bastard… Say the word, my lady, and I will kill him." His voice was a low growl.

Lady Haldren gave him a dry, bitter smile that did not reach her eyes. "No, Sir Tolman. And besides—your honor would not allow it."

He paled slightly, his head lowering in acknowledgment. "No, my lady." A beat passed, filled only by the crackle of the hearth. "Then… have Belaric do it."

Belaric blinked, genuinely surprised. "What? Why me?"

All three of them looked at him with the same knowing, pointed expression.

He sighed, running a hand over his face. "Fair point. But I was told, 'No killing.'"

"There will be no killing Lord Halmor," Lady Haldren said firmly, emphasizing the specific target, before adding, "not yet, at least. Your methods are for desperate times." Though she was putting on a brave face, her grip on the wineglass now trembled slightly, betraying how thin her patience was wearing. She drained the glass, then set the cup aside with a decisive thump. "Prepare the men, Sir Tolman. We leave at first light. I do not trust what Lord Halmor may try next, and I will refuse to be a pawn in his monstrous schemes."

Sir Tolman bowed, his face grim. "It will be done, my lady. We will be ready."

As the two men turned to leave, she turned toward Lyra. "And you, young lady—what is this I hear about insulting Lady Halmor? What did I say about that?"

Lyra shifted awkwardly. "She insulted Belaric—said he was not fit to be a proper bodyguard. I told her she was wrong. That he could even beat Sir Tolman."

Sir Tolman froze mid-step. "You said what now?"

Lady Haldren and Lyra turned to him with that familiar, knowing look—the one that said they saw right through his bluster.

He sighed in resignation. "Fine. Yes, he would. But there is no need to say it. I have a reputation to maintain."

Laughter broke the tension, warm and genuine. Even Lady Haldren cracked a smile as she waved them off.

"I need to finish speaking with my daughter. See to the preparations," she told them.

Belaric and Tolman bowed and stepped into the hall, the heavy door closing behind them like punctuation at the end of an ugly chapter.

The remaining hours of the day passed quickly, filled with quiet preparation. Belaric and Tolman made sure the men were ready—horses fed, saddlebags secured, weapons oiled and sharpened. The Halmor estate was still and watchful, the servants polite but reserved, as if they too sensed the weight hanging in the air.

Dinner that evening was tense.

Lord Halmor played the gracious host, but his charm had soured. His smile stretched too wide, his words too eager. He practically begged them to stay another night. Lady Haldren declined with calm civility, offering a diplomatic excuse about the need to defend her home. Her tone never wavered, but Belaric could see Halmor growing colder with every sentence.

He watched the man closely, noting the clenched jaw, the flicker in his eyes. Halmor had made his move—and it had failed. Belaric was not sure what he would try next, but he knew this was not the end.

That night, it was decided that Belaric would stay in Lady Haldren's room, guarding her and Lyra from the shadows. He did not expect an attack, but neither did he discount one. He remained near the balcony doors, seated in the dark, watching the flicker of the candle and listening to every creak and whisper in the stone.

As the two women slept, he let his gaze settle on them for a quiet moment. He had guarded nothing so fragile in years. It felt… unfamiliar. And in that unfamiliarity, something like purpose stirred beneath the discipline.

The night passed without incident.

At dawn, the group rose before the sun. They moved quickly and without ceremony, assembling in the courtyard as a thin mist clung to the stones. The farewell was brief, thanking Lord Halmor for the information and food and the promise to write with Lady Haldren's answer. The men moved quickly, tightened straps, mounted saddles, and with the clatter of hooves as they departed the estate without looking back.

They took the same road home. It was a path they knew now, with clearings they trusted and watch rotations already set. The men were alert, disciplined, and no one questioned the pace. Fires were kept low at night. Sleep came in shifts.

On the third day, just past midday, Brookhaven appeared through the trees.

Its outer walls, its distant rooftops, the rippling banners—all familiar now, all a welcome sight. As the group crested the last rise, a breeze swept down the road and rustled through the trees.

Lyra pulled her cloak tighter and murmured, "It is good to be home."

But even as she said it, her eyes lingered on the horizon.

Within minutes, they passed through the gates and rode up the lane toward the estate house. No orders were needed. The men dismounted and moved into their tasks with practiced ease—some leading horses to the stables, others vanishing toward their quarters.

The last light of the day stretched golden across the fields. For the first time in days, the pace of life began to slow.

Belaric remained still in his saddle a moment longer, his gaze turned south—toward a stone house tucked into a mountain, and the man who had smiled too tightly at dinner.

He was not sure what Lord Halmor would try next.

But he knew the man was not finished.

23

Belaric dismounted and ran a gloved hand along Eddaross's flank, the stallion's coat damp with sweat and dust from the road. He quickly unstrapped his pack, tossing it to Staven with a request to place it on his bed, before turning back to Eddaross.

"You have done well, old boy," he murmured. "If Rusk has not run out of apples, I would say you have earned one."

Eddaross gave a soft snort in reply, ears flicking at the clamor of steel-shod hooves and men dismounting behind them.

The stable was alive with noise and motion. Rusk moved like a man possessed, wrangling reins and shouting half-coherent orders to the young stable hand who was too slow or too green to be of much use. The stables had never been meant for this many horses—certainly not warhorses—but somehow Rusk made them fit. He always did. A man born in chaos, thriving in it.

As Rusk took Sir Tolman's horse, he paused, offering a quick gaze at Belaric. "Do not mind waiting, do you?" Rusk asked. "Gotta pen these bastards first. I will take Eddaross last," he said as he moved back towards the stable.

Belaric nodded. "No rush. Got any apples left?"

Rusk glanced back his way, eyes flashing under sweat-damp hair. "Sack's over there," he grunted, jerking his chin toward a bundle propped against the stable wall. "Figured you would want them."

Belaric offered a faint smile and led Eddaross over. He reached into the sack and pulled free a pair—one for him, one for the horse. They stood in the quiet shade, crunching side by side. Eddaross devoured his in savage, contented bites, the sound loud against the background of stamping hooves and Rusk's curses. Belaric chewed slower, jaw aching from fatigue, eyes half-closed as he breathed in the scent of hay, sweat, and damp wood.

For a moment, he let himself believe that all these secret plots were far away.

Then something moved.

A flicker—quick, sharp—just beyond the treeline. Without thought, Belaric's hand dropped to the hilt of his blade, his body already shifting into a low, defensive crouch. The forest stood still now, but something had been there. Not wind. Not a bird. It had shape. Intent.

He scanned the treeline, slow and deliberate, his gaze dissecting every patch of shadow, every clump of brush. No movement. No sound. No reason for his skin to crawl the way it did.

A bird should have flown. A squirrel should have scattered. But the forest held its breath—and that was worse.

He narrowed his eyes and waited.

The last shadow had brought a blade bared for Lady Haldren and Lyra. He would not let another come close enough to strike.

"Alright, bring him in!" Rusk called out, bringing him back.

Belaric stood and pulled his hood up without thinking, shadows swallowing the sharp lines of his face. The instinct had outlived the Order, but it served him still. He took the reins and led Eddaross into the stables.

"Be gentle with him," he said as he passed the reins over. "He has earned it."

Rusk gave a snort that might have been a laugh. "He is better fed than I am, that beast."

Belaric nodded, a nagging unease still prickling his skin from the encounter at the treeline. He decided a quick check-in with Lady Haldren and Sir Tolman was necessary before fully relaxing. He then turned toward the estate. The warmth of the day had already begun to bleed from the stones. Evening crept in slowly, quietly, and watchful.

Inside, he found Lady Haldren and Sir Tolman in the front room. She sat at the table, pale fingers rifling through parchment. Dozens of letters lay strewn before her—seals cracked, inks still fresh. Messages from potential allies and some potential enemies had arrived while they had been away. It seemed Lady Haldren was keen on answering every letter.

Sir Tolman stood nearby, arms crossed, watching her without speaking. His posture indicated fatigue, but his eyes were sharp. Alert.

Belaric stepped beside him, voice low. "Extra guards tonight," he whispered. "One at every door. Rotate them often. I want one in Lady Haldren's and Lyra's room—hidden and watching the windows. I will be moving around."

Sir Tolman glanced at him, concern deepening the lines on his brow. "What is it?"

Belaric's eyes flicked toward Lady Haldren, then back, his jaw tight. "Might be nothing," he said. "But it did not feel like nothing."

Sir Tolman studied him for a long moment, then gave a single nod. "I will tell the men. Those on first watch should get what sleep they can."

"Thank you," Belaric said, and turned away.

He reached his room and closed the door with a quiet click. The bed waited like a promise he did not quite trust. He stripped off his clothes piece by piece, each layer peeling away the weariness, the suspicion, the guilt that never quite washed off. He slipped beneath the blanket and lay still, muscles tight beneath the surface.

Sleep did not come easily these days.

But tonight, he prayed it would come quickly.

Even if it did not stay.

Hours later, a hand gripped his shoulder and shook.

Belaric's eyes snapped open, the dark room sharpening into focus in a breath. Kedd stood above him, already armored, face carved from iron. "Time to go."

Belaric nodded and swung his legs over the edge of the bed as Kedd turned and left. He rose slowly, stretching each muscle until the tension cracked and gave. The air was cold on his skin.

He knelt and pulled the pack from under the bed. The assassin's outfit stared back at him. Worn leather, black cloth, old blood worked into every crease. It was not a disguise anymore. It had not been for a long time. With a breath through his nose, he pulled each piece free and dressed in silence. The leather gripped him like memory, each strap pulling him deeper into who he used to be. When the last buckle was fastened, he raised the hood and let it settle low over his brow, casting his face in shadow. He studied himself once in the mirror—just long enough to recognize the man he hated—then stepped into the hall.

Sir Tolman waited at the bottom of the stairs, arms crossed. "I will never get used to that," he muttered, giving Belaric a sideways glance.

Belaric gave a faint chuckle. "No one ever does."

Sir Tolman stepped forward, voice low and focused. "Staven and Nollan are on patrol outside. Lady Haldren and Lyra are in her chambers. Jass is inside—hidden, crossbow aimed at the window. I will stay in the hall outside their door. Kedd's at the front entrance. Knoll at the back. When it is time to switch, wake the others. I do not want a single entry left unguarded."

Belaric nodded. "Smart. Let us hope we do not need any of it."

"Hope is a luxury," Sir Tolman said, already turning. "We have got people to protect."

"Yes, sir," Belaric said, and walked into the dark.

Two hours passed like smoke. Belaric moved from corner to corner, shadow to shadow, never still for long. He watched. Listened. The house slept, but his blood did not. The wind whispered across the roof. Timbers creaked in protest. The silence felt unnatural. Like something holding its breath.

Maybe it was a bird, he told himself. Maybe you are chasing ghosts again. Still, the unease gnawed at him. His instincts had never left him. They waited, quiet, until they were needed.

It was nearly time to wake Tarnel for the next shift when he heard it—a sound like a fingertip on glass. Soft. Deliberate. Belaric stopped mid-step. Another sound followed—quieter still. A scrape. A tool at work. Someone was testing the window.

He pressed himself against the wall, heartbeat slowing, body sharpening like a blade being drawn. His hand slid to the dagger at his belt. The shadow outside was still. Listening. So was he.

Then movement. The window began to slide open. Slow. Cautious. A leg came through. Then, a hand gripping the frame. The figure moved like a ghost trained to kill.

So did Belaric.

The lunge came without thought—the body remembered what the heart tried to forget. He seized the man with one arm, dagger raised. The assassin flinched, startled, and lost his grip and fell back. They crashed through the window together in an eruption of glass and wind.

For a breath, all was still.

Then pain. Cold. Dirt beneath his hands. The dagger was gone, lost in the fall. Belaric recovered first, driving the assassin's arms to the ground beneath his knees.

"Staven! Nollan!" he shouted into the dark. No answer.

From inside came the thunder of boots—Sir Tolman, already barreling down the stairs. Belaric's eyes swept the yard—and caught it.

A shape in the brush. A figure slumped halfway out of cover. The outline was all wrong—too still, too soft. One pale hand hung in the weeds, fingers limp.

Staven.

His voice caught. "No..." He started to rise. "Staven, get up!" he shouted, his voice cracking.

No movement. Just the hush of wind and the pounding in his ears.

The assassin saw his opportunity and struck. The man's elbow lashed out at Belaric's head. Belaric's grip had loosened as the impact connected—rage had robbed him of caution. The strike had cracked into his skull, and he hit the dirt hard, vision flaring white.

Sir Tolman burst from the doorway, sword drawn. He scanned the scene in a blink, saw Belaric on the ground and the assassin fleeing. He did not speak—just roared and charged. But the assassin ran on. A blur in black, fast and fluid. He vaulted the fence like mist on stone and vanished into the trees.

Belaric shoved himself to his feet, staggered, then locked his eyes on Staven's body again. "Tolman! See to Staven!" he shouted, voice fraying.

Sir Tolman froze mid-run and turned. He followed Belaric's gaze—and the anger left him like breath in winter. He staggered to the brush, dropped beside the boy, hands already moving.

Belaric did not wait.

He turned and ran.

"BELARIC!" someone called after him, but it was already too late.

He reached the steel fence and climbed it in a fluid surge. Pain followed him. Grief gave it wings. He hit the ground running. They had taken one of his own.

He would find them.

And they would die for it.

Belaric ran harder.

The forest swallowed light and sound, but he pushed through, branches clawing at his cloak, roots threatening every step. He caught glimpses of movement ahead—the faint silhouette of the assassin ducking low, weaving between trees. The bastard was fast, but Belaric was closing the distance.

They pressed deeper into the woods. The assassin's pace faltered, navigating uneven ground and jutting roots, and Belaric's did too—less from fatigue than from caution. He lowered his eyes for just a second to avoid a snarl of roots, then looked up.

Gone.

The forest ahead was still. Empty.

Belaric slowed to a stop, breath steaming in the cold. The silence felt wrong, forced. The kind of quiet that masks a trap. He moved forward slowly, trying to soften each step, but every twig seemed to snap like bone beneath his boots, every leaf a drumbeat.

Then—behind him—there was a sound.

Soft. Familiar. The hiss of a blade sliding free.

He dropped flat onto the ground. A heartbeat later, something sliced the air above him and embedded in the ground with a heavy thunk. Belaric rolled, kicked to his feet, and drew his second dagger in a smooth, practiced motion.

A figure moved above—just ahead, perched on a low branch. Moonlight caught the glint of a mask—matte black, featureless, shaped to erase the man beneath it. The same kind Belaric once wore. It stripped identity, replacing it with duty.

The man rose to full height, half-hidden by the shadows, and looked down on him.

"It really is you," the assassin said, voice muffled through the mask.

Belaric's grip tightened. "If you know who I am, then you know I will not let you leave this forest alive."

The man chuckled darkly. "Just like that boy? What did you call him—Staven?" A pause filled with venom. "He cried for you. Begged like a coward. Died alone."

Rage twisted through Belaric like wire drawn tight, but he held it down, deep beneath the surface. The man wanted emotion. Emotion made you stupid. Made you bleed.

Belaric's sneer was cold. "The only coward I see is the one hiding in a tree. Come down and meet death, or are you too scared to face it?"

The assassin stood tall, then dropped to the forest floor in a crouch. The sound of his landing echoed like a challenge. He straightened slowly, drew another dagger, and leveled it toward Belaric.

Belaric spat at the man's feet. He needed calm.

They closed the distance in silence. Footfalls careful, eyes locked. The wind hissed between them like a warning.

Then they moved.

Steel flashed. The assassin struck low—Belaric pivoted, blade catching the strike and redirecting it wide. He answered with a slash meant to bleed, but the man ducked and countered with a thrust to the gut. Belaric twisted aside, dirt kicking up as he moved.

They circled. Again. Then clashed.

Metal rang against metal, quick strikes and sharper counters. They moved around trees, ducked beneath branches, and danced over roots like men who knew the price of tripping. Neither gave ground easily. Belaric aimed for tendons, for the throat, for the heart—but the man was well trained. Fast.

Belaric knew the rhythm of it—the footwork, the angles, the cold precision. It was their style, unmistakable and deadly. Every feint, every angle of pressure, every silent shift of weight–he knew them all, for he had trained alongside this very discipline for years. A chilling thought pierced through the combat haze: had fate turned a day differently, it could have been him on the other end of that blade.

But where the assassin fought with speed, Belaric fought with purpose. He had been forged in the same mold—but he had shattered it.

A slash missed Belaric's ribs by inches. He kicked a fallen branch up into the man's path, forcing a stumble, then pressed forward. The assassin met him, their blades crashing together, locking in a deadly grip. They strained, breath fogging between them, arms trembling with effort.

"You are too late," the assassin hissed. "He was still warm when I—"

Belaric roared. Fury overtook restraint.

He shoved the assassin back with brutal force. The man stumbled—but too cleanly. Too balanced. The shift in his weight, the readiness of his stance—it was not retreat. It was bait.

The slash came down fast and vicious, angled to kill, not to wound. But Belaric was ready.

He sidestepped cleanly; the blade whistling past his shoulder, and countered with a vicious upward cut that tore through the assassin's arm. Steel clattered as the dagger dropped. The man shouted in pain, staggering back.

Belaric did not stop.

He surged forward and drove his knee into the man's gut. The assassin choked, breath leaving him in a sharp grunt. Belaric seized him by the head, wrenched it down, and slammed him hard into the ground. The forest floor trembled with the impact.

Without pause, Belaric grabbed the man's uninjured arm, pinned it down, and pressed his dagger to the soft flesh beneath his chin. The blade kissed skin, steady and cold, drawing a sharp line of blood. The assassin's breath hitched.

He froze beneath him.

They were close now, tangled in breath and blood. Belaric could not see the man's eyes through the mask, but he could feel the recognition—the shift in tension, the breath held between two men trained by the same ghosts. He knew this stance. Knew this stillness. He had shared kills with it once. Shared silence.

The Black Vow.

One of his own.

Or what used to be.

The quiet between them was not just stillness—it was memory. Belaric stared down at him, fury simmering beneath his skin.

"You were one of us, Varros. But now you are nothing but a coward who ran from the Order," the man rasped. "Your traitorous face is known to all of us now. And now that I have found you, every blade the Order has will come for you."

Belaric's jaw tightened. "No, I was not, not really. I am not scum like you."

The assassin laughed behind the mask. "Keep telling yourself that, Varros, you are nothing more than a killer like the rest of us. "

Belaric leaned in, voice like ice. "Shut the fuck up." The knife pressed deeper.

"This is how it is going to go," Belaric said, his voice low and sharp enough to cut. "I ask a question. You answer. If you lie—or if I even think you lied—I stab you."

The assassin remained utterly still. "I will tell you nothing," he rasped, a faint, defiant chuckle following.

Belaric did not wait. He drove the dagger into the man's bicep—deep enough to tear through the flesh and scream actual pain into his bones, but not deep enough to do lasting harm. The man cried out, jerking beneath him.

"You are a fool, Varros," he spat, breath ragged but defiant. "You will die. Soon."

Belaric's tone did not shift. "I already killed Aeryn. And now you. I will kill the rest, one by one."

He yanked the blade free and drove it again, this time into the meat of the man's thigh. The assassin groaned, leg twitching.

Belaric growled, twisting the hilt. "Where is the Vowkeeper?"

The man grunted, then laughed again. "No one knows where he is, you stupid bastard, and even if I did, I would never tell a cowardly traitor like you. You will die screaming like the pathetic retch you are."

Belaric knew the man was not lying about the Vowkeeper's location. But he did not care. He grabbed the man's arm, forced it down flat, and plunged the dagger through the web of his hand. The assassin screamed, a broken, startled sound this time. His body flinched, breath catching in his throat. Fear, finally.

"Insult me again," Belaric said, his voice ice. "And I will cut your cock off and feed it to you."

The assassin froze. The mask offered no expression, but the silence told Belaric enough.

"Why are you here?" he asked.

"Why do you think?" the man gasped. "Aeryn's dead. I was sent to find out how. They knew that oaf could not have done it. When I saw you at the stables…" He coughed a laugh. "I knew. Sent a bird the second I laid eyes on you."

Belaric held his breath. Kept his hand steady.

"Then why attack?" he asked. "You knew we had the numbers. You knew I was there. Did you really think you could kill us all?"

The assassin tilted his head against the dirt. "The Order suffers no weakness. I saw my chance and took it. I knew I might die. But if I had the chance to kill you—and those two whores—I would take it every time."

Belaric did not speak.

He leaned in close. Pressed the dagger tip against the man's stomach—and kept pressing. Slow, relentless.

The man screamed again, his limbs trembling. "WAIT—!"

Belaric's whisper was almost gentle.

"You speak of them again," he said, "and I will cut you a thousand times. I will make your death so slow you will beg me to flay you just to end it."

He slid the blade back out, and the assassin whimpered. His free hand darted to the wound, trying to stop the bleeding, but Belaric just shook his head. It would not be enough.

"JUST KILL ME, YOU BASTARD!" the assassin roared, voice breaking as he buckled under the pain.

Belaric placed the blade against his throat again, steady as stone.

"The gods know I want to," he muttered. "But your judgment will not come from me."

He rose, looming over the man. "She will decide," he told him, voice flat.

The assassin writhed at his feet. Belaric grabbed him by the throat, forced him upright, turned him roughly, and pressed the dagger to the back of his neck.

"Walk," he commanded.

The man limped forward. Several times he tried to stop, to fall, to crawl instead—but each refusal earned him a brutal elbow to the ribs, a knee to the back, a reminder that pain was always an option.

The forest gave way to firelight.

Torches burned at the perimeter of the estate, casting flickering halos across the trees. Guards stood in a full circle around the manor now, armed and waiting, blades drawn against the night. When Belaric emerged from the treeline with the masked figure in tow, silence swept the line of men.

Then a voice called out.

"TOLMAN!"

The gate swung open in seconds. Belaric forced the assassin through it. The man stumbled, a grotesque shadow, leaving a trail of dark, glistening blood across the trampled grass. His left bicep was a pulped mess, crimson soaking the dark fabric, and his thigh streamed a fresh, steady flow. He was bloody and limping, but Belaric kept the dagger pressed to his back.

The guards stepped aside without a word. None spoke. None dared.

The front doors opened.

Sir Tolman stepped out into the firelight, sword still in hand. Lady Haldren was behind him, pale in the torch glow. They saw Belaric—his cloak torn, his arms streaked with the assassin's blood, a dagger to the prisoner's back—and their faces went tight with shock.

Sir Tolman took a step forward, his voice low. "Holy hell, man. What did you do?"

Belaric looked at him, dark eyes heavy with something more than anger. He spoke one word.

"Staven."

Sir Tolman let out a slow breath, his shoulders heavy.

"He was stabbed low in the gut," he said. "He lost a lot of blood before we found him. We sent for Bramley—the town healer—and he got here fast, but... he does not know if the boy will live."

Before anyone could speak, the assassin chuckled.

"He will be dead by—"

Belaric stepped forward and struck him across the back of the head with the hilt of his dagger. The blow landed hard. The assassin grunted, body jerking, then crumpled to the dirt without another word.

Lady Haldren flinched. Her eyes widened, but she did not speak right away. Her gaze lingered on the unconscious body, then flicked to Belaric—his bloodied hands, the clenched jaw. Something unreadable passed across her face. Not fear. Not quite disapproval. Something quieter. Unsettled.

Belaric exhaled and looked at her. "My apologies, my lady. I have heard enough of him for one lifetime."

She steadied herself and took a step forward, voice calm again. "I am surprised you let him live."

"I gave my word," Belaric replied. "I will not kill unless I must. But I hoped he might still be useful. He may have the answers we need."

Sir Tolman stepped beside him, glancing down at the unconscious figure. "Looks like you already interrogated him."

Belaric nodded. "He talked. Some of it was worthless, but I got enough. We may get more when he wakes."

Lady Haldren tilted her head, intrigued. "What did you learn?"

Belaric hesitated, voice quieter now. "They know I am here. He sent a bird when he saw me at the stables. It is done. There is no more hiding."

A shadow crossed his face, and for the first time, his voice held something besides steel—weariness, laced faintly with guilt.

Lady Haldren nodded slowly. "We expected this. Now we act. For now, let us focus on the moment." She turned slightly, eyes sharp again. "Sir Tolman—secure the prisoner. I want him bound and guarded at all hours."

Sir Tolman was already moving. "Kedd," he called out, "get irons and rope. And keep that bastard breathing."

Lady Haldren turned back to Belaric. "Are you hurt?"

He shook his head. "He was skilled," he admitted. "Fast. But he had not survived what I have."

Then his eyes shifted toward the manor. His next words came slower, heavy.

"I would like to see Staven," he said.

She studied him for a moment—his posture, the tight set of his jaw—and gave a small nod. "Go. I am sure he will be glad to know you are still walking."

Her voice rose slightly as she addressed the others. "Everyone else—return to your posts. Keep your eyes sharp."

Her command moved through the courtyard like wind through leaves. The guards snapped to action, some pulling away, others reinforcing the perimeter. Tolman barked fresh orders, already shifting focus, while Kedd hurried off to fetch what was needed.

Belaric followed Lady Haldren toward the doors. As they reached the steps, she glanced over at him.

"He is in the room. Bramley's still with him," she told him.

Belaric gave a slow nod. "Thank you."

Then he turned and walked the familiar hallway alone.

The hallway was silent, but Belaric's thoughts were not.

Each step rang louder in his head than it did on stone. Guilt clawed at him with every breath. He had seen something—felt it in his bones. The shadows were shifting before the attack. He should have been outside. Watching. Waiting. Not hiding like he always did. If he had been, maybe Staven would not be lying in a bed, pale and bleeding.

He paused before the door, his hand on the handle.

A deep breath. Then another.

He turned it and stepped inside.

The room was dim, lit by a single oil lamp on the far table. The air smelled of sweat, blood, and crushed herbs. Outside, the wind hissed softly against the shutters, as if the forest still breathed just beyond the walls.

Staven lay motionless on the bed, stripped down to his undergarments, his body pale against the linen. His stomach was bound in layers of cloth, and though the healer had done his work, red still bloomed faintly beneath the wrapping. It had not stopped. The bleeding had not stopped.

A figure sat beside the bed, leaning over him with practiced care. He turned when Belaric entered.

The healer was older, his face a map of hard years and sleepless nights. Deep wrinkles creased his brow and cheeks, and what little hair remained clung in wisps of white around a balding crown. His simple grey robe was stained with herbs and wear, the sleeves rolled to his elbows, hands calloused from long labor and smelling faintly of dried lavender and wood smoke. His movements were slow but precise, the way a master carpenter works a piece of wood, each touch deliberate and confident.

"Who the hell are you?" he asked, his voice a low gravel, edged with weary defensiveness.

Belaric raised his hands. "I am Belaric. One of Lady Haldren's guards."

The man looked him over, his gaze sharp and assessing. "You are the one who patched up Sir Tolman?"

"I am," Belaric replied.

The healer gave a curt nod and turned back to his patient. "Name's Bramley. That bastard got the boy good."

Belaric stepped closer, eyes fixed on the blood-stained bandages. "How is he?"

Bramley sighed, his voice dipping low. "The cut was deep. Blade went through the outer stomach wall and tore into the small intestine—it was not clean either, more like it chewed its way in. Took me too long to stop the internal bleeding. I sealed what I could with fire-wort and stitched the gut, but he is still bleeding from inside. Slowly."

He reached for a cloth, dabbed it along Staven's brow. "I gave him bloodroot to thicken the flow, and night blossom to dull the pain. But he is weak. He is burning up. If the bleeding does not stop by morning, or if infection sets in…" Bramley did not finish the thought. He did not need to.

Belaric nodded slowly and knelt beside the bed, his knees protesting as they hit the floor. Staven's skin was clammy with sweat. His chest rose and fell in a shallow, uncertain rhythm. His hands trembled faintly.

The boy looked small like this. Fragile.

He is a good man. This… he did not deserve an assassin's blade in the gut.

Bramley glanced down at Belaric. "Can you sit with him? I need to fetch more herbs, clean bandages—maybe something stronger for the fever. If he worsens, pour cold water over his chest and call for me."

Belaric did not take his eyes off Staven. "I will."

Bramley nodded once and moved with surprising speed, gathering up his sack of different herbs. His grey robe whispered as he left, closing the door gently behind him.

The silence that followed was heavy. Belaric dipped the cloth into the basin and wrung it out. He leaned forward, gently pressing it to Staven's brow. The heat radiating from the boy was unnatural.

"I am sorry, Staven," Belaric whispered, voice cracking at the edges. "I should have been there. I should not have been hiding in the shadows like I always do. I could have stopped it. I should have. I failed you… just like I failed them."

His hand dropped to the edge of the bed, cloth still damp between his fingers. A tear welled in his eyes but refused to fall. He blinked it back, jaw clenched.

Then—something touched his hand.

He looked up.

Staven's fingers, shaking and pale, had closed over his. Weak, but firm enough to feel.

Belaric froze for a moment, then reached back and gripped the hand gently but firmly.

"I will not leave your side," he said, his voice a breath.

And though the boy did not speak, his fingers tightened in answer.

The hours passed slowly. The kind of slow that settled into the bones and stayed there.

Bramley had returned once already, quiet and focused. He re-wrapped Staven's bandages, gave him more herbs to fight the fever and slow the bleeding, and worked without wasting breath. The old man had been woken in the dead of night, and his limbs moved with weariness, but his hands were steady. When he finally admitted that he needed rest, Lady Haldren offered him one of the upstairs rooms. Bramley hesitated, but Belaric insisted.

"I will stay with him," he said. "If anything changes, I will come find you."

Now Belaric sat on the floor, back against the bedframe, eyes locked on nothing, ears tuned to the sound of Staven's breathing—slow, wheezing, each one sounding more fragile than the last. The air in the room felt thick and motionless. Outside, the wind had fallen still, as though the world beyond the walls was waiting for something. He tried to silence his thoughts, but they clawed at him all the same. He kept seeing it differently—him outside, catching the assassin first, striking before the boy was ever touched. He imagined dragging the killer down before a blade was drawn. If he had done anything differently, Staven would not be dying. It should be me in that bed, he thought.

Then, a sound broke the stillness.

"Belaric."

He spun. Staven's eyes were open—clouded and glassy, but aware. They searched for him in the dark. Belaric scrambled around, falling to his knees beside the bed, taking the boy's trembling hand.

"You are awake," he said, voice roughened by fatigue and something deeper.

Staven's lips moved slowly. "I am sorry, Belaric… I failed you… and Lady Haldren."

"No," Belaric said, shaking his head. "No, you did not. I failed you. I should have been there. I should have killed him before he even got close."

Staven tried to move his head, but the motion sent a shudder through his frame. "It is not your fault. I thought I heard something… I did not call out. I went to the bush. I knew it was foolish… but I still went."

He was taken by a fit of coughing—wet, sharp. Blood stained his lips. Belaric reached for the cloth and gently wiped it away, keeping his touch steady.

"You need to rest. I will go get Bramley—"

But Staven did not let go of his hand.

"No," he whispered. "It is too late. I have accepted it. Just… tell Lady Haldren I am sorry."

Belaric froze, his heart thudding like a war drum.

"No," he said again, more fiercely. "You are not allowed to die. Lady Haldren ordered you to live. You do not disobey orders."

Staven's mouth twitched into something like a smile. "Well… I am sorry. It is one order I cannot follow."

He tried to laugh, but it came out as a breathless wheeze. "I will miss our sword training. You are… a master with that blade."

Belaric lowered his head, the shame rising like bile in his throat. "You would have surpassed me in no time."

Even near death, Staven managed another faint grin. "Even I am not that foolish."

His breathing grew shallower with every word. His eyes drifted, fighting to stay open.

"Thank you, Belaric. Please… keep them safe."

"I will," Belaric said, barely above a whisper. "I swear it."

Staven nodded weakly, then looked up toward the ceiling, his gaze going distant. "It will be good... to see my father again. I hope he is proud of me."

Belaric held his hand tighter, the ache in his chest threatening to crush him. "I am sure he is."

The boy gave a shallow breath. Then another. A faint rattling sound from deep within his chest. And then, silence.

The candle on the bedside table flickered. Somewhere beyond the walls, an owl cried once, and then the night returned to stillness.

Belaric leaned in, staring. "Staven?" He shook him gently. "Staven—wake up."

He shook him again, harder now. "Lady Haldren ordered you. We need you—I need you. Damn it, wake up!"

He stood up and strode to the door, yanking it open with shaking hands. "Bramley!" he shouted down the hallway. "Bramley!"

No answer.

He shouted again, louder this time. "Bramley!"

Footsteps came quickly. Bramley appeared moments later, cloak thrown over his shoulders, eyes wide and urgent. He brushed past Belaric without a word and dropped to his knees beside the bed. He pressed an ear to Staven's chest, checked his pulse, then his throat. Lifted the boy's wrist and let it fall.

He tried to bring the breath back—hands working with what strength age had left him. But it did not come.

After long minutes, Bramley sat back slowly. He looked up at Belaric, and though his voice was soft, it hit like a blade.

"I am sorry," he said. "Staven is dead."

Belaric stood still, staring at the boy who had once grinned at him during drills and asked too many questions. His hand clenched slowly at his side, fingers trembling. He did not speak. Did not move.

The candle beside the bed burned on.

24

Belaric gave a stiff nod. "Thank you for trying to save him, Bramley," he said, voice clipped, the words like stones in his throat.

Before the old healer could speak, Belaric turned and walked out. He did not trust himself to hear any more.

He moved through the house like a blade unsheathed—silent, sharp, aching to cut. His thoughts roared behind his eyes, a storm he could barely keep contained. He passed Dross in the hall; the man opened his mouth, concern plain on his face.

Belaric did not stop.

He pushed into the kitchen.

Lady Haldren stood by the far wall, posture taut, arms crossed, annoyance flickering in her eyes. Sir Tolman was there too, stationed before the captive like a watchtower of muscle and quiet fury. The assassin sat bound to a chair, stripped of hood and mask. He was young. Short black hair, a shallow wound on his cheek, and green eyes that gleamed with something Belaric knew far too well: pride dressed up as contempt.

As soon as Belaric entered, the assassin's gaze locked onto him, and he smiled.

A bloody thing, all teeth and malice.

Tolman and Lady Haldren turned at the sound of the door. Something in Belaric's expression must have warned them, because Lady Haldren took a careful step toward him.

"Belaric?" she asked. "What is wrong?"

The assassin laughed.

"He is dead, is he not?" The words oozed out, thick with mockery. "Poor fool thought he could outrun death."

Belaric did not speak.

He crossed the room and struck the man square across the face.

The force knocked the chair sideways. Wood scraped. Bone cracked. The assassin's laughter deepened, wet and gurgling, but still laughing.

And Belaric saw red.

He stood over him and drove his fist down again. And again. He felt the skin on his knuckles split. He did not care. He welcomed the sting. The assassin's head snapped back with each hit, blood splattering in a thin arc across the kitchen floor. Still, he laughed.

Sir Tolman swore and lunged, but before he could intervene, Belaric was already drawing his dagger.

In one brutal motion, he grabbed the man by the throat, fingers digging into the slick heat of his skin, and drove the blade forward until the tip kissed the wet white of the man's eyeball.

"Stop laughing," Belaric growled, voice low and flat. "Stop laughing, or I will hollow your skull."

The kitchen froze. Even the fire in the hearth seemed to quiet.

"I am going to kill you," Belaric whispered. "And not quickly. You will suffer. You will scream Staven's name, and I will make sure the last sound you hear is your own voice choking on blood."

The assassin gasped, not laughing now.

For a heartbeat, his smile faltered. He looked up, blood on his lips, and for the first time, his eyes wavered—not with defiance, but fear.

"Staven is dead?" Sir Tolman said behind him, the words a dull echo. His voice was already breaking.

Belaric did not turn. "He is. He asked me to tell you he was sorry, my lady. He died thinking he had failed."

The memory struck with cruel sharpness. Staven's eyes dimming, voice rasping, "Tell her I am sorry." Belaric had reached for his hand, but the life had already slipped away.

A silence followed, too large to fill with anything human.

Lady Haldren's face fell, her composure cracking just slightly. Her jaw trembled. She looked to the assassin, then to Belaric—her eyes wet, her voice barely rising above a whisper.

"No, he did not fail." She stepped forward, her tone gaining strength. "Staven was brave. He held the line when others would have fled. I suffer with you, Belaric, I do. But this—" her eyes flicked to the knife, "—this is what he wants. This is what they want. To turn you into something you are not."

Belaric's grip tightened around the man's throat. He could feel the thrum of the pulse beneath his fingers, quick as a rabbit's.

It would be easy. One push. With one flick of the wrist and it would be over. Justice. Vengeance. Whatever word dulled the edge.

But then he saw Staven's face again—bloodied, pale, smiling despite it all.

He would not want this. The thought hit like a cold wind.

Lady Haldren's hand landed on his shoulder, warm and steady. "We need this man alive. Not for mercy. For answers."

Sir Tolman added quietly, "Come on, lad. Let the gods weigh him later. We still have a use for him."

Belaric's jaw clenched. Slowly, he withdrew the blade. The tip glistened red. The assassin gasped, coughing, blood spattering across his chin.

Belaric stood, eyes burning. "I want a funeral for him," he said hoarsely. "A proper one. He died a man of honor."

Lady Haldren nodded solemnly. "We will bury him as the hero he was."

Belaric's voice tightened further, almost breaking. "It will be today. I will dig the grave myself. Just tell me where."

For a moment, no one spoke. Then, Lady Haldren placed a hand gently over her heart. "There is a tree on the north hill. A lone birch. That is where we buried my father's steward. It is quiet there. Peaceful."

Belaric nodded once. Digging the grave himself—it was all he had left to offer. A blade could not fix this. But maybe sweat, soil, and silence could.

No more words. He turned and walked out of the kitchen; the assassin choking on breath behind him, and rage still coiled like wire in his chest. Blood dripped from his knuckles in slow, warm taps as he walked. He did not bother wiping it away.

Belaric returned to his room, his steps slow and deliberate. The old healer sat resting, half-slumped in a chair, weariness clinging to his face like a second skin. His eyes opened at the sound.

"Can you prepare Staven's body?" Belaric asked quietly, voice rough from disuse.

Bramley nodded, the lines around his mouth deepening. "I will. He will be ready when the time comes."

Belaric gave a curt nod and turned without another word, making his way through the estate toward the back door. His hand paused on the handle when he saw Kedd standing in the hallway, shoulders stiff, face pale.

"Is it true?" Kedd asked.

Belaric met his eyes. "I am sorry, Kedd."

He did not respond. Grief had settled into him like a weight. His lips trembled once, but whatever words he meant to say were swallowed. As Belaric stepped past, Kedd reached out and touched the stone wall beside him—just barely, as though trying to steady himself. A small, broken gesture. Belaric did not look back.

He stepped out into the morning. The sun was just beginning to crest the hills, gilding the sky in soft gold. A breeze carried the scent of hay, earth, and summer bloom. It should have been beautiful. But all Belaric felt was the cold inside his chest.

He found a shovel leaning against the stable wall. The wood was old, worn smooth by years of use; the blade was nicked and rusting. As he passed the stables, Rusk poked his head out from a side door, hay sticking to his tunic. When he saw the shovel, his expression darkened.

"Do you need help, lad?" he asked.

Belaric shook his head. "This is my burden to bear."

From inside the stall, Eddaross gave a low, restless snort. Belaric stepped closer and ran a hand across the stallion's flank. "I will be back, old boy. Do not worry." The horse huffed and stamped once, but said no more.

Belaric walked up the hill in silence, shovel over his shoulder. At the top, he found the lone birch Lady Haldren had spoken of. A single grave rested at its base—weather-worn stone, moss gathered at the corners. Her steward, buried years ago. A few feet beyond it, the morning sun cut clean across the grass. It was a good place. Peaceful. The light touched the ground gently here.

He shrugged off his tunic, leaving only his undershirt; the burden of it was too much to bear. The leather was stiff with dried blood, the scent of smoke still clinging to it. He stared at the armor for a long moment. This was what he had worn when Renna's body was burned. What he wore when the Vowkeeper escaped with Eryndorr. What he wore when Staven fell. It sickened him. He threw it aside and drove the shovel into the soil.

Each thrust was deliberate. His muscles burned early, but he did not stop. Could not. Every breath came with Staven's final words, playing again and again in his head. "Tell her I am sorry..." Their time had been short, but in that time, Staven had shown more courage, more loyalty, than men three times his age. He never wavered. Never once looked for a way out.

Belaric had buried others before. Too many. But this felt different. This felt like burying hope itself.

The hours passed slowly. Dirt piled high beside the grave. Sweat clung to his back and shoulders, dust caked his arms, and the shovel's handle bit into his palms. He paused once, leaning on the wood, glancing back at the estate. The ground was still. No one stirred. But carried faintly on the wind, he thought he heard it—the sound of weeping.

Lyra, he thought.

He swallowed the ache and dug deeper.

He was nearly finished when he heard the footsteps—slow, measured, someone approaching from behind. He looked up. Sir Tolman stood at the edge of the grave, a wooden marker held across both arms like a sword. Belaric climbed out of the hole as the knight approached him.

"Lady Haldren had it made in time," Tolman said, stepping past him. "Now they will all know where the hero Staven Hollard was laid to rest." He knelt and placed the marker into the earth with careful hands.

Belaric moved beside him and read the words carved into the wood: Staven Hollard–A Man of Honor. He stared at it for a moment, then lifted his gaze to the sky. A gust of wind stirred the grass, tugged gently at the birch leaves.

"Your father would be proud, Staven," he whispered.

Sir Tolman watched him in silence, then held out a hand. "Hand me the shovel, lad."

Belaric hesitated, grip tightening on the handle out of instinct. Reflex. Possession.

Sir Tolman sighed. "You need to clean up. Get changed. This is not just your burden. I was meant to train him. I put him on watch, knowing the risk. If anyone failed, it was me. I will finish it. Because it should be my hands that bury him."

His voice did not shake, but it carried the weight of a man who had buried too many things—and now added one more to the list.

Belaric stepped forward and handed him the shovel. Then he placed a hand on Sir Tolman's shoulder. "We failed," he said. "But we will not fail again. I will not let them take another soul from that house. Not while I still breathe."

His voice hardened. "I will hunt them. One by one. For Renna. For Eryndorr. For Staven."

Sir Tolman stood straighter. "We will hunt them," he corrected.

Belaric offered a tired half-smile. A rare thing. He nodded.

Sir Tolman nodded back. "Go. Get clean. I have work to do, and you smell like an old dirty beggar."

Belaric retrieved his gear—the leather hot from the sun, the edges stiff and dry with a faint, metallic scent—and slung it over his shoulder. He turned toward the estate, walking slowly, shoulders raw but his spine unbent. The grave behind him was not filled yet.

But the promise had been made.

Belaric moved slowly, a single thought a brand in his mind: I will find him. He would not fail his son. Not like he had failed his wife. Not like he had failed Staven.

The estate loomed ahead. As he entered through the back door, he heard the soft clatter of spoons and bowls, the low scrape of chairs—some men were eating, but none were talking. The silence in the air was heavier than any storm.

He made his way to his room. Staven's body had been moved, but the bloodstains remained—dark smears on the sheets where the man had bled through the night. Belaric sat on the edge of the bed and ran his hand over the dried blood, fingers brushing the edge of one stain.

He must have been in so much pain, Belaric thought. But he held on for hours. A testament to his strength... to his will.

He sighed, stood, and began stripping out of the rest of his assassin's garb. The black leathers had served their purpose, but today was not a day for shadow. He pulled on a simple linen shirt and grey pants, planning to wash before donning anything finer.

At the washroom door, he knocked once—grateful when no one answered. He stepped inside and locked the door behind him. The wooden tub had already been filled, the water cool to the touch, but he did not flinch as he lowered himself in. The cold grounded him.

He washed slowly, letting the water carry away the dirt and sweat from the grave. He scrubbed the blood from his arms and chest, ran wet fingers across his face. His beard had thickened—he would need to shave soon, he thought distantly. He stretched, feeling the ache in his shoulders, the deep weariness from hours of digging still clinging to his bones. When he finally finished, he stepped out, dried quickly, and dressed in the clean, simple clothes.

His stomach growled. He had not eaten since the day before.

When he stepped into the kitchen, Wess was there, stirring a large pot over the fire. The smell of roasted meat and herbs wrapped around him like a blanket. Wess looked over his shoulder and nodded once. Words did not belong to today. Not yet.

Belaric sat at the long table, and Wess brought him a bowl. The stew steamed gently in the morning light. He blew on it and ate in silence, the only sound the soft clink of Wess's ladle tapping against the pot.

His mind wandered as he ate, a hundred faces flashing behind his eyes. He forced the thoughts back, drove them down into silence.

He stood and quietly thanked Wess before returning to his room to dress in the finest clothes he owned. When he emerged into the hall, the others were gathering near the staircase.

As he approached, the men shifted aside to make room, each nodding solemnly as he passed. Only Jass and Hasker were absent; they had volunteered to guard the captured assassin. Belaric did not like the arrangement, but Sir Tolman had assured him the man could not move.

Near the base of the stairs stood a stretcher bearing Staven's body, now wrapped in clean white sheets. Sir Tolman, Kedd, Tarnel, and Dross stood at its corners, solemn and ready. Dross gave a small wave when he saw Belaric and motioned for him to join them. Belaric took his place silently.

Lady Haldren stood nearby, dressed in deep violet, with Lyra at her side. The girl's eyes were already wet with tears, her small hand clinging tightly to her mother's.

Once Belaric was in position, Lady Haldren gave a single nod, and the group began to move.

They trudged through the estate and out into the courtyard, then down the path toward the hill. Belaric was surprised to see dozens of townsfolk gathered ahead, circling the grave. Men, women, even children—many he did not know—all came to pay respect. The march up the hill stretched on, not because of the distance, but because of the weight pressing on his chest.

His mind screamed at him the entire way.

It should have been me.

When they reached the crest of the hill, a man in white robes stepped forward from the side. A priest—Belaric had not known one had been summoned. The four of them set Staven's body gently beside the open grave and stepped back.

Belaric stood beside Lady Haldren, Lyra on her other side. The girl's quiet sobs filled the still air as the priest stepped forward.

He raised his arms. His voice was calm, low, but strong.

"Veyrith, Father of the Gods, we ask you to open your home to this man. Let him sit at your table, let him eat the bread of peace and drink from the cup of rest."

"Seyra, Mother of the Living, guide him gently through the veil. Let your hands be soft upon his soul."

"This was a man who kept his word. A man who stood his ground. Though no crown lay upon his brow, he was noble in his heart. He gave his strength so others could live. He gave his blood so others would not bleed."

"He was not born into greatness, but he walked with it. May he rest among heroes."

As the priest spoke, Lyra's sobs grew louder. Her small hand reached for Belaric's, and without thinking, he took it. Her fingers were trembling. He looked down at her, then squeezed her hand gently.

Several of the townsfolk had tears on their cheeks as well, silent and sincere.

When the priest finished, the four men stepped forward once more and lowered Staven into the earth.

Quiet fell over the hill.

A group of townsmen approached, each holding a shovel. They bowed first to Lady Haldren, who stepped forward with tears in her voice.

"We thank this man for everything he gave us. For the smiles. For the laughter. For the moments we forgot the world was broken."

"He was a good man. A man I am proud to call my friend. I will never forget him, and I pray to the gods that I will see my friend again one day."

The townsmen nodded and began to work. Dirt thudded into the grave with a soft, solemn rhythm. Belaric stood still, watching as the white cloth vanished beneath the earth. He lowered his head, whispering a quiet prayer.

"Renna… if you see him, give him one of your apples."

Belaric stayed until the last shovelful of dirt had been placed. Lyra never left his side. Even after the others returned to the estate and the townsfolk made their way down the hill, she remained, her small hand clinging to his. The sun was dipping below the distant hills now, casting long shadows across the grave. He glanced down at her. Her eyes were red and swollen, her cheeks streaked with the lines of dried tears. He offered a faint smile—not out of joy, but out of duty, a slight comfort for someone who needed more than he could give.

"Time to head inside, Lyra," he said gently.

She nodded and reached for his hand again. They walked together down the slope toward the estate, slowly and silently.

"I do not want anyone else to die," she said, her voice quiet but thick with grief.

Belaric looked down at her. "We all die eventually," he said after a moment, "but I will not let them hurt anyone else here. Not while I am breathing."

"I want you to train me," she said.

He blinked, caught off guard by the resolve in her tone. "What? Why?"

"They will come again," she said, eyes forward. "And when they do, I will not hide behind others. I want to fight those who seek to hurt me... or my family."

Belaric sighed. "Your mother will not approve."

"It is not her choice," she said, steel in her voice. "I will be the ruler of this house one day. I need to know how to defend it. You know how assassins think—how they move. You are the best man for the job."

"You are too young," he countered. "And you are a noble girl. What do you think people will say?"

She stopped, turning toward him with narrowed eyes. "I do not care what they say. If they want to challenge me, they can face me in a formal duel. And besides... you were younger than me when you started."

Belaric exhaled slowly. "I did not have a choice. I was not trained to duel. They trained me to kill. Quietly. Quickly."

"I do not care," she repeated, fire in her tone. "You will train me."

She released his hand and strode ahead toward the estate. Belaric watched her go and ran a hand through his hair, sighing. "Fine," he called after her. "Only if your mother agrees."

Lyra turned, grinning. "Thank you, Belaric," she said, giving him a determined nod, and disappeared inside. He shook his head and followed at a slower pace.

That night, many gathered at the tavern to honor Staven—Lady Haldren, Lyra, the guards, and much of the town. They drank to his memory, told stories, and shared laughter through tears. Belaric remained behind. He needed silence more than company. When the house had finally fallen quiet, he slipped beneath the thin blanket and let his eyes close.

"Belaric."

He tried to move but found himself bound—arms twisted behind him, wrists locked in rusted iron, the cold metal biting deep into his skin. His legs were shackled to the cold stone beneath him, each chain link pressing raw against his ankles. He strained, muscles trembling, metal biting into flesh.

"Belaric."

The voice came again, low, mocking.

"Who is there?" he demanded, his voice sharp, ragged. "Show yourself!"

A sickening laugh echoed through the dark. Then—light. A faint orange flicker in the distance drew closer. Torchlight, he realized.

A figure emerged from the void, walking slowly, dragging something behind him. As the torchlight grew, Belaric saw the mask, the cloak—the silhouette of a Black Vow assassin. His breath caught. The body being dragged scraped across the stone, arms limp, blood streaking behind.

Staven.

"You bastard!" Belaric roared. "Release him!"

The figure let out a low chuckle. "I told you he would die," the voice sneered. It was unmistakable. The assassin he had captured.

Belaric struggled harder, veins straining against the iron. "I will kill you."

"You let him die," the man whispered. "You could have killed me. You had a chance. More than once. But you hesitated. Some friend you are."

More laughter echoed from the shadows behind him.

He turned as best he could, eyes wide, and saw more figures stepping forward from the dark. Each carried a torch. Their faces were hidden, but their presence was undeniable—Black Vow, one and all.

"Oh, Belaric," one crooned. "How many more have to die before you realize what you really are?"

"You are a failure," another hissed.

The first assassin stepped closer. "Here," he said mockingly, "thought you might want this."

It landed with a wet thud, rolled once, and came to rest beside Belaric, a soft squelch accompanying its final settle.

Staven's head.

Blood soaked his hair. His eyes were still open, glazed, mouth frozen mid-scream.

Belaric's heart stopped. His breath turned shallow. The man cackled.

"First Renna," one said. "Then Staven."

"Who is next?" another called.

"I know," said a voice like oil. "Let us kill Lyra next. That brat has had it coming."

Rage exploded through him. He screamed and thrashed, chains digging into his flesh.

"I will kill you! I will kill every last one of you!"

The voices pressed closer, circling, whispering.

"Poor Belaric," one said near his ear. "You cannot save anyone."

"You are not a protector," another added. "You are a weapon. A killer. That is all you will ever be."

A shape moved near the edge of his vision and tossed something. Another head. Renna.

Then Sir Tolman.

Then Lady Haldren. Her eyes were vacant. Her neck twisted at an impossible angle.

More followed—Kedd. Then, finally, Lyra.

Her face was small, pale. Her braids were stained red. Her eyes closed forever.

Belaric collapsed to his side, gasping, bile rising in his throat. "No... please... stop," he sobbed, his voice barely audible.

The figures only laughed louder.

"You are death, Belaric," one whispered. "That is all you bring."

He squeezed his eyes shut. The world cracked around him and shattered.

He jolted awake, a dull ache throbbing behind his eyes, drenched in sweat, breath ragged. The room was dark. His blanket was tangled around his legs. He pressed a hand to his face and felt wetness—tears he had not realized he had shed.

It had only been a dream.

But it felt real. Too real.

He lay in silence as the others returned from the tavern. He kept his eyes closed, pretending to sleep. No one stirred him. No one spoke.

He dared not close his eyes again.

He would not risk another dream.

The days passed quickly in the wake of Staven's funeral. Though the weight of his loss still lingered in every corner of the estate, there was work to be done, and none felt that more than Belaric. He met with Lady Haldren, and together they agreed: the assassin needed to be housed somewhere more secure. The estate's interior was no place to hold a killer.

With the help of Oswin, the town blacksmith, and Tebbick, the lumber master, they constructed a small, fortified prison just beyond the estate's eastern wall. Belaric designed it himself—a narrow, shed-like structure built from thick hardwood boards, reinforced at every joint with iron brackets and bolts. The roof sloped low enough that a man could not fully stand inside. The single door was triple-locked, iron-banded, and reinforced from the inside with a bar. Inside, four circular hooks were bolted into the floor and walls, each one chained to the assassin's limbs and waist. The floor was packed earth over stone. There were no windows. No light except for what crept in when the door opened.

Belaric had checked every link himself. He tugged at the shackles, studied the angles of the iron, tested each bolt with the heel of his boot. He even circled the shed three times, looking for weaknesses no one else would consider—cracks in the wood grain, gaps near the hinges, anything a trained man might exploit. He tried the door from the outside once Oswin sealed it, leaning his full weight into the frame. It did not budge. Not even a creak—the impact deadened by stone and thick wood.

Meanwhile, Lyra's determination had not waned. After several days of increasingly pointed arguments, Lady Haldren relented. Belaric agreed to train her, but cautiously. They began with the basics—footwork, stance, posture, and how to hold a blade without losing a finger. He noticed her hands trembled on the first day, but by the third, they were steady. She absorbed every lesson like dry cloth soaking water, never once complaining.

Belaric also doubled his efforts with the estate guard. He and Sir Tolman drilled the men morning and night, pushing them harder than ever. Belaric taught them how the assassins of the Black Vow moved, how they struck unseen, how they exploited silence and timing. They learned to fight from the ground, to check their blind spots, to react on instinct when their eyes failed. The estate was no longer just a noble's home. It was becoming a fortress.

Lady Haldren continued to send letters, and more responses came. A few nobles visited in person. All claimed it was business—but none could hide their curiosity. They wanted to see the captured assassin for themselves. Some doubted the story. Most left unsettled. Whispers followed them. Tales spread. Lady Haldren had survived two attempts on her life, so people questioned who controlled these assassins and what their motives were.

Brookhaven was changing. Belaric could feel it in the dirt, in the way people lingered too long near fences, in the cautious way guards now greeted even familiar faces. The tavern grew loud at night. Markets were busier. Strangers walked the streets with questions in their mouths and blades at their hips. People whispered in corners. Guards glanced over shoulders more often. Trust was thin. But the interest was high.

Belaric and Sir Tolman hated it. More people meant more masks, more daggers, more risks.

A few men came offering their services as guards. Belaric would have turned them away, but Lady Haldren saw an opportunity. Though the estate was well-defended, she hired the newcomers to patrol the village. Sir Tolman grumbled about giving swords to strangers, but Lady Haldren insisted the town needed protection too. Belaric said nothing, though his gaze lingered on each of the newcomers longer than it used to. He watched their stances, the subtle way they held their shoulders, and the easy familiarity with which they gripped their sword hilts. Every motion spoke a language, and Belaric had learned to read it fluently.

Late one afternoon, the men were in the yard training when a carriage appeared on the road leading toward the estate. It was not lavish, but well-built—lacquered trim, clean wheels, a matched pair of gray mares. Not royal, but not poor.

Everyone paused. Belaric and Sir Tolman moved toward the gate, their steps calm but deliberate, the guards following suit. Hands drifted near hilts. Shoulders lowered instinctively into looser, readier stances.

The carriage rolled to a stop. The driver pulled the reins and called back, "We have arrived, my lord."

Belaric and Sir Tolman shared a glance. The crest was unfamiliar.

Dross spat on the ground. "Look at the paint on that carriage," he muttered. "More money than sense."

Sir Tolman gave him a warning glare, but said nothing.

The door creaked open.

A man stepped out, balancing a bottle of wine in one hand as he steadied himself on the carriage frame. He wore fine black trousers and a dark tunic with polished silver buttons, not noble finery, but just close enough to be a mimicry of power. His face was smooth, freshly shaven, his expression disarmingly casual, but his eyes held a glint of something sharp and calculating.

"By all the gods, Rulmar," he sighed, inspecting the bottle, "I told you to avoid the ruts. This wine cost me three gold, and I would rather not waste it on road dust."

"My apologies, my lord," the driver replied flatly.

The man turned and approached the gate with unhurried grace. He did not walk so much as glide, a predator who knew there was no reason to hurry. His eyes moved over the guards as if he were cataloging them, a calm, impersonal assessment of assets. When he spotted Tolman, his smile broadened—a wide, practiced flash of white teeth that did not reach his eyes.

"Sir Tolman," he said warmly, "so good to see you again. I believe your lady received my letter?"

Sir Tolman's jaw tensed. "Lord Talveth. What a... lovely surprise."

Lord Talveth laughed, the sound easy and pleasant. "You were always a terrible liar, Tolman. No need to pretend." He paused dramatically, lifting the bottle. "Now, be a good man and open this gate. I would hate to see the wine sour before I have had a chance to impress your lady with it."

Sir Tolman exhaled hard, exchanged a last look with Belaric, and motioned for the guards to open the gate. The hinges groaned.

Lord Talveth strolled in as if he belonged there, his gaze sweeping over the grounds with a possessive air. As he passed, his eyes flicked briefly to Belaric—no pause, no greeting. Just a glance, like weighing a stone before pocketing it. He did not smile this time. His expression flattened into something unreadable—just for a moment—and then the charm snapped back into place like a mask.

Belaric felt his shoulders tighten.

Men like Lord Talveth smiled too easily.

And meant none of it.

25

As Lord Talveth made his way to the door, he called back over his shoulder, "Sir Tolman, are not you going to show me the way?" His voice was wrapped in velvet, the mockery barely hidden beneath.

Sir Tolman sighed, jaw tight, and stepped forward. "Of course, my lord."

But Lord Talveth halted with a spin, one arm swinging wide in a theatrical gesture. "Ah, but on second thought—I think two escorts would suit me better. A man of my standing should not wander halls half-guarded. Appearances and all that."

He turned, surveying the room, then pointed directly at Belaric. "You, my good man. Come along."

Belaric did not move. He stood as he was, arms folded, eyes fixed on the man with unreadable intent. A colder silence fell across the room, the kind that hinted someone had said too much without knowing it.

Sir Tolman frowned, confusion flickering across his face. "Two guards to walk you twenty paces to Lady Haldren?" he asked.

Lord Talveth gave a bright, shameless smile. "Indulgent, I know. But I rather like the look of this one." He glanced again at Belaric. "Strong build. Steady eyes. A man accustomed to violence, would not you say?" He turned slightly, gesturing vaguely to another nearby. "No offense, of course."

Kedd scowled but said nothing.

Sir Tolman stepped forward, his voice hardening. "If two are needed, Kedd will accompany me. Belaric stays and continues the training," he said flatly.

Lord Talveth let out a disappointed hum, head tilted. "Oh no, I much prefer—"

"What are you playing at, Lord Talveth?" Sir Tolman asked, cutting him off.

There it was. The shift. For a moment, something passed behind Lord Talveth's eyes—too quick to catch. Then he smiled again, wide and gracious. "Such hostility, dear Sir Tolman. Is that the tone Lady Haldren teaches her men to take with her guests? I should hope not. Perhaps I will mention it to her, just in passing."

Sir Tolman stared at him, breathing slowly, before giving a curt nod. "As you wish. Belaric—assist me."

Belaric's eyes never left Lord Talveth's. He did not like the man's smile, nor the way it never quite reached his eyes. But a game was unfolding, and he had learned long ago that the best way to see the board was to play along. He stepped forward without a word.

Lord Talveth clapped his hands once. "Splendid. Lead on, gentlemen."

They led him inside. Lord Talveth trailed behind, whistling some half-remembered tune like a man on a stroll through a garden instead of an estate braced for knives in the dark.

They found Lady Haldren and Lyra seated in the front room at the table, letters and half-opened scrolls scattered across the surface. The moment Lady Haldren looked up and saw Lord Talveth, her smile faltered.

Belaric thought he heard a sigh escape her lips before she masked it behind a polite curve.

"Ah, Lord Talveth," she said, standing. "What a surprise. I said in my letter there was no need for a visit."

Lord Talveth stepped past Sir Tolman and Belaric without hesitation. "Oh, my lady, I had to come. You warned me about that bastard Lord Halmor's plotting—how could I not thank you in person? I am truly in your debt."

She tried to wave him off with a smile that did not quite reach her eyes. "There is no debt to speak of. I did only what was right."

"Nonsense," he said, taking her hand and bowing low. "And I have come to repay that debt. I bring valuable information."

She did not hide her skepticism. "I am sure you do. But as you can see, I am quite busy at the moment. Perhaps we can speak later."

Lord Talveth shook his head, insistent. "No, my lady. You need to hear this now. I swear it."

Lady Haldren studied him for a beat. Whatever she saw made her curiosity outweigh her caution—barely. "Very well. But be brief. Lyra, Sir Tolman, Belaric—leave us."

Before any of them could move, Lord Talveth raised a finger. "Ah, no. I would prefer if they all stayed. This is not something I wish overheard... but I trust the ones in this room."

He gave a wink toward Lyra that made Belaric's hand twitch.

"Just have Sir Tolman shut the door," he added with a casual wave. "We must not have stray ears."

Lady Haldren hesitated. Belaric could see she did not like the idea, but her eyes narrowed slightly—she sensed he knew something worth hearing.

Sir Tolman closed the door.

Lord Talveth wandered toward the table and, without asking, poured himself a cup of wine. Then one for her. He hummed to himself as he worked, a low, tuneless whistle. Belaric's gaze did not leave his hands.

Lord Talveth turned and handed her the cup. She took it slowly, but did not drink—her eyes locked on his.

He smiled and drank deeply from his own.

"Oh, Lady Haldren. Come now. You do not think I would come all this way to harm you, do you?" he told her.

She did not blink. "I have had two assassins try already. Forgive me if I have become cautious," she said flatly.

"Quite right," he said brightly, turning toward the bookshelf and running a finger along the spines, reading titles like a man browsing a market stall. "Caution is the armor of the wise."

Lady Haldren cast a glance at Sir Tolman and Belaric. The knight shrugged. Belaric remained silent, coiled like a spring.

"My lord," she said, voice edged in steel, "you said you had something important to share. So share it."

Lord Talveth chuckled. "Indeed, I do."

He turned, wine in hand, and looked at all of them—Lyra, Lady Haldren, Tolman, and finally Belaric. The smile on his lips was playful. The glint in his eyes was not.

"The information I have for you," Lord Talveth said, drifting along the edge of the room like a man walking a cliff's edge, "I know you will not believe." He tapped a finger to his lips, tilting his head in mock contemplation. "So... how do I convince you?"

The room watched him in silence. Belaric stood motionless, but alert. Lyra leaned forward, wary. Lady Haldren folded her arms, more annoyed than intrigued—though a sliver of unease had already crept into her gut. Lord Talveth moved to the center of the room, arms swinging loosely at his sides. He looked at each of them, then smiled.

"Ah yes. That is how I will do it." He turned to Sir Tolman. "You, good knight. You are known for your honesty, are you not?"

Sir Tolman gave a slow nod. "Among other things."

"Wonderful. Then tell me—what do people say about me?" he asked.

Sir Tolman hesitated. Lady Haldren gave him a short, resigned shrug. "They say you drink too much," Tolman said. "They say you waste coin on brothels and wine, that you are a fool with a title, nothing more."

Lord Talveth threw his head back and laughed. "Yes! Beautiful! All the old songs. The drunkard. The lecher. The buffoon. I have heard them all." Then, with a speed that startled everyone, the laughter vanished. His back straightened. Shoulders squared. His smile died, and something hard stared out through his eyes.

"They are all lies," he said, his voice leaving little room for doubt.

A silence dropped over the room like a curtain. Lady Haldren tensed. She had known many men who wore masks—lords who played games to hide their ambition, or cowards who cloaked weakness in charm. But this was not that. It was like watching a man take off his mask mid-sentence. And what stood beneath it was not safe.

"Some truths, yes," he continued. "But mostly lies. Crafted tales. You see, people let down their guard around fools. They speak more freely when they think the listener is too drunk to remember." He turned slowly, sipping from his wine. "It is a role. One I have played very well."

Belaric narrowed his gaze. The shift in Lord Talveth's posture had not gone unnoticed—and neither had the precision behind his words.

"I do not have armies. I do not sit on a pile of gold. But I hold secrets. I knew of Lord Halmor's plot weeks before your letter reached me. Lord Danvar told me himself," he said smugly.

The room stilled. Even Lyra blinked at that. "You expect us to believe you?" Sir Tolman asked, though there was less certainty in his voice now.

"I know things about Lord Danvar that would ruin him. That is why he does as I command. That is why many do." Lord Talveth turned back to them, and for a moment, the noble mask returned—just enough charm to unsettle. "When I received your letter, my lady, I was already watching. And I was impressed. You refused a pig like Halmor. Smart," he told her.

Sir Tolman stepped forward. "He is lying. He spins stories, nothing more."

Lord Talveth feigned a wounded gasp, placing a hand to his chest. "Harsh words, Sir Tolman. But let us not ask me if I speak the truth." He paused. Let the silence breathe. Then his gaze slid, unhurried, toward Belaric. "Let us ask Varros."

The name struck like a blade across stone. Belaric moved instinctively. His hand gripped the hilt of his sword, and his voice came low, dangerous. "What did you just call me?"

Sir Tolman turned, eyes wide. Lady Haldren's face hardened with alarm. Lyra sat frozen. Lord Talveth raised both hands, palms up, stepping back slightly. "Peace. I mean no threat. Only the truth, and before you ask, no, I am not a member of the Order."

He spoke softly now, each word deliberate. "I know what you are. Or rather, what you were. A shadow of the Black Vow. A traitor now, hiding among allies. Protecting Lady Haldren and her daughter... because they have been marked." His eyes found Lyra. She flinched and looked away.

Lady Haldren stepped forward. "How do you know this?"

Lord Talveth's smile returned, though colder now. "I have already given one secret today. Do not expect another. But now, at least... perhaps you believe me."

No one spoke. Then Lyra did. "This is not why you came. You want something."

Lord Talveth turned to her with a glint of admiration. "Sharp as they say. Yes. I come with a proposal. A simple one."

Lady Haldren crossed her arms again. "Marriage?"

He chuckled. "Gods, no. I love my wife." His face sobered. "A military alliance. Nothing more."

She did not respond. So he continued. "If Halmor rides against me, you come to my aid. If he comes for you, I will return the favor."

"Halmor has no reason to attack her," Sir Tolman said.

Lord Talveth tilted his head. "Does he not? She rejected him. And he will learn of her warning to me. His ambition stretches further than his reach." He told him.

Belaric nodded. "He is right. Lord Halmor does not let things go. He waits... and then he kills."

Lord Talveth snapped his fingers. "Exactly. But this alliance... it is only for Halmor. I will not help you with the Vowkeeper."

Belaric took a step forward. "You know where he is?"

"I do not," Lord Talveth said, tone flat. "And if I did, I would keep it buried. That man terrifies me more than you ever could."

He turned back to Lady Haldren. "So... do we have an agreement?"

Before she could answer, Lyra spoke again. "If you stay silent. No leaks. No manipulation. You hear nothing. You say nothing. That is the condition."

Lord Talveth beamed. "You honor the Valasar, Lyra. Very well. I agree. And I suggest we keep the alliance hidden until the right moment."

Lady Haldren arched a brow. "Why?"

Lord Talveth chuckled. "Because that is the only hand worth holding. You do not lay it down until it wins you the table."

She looked at the others—Belaric, Sir Tolman, Lyra. None objected.

"I will give you my answer tomorrow," she said.

"Excellent," Lord Talveth replied. "I will stay at the inn."

"You may stay here," she offered.

He shook his head. "No. I wear the mask, my lady. Like our friend Belaric once did." He glanced toward the former assassin. "He took his off. I leave mine on."

He turned to the door, paused.

"One last thing." He looked back, eyes too calm. "There is a rumor," he said softly. "Of a noble house that could not produce an heir. Then, suddenly... a healthy baby boy. No one knew the lady was even with child. They said it was a true miracle." Belaric's blood turned to ice.

Lord Talveth's next words cut deep. "They say the child bears a strange sign. Something whispered to be a gift from the gods. On his back."

Belaric stepped forward, voice low and shaking. "Where is my son?"

Lord Talveth offered a thin smile. "It is only a rumor. And that, Belaric... is your fight. Not mine."

He left, closing the door behind him.

Belaric turned to the window, though he saw nothing through it. His hand trembled slightly at his side. A noble house. A boy. A mark on his back. He had not let himself hope for weeks. Hope was a blade turned inward. But now...

He clenched his jaw. "I will find him," he murmured.

Not to them. Not to the room.

To the gods. Or whatever listened in the dark.

Every muscle in Belaric's body tightened. His jaw clenched, his fists balled so tightly that the leather of his gloves groaned in protest. Someone else was raising his son. Someone else—some noble bastard with silken sheets and soft hands—was whispering lies into his boy's ears. Telling him they were his mother. His father. The thought was enough to make him sick.

His mind raced. He began sifting through the web of noble houses, trying to recall every name, every lineage he had ever studied or heard spoken of in passing. Which family had long struggled to bear an heir? Which had suddenly, quietly, produced a miracle child? There were too many—hundreds of them, spread across provinces and valleys. Even with everything he had learned as a Black Vow assassin, it was a needle in a thousand haystacks.

Frustration boiled behind his ribs. He wanted to tear the room apart, to scream, to run until his legs collapsed under him—but he exhaled hard and forced himself to turn back around.

Lady Haldren, Lyra, and Sir Tolman were all watching him. None of them spoke. The silence between them felt fragile, ready to break.

"Do we believe him?" Belaric asked at last, his voice stripped of strength. It sounded distant, defeated.

"Belaric—" Lady Haldren began gently, but he raised a hand to stop her.

"Please. Let us speak of Lord Talveth for now. I knew he was playing some game, but this?" He shook his head, pacing once more. "Claiming to have powerful nobles in his pocket, yet coming to us for aid? If he holds their secrets, why not force their hand? Compel them to fight Halmor on his behalf?"

"I do not believe it is that simple," Lyra said quietly.

They all turned toward her. She stood with arms crossed, her brow knit in thought. There was no hesitation in her voice—only reason.

"I believe he has ulterior motives," she continued, "but I also think he intends to be our ally."

Lady Haldren's eyes narrowed slightly. "Why, Lyra?"

Lyra paused for a moment, choosing her words. "Because if I were being blackmailed by someone, and I discovered others were moving against them, I would be tempted to let it happen. Maybe even help, in secret. If Lord Talveth forces his blackmail targets into open battle, he risks their wrath. The moment they no longer fear him, they will destroy him. If I were one of those lords, I would ride to battle beside him... and stab him in the back the first chance I got."

She let the thought hang in the air before continuing.

"Lord Talveth knows that. Forcing them would only deepen their hatred. And some nobles—especially the powerful ones—do not tolerate having their egos bruised. But us? He is not blackmailing us. Yes, he knows about Belaric. But he revealed something of himself too. He put us on an even footing. And the rumor about the child—it may be true, but it was also a message. He is trying to draw us in."

Lady Haldren listened in silence, her fingers absently toying with the edge of one of the open letters before her. The words struck a chord—Lord Talveth had not cornered them. He had invited them to step into the shadows with him. And though every part of her wanted to remain above such games, the truth clawed at her reason: they were running out of time, and faster still, running out of options.

She did not trust Lord Talveth. But she trusted desperation, and desperation was outweighing caution.

Sir Tolman's jaw tightened, but he gave a reluctant nod. "I agree with part of that. He is still playing games. And he wants something else. We cannot trust him. I say we refuse his offer."

Belaric's temper flared. "He may hold answers about the Vowkeeper. About my son."

"He already said he will not help with that," Sir Tolman interrupted sharply.

Belaric's hands opened and closed at his sides. "Then why mention my son at all?" he asked bitterly. "Why drop that rumor now, after everything?"

"To distract us," Sir Tolman snapped. "To draw our eyes from his real motive. For all we know, he lied, and he is part of the Black Vow—or worse. He could be the Vowkeeper himself."

"That is enough," Lady Haldren said, stepping between them with a raised hand. Her gaze fixed on Belaric. "Is that possible? Could he be one of them?"

Belaric exhaled slowly, the fury dimming into cold calculation. "Faces are never known. We used false names, false origins. But I do not recognize his voice. And no, he is not the Vowkeeper. I saw that man the night they took my son. He was taller. Broader. His voice was deeper."

Sir Tolman gave a tight nod. "So he is not the Vowkeeper. That does not mean he is not part of the Order. You have said the Vowkeeper is powerful. That nobles protect him. How did Lord Talveth get one of those nobles to open their mouth?"

"We do not know," Belaric admitted. "And that is the risk. If he is part of the Order, then he is playing a dangerous game. He must know that if I find out, I will kill him."

Sir Tolman's voice softened slightly. "Killing is not always the answer."

"And neither is doing nothing," Lyra said firmly. Her eyes locked on Sir Tolman. "We cannot win this alone. More nobles are turning up dead. More are asking questions. How long before the sparks of rebellion turn to flame? We will need allies."

"Then let us find better ones than Lord Talveth," Sir Tolman said, his tone sharp again.

Lyra shook her head. "You know as well as I do, most nobles are corrupt. Self-serving. Ours is one of the few that are not. And trying to find others like us would take time we do not have. And what could we even offer them? Why would they risk war for us?"

Sir Tolman did not answer.

"At least with Lord Talveth," Lyra continued, "we know what he is. A liar. A schemer. But one we can watch. One we can prepare for. I would rather deal with the viper I can see than stumble into the fangs of one I cannot."

Sir Tolman looked at Lady Haldren. "I do not agree, my lady."

Lady Haldren raised her hand, silencing them both. "I have heard enough. I will consider what has been said and give my answer in the morning. For now, I need quiet. Please—leave me."

The three nodded, turning to the door. But as Belaric stepped forward, she spoke again.

"Belaric—stay a moment, if you would," she asked.

He paused. Of course, she wanted to speak to him alone. He turned back slowly, nodding once.

Sir Tolman and Lyra exited the room without another word, the door closing softly behind them.

Lady Haldren motioned for Belaric to join her at the table. He obeyed, settling into the chair across from her as she crossed the room, fetched another cup, and poured wine into it with careful, measured movements. She set both cups on the table, sliding one across to him. For a long moment they sat in silence, drinking, the clink of the cup against the wood the only sound between them.

Finally, Lady Haldren set her cup down and spoke. Her voice was soft, but laced with sorrow. "It may not be true, you understand that, do you not? Sir Tolman could be right. It could all be a trap."

Belaric tried to meet her gaze, but she refused to lift her eyes to his. He sighed, setting his cup aside.

"It is very possible," he admitted, his voice low. "It could be false. A ploy to distract me. But I still hold on to a tiny sliver of hope that it is true. That I can still find him. That I can still save my son."

At last, she looked up. There was a quiet ache in her expression, a deep and shared grief. "I cannot imagine the pain you feel. I was broken when my husband died... but I had Lyra. She held me together." A small, sad smile crossed her lips. "She still does."

Belaric smiled faintly in return. "And Eryndorr is mine. I will do everything in my power to bring him home." His gaze lowered, shadows creeping into his voice. "But... there is a part of me that wonders if he is not better off without me. You know what I am. Can a man like me ever be a real father? Sir Tolman would teach his son honor. What would I teach mine? How to poison a man? How to vanish into a crowd?" His hand tightened around his cup. "Maybe he would live a better life under a noble house."

Without hesitation, Lady Haldren reached across the table and gripped his hand firmly.

"You cannot think like that," she said. Her voice, though gentle, left no room for doubt. "He is your son. No one—no one—will ever love him the way his true father can. You will teach him what he needs to survive. To endure. You are not the man you once were, Belaric. We all see that. You have a heart. You care for others. And I promise you—we will find Eryndorr."

Belaric stared at her for a long moment, the iron certainty in her words striking something deep inside him. Slowly, he smiled.

"Thank you, my lady. You truly have a kind soul," he whispered.

Lady Haldren laughed, releasing his hand and leaning back in her chair. "Oh, I must have the patience of a saint after dealing with you and Sir Tolman all day."

Belaric chuckled—a genuine laugh, rare and unexpected. It felt good, like the sun cutting through a long night. For a fleeting second, he simply basked in it, grateful for her strength. Maybe she truly was a saint, he thought. Or at least as close to one as this brutal world could allow.

The wine chased some of the tension from their shoulders, but not the burden from their minds. The laughter faded quickly, leaving only the faint warmth of a brief reprieve.

He tilted his head. "Do you know of any houses that struggled to have children?"

Her laughter faded, replaced by a more somber expression. She shook her head. "I am sorry, Belaric. I never socialized much with the other noble houses. That was my husband's duty. After he died, I withdrew even further. I am rarely summoned by the major families, and I saw no need to chase invitations that were never sent."

Belaric nodded slowly. "I could not think of any either." He leaned back in his chair, his mind churning. "I assume Lord Talveth expects me to lose control tonight. To come hunting him for answers."

Lady Haldren's gaze sharpened, her voice firm. "Then he will be disappointed. You have duties here. People to protect. You will not abandon them."

Belaric smiled at the steel in her tone. "Will you accept his offer?"

Lady Haldren sighed, swirling the wine in her cup. "I am not sure. I know you and Lyra believe we should. The logic supports it. But what if Sir Tolman is right?"

Belaric turned his gaze toward the window, the sunlight streaming through in thin golden beams. "He may be. Sir Tolman's nature is to protect at all costs. He wanted me arrested, remember?" He smiled, glancing back at her. "And yet, look at us now. We understand the need for one another. Maybe in time we will come to see Lord Talveth the same way."

He hesitated, then continued, his voice steady. "I think Lord Talveth wants to tell us more. He knows it will drive me to hunt the Vowkeeper—the only man he truly fears. If I kill the Vowkeeper, Lord Talveth gains power. That is his real motive."

Lady Haldren tapped a finger against the rim of her cup, thoughtful. "The logic is there. But can we really invite a snake into our house?"

Belaric shook his head. "By his terms, he is not invited in. Only an ally if battle comes. And besides, we have barely enough fighting men to be of proper use to him."

She nodded slowly. "That is true. Which... is part of why I hesitate."

Belaric frowned. "Why, my lady?"

"Because we are small. Weak. We have little to offer. There are stronger houses he could make deals with. Yet he chose us." She leaned forward slightly. "I believe he intends to watch us. He knows our secret about you. This alliance gives him a foot in the door."

Belaric considered that. "You may be right. And I am certain he will try. But he will find it harder than he thinks. He cannot send spies—I would find them. He cannot come himself—we do not trust him. And Lyra would see through any puppet he sent."

He paused, exhaling slowly. "But perhaps he already expects that. Perhaps he has plans layered behind plans. There are too many unknowns. We need more information."

Lady Haldren gave him a pointed look. "And as I commanded—you will be here, guarding us tonight. No creeping after Lord Talveth."

Belaric chuckled, bowing his head slightly. "Of course, my lady."

He grew serious again. "We need our own eyes, though. Our own network. I know people. Mercenaries. Couriers. Those loyal only to coin, not crowns or vows. I could write to a few."

Lady Haldren nodded immediately. "Do it. Any information we can gather will help."

She lifted her cup again, taking a long sip. "Why," she muttered, half to herself, "did life have to become so damned complicated?"

Belaric smiled grimly. "Because life is rarely fair. And rarely gives us much choice."

She raised her cup slightly toward him. "I will drink to that."

Belaric lifted his own cup, tapping it lightly against hers. They both drank, and for a fleeting moment, the world seemed simpler.

Lady Haldren put her cup down and exhaled. "Now go. Train the men. I have thinking to do."

Belaric stood and bowed slightly. "Thank you, my lady."

He stepped out into the courtyard. The sun greeted him with its warm light, bright against his face. He paused, breathing it in. The darkness was always waiting—but for now, for a little while, there was still light.

"Soon," he whispered under his breath. "I will drag you into the light too."

With that, he squared his shoulders and strode across the courtyard toward Sir Tolman and the other guards, ready to face whatever waited next.

Belaric rejoined the men in the courtyard, the afternoon sun already sagging toward the distant hills. He and Sir Tolman pushed the men hard, driving them through drill after drill until sweat matted their hair and dust clung to their tunics. Belaric corrected Kedd sharply when he overextended his strike, forcing him to repeat the movement again and again until it became instinct. "You are telling them exactly what is coming, boy," he barked at Jass to mask his feints better. He watched Ruthan closely, noting how the man's eyes flickered to the ground every time he parried, a bad habit that would get him killed in an actual fight.

There was little patience left among any of them, but none dared complain. They all understood now. The danger was no longer a whisper or a rumor. Staven's grave was proof enough. They had lost one of their own, and not a soul among them would allow it to happen again.

As dusk fell, the estate took on a new shape. Torches were lit along the iron fence that encircled the grounds, placed every few feet at Sir

Tolman's orders. The Black Vow thrived in darkness; they would give them no shadows to hide in tonight.

Belaric took up his post inside Lady Haldren's chambers, standing silently in the corner as night settled fully. He had forgone his assassin's garb, choosing instead the plain uniform of a house guard. His daggers remained hidden beneath the folds, but he wore no mask, no cloak. If an enemy came, they would see him—and it would be the last thing they saw.

The night passed in uneasy silence. Only the sound of Lady Haldren and Lyra's breathing filled the room, a quiet reminder of what he stood to protect. No threat came. Belaric had not expected one yet; the Black Vow rarely moved so swiftly after failure. They would regroup, plot anew. A few days at least before another blade slipped through the dark.

When morning came, Lady Haldren summoned Lyra, Sir Tolman, and Belaric to the main hall. She wanted them present at the meeting with Lord Talveth. They seated themselves around the long oak table, tension coiled in the air like a drawn bowstring.

It was not long before they heard shuffling footsteps outside the door. The heavy wood creaked open, and Lord Talveth stumbled in, a bottle of wine clutched loosely in one hand. His fine clothes were rumpled and stained, his hair mussed as if he had fallen asleep in a gutter. He slurred his words loudly to the guard at the door, waving the bottle for emphasis.

Belaric's fingers twitched instinctively toward the dagger hidden at his belt—old reflexes stirred by sudden movement. Across the table, Sir Tolman's jaw locked in visible disgust.

But the second the door closed, Lord Talveth's entire posture shifted. He straightened, smoothed his tunic with a few casual sweeps of his hands, and turned to them with clear, sober eyes.

"Forgive me," he said lightly, voice crisp and free of any slur. "Appearances must be maintained."

Lady Haldren rolled her eyes but motioned for him to join them. Lord Talveth sauntered to the table and dropped into a chair at the far end, a wide grin stretching across his face.

"I have considered your proposal, Lord Talveth," Lady Haldren said, her voice measured. "And I will accept."

Lord Talveth beamed with excitement and clapped his hands. Sir Tolman sighed and lowered his head, pinching the bridge of his nose as if trying to stave off a headache.

Lady Haldren motioned for silence before Lord Talveth could speak again. Her voice turned sharp, cutting through the pleasantries like a blade.

"We will come to your aid, and you to ours. Beyond that—you are on your own. Your secrets are yours to keep. We want no part in them, no hand in the games you play." She leaned forward slightly, her gaze turning cold as steel. "But know this, Lord Talveth: if you betray us, or if I even suspect you have, I will send Belaric and Sir Tolman after you. And there will be no inn, no shadow, no rock you can hide under. They will find you—and you will learn why it is them you should fear."

A flicker of surprise crossed Sir Tolman's face, quickly masked by a tight, satisfied smile. Even Belaric allowed himself the faintest curl of a grin.

Lord Talveth only chuckled, unbothered. "Of course, my lady. Entirely understood. I would expect nothing less."

He reached into his tunic and, with a flourish, pulled out a folded sheet of parchment. He tossed it lightly across the table. Belaric's hand shifted slightly, another instinctive movement toward his blade, before he forced himself still. Old habits, never fully unlearned.

Lady Haldren and Lyra both leaned over the contract, reading it carefully. Lord Talveth leaned back in the chair, sipping his wine, watching them with lazy satisfaction.

Lady Haldren's fingers hovered over the quill for just a moment too long. Belaric saw the hesitation—the calculation. She knew she was striking a deal with a snake. But slowly, deliberately, she signed her name. Lyra followed, adding her mark beneath.

Lord Talveth sprang to his feet with a grin, tucking the parchment away with a casual flair. "Splendid. Well, I have others to meet, plots to weave, wine to spill. I bid you all farewell."

With a jaunty bow, he swept from the room; the door closing heavily behind him.

The silence that followed was thick.

Lady Haldren exhaled slowly, rubbed her eyes, and sank back into her chair. "Now that he is gone," she muttered, reaching into her pocket, "we have another problem."

She placed a heavy letter on the table, sealed in deep red wax stamped with the unmistakable crest of the king.

Belaric leaned forward, dread curling through his gut like smoke.

The king's seal.

He exchanged a grim look with Sir Tolman.

"What does the king want?" Belaric muttered under his breath.

26

They all stared at the letter, the broken seal lying like a dead thing between them—the crest of King Aelion Valebran torn clean through.

It was Lyra who broke the silence. "What does it say, Mother?" she asked, her voice quieter than usual, as if afraid the parchment itself might answer.

Lady Haldren let out a breath that seemed to carry more years than it should. "The king has summoned us to the capital," she said. A pause. A tightening of her hand around the letter. "He demands we bring the assassin. They intend to question him." She set the letter down on the table with a firm, final sound.

Belaric's eyes, ever-vigilant, followed the movement, and as Lady Haldren turned away for a moment, he saw it—another letter beneath the king's, its parchment a shade darker. The seal was broken, but he thought he recognized the shape. He could only make out the last line of the script: "... I look forward to speaking with you, my lady."

Lady Haldren turned back, her hand moving with a casual grace to pick up the letter, tucking it away into the folds of her dress. "Do not worry about that one, Belaric. It is just... an old friend."

"Of course, my lady," he replied, but the broken seal, and the final line of the letter, were burned into his memory.

The quiet that followed was a brittle thing, ready to shatter.

Lyra, her brow furrowed, looked up from the letter. "But how could he know so quickly?" she asked, her voice tight with a confusion that sharpened into something else. "It has only been days. Even with the fastest riders, a message to the capital and a reply... I cannot believe it would be possible."

Sir Tolman's eyes widened slightly, a sudden understanding dawning. "Spies," he rasped, his voice rough. "They must have eyes here, watching us maybe even in the town." He slapped a fist onto the table, hard enough to rattle the inkpot. "They expect us to drag a killer halfway across the kingdom just to hand him over for answers they will never get?" he barked, his anger a wounded thing trying to roar.

Lyra's gaze flicked to Belaric, a new, unsettling thought forming in her eyes. "Or," she said, her voice dropping to a near whisper, "what if the king already knew the assassin was coming?"

Belaric leaned back and folded his arms, studying the cracked ceiling as if someone might have carved the answer there. His own eyes, cold and hard, met Lyra's. "He is involved," Belaric said, his voice flat and certain, drawing their full attention. "The king knows more than we can imagine. This is another scheme."

A shiver seemed to pass through the room.

"They will not question him. The moment the doors close, his throat will be slit. They know I am here now—and they are afraid of what he might tell me," Belaric stated.

His brow furrowed. "But it does not fit," he muttered, almost to himself. "They know I would see the trap. They knew I would expect it. So why offer such an obvious snare? Where are the real teeth?"

The room sank into thought. Even the fire in the hearth seemed to crackle more softly, as if listening.

"They will attack on the road," Lyra said at last, her voice quick and sure. "But not right away. Not while we are sharp. It will be near the end of the journey, when we are tired... when we are close enough to think we are safe."

Lady Haldren gave a slow nod, her fingers tapping a restless rhythm against the table. Sir Tolman grunted. "It is what a clever bastard would do," he agreed.

"No," Belaric said, cutting across them.

They turned toward him; the firelight throwing hard shadows across his face.

"They know better. They know that a former assassin rides with them. And a Valasar gifted child sharp enough to see through any ruse. They expect us to see it coming." His gaze moved across the room, weighing them all. "The actual attack will not come on the road. Or in the capital. It will come after we return. After days of waiting for a knife that never falls. We will be tired. Relieved. Grateful that no blade found us... and then it will."

Lyra's eyes flickered, racing ahead of the words. "Or... would they expect us to think that too?" she said softly.

Sir Tolman let out a heavy breath and shoved a hand through his hair. "This is madness. They are playing games with our expectations, and they know we are doing the same to theirs." He scowled. "Fine. Let them play their games. We stay ready. We never drop our guard. Problem solved."

For a heartbeat, no one moved. Then, against all odds, they chuckled—even Lady Haldren, though the sound was grim and with little warmth.

"You are right, Sir Tolman," Lady Haldren said, rising to her feet. There was a new steel in her voice, the sound of someone making peace with the weight they had to carry. "An attack will come. We need to prepare."

She looked to him and Belaric. "We cannot refuse a royal summons. Prepare the men. We depart in two days. That should be enough to plan and gather supplies?"

Sir Tolman straightened, the faintest grin tugging at his mouth. "Of course, my lady."

"Good," she said. She turned to Lyra, extending a hand that the girl took with a rare, calm smile. "Come, Lyra. We have outfits to choose from. I will not have us looking like commoners before the king."

The two of them swept from the room, leaving Belaric and Sir Tolman standing amid the maps and broken seals.

Sir Tolman gave a grunt, pulling a roll of parchment from a nearby shelf and unfurling it across the table—a rough map of the region, marked with ink stains and travel lines.

He met Belaric's gaze, all trace of humor gone. "Let us begin," he said.

Belaric and Sir Tolman leaned over the map, their heads nearly touching, the battered parchment spread across the long oak table. Faded ink traced the winding roads leading north toward Draskmarr, the king's city.

"We will stop here in Holmark the first night," Sir Tolman said, tapping the map with a calloused finger. "Good walls, decent inn. We can lock the wagons inside the yard."

Belaric nodded, scratching notes onto a scrap of paper. "Avoid Threston," he said. "Too many mouths. Too many eyes."

"Aye," Sir Tolman agreed. "We will camp off the road that night. Rotate the men, four on watch at all times."

They moved slowly, deliberately, marking towns to pass by and those where they could safely rest. The journey would take days, longer if the weather turns foul or trouble found them early. They had to be ready for either.

Belaric made a list as they worked: grain for the horses, dry stores for the men, replacement tack, sharpened steel. And chains, heavy, iron forged, and strong enough to hold a man who would kill with his bare hands if given the chance.

"I will see Oswin about the chains," Belaric said. "Each wrist, each ankle. A band at the waist. Another at the neck. I will give him just enough movement to walk, nothing more."

Sir Tolman snorted. "Bastard will jangle like a sack of pots."

"Good," Belaric said flatly. "Let every mile remind him who holds the keys."

They planned for three wagons: one wagon to carry the prisoner, chained and bolted to the bed itself; one wagon for supplies and a place where off-shift guards could catch a few hours of sleep; and a carriage, reinforced with lumber, to protect Lady Haldren and Lyra from arrows or worse.

"I want the carriage plated from within," Belaric said, pointing to a rough sketch he had drawn beside the map. "Half-inch boards, nailed flush against the frame. Stronger than canvas but still light enough to move."

"You think it will hold against a crossbow?" Sir Tolman asked.

"Possibly; depends on the distance. It will slow them down, if nothing else." He offered a thin smile. "And if they have crossbows, we will have worse problems anyway."

Sir Tolman grunted and rolled the map closed. "Then let us get to it."

They parted ways with little ceremony. The day was already slipping away from them.

Belaric made his way into Brookhaven, the town buzzing louder than a hornet's nest in summer. The main road bustled with carts, tradesmen hawking their wares, and townsfolk gossiping in tight knots. It seemed every face in the crowd turned to watch him pass, some with awe, some with fear, others with that predatory gleam that always came when folk scented blood on the wind.

Oswin stood hammering away when Belaric arrived at his forge. The man wiped his brow and grinned. "Figured you would come calling," he said.

"I need chains," Belaric said without preamble. "Heavy ones. Wrist to ankle, waist to neck. I want the bastard trussed tighter than a hog at slaughter."

Oswin whistled low. "You planning to hang him or haul him?"

"Both, if it comes to it," Belaric replied.

Oswin chuckled and nodded. "I will work through the night. They will be ready by sunrise."

From there, Belaric sought Tebbick, the lumber master, who greeted him with a firm handshake and a shrewd eye. They agreed on thick-cut planks, measured precisely to reinforce the carriage from within without overburdening the horses.

"I will have the wood delivered by midafternoon," Tebbick promised. "Best oak I have got."

Belaric nodded his thanks and moved on, bartering for grain, salted meat, hard cheese, dried fruits—enough to keep them fed until the road grew meaner.

The town teemed with more bodies than he liked. There are too many unfamiliar faces. Any of them could belong to the Order, and he would never know—not unless they spoke, and by then, it might already be too late.

Lady Haldren had been wise to restrict access. Only Belaric and the guards were permitted near the prison, the timbered structure built just next to the estate. No curious townsman would get close enough to slip a blade through the bars or whisper a warning.

Still, the attention gnawed at him.

He pushed the thought aside. Paranoia would gut him quicker than any knife if he let it.

By the time he returned to the estate, Tebbick's men were unloading lumber by the carriage house. Belaric stripped off his cloak and set to work without a word, hammering heavy planks into the carriage walls. They reinforced the sides first, then braced the doors from within. Extra slats covered the undercarriage, tied to the frame with thick iron nails. They layered the windows last—thin slits left open for breathing, but too narrow to fire an arrow through.

It was slow, brutal work. But it kept his hands busy, and for now, that was enough.

By the time he set the last plank and the hammer slipped from his aching fingers, the moon was high and cold above the estate.

Belaric ate little that night, a bowl of stew, half-forgotten in front of him, before staggering to bed. For once, he was grateful when the other guards insisted he rest. No watch tonight. No dark corners to haunt.

He was grateful to the men. He would need his strength soon enough.

The following days passed in a blur of preparations. Oswin brought the chains by noon—thick, blackened iron links, heavy enough to hobble an ox. Belaric ran his fingers over them, feeling the weight, the strength. Brutally simple things, made for one task and no mercy.

With a hammer and thick iron nails, Belaric fastened the chains to the prison wagon, securing them into the oak frame with bolts the size of a man's thumb. Oswin had promised him they would not give, no matter how hard the prisoner struggled. "You could hook a warhorse to them and they would hold," the blacksmith had said with a grin.

Belaric made sure of it himself, testing each anchor point until he was satisfied.

The extra supplies arrived in the meantime—barrels of grain, sacks of oats, crates of dried fruits and hard cheese. Tebbick sent fresh vegetables bundled in burlap, and another merchant brought smoked meats wrapped tightly against the heat. Someone had even thought to include a small box of sweet pastries, glazed and dusted with sugar—a rare luxury for the road.

Belaric and Sir Tolman left nothing to chance. They checked and rechecked every list, every wagon, every bolt of gear. They spent every moment they could spare ensuring they would shield Lady Haldren and Lyra from harm, at least as much as mortal men could manage.

On the morning of the third day, the estate buzzed with quiet energy. The sun was only beginning to climb over the hills, its light a pale, uncertain thing.

Belaric made one final round, reinspecting everything himself. The horses were saddled and harnessed—sturdy beasts, chosen for endurance over speed. The wagons were loaded and secured, their wheels checked twice over. They shackled the prisoner's hands, feet, waist, and throat, and bolted the chains tight to the wagon's iron frame.

Belaric had done the binding personally. He had looped the chains around each wrist and ankle, a heavy band around the waist, another across the throat just loose enough to breathe. The man could shift his weight slightly, but that was all. There would be no slipping free, no sudden lunges for a guard's throat.

He finished bolting the last chain, double-checked every shackle. For a moment, he just stood there, staring at the man—bound, broken, silent.

This is what they had made of him too, once.

He shoved the thought aside and mounted Eddaross without a word.

Hasker and Jass sat on the prison wagon's bench beside him, swords and daggers within easy reach, their faces set in grim determination. Nollan held the reins, his jaw tight as he kept one eye always flickering back toward the prisoner.

Sir Tolman rode at the head of the column, his grey charger setting a steady pace. Behind him rumbled Lady Haldren's carriage, Dross perched atop the driver's seat, reins firm in hand. The supply wagon followed next, driven by Kedd, its bed piled high with provisions and spare arms. The prison wagon came after, the prisoner locked in chains and watched by Hasker and Jass with blades bare and ready. And at the rear, Belaric rode Eddaross, his storm-grey stallion restless beneath him, his gaze sweeping the road ahead and the woods beyond, never lingering, never trusting. The remaining guards were spread out in a loose formation around the wagons and carriage.

Belaric's gaze never rested. Every shifting shadow, every whisper of movement beyond the road's edge, pulled his attention. He did not expect an attack—not yet, at least. The king would want Lady Haldren's secrets first. Only then, when she had no further use, would the command be given to destroy them.

Still, he knew better than most: expecting safety was the surest way to invite death.

They had to remain sharp.

When the last checks were complete and the men mounted up, Sir Tolman lifted his sword in a simple salute and barked the command.

"Move out!"

His voice cracked across the courtyard, echoing against the stone walls. One by one, wheels creaked into motion, hooves clattered, and the caravan rolled forward.

A crowd had gathered along the estate's fence to watch them go. Farmers, merchants, craftsmen —men and women who had made Brookhaven their home. Some spat curses at the chained assassin, shouting oaths to whatever gods would listen. Others lifted prayers for Lady Haldren and Lyra, calling for their safe return.

Belaric watched them as they passed. Old faces, youthful faces, hard faces weathered by years of toil and survival. He was glad that they wished her well.

Wishes would not stop knives, though.

The road grew narrower with each passing mile, the wild pressing in from both sides. Thick pines and gnarled oaks leaned in as if listening, their branches clawing at the sky. The air grew damp and sour, heavy with rot and unseen things slithering through the underbrush.

Belaric kept his hand near his sword hilt, his eyes roving the treeline.

Twice he thought he saw shapes—flashes of movement too large to be deer, too purposeful to be the wind. Both times when he turned, there was nothing but empty branches and the slow whisper of leaves.

The others felt it too.

Hasker muttered prayers under his breath.

Jass kept darting glances over his shoulder.

Ruthan rode close behind, shifting uneasily in his saddle, hand tight around the haft of his axe.

They made good time the first day, reaching Holmark just as the sun bled down past the trees. The town had high wooden walls, stout gates, and an inn large enough to hold the guards and Lady Haldren's household.

Already, word had traveled ahead of them. As they rode through the gates, heads turned, voices whispered behind cupped hands.

A few bold souls crept closer, trying to glimpse the chained man slumped in the prison wagon.

Sir Tolman barked an order sharp enough to cut through stone. "Back! Keep your distance!"

His glare was enough to send most scurrying.

Belaric watched the crowds thin out, but he kept his hand close to his sword all the same.

Belaric and Sir Tolman spoke with the stablemaster, a round-shouldered man who squinted at them as if afraid of what bringing such travelers inside might cost him.

"We will stable the horses inside the walls," Sir Tolman said, voice flat and firm. "And the prisoner stays chained to the wagon. No arguments."

The man nodded quickly, eager to be rid of them.

Belaric took first watch that night, prowling the edges of the inn yard. The prisoner slept in chains inside the wagon, Hasker and Jass stationed close enough to kill him if he so much as coughed wrong. Knoll and Ruthan kept the perimeter, walking slow circles through the night with torches in hand, the flickering light making long shadows leap across the inn walls.

Belaric trusted the guards. Trusted their steel.

It was the others he worried about—the faces in the darkness, the hands that might reach through the slats of the fence if the watch wavered for even a breath.

The night passed without bloodshed.

The second night, they had no town to shelter them. Sir Tolman ordered the camp to be hidden in the woods, the fires kept low and shielded behind rocks and fallen logs. The men took turns on watch, weapons close at hand. Sleep came lightly, broken by the hoot of owls and the distant crack of unseen branches.

Dinner was whatever could be eaten cold—strips of smoked meat, hard cheese, dried apples pulled from rough sacks. The bread was already beginning to harden.

They trained when they could—small sparring drills by firelight, enough to keep the edges of their swords and their wits sharp. Tarnel and Jass clashed wooden blades quietly under Belaric's watchful eye, while Ruthan worked through slow, deliberate axe forms. Even exhausted, they obeyed. Complacency was a quicker killer than steel.

By the third day, they rode into Dornstead, a small valley town, a half-forgotten place clinging stubbornly to the green hills.

Here too, word had spread.

Townsfolk lined the muddy main street, whispering and pointing as the small convoy clattered through. A few men even moved as if to approach the prison wagon before Sir Tolman's voice cracked out like a whip.

"Stay back! Move aside!" Sir Tolman commanded.

The guards closed ranks, their faces grim.

They spent the night in the open field beside the town's crumbling shrine, ringed by torches and steel.

Late that evening, Belaric found deep tracks in the mud. Hoofprints, dozens of them. Hooves shod for war, not travel. He crouched low, tracing one with his fingertips.

Knoll knelt beside him, grimacing. "Too many to count," he muttered.

"Soldiers," Belaric said, voice low and certain.

Sir Tolman said nothing, but the guards moved slower after that, every man checking his gear twice.

The fourth day brought a gentler road. They reached Thesselbrook by nightfall—a quiet farming village of whitewashed cottages and neat stone fences. No crowds here. No shouts. Only a few wary eyes peeked from behind shutters.

The villagers gave them bread and water and kept their distance.

It rained that night, cold and miserable.

By morning, the road was a mire, and their progress slowed to a crawl. Cloaks soaked through. Boots squelched with every step. The prisoner coughed constantly, shivering where he was chained, but Belaric gave him no more slack than the wagon wheels allowed.

On the fifth day, they stumbled into Brynloch—a town much like Brookhaven, snug against the hills, the roofs steaming under the steady rain.

Whispers greeted them even before they reached the main square.

Children darted along the roadside, pointing at the chained figure in the wagon.

An old woman shouted something Belaric could not catch.

When a few of the bolder ones moved as if to draw closer, Sir Tolman wheeled his horse around and barked, "Stand clear!"

Faces vanished behind shutters.

The streets emptied as if a plague had ridden into town.

Belaric argued for camping in the woods again, unwilling to risk the crowds.

Sir Tolman shook his head. "The ladies will not sleep in the mud," he said simply, and that was the end of it.

They took rooms at a crowded inn while the guards kept close watch over the wagons outside. The rain drummed steadily against the windows, and the walls seemed too thin to hold out the world.

Belaric barely slept.

Every time he closed his eyes, he heard things moving—soft footfalls, whispered voices, the rustle of unseen things just beyond reach.

Tarnel sharpened his dagger by firelight, the rasp of stone on steel.

Kedd tended the horses, his voice low and calming even as the animals trembled.

At dawn, they found more tracks in the mud—boot prints circling their wagons.

Someone had come close.

Watched them.

Hasker cursed under his breath.

Sir Tolman tightened his sword belt and ordered them moving without breakfast. No one dared argue.

The rains broke on the sixth day, leaving behind a grey, dripping world.

They reached Bracken reach by late afternoon—a merchant town bustling with life. Fresh thatch crowned the buildings, and colorful banners snapped from spires above the main square. Traders shouted their goods, children laughed in the alleys, and the scent of roasting meat filled the air.

But even here, eyes followed them.

The whispers traveled faster than the wagons themselves.

Belaric saw a merchant's boy crane his neck for a better look at the prisoner before Sir Tolman's hard stare sent him scurrying back behind a stall.

For a moment, it almost felt normal.

Belaric did not trust it.

They quartered the ladies at a well-guarded inn and doubled the guard at the wagons. The prisoner remained chained, watched day and night.

That evening, Belaric drilled the men harder—short, brutal rounds with wooden swords and blunted axes, each bout ending quickly in bruises and sweat.

The seventh night brought them to a lonely hill overlooking the river lands beyond. No village this time. Only wet grass, rough stones, and a wide sky full of wheeling black clouds.

They camped high, torches set wide around their perimeter.

The fire sputtered in the damp wind.

The guards rotated every few hours, but sleep came only in fits and starts.

The meals were growing thin—smaller slices of dried venison, heels of stale bread, cold cheese that tasted more of wax than milk.

Still, they pressed on.

Silent. Watchful. Grim.

Their bodies ached. Their eyes burned. Their supplies dwindled.

But the road stretched onward, and so they followed it.

The towers of Draskmarr loomed ahead through the haze—jagged, vast, and unwelcoming.

And the worst of the journey, Belaric knew, was still to come.

They pressed onward, the road narrowing into a single, rutted path crowded with merchants, pilgrims, and the desperate. Draskmarr grew with every mile. Belaric's stomach tightened as he glimpsed the black, broken crown rising from the mist, promising little mercy to those foolish enough to seek it.

At first, it was just the towers—thin and sharp like broken spears.

Then the walls—massive slabs of stone, taller than any fortress he had ever seen, layered with walkways and arrow loops, bristling with banners of black and gold that snapped in the rising wind.

The city sprawled like a living beast across the horizon, smoke rising in thick tendrils from thousands of chimneys. A hundred spires pierced the grey sky, some new and gilded, others ancient and crumbling. The streets twisted through it like veins, carrying the lifeblood of a kingdom, and the rot that festered beneath.

Ahead of him, Belaric saw Ruthan shift in his saddle, muttering a low curse under his breath. Tarnel straightened, his hand tightening unconsciously around the hilt of his sword. Even Jass, usually quick to grin, rode silently, his face pale as the first sight of the city towers loomed fully into view.

Belaric said nothing. He simply adjusted his grip on Eddaross's reins and kept moving, eyes forward.

Cities ate men alive. This one would be no different.

The closer they came, the more overwhelming it grew. Merchants shouted from wagon beds, hawking bolts of cloth, leather goods, and spiced meat pies. Pilgrims knelt in the mud along the roadside, pressing their foreheads to crumbling stones, murmuring prayers too soft to hear. Soldiers on patrol rode past, armor polished bright, visors down, spears upright like an iron forest. Packs of ragged children darted between carts and wagons, slipping deft hands into saddlebags and pockets before vanishing into the crowd.

The air reeked of smoke, sweat, manure, and roasting meat—the stink of a thousand lives crammed too close together.

Belaric watched it all from the saddle, his face unreadable. His hand never strayed far from the hilt of his sword.

On the morning of the eighth day, they reached the outer walls.

At a crossroads a mile from the gates, Sir Tolman called a halt. Horses stamped and snorted; the prisoner slumped silent and soaked in chains.

Sir Tolman addressed them all in a low, fierce voice. "We ride through the gates together. Tight formation. No splitting. If anyone tries to approach, we ride past or through them. No questions, no slowing. Understood?"

A chorus of grim nods answered him. Even Dross, normally cracking jokes, gave a firm nod as he tightened the reins on Lady Haldren's carriage.

Belaric checked the straps on his weapons one last time. His muscles ached from days of riding, but his mind was sharper than it had been in weeks.

Danger had a way of clearing the fog.

They rolled forward as one—a grim convoy pushing toward the jaws of the kingdom's beating heart.

The gates of Draskmarr loomed above them, black iron and towering stone. Guards stiffened at their approach, hands drifting to spear shafts, voices murmuring behind helmets.

Word would already race ahead of them—up stone towers, through winding alleys, into noble halls.

They had arrived.

And whatever waited inside, there would be no turning back now.

The convoy drew to a halt before the outer gates of Draskmarr.

The iron portcullis loomed overhead, blackened by smoke and age, spears of metal stabbing down from the heavy frame. Guards lined the walls above, crossbows ready, their eyes sharp with suspicion.

A single man approached from the guard post—a sergeant, by the cut of his armor. His face was weathered, serious, with a grizzled jaw and the deep-set eyes of a man who had seen his share of blood and betrayals.

Sir Tolman rode forward to meet him, reining his horse in with a tug.

"We come by order of the king," he called out, voice carrying in the crisp morning air. "Lady Marvella Haldren brings the prisoner his majesty commanded delivered."

The sergeant eyed the group warily—the grim-faced guards, the battered wagons, the prisoner slumped and shackled in iron.

Skepticism twisted his mouth. "A bold claim," he said, voice rough with doubt.

Belaric watched as the man's eyes swept the convoy, lingering on the wagons, the weapons, the hard faces among them. The sergeant did not believe it.

Sir Tolman reached into his cloak and withdrew a heavy parchment sealed in black wax—the royal sigil of King Aelion Valebran stamped deep into its surface. He offered it down with two fingers.

The sergeant accepted it with a wary hand. He unfolded the letter. His eyes roamed the page slowly—and widened.

He snapped the parchment shut, giving a sharp nod. "Wait here," he barked, then turned on his heel and strode off at a near run.

Belaric shifted in the saddle, his hand resting lightly on Eddaross's reins.

The city walls pressed close, the eyes of the guards above heavy on them.

It felt too much like waiting for judgment.

After several tense minutes, the sergeant returned, and he was not alone.

He came leading a man clad head to toe in polished steel, his armor a masterpiece of craftsmanship. Blackened plates overlapped in a style both functional and terrifying, each etched with the faint sigil of the king's crown and crossed blades. Thick pauldrons rose like the shoulders of a beast, and the full chest plate gleamed with the dull sheen of worn battles, not parade ground polish. Every movement whispered authority.

The man's horse was a beautiful beast—a black war stallion taller than any Belaric had ever seen, its coat gleaming like oil, its breath misting in the cold morning air. A massive two-handed sword, nearly as long as a man was tall, hung strapped to the saddle within easy reach. The sword was old, its leather-wrapped hilt worn smooth, its pommel a simple, unadorned piece of iron, and its blade bore the faint nicks of countless clashes.

The knight removed his helmet, tucking it under one arm.

Belaric felt his chest tighten.

Sir Vaeldin Kesteren.

The finest blade in the kingdom, the king's own hammer, a man undefeated in duel or battlefield challenge. His dark hair, cropped short, ruffled in the breeze, and his neatly trimmed beard framed a mouth set in a line of grim resolve. His piercing blue eyes swept the company with a soldier's precision, reading strength, weakness, and intent all in a glance. He did not move with the casual grace of a noble, but with the coiled stillness of a man who could turn an insult into a fight in a heartbeat.

It was widely known that he bore the Valasar blessing of strength on his left arm. Belaric knew the stories well enough. Sir Kesteren could wield that massive blade one-handed if need be. People said he could shatter a shield with a single blow. He carried himself not with arrogance, but with the quiet, weary confidence of someone who had faced death too many times to be afraid of it anymore.

Sir Tolman dismounted smoothly and crossed the small gap to him.

The two men shook hands—not the light clasp of courtiers, but the firm grasp of warriors who knew the weight of steel and death.

"Sir Tolman," Kesteren said, his voice a deep rumble. "It has been too long."

"Too long indeed, old friend," Sir Tolman replied dryly, but with the ghost of a smile.

Sir Kesteren turned next to Lady Haldren's carriage. He dismounted in a fluid motion, leaving the stallion standing unattended. He approached the door and bowed respectfully as Lady Haldren stepped down, Lyra close behind.

"Lady Marvella Haldren," he said, voice softening. "You honor the king with your loyalty."

Lady Haldren offered him a gracious nod, Lyra dipping a small curtsy at her mother's side. For all the knight's reputation for ruthlessness, Belaric saw now the glimmer of kindness buried beneath the steel.

After a brief exchange, Sir Kesteren turned sharply.

"Form ranks!" he barked.

His men moved at once, riding out in disciplined lines, surrounding Lady Haldren's group on all sides.

"The city has heard you are coming," Sir Kesteren said grimly, swinging into the saddle with ease. "Fools pack the streets, wanting a glimpse of the assassin. We will clear a path."

He rode at Sir Tolman's side, his presence a living wall.

At his signal, the convoy moved forward.

The streets beyond the gate surged with humanity. Hundreds of people moving about, some staring openly at them. Belaric took it all, his face a mask, unwilling to show anything. The streets twisted like a gut, and his stomach along with it. His hand on the hilt of his sword.

Sir Kesteren's voice cracked over the noise.

"Clear the way!"

When the crowds hesitated, his riders lowered spears, a soundless, practiced motion, and people scattered in a sudden tide of fear.

Belaric watched from the saddle, Eddaross steady beneath him.

Every head turned. Every eye followed them.

Even in the lower quarter, Draskmarr was impressive—the streets wide and paved in rough cobblestones, the buildings tall and closely packed, their faces clean and newly plastered. Merchants hawked their wares from heavy stalls draped in bright colors. The scent of fresh bread, horse dung, and spice drifted thick in the air.

It took longer than expected to reach the middle district. Twice they had to halt, waiting for crowds to scramble aside.

When they finally passed through the gate into the middle quarter, Belaric took in the sights with muted awe. Here, the streets widened. The buildings stood taller still—fine shops and merchant houses, their windows framed in carved stone. Fountains splashed clear water into tiled basins, and armored guards in silver tabards patrolled the streets on foot.

Well-dressed nobles rolled past in polished carriages, their faces turning away in disgust as they glimpsed the prisoner slumped in chains. A few sneered openly, as if the very sight of Lady Haldren's grim convoy offended them.

Fewer commoners lived here. Only those with coin enough to afford it.

They pressed on.

Finally, they reached the great gate leading into the upper district—the domain of the nobles, the king's favorites, the untouchable elite.

The heavy gate swung open the moment Kesteren barked a command. No questioning here. No delay.

They passed through, their convoy now moving under the shadow of true power.

In the distance, the palace rose—a mountain of gleaming white stone veined with gold, its towers thrusting high into the clouds. Balconies and bridges wove between its spires like threads of silk. Pennants snapped from every parapet, displaying the black and gold of House Valebran. It was not a castle built to repel sieges. It was a fortress of wealth, a monument to unchallenged rule.

Belaric swallowed the knot rising in his throat.

It hardly seemed possible that men had built it.

Finally, they reached the last barrier—a massive iron-bound gate, a foot thick with layered wood and blackened steel. A dozen men waited inside to haul it open at Kesteren's signal.

When the great gate creaked wide, the convoy rolled through into the palace courtyard.

The space was vast—stables flanking the left, a barracks rising to the right, and the main palace doors looming ahead like the mouth of a giant beast.

Servants hurried forward to take the horses, but Belaric dismounted warily, soothing Eddaross with a few steady strokes along the stallion's neck.

One of Sir Kesteren's men moved toward the prisoner's wagon, clearly intending to take the assassin into custody.

Belaric stepped in sharply.

"I will take him," he said, his tone flat.

The guard hesitated, glancing at Sir Kesteren.

The knight studied Belaric with his piercing blue eyes—a long, weighing look.

At Sir Tolman's small nod, he gave a curt jerk of the head.

Belaric moved quickly, unchaining the prisoner from the wagon and securing him under his own hand. A dagger sat hidden in his belt, the point pressed lightly against the man's back.

One wrong move would be his last.

They formed up before the palace doors—Sir Tolman and Sir Kesteren at the front, Lady Haldren and Lyra behind them, and Belaric's guards forming a tight circle around him and the prisoner.

The palace doors groaned open with a heavy sound of iron on stone.

Belaric shifted his grip on the prisoner's chains, his eyes narrowing.

He could not shake the feeling that they were walking into a trap.

And there would be no easy way out.

27

Sir Kesteren led them through the towering palace doors, the great iron hinges groaning softly as if resenting the interruption. Polished boots struck marble with every step—smooth white stone veined with grey, each slab cut so precisely it might have offended the gods had they not lived above such things.

Belaric kept a firm grip on the assassin's bound arms, guiding him forward with just enough pressure to remind him of his place. The man walked with the stiff pride of a cornered predator, head high, but it did not fool Belaric. As they crossed the threshold into the inner halls, the assassin leaned close, his voice a whisper thick with mockery.

"You know what happens here, Varros. They will demand you hand me over. I will be returned to the Order. They will patch me up, give me a new target. It will be you, and I will slit your throat in the darkest hours of the night."

Belaric leaned in, his tone flat and cruel.

"They will demand it, yes. But the Order does not take back failures. Now, everyone knows your face. The people know your face. You are spoiled meat now. All that awaits you is a slow death in the dark—if you are lucky. So, enjoy the walk. It is your last one with a spine intact."

The assassin tensed, a ripple of fury passing through him. He jerked against Belaric's grip—a mistake. Belaric wrenched his arm, drawing a grunt from the man's throat. A few guards ahead turned at the sound, hands drifting toward hilts. Belaric offered them a smile and kept walking.

Behind the assassin's scowl, Belaric caught it—the twitch of his jaw, the faint rise in his breathing. He was rattled. Not broken, not yet, but the cracks were forming. Good.

The palace was a temple of wealth and legacy—every surface carved, etched, or embroidered to remind the viewer who ruled and how long they had done so. Towering stone walls rose high above, cut and polished with such artistry that they caught reflections like still water. Gold filigree ran along the borders of the ceiling beams. Tapestries hung like memories across the walls—woven tales of kings long dead, battles long won, and saints no one truly believed in anymore. Portraits of noble bloodlines glared down from gilded frames, each pair of painted eyes watching with the cold scrutiny only the dead could master.

A few of the guards slowed their pace, awed by the sheer magnificence. Sir Tolman gave one a firm nudge, reminding him with a glance that the King did not tolerate being made to wait—not even from those bearing chained assassins.

After several long corridors and a staircase wide enough to fit a siege tower, Sir Kesteren led them to a towering oak door, banded in black steel. He paused and turned, face unreadable but voice edged with something personal.

"My lady," he said with a respectful bow, "I must ask that you and your men surrender your weapons. By decree, only the Royal Guard and the Blood of the Crown may carry steel in the presence of His Grace. I hope you understand."

Lady Haldren inclined her head. "Of course."

She turned to her men, and the message passed wordlessly. Each one stepped forward, offering their weapons to the guards. They had expected this—custom, after all, custom and tradition was more binding than iron.

Belaric handed over the sword at his side, and the dagger strapped beneath his belt. But he did not reach for the slim blade hidden beneath his belt—the one fashioned for quiet murders and last chances.

"You will receive your weapons once the King is finished," Sir Kesteren said. His tone was polite, but a flicker of contempt tightened the corner of his mouth. "We would not want... misunderstandings."

He turned, about to push the door open—then stopped. His eyes fell on Belaric.

"Do not take me for a fool," Sir Kesteren said, voice like the edge of frost. "The hidden blade. Now. Or I will take it myself."

The air shifted. All eyes fell on Belaric.

Lady Haldren's expression soured into something tight and unimpressed. Sir Tolman looked as if he might burst trying to suppress a grin.

Belaric chuckled, slow and unconvincingly. "My apologies, Sir Kesteren. I had forgotten it was there."

He drew the slim blade from beneath his belt and handed it to one of the waiting guards. Sir Kesteren did not respond. His narrowed eyes said enough.

With the last act of surrender complete, Sir Kesteren turned and pushed the great oak door open. It creaked on old hinges and revealed the seat of power—the throne room of Draskmarr.

It was a cathedral of politics and silence. Vaulted ceilings rose into the heavens, painted with scenes of war and prophecy. The floor was a mirror of polished obsidian, cut to reflect every motion, every lie. Pillars flanked either side of the hall, carved from white stone and inlaid with veins of gold, rising like judgment made manifest. Between them stood the royal guards—unmoving, encased in full suits of steel polished to the brightness of ice, their helms crested with silver feathers. Eyes like stone beneath.

Nobles lingered across the sides of the room, whispering in small, strategic knots. Each wore robes dyed in deep crimsons, forest greens, and ocean blues; the colors of their houses, loud as trumpets. Rings shone on every finger, tokens of birthright and bribery.

And at the far end, seated atop a pair of thrones carved from dark-hued oak and lacquered to perfection, sat the King and Queen of Nareth.

King Aelion Valebran looked every bit the portrait made flesh—tall and lean, with golden hair that fell to his shoulders in neat waves. His posture was not that of a man at ease, but of one who had learned to hold himself in a specific, heavy silence. His eyes, deep and cold and blue as the northern sea, surveyed the room with the tired patience of a man who had been born to watch others disappoint him. He wore a robe of deep sapphire, belted in silver, with a heavy fur cloak draped over his shoulders like a mantle of winter. His hands, resting on the arms of the throne, were long and slender, but the knuckles were white beneath the skin, a subtle tell of a tension he never allowed himself to show.

Queen Calenna Valebran sat to his right, radiant and still. Her dress mirrored his colors, a slimmer, elegant cut that clung to her form without daring to reveal too much. Her black hair was braided into a crown across her brow, and her pale eyes—lighter than her husband's but no less cold—studied the approaching group with the grace of a knife watching its next meal. She did not move, but her stillness was more dangerous than a wild thrashing. It was the absolute calm of a spider in its web.

As they walked, the length of the hall, all eyes turned to the prisoner. Even the nobles, usually far too proud to notice commoners, seemed drawn to the chained man. Whispers passed like a fever through the chamber. An assassin captured. A member of the Black Vow, shackled and brought before the King.

As they reached the obsidian floor before the thrones, Belaric glanced down and saw himself reflected there, dim and warped. So too did the assassin beside him, his face twisted by the glossed stone. A ghost of what they were. A warning of what power could make them.

Ten feet from the steps, Sir Kesteren raised his hand. The group halted as one.

Sir Kesteren stepped forward, dropped to one knee, and bowed his head.

"My King," he said, "I present Lady Marvella Haldren and Lady Lyra Haldren of Brookhaven."

Behind him, the rest of the group followed suit, some slower than others. Belaric forced the assassin to his knees, one hand still gripping the man's shoulder.

The king stood, his voice carrying easily across the chamber.

"Please," he said, sweet as honey. "Rise."

Belaric did so with a soft breath. His bones ached, but it was the eyes on him that weighed the most.

Time to play the game.

As the group rose, so did the King. He extended his arm without looking, and Queen Calenna took it with practiced grace. Together, they descended the steps—regal, poised, and utterly in control. When they reached the base, their steps curved toward Lady Haldren.

"My lady," the king said, his voice smooth as silk warmed over fire, "we are so grateful you braved the journey."

His smile was charming, measured, and hollow. "And more grateful still," the queen added, her tone velvet-wrapped steel, "that you and your daughter are alive and well."

"How right you are, my dear," the king replied, flashing his wife a loving smile that never reached his eyes.

"We are honored that you have granted us an audience, Your Grace," Lady Haldren said, bowing her head.

The king waved the formality aside with a flick of his wrist. "Oh, my lady, it is you who honor me. You have dragged a truth into daylight—that a festering order of shadows still dares strike at those under my protection." His gaze shifted toward the assassin still bound in Belaric's grip. "Such vermin must be dealt with."

Then he turned to Lyra, gently releasing his wife's arm as he stepped forward. His smile widened, though his eyes did not. "Ahh, young Lyra. I have not seen you since you were a child wrapped in blue silks, more curiosity than girl. And now look at you—nearly grown. Even your mark shines brighter than many full-grown Valasar blessed."

His gaze lingered on the swirl of pale light at her temple.

Lyra bowed gracefully despite her nerves. "I am still learning to use it, Your Grace. But I have heard that you have mastered your chest mark."

The king laughed loud enough to echo. "Ah, well, the mark stretches across most of my chest—but even now, there is always more to learn. That is what keeps a man dangerous."

He leaned forward and kissed her brow, where the mark shimmered faintly. She bowed again, murmuring, "You honor me, my king."

He chuckled and patted her shoulder before pivoting toward Sir Tolman. "And Sir Tolman. The Grand Protector," the king said with a grin too sharp to be friendly. "Even in your twilight years, you have not lost your step."

It was meant to be a compliment. It was not.

Sir Tolman bowed low, steady and proud. "I will always protect House Haldren, Your Grace. I know of no greater honor."

The king's grin faltered—just for a moment—before he forced it back into place. He had heard the sting in Sir Tolman's words, though he chose not to bite back. Yet.

Instead, he clapped his hands. "Now then… let us see the assassin."

Sir Kesteren gave a sharp nod and stepped toward Belaric. The two men faced each other, the tension thick between them. Sir Kesteren reached for the chains, and for the briefest moment, Belaric resisted. Just enough to make it known. Then he released his grip.

Sir Kesteren had noticed. His hand tightened on the chain as he dragged the assassin forward and threw him down before the king's feet. The man hit the marble with a grunt. The throne room fell deathly quiet—even the nobles held their breath.

King Valebran crouched, one hand gripping the assassin's jaw, forcing their eyes to meet. "You are a fool," the king whispered.

Whispers broke out. Eyes darted to one another—confusion writ clear. No one understood what the king meant.

"You send one, and she dies. So you send another. Foolish," he muttered. "Tell me—did you challenge Sir Tolman to a duel, like the last one?"

The assassin chuckled, venom behind his teeth. "Had I done so, the old ox would be dead."

King Valebran tilted his head, smile twitching. "And yet... here you are in chains, and there he stands unbloodied. Curious."

The assassin turned toward Belaric, hate flaring. "Only because he did not finish the job. Even after I gutted the boy." He smiled—a cruel, rotten thing.

Belaric's fingers flexed. Rage, hot and sudden, pulsed through him at the mention of Staven. It took every ounce of restraint not to strike him.

The king caught the shift in tone. Interest flickered across his features. He rose and turned to Belaric, who stood straighter as Sir Kesteren returned to his side.

"You captured this man?" the king asked, gesturing toward the kneeling figure.

Belaric bowed. "Yes, my king."

"And your name?" The king asked.

"Belaric Kelmore," he replied smoothly.

The king raised a finger to his lips and hummed, as though considering something deeply irrelevant. "Kelmore... sounds like a merchant's name."

Belaric kept his face composed, though it took effort. "I wish I had been so fortunate, Your Grace. But the gods chose another path for me."

"And what path is that, I wonder?" the king questioned.

Belaric smiled without warmth. "Protecting House Haldren. And killing anyone who dares threaten them."

The chamber stilled. A murmur rose—nobles shifting, lips parting. A commoner had spoken bold words to a king. Too bold.

The king only chuckled. "Well said, Master Kelmore. Then I wish you good luck—it sounds like you will need it."

"I thank you for your wisdom, my king. I will prepare for whatever comes," he replied flatly.

Sir Kesteren's jaw tightened, but the king merely laughed. "I like this one," he said, turning back toward Lady Haldren.

"My sweet lady, you must be exhausted from your journey. Allow me to offer you and your daughter rooms here in the palace. We will speak more tonight. Your men may rest in the barracks."

Lady Haldren bowed her head. "You are generous, Your Grace. I have one request—that Sir Tolman and Belaric remain with us. They bring Lyra comfort in these dark times."

Belaric nearly smiled. A blade of her own, slid between silk.

The king's lips twitched, clearly ready to deny it—but the queen stepped forward instead.

"Of course," she said smoothly. "We want our guests to feel safe at all times. We will arrange for a room."

Lady Haldren bowed again. "Thank you, my queen."

The queen smiled—and it was real, or at least well-practiced.

"Yes, yes," King Valebran said, clearly irritated but unable to contradict his wife. "Before I forget—this prisoner is now ours. My interrogators will question him. Thoroughly."

His smile twisted into something colder. "They have been rather... restless."

They all knew this was coming. They had no say in it.

Lady Haldren nodded. "Of course. We hope he leads us to whomever is behind these attacks."

"Oh, I am sure he will," the king told her.

The king turned toward Sir Kesteren. "Escort her men to the barracks."

Sir Kesteren bowed, handed the prisoner to two armored guards, and began ushering the others away. The men turned to bow—to the king, to Lady Haldren. As they filed out, Hasker gave Belaric a hard, low nod, a silent promise to stay alert even in the barracks.

King Valebran clapped once. "Sennith!"

A well-dressed servant appeared with speed, kneeling before the thrones.

"Have rooms prepared for Lady Haldren, Lady Lyra, and their protectors. The finest we have," he commanded.

"Yes, my king," Sennith replied, rising quickly and approaching to escort them.

As the four were led toward the far exit, the king's voice called after them.

"I look forward to hearing the tale of how you captured the assassin, Belaric," the king called out.

His tone was mocking—a grin beneath a dagger.

He could feel the king's smile behind him.

But what lingered most was the assassin's stare—unblinking, hateful—as the guards dragged him away.

It was not the venom that unsettled Belaric.

It was the patience behind it.

As they emerged from the throne room, a royal guard stood waiting with their weapons. Belaric took his sword and daggers, the familiar weight a comfort, while Sir Tolman's hand wrapped tightly around the hilt of his own sword. The guard gave a curt nod before returning to his post.

Sennith led the four of them—Lady Haldren, Lyra, Sir Tolman, and Belaric—through the winding corridors of the palace. Belaric said nothing, but his eyes missed little. Every shadow was a hiding place. Every alcove a trap. He mapped each turn, noted which walls bore mounted steel torches and which did not, and memorized the number of guards they passed. He also noted the pairs of guards posted outside specific rooms, their posture rigid and unmoving. Their eyes, cold and sharp, followed the group for a beat too long before looking away. This was not a sanctuary. It was a gilded cage—and cages always had keys.

After several long minutes, Sennith came to a halt at a polished stone archway.

"This room will be for Lady Haldren," he said, gesturing to the door on the right. Then he pointed across the corridor. "And that one, for Lady Lyra. I will have fresh sheets and food sent up shortly."

He turned to Belaric and Sir Tolman, his gaze condescending. "The next two doors are for you… fine gentlemen."

Sir Tolman nodded once. "Thank you, Sennith."

The servant did not respond. Instead, he turned back to Lady Haldren, his eyes sweeping her and Lyra from head to toe with quiet disdain. "The king will summon you for dinner later this evening. Please ensure you are dressed appropriately."

The implication landed like a slap.

Sir Tolman stepped forward, his voice low and dangerous. "You may serve the king, but insult my lady again and you will be wearing the white funeral robes."

Sennith blanched, clearly not expecting the threat. Before he could gather a reply, Belaric stepped in with a smile that did not reach his eyes.

"Sennith, I am sure you have duties to attend to. We will see ourselves in," Belaric said, forcing a smile.

The man glanced between them, then straightened his spine with as much dignity as he could muster. "Yes. I will see to it," he muttered, turning on his heel and disappearing down the hall.

Belaric turned to Tolman with a grin. "Must you scare everyone, old man?"

Sir Tolman snorted, narrowing his eyes. "I will show you old."

Lyra giggled, but Lady Haldren raised a hand. "Enough, boys."

She opened her chamber door and motioned for them all to step inside. Once they had, she closed it behind them with a quiet click.

She opened her mouth to speak, but Belaric raised his hand. The others stilled as he crossed the room. He ran his fingers along the walls, pressed gently at seams in the stone, tested the corners near the ceiling and floor. He inspected the fireplace, the window, and the underside of a wooden chair. When he passed the window, he paused and looked through the glass—not at the view, but at the shadows just beyond it.

Only when he turned back did he speak. "It is safe. We can speak freely."

They all watched him with a mix of respect and unease.

"He knows who you are," Sir Tolman said.

"I expected he would," Belaric replied. "They will be watching closely. Every step we take, every word."

"What will you do?" Lyra asked.

Belaric sighed. "We will probably be here for a few nights. I need to scout, but I cannot move alone. That would draw attention. So tomorrow, Lyra and I will explore the palace—openly."

Lady Haldren tilted her head. "Do you not already know the layout?"

He shook his head. "I have only been here once before. Entered through the servant's quarters. I need to learn the noble wings—where guards are posted, which halls loop back on themselves, which do not."

"And after that?" Sir Tolman asked.

Belaric's smile was faint but sharp. "Then I do what I was made for. Find their secrets. There is always something hidden in a place like this."

"Will it not be too dangerous?" Lady Haldren said. "Surely they will expect it."

"Of course they will. That is what makes it fun." He paused. "But we need answers, and no one here is better suited to dig for them than me."

None of them argued that point.

"And tonight?" she asked. "The king may not allow you or Sir Tolman to join us at dinner."

Belaric nodded. "I expect as much. That is where Lyra comes in. She can out think anyone in this palace. Even him."

Lyra grinned. "It was irritating. The king kept channeling into his forehead and mouth the entire time."

Belaric's brow furrowed. "What?"

"He was channeling," she said again, laughing. "Not sure why. It is not like he could out think me or sweet-talk us into anything. Waste of energy if you ask me."

"Wait—he is chest-marked. Are you saying he can use Valasar elsewhere?" he asked.

Lyra looked puzzled. "Yes? We all can."

Belaric's expression darkened with confusion. "I thought you could only use Valasar on the part of the body where the mark is."

She shook her head. "No. The mark grants access to Valasar. The location determines your strongest channel, but you can direct it elsewhere. I can draw power into my hands, my legs, even my eyes."

"Then why not do that all the time?" he asked, confusion building.

"Because it burns too much energy," she said. "I can channel to my forehead for hours. Into my arms? Maybe minutes. And only briefly. Someone like the king—whose mark covers most of his chest—has enough reserve to sustain it longer."

Belaric was stunned. How have I never heard this before, he wondered.

Lyra, seeing his confusion, continued.

"We are told to keep the full extent of our abilities hidden," Lyra said with a shrug. "So no one can use it against us. It is not something we talk about openly."

Belaric shook his head. "There are more secrets in this kingdom than shadows."

Lady Haldren let out a breath. "Well, as enlightening as this Valasar lesson is, we have more pressing matters."

She turned to Lyra. "You said he was channeling?"

Lyra nodded. "He shifted between his head and mouth. It was not effective. He must not realize I learned to sense the Valasar, meaning he underestimates me."

Sir Tolman smirked. "That will be his downfall."

"Yes," Lyra said, smiling. "It will."

They all laughed—softly—and then set about the rest of their planning. They discussed what Lady Haldren and Lyra would say during the evening meal, and how Belaric and Lyra might explore without drawing suspicion. Servants came and went, delivering food, wine, fresh sheets, and fine blue gowns. Belaric kept their conversation mundane whenever others were present.

Eventually, Lady Haldren moved to the window, peering out at the sinking light. "It is time. Lyra and I need to change."

She turned to the bed and lifted one of the dresses, examining it. As the others stood to leave, she glanced over her shoulder.

"Dress quickly, all of you. Even if you are not invited to dine, I expect you to escort us to the door. It will give the impression of unity—and, it may grant you a better chance to map the royal wing Belaric."

Belaric nodded. "Understood."

"Check your rooms," he added, voice quiet. "Every corner. Every gap."

Sir Tolman and Lyra both agreed. No further words were needed. The three slipped into the hallway, the palace swallowing each of them into its stone-lined silence.

Belaric entered his room and took it in at a glance—nearly identical to Lady Haldren's in structure but fitted for a man of status. A massive bed sat against the far wall, framed in master-crafted dark wood carved with cresting waves and curling leaves. A hearth smoldered opposite, low embers casting flickering shadows across the stone floor. A large writing table stood beside the window, its surface bare but inviting, and several towering wardrobes loomed near the wall, each one tall enough to make Belaric feel small beside them. He opened the nearest and found several sets of fine clothing arranged with ceremonial care—dark tunics, embroidered coats, and trousers in shades meant to impress. Sennith, it seemed, intended to remind them of their place through fabric alone.

His eyes flicked to the bookshelves—three of them, filled edge to edge with thick tomes and gilded spines. Political histories, noble bloodlines, and a few volumes Belaric suspected were more for show than use.

He moved quickly, checking the room for signs of tampering. He tested the fireplace, peered behind tapestries, ran fingers along the seams of the stone. When he was certain it was clear, he let out a breath and turned toward the bed.

Belaric dressed in one of the more functional outfits from the wardrobe: black wool trousers, a fine black tunic with silver threading that sported more buttons than any sane man would wear, and a pair of polished leather boots—soft-soled and tight-laced. He strapped one dagger to his left side, the sword to his right, and secured the last blade against his forearm beneath the sleeve. A flick of the wrist confirmed it was secure and would not cut him by mistake.

He caught a glimpse of himself in the mirror beside the hearth. His beard had grown again, coarser than usual, trailing past his jaw. I need to find time to trim that, he thought, knowing he would not. Not while war whispered beneath every quiet moment.

Satisfied, he stepped into the hallway and found Sir Tolman already waiting.

"What, could not decide which outfit made you look the prettiest?" Sir Tolman asked, chuckling.

Belaric gave him a slow once-over, noting the man's grey linen pants and a deep blue tunic that clashed magnificently. "Bold choice—dressing like the losing side of a tavern brawl. What happened? Did your wardrobe surrender before sunrise?"

Sir Tolman's grin died instantly. "I will show you a brawl."

Belaric snorted. "I am terrified. Shall I send a runner to fetch Dross? You might need him again. I would hate for your knees to give out mid-charge."

Sir Tolman stepped forward with mock threats. "Oh, I am going to beat you worse than that wardrobe beat you."

They squared off, still laughing, when a voice cut through the corridor.

"Is it possible for you two not to act like children wherever we go?" Lady Haldren asked.

She stood with arms crossed, a faint scowl on her face. Lyra was just behind her, giggling despite her mother's tone. Both wore flowing light blue gowns that shimmered softly in the torchlight—elegant, refined, and stately. Lyra moved with surprising grace, her posture poised, her chin high. She looked more like a young noblewoman than the girl Belaric had first met back in Brookhaven.

Both men straightened and bowed. Lady Haldren rolled her eyes.

At that moment, Sennith rounded the corner and froze, chin raised as if preparing to deliver judgment. "My lady, if you will follow me," he said curtly, not sparing a glance for the men.

The four exchanged a brief look—Lyra rolled her eyes this time—and followed. Sennith moved fast, his steps sharp and rehearsed. As they walked, Belaric memorized the path. Every turn. Every stair. Every noble crest along the walls. He noted several guards standing posted outside closed doors. Nobles, perhaps. Secrets, more likely. He also noticed pairs of guards stationed at every intersection and stairwell, their gazes following their group with silent scrutiny.

Eventually, the corridor narrowed, leading to a single door at its end. Sir Kesteren stood before it, a steel sentinel, his armor catching the firelight in quiet glints. He looked as if he had been carved from iron and discipline both.

"This is the royal family's private dining room," Sennith said over his shoulder. "You should feel honored."

As they approached, Sennith addressed the knight. "Lady Haldren and Lady Lyra are here for their dinner with the royal family."

Sir Kesteren ignored him entirely, his eyes shifting to the women. He bowed, deep and respectfully. "My ladies, it is a pleasure to see you again. The gods have truly blessed us with such beauty at court."

Belaric resisted the urge to sigh. Must the man be so likeable?

Lady Haldren and Lyra bowed politely. "Thank you for your kind words, Sir Kesteren," Lady Haldren replied.

He nodded and then opened the door for them. The women entered without hesitation—Lady Haldren with quiet elegance, Lyra with subtle confidence that hinted at growing awareness of her place in this game.

Belaric and Sir Tolman stepped to the side, taking up guard positions at either end of the door.

Sir Kesteren looked at them with mild confusion. "What are you doing?"

Sir Tolman blinked. "Guarding the hallway?"

Sir Kesteren exhaled sharply. "Get in the room, or you will not be having dinner with the royal family."

Sennith made a sound of disgust. "What? Them? They are not worthy—"

Sir Kesteren turned to him, expression cold and sharp. "The two men who stopped not one but two assassins and kept Lady Haldren and her daughter alive? Tell me, Sennith—how many assassins have you stopped?"

Sennith's mouth opened, then closed.

Sir Kesteren did not wait. "That is what I thought. Now go change the sheets on a bed. Maybe one day, you will be worthy to share a meal with the king."

Sennith's face went red, but he held his tongue. He spun on his heel and stormed off, dignity shattered behind every stiff step.

Belaric and Sir Tolman exchanged a glance, both struggling not to laugh. They nodded their thanks to Sir Kesteren.

"I will still need your weapons," he said, tone flat. "All of them."

They obeyed, removing sword and dagger alike. Belaric even gave up the blade hidden in his sleeve, handing it over without protest. Sir Kesteren accepted them silently and motioned them inside.

The dining room was simpler than expected. A modest hearth crackled in the side wall, its warmth welcome against the palace chill. A long wooden table stretched down the center of the room, its surface smooth, its legs thick with ornate carving. Several chairs, each finely made, surrounded it. The scent of pine resin and lemon oil clung faintly to the polished wood.

As Belaric stepped further in, he took another glance around. Something about the room—it felt too perfect. The chairs placed just so; the fire crackling a little too neatly. A room dressed for guests, but not entirely private. His instincts stirred, but nothing moved.

Sir Kesteren followed them in and placed their weapons against the far wall. "The food will be brought out when the royal family arrives. When they enter, you stand and bow. The king prefers these meetings to be… less formal."

Belaric was surprised. Not just that they had been allowed in, but that even the king loosened tradition here. That meant something.

They nodded, took their seats, and waited.

Sir Kesteren moved to a side door, cracked it open, and kept watch through the hallway beyond.

The king and his family would arrive soon.

28

The room was quiet enough to hear the breath of the fire behind them. None of the four spoke. The silence was not tense—it was worse than that. It was expectant.

Belaric heard it first. The sound of boots on marble—slow, deliberate. Each click echoed like a gavel striking judgment.

Sir Kesteren straightened his shoulders and motioned with a gloved hand. "On your feet."

They rose as one.

He turned, his voice carrying the weight of practiced ceremony. "My king," he said, bowing deeply. As he straightened, he faced the table. "I present His Lordship and Ruler of the Realm—King Aelion Valebran."

The king entered without fanfare, as though royalty was a burden best carried quietly. He wore a robe of deep forest green, soft and unadorned. Beside him, Queen Calenna matched his stride, her dress form-fitting, dyed the same shade.

They matched, Belaric noted. Not by coincidence.

More footsteps followed. A young man entered, barely older than Lyra—tall, golden-haired, with eyes the color of clear sky over snow. The resemblance to the king was unmistakable, but the weight of a crown still unburdened his face, and his movements held the loose-limbed energy of a boy, not the coiled stillness of a man.

Then came the last. A young woman, early twenties moved with a poise that had been trained into her bones. She did not walk with grace, but with a deliberate, confident step that seemed to measure every inch of the hall. She wore an elegant red gown, her hair tied back to show off a face sculpted for thrones and war tables alike. Her eyes, cool and intelligent, took in the scene with a cold detachment, and a single gemstone hung from her neck—its cut and shimmer far too deliberate to be decoration alone.

Tessara Valebran, Belaric thought. And the boy—Davin Valebran.

But there were three children.

Their eldest was missing.

He caught a flicker of movement—Princess Tessara's gaze meeting Sir Kesteren's. A moment too long. A moment too intentional. Sir Kesteren looked away, but not fast enough. The glance was a silent conversation, a quick, sharp message passed between two people who understood each other on a level beyond words.

Dangerous, Belaric thought. Not the glance—the implications. If others saw what he had just seen, Sir Kesteren's neck would soon find itself beneath a noose… or a marriage crown.

The royal family lined up—a perfect, composed, inscrutable tableau. Each member held themselves with a specific, practiced stillness, like pieces on a chessboard.

Belaric, Sir Tolman, Lady Haldren, and Lyra bowed in unison.

"Oh, please," the king said, waving a hand. His voice was smooth, too smooth. "Let us spare the formalities tonight. We have all endured enough solemn halls and sharpened words. Sit, all of you."

Lady Haldren bowed her head again. "You honor us, my king. We are grateful for this invitation—to sit with your family is no small thing."

"The honor is mine," King Valebran said. "I have been looking forward to this meal more than any council session I have suffered through today."

He took his seat. The others followed suit.

"Sir Kesteren," the king said, glancing toward the knight. "Call for the wine."

Sir Kesteren bowed. "At once, Your Grace."

He stepped to the door and clapped his hands. "First course." His voice echoed like steel on stone.

The soft patter of feet followed—servants entered carrying bowls of steaming soup and pitchers of deep red wine. Each movement was rehearsed, silent, and fleeting. Bowls were placed, goblets filled, and then they were gone.

"Rabbit stew," the king said, lifting his spoon. "Roasted with mountain thyme, black root, and a drop of cherry vinegar. Gods, I love when the kitchens get it right."

A quiet throat-clear from the queen stopped him. She tilted her head slightly. Expectant.

King Valebran sighed, smiling faintly. "Ah. My manners."

He gestured across the table. "Lady Haldren, allow me to introduce my daughter, Princess Tessara, and my son, Prince Davin."

Both inclined their heads with measured grace.

Lady Haldren returned the gesture. "Your Highnesses. May I present my daughter Lyra, and my two most trusted protectors—Sir Marius Tolman and Belaric Kelmore."

Prince Davin tilted his head. "Not Sir Belaric? Odd... for a commoner to be a personal guard for a noble."

The words dropped like pebbles in a still pond.

"Davin." Queen Calenna's tone was clipped, a blade's edge wrapped in silk. "You will not disrespect our guests. Belaric has risked his life for Lady Haldren and Lyra. That alone deserves nobility."

The prince flushed, stiffened, then turned. "I apologize, Belaric. I meant no offense. I am simply unfamiliar with situations such as yours."

Belaric offered a faint smile, keeping his tone even. "No apology needed, my prince. I am an odd sight at any table—especially one like this."

The king chuckled, clapping his son's shoulder. "Good. A man who can admit fault may one day lead with strength, rather than stubbornness."

Prince Davin nodded. "Yes, father."

Lady Haldren shifted the conversation. "Forgive me, Your Grace, but I believed you had three children?"

The king's spoon paused mid-air. Then he smiled again. "Indeed. Venricel is away—he sailed for Moraketh three weeks ago. High King Solkrath has a daughter of age, and our court sees… potential in the match. I do not share all their enthusiasm, but I see no harm in letting the boy measure what might be gained."

He resumed eating, more slowly. "Tessara will follow suit soon enough. We have had no shortage of noble hopefuls."

Again, Belaric caught it—Princess Tessara's glance toward Sir Kesteren. A flicker of longing? Guilt? Defiance? He could not read it all. He knew it meant something.

The queen laid a gentle hand on the king's wrist. "My love… perhaps not tonight. We are here for Lady Haldren and Lyra."

The king softened, just slightly. "Yes. Of course." He turned back to his guests. "How was your journey, my lady?"

Lady Haldren dabbed her lips with a cloth. "Swift and quiet. Sir Tolman and Belaric saw to everything. I daresay I have never felt safer."

The king nodded, then looked toward Sir Tolman with something sharper in his gaze. "I remember the first tale I heard of you, Sir Tolman. A border dispute—western lands, was it not? Three-to-one odds against your line. They said you broke the charge yourself. Cut down men like wheat, drove them back single-handedly."

The king leaned forward. "They gave you a name, did not they?"

Sir Tolman cleared his throat. "Yes, my king. Though I have not heard it in years."

"What was it?" Prince Davin asked, eyes wide.

Sir Tolman gave a rueful smile. "The Raging Bear."

Davin grinned.

King Aelion chuckled, a sound without warmth. His gaze shifted to Belaric. "A fitting name for a legend, Sir Tolman. But legends, like all things, eventually meet their match. Even the Raging Bear might struggle against a truly exceptional blade, would not you agree, Master Kelmore? Someone like, say... Sir Kesteren?" The king's eyes shifted to Belaric—just slightly, but with intent. "Could you best him?"

The room stilled.

Belaric met the king's gaze. Unblinking. "My king, Sir Kesteren is one of the finest blades in the kingdom. I have no doubt that he would win. And unlike Sir Tolman, I have never been foolish enough to find out."

King Valebran stared a moment longer... then smiled. "Well spoken. Modesty and wisdom—rare in men who wear blood on their boots."

Belaric forced a smile. But in his gut, the warmth drained.

The food cooled slowly in their bowls. No one noticed.

From somewhere behind the great hall doors, a soft knock echoed—once, then again. Sir Kesteren rose without waiting for the king's leave, already sensing something was off.

The king turned toward the sound, frowning. "I gave the order that we were not to be disturbed."

Sir Kesteren opened the door—just a crack. A servant stood beyond, pale and trembling. He handed something through the opening: a folded slip of parchment, the seal already broken.

Sir Kesteren read it once. His jaw tensed.

He crossed the room with careful steps and handed it to the king. The king unfolded it, eyes scanning the lines.

Whatever he read, it killed the humor on his face.

The candlelight suddenly felt colder.

The king exhaled through his nose, the sound too composed to be called a sigh. "It seems our questioners were... overzealous," he said, sighing. "The assassin has died. Blood loss."

The words fell flat. Almost careless. But his gaze told a different story—locked on Belaric like a trap half-sprung.

Belaric did not blink. He knew a test when he saw one. The timing of the message, the casual delivery, the probing eyes—this was no accident.

"A shame," the king went on, lifting his wine. "They managed only a name before he bled out. Vellis Sorn." His eyes slid to Lady Haldren. "Does that name mean anything to you, my lady?"

Lady Haldren waited a breath too long before answering—just enough to suggest deep thought rather than delay. "No, my king. I do not believe I knew anyone by that name."

Belaric turned the name over in his mind like a stone in the hand. It meant nothing to him. Not truly. But that did not mean it was false. The Order used many names, and buried more.

The king gave a slow nod. "Resilient, then. Hours under the knife, and all he gave was his name." A pause. "I am told he never screamed. Men like that are... forged, not born."

The line hung in the air like smoke.

"I assume you questioned him as well?" the king asked, tone mild. But his eyes stayed on Belaric. "Did you learn anything of worth?"

Lady Haldren set her spoon down gently. "We learned little. But we were interested in the name of the person who sent him. That man's fate was sealed the moment he crossed my gate with murder in his heart. I cared more for the hand that sent him than the blade he carried."

Belaric felt the corner of his mouth twitch. She did not flinch. Not once.

The king studied her. "And did he mention anything?"

Lady Haldren shook her head. "Only curses. Sadly, we lack the refinements of your questioners."

The queen smiled faintly at that, but said nothing.

The king leaned back, swirling the wine in his goblet as if the sediment might reveal something deeper. Belaric could feel the weight of the next move gathering like storm clouds over still water.

The king took another sip of wine, slow and measured. "Two assassins dead," he said, voice soft as falling ash. "And I imagine more will follow. They do not strike me as the kind to give up easily." Though he addressed the table, his pale eyes never left Belaric.

Before Belaric could respond, Lyra's voice rang out clear and sharp. "Yes, more will come. And we will be ready."

The room quieted as all eyes turned to her. "They are cowards who skulk in shadow, like the ones who command them," she continued, chin held high. "We will drag them into the light and let the world see what they really are."

The king's lips curled slightly, but there was no warmth in it. "Ah, the confidence of youth—"

"Why would I not be confident, my king?" Lyra cut in. "The only men ever to kill one of these assassins stand at my side. My mother is beloved by the people, and they would die for her. And me..." She straightened further. "You said it yourself—my Valasar surpasses those of grown adults who bare the Valasar blessing. And it has only just begun. We will stand. We will not falter."

An uneasy silence followed. The queen raised a brow, and Belaric spared a glance at Lady Haldren, but her expression remained perfectly composed. The king, still smiling, let the quiet stretch a moment longer before the queen intervened.

"Well said, my dear," Queen Calenna broke in with practiced grace, lifting her glass. "To strength. And to conviction."

One by one, the others raised their wine. Lyra beamed, pleased with herself, while the king drank last, his smile restored but thinner.

Sir Kesteren stepped forward with a sharp clap. At his signal, the servants glided in with quiet urgency. The scent arrived first—warm spices, caramelized glaze, roasted meat.

A servant bowed. "My king. Tonight's main course is roasted boar, slow-cooked and glazed in wild honey. It is seasoned with cinnamon bark, sun-pepper from the southern isles, and cloves from the merchant coast. Served with it are roasted root vegetables—parsnip, carrot, and gold beet—charred at the edges for flavor, a mash of onion and barley softened with cream and stock, and pilaf with lemon thyme, wild garlic, and black grain."

The rich aroma filled the room as plates were set, and wine replenished. Once the servants withdrew, the king breathed in deeply. "Excellent. Let us eat."

For a while, the only sounds were the scrape of cutlery and the quiet rhythm of chewing. Then, with the same casual tone a hunter might use to speak of snares, the king spoke again.

"We have heard the tale of Sir Tolman's killing the first assassin. But Belaric... your story remains untold. Will you not share it?"

Belaric dabbed at his mouth with exaggerated slowness. He let the silence stretch, made the king wait for the answer he already believed he owned. There it was, Belaric thought, the test within the test. The king did not want a story. He wanted a crack.

Finally, he set the cloth aside and met the king's gaze evenly. "Sadly, my king, there is little to tell. I heard him before I saw him—clumsy, making noise as he tried to slip through a window. I tackled him. He ran, and I gave chase. We fought in the woods, but he was poorly trained. Kept stumbling over roots. It was not difficult to bring him down."

Belaric shrugged lightly. "Whoever sent him either overestimated their reach... or underestimated me."

The king chuckled, low and empty. "Perhaps your next encounter will be more... entertaining."

The room chilled. Even the queen turned her eyes briefly toward her husband. Belaric sat motionless, the fork resting in his hand. This was not dinner, he thought; it was war drenched in wine and velvet.

Again, it was the queen who shifted the current. "Lady Haldren," she said with a smile, "forgive the forwardness, but have you given thought to Lyra's future match?"

Lyra stiffened, clearly about to protest, but Lady Haldren interjected smoothly. "Not yet, my queen. There have been offers—sons, brothers. But I still hope she might choose someone for love, not alliance."

A beat passed. Across the table, Belaric caught a glance exchanged between Princess Tessara and Sir Kesteren. Quick. Subtle. But there. So, he thought, it is not just an accident. That fire burns hot on both ends.

And as if reading his thoughts, Sir Kesteren turned and locked eyes with him. For a breath, they measured one another in silence—not as rivals, not as enemies, but as men who understood what it meant to love something they could not have.

"Ah, love," the queen mused, her voice softening. "Did you know that when Aelion and I were matched, we could scarcely tolerate each other?" She reached across and took the king's hand. "But after a few months... we began to speak. To share. And in time, we were lucky enough to fall in love."

The king gave her a smile—the kind polished by years of public life. "Very lucky indeed, my love."

He set down his fork and clapped once. "Now, I believe I have had enough boar. Shall we enjoy dessert? Another of my favorites."

His eyes flicked to Belaric, just long enough to press the blade in deeper.

Sir Kesteren clapped again. The servants returned, clearing the plates with quiet precision and refilling the wine. Then came the scent.

Belaric knew it before he saw it. Apple. Cinnamon. A crust browned to perfection. Butter and sugar layered over memory like salt on a wound.

Each plate bore a perfect slice of apple pie.

"I love apple pie," the king said. "Had the apples brought in special. From Vorinfall."

Belaric did not move. Did not blink. Inside, the name echoed like a fist pounding on a coffin lid. He remembered Renna's hands dusted with flour, her laugh as she pulled a golden pie from the oven.

The king watched him as he took a slow bite. Belaric did the same. Each mouthful was ash and grief.

The servers cleared the plates in silence. The king rose, smiling as though nothing had been spoken in malice. "A fine meal. Would not you all agree?"

They nodded, each in turn. Some more slowly than others.

"Well then," he said. "We have got a full day ahead tomorrow. Let us rest."

Chairs scraped. They exchanged words of gratitude. Lady Haldren thanked them both once more. The queen responded graciously, promising further conversation. Princess Tessara lingered, stealing a last look at Sir Kesteren. Prince Davin gave a curt nod and followed.

Once the last of the royal family had left, Sir Kesteren stepped forward and returned Belaric and Sir Tolman their weapons. He said nothing as he led the four of them through the quiet corridors of the palace.

At the guest chambers, Lady Haldren turned. "We will speak in the morning."

Belaric nodded. "We will."

He entered his room and closed the door behind him. The silence pressed in like a closing fist. He leaned against the wood for a long moment before moving to the hearth. The fire had dwindled to embers. He added two logs and watched the flames rise.

He stripped off the fine clothing, folded it carefully, and placed it over the back of a chair. Then he sat on the edge of the bed and lowered his head into his hands.

"Renna."

He said her name like a confession—quiet, bitter, honest.

If the gods still listen, he thought, let me not dream tonight.

Belaric considered it a blessing that his mind refused to obey him. Sleep did not come without dreams—but for once, they were not nightmares. He was back in the garden. Renna sat on the old stone bench, sunlight painting her hair gold as she rocked their son gently in her arms. She hummed a soft melody, one she had only ever sung when she thought no one was listening. Belaric moved through the rows, pulling weeds, gathering fresh fruit, glancing back more often than he needed to. Her smile met his each time. The boy cooed and kicked in her lap. Peace hung over it all, too perfect to be real.

When the light of dawn finally broke through the window, the dream faded like mist. Belaric opened his eyes and lay still. The warmth was gone. The garden was gone. And she... was gone.

He sat up slowly; the ache settling in his chest as familiar as breath. He wished he could fall backward into that vision and stay there—to tell her what he had not said in life. To apologize. To beg. But the waking world offered no such mercy.

Rising, he crossed to the window and opened the shutters. The city below was stirring—market carts creaked into motion, vendors called faintly, a child laughed somewhere beyond the stone walls. He looked up toward the sky, past the rooftops, and whispered.

"You are watching me, are you not?" His voice was low, uncertain. "You have seen it now. The things I have done. I am sorry I lacked the courage to tell you. I was afraid. I thought if you knew, you would leave. And maybe... maybe you should have," he whispered.

He closed his eyes briefly. "But I will find him, Renna. I will save our son. And I will raise him to be everything I am not. To this—" his voice cracked slightly, "—I swear."

A soft gust rolled through the window, brushing his cheek. For a heartbeat, he caught it—the barest trace of her perfume. Lavender and jasmine. He almost laughed. Almost wept.

A knock at the door stirred him. He pulled on a pair of grey linen trousers and crossed the room. When he opened the door, Lady Haldren, Lyra, and Sir Tolman stood in the hallway, two breakfast trays in hand.

"See?" Sir Tolman grinned. "Told you old men like to sleep in."

Belaric rolled his eyes and stepped aside, letting them enter. He moved to the wardrobe, reaching for a shirt. When he turned back, all three were staring—shock plain on their faces.

"What?" he asked.

Sir Tolman let out a low whistle. "Holy hells. I knew you were good with a blade, but what in the gods' names happened to you?"

Belaric looked down. His torso was a tapestry of scars—slashes, burns, broken bones that had never quite healed right. He ran a hand across his chest and sighed. "The Order does not believe in second chances. Every failure was punished. I have lost count of the bones I have broken."

For a moment, no one spoke. Then Belaric slipped the shirt over his head and moved to the table. Sir Tolman and Lyra set the trays down while he fetched plates and cups from a nearby shelf. Tolman served thin slices of peppered meat, soft scrambled eggs, and warm biscuits still wrapped in cloth. Lyra poured cool water from the jug into each cup.

They ate in silence for a time. The food was simple, but warm and grounding. When they finished, Lady Haldren dabbed at her mouth with a cloth and looked at Belaric.

"First, I want to thank you. Last night was difficult, but you kept your composure. I was proud of you," she said.

Belaric gave a slight nod and glanced at Lyra and Tolman, both of whom met his eyes with quiet approval.

"Thank you, my lady. The king is clever. I expected him to provoke me. That pie was—" He paused, clearing his throat. "You helped. Especially you, Lyra. Your words struck him deeper than you know."

Lyra lowered her head. "I was angry. I hated the way he looked at you."

Lady Haldren reached out and took her daughter's hand. "You spoke the truth. And from the heart. Just be cautious next time. We face foes with armies, influence, and coin. A single misstep could undo everything."

Lyra nodded. "I will, Mother. I promise."

Belaric set his cup down and leaned forward slightly. "There is something else you should know. Something I noticed during dinner."

The room stilled again.

"Princess Tessara and Sir Kesteren. Their eyes kept finding each other. Not once or twice—again and again. It was not a polite acknowledgment. It was... familiar. Intimate. I would wager they are in love."

Sir Tolman's brow furrowed. "Are you sure it was not just courtly politeness?"

"I spent most of my life reading people without ever speaking to them," Belaric replied. "It was not politeness. There is something between them."

Lady Haldren exhaled through her nose. "That could be dangerous."

"Agreed. We do not know where either of them truly stands. Sir Kesteren is loyal, but how loyal? And Princess Tessara..." she paused, "if she shares her father's ambitions, any misstep could be fatal."

"I am not saying we act on it," Belaric said. "Only that we remember it. If things change—if alliances shift—it might be something we can use."

They sat in silence for a beat, each weighing the value of love in a court ruled by fear.

Then Lady Haldren straightened. "Now, to the matter at hand. The king knows who you are, Belaric. We must assume we are being watched constantly. Do you have a plan?"

Belaric nodded. "I want to walk through the palace first. Observe the halls, the guards, the shadows. Lyra will come with me. If we are questioned, we will say we are looking for the library. I have heard it is one of the best in the kingdom."

Lyra brightened. "A day at the library sounds perfect."

Lady Haldren smiled. "Good. It fits well. The queen has invited me to a private lunch—just the two of us. I do not know her intent, but I will treat it as a chance to gather information."

"I am not sure whether she is complicit or simply playing her own game," Belaric said. "But if she is truly separate from the king's designs, it could be our best opening."

They turned to Sir Tolman.

"And you?" Belaric asked.

Sir Tolman shrugged. "I will check on the men. Make sure they are not growing soft. I am sure the other guards will be there, too. Soldiers love to talk. With any luck, I will hear something useful."

Lady Haldren nodded. "Good. Then we each have our paths. But remember—we are surrounded by courtiers and blades. We speak freely here, but outside this door, every glance might be a knife."

She looked at them, each eyes sharp. "This court thrives on secrets, not steel. So we will play their game—but we play it on our terms."

They all agreed, finishing the last of their water. Belaric dressed in his guard uniform while Lyra waited just outside. Once he joined her, they wished Lady Haldren well and parted ways. She walked alone toward her meeting with the queen; her back straight and head high. Sir Tolman bowed once and set off for the barracks, already muttering about idle recruits and sharpening drills.

Lyra turned to Belaric with a smile that, for a moment, held none of the day's weight.

"So... should we go find this library?" she asked.

Belaric smiled back. "Yes, we shall."

And together, they set off—into marble corridors that whispered lies and secrets with every step.

They walked the palace halls with purpose masked as aimlessness—Lyra a few steps ahead, Belaric shadowing her with one hand resting on the hilt of his sword. The image was important: the curious young noblewoman, and the silent, watchful guard.

They took their time. Every corridor was a puzzle to be solved—columns to be counted, windows to be noted, side passages committed to memory. Belaric made sure to lag slightly at turns, just enough to catch glimpses of other wings or adjacent stairwells.

They passed several guards along the way. Each one offered a courteous nod, some even addressing Lyra by title. But none of them looked at her for long. Their eyes always returned to Belaric—watching him, weighing him. A few tried to hide it, but most did not bother. Whatever rumors the king had sown were already blooming. He was no mystery to them. He was a threat.

Once, a servant paused to offer directions. Lyra smiled sweetly and told her they were "a bit turned around." The servant offered to escort them to the library, but Lyra politely declined, insisting they would find their way.

And they did. Eventually.

After two hours of quiet exploration, careful observation, and pretending to be lost, Belaric decided it was time. Any longer, and someone might grow suspicious. They changed direction and allowed themselves to be "guided" toward the true destination.

The library doors stood like sentinels—tall oak slabs veined with age and brass-bound at the hinges. As they reached it, Belaric paused for a moment. Every stone in this place was built to make common men feel small. But Belaric had killed kings. He was not impressed.

The doors opened with a low groan. Inside, the room was immense. Two floors of shelves towered up around them, books stacked from ground to vaulted ceiling. A few long tables lined the central aisle, oil lamps positioned to provide warm light to those who wished to read in quiet. Spiral staircases curled into the upper gallery, where still more shelves waited, packed tightly with the weight of centuries.

A man in a gray robe shuffled between aisles with a feather duster and a stack of tomes. He turned as they entered, blinking behind spectacles, and broke into a wide grin.

"Ahhh, Lady Lyra Haldren," he said, bowing low. "I heard you had arrived at the palace. I suspected it was only a matter of time before you found your way here."

Lyra blinked, surprised. She glanced at Belaric, then back at the man. "You... you know who I am?"

The man chuckled and straightened. "Of course, my lady. At fifteen, you have advanced your mark further than many achieve in their whole lives. And on the forehead, no less—the most difficult to refine. Quite the feat."

Lyra's face lit up with a mix of pride and curiosity. "Why, thank you, sir...?"

"Fenro," the man said with a bow. "Fenro Alnoth, librarian and archivist of the Royal Athenaeum."

Lyra bowed in return, her voice softening. "Well, Fenro, would you be able to show me anything written about my Valasar mark? I am especially interested in reading about others who bore it—what they were capable of."

Fenro beamed, as though she had just offered him a lifelong wish. He glanced about the room, lowering his voice.

"Lyra," he said conspiratorially, "follow me."

He turned and led them up one of the spiral staircases to the second level. The floorboards creaked faintly beneath their feet. He brought them to a long shelf lined with thick, leather-bound volumes.

"These," he said with a flourish, "are first-hand accounts—journals and recollections—from some of the most gifted individuals that bore the Valasar mark on their foreheads. Scholars, philosophers, strategists... even a few prophets." He looked over his shoulder with pride. "Their talents went far beyond memory and thought—they shaped history."

Lyra smiled and thanked him with a bow. Fenro returned the gesture, then made himself scarce, drifting back down the stairs to resume his quiet tending.

Lyra moved along the shelf, her fingers trailing across spines worn with age and use. She pulled a few out, flipped through the pages, then returned them in search of something more personal.

Belaric, meanwhile, browsed the shelf adjacent. One title caught his eye: The Blade of Arthen Corven. He pulled it free.

The name was familiar. A legendary swordsman from over a century ago—his duels still spoken of in hushed tones by blade's men and dreamers alike. Belaric had heard the stories, even doubted a few. But the spine of the book read of a personal account. Curiosity outweighed cynicism.

He opened it, thumbed past the first few pages, and sat down on a bench beneath a lamp. No harm in learning what Corven had thought of himself—great men often told the most interesting lies.

Beside him, Lyra had settled with a thick volume of her own, the pages already turning beneath her careful hands.

The library, for now, was quiet.

But in a place like this, silence was never innocent.

After several hours of reading, the sun had shifted across the high windows and begun to cast long shadows through the library's upper arches. Lyra had moved from book to book, her curiosity unrelenting. She flipped pages with focused fingers, sometimes reading aloud a line that caught her attention, sometimes falling into long stretches of silence.

Belaric had remained mostly quiet, thumbing through The Blade of Arthen Corven. The swordsman's own words were blunt, precise, and filled with the kind of grim clarity that only came from men who had survived too many battles. Belaric found himself surprised by how much rang true.

Eventually, Lyra closed her current tome and let out a breath. "We should head back," she said, rising and stretching her arms.

Belaric stood as well, sliding Corven's journal back onto the shelf. "Let us not take the direct path," he murmured.

As they descended the stairs, Fenro appeared from behind one of the shelves, a wide smile already in place. "I hope you found something worthwhile, my lady?"

"I did, thank you," Lyra said, offering him a bow. "I will be back soon."

Fenro bowed deeply. "It would be my honor. And thank you both for visiting. May your thoughts remain sharp."

Belaric gave the man a brief nod and followed Lyra out into the corridor. They took a long route back—intentionally winding through sections they had already mapped earlier. Belaric was not looking for new passageways this time. He was looking for eyes.

And they were still there.

Every hallway they had passed that morning still bore a guard. Not crowded, not obvious—just one man watching their every move. Stationed casually near archways, standing by doors with a hand on the pommel of a blade, watching without watching. The palace was not guarding itself. It was watching him.

He said nothing, but Lyra caught his look once and nodded, lips pressed tight. She saw it too. The brightness she had carried in the library dimmed into something quieter. Her steps slowed. She walked beside him now, rather than ahead.

By the time they reached their rooms, the sky beyond the palace windows had turned the color of old brass. They approached Lady Haldren's door and gave a single knock.

"Enter," came her voice through the wood.

Belaric pushed the door open. Inside, Lady Haldren sat at a small table beside the hearth, a porcelain cup in hand. Sir Tolman was beside her, sipping tea and looking irritated in a way only Sir Tolman could.

"Why would you spend so long in the library?" he asked, lifting his brow. "You cannot even read."

Belaric grinned. "Maybe not. But at least I can climb stairs without wheezing, old man."

Sir Tolman's laughter died on the spot. Lyra snorted. Lady Haldren tried and failed to hide her smile.

Sir Tolman narrowed his eyes at both of them. "Keep laughing. One day I will drop you both in the river and pretend it was justice."

"Well," he said after a pause, glancing toward Lady Haldren, "seems none of us found much today. No fruit on this tree." He turned to Belaric. "Do you have a plan for tonight?"

Belaric's smile returned—wry, calm, dangerous. "Of course I do."

He just had not decided whether it would be quiet or bloody.

29

"You want us to do what?" Sir Tolman asked, louder than necessary. He crossed his arms as if he meant to block the very idea.

Belaric did not move. He stood near the hearth, arms behind his back, firelight licking the edges of his cloak. When he spoke, his voice lacked emotion.

"I need you all to pretend to be drunk. Loud, staggering, annoying. Then I need you to disable as many of the palace guards as you can without making it obvious."

"You mean poison," Lady Haldren said.

"No deaths," Belaric replied. "Just sleep. Four to six hours. And when they wake, they will not remember a thing."

Sir Tolman's face darkened. "And if one of them stumbles into someone like Sir Kesteren before collapsing? What then? What happens when we are caught with poison on our hands and half the guard unconscious?" Sir Tolman demanded.

Belaric met his gaze.

"Then we have already failed. They will charge us with treason and hang us for it. But make no mistake—our deaths are already written. These people do not play by the rules, and if we cling to the high road, they will bury us on it. Let them write the next chapter of your life, Lady Haldren, and it ends in a grave."

He turned to her. "Do you truly believe the king brought us here for goodwill and reconciliation? He is no fool. He knows who I am. He knows I killed the assassins he sent—and you think he will forget that? Let us leave in peace after we have challenged him openly? No, he is a wolf cloaked in velvet. That smile he wears—it does not differ from the mask I used to hide behind."

Lady Haldren narrowed her eyes. "You believe there is something hidden here."

"I know there is. Guards at every door. Eyes are on us at all times. The servants barely speak—they have been warned, and failure is not tolerated. The king controls everything here. Every word, every glance. This is the heart of the kingdom, and behind every door, something's being hidden."

Lyra spoke softly. "So they act drunk. Cause a scene. Meanwhile, you disappear?"

"They do not just act drunk," Belaric said. "They must sell it. Get noisy. Be a problem. Enough of one that they stop watching me and start watching them."

She hesitated. Just a breath, but he saw it. Her hand gripped the edge of the table, knuckles pale.

"And the guards?" she asked. "Will they wake up? They will be alright?"

Belaric nodded. "It is not lethal. Just quiet."

Sir Tolman still looked unconvinced, but Lyra slowly pushed herself to her feet. "I can get the pins," she said. "Mother keeps a dozen for her hair."

Lady Haldren turned toward her daughter, expression unreadable. There was no command, no refusal—only a moment's stillness, then a slow nod.

"Very well," she said. "I will help you find more."

"We will need sharp ones, thin enough to pierce but thick enough not to bend," Belaric told them.

The two stood. Lady Haldren went to her trunk and began searching while Lyra quickly went back to her room.

Lyra returned with a velvet pouch of ivory-handled pins. Lady Haldren produced another handful—simpler, utilitarian things used by palace maids. Belaric dumped them on the table, sifting through them like a jeweler sorting gemstones.

"These five will work," he muttered. "The others are too thick, or they will bend when shaved down."

"And the poison?" Lady Haldren asked.

Belaric gave a nod. "I have enough. But there is one more thing we need. Summon the others. I will return shortly." The others looked at him, confusion plain on their faces.

Without another word, he rose and left the room, descending two levels to the servant's quarters. The boy he found there was no older than twelve, elbows deep in a bucket of dirty water, scrubbing boot tracks off the stone.

"I need wine," Belaric said. "Twelve bottles. No delay. Bring them to my chambers. And not a word."

The boy looked ready to bolt. Belaric held out a silver piece.

"Understand?" Belaric asked.

The boy nodded and ran so fast he left the bucket behind.

When Belaric returned, Sir Tolman had already fetched the full complement. The guards filled the room—Dross, Hasker, Knoll, Ruthan, Nollan, Kedd, Tarnel, and Jass. Some leaned on walls, some sat cross-legged on the rug, but all wore the same expression: wary, coiled.

They were not used to being inside stone palaces or playing games with kings. But they trusted Belaric. That was enough.

They stayed long enough to exchange sharp glances and murmur in low tones, their eyes flicking from the strange sight within to each other, before leaving.

One of them looked back just before the door closed. His eyes lingered on the weapons, the men, the strange silence beneath the laughter. Then the latch clicked.

"They will talk," Ruthan muttered.

"Let them," Belaric said. "By the time anyone listens, this will be done."

"Or all of us will be," Nollan added under his breath.

Belaric pulled out a small steel-bladed knife from his belt. "Start drinking. Not much. Just enough to look it. Then spill the rest on your clothes."

Jass grinned. "Finally. A plan I can live with."

"Do not get too comfortable," Belaric said. "The rest of this requires precision."

He knelt by the fire with the pins and began to shave one end down on each. It was slow work—grinding the metal to a thin edge, flattening it just enough that it could slip beneath the skin with barely a mark. The process required patience. But it was one he had stored in his memory long ago.

This was old training. Tools of the trade meant for silencing, for disabling. The Order had taught him many things. He found he remembered every lesson.

Once the pins were ready, Belaric unwrapped a small pouch of powders and ground herbs. They were pale green and smelled faintly of crushed mint and something sour underneath.

"Do not touch the coated ends," he warned, mixing them into a bit of heated wine. "It will not kill you, but it will drop you. Fast."

Using a small brush, he dipped the sharpened ends and waited for them to dry before wrapping the other ends in linen thread.

He handed them out. "Hold it between these fingers," he said, demonstrating. "Like you are hiding a coin. Aim for soft spots—neck, thigh, inside of the elbow. One prick and they will be on the floor before they know they have been touched."

Knoll studied his with a raised brow. "Palace guards taken down by a hairpin. Who would believe it?"

Hasker let out a quiet chuckle. "Hope they do not make us pay the cleaning fee."

Kedd nodded. "If it works, they will think the gods sent us."

"Or devils," Ruthan muttered.

The first bottle of wine was half-emptied, and the rest was poured onto tunics, cuffs, and the floor. The men began to act the part—shoulders slouching, speech thickening, laughter swelling. Jass had the loudest laugh, a deep belly roar that echoed in the hallway. Tarnel kept hiccupping on purpose, while Kedd spilled half a bottle over Ruthan and blamed it on "slippery fingers."

More wine arrived. The second delivery drew a raised brow from the servant, who now gave a faint, uneasy glance to Lady Haldren. She did not smile. She did not speak. The man bowed stiffly and left without a word.

Lady Haldren sat beside Lyra, quiet but alert. She nursed a half-cup of wine, more for show than for pleasure. Her hand never left the crossbow Jass had brought her earlier in the day.

When Belaric nodded, the men moved.

They filed out in pairs, some arm in arm like old friends staggering from a tavern. They cursed, bumped into walls, spilled their voices across the stone corridors. Dross and Hasker began singing a hunting song with the wrong lyrics. Knoll's hand, holding a pin like a hidden splinter, brushed a passing guard's neck. A faint, almost imperceptible flinch, then the guard continued his walk, a beat behind the others. Ruthan walked with exaggerated care, as if the floor might betray him at any moment. Nollan kept stopping to adjust his boots and shout about "uneven stairs."

Belaric watched from the doorway. One by one, the guards vanished down the corridor.

He turned back to the room. "Lock the door behind me."

Lady Haldren stood. "Anyone who tries to come in who is not you, I will put a bolt through his or her eye."

She meant it.

Lyra stepped forward, her voice trembling despite the strength behind it.

"Please… be careful. Do not let them catch you. Or the others. I know you are good at this, but they are watching everything. If something happens—" She bit her lip, unable to finish.

Belaric turned to her fully, and for a moment, the assassin fell away. What remained was a man burdened by promises he had already broken too many times.

"I will be careful," he said quietly. "And I will let nothing happen to them. Or to you. That is not just a promise—it is a vow," Belaric stated, his voice leaving little room for doubt.

He moved to the door and stepped out.

The door shut with a soft click. A turn of the key locked it tight behind him.

He stood in the hall for a moment, letting his eyes adjust, listening to the muffled echoes of laughter down the far corridor.

A groan followed. Then a heavy thud.

The first guard down.

Belaric drew his hood and melted into the dark.

Belaric moved down the hallway, steps soft, weight on the balls of his feet. He kept close to the wall, skirting the pools of torchlight, breath slow and even. When he rounded the corner, he found the first body—one of the king's guards slumped against the stone, head tilted, mouth slack.

Belaric crouched beside him and pressed two fingers to the man's neck. Still breathing. Pulse steady.

"I am sorry," he murmured under his breath. The man was not the enemy. Just another pawn on a board he did not know he was standing on.

The door beside the guard stood silent. Belaric leaned in, placing his ear near the wood, and listened. Nothing. No breath, no shift, not even the creak of a bedframe. He tested the handle. It gave with barely a whisper. He opened it a finger's width and peered through. A well-furnished room—elegant, expensive, but untouched. No fire lit, no clothes disturbed. The bed had not been slept in.

Empty. The guard had not been protecting a guest. He had been stationed there to watch Belaric and his companions.

Belaric closed the door gently and moved on.

He drifted between shadows, past alcoves and high-arched windows. The palace was quiet. Too quiet. He found more guards—two slumped outside a study, another sitting with head bowed like he had fallen asleep in prayer. He checked them all. Still breathing. His poison had worked—fast, clean, and, if the dose was right, forgetful.

The doors they guarded revealed nothing. Empty rooms. Guest quarters. Unused offices with neatly arranged scrolls and untouched wax seals.

Frustration crept in. He was wasting time. Every second risked one of the guards being found, the entire act unraveling.

At the end of a narrow corridor, he found a door with no guard posted. That alone made him pause. Every other room had been watched. This one stood unprotected. A trap? Or overlooked?

He tested the handle. It turned easily. Inside was a bare office—just a desk, two chairs, and a pair of bookshelves half-filled with dusty volumes. A quill lay on the desk beside a dried-up inkwell. The air smelled of old paper and stone.

Belaric stepped in slowly, gaze scanning corners, under the desk, around the shelves. Nothing. He turned to leave—then stopped.

Voices.

Faint. Muffled. But close.

He turned his head and followed the sound. There—a thin line of warm light glowed at the base of one bookshelf. He knelt and leaned close, careful not to touch the shelf. The light flickered faintly. A secret door. He adjusted his weight and tilted his ear near the seam.

"...why would he summon them to the palace?" said the first voice—frustrated, sharp. "He knows who that man is. He knows what he is capable of. It is foolish."

"I have told you," a second voice answered. Calm. Measured. "He had to. Two failed attempts already. If the king did nothing, the whispers would grow."

"He is acting too rashly," the first snapped. "He wants to send Kesteren with two dozen men and kill them in their sleep. But the queen will not allow it."

"Thank the gods for the queen," the second muttered. "She keeps him leashed, at least for now. We cannot afford mistakes this late."

The first chuckled. "I heard once they confirmed it was him—since then the king has not let Sir Kesteren out of his sight. Man jumps at every shadow."

"I would too," the second said. "He is not just another killer. He was one of the Order's best. Second to none with poisons. The king has every right to be afraid. All it takes is one drop in his wine, and he dies screaming."

Belaric stayed still. The shelf radiated warmth. The voices were real. They knew who he was. All of them did. The queen, too. She was not resisting the king's madness. She was helping to guide the blade.

"What will he do next?" the first asked.

"I do not know. The queen has plans of her own, but she will not reveal them yet."

Footsteps sounded behind him. Belaric turned, dagger drawn in a heartbeat.

The door cracked open. A shadow entered—slow, cautious. Then, there was a familiar shape.

Sir Tolman.

Belaric raised a finger to his lips. Tolman stilled, read the room in seconds, and shut the door quietly. He joined Belaric near the shelf. Belaric pointed to the light, then leaned closer. Tolman followed, face pale in the candle-glow.

"...just to think," the second voice said, more bitter now. "All this over one girl. One stupid girl who could not keep her mouth shut."

The first laughed. "I heard the queen is planning something special for her. Says the little brat disrespected the king. Now she will suffer for it."

"I am not sure," the second replied. "The king wants her dead, but I heard whispers. The queen wants her married off—then ambushed on the road. A hired group of men. The kind who take their time," he paused. "Still untouched, they say. That will draw out the worst of them."

Belaric's grip on his dagger tightened. His mind flickered—to Lyra, sitting by the hearth earlier that evening, her laugh echoing in the chamber. And then the image shifted. Her screaming. Blood on cobblestones.

Sir Tolman lurched forward, hand on his sword.

Belaric caught his arm fast.

The old knight turned, eyes wide and burning. Fury contorted his face, a raw, protective instinct surging to cut down the unseen voices that dared to threaten his ladies.

"…and the mother too," the first voice added, laughing again. "That one's got fire. She will scream loudly."

Sir Tolman jerked against Belaric's grip.

Something was wrong. Too wrong. Why speak so plainly? No guard. Door unlocked. A hidden room designed to leak secrets. Every detail, every cruelty, laid out in the open.

No, not a mistake.

Belaric leaned in to Sir Tolman's ear.

"Think," he whispered. "Why no guard? Why leave the door unlocked? Why speak loud enough to hear but never show themselves?"

Sir Tolman's brow furrowed. His rage dulled, replaced by dawning clarity.

"They want us to listen," Belaric said, barely audible. "But not see."

Sir Tolman's jaw clenched. "A trap."

Belaric nodded.

They backed away together. Belaric cracked the door open and slipped into the hall, Tolman close behind. He eased the door shut and released a slow breath.

Sir Tolman rounded on him. "Are you certain?"

"It is too perfect," Belaric said. "Every detail was meant to draw us in. To make us act. Those men were not alone. I would wager steel waits behind that shelf for anyone who opens it."

Sir Tolman's fists clenched. "Those bastards."

"We can worry about them later," Belaric said. "The entire show might have been to pull us away."

Sir Tolman froze. "Lady Haldren and Lyra," he breathed.

They ran.

Boots striking stone. Shadows whipping past. The corridor stretched longer than it should have. A wrongness gnawed at Belaric's instincts—the rhythm was off, too quiet.

Then he saw it.

The guards he had passed earlier, the ones unconscious—gone. Every last one. No sign of a struggle. Just empty halls and the distant sound of raised voices.

Sir Tolman slowed beside him. "This is not good, Belaric."

As they rounded the last corner, the voices sharpened. The scene ahead stopped them in their tracks.

Belaric's room was blocked. His eight men—Dross, Hasker, Knoll, Ruthan, Nollan, Kedd, Tarnel, and Jass—stood shoulder to shoulder before the door, weapons sheathed but hands resting on hilts. Opposite them, four palace guards faced them down, tension coiled tight. The lead guard, red-faced and shouting, stood inches from Dross, fury in every line of his stance.

"You assaulted the king's men! You will hang for it!" he shouted.

Dross stood like a stone pillar. Arms crossed. Unmoving. "We did no such thing," he said calmly. "It was the assassin you failed to stop. Some guard you are!"

The guard stepped closer, nostrils flaring. His hand dropped to his sword.

"ENOUGH!" Sir Tolman's voice cracked across the hall. The words slammed into the moment like a hammer. All heads turned.

"What is the meaning of this?" Sir Tolman demanded, his gait unshaken as he approached.

The lead guard pointed a finger toward the door. "Your men attacked the king's guards. We are placing them under arrest—and you as well."

Sir Tolman marched straight up to him, eyes hard as stone. Belaric moved behind him, quiet and steady, like a shadow drawn to the storm.

"We have done no such thing," Sir Tolman said, nearly nose-to-nose now.

"Liar," the man spat at him.

"Is this how the king's men act?" Sir Tolman growled. "Fail to stop an assassin, then blame the men protecting the king's guests? How disgraceful."

The palace man grabbed the hilt of his sword, steel sliding an inch free.

"You are all coming with me," he hissed, "or you can die where you stand."

Sir Tolman let out a dry, humorless laugh. "I am a knight of the realm. You have no authority to arrest me. And if you try—" he drew his blade an inch more "—I will cut you down, and your men with you."

But a new voice rang out behind them—cold, commanding.

"I can arrest you."

They turned.

Sir Kesteren strode into the hallway clad in full steel. His helmet was tucked under one arm, his expression sharp as drawn iron. A dozen guards followed behind him in perfect formation.

They stopped just short of Sir Tolman and Belaric, forming an unyielding wall of steel.

"Several of my men were found unconscious," Sir Kesteren said. "And word reached me your guards were seen drunk in the halls, while this man—" he pointed at Belaric "—was nowhere to be seen. Explain that."

Sir Tolman stepped forward, unflinching. "My men were relaxing. They have not had a full night's rest in weeks. I assumed with so many palace guards there was no risk."

He paused, then added with venom, "Clearly, I was wrong. Your men failed. If not for Belaric, Lady Haldren and Lyra would be dead. He chased the assassin off while your guards lay useless."

Belaric blinked. The lie hit him harder than the accusation had. He had not expected that—Sir Tolman lying for him without hesitation. His chest tightened, a quiet ache buried under iron instinct.

One of the palace guards behind Sir Kesteren started to speak, but Sir Kesteren raised a hand, silencing him.

He stepped closer to Sir Tolman, nearly nose to nose. "You expect me to believe that farce?" His voice turned bitter. "I know a killer when I see one."

His finger jabbed toward Belaric again. "And this one reeks of blood."

Sir Tolman did not blink. "You dare question my honor, boy?"

"I am no boy," Sir Kesteren snapped. "You and your men are all coming with me. Now."

Sir Tolman's lips curled into a faint smile. "No," he said. "We are not."

A second passed. Then another.

And then Sir Kesteren moved.

His sword flashed free in a single motion—steel singing in the fire-lit corridor. The sound was met by two dozen more. Every man in the hallway, both sides, drew steel. Torchlight danced across the blades.

Belaric exhaled once.

Then moved.

The hidden blade whispered from under his sleeve as he stepped forward. In a single, fluid motion, he slid past Sir Tolman and brought the point of the blade to rest in the narrow seam between Sir Kesteren's helmet and shoulder guard—just above the artery. Cold steel touched skin.

Everyone froze.

"As Sir Tolman said," Belaric murmured, calm and quiet, "we are not going anywhere. And if you try to force us..." he leaned in, close enough only Kesteren and Tolman could hear him, "I will not hesitate to open your throat. I imagine the princess will be very sad when she hears how easily you died."

He felt a change. Sir Kesteren did not waver, but the silence was different now—fear beneath the armor.

Then—another voice.

"What the hell is going on here?"

It was not a question. It was a command.

They turned.

A tall man marched toward them down the corridor, wrapped in shadows and authority. Long grey hair swept back from a weathered brow. A white beard, perfectly trimmed. His black military uniform shimmered with silver trim, a black cape trailing behind him. The sword at his side looked ceremonial—but it was not.

Lord General Drekken Storn.

A legend. The man had never lost a battle, not in thirty years. Rumor said he bore a hidden forehead mark—that he remembered everything, every formation, every enemy weakness.

Belaric's eyes fell to the man's hand, and there it was—a heavy silver ring, the sigil of his house etched into it. The same broken seal from the letter Lady Haldren had been so quick to hide. He must have been on his way to speak with Lady Haldren, Belaric realized, and walked right into this mess.

The corridor fell silent.

Sir Kesteren stepped back from Belaric's blade and bowed stiffly. So did his men. Even the guards, who had been ready to spill blood seconds ago, backed away.

Belaric lowered his blade. Few men could command a room with such a silent force. Drekken Storn was one of them.

"Lord General," Sir Kesteren began, "I was just questioning Sir Tolman and his men about the attack—"

"Then why," the general interrupted, voice steady and sharp, "do I see blades drawn? Why is there about to be a bloody fight in my fucking hallway?"

Sir Kesteren did not flinch. "My men believed Sir Tolman's men assaulted palace guards. When they refused to come with us, weapons were drawn."

"What proof do you have?" The Lord General demanded.

Sir Kesteren hesitated. Just long enough.

"You have none, do you?" the Lord General snapped. "I spoke with the unconscious guards. They remember nothing. You saw nothing. And now you confront the king's guests—who have been targeted by assassins—and draw blades on them? Is that right?"

Sir Kesteren opened his mouth. "Lord General, this man—"

"Silence." The word cracked like a whip. "I do not want excuses. Get your men and get the fuck out of my sight. You have disgraced the uniform. I will deal with you later. Understood?"

Sir Kesteren's face did not move, but he nodded. After a moment, he turned and led the others away. The corridor remained thick with tension until their footsteps vanished entirely.

Only Belaric, Sir Tolman, the eight guards, and the Lord General remained.

He sighed. "Sir Tolman, I apologize for that disgrace. Can you tell me what happened?"

Sir Tolman bowed. "Lord General, we—"

Click.

The door behind them opened.

Every head turned.

Lady Haldren stepped into the hall with deliberate poise. Her expression was calm, her posture regal, but Belaric saw it in her eyes—the fire, barely contained.

"Lord General," she said smoothly. "I believe I can answer that."

The Lord General stepped forward and offered a shallow bow.

"Lady Haldren," he said with controlled warmth, "I apologize for not coming to see you sooner—and for the disturbance my men caused tonight. I am still gathering the full account of what happened."

Lady Haldren offered him a soft smile, all grace and polish. "Drekken, it is good to see you again. It has been far too long. And there is no need to apologize. Some of your men were attacked tonight—tempers ran high. I understand it well. When I was attacked, I was angry too."

The general nodded slowly, watching her with a tactician's eye—measuring, noting, reading between the lines. But as he did, his gaze lingered on her for a breath, a fleeting flicker of something that Belaric could not quite name—recognition, perhaps, or a shared history that ran deeper than courtly pleasantries. It was gone almost as quickly as it appeared, but Belaric caught it, filed it away.

"I have been told your men claim it was an assassin. Is that true?" he questioned.

She sighed and lowered her gaze for a beat. "Sadly, yes. Earlier today, I gave most of my men the night to rest. They have had little of it in recent weeks. Only Belaric remained behind. We heard a noise outside the door. When he opened it, there was a woman—just a flash of her before she fled. He told us to lock the door and went after her. Not long after, the other men returned. I told them what had happened, and they took up positions outside to protect us."

The general folded his arms as he listened, nodding thoughtfully. His gaze shifted.

"You are Belaric, are you not?" he questioned.

Belaric stepped forward and gave a curt bow. "Yes, Lord General. I am."

"What happened after you gave chase?" he asked.

"I followed her down the hall," Belaric said. "I passed several guards—already unconscious. I wanted to stop and check on them, but I could not risk losing her. She turned down a side passage, and as I went to follow, I collided with Sir Tolman coming from another corridor. He had seen her too."

He paused. "I hit the ground. Sir Tolman helped me up, but by the time we gathered ourselves, she was gone. We searched briefly, but there was no sign of her. We did not want to leave Lady Haldren and Lyra alone for long, so we turned back. On our return, we saw that the guards were no longer where they had fallen. Then we found your men confronting ours outside the room."

The Lord General absorbed it all, face unreadable. Then he turned to Sir Tolman.

"You were with your men but left him alone. Why?" he asked.

Sir Tolman bowed his head. "Because it did not sit right with me. Belaric may be skilled, but exhaustion is a heavy weight—and he has carried more than most. I turned back because no man should carry that alone."

The general nodded, slow and thoughtful, and turned to the others.

"And the rest of you? Why did you return?" he questioned.

Dross stepped forward and lowered his head. "We ran out of wine, Lord General," he said, voice low with staged shame. "We came back for more. That is when we found out what happened."

"I see." He looked at each of them in turn, then finally at Lady Haldren. "Then we were lucky your men were here tonight. I thank them for keeping you safe. I swear I will find the assassin who did this and hang them myself."

Lady Haldren gave him a weary smile. "Thank you, Drekken. You were always a kind man."

He bowed again. "I will place my best men outside your chambers from now on."

But she lifted a hand gently, her tone soft. "Please, no disrespect—but it was my men who saved me tonight. I would prefer to keep them close."

There was a quiet sorrow beneath her words, and it hung in the air.

The general dipped his head. "I understand, my lady. Is there anything else I can do?"

She stepped forward and lightly took his hand in hers. "Yes. Could you ask the king to grant me an audience in the morning? And... have our horses prepared. I do not feel safe here, Drekken. I need to return home."

The general looked down, jaw clenched, eyes heavy with regret. "I understand," he said. "I am sorry I failed you."

She embraced him briefly, gently. "You did not fail me, old friend. The gods just play cruel games."

He held her for a heartbeat longer, then nodded solemnly. "Yes. They do." He stepped back. "I will go now and speak to the king. My men will not trouble you again tonight. Please—get some rest."

"Thank you, Drekken," she told him.

They bowed to one another, and he turned without another word, cloak trailing behind him like an omen. They waited until the sound of his boots faded entirely.

Lady Haldren let out a long breath. "Let us all rest. We will speak more in the morning." Her voice was calm but firm. "We have had enough excitement for one night."

The men gave nods of agreement and began peeling away toward their quarters. Lyra lingered for a moment beside her mother, eyes shadowed, lips pressed in a line. She had not spoken since the door opened, but her fingers trembled faintly where they clutched her sleeve. Belaric saw it—and remembered the trap, the voices, the cruelty behind the wall.

He watched until they vanished into their room. Then, with nothing left to do, he turned toward his own.

Inside, the chamber was cold and still.

Belaric sat on the edge of the bed for a long while, staring at the door, expecting it to open again. Expecting a soldier, a blade, another game. None came.

Eventually, he lay back and stared at the ceiling.

He still could not believe the lie had held. Or at least... seemed to. The Lord General had sounded sincere, but a man like that always kept a layer hidden beneath whatever mask he wore. Whether he had believed the tale or simply played along—it was impossible to say.

He had lied before. Killed for less. But something in him twisted at the sound of Sir Tolman's voice defending him.

Not regret. Not yet. But something dangerously close to it.

He closed his eyes.

The morning sun crept into Belaric's room like a quiet intruder, slipping past the curtains to lay warm fingers across his face. He blinked, groaned, and forced himself upright with a sigh. Sleep had come quickly, but it had not washed the weight from his limbs.

They would leave soon. He doubted the king would let them go without a last word—perhaps a farewell, perhaps a threat dressed as civility. Then came the road. Days of hard riding. He hoped that the horses had recovered enough to carry them without injury. They would need to check their supplies. Food, water, spare arms. Anything not locked away or stripped in the night.

Belaric dressed quickly in his guard attire; the familiar weight of it grounded him. He strapped his sword to his hip and slid two daggers into the sheaths beneath his tunic; the others tucked into his pack with the precision of a man who had done this a hundred times. He slung the pack over his shoulder and took one last look around the room.

It was easily the finest he had ever stayed in. Clean stonework, thick carpets, silk sheets. A carved headboard and a view that reached the distant river. A room not meant for men like him. He wondered if he had ever sleep in a place like this again.

He stepped into the corridor and made his way to Lady Haldren's chamber.

A single knock.

"Enter," came her voice through the door.

He stepped inside. Lady Haldren and Lyra were already seated at the table, drinking tea. They looked composed—too composed, given the night they had.

"Good morning, my lady," he said, setting his pack down beside the door and closing it behind him.

"Good morning, Belaric," she said warmly. "Please join us. How did you sleep?"

"Well enough," he replied, crossing the room and taking a seat beside Lyra.

She glanced at him, offering a faint smile, but there were dark circles under her eyes. Her hands, though still, were clenched around the rim of her cup, the tea inside growing cold. She had not touched it. Her gaze seemed fixed on something beyond the walls, with a haunted quality in her usual bright eyes. Her silence felt heavier than usual. Belaric saw it, an icy knot forming in his gut. The whispers from that hidden room had been meant to wound, and Lyra, with her sharp mind, had likely replayed every cruel word about her fate.

"I have sent for breakfast," Lady Haldren said. "We will eat before meeting the king. Best to ensure we are all on the same page."

Belaric nodded, and the conversation drifted into idle chatter. The sort spoken to fill silence. Lyra made a tired joke about one guard snoring like a dying bear. It earned a weak laugh from Lady Haldren. Belaric said little.

Strange, he thought. There was a time he would have trusted no one at this table. Now, their silence felt like armor.

A knock at the door interrupted them.

Two young servant girls entered, heads bowed, and set trays on the table before withdrawing without a word. Fried eggs, a bread trencher piled with spiced sausage, wild greens glistening in garlic oil, and a jug of cold water.

Moments later, the door opened again. This time, slower.

Sir Tolman stepped in, looking like he had not slept at all. His shoulders sagged, and his eyes were red and dull. He shut the door quietly.

"What happened to you?" Belaric asked, watching him approach.

Sir Tolman sighed and rubbed a hand through his gray-streaked hair. "I was worried they would come again in the night. I stayed up listening. Ear to the door for most of it."

Lady Haldren exhaled. "Thank you, Sir Tolman. I only hope you have the strength to ride today."

"I will manage," he muttered, sitting down at the table.

They filled their plates in silence. The smell of warm food filled the room, but no one ate quickly. Weariness had replaced their hunger.

After a few bites, Lady Haldren raised her cup. "First, I must thank you again, Sir Tolman. I know it was difficult—what you said last night. But it may have saved us all."

Tolman stared at his plate. "It went against everything I stand for. I was taught to speak the truth, no matter the cost. But last night... truth would have gotten us killed. I hated lying. But I understand now why it was necessary."

He looked around the table. "We are surrounded by enemies. If we do not hold together, we will be torn apart. The less others know, the better. I just hope we do not make a habit of it."

There was a quiet murmur of agreement. Even Lyra nodded, still clinging to her untouched cup.

"We are not the ones who should feel shame," she whispered. "They are."

Lady Haldren placed a hand gently over her daughter's.

Then she set down her cup and straightened in her chair. Her voice was firm.

"The king will ask questions," she said. "We need to agree on the answers before he does."

30

The corridor stretched before them like a throat waiting to swallow. Lady Haldren led the way, her stride sharp, her chin high. She moved with the calm of a woman who had already decided what must be done and would not be swayed. Belaric followed just behind, his hand never straying far from the hilt of his hidden blade. They would leave soon—if the gods permitted. He could feel the lie hardening inside him, a bitter taste he was already growing accustomed to. Their lives now hung on threads of deception and the shifting winds of royal whim.

He had already dispatched a servant to check the horses, ensure they were fed and saddled and that someone had loaded their packs. Sir Tolman had made one last round to ensure Dross, and the men were prepared. Brookhaven awaited. If they were lucky, they would reach it before another blade found their throats.

When they reached the great doors of the throne room—the same ones that had opened on their arrival—Belaric felt the tension thicken. Sir Kesteren was notably absent, replaced by two unfamiliar guards in polished breastplates. Silent, statuesque. He and Sir Tolman relinquished their weapons without protest. Rituals mattered in these halls, and survival often depended on appearances.

Inside, people already crowded the hall. Nobles in embroidered silks stood in clusters, murmuring like vultures deciding who would die next. Royal guards lined the walls. Too many eyes. Too many blades.

The king sat slumped on his throne, like a man burdened by his own crown. His face, however, held no weariness—only annoyance, sharpened by something deeper. Something hungry. The Lord General stood a few paces to his right, hands folded neatly behind his back, offering Lady Haldren a smile that did not reach his eyes. Belaric caught a fleeting, analytical glint in the Lord General's gaze as it passed over him, assessing everything, missing nothing. This was a man who understood the unseen forces at play.

The four stopped short of the dais and dropped to their knees. The stone was cold beneath Belaric's joints.

"Ah, Lady Haldren," the king said, his voice edged with disdain. "I hear you had a rather eventful night."

He did not tell them to rise.

"Yes, my king," Lady Haldren answered, her tone level. "Another assassin came for us. This one slipped past the palace guards."

A ripple moved through the nobles like wind through dry leaves. Gasps. Murmurs. A few exchanged knowing glances. Blood was always more interesting when it spilled in court.

Belaric closed his eyes. Say too much and you risk a cell—or worse. Say too little, and the game continues with sharper stakes.

"Is that so?" the king said, contempt thickening his voice. "I find it difficult to believe that a lone assassin whose aim was your death—and your daughter's—undid the finest guards in the realm."

Lady Haldren rose. The silence that followed crackled with disapproval and expectation.

"Yes, my...king," she said, biting each word. "An assassin passed several of your guards and attempted to enter my chamber. My men drove her off. And then your guards—the same men who failed—threatened my men and accused them of assaulting them with no proof. One so bold even threatened to arrest Sir Tolman. I was unaware a simple soldier had the right to arrest a knight, or question the honor of a guest of the crown."

Belaric lifted his gaze slightly. The king's knuckles had gone white against the armrest. His breath was shallow, controlled rage waiting to rupture. Around them, the nobles watched like wolves sniffing out weakness.

"You dare insult me?" the king roared, rising from the throne and descending the steps like a drawn sword.

"My king—" the Lord General began.

"SILENCE!"

The Lord General's jaw tightened, a muscle in his cheek twitching once before his expression settled back into impassive stone. His eyes, however, briefly met Lady Haldren's—a silent, almost imperceptible flicker of understanding or warning that passed between them before the king's next breath.

The king halted just before Lady Haldren, close enough to strike. She did not flinch.

"I speak only the truth," she said. "There was another attempt on my life. Your men failed in their charge. Mine did not."

With a single step closer, Belaric was already shifting his weight—calculating distance, checking angles. He could strike the king once, maybe twice. Then, they would all die. Kings, queens, masks of civility. The crown was just another blade—worn at the throat instead of the hip.

But a voice, sharp as steel, cut through the air.

"Husband."

The queen strode in like a storm given flesh. Her gown swept behind her like banners in retreat. She placed herself between the king and Lady Haldren with the grace of someone used to stopping wars.

"We are all tense," she said, her voice calm and cold. "Yes, an assassin reached our guests. Yes, our men failed. And yes, we have shamed ourselves in the eyes of those we vowed to protect."

She turned to Lady Haldren and offered a slight bow.

"Rise, all of you. Please."

Belaric, Lyra, and Sir Tolman stood. Lady Haldren bowed low.

"My queen... I let fear rule my tongue. I wished only to protect my daughter." She told her.

The queen stepped forward and embraced her.

"If I were in your place, I would have done worse," she said.

Behind them, the king exhaled sharply.

"My wife, ever the peacemaker," he muttered. "She is right, of course. I apologize—for my outburst and for the actions of my men."

"There is no need for apology, my king," Lady Haldren said, though her voice carried iron beneath the silk.

He tilted his head. "Why do I get the sense there is more you have to say, Lady Haldren?" the king asked.

"I fear it is time we returned to Brookhaven," she said. "The longer we remain, the greater the risk. They will come again, and I would rather greet them on ground I know."

Before the king could respond, the queen spoke.

"Then let us help. We can have an escort prepared within minutes."

Lady Haldren shook her head. "Too many swords will draw eyes. We intend to ride hard and fast."

"At least let us provide supplies," the king offered, his voice quieting. "You will need them."

Lady Haldren inclined her head. "We appreciate your generosity."

After a few more brittle farewells, the four turned and walked from the hall. The nobles watched them go with the quiet hatred of those who had just witnessed someone win.

The courtyard was already in motion. Dross stood with his men, armor gleaming, horses saddled, the carriage hitched and waiting. Belaric exchanged nods with the captain. No words. They had no more to waste.

The supplies arrived shortly after—sacks of dried meat, flasks of water and wine, a few cloaks for the road.

They mounted.

Brookhaven lay far to the south. Home, if any place still earned the word.

The wind came from the south, strange and warm. It carried the scent of distant fires.

Belaric adjusted his reins.

He did not look back.

The journey home stretched like a taut wire—tight, fraying at the edges. Every man rode with his hand near steel, eyes scanning the hills, minds full of ghosts. More than once, Belaric expected to hear the thunder of hooves behind them and see the king's banners tearing down the road in pursuit. But the only sounds were the wind and the groans of tired horses.

They followed the same road they had taken days before, though it felt longer now, narrower somehow. The carriage could not keep pace, but they pushed it anyway, as if speed might outrun fate. Belaric rode near the back, always watching the trail behind them. Twice he thought he saw movement—shadows darting between the trees, figures at the edge of vision. But each time he turned, there was nothing.

Still, the feeling of being watched never left him.

He spoke of it to Sir Tolman that night beside the fire, and the old knight did not scoff. Instead, he checked his sword and whispered to Dross. The men doubled their vigilance, hands resting on hilts even as they slept. But the attack never came.

When they finally passed under the worn wooden archway into Brookhaven, the sun already slanting from its highest point, their weariness hung on them like a second cloak. The guards at the gate stood tall. The townsfolk gathered in the streets to cheer their return—though the joy felt strange, distant. Belaric had not expected it. He did not know whether they deserved it.

The town had changed. There were more people now—unfamiliar faces, unfamiliar eyes. The air, once filled with the familiar scents of wood smoke and hearth fires, now carried the clamor of strange tongues and the unwashed smell of desperation. Over a dozen merchant carts choked the alleys, their wares stacked high. Travelers, refugees, opportunists. And more men had arrived asking to join the guard. Some looked eager. Others… too eager.

One man caught Belaric's eye. He stood near the stables, lean and weathered, his tunic plain, sword belted low. He smiled too easily. When he noticed Belaric watching, he looked away too quickly.

Belaric narrowed his eyes. "Too many eyes," he muttered. "Too many knives."

It would be a problem for tomorrow.

They reached the estate within minutes. Rusk and his stable hand took the reins wordlessly, leading the horses away as the riders dismounted with groans and stiff limbs. Lyra and Lady Haldren said little. As they reached the doors of their chamber, Lyra leaned her head briefly against her mother's shoulder, a silent acknowledgment of the tightrope they had just walked. Both vanished quickly into the estate, seeking hot water and silence.

Belaric and Sir Tolman lingered at the doors. The men were told to rest. There would be no rest for them.

As they stood watch beneath the slow-dimming sky, Belaric leaned close.

"We were followed," he said. "On the road, maybe even before. I felt eyes on us the moment we crossed the gate—and not the kind that cheer."

Sir Tolman nodded grimly. "I know. If they are watching, they are waiting for something."

Belaric did not answer. He did not need to.

"We spring the trap before they do," Sir Tolman whispered.

And so they laid it. Belaric spoke low, and quickly, drawing rough lines in the dirt with the tip of his knife. Sir Tolman nodded with each detail, offering a few refinements of his own. They would use the estate's walls, the stable paths, even the blind spots. Tonight, the hunters would become prey.

As the sun sank, they roused the men. Quiet words, steady hands. Positions were taken under the cover of darkness. Torches were lit in some places, left cold in others. Shadows stretched long over Brookhaven.

Later, in his room, Belaric stood before the hook where his assassin's garb still hung. It looked heavier than he remembered. A second skin, black as night and twice as cruel.

He sighed and ran his fingers over the fabric, the worn edges, the silent seams that had once made him a ghost in the dark.

He prayed he would never have to wear it again.

But prayers were for men who had not already damned themselves.

He dressed slowly, each strap and buckle a memory. He remembered the first time he had worn it—young, eager, unknowing. Back when it had been a tool. Before it became a mirror.

Now it reminded him only of the monster he used to be.

When he stepped outside, the air had turned cold. The estate was quiet, unnatural in its stillness. But the men were ready. They waited in silence. Eyes open. Blades drawn.

Belaric moved to his position.

And then they waited.

They stood by in silence, each breath stretched thin by anticipation. Shadows clung to the walls like ghosts unwilling to leave. The hearth crackled in the corner, its fire gnawing at half-burnt logs. Across the room, Lady Haldren and Lyra sat cross-legged near the flames, playing Crowns Fall in near silence—each move more distraction than strategy. Sir Tolman stood with his back to the door, one hand resting on the pommel of his sword, still as stone.

Belaric crouched behind a bookcase, blade drawn, eyes narrowed to slits. He had begun to wonder if he had been wrong—if the trap had been set for no one. Then he heard it. Soft. Measured. The faint whisper of footfalls gliding over the woven rug.

He leaned forward, silent. Two shadows slipped inside—quick and low. A third followed moments later, slower, but more assured. He waited. They needed to be deep enough. No chance to flee. When they were only a few strides from Sir Tolman's back, Belaric hissed, "Now."

The trap sprang.

Dross and Hasker lunged from either side of the entrance, slamming the doors shut with a thunderous boom. A thick wooden bar dropped into place behind them. Torches blazed to life from the upper balcony—Jass, Kedd, and Tarnel lighting pitch-soaked cloth and leveling crossbows downward. From behind, Knoll, Ruthan, and Nollan emerged from the gloom, torches in hand, flanking the assassins in a semicircle.

Sir Tolman turned, calm and grim. "Welcome," he said.

Belaric stepped from the shadows, his boots silent on the wood, sword already drawn. The three intruders froze. One of them—tall, thick-shouldered—let out a low, rasping laugh.

Belaric's grip tightened. "Dainrik."

The laughter stopped. "I knew you would be ready," Dainrik said. "Told them so. They did not listen. Thought you would be asleep, or stupid. Turns out, only they are."

The two beside him turned sharply. "You knew?" one hissed.

Dainrik did not flinch. "Quiet."

"It was foolish to come here," Belaric said.

"Maybe," Dainrik replied, giving a one-shouldered shrug. "But we came to kill you."

"And now you will die instead," Belaric replied.

"I knew the moment I walked through the door. It stank of torches and death."

Belaric paused, eyes locked onto Dainrik's. "You were always smarter than the rest. So tell me—why?"

"Why, what?" he asked.

"You let me live. You saw the blade tucked in my belt when I was bound. You looked right at it—and said nothing. Why?" he demanded.

The two assassins beside Dainrik stiffened. "You what?" one snapped.

"I said quiet," Dainrik snapped back, before turning to Belaric again. His laugh was a dry, rasping sound. "Because Orris was filth. And you were my key."

Belaric said nothing. Dainrik continued, his voice rough with bitter resentment.

"For years, they made me their hound. Guard the doors. Train the children. Kill the weak. While you were out there, a shadow amongst the darkness, doing proper work. I watched Orris. Saw the things he did when he thought no one was watching. And when you landed in his cage, I saw my chance to finally get free of that damned hall."

"They blamed me for your escape," he continued. "Knew they would. But I offered a solution—let me fix it. Let me finish the job. Said you were my failure to fix. So they did. My ticket out."

Belaric's gaze hardened. "You begged them to let you come here only to die."

"Better than dying there," Dainrik stated flatly. He glanced around the room at the weapons trained on him. "So this is how it ends? A bolt to the chest? Hah. Still wondering, are you not?"

Belaric did not move. Sir Tolman glanced his way. "What is he saying?"

"He wants to know," Dainrik answered, eyes still on Belaric.

Lady Haldren stood. "Know what?"

"Which one of us is better," Dainrik said. "We were always rivals. I won the last fight—but he was injured. Now he is not. He is wondering whether he can beat me."

Lady Haldren scoffed. "He is not that foolish. Just kill this filth and be done with it."

Around the room, fingers hovered near triggers—but Belaric raised his hand. Everyone froze.

He looked around—Sir Tolman's disapproval, Lyra's wide-eyed fear, the flicker of disbelief in Dross's face—and settled back on Dainrik. This had always been coming. There was no escaping the shadow of his past. Not while Dainrik still lived.

"Just me and you," Belaric said, voice cold.

Sir Tolman stepped forward. "You cannot be serious."

"I am." He drew his sword. "This is my fight."

Lady Haldren took a step toward him. "You have already proven yourself. Do not let him drag you back into that world."

Belaric looked at her—truly looked—then turned back to Dainrik. "It is already too late."

Dainrik nodded and stepped toward Dross, slowly and deliberate. Dross tensed, confused, as Dainrik extended a hand—not for a strike, but toward the sword at Dross's waist. Dross looked to Belaric, uncertain.

Belaric gave a small nod.

Reluctantly, Dross unsheathed the blade and handed it over. Dainrik tested the weight, spun it once in his hand, then returned to stand several paces from Belaric.

The fire crackled in the hearth. No one moved.

Belaric stepped forward, sword held low, breathing steadily. This was it. No more shadows. No more masks. Only steel—and whatever truth lay waiting at the edge of it.

The two men blurred into motion.

They struck fast and hard, blades flashing in torchlight, each movement a calculated test of the other's guard. Belaric lashed out with honed precision, but Dainrik was faster than memory. Dainrik answered every strike. Every parry countered. Sparks leapt from clashing blades, and blood began to trace thin lines down arms and ribs. The cuts were not deep—but they were reminders that the margin for error was shrinking with every breath.

After a minute of this deadly dance, Belaric exhaled sharply. "Can we stop pretending?"

Dainrik barked a ragged laugh, blood running from a nick above his eye. "Finally."

They exploded into full combat. No caution now—only fury. Dainrik came forward with brute force, his sword carving through the air. Belaric answered with speed, ducking and weaving, blades screaming as they collided. Every blow came intending to kill. Their blades locked, twisted, broke apart, only to crash together again. Belaric turned a low strike and countered with a slash to the thigh, but Dainrik caught it with the flat of his blade and shoved back.

The second lock nearly broke him. Dainrik bore down with brute strength, and Belaric could feel the strain in his arms. With a violent push, Dainrik threw him off. Belaric stumbled. He lifted his blade to block the follow-up, but the angle was off. When their swords met again, Dainrik's power shattered the guard. Belaric's sword flew from his hands, skittering across the stone floor.

Dainrik surged forward with another killing blow, but Belaric dropped to a roll, avoiding the strike by inches. He came up on one knee, breath tight, ribs aching. Dainrik laughed, circling now.

Without a word, he tossed his own blade aside. It spun point-first into the floor.

"No tricks. Even ground," he said, spitting blood.

He charged.

They slammed together like beasts. Fists crashed into ribs, elbows into jaws. Dainrik's size gave him power, but Belaric moved like a coiled serpent—fast, reactive, relentless. He ducked under a wide hook and drove his shoulder into Dainrik's chest, staggering him. But Dainrik recovered, throwing a heavy knee into Belaric's side that made the world flash white. They broke apart only to clash again. A headbutt from Belaric cracked Dainrik's nose; blood gushed freely. Dainrik grinned through it.

They circled again, both swaying, bruised and heaving. Belaric reached behind his back and drew his daggers—one in each hand. The blades glinted in the firelight.

Dainrik grinned. "Finally."

He mirrored the motion, pulling twin blades of his own.

They collided once more. This time, there was no finesse—only murder. Steel flashed in tight arcs, hands moving in bursts of precision. Belaric gave ground and absorbed minor cuts to stay alive—a slice across the forearm, a graze along the ribs. He could not afford to meet Dainrik's strength head-on. Instead, he dodged wide swings and punished every mistake with stabs of his own. Both men bled freely, their steps smearing red across the floor.

Then Belaric feinted. He dipped low, flicked his left-hand blade forward in a fast throw. Dainrik reacted instantly, knocking it from the air.

That was the mistake Belaric needed.

He surged in. The dagger in his right hand drove deep into Dainrik's stomach. The larger man gasped, staggered. Before he could recover, Belaric hooked his leg and slammed him to the ground. The impact shook the hall. Dainrik's daggers flew from his hands as his body hit the floor in a spray of blood.

They both lay still for a moment.

Then Dainrik coughed, wet and sharp, and laughed.

"You were always faster than me," he rasped, voice trembling. "You little shit."

He coughed again—blood trickling from the corner of his mouth.

"Do me one favor. Do not bury me like the rest of those fools. Burn me. Old friend."

Belaric stared down at him for a long second. Then he nodded.

Dainrik's chest rose once. Shuddered.

Then it stopped.

Belaric stood, bleeding and breathless. The room was silent. Not even the fire cracked. All eyes were on him. Lyra stood pale near the hearth, frozen in place, tears slipping silently down her cheeks. Lady Haldren stepped beside her, placing a steadying hand on her shoulder. Sir Tolman's jaw was clenched. No one moved.

Belaric turned to the two remaining assassins.

"You will get no mercy," he said, voice like stone.

He gave the order with a single word.

"Fire."

Crossbows thudded. The assassins dropped where they stood, bolts buried deep. A second later, the guards rushed in and finished the job with steel. Quick. Merciless. Done.

Belaric let out a breath. His tunic clung to him, soaked through. Blood ran down both arms, along his ribs, into his boots. He needed stitching. He needed rest. But not yet.

He crossed to the table, sat slowly in one of the chairs, and grabbed the nearest bottle of wine. He drank straight from the neck, the liquid spilling a little across his chin. Still, no one spoke.

Finally, he lowered the bottle and stared at the room.

"Put their bodies on display," he said. "Let the world see."

The guards nodded and moved—but when they reached Dainrik's body, Belaric's voice stopped them.

"Not him," he stated flatly.

They turned, confused.

Lady Haldren frowned. "Why?"

Belaric looked at her, then at Sir Tolman, then at Lyra.

"I am alive because of that man," he said. "You are too. He was cruel. A killer. But he made a choice—and because of it, we are standing here. He asked for one thing."

His voice hardened.

"I will honor it," he whispered.

Lady Haldren gave a slow nod. No one argued. No one touched Dainrik again.

Outside, the wind scraped against the windows.

Belaric sat still, the warmth of the fire barely touching him. He stared into the flame, the wine bottle still in his hand, its label stained with blood.

Belaric sat at the table for hours, unmoving. Around him, the others moved with quiet purpose—removing the bodies, scrubbing blood from the stone, extinguishing torches. No one spoke to him, and he did not offer a word in return. The wine bottle rested in his hand, half-empty, forgotten.

When the sun finally crept through the high windows and brushed pale gold across the hall, Belaric stirred. He set the bottle down with a soft clink, stood, and stretched his aching limbs. Pain flared through his body—stiff joints, torn muscle, shallow cuts that burned from dried sweat and blood—but he ignored it.

He crossed the room and bent beside Dainrik's body. With a grunt, he hoisted the man onto his shoulder. His body screamed in protest, but he did not stop. One foot in front of the other, he carried Dainrik outside.

The morning was quiet. Cold.

He found a small clearing just beyond the edge of the estate, where the trees broke enough to let in light, but still offered solitude. There, he laid Dainrik down. He returned to the estate and gathered wood from the storage stacks—thick pieces for the base, smaller ones for kindling. He built a pyre with slow, deliberate care, stacking the wood in tight, clean layers.

Once it was ready, he looked down at the body.

Then he turned and walked back inside.

He changed out of his blood-soaked clothes, standing shirtless before a cracked mirror in the hall. Bruises bloomed across his ribs and shoulders. His arms were sliced and swollen. He washed what he could, then forced himself to dress—simple clothes, plain and honest. No armor. No knives.

He returned to the pyre and placed Dainrik's body atop the wood. Then, without ceremony, he took his assassin's garb—black leather worn thin from years of use, blades still tucked into the folds—and laid it over the corpse.

He retrieved a small flask of oil, poured it across the body and the garb, then lit a lantern from the estate wall and carried it back to the clearing. With one final breath, he lit a stick from the flame and tossed it onto the pyre.

The oil caught immediately. Fire surged to life with a roar, devouring cloth, wood, and flesh alike.

Belaric did not flinch. He felt a strange, cleansing heat rise from the pyre, burning away not just the fabric, but years of clinging darkness. He stood there, watching as the flames licked higher, feeding on his past.

He did not hear Lyra approach until she was beside him.

"You honor a man you hated?" she asked, her voice soft, uncertain.

Belaric nodded, eyes still on the flames. "We knew each other for fifteen years. Most days we fought—sparring, dueling, always trying to prove who was better. In the end, we both knew the truth. He just wanted to choose how it ended." His voice dropped quiet. "And I owed him for that night. He gave me a chance. He did not have to."

Lyra was quiet for a moment. "And the armor?"

"It is a symbol," Belaric said. "Of who I was. I am not that man anymore. I cannot keep dragging it behind me. If I want to bring them into the light—I cannot still live in the shadows."

His tone was resolute. Final.

Lyra nodded. "I am proud of you, Belaric. You have proven time and again that you are a good man. We would be lost without you."

He glanced at her, then let a faint smile tug at the corner of his mouth. "I would not go that far. You are clever. Your mother's fearless. And Sir Tolman is the stubbornest knight I have ever met. You would have been fine."

She reached out and took his hand. "We both know that is not true."

Their eyes met for a moment, and the silence between them said the rest.

Belaric turned back to the fire. The flames were lower now, the body half-consumed. The assassin's garb had vanished in the blaze, reduced to drifting smoke and ash.

They stood in silence as the pyre burned down to coals. An hour passed. Neither spoke.

"Goodbye, old friend," Belaric whispered when only ashes remained.

Belaric turned. Lyra followed. Together, they walked back to the estate.

And behind them, the smoke of another life curled into the morning sky.

The bathwater had long gone cold, but Belaric remained still beneath the surface. The warmth had helped briefly, easing the knots in his back and softening the sting of his bruises. But it had not lasted. Pain clung to him in quiet places—beneath the ribs, along the shoulder, behind the eyes. He scrubbed away dried blood, flakes of ash, and the soot that still clung to his skin from the pyre. The scent of smoke had soaked into him, as if the fire refused to let him go.

He ran a cloth down the fresh cuts that lined his arms and chest, flinching only slightly as the linen met raw skin. Some wounds were shallow, but a few would need tending. He rose out of the water slowly and dried himself in silence. Once dressed, he sat before a small table near the window and stitched the worst of the gashes himself—jaw clenched, hands steady from years of practice. He had learned long ago not to wait for someone else to patch him up.

A quiet knock interrupted his thoughts. He did not answer, but a moment later he heard the soft thud of something being slipped under the door. When he opened it, he found a single folded letter—no name on the front, just a black wax seal stamped with a sigil he had not seen in years.

He opened it slowly.

The handwriting was unmistakable: clean, deliberate, sharp as a blade. It belonged to a man named Lurell Vane—an old acquaintance from his old life, a former informant turned schemer. The letter was brief, but dense. Belaric had offered payment for information. He knew he could not trust him; the man was only loyal to coin, but he needed information. He read the letter slowly.

The first one is on the house for an old friend; anything more than the normal rate, you know where to find me.

Belaric read it twice, then folded it and tucked it into the inside pocket of his coat. He was not ready—not yet. But the world was moving, and he would need eyes when it did.

Later that day, as the sun slanted westward, he walked the perimeter of the estate, taking quiet note of how much had changed. Brookhaven had grown—more than he expected. The streets were busier now, crowded with merchants and craftsmen and refugees who had heard whispers of safety. The sound of hammering echoed from the south end, where workers were building new homes, their frames rising like skeletal arms toward the sky. Barracks were being erected near the main gate, and walls reinforced with timber and stone. Dozens of new recruits were drilling in the dirt yard—Sir Tolman's voice barked orders from the center.

Belaric nodded to him as he passed, and Sir Tolman gave a small salute in return.

Along the eastern tree line, the bodies of the assassins still hung from a twisted oak—a warning to any who would come in the night. Some townsfolk turned their eyes away when they passed. Others did not.

Word had spread. Brookhaven was becoming more than a village. It was becoming a symbol. A place that defied silence. A place that had bled and survived.

By the time the sun had reached the horizon, Belaric had made his way to the top of a small grassy hill just outside the northern edge of the town. From there, he could see everything—the rooftops catching firelight, the smoke curling from chimneys, the outline of the Hollowood in the distance.

He stood there as the sky dimmed, turning orange, then deep red, then violet. The light touched his face, warm and soft. His arms were crossed, his thoughts heavier than the armor he no longer wore.

He thought of Renna. Her laugh. Her stubbornness. The way she had looked at him with eyes that saw the man beneath the shadow. He could still see her holding Eryndorr in her arms, breath shallow, skin pale, whispering his name before the gods took her.

Belaric closed his eyes. He did not speak her name aloud. He did not have to. The silence between them had said enough.

He mourned her still—every morning he woke and every night he did not die. That would not change.

But now there was only one promise left to keep.

He would find Eryndorr.

No matter where the Vowkeeper had hidden him, no matter what lies the masters wove to keep the child from the truth—he would find his son.

He had failed once. He would not do it again.

Belaric turned, the last light of the sun brushing against his back, and made his way down the hill—back toward Brookhaven, back toward the firelight.

And behind him, the sky burned like a vow unbroken.

Epilogue

Belaric stood at the edge of a cobbled lane, the salt-bitten wind catching the edge of his cloak. Before him, Avenmar sprawled in dusky layers, the town carved into the sloping cliffs where the eastern sea beat itself against stone. A few thousand called it home—fishermen, merchants, petty nobles clinging to titles worth less than the silver used to mint them. The city had grown in halves: to the south, timber homes stacked like driftwood, narrow alleys crawling with hawkers and smoke. To the north, the noble quarter crowned a series of stepped terraces, dotted with manicured hedges and wrought-iron gates that did little to keep rot from seeping in.

He had always liked it here. A town big enough to disappear in, but not so large that your enemies vanished first. He once dreamed of boarding a ship from Avenmar's harbor with Renna and Eryndorr—any vessel heading west, away from the blood and the vows. He pictured Renna laughing, her red hair torn loose by the sea wind. He imagined Eryndorr wrapped in a woolen blanket, reaching for the gulls overhead with clumsy, eager hands. The boy would be eight months old now. Likely crawling. Maybe pulling himself upright on a table leg, wide-eyed and full of wonder.

If the gods had not turned cruel.

He remembered how Renna had held Eryndorr that first night, the child's breath shallow, his fingers no thicker than a reed. She had cried—not from pain, but wonder.

"He is perfect," she had whispered.

Belaric had said nothing. He had not trusted the world not to steal that moment. And it had.

He exhaled slowly. There was no room for dreams anymore. Renna was ash. Eryndorr had been taken by wolves dressed in men's robes. But he would find the boy. No matter how deep the pit or how sharp the teeth waiting within. And today, he would drag those teeth into the light.

This was no coincidence. He had planned for weeks, and Lady Haldren had given her blessing. She understood what had to be done.

The Order Hall in Avenmar had kept quiet since Dainrik's death a few months ago. No whispers. No sightings. No retaliation. It was not weakness. It was patience. And Belaric had run out of his.

So he would force their hand.

Brookhaven had grown in the meantime. What had been a quiet hamlet with a few dozen souls now swelled with over three hundred. New homes were being raised, timber wagons rolling in by the week. A barracks stood behind Lady Haldren's estate, home to thirty trained guards loyal to her and her alone. Trade followed the coin, and coin followed her name—merchants now came willingly, drawn by the promise of safety and the favor of a noble unbound by the king's leash. Salted meats, fine cloth, tools, and grain all passed through Brookhaven's gates. The markets bustled where once there had been silence. Children played in the fields near the orchard now, shouting names he did not know. Wess the baker rose before the sun to fill the square with the scent of cinnamon and ash. Even the guards had begun to laugh again—some with scars from battles fought under torchlight. Brookhaven lived. And living things were worth protecting.

Other lords and ladies—disillusioned with the crown, drawn by Haldren's defiance—continued to arrive, cloaking their ambition in courtesy. They drank her wine, nodded to her cause, and whispered her name in halls far beyond Brookhaven's borders.

But none of them had brought him closer to the Vowkeeper. Or to his son.

So tonight, Belaric would stoke the fire himself.

He had spent the last hours leaning in shadow, eyes fixed on the narrow three-story house that passed for a spice merchant's storehouse. None of the townsfolk paid him any mind—a guard off-duty, a traveler loitering. He watched the flow of people thin as dusk fell; the light fading to a copper wash over slate roofs. He needed the crowd to vanish just enough to move, yet remain just enough to witness.

A guardsman paused five feet from him, armor creaking as he turned to scan the square. Belaric did not move. He had spent years learning how to be unseen without vanishing. The trick was not in hiding—it was in blending.

"Evening," the man muttered to no one in particular, then turned and walked on.

Belaric allowed himself to breathe again.

Six hours earlier, he had barred the secret exits beneath the Order Hall. Locked them with iron pins. Buried some. Jammed others. If they tried to flee below, they would find nothing but stone and silence.

The assassin he had killed last night was still down there. Slumped in the passage, garbed in black, the blood crusted around his throat where Belaric's knife had gone in. No one had come for the body. No one would risk daylight. Even ghosts knew better than to rise under an open sky.

As the last sliver of sun kissed the rooftops, Belaric moved.

He passed the grocer's stall and stepped into the abandoned shop beside it. Dust coated every shelf. Crates of rotted fruit sat forgotten. The trapdoor behind the counter opened with a groan, and he knelt to stare into the dark. The smell of death greeted him.

He poured oil in slow, practiced sweeps—over the floorboards, the walls, across curtains and crates. When the last drop fell, he lit a torch and stood at the doorway.

"Let them crawl up into the fire," he muttered.

Flame bloomed behind him as he slipped into the alley, the torch tossed to the floor like a curse cast backward. Within minutes, orange light clawed through the windows, smoke curling up toward the noble quarter. Screams rang out. A woman called for water. A child cried. Boots thundered on the street. The town's guards arrived in droves, buckets in hand, forming lines as they tried to save a building already too far gone.

They doused half the structure before the roof collapsed inward with a groan. That was enough.

Belaric watched from the dark, unseen as ever. They would search. They would find the passage. And the body. And the truth. The Black Vow was here, buried beneath their streets, dressed in merchant's garb and hidden behind false doors.

Let them explain that.

He turned from the fire as more guards arrived, shouting orders, blades drawn. They would dig deeper. They would uncover things meant to stay buried.

Good.

Let the world see.

Let the Vowkeeper squirm.

And when they came for him—and they would—he would be waiting.

Not just for blood. Not just for vengeance.

But for the boy the gods had stolen.

The boy, whom he would not fail.

He turned away as the cries grew louder; the flames roaring high enough to catch the attention of the noble quarter. No one noticed the man in the alley vanish.

He walked into the night like a blade returned to its sheath—silent, sharp, and waiting to be drawn. A single focused instrument. For his son.

www.ingramcontent.com/pod-product-compliance
Lightning Source LLC
Chambersburg PA
CBHW060808120726
47909CB00006B/1825